Library of America, a nonprofit organization,
champions our nation's cultural heritage
by publishing America's greatest writing in
authoritative new editions and providing resources
for readers to explore this rich, living legacy.

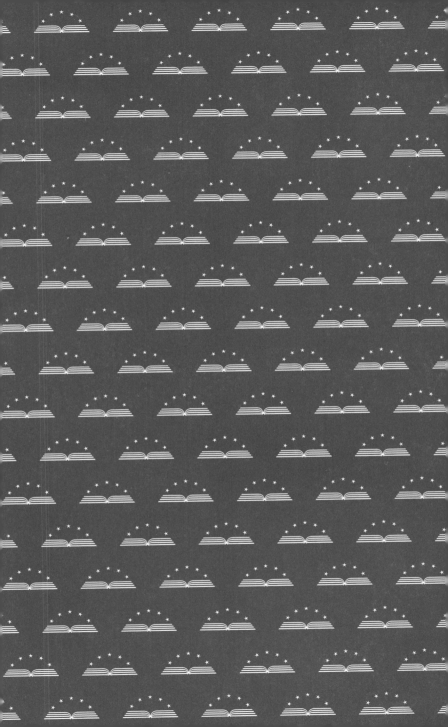

PETER TAYLOR

PETER TAYLOR

COMPLETE STORIES
1938–1959

Ann Beattie, *editor*

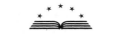

THE LIBRARY OF AMERICA

Visit our website at www.loa.org.

All texts published by arrangement with the Estate of Peter Taylor.

This paper meets the requirements of
ANSI/NISO Z39.48–1992 (Permanence of Paper).

Distributed to the trade in the United States
by Penguin Random House Inc.
and in Canada by Penguin Random House Canada Ltd.

Library of Congress Control Number: 2016959018
ISBN 978–1–59853–542–6

First Printing
The Library of America—298

Manufactured in the United States of America

Peter Taylor: The Complete Stories
is kept in print with a gift from

THE GEOFFREY C. HUGHES FOUNDATION

to the Guardians of American Letters Fund,
established by the Library of America
to ensure that every volume in the series
will be permanently available.

Contents

UNDERGRADUATE STORIES 1936–1939

Introduction

BY ANN BEATTIE

MATTHEW HILLSMAN TAYLOR JR., nicknamed Pete, decided early to become simply Peter Taylor. The name has a certain directness, as well as a hint of elegance. Both qualities were also true of his writing, though his directness was reserved for energizing inanimate objects, as well as for presenting physical details. (His sidelong psychological studies, on the other hand, take time to unfold.) It was also his tendency to situate his characters within precisely rendered historical and social settings. His stories deepen, brushstroke by brushstroke, by gradual layering—by the verbal equivalent to what painters call atmospheric perspective. Their surfaces are no more to be trusted than the first ice on a lake.

Born in Trenton, Tennessee, in 1917, Taylor was a self-proclaimed "mama's boy," though he said his mother never showed favoritism among her children: he had an older brother and two older sisters. She was old-fashioned, even for her day. Still, he adored her, and women were often the objects of his fictional fascination. The women in Taylor's stories are capable, intelligent, if sometimes unpredictable in their eccentricities as well as in their fierce energies and abilities. Obi-Wan Kenobi wouldn't need to wish them anything: they already have the Force.

How wonderful that all the stories are now collected in two volumes in the Library of America series. A reader unfamiliar with Taylor's work will here become an archaeologist; American history, especially the Upper South's history of racial divisions and sometimes dubious harmonies, is everywhere on full display. Taylor was raised with servants. The woman who was once his father's nurse also cared for him. Traditions were handed down, as were silver and obligation. Though he seldom writes about people determined to overturn the social order, Taylor never flinches when presenting encounters between whites and blacks—whether affectionate, indifferent, or unkind—and dramatizes them forthrightly.

The stories, rooted in daily life, use the quotidian as their point of departure into more complex matters. Writers have little use for the usual. Whenever a writer takes the pose that the events of his story are typical and ordinary, the reader knows that the story would not exist if this day, this moment, were not about to become exceptional. (*Of course* things will not go smoothly at the Misses Morkan's annual dance in James Joyce's "The Dead.") Taylor mobilizes his characters and the plots that they create as if merely observing, as if capably invoking convention and happy to go along with it. To add to this effect, he sometimes creates a character, often a narrator, that the reader can take for a Peter Taylor stand-in: a child, a college professor, or a young man like Nat, the protagonist of "The Old Forest," whose thwarted desires and covertness about tempting fate are at odds with what society condones and also with his inexperience. It is a woman who, in that particular story, turns the tables, and another woman—Nat's fiancée, Caroline—who, in the closing lines, kicks the table right out of the room, so to speak. It is one of the most amazing endings in modern fiction, with a revelation that rises out of the subtext: "Though it"—says Nat, referring to leaving home and rejecting an identity determined by others—"clearly meant that we must live on a somewhat more modest scale and live among people of a sort she [Caroline] was not used to, and even meant leaving Memphis forever behind us, the firmness with which she supported my decision, and the look in her eyes whenever I spoke of feeling I must make the change, seemed to say to me that she would dedicate her pride of power to the power of freedom I sought."

The present tense of "The Old Forest" is the early 1980s, when Nat is a man in his sixties. The story's action, however, takes place in a remembered 1937, just before Nat, then a college undergraduate, is to marry Caroline. His wedding plans go astray when, while driving near Overton Park with another young woman, he has a minor car accident, after which the woman flees into the forest and disappears. The mystery of her disappearance must be solved before the marriage can take place. Nat, as narrator, has alerted us early on (no doubt so we might forget about it) that the story we're about to read happened in the Memphis of long ago. It ends in an epiphany we never see play out. The future—the "now" of the story—is only eloquently suggested. The story of the forty intervening years is barely, glancingly told—shocking as some of the few offered details are. Virginia Woolf's surprising use of parentheses to inform the reader of the death of Mrs. Ramsay in *To the Lighthouse* was stunning; Taylor's narrator, who hurries through his account of family tragedies, is equally shocking, as the information he relays appears to be but a brief aside to the story he wishes to tell.

Every writer thinks hard about the best moment for a story to begin and end. Taylor does, too, but his diction—his exquisite and equivocal choice of words—often suggests that beneath the surface action of the story dwells something more, something uncontainable. With "pride of power" comes the hint that Caroline is fiercely leonine (pride of lions) as well as heroically self-sacrificing. This, however, is projected onto her by Nat: it "seemed to say to me." In other words, it's worth noting that an idea has been planted, both in Nat's mind and the reader's, yet is unverifiable; we do not get to read the story of a lifetime that might otherwise inform us or offer a different interpretation of what we're asked to understand. Elegant prose, calculated to convince, appears at story's end—a literary high note, nearly one of elation, on which to conclude. But I wouldn't be sure. In retrospect, the story tells us a lot about Nat (perhaps that he can be as annoying as a gnat), who intermittently interrupts the narrative to inform us with disquisitions about the historical significance of the old forest. It's a ploy to distract our attention from all that's forming below the surface (as in the cliché "Miss the forest for the trees"). Nat writes in the present, from the perspective of maturity. Nat knows himself, yet not entirely; he feels he must do the right thing, but does so only when prodded by Caroline, a strong woman; he is adamant that he and she must find another way, a new way, a way forward in which something is lost (Memphis, his family, and their expectations of him) but something also gained (autonomy and the ability to pursue one's passion). All this leaves the lioness a little on the sidelines, and the present-day reader might be saddened that the Caroline of 1937 understands that her only way forward is to attach herself to Nat, a man—but at the moment the story concludes, the two characters are united by the writer in their own version of triumph.

With apologies to the New Criticism (originated and practiced by some of Peter Taylor's most important teachers, including Allen Tate, John Crowe Ransom, Cleanth Brooks, and Robert Penn Warren), here is where I conflate the life of the writer with the actions and thoughts of his stand-in character. The tension that arises from a psychological or emotional conflict within the protagonist is a common theme of Taylor's stories. As is the idea of a trade-off, or compromise. As is ambiguity, a feeling of unease that can creep over the reader like a shadow, so slow moving that it's accepted without question. It's not until later that one looks for its source. There, at the source of our unease, is where Taylor always outfoxes the reader. Taylor often purposefully disrupts a story's forward momentum to delve into the narrator's past, making what might seem to be equilibrium, when jammed up against the story's present moment, cause disequilibrium. What makes me so admiringly queasy is not this juxtaposition and the discordant tone it sounds but what the methodology evokes more broadly: Peter Taylor, as writer, occupying the role of both Orpheus and Eurydice. He repeatedly creates narrators who guide the reader through the story toward an expected and just resolution but who then hesitate, or momentarily lose their moral focus, and so scuttle that resolution. Taylor's characters want to come out into the light, but the person who can best guide them, the writer himself, is impelled to make them look over their shoulder and face the omnipresent past, with all its implied demands. The possibility of faltering, the *probability* of it, is a recurring undertow in this writer's stories. It's as if, in his worst fears, Taylor, relegated to Eurydice's powerless and inescapable position, might himself need rescuing. The way out is never easy or clear, even with a narrator's guidance, and so daunting one can't go it alone. Taylor's main characters always need to bring someone with them; individuals, in Taylor's fiction, must exist in pairs. After all, his narrators are mortal.

The writer's use of intrinsic doubt—of *aporia* as a rhetorical strategy—is also fascinating. Just when we're almost hypnotized by the narrative abilities of some of his eloquent yet dissembling characters, there comes a shift in tone, really a *sotto voce* moment, in which the narrator second-guesses himself or the tale he is telling, thereby indicating that everything the reader hears must not be taken at face value. Quite a few of the stories verge on being mysteries ("The Oracle at Stoneleigh Court," "First Heat"), though not the conventional kind that pose suspense-filled puzzles that will eventually be solved. Rather, Taylor's puzzles are articulated so that some potential accommodation, some new way to go on with one's life, may become apparent. Though the reader may not register it immediately, at the end of a Peter Taylor story some essential riddle remains.

Peter Taylor embodied contradictions. He often explored them in his fiction, though rarely does he leave us with a feeling that things have been comfortably reconciled for himself or his characters. There remains an oscillation, an internal push/pull, as if the mind were a vibrating tuning fork. Currently, in the age of memoir, there's a lot of self-important talk among writers about writing as a means to self-salvation. To the extent that this applies to Taylor, his characters are proof that the energy generated by inner turmoil is synonymous with really living. Take "Je Suis Perdu" as a beautiful example. Its real-life point of departure is that the Taylors, in the mid-1950s, went to France with their two young children. The story chronicles a day in the life of an unnamed American husband and father (he is thirty-eight) who is morbidly preoccupied with aging and mortality. Our protagonist goes to the Luxembourg Gardens, where Taylor begins to expose him to various backdrops, beginning with Poe-like monstrous façades. His thoughts turn to the French painter David and his only landscape, an oil-on-canvas view from the building in which he was imprisoned. We can't fail to understand the import of this implied link between the two men. The character also considers the Panthéon, a mausoleum for France's secular saints, projecting his dark mood so that it, too, is personified into monstrousness. Late in the story, our protagonist seems to be suddenly overwhelmed with a kind of emotional vertigo, along with the disoriented reader: "When the mood was not on him, he could never believe in it." The writer is always aware of individual words, and all they might convey: significantly, it is "the" mood, not "his mood." It becomes "his"—it is personalized—only on the last page of

the story. Yet again, the writer provides us with a psychological study (this one more explicit than most) not to solve the
mystery of his protagonist's conflicting moods but rather to
create anxiety with its articulation: it is a beautiful day in Paris;
he loves his wife and children; he's been away from his job in
America, working on a book he has just finished. Aha. So this
is also a story about writing, and about one writer's personal
demons being projected onto the external world. Consider the
"cute" antics of his baby son, which impress the reader as more
grotesque than humorous, the boy's spinning reminiscent of
the devil's; also his wife, who, in her slip, does not disrobe but
instead gives him the slip (as one would say colloquially) as she
goes off to dress; and his daughter, who is too tightly wound,
her shrieking portending the nightmarish perceptions that will
soon overwhelm her father.

The story is divided into two sections, titled after Milton's
pastoral poems "L'Allegro" and "Il Penseroso." Sometimes
described as paired opposites, the poems actually embody
their own contradictions in an embedded complexity that
would appeal to Taylor, who never thought in terms of either/
or. Also, Taylor would never invoke Miltonic high seriousness
if not to alter it—in this case, by wittily playing against it.
This is a story about a man who should be all right, but who
isn't. (How many of us have admonished ourselves privately
for not appreciating our good fortune?) Its ending is qualified
by the indelibility of every revelation that, earlier in the story,
we've been so immediately immersed in; Taylor overwhelms
both reader and character with the intensity of the character's
inner conflict. Our own moods plunge as we read. Here's what
the writer depends on: once we see something, we can't *not*
see it; once we feel something, we can't be told we don't. It
sounds so obvious, but few writers have the mastery to haunt
the reader long after their characters have ostensibly shaken off
their demons. The story's final paragraph, with ellipses that
convey what must remain unspoken, the "buts" still too painful to articulate, expresses a tentativeness that purports to end
with enlightened awareness: "But this was not a mood, it was
only a thought." This sounds like an important distinction,
yet it's more likely the character is grasping at straws—word

straws—desperate to regain (or at least feign) equilibrium. We, however, have felt the bleakness of his mood; we retain the afterimage of the Panthéon transformed into a glaring monster. Near story's end, Taylor expands his horizons: we find ourselves reading an unexpected parable about America, and furthermore this consideration—which we now understand has been a significant part of the subtext—mitigates the ending's potential upswing. We're taken aback, just as we are at the end of *The Great Gatsby*, though without the enlightened exhilaration. In Taylor's story, as in Fitzgerald's novel, one has gone to a foreign land (in *Gatsby* we hear about the Dutch sailors; the characters' predecessors have also moved, in Taylor's story, to a new frontier); the protagonist of "Je Suis Perdu" has become something of an actor (he grows, then shaves off, his moustache; Gatsby, with his rainbow of colorful shirts, has nothing on this guy). Time and again in Taylor, the visitor is never, ever, truly accepted, however well he tries to act the required role. It's the status quo that our protagonist desperately returns to—or tries to—at the end of "Je Suis Perdu," words his daughter utters that, we come to understand, expand in their connotations so that, metaphorically, we see it is he, the father, who is lost. We know "the mood" will descend again.

An admirer of Hemingway (*there* we see shadows before we suspect the source), Taylor, as his talent matured, increasingly turned toward another early influence, Henry James. Taylor has been compared (too often and too easily) to Chekhov. He admitted that he learned a lot from him, particularly how to consider things from many perspectives. But in reading or re-reading Peter Taylor's work after many years, I was struck not by these but rather by certain other influences that I'd previously passed over: Freud, for example. (Taylor, on being sent students' analyses of his story "A Walled Garden": "As I read their papers, I began to think, 'Well, you know, that didn't occur to me while I was writing it, but in a way that's why it works as well as it does.'" It's not unusual for writers to write from an unconscious level, though Taylor's level-headedness—at least in interviews—seems so atypically rational, one wonders whether he isn't being a bit coy in his modesty.) I was surprised at the number of times the progression of a story and its symbols seemed so obviously Freudian, or to hint at allegory. When Taylor began writing, psychoanalysis and Freud's surprising new ideas were in the air. Freud and Jung's ways of thinking were part of the cosmology of some of his closest friends and fellow writers, such as Robert Lowell.

Taylor did not compose in a white heat, though, or dash off rough drafts. He was an urbane, educated man, as well as someone who clearly perceived the world intuitively, and through his senses. He was keenly attuned to tone, timing, gestures, and subtleties. Peter Taylor was also a playwright, which informed his fiction writing. Time and again he lets us *see* people acting, whether they're gazing into a foggy mirror, as in "Je Suis Perdu," or rationalizing aloud a bit too much, as Nat does in "The Old Forest." When a text is composed over many months—as was his usual working method—I wonder how often he must have stared at the wallpaper, only to suddenly see an alternate, hidden pattern emerge. Like other highly visual writers such as John Updike and Elizabeth Bishop, his involvement in art began in a childhood desire to paint. *He drew his dreams.* Perhaps more than he let on, he trusted unconscious forces. A case could be made that his writing conveyed so much immediacy because, awake, the writer was trying to connect the dots, flashes of a dream that lit up here and there unexpectedly, in the moment of its being dreamt. Though the dreamer cannot be both dreamer and interpreter of the dream, there's no prohibition against waking up, remembering, pondering, and incorporating the dream's meaning in its re-take, its re-shaping into a story. What I'm suggesting is that Taylor often deliberately immerses the reader in the illogic of a dream ("Demons," "A Cheerful Disposition," "The Megalopolitans") and gives us a visceral sense of how that feels. With guidance (his conscious mind perfects the story), its symbols, when they have their dots connected, form the character's personal psychological map—one that at times we are better able to understand than the character can.

Taylor was also interested, at least as a subject of fiction, in the occult, in the Tarot, in ghosts—as was Henry James. Reading Taylor, one is reminded more than once of James's "The Jolly Corner." Of course this story would appeal to him, with its hints of what is unseen becoming manifest, and the implied question of what one's life would be like if it could be re-lived. Taylor's early story "The Life Before," which appeared in the Kenyon undergraduate magazine *Hika* and is included here in book form for the first time, shows his interest in characters who are haunted: the protagonist and his wife conjure up their guardian angel, a seemingly ageless man named Benton Young, who appears in the doorway of the hotel in which they live to remind them of the power of his love, which comes as a kind of blessing to these two people who each love him in different ways. There is much more to the story, but placed in a context of his other "ghost" stories, and his collection of one-act plays titled *Presences* (1973), this early story is a little unsubtle in technique, yet also significant. (One can understand why plays appealed to Taylor: "In fiction you've got to prepare for the ghost for pages and make it right, whereas in a play you just say, 'Enter ghost.'" Taylor could be quite witty.)

Socially, Taylor was a raconteur who never told stories for easy laughs any more than he let them inflate into tragedies. I met him in 1975 and remained his and his wife Eleanor's friend for the rest of their lives. Peter Taylor and his former student John Casey were the people who got me hired at the University of Virginia when I was twenty-five. Was I awestruck? Not really, because he made anyone he befriended feel so comfortable. Was I intimidated by his wizardry in constructing a story? I just assumed anyone who could write them was a genius. Do I wish I'd asked him questions about everything from what books to read (his students were treated to this, because he read aloud in class) to how certain effects were achieved in his own fiction? At the very least, couldn't I have interviewed him? I'd like to go back in time—which I think Taylor would sympathize with—and give my younger self a shove. But I got from him, because of his attention as well as his talent, what some other lucky people also received: the idea of how a person might have a life in writing.

In the early stories, and even more so in the later ones, his narratives zig and zag through time as he gestures to other literary texts, and sometimes to works of visual art, with which his writing is in dialogue. Many of the stories (particularly the longer ones) are intended to approximate oral storytelling, rich in episodic digressions and a mixing of the important with the seemingly unimportant. Readers perceive different connotations, different connections, depending on their level of literary awareness. "A Walled Garden," for instance, is a prolonged apostrophe that sounds more than a little like one of Robert Browning's dramatic monologues, though anything Taylor took in was made his own.

"Venus, Cupid, Folly and Time," written in the indirect third person (until the anonymous narrator, having cleared his throat for twenty-five pages, at last steps forward and says "I"), asks us to believe a narrator who casually assumes that his views and the reader's coincide, yet who also informs us of things no one else would realize or put together in the same way. At the heart of the story is an account of the last of the annual parties given by Mr. Alfred Dorset and "his old-maid sister," Miss Louisa Dorset, for the children of provincial Chatham, Tennessee. Brother-sister incest, the story's subtext, is never observed but instead is displaced, prismatically: we see many puzzling points of light before the picture that the narrator is painting comes into focus. We "see" it in its pictorial or visual equivalents—lovemaking stopped in time (an echo of Keats?) as depicted in Rodin's sculpture "The Kiss," as well as in the busy Bronzino canvas that gives the story its name: there the naughty Cupid fondles his mother's breast, while the child Folly, rushing up behind them, prepares to shower them with a fistful of rose petals. These images—together with a plaque of Leda and the Swan—hang on the walls of the Dorsets' home. Into this highly sexualized setting comes an adolescent named Tom, whose actions disrupt the children's party and upend the lives of its hosts. If the reader hasn't suspected before, the "uninvited guest" of Taylor's story is played against that of Poe's "The Masque of the Red Death," though the stakes are not quite so sensational, or so deadly; instead, they remain murky and hauntingly disturbing, since there is no one form of evil to unmask. "Venus, Cupid, Folly and Time" also, in places, mimics a fairy tale. By extension, it might be America's fairy tale about itself, gone wrong: "The wicked in-laws had first tried to make them [brother and sister] sell the house, then had tried to separate them . . ." These references are gestures tossed out by Taylor's sleight of hand that reappear in his literary layering by way of double exposure.

Taylor is a writer who so loves to keep our senses sharp; our eye is forced to work like a borer bee as it moves closer to the deeper meaning below the intricately contrived surface pattern. In this story, the calculated miscalculation of a teenager's joke—a mock seduction—echoes the off-the-page "real" seduction (the incest of the Dorsets, who, as Miss Louisa tells us, "have given up everything for each other"). All this is played against a backdrop of sexually evocative sculpture and painting—to which is added the suggestion that time (and sexual maturity) does, and does not, change everything. The old couple being teased, in the reader's presence, have already been relegated to twisted figures depleted by time: the sister, symbolically wearing (like a wedding dress) a "modish white evening gown, a garment perfectly fitted to her spare and scrawny figure . . . never to be worn but that one night!"; her brother, like a Tennessee cousin of Gustav von Aschenbach, "powdered with the same bronze powder that his sister used."

The use of exclamation points in this story is purposeful: they indicate *faux* surprise and mock the Southern Gothic horror genre, which insistently telegraphs its shocking revelations. In the claustrophobic funhouse Taylor has orchestrated, his narrator blithely tells us things as if telling a conventional story, the author withholding many metaphorical exclamation points of his own. This amazing tour de force, which was published in *The Kenyon Review* and awarded First Prize in the 1959 *O. Henry Awards* collection, has been much anthologized. It must have gone over many of its first readers' heads like a shooting star. It's meant to read like the transcript of a spoken story; it's a bit meanderingly and imperfectly told. The repeated use of the conjunctions "and" and "but" to begin sentences says everything: *and* means there is a connection between things; *but* means that that connection is not absolute. Also, the story's location, the fictional town of Chatham—described by some as "geographically Northern and culturally Southern," by others as "geographically Southern but culturally Northern"—puts us on a fault line, in troubled and troubling territory that makes everything liminal. With a historical perspective introduced only in the last pages of the story, we're made to understand that the mercenary, mercantile Dorset family opportunistically settled Chatham "right after the Revolution" and then, in the early twentieth century, abandoned it—"practically all of them except the one old bachelor and the one old maid—left it just as they had come, not caring much about what they were leaving or where they were going." The rape of the town echoes the rape Taylor has earlier alluded to in "Leda and the Swan"; it also keeps the suggestion of incest ambient. Heedless people. Opportunists, Taylor intends us to see—analogous to those who grasp for what serves *their* purposes to embrace.

One doesn't look for consistencies in writers' lives because few are to be found. Peter Taylor married a poet, and both his son and daughter wanted to write. It made him worry about their futures—a recognizable worry of many fathers. As for himself, he took the position that if the conservative path was nonetheless the right one, however unglamorous (or because it *was* unglamorous), he was perfectly fine with it. For a limited time. A certain number of clichés, or banal assumptions in conversation, are helpful in orienting one's audience, forging a bond in either friendship or literature. It could be said—it must be said—that how he conducted himself personally has nothing to do with his work. I don't mean to suggest that he gave advice he disbelieved. Yet being aware of some of his contradictions offers a helpful orientation for understanding stories in which a turn of phrase, or a character's casually uttered misgivings (heard as loudly as a shout), serve to make the reader listen not to what's off the page, as we do when reading Hemingway, but to the levels of meaning embedded in the carefully chosen words or cagey digressions that *are* there.

Peter Taylor was a Southerner whose best friend was Robert Lowell, a Boston Brahmin. It's possible that, for reasons of his own, he put a positive spin on some of Lowell's pointed needling and, ultimately, neediness. (Taylor once told an interviewer that Lowell "invented facts and stories that made his dearest friends out as clichés . . . cliché Jews, cliché Southerners, cliché Englishmen. Naturally this was irksome sometimes—even mischief-making. He was fond of representing me as a Southern racist, though of course he knew better—knew it from the hours of talk we had had on the subject, as well as from my published stories. . . . His teasing was always rough

[but] it was his way of drawing closer to his friends, rather than putting them off.") It seems equally possible that sometimes he was hurt, though he always remained Lowell's loyal friend. Peter Taylor was in some instances quite sure of his feelings: he knew, for example, that as a young man he must stand up to his father and—even if it meant forgoing his acceptance at Columbia—refuse to attend Vanderbilt, his father's choice of university for him. (Peter Taylor *did* later attend Vanderbilt, but for his own reasons and on his own terms.) He knew the first time he saw Eleanor Ross that he would marry her and waited only six weeks to do this. Their long marriage lasted until his death. As for finally wearing a somewhat ironic crown, in 1987 he received the Pulitzer Prize for a novel, *A Summons to Memphis*, yet thought of himself as primarily a short story writer. Like all of us, at times he revealed more than he knew. He explained his election to the American Academy of Arts and Letters by mentioning that there were "no dues, or anything like that." I love the slight naïveté, as well as everything implied in the phrase "anything like that."

In Charlottesville, one didn't see Peter Taylor on the golf course or riding with the horsey set. Though he taught at a great many colleges and universities—in the East and the Midwest as well as in the South—he returned in the end not exactly to the foul rag and bone shop of his heart, but, with fondness, to a place he thought of as a prestigious known entity: the University of Virginia. In what might or might not be a contradiction, he taught creative writing while remaining skeptical about whether there should *be* a creative writing program. When he retired, he and Eleanor continued to live in town. Eleanor liked to garden. If she'd written a poem during the day, no visitor was told. Quite a few of his students and former students became his friends. Robert Wilson, who later became a distinguished writer and editor, accompanied him to Paris to receive the Ritz Paris Hemingway Award. Dan O'Neill, a student who later became his real estate agent, drove a rented van to Long Island to fetch Jean Stafford's settee (a wonderful Tayloresque word that has vanished from the current vocabulary), which she'd willed to Peter and Eleanor. (Only after her husband's death did Eleanor say she didn't much like it.) A former student routinely drove the couple to Florida in the winter.

They bought a house in Gainesville near Eleanor's sister, Jean, who had married the poet Donald Justice; earlier, they'd lived in Key West. Oddly—or maybe significantly—while wild tales of Tennessee Williams and, more recently, the bon mots of James Merrill are as essential to the residents of Key West as the literary air they breathe, there is no plaque on the Pine Street house where the Taylors lived, nor is there any Peter Taylor lore.

Peter and Eleanor were real estate enthusiasts. They bought and sold and repurchased a house, only to later sell it again. They came for dinner and, if you were renting, asked if you knew whether the house was for sale. Taylor showed pictures of properties they were considering when Eleanor left the room. Eleanor, in the kitchen, would earlier have laid out on the breakfast table photographs of her own recent house fascinations. (In an echo of life imitating art, might he have thought of them as analogous to having Tarot cards read?) They rented Faulkner's house in Charlottesville but were unable to buy it. They bought the house next door. Later, they moved a bit closer to the university. But I don't believe they ever owned only one house, even when limited to one location when Taylor's heart trouble worsened.

Enough background. I bring it up because their preoccupation with houses was surprising and a bit eccentric, but also because houses and their home-obsessed inhabitants are everywhere in his fiction. Never props, houses (apartments and hotels, as well), along with their furnishings (think of the wardrobe in "In the Miro District"), are given the stature of characters. The characters are an outgrowth of the life lived within, as well as the houses' being significant because of where they're located, how they're used, and what details have been described in such highly visual terms that they convey indelible meaning throughout the story (Alice Munro and William Maxwell are also brilliant at this). The houses are as integral to the story as a shell is to a turtle. And, like a turtle, they suggest that no one's going anywhere fast. In spite of life's flux, houses give the impression of being constant.

Taylor isn't Hawthorne or Poe (he admired them, but their pyrotechnics didn't reflect his sensibility; if they were the fireworks, his stories would be the just-struck match). He did have the ability to create his own sort of visceral scariness—one that rarely had anything directly to do with obvious projection or personification ("Je Suis Perdu" is an exception that proves the rule). Here is Peter Taylor, talking to interviewer J. William Broadway in 1985: "I like to do landscaping. On the last place I had I built three ponds, one spilling into the other—eighteenth-century style. And that's what I've done to this place. It's got great boulders on the side of the hill, rocks as big as this room. And it's very beautiful. I was even building an imitation graveyard, a topiary graveyard, with carvings and shrubbery. It was pure folly. And Eleanor's planted acres of trees. Then there are a lot of blackberries, persimmons to be gathered and that sort of thing." Of course, his saying this, and making the "folly" we'll never see so vivid, remind me of how important his dreams were to him, how Freudian the implications of some of his stories are, as well as of his own use of allegory. It's almost astonishing how easily we can read into his words and understand that he is speaking simultaneously about a literal and symbolic landscape (as in dreams). When he described his property, he was already suffering from heart problems. He doesn't reflect on his statement or in any way let on that he knows what he's said, but it's easy to see that the topiary graveyard conveys both his concern with mortality and the careful artistry, the pruning/writing that he undertakes; landscaping is an inherent metaphor by which, in creating an ideal world, he wishes to prove he's powerful—still alive.

To read a great number of his stories is to sense an invincibility about Taylor's dwellings that make them a force to be reckoned with. His writerly interest in myth, palmistry, superstition, and ghosts is also obvious. A house, though, is the opposite of a ghost, entirely apparent. But within them—as within all of us—must be secrets, areas of disrepair, covert demands exerted. One of his major considerations as a writer is the clash of past and present, the old order versus the changing world, Nashville versus Memphis. This evolution asks important questions about who we are, where we belong (and whether we can ever really leave those places), and what meaning to ascribe to exteriors, compared with (I'm speaking psychologically) interiors. In the stories, we sometimes hear angry words from a character, a roar, occasionally hysteria—though no reader would typify his material by these outbursts. When things go out of control, in life or in fiction, they rarely devolve into complete chaos (war zones excepted), though it's true that Taylor tends to play in quieter territory.

Has he not had the reputation he's so long deserved because it takes a while for his subtle, disturbing stories that gestate below the surface to settle in? Was his magic act of Now-You-See-It, Now-You-Don't a bit too successful, a ruse that ultimately became counter-productive? His proclivity toward selecting narrators who have a cordial, confiding tone was trickery, but may have misled some readers into thinking that he was a nice Southern gentleman, indistinguishable from his fictional creations. (He *must* have read Ford Madox Ford's *The Good Soldier*—though none of Taylor's characters ever blow their cover.)

It's also possible that his reputation is a rare case of a short story writer being eclipsed by the poets of his generation, Lowell foremost among a group that also included Randall Jarrell and the now iconic Elizabeth Bishop. Another factor may be that once upon a time Southern writers, with notable exceptions such as William Faulkner or, more recently, William Styron, were considered regional writers, whose voices did not rise to universal truths. This is not the case today, if it ever was, so it can be easy to forget that there was a time when the term "regional writing" carried negative associations, and things Southern were thought a bit unsophisticated. In some ways, Peter Taylor's discursive, chatty stories played into a stereotype about pawky storytellers whose horizons were obscured by the hills of home. His contemporary, Eudora Welty—she was of his generation, eight years older than he—has more admirers for her stories than for her novels. At least in the academic world Welty's novels are rarely taught (she won the Pulitzer Prize in 1972 for *The Optimist's Daughter*), though her stories are. Taylor very much liked her writing. I might be overstating the case, but it's as if the audience already had their cherished Southern short story writer in Eudora Welty. In the 1990s, during Peter Taylor's last years, it was *her* work that was celebrated as the example of the quintessential Southern short story. Meanwhile, he struggled to get his stories and books into print (in any case, he was never prolific) and his critical reputation became wobbly; had it not been for the admiration of such distinguished writers as Anne Tyler and Joyce Carol Oates, his reputation might have dipped further—that and the unwavering support he received (he was often agentless, by choice) from so many former students in the world of writing and publishing. Jonathan Yardley, former book critic at the *Washington Post*'s *Book World*, did much to spread the word about Peter Taylor's singular talent; a former student, the book editor Jonathan Coleman, persuaded Peter to assemble *In the Miro District* for Knopf. It's rarely easy to find and keep an audience when a writer is writing only intermittently, especially when that writer is not easily categorizable: Taylor alternated between genres; he composed stories in verse (some of his rough drafts—in fact, every story in *In the Miro District*, he once said—initially took this form); he did not write essays and seldom reviewed books. He did not live in New York City. When his career was on the ascent, during the Thomas Wolfe and Maxwell Perkins era, writers and editors took each other very seriously. Writing wasn't the business it has become, in a time when corporations own the publishing houses and issue a mandate to make money. (If today's talented young book editors were Peter Taylor characters, they, like Nat, might do better to go off to study Latin.) Taylor advised writers to find a teaching job that would allow them time to write—conservative, no doubt practical advice, though having done that, he, himself, moved from job to job. Having one's peers admire you (he certainly had that) was valued by Peter Taylor as the greatest compliment. He thought small literary magazines were where a beginning writer could attract an audience and be encouraged as one built a reputation. Now, with few magazines printing fiction, and *The Kenyon Review* and *The Southern Review* (among other magazines where he first published) still going strong, he turns out to be right, again.

Peter Taylor once remarked, "Flaubert says, 'Madame Bovary, c'est moi.' How can you write fiction if you can't imagine it? And how can you imagine it if you don't link your psychology to your characters? Writing starts with events and experiences that worry me, and I put them together. You write a story in which you are the protagonist, but you have to change him for the theme's sake."

As always, he's very clear about what he believes. It is the reader's good luck that he worried. His best stories rise to the level of transcendent worry. When we finish reading one of his more complex stories, he's capable of making us look upward from planet Earth, and from the South, in particular, to a blue sky, or a dark sky, just waiting to be projected upon.

COMPLETE STORIES
1938–1959

A Spinster's Tale

M Y BROTHER would often get drunk when I was a little girl, but that put a different sort of fear into me from what Mr. Speed did. With Brother it was a spiritual thing. And though it was frightening to know that he would have to burn for all that giggling and bouncing around on the stair at night, the truth was that he only seemed jollier to me when I would stick my head out of the hall door. It made him seem almost my age for him to act so silly, putting his white forefinger all over his flushed face and finally over his lips to say, "Sh-sh-sh-sh!" But the really frightening thing about seeing Brother drunk was what I always heard when I had slid back into bed. I could always recall my mother's words to him when he was sixteen, the year before she died, spoken in her greatest sincerity, in her most religious tone: "Son, I'd rather see you in your grave."

Yet those nights put a scaredness into me that was clearly distinguishable from the terror that Mr. Speed instilled by stumbling past our house two or three afternoons a week. The most that I knew about Mr. Speed was his name. And this I considered that I had somewhat fabricated—by allowing him the "Mr."—in my effort to humanize and soften the monster that was forever passing our house on Church Street. My father would point him out through the wide parlor window in soberness and severity to my brother with: "There goes Old Speed, again." Or on Saturdays when Brother was with the Benton boys and my two uncles were over having toddies with Father in the parlor, Father would refer to Mr. Speed's passing with a similar speech, but in a blustering tone of merry tolerance: "There goes Old Speed, again. The rascal!" These designations were equally awful, both spoken in tones that were foreign to my father's manner of addressing me; and not unconsciously I prepared the euphemism, Mister Speed, against the inevitable day when I should have to speak of him to someone.

I was named Elizabeth, for my mother. My mother had died in the spring before Mr. Speed first came to my notice on that late afternoon in October. I had bathed at four with the aid of Lucy, who had been my nurse and who was now the upstairs maid; and Lucy was upstairs turning back the covers of the beds in the rooms with their color schemes of blue and green and rose. I wandered into the shadowy parlor and sat first on one chair, then on another. I tried lying down on the settee that went with the parlor set, but my legs had got too long this summer to stretch out straight on the settee. And my feet looked long in their pumps against the wicker arm. I looked at the pictures around the room blankly and at the stained-glass windows on either side of the fireplace; and the winter light coming through them was hardly bright enough to show the colors. I struck a match on the mosaic hearth and lit the gas logs.

Kneeling on the hearth I watched the flames till my face felt hot. I stood up then and turned directly to one of the full-length mirror panels that were on each side of the front window. This one was just to the right of the broad window and my reflection in it stood out strangely from the rest of the room in the dull light that did not penetrate beyond my figure. I leaned closer to the mirror trying to discover a resemblance between myself and the wondrous Alice who walked through a looking glass. But that resemblance I was seeking I could not find in my sharp features, or in my heavy, dark curls hanging like fragments of hosepipe to my shoulders.

I propped my hands on the borders of the narrow mirror and put my face close to watch my lips say, "Away." I would hardly open them for the "a"; and then I would contort my face by the great opening I made for the "way." I whispered, "Away, away." I whispered it over and over, faster and faster, watching myself in the mirror: "A-way—a-way—away-away-awayaway." Suddenly I burst into tears and turned from the gloomy mirror to the daylight at the wide parlor window. Gazing tearfully through the expanse of plate glass there, I beheld Mr. Speed walking like a cripple with one foot on the curb and one in the street. And faintly I could hear him cursing the trees as he passed them, giving each a lick with his heavy walking cane.

Presently I was dry-eyed in my fright. My breath came short, and I clasped the black bow at the neck of my middy blouse.

When he had passed from view, I stumbled back from the window. I hadn't heard the houseboy enter the parlor, and he must not have noticed me there, I made no move of recognition as he drew the draperies across the wide front window for the night. I stood cold and silent before the gas logs with a sudden inexplicable memory of my mother's cheek and a vision of her in her bedroom on a spring day.

That April day when spring had seemed to crowd itself through the windows into the bright upstairs rooms, the old-fashioned mahogany sick-chair had been brought down from the attic to my mother's room. Three days before, a quiet service had been held there for the stillborn baby, and I had accompanied my father and brother to our lot in the gray cemetery to see the box (large for so tiny a parcel) lowered and covered with mud. But in the parlor now by the gas logs I remembered the day that my mother had sent for the sick-chair and for me.

The practical nurse, sitting in a straight chair busy at her needlework, looked over her glasses to give me some little instruction in the arrangement of my mother's pillows in the chair. A few minutes before, this practical nurse had lifted my sick mother bodily from the bed, and I had the privilege of rolling my mother to the big bay window that looked out ideally over the new foliage of small trees in our side yard.

I stood self-consciously straight, close by my mother, a maturing little girl awkward in my curls and long-waisted dress. My pale mother, in her silk bed jacket, with a smile leaned her cheek against the cheek of her daughter. Outside it was spring. The furnishings of the great blue room seemed to partake for that one moment of nature's life. And my mother's cheek was warm on mine. This I remembered when I sat before the gas logs trying to put Mr. Speed out of my mind; but that a few moments later my mother beckoned to the practical nurse and sent me suddenly from the room, my memory did not dwell upon. I remembered only the warmth of the cheek and the comfort of that other moment.

I sat near the blue burning logs and waited for my father and my brother to come in. When they came saying the same things about office and school that they said every day, turning on lights beside chairs that they liked to flop into, I realized not that I was ready or unready for them but that there had been, within me, an attempt at a preparation for such readiness.

They sat so customarily in their chairs at first and the talk ran so easily that I thought that Mr. Speed could be forgotten as quickly and painlessly as a doubting of Jesus or a fear of death from the measles. But the conversation took insinuating and malicious twists this afternoon. My father talked about the possibilities of a general war and recalled opinions that people had had just before the Spanish-American. He talked about the hundreds of men in the Union Depot. Thinking of all those men there, that close together, was something like meeting Mr. Speed in the front hall. I asked my father not to talk about war, which seemed to him a natural enough request for a young lady to make.

"How is your school, my dear?" he asked me. "How are Miss Hood and Miss Herron? Have they found who's stealing the boarders' things, my dear?"

All of those little girls safely in Belmont School being called for by gentle ladies or warm-breasted Negro women were a pitiable sight beside the beastly vision of Mr. Speed which even they somehow conjured.

At dinner, with Lucy serving and sometimes helping my plate (because she had done so for so many years), Brother teased me first one way and then another. My father joined in on each point until I began to take the teasing very seriously, and then he told Brother that he was forever carrying things too far.

Once at dinner I was convinced that my preposterous fears that Brother knew what had happened to me by the window in the afternoon were not at all preposterous. He had been talking quietly. It was something about the meeting that he and the Benton boys were going to attend after dinner. But quickly, without reason, he turned his eyes on me across the table and fairly shouted in his new deep voice: "I saw three horses running away out on Harding Road today! They were just like the mules we saw at the mines in the mountains! They were running to beat hell and with little girls riding them!"

The first week after I had the glimpse of Mr. Speed through the parlor window, I spent the afternoons dusting the bureau and mantel and bedside table in my room, arranging on the chaise longue the dolls which at this age I never played with and rarely even talked to; or I would absent-mindedly assist Lucy in turning down the beds and maybe watch the houseboy set the dinner table. I went to the parlor only when

Father came or when Brother came earlier and called me in to show me a shin bruise or a box of cigarettes which a girl had given him.

Finally, I put my hand on the parlor doorknob just at four one afternoon and entered the parlor, walking stiffly as I might have done with my hands in a muff going into church. The big room with its heavy furniture and pictures showed no change since the last afternoon that I had spent there, unless possibly there were fresh antimacassars on the chairs. I confidently pushed an odd chair over to the window and took my seat and sat erect and waited.

My heart would beat hard when, from the corner of my eye, I caught sight of some figure moving up Church Street. And as it drew nearer, showing the form of some Negro or neighbor or drummer, I would sigh from relief and from regret. I was ready for Mr. Speed. And I knew that he would come again and again, that he had been passing our house for inconceivable numbers of years. I knew that if he did not appear today, he would pass tomorrow. Not because I had had accidental, unavoidable glimpses of him from upstairs windows during the past week, nor because there were indistinct memories of such a figure, hardly noticed, seen on afternoons that preceded that day when I had seen him stumbling like a cripple along the curb and beating and cursing the trees did I know that Mr. Speed was a permanent and formidable figure in my life which I would be called upon to deal with; my knowledge, I was certain, was purely intuitive.

I was ready now not to face him with his drunken rage directed at me, but to look at him far off in the street and to appraise him. He didn't come that afternoon, but he came the next. I sat prim and straight before the window. I turned my head neither to the right to anticipate the sight of him nor to the left to follow his figure when it had passed. But when he was passing before my window, I put my eyes full on him and looked though my teeth chattered in my head. And now I saw his face heavy, red, fierce like his body. He walked with an awkward, stomping sort of stagger, carrying his gray topcoat over one arm; and with his other hand he kept poking his walnut cane into the soft sod along the sidewalk. When he was gone, I recalled my mother's cheek again, but the recollection this time, though more deliberate, was dwelt less upon; and I could only think of watching Mr. Speed again and again.

There was snow on the ground the third time that I watched Mr. Speed pass our house. Mr. Speed spat on the snow, and with his cane he aimed at the brown spot that his tobacco made there. And I could see that he missed his aim. The fourth time that I sat watching for him from the window, snow was actually falling outside; and I felt a sort of anxiety to know what would ever drive him into my own house. For a moment I doubted that he would really come to my door; but I prodded myself with the thought of his coming and finding me unprepared. And I continued to keep my secret watch for him two or three times a week during the rest of the winter.

Meanwhile my life with my father and brother and the servants in the shadowy house went on from day to day. On week nights the evening meal usually ended with petulant arguing between the two men, the atlas or the encyclopedia usually drawing them from the table to read out the statistics. Often Brother was accused of having looked-them-up-previously and of maneuvering the conversation toward the particular subject, for topics were very easily introduced and dismissed by the two. Once I, sent to the library to fetch a cigar, returned to find the discourse shifted in two minutes' time from the Kentucky Derby winners to the languages in which the Bible was first written. Once I actually heard the conversation slip, in the course of a small dessert, from the comparative advantages of urban and agrarian life for boys between the ages of fifteen and twenty to the probable origin and age of the Icelandic parliament and then to the doctrines of the Campbellite Church.

That night I followed them to the library and beheld them fingering the pages of the flimsy old atlas in the light from the beaded lampshade. They paid no attention to me and little to one another, each trying to turn the pages of the book and mumbling references to newspaper articles and to statements of persons of responsibility. I slipped from the library to the front parlor across the hall where I could hear the contentious hum. And I lit the gas logs, trying to warm my long legs before them as I examined my own response to the unguided and remorseless bickering of the masculine voices.

It was, I thought, their indifferent shifting from topic to topic that most disturbed me. Then I decided that it was the tremendous gaps that there seemed to be between the subjects that was bewildering to me. Still again, I thought that it was the equal interest which they displayed for each subject that was dismaying. All things in the world were equally at home in their arguments. They exhibited equal indifference to the horrors that each topic might suggest; and I wondered whether or not their imperturbability was a thing that they had achieved.

I knew that I had got myself so accustomed to the sight of Mr. Speed's peregrinations, persistent yet, withal, seemingly without destination, that I could view his passing with perfect equanimity. And from this I knew that I must extend my preparation for the day when I should have to view him at closer range. When the day would come, I knew that it must involve my father and my brother and that his existence therefore must not remain an unmentionable thing, the secrecy of which to explode at the moment of crisis, only adding to its confusion.

Now, the door to my room was the first at the top of the long red-carpeted stairway. A wall light beside it was left burning on nights when Brother was out, and, when he came in, he turned it off. The light shining through my transom was a comforting sight when I had gone to bed in the big room; and in the summertime I could see the reflection of light bugs on it, and often one would plop against it. Sometimes I would wake up in the night with a start and would be frightened in the dark, not knowing what had awakened me until I realized that Brother had just turned out the light. On other nights, however, I would hear him close the front door and hear him bouncing up the steps. When I then stuck my head out the door, usually he would toss me a piece of candy and he always signaled to me to be quiet.

I had never intentionally stayed awake till he came in until one night toward the end of February of that year, and I hadn't been certain then that I should be able to do it. Indeed, when finally the front door closed, I had dozed several times sitting up in the dark bed. But I was standing with my door half open before he had come a third of the way up the stair. When he saw me, he stopped still on the stairway resting his hand on the banister. I realized that purposefulness must be showing on my face, and so I smiled at him and beckoned. His red face broke into a fine grin, and he took the next few steps two at a time. But he stumbled on the carpeted steps. He was on his knees, yet with his hand still on the banister. He was motionless there for a moment with his head cocked to one side, listening. The house was quiet and still. He smiled again, sheepishly this time, and kept putting his white forefinger to his red face as he ascended on tiptoe the last third of the flight of steps.

At the head of the stair he paused, breathing hard. He reached his hand into his coat pocket and smiled confidently as he shook his head at me. I stepped backward into my room.

"Oh," he whispered. "Your candy."

I stood straight in my white nightgown with my black hair hanging over my shoulders, knowing that he could see me only indistinctly. I beckoned to him again. He looked suspiciously about the hall, then stepped into the room and closed the door behind him.

"What's the matter, Betsy?" he said.

I turned and ran and climbed between the covers of my bed.

"What's the matter, Betsy?" he said. He crossed to my bed and sat down beside me on it.

I told him that I didn't know what was the matter.

"Have you been reading something you shouldn't, Betsy?" he asked.

I was silent.

"Are you lonely, Betsy?" he said. "Are you a lonely little girl?"

I sat up on the bed and threw my arms about his neck. And as I sobbed on his shoulder I smelled for the first time the fierce odor of his cheap whiskey.

"Yes, I'm always lonely," I said with directness, and I was then silent with my eyes open and my cheek on the shoulder of his overcoat which was yet cold from the February night air.

He kept his face turned away from me and finally spoke, out of the other corner of his mouth, I thought, "I'll come home earlier some afternoons and we'll talk and play."

"Tomorrow."

When I had said this distinctly, I fell away from him back on the bed. He stood up and looked at me curiously, as though in some way repelled by my settling so comfortably in the covers.

And I could see his eighteen-year-old head cocked to one side as though trying to see my face in the dark. He leaned over me, and I smelled his whiskey breath. It was not repugnant to me. It was blended with the odor that he always had. I thought that he was going to strike me. He didn't, however, and in a moment was opening the door to the lighted hall. Before he went out, again I said: "Tomorrow."

The hall light dark and the sound of Brother's footsteps gone, I naturally repeated the whole scene in my mind and upon examination found strange elements present. One was something like a longing for my brother to strike me when he was leaning over me. Another was his bewilderment at my procedure. On the whole I was amazed at the way I had carried the thing off. It was the first incident that I had ever actively carried off. Now I only wished that in the darkness when he was leaning over me I had said languidly, "Oh, Brother," had said it in a tone indicating that we had in common some unmentionable trouble. Then I should have been certain of his presence next day. As it was, though, I had little doubt of his coming home early.

I would not let myself reflect further on my feelings for my brother—my desire for him to strike me and my delight in his natural odor. I had got myself in the habit of postponing such elucidations until after I had completely settled with Mr. Speed. But, as after all such meetings with my brother, I reflected upon the posthumous punishments in store for him for his carousing and drinking, and remembered my mother's saying that she had rather see him in his grave.

The next afternoon at four I had the chessboard on the tea table before the front parlor window. I waited for my brother, knowing pretty well that he would come and feeling certain that Mr. Speed would pass. (For this was a Thursday afternoon; and during the winter months I had found that there were two days of the week on which Mr. Speed never failed to pass our house. These were Thursday and Saturday.) I led my brother into that dismal parlor chattering about the places where I had found the chessmen long in disuse. When I paused a minute, slipping into my seat by the chessboard, he picked up with talk of the senior class play and his chances for being chosen valedictorian. Apparently I no longer seemed an enigma to him. I thought that he must have concluded that I was just a lonely little girl named Betsy. But I doubted that his nature was so different from my own that he could sustain objective sympathy for another child, particularly a younger sister, from one day to another. And since I saw no favors that he could ask from me at this time, my conclusion was that he believed that he had never exhibited his drunkenness to me with all his bouncing about on the stair at night; but that he was not certain that talking from the other corner of his mouth had been precaution enough against his whiskey breath.

We faced each other over the chessboard and set the men in order. There were only a few days before it would be March, and the light through the window was first bright and then dull. During my brother's moves, I stared out the window at the clouds that passed before the sun and watched pieces of newspaper that blew about the yard. I was calm beyond my own credulity. I found myself responding to my brother's little jokes and showing real interest in the game. I tried to terrorize myself by imagining Mr. Speed's coming up to the very window this day. I even had him shaking his cane and his derby hat at us. But the frenzy which I expected at this step of my preparation did not come. And some part of Mr. Speed's formidability seemed to have vanished. I realized that by not hiding my face in my mother's bosom and by looking at him so regularly for so many months, I had come to accept his existence as a natural part of my life on Church Street, though something to be guarded against, or, as I had put it before, to be thoroughly prepared for when it came to my door.

The problem then, in relation to my brother, had suddenly resolved itself in something much simpler than the conquest of my fear of looking upon Mr. Speed alone had been. This would be only a matter of how I should act and of what words I should use. And from the incident of the night before, I had some notion that I'd find a suitable way of procedure in our household.

Mr. Speed appeared in the street without his overcoat but with one hand holding the turned-up lapels and collar of his gray suit coat. He followed his cane, stomping like an enraged blind man with his head bowed against the March wind. I squeezed from between my chair and the table and stood right at the great plate glass window, looking out. From the corner of my eye I saw that Brother was intent upon his play. Presently, in the wind, Mr. Speed's derby went back on his head, and his hand grabbed at it, pulled it back in place, then returned to hold his lapels. I took a sharp breath, and Brother looked up. And just as he looked out the window, Mr. Speed's derby did blow off and across the sidewalk, over the lawn. Mr. Speed turned, holding his lapels with his tremendous hand, shouting oaths that I could hear ever so faintly, and tried to stumble after his hat.

Then I realized that my brother was gone from the room; and he was outside the window with Mr. Speed chasing Mr. Speed's hat in the wind.

I sat back in my chair, breathless; one elbow went down on the chessboard disordering the black and white pawns and kings and castles. And through the window I watched Brother handing Mr. Speed his derby. I saw his apparent indifference to the drunk man's oaths and curses. I saw him coming back to the house while the old man yet stood railing at him. I pushed the table aside and ran to the front door lest Brother be locked outside. He met me in the hall smiling blandly.

I said, "That's Mr. Speed."

He sat down on the bottom step of the stairway, leaning backward and looking at me inquisitively.

"He's drunk, Brother," I said. "Always."

My brother looked frankly into the eyes of this half-grown sister of his but said nothing for a while.

I pushed myself up on the console table and sat swinging my legs and looking seriously about the walls of the cavernous hallway at the expanse of oak paneling, at the inset canvas of the sixteenth-century Frenchman making love to his lady, at the hat rack, and at the grandfather's clock in the darkest corner. I waited for Brother to speak.

"You don't like people who get drunk?" he said.

I saw that he was taking the whole thing as a thrust at his own behavior.

"I just think Mr. Speed is very ugly, Brother."

From the detached expression of his eyes I knew that he was not convinced.

"I wouldn't mind him less if he were sober," I said. "Mr. Speed's like—a loose horse."

This analogy convinced him. He knew then what I meant.

"You mustn't waste your time being afraid of such things," he said in great earnestness. "In two or three years there'll be things that you'll have to be afraid of. Things you really can't avoid."

"What did he say to you?" I asked.

"He cussed and threatened to hit me with that stick."

"For no reason?"

"Old Mr. Speed's burned out his reason with whiskey."

"Tell me about him." I was almost imploring him.

"Everybody knows about him. He just wanders around town, drunk. Sometimes downtown they take him off in the Black Maria."

I pictured him on the main streets that I knew downtown and in the big department stores. I could see him in that formal neighborhood where my grandmother used to live. In the neighborhood of Miss Hood and Miss Herron's school. Around the little houses out where my father's secretary lived. Even in nigger town.

"You'll get used to him, for all his ugliness," Brother said. Then we sat there till my father came in, talking almost gaily about things that were particularly ugly in Mr. Speed's clothes and face and in his way of walking.

Since the day that I watched myself say "away" in the mirror, I had spent painful hours trying to know once more that experience which I now regarded as something like mystical. But the stringent course that I, motherless and lonely in our big house, had brought myself to follow while only thirteen had given me certain mature habits of thought. Idle and unrestrained daydreaming I eliminated almost entirely from my experience, though I delighted myself with fantasies that I quite consciously worked out and which, when concluded, I usually considered carefully, trying to fix them with some sort of childish symbolism.

Even idleness in my nightly dreams disturbed me. And sometimes as I tossed half awake in my big bed I would try to piece together my dreams into at least a form of logic. Sometimes I would complete an unfinished dream and wouldn't know in the morning what part I had dreamed and what part pieced out. I would often smile over the ends that I had plotted in half-wakeful moments but found pride in dreams that were complete in themselves and easy to fix with allegory, which I called "meaning." I found that a dream could start for no discoverable reason, with the sight of a printed page on which the first line was, "Once upon a time"; and soon could have me a character in a strange story. Once upon a time there was a little girl whose hands began to get very large. Grown men came for miles around to look at the giant hands and to shake them, but the little girl was ashamed of them and hid them under her skirt. It seemed that the little girl lived in the stable behind my grandmother's old house, and I watched her from the top of the loft ladder. Whenever there was the sound of footsteps, she trembled and wept; so I would beat on the floor above her and laugh uproariously at her fear. But presently I was the little girl listening to the noise. At first I trembled and called out for my father, but then I recollected that it was I who had made the noises and I felt that I had made a very consider-able discovery for myself.

I awoke one Saturday morning in early March at the sound of my father's voice in the downstairs hall. He was talking to the servants, ordering the carriage I think. I believe that I awoke at the sound of the carriage horses' names. I went to my door and called "Goodbye" to him. He was twisting his mustache before the hall mirror, and he looked up the stairway at me and smiled. He was always abashed to be caught before a looking glass, and he called out self-consciously and affection-ately that he would be home at noon.

I closed my door and went to the little dressing table that he had had put in my room on my birthday. The card with his handwriting on it was still stuck in the corner of the mirror: "For my young lady daughter." I was so thoroughly aware of the gentleness in his nature this morning that any childish timidity before him would, I thought, seem an injustice, and I determined that I should sit with him and my uncles in the parlor that afternoon and perhaps tell them all of my fear of the habitually drunken Mr. Speed and with them watch him pass before the parlor window. That morning I sat before the mirror of my dressing table and put up my hair in a knot on the back of my head for the first time.

Before Father came home at noon, however, I had taken my hair down, and I was not now certain that he would be unoffended by my mention of the neighborhood drunkard. But I was resolute in my purpose, and when my two uncles came after lunch, and the three men shut themselves up in the parlor for the afternoon, I took my seat across the hall in the little library, or den, as my mother had called it, and spent the first of the afternoon skimming over the familiar pages of *Tales of ol' Virginny*, by Thomas Nelson Page.

My father had seemed tired at lunch. He talked very little and drank only half his cup of coffee. He asked Brother matter-of-fact questions about his plans for college in the fall and told me once to try cutting my meat instead of pulling it to pieces. And as I sat in the library afterward, I wondered if he had been thinking of my mother. Indeed, I wondered whether or not he ever thought of her. He never mentioned her to us; and in a year I had forgotten exactly how he treated her when she had been alive.

It was not only the fate of my brother's soul that I had given thought to since my mother's death. Father had always had his toddy on Saturday afternoon with his two bachelor brothers. But there was more than one round of toddies served in the parlor on Saturday now. Throughout the early part of this afternoon I could hear the tinkle of the bell in the kitchen, and presently the houseboy would appear at the door of the parlor with a tray of ice-filled glasses.

As he entered the parlor each time, I would catch a glimpse over my book of the three men. One was usually standing, whichever one was leading the conversation. Once they were laughing heartily; and as the Negro boy came out with the tray of empty glasses, there was a smile on his face.

As their voices grew louder and merrier, my courage slackened. It was then I first put into words the thought that in my brother and father I saw something of Mr. Speed. And I knew that it was more than a taste for whiskey they had in common.

At four o'clock I heard Brother's voice mixed with those of the Benton boys outside the front door. They came into the hall, and their voices were high and excited. First one, then another would demand to be heard with: "No, listen now; let me tell you what." In a moment I heard Brother on the stairs. Then two of the Benton brothers appeared in the doorway of the library. Even the youngest, who was not a year older than I and whose name was Henry, wore long pants, and each carried a cap in hand and a linen duster over his arm. I stood up and smiled at them, and with my right forefinger I pushed the black locks which hung loosely about my shoulders behind my ears.

"We're going motoring in the Carltons' machine," Henry said.

I stammered my surprise and asked if Brother were going to ride in it. One of them said that he was upstairs getting his hunting cap, since he had no motoring cap. The older brother, Gary Benton, went back into the hall. I walked toward Henry, who was standing in the doorway.

"But does Father know you're going?" I asked.

As I tried to go through the doorway, Henry stretched his arm across it and looked at me with a critical frown on his face.

"Why don't you put up your hair?" he said.

I looked at him seriously, and I felt the heat of the blush that came over my face. I felt it on the back of my neck. I stooped with what I thought considerable grace and slid under his arm and passed into the hall. There were the other two Benton boys listening to the voices of my uncles and my father through the parlor door. I stepped between them and threw open the door. Just as I did so, Henry Benton commanded, "Elizabeth, don't do that!" And I, swinging the door open, turned and smiled at him.

I stood for a moment looking blandly at my father and my uncles. I was considering what had made me burst in upon them in this manner. It was not merely that I had perceived the opportunity of creating this little disturbance and slipping in under its noise, though I was not unaware of the advantage. I was frightened by the boys' impending adventure in the horseless carriage but surely not so much as I normally should have been at breaking into the parlor at this forbidden hour. The immediate cause could only be the attention which Henry Benton had shown me. His insinuation had been that I remained too much a little girl, and I had shown him that at any rate I was a bold, or at least a naughty, little girl.

My father was on his feet. He put his glass on the mantelpiece.
And it seemed to me that from the three men came in rapid succession all possible arrangements of the words, Boys-come-in.
Come-in-boys. Well-boys-come-in. Come-on-in. Boys-come-
in-the-parlor. The boys went in, rather showing off their breeding and poise, I thought. The three men moved and talked
clumsily before them, as the three Benton brothers went each
to each of the men carefully distinguishing between my uncles'
titles: doctor and colonel. I thought how awkward all of the
members of my own family appeared on occasions that called
for grace. Brother strode into the room with his hunting cap
sideways on his head, and he announced their plans, which the
tactful Bentons, uncertain of our family's prejudices regarding
machines, had not mentioned. Father and my uncles had a
great deal to say about who was going-to-do-the-driving, and
Henry Benton without giving an answer gave a polite invitation to the men to join them. To my chagrin, both my uncles
accepted with-the-greatest-of-pleasure what really had not been
an invitation at all. And they persisted in accepting it even after
Brother in his rudeness raised the question of room in the five-
passenger vehicle.

Father said, "Sure. The more, the merrier." But he declined
to go himself and declined for me Henry's invitation.

The plan was, then, as finally outlined by the oldest of the
Benton brothers, that the boys should proceed to the Carltons'
and that Brother should return with the driver to take our
uncles out to the Carltons' house which was one of the new
residences across from Centennial Park, where the excursions
in the machine were to be made.

The four slender youths took their leave from the heavy men
with the gold watch chains across their stomachs, and I had
to shake hands with each of the Benton brothers. To each I
expressed my regret that Father would not let me ride with
them, emulating their poise with all my art. Henry Benton was
the last, and he smiled as though he knew what I was up to. In
answer to his smile I said, "Games are *so* much fun."

I stood by the window watching the four boys in the street
until they were out of sight. My father and his brothers had
taken their seats in silence, and I was aware of just how unwelcome I was in the room. Finally, my uncle, who had been a

colonel in the Spanish War and who wore bushy blond side-burns, whistled under his breath and said, "Well, there's no doubt about it, no doubt about it."

He winked at my father, and my father looked at me and then at my uncle. Then quickly in a ridiculously overserious tone he asked, "What, sir? No doubt about what, sir?"

"Why, there's no doubt that this daughter of yours was flirting with the youngest of the Messrs. Benton."

My father looked at me and twisted his mustache and said with the same pomp that he didn't know what he'd do with me if I started that sort of thing. My two uncles threw back their heads, each giving a short laugh. My uncle the doctor took off his pince-nez and shook them at me and spoke in the same mock-serious tone of his brothers: "Young lady, if you spend your time in such pursuits you'll only bring upon yourself and upon the young men about Nashville the greatest unhappiness. I, as a bachelor, must plead the cause of the young Bentons!"

I turned to my father in indignation that approached rage.

"Father," I shouted, "there's Mr. Speed out there!"

Father sprang from his chair and quickly stepped up beside me at the window. Then, seeing the old man staggering harmlessly along the sidewalk, he said in, I thought, affected easiness: "Yes. Yes, dear."

"He's drunk," I said. My lips quivered, and I think I must have blushed at this first mention of the unmentionable to my father.

"Poor Old Speed," he said. I looked at my uncles, and they were shaking their heads, echoing my father's tone.

"What ever did happen to Speed's old-maid sister?" my uncle the doctor said.

"She's still with him," Father said.

Mr. Speed appeared soberer today than I had ever seen him. He carried no overcoat to drag on the ground, and his stagger was barely noticeable. The movement of his lips and an occasional gesture were the only evidence of intoxication. I was enraged by the irony that his good behavior on this of all days presented. Had I been a little younger I might have suspected conspiracy on the part of all men against me, but I was old enough to suspect no person's being even interested enough in me to plot against my understanding, unless it be some vague personification of life itself.

The course which I took, I thought afterward, was the proper one. I do not think that it was because I was then really conscious that when one is determined to follow some course rigidly and is blockaded one must fire furiously, if blindly, into the blockade, but rather because I was frightened and in my fear forgot all logic of attack. At any rate, I fired furiously at the three immutable creatures.

"I'm afraid of him," I broke out tearfully. I shouted at them, "He's always drunk! He's always going by our house drunk!"

My father put his arms about me, but I continued talking as I wept on his shirt front. I heard the barking sound of the machine horn out in front, and I felt my father move one hand from my back to motion my uncles to go. And as they shut the parlor door after them, I felt that I had let them escape me.

I heard the sound of the motor fading out up Church Street, and Father led me to the settee. We sat there together for a long while, and neither of us spoke until my tears had dried.

I was eager to tell him just exactly how fearful I was of Mr. Speed's coming into our house. But he only allowed me to tell him that I *was* afraid; for when I had barely suggested that much, he said that I had no business watching Mr. Speed, that I must shut my eyes to some things. "After all," he said, nonsensically I thought, "you're a young lady now." And in several curiously twisted sentences he told me that I mustn't seek things to fear in this world. He said that it was most unlikely, besides, that Speed would ever have business at our house. He punched at his left side several times, gave a prolonged belch, settled a pillow behind his head, and soon was sprawled beside me on the settee, snoring.

But Mr. Speed did come to our house, and it was in less than two months after this dreary twilight. And he came as I had feared he might come, in his most extreme state of drunkenness and at a time when I was alone in the house with the maid Lucy. But I had done everything that a little girl, now fourteen, could do in preparation for such an eventuality. And the sort of preparation that I had been able to make, the clearance of all restraints and inhibitions regarding Mr. Speed in my own mind and in my relationship with my world, had necessarily, I think, given me a maturer view of my own limited experiences; though, too, my very age must be held to account for a natural step toward maturity.

In the two months following the day that I first faced Mr. Speed's existence with my father, I came to look at every phase of our household life with a more direct and more discerning eye. As I wandered about that shadowy and somehow brutally elegant house, sometimes now with a knot of hair on the back of my head, events and customs there that had repelled or frightened me I gave the closest scrutiny. In the daytime I ventured into such forbidden spots as the servants' and the men's bathrooms. The filth of the former became a matter of interest in the study of the servants' natures, instead of the object of ineffable disgust. The other became a fascinating place of wet shaving brushes and leather straps and red rubber bags.

There was an anonymous little Negro boy that I had seen many mornings hurrying away from our back door with a pail. I discovered that he was toting buttermilk from our icebox with the permission of our cook. And I sprang at him from behind a corner of the house one morning and scared him so that he spilled the buttermilk and never returned for more.

Another morning I heard the cook threatening to slash the houseboy with her butcher knife, and I made myself burst in upon them; and before Lucy and the houseboy I told her that if she didn't leave our house that day, I'd call my father and, hardly knowing what I was saying, I added, "And the police." She was gone, and Lucy had got a new cook before dinnertime. In this way, from day to day, I began to take my place as mistress in our motherless household.

I could no longer be frightened by my brother with a mention of runaway horses. And instead of terrorized I felt only depressed by his long and curious arguments with my father. I was depressed by the number of the subjects to and from which they oscillated. The world as a whole still seemed unconscionably larger than anything I could comprehend. But I had learned not to concern myself with so general and so unreal a problem until I had cleared up more particular and real ones.

It was during these two months that I noticed the difference between the manner in which my father spoke before my uncles of Mr. Speed when he passed and that in which he spoke of him before my brother. To my brother it was the condemning, "There goes Old Speed, again." But to my uncles it was, "There goes Old Speed," with the sympathetic addition, "the rascal." Though my father and his brothers obviously found me more agreeable because a pleasant spirit had replaced my old timidity, they yet considered me a child; and my father little dreamed that I discerned such traits in his character, or that I understood, if I even listened to, their anecdotes and their long funny stories, and it was an interest in the peculiar choice of subject and in the way that the men told their stories.

When Mr. Speed came, I was accustomed to thinking that there was something in my brother's and in my father's natures that was fully in sympathy with the very brutality of his drunkenness. And I knew that they would not consider my hatred for him and for that part of him which I saw in them. For that alone I was glad that it was on a Thursday afternoon, when I was in the house alone with Lucy, that one of the heavy sort of rains that come toward the end of May drove Mr. Speed onto our porch for shelter.

Otherwise I wished for nothing more than the sound of my father's strong voice when I stood trembling before the parlor window and watched Mr. Speed stumbling across our lawn in the flaying rain. I only knew to keep at the window and make sure that he was actually coming into our house. I believe that he was drunker than I had ever before seen him, and his usual ire seemed to be doubled by the raging weather.

Despite the aid of his cane, Mr. Speed fell to his knees once in the muddy sod. He remained kneeling there for a time with his face cast in resignation. Then once more he struggled to his feet in the rain. Though I was ever conscious that I was entering into young womanhood at that age, I can only think of myself as a child at that moment; for it was the helpless fear of a child that I felt as I watched Mr. Speed approaching our door. Perhaps it was the last time I ever experienced the inconsolable desperation of childhood.

Next, I could hear his cane beating on the boarding of the little porch before our door. I knew that he must be walking up and down in that little shelter. Then I heard Lucy's exasperated voice as she came down the steps. I knew immediately, what she confirmed afterward, that she thought it Brother, eager to get into the house, beating on the door.

I, aghast, opened the parlor door just as she pulled open the great front door. Her black skin ashened as she beheld Mr. Speed—his face crimson, his eyes bleary, and his gray clothes dripping water. He shuffled through the doorway and threw his stick on the hall floor. Between his oaths and profanities he shouted over and over in his broken, old man's voice, "Nigger, nigger." I could understand little of his rapid and slurred speech, but I knew his rage went round and round a man in the rain and the shelter of a neighbor's house.

Lucy fled up the long flight of steps and was on her knees at the head of the stair, in the dark upstairs hall, begging me to come up to her. I only stared, as though paralyzed and dumb, at him and then up the steps at her. The front door was still open; the hall was half in light; and I could hear the rain on the roof of the porch and the wind blowing the trees which were in full green foliage.

At last I moved. I acted. I slid along the wall past the hat rack and the console table, my eyes on the drunken old man who was swearing up the steps at Lucy. I reached for the telephone; and when I had rung for central, I called for the police station. I knew what they did with Mr. Speed downtown, and I knew with what I had threatened the cook. There was a part of me that was crouching on the top step with Lucy, vaguely longing to hide my face from this in my own mother's bosom. But there was another part which was making me deal with Mr. Speed, however wrongly, myself. Innocently I asked the voice to send "the Black Maria" to our house number on Church Street.

Mr. Speed had heard me make the call. He was still and silent for just one moment. Then he broke into tears, and he seemed to be chanting his words. He repeated the word "child" so many times that I felt I had acted wrongly, with courage but without wisdom. I saw myself as a little beast adding to the injury that what was bestial in man had already done him. He picked up his cane and didn't seem to be talking either to Lucy or to me, but to the cane. He started out the doorway, and I heard Lucy come running down the stairs. She fairly glided around the newel post and past me to the telephone. She wasn't certain that I had made the call. She asked if I had called my father. I simply told her that I had not.

As she rang the telephone, I watched Mr. Speed cross the porch. He turned to us at the edge of the porch and shouted one more oath. But his foot touched the wet porch step, and he slid and fell unconscious on the steps.

He lay there with the rain beating upon him and with Lucy and myself watching him, motionless from our place by the telephone. I was frightened by the thought of the cruelty which I found I was capable of, a cruelty which seemed inextricably mixed with what I had called courage. I looked at him lying out there in the rain and despised and pitied him at the same time, and I was afraid to go minister to the helpless old Mr. Speed.

Lucy had her arms about me and kept them there until two gray horses pulling their black coach had galloped up in front of the house and two policemen had carried the limp body through the rain to the dreadful vehicle.

Just as the policemen closed the doors in the back of the coach, my father rode up in a closed cab. He jumped out and stood in the rain for several minutes arguing with the policemen. Lucy and I went to the door and waited for him to come in. When he came, he looked at neither of us. He walked past us saying only, "I regret that the bluecoats were called." And he went into the parlor and closed the door.

I never discussed the events of that day with my father, and I never saw Mr. Speed again. But, despite the surge of pity I felt for the old man on our porch that afternoon, my hatred and fear of what he had stood for in my eyes has never left me. And since the day that I watched myself say "away" in the mirror, not a week has passed but that he has been brought to my mind by one thing or another. It was only the other night that I dreamed I was a little girl on Church Street again and that there was a drunk horse in our yard.

Cookie

TWO NIGHTS a week, he *had* to be home for supper, and some weeks, when his conscience was especially uneasy, he turned up three or four times. Tonight, she had a dish of string beans, cooked with cured side meat, on the table when he came in. The smoky odor of the fat struck him when he opened the front door, but he couldn't believe it until he went back to the dining room and saw the dish on the table. "Good God!" he said to himself. "That's fine. Where did she get fresh beans at this time of year?"

Presently his wife, who was, like himself, past fifty, came through the swinging door from the pantry.

"Ah," she said, "my husband is right on time tonight." She came to him and undid the buttons of his overcoat, as she used to undo the children's. It was his lightweight "fall coat," which she had brought down from the attic only two weeks before. She took it and folded it over the back of a dining-room chair, as she would have a visitor's. She knew that he would be leaving right after coffee.

He leaned over the dish and smelled it, and then sat down at the place that was set for him. It was directly across the round dining-room table from her place. She stepped to the pantry door and called: "Cookie, we're ready when you are." She pulled out her chair and sat down.

"Shall we have the blessing tonight?" she said, with some small hope in her smile.

"Oh, let's not." He smiled back. It was a cajoling smile.

"All right, then." She smoothed the tablecloth with her fingers.

He served himself from the dish of beans and selected a piece of the side meat. He bent his head over and got one whiff of the steaming dish. "You're too good to me," he said evenly. He pushed the dish across the table to within her reach.

"Nothing's too good for one's husband."

"You're much too good to me," he said, now lowering his eyes to his plate.

Cookie came through the swinging door with a vegetable

dish in each hand. She was a brown, buxom Negro woman, perhaps a few years older than her mistress. She set the dishes on the table near her mistress's plate.

"Good evenin', Cookie," he said to her as she started back to the kitchen.

"Yessuh," she said, and went on through the doorway.

His wife was serving herself from a dish. "Here are some of your baked potatoes," she said.

"Ah!" he said. "You *are* too good . . ." This time he left the sentence unfinished.

She passed him the dish. "And here are simply some cold beets."

"Fine . . . fine . . . fine."

"Do you think we would like a little more light?" she said. She pushed herself back from the table.

"We might. We might."

She went to the row of switches by the doorway that led to the hall. She pushed the second switch, and the light overhead was increased. She pushed the third, and the wall lights by the sideboard came on. With each increase of light in the room her husband said, "Ah . . . fine . . . ah . . . fine." It was a small dining room—at least, it seemed so in the bright light, for the house was old and high-ceilinged. The woodwork was a natural pine, with heavy door facings and a narrow chair rail. The paper above the chair rail was a pale yellow, and no pictures were on the walls. There were two silver candlesticks and a punch bowl on the sideboard. Through the glass doors of the press the cut glassware showed. The large light fixture, a frosted glass bowl, hung from a heavy "antiqued" chain low over the table, and the bright light brought out a spot here and there on the cloth.

She was taking her seat again when Cookie pushed through the door with the meat and the bread.

"What's this? A roast? You're outdoing yourself tonight, Cookie," he said.

"Y'all want all iss light?" Cookie said, blinking, and she set the meat down before him.

"Well, it's—well, it's cold-water cornbread!" He took two pieces of bread from the plate that Cookie held to him.

"Y'all want all iss light?" Cookie said to her mistress, who was selecting a small piece of bread and smiling ingenuously at her husband.

"Yes, Cookie," she said, "I think so. I thought I'd turn 'em up some."

"Wull, I could a done it, Mizz."

"It's all right, Cookie. I didn't want the bread burned."

"Wull, it ain't Judgment Day, Mizz. Y'all could a waited. I'd a done it, stead of you havin' to do it." She put the bread on the table and covered it with the napkin that she had held the plate with.

"It's all right, Cookie."

Cookie opened the door to go back to the kitchen. As she went through, she said, "Lawd a *mercy*!"

His wife pushed her plate across the table, and he put on it a slice of roast that he had carved—an outside piece, because it was more done. He cut several slices, until he came to one that seemed rare enough for himself. "Any news from the chillun?" he said.

"Yes," she said. "Postcards from all three."

"Only postcards?"

She began to taste her food, taking so little on her fork that it was hardly visible.

"Now, that's just rotten!" he said. He brought a frown to his face. "They ought to write you letters. They ought to write you at least once a week! I'm going to write the boys tomorrow and tell 'em."

"Now, please, honey! Please don't! They're well. They said so, and that's all I need to know. They're just busy. Young people don't have time for letters." She eased her knife and fork down on her plate. "They're young!"

"What's that got to do with it?" he said. "They ought always to have time for *you*." He went on eating and talking at the same time. "These beets are fine," he said. Then, after swallowing, "I won't have that! They ought to write their mother once a week. When I was in med school, you know how much I wrote Mama. Father would have beaten me, I believe, and taken me out, if I hadn't. I ought to take them out just once."

He stopped eating for a moment, and shaking his fork at her, he spoke even more earnestly: "And just one month I should forget to send *her* that check."

His wife sat, somewhat paled, making no pretense of eating. "Now, please, honey," she said. "She has two little children and a husband who is far from well. I had a letter from her last week, written while the children were taking a little nap. Remember that she has two little children to look after." Her lips trembled. "There's nothing for the boys to write. They say on every single card they miss being home."

He saw that her lips were quivering, and he began eating again. He frowned. Then he smiled suddenly and said, as if with relief, "I'll tell you. Yes. You ought to go up and see 'em. You haven't been to Nashville since they were *both* in med."

She wiped her mouth with her napkin and smiled. "No, there's no need in my going," she said. And she began to eat her dinner again.

Cookie came in with a small pan of hot bread, holding it with a kitchen towel. She uncovered the plate of bread on the table and stacked the hot bread on top of what was there. With her free hand, she reached in front of her mistress and felt the untouched piece of bread on her plate. "'S got cole on ya," she said. She picked it up in her brown hand and threw it on the cooking pan. She placed a piece of hot bread on her mistress's plate, saying, "Now, gwine butter't while 't's hot."

Her mistress pushed the bread plate across the table toward her husband. She said to him, "Cookie and I are going to get a box of food off to 'em next week, like we used to send 'em in military school. Aren't we, Cookie?"

"Fine . . . fine . . . fine," he said. He took a piece of the cornbread and began to butter it.

Cookie nodded her head toward him and said to her mistress, "*He* hear from 'em?" Then she took several steps around the table, picked up the bread plate, and returned it to its former place. She was tucking the napkin about its edges again.

"No, I have *not*!" He brought the frown to his face again. "They ought to write their mammy, oughtn't they, Cookie?"

"Sho-God ought. 'S a shame," Cookie said. She looked at her mistress. And her mistress put her knife and fork down again. Her lips began to quiver. She gazed tearfully at her husband.

He looked away and spoke out in a loud voice that seemed almost to echo in the high-ceilinged room: "What are you goin' to send 'em? What are you going to send them young'ons, Cookie?"

Cookie looked at him blankly and then at the butter plate, which was in the center of the table. "Whatever she say."

"Well, what do you say, Mother?"

She cleared her throat and ran her hand in a series of pats over her thick and slightly graying hair that went in soft waves back over her ears. "I had thought that we might get hold of two fat guinea hens," she said.

"Fine . . . fine."

"I thought we might get some smoked sausage, not too new and—"

"Ah . . . fine."

"And we might spare one of the fruitcakes we've got soaking."

"How does that suit you, Cookie?" he said.

Cookie was on her way toward the kitchen again. "Yessuh," she said.

He ate in silence for several minutes, took a second helping of string beans, and another piece of bread. She nibbled at a piece of bread. She put more salt and pepper on her meat and ate a few bites. And then she arranged her knife and fork on her plate. Finally, he put his knife and fork down on his empty plate and, with his mouth still full, said, "There's not more, surely?"

She smiled, nodding her head. "Pie."

"No! What kind!"

"I cooked it myself." She picked up a little glass call bell beside her plate and tinkled it. He sat chewing his last bite, and presently Cookie appeared in the doorway with two plates of yellow lemon pie topped with an inch of white meringue.

"This is where she can beat you, Cookie," he said as the cook set the piece of pie before him.

Cookie made a noise that was somewhat like "Psss." She looked at her mistress and gave her a gold-toothed smile. She started to leave with the dinner plates.

"Wait a minute, Cookie," he said. She stopped and looked at him, with her lower lip hanging open. He was taking big bites of the pie. "Cookie, I've been wantin' to ask you how your 'corporosity' is."

"M'whut, Boss-Man?"

"And, furthermore, I understand from what various people are saying around that you have ancestors." He winked at his wife. She dropped her eyes to her plate.

"Whut's he mean, Mizz?" Cookie asked, standing with the two dinner plates in hand.

"Just some of his foolishness, Cookie," she said, with her eyes still on her plate.

He thought to himself that his wife was too good to tease even Cookie. He said to himself, "She doesn't realize that they really eat it up."

"M' coffee's bilin'," Cookie said, and she went through the swinging door.

His wife looked up from her plate. "You know Cookie never has liked to joke. Now, please, honey, don't tease her. She's getting along in her years now. Her temper's quicker than it used to be."

He had finished his pie when Cookie brought in the coffee. She brought it on a tray—two cups and a kitchen pot. She set a cup at each place, filled them, and set the pot on the tablecloth.

"How's that church of yours comin', Cookie?" he said.

"It's makin' out, Boss-Man."

"Haven't you-all churched nobody lately?"

"No, suh, not us."

"How about Dr. Palmer's cook, Cookie? Is she a member in standing?"

"Sho. Mean 'at gal Hattie?" She looked at her mistress and smiled.

He looked at his wife, who he thought was shaking her head at Cookie. Then he looked at Cookie. "Yes," he said, almost absent-mindedly. "He brought her in from the country. That's it—Hattie! That's her name."

"Yessuh. She's from out on Pea Ridge."

"She's givin' 'im some trouble. Drinkin', ain't she, Cookie?"

"'Cep' *he* didn't get her from Pea Ridge."

"No, Cookie?"

"She put in a year for some ladies he know out near the sand banks, and—"

"She's a drinker, ain't she, Cookie?"

"Yessuh. I *reckon* she is." She tilted her head back and gave him her gold-toothed laugh, which ended in a sort of sneer this time. "She uz dancin' roun' outside chuch las' night an' say to me she want to teach me how to do dat stuff. I tell huh she's drunk, an' she say, 'Sho I is. I teach you how to hit de bottle, too!' "

He pushed his chair away from the table, still holding his coffee, and laughed aloud. He saw that his wife was looking threateningly at Cookie. "What else did she say, Cookie?" he pressed her.

"Oh, dat gal's a big talker. She's full of lies. De way she lies 'bout huh boss-man's terble. She lie 'bout anybody an' everybody in Thornton. She call names up an' down de street."

"What sort of lies?" He leaned forward, smiling, and winked at his wife.

"Them ladies from the sand banks—she say they's in an' out his place mos' any night. Doc Palmer's a bachlorman, sho, but Hattie say hit ain't jus' Doc Palmer! They comes there to meet the ladies—all sorts of menfolks, married or not. She say she see 'em *all* 'bout his place sooner later."

His wife had quit sipping her coffee and was staring at Cookie.

"Who, for instance, Cookie? Let us in on it," he said.

The cook turned to him and looked at him blankly. "You, Boss-Man."

His wife stood up at her place, her napkin in her hand. Her eyes filled with tears. "After all these years!" she said. "Cookie, you've forgotten your place for the first time, after all these years."

Cookie put her hands under her apron, looked at her feet a moment, and then looked up at him, her own eyes wet. Her words came almost like screams. "Hattie say she *seen* ya! But she's a liar, ain't she, Boss-Man?"

Her mistress sat down, put one elbow on the table, and brought her napkin up to cover her face. "I'm disappointed in you, Cookie. Go to the kitchen."

Cookie went through the swinging door without looking at her mistress.

In a moment, his wife looked up at him and said, "I'm sorry. I'd not thought she was capable of a thing like that."

"Why, it's all right—for what she said. Doctors will get talked about. Even Cookie knows the girl's a liar."

His wife seemed, he thought, not to have heard him. She was saying, "A servant of mine talking to my husband like that!"

"It's only old-nigger uppitiness," he reassured her.

"I shall speak to her tonight," she said. "I promise you."

"Oh, I suppose you'll think you have to fire her."

She looked at him, her features composed again. She ran her hand over her hair in a series of pats. "No, no," she said. "I can't fire Cookie. I'll speak to her tonight. It'll never happen again."

"Now I think of it, perhaps she ought to be sent on her way after talking like that."

"I'll look after the matter."

He poured himself a second cup of coffee and, as he drank it, he watched his wife closely. He frowned again and said, "Why, she might talk to *you* that way some day. That's all I thought."

She smiled at him. "There's no danger. I'll have a talk with her tonight."

She helped him on with his overcoat. He said, "Got to see some country people tonight. Might even have to drive over to Huntsboro." She was buttoning his coat. "There's a lot of red throat over there."

"I can't have her talking that way to my husband," she said aloud, yet to herself. "But I won't fire her," she told him. "She's too much one of us—too much one of the family, and I know she'll be full of remorse for speaking out of turn like that."

He looked directly into her eyes, and she smiled confidently. She told him she would leave the back light on, because lately the nights had been cloudy and dark. As he stopped in the hall to pick up his hat and his case, he heard Cookie come through the swinging door.

"Now, Cookie, I want to have a little talk with you," his wife said, and Cookie said, "Yes'm, Mizz."

He went out, closing the door softly behind him, and as he crossed the porch, he could still hear their voices inside—the righteousness and disillusion of Cookie's, the pride and discipline of his wife's. He passed down the flight of wooden steps and stepped from the brick walk onto the lawn. He hesitated a moment; he could still hear their voices indistinctly—their senseless voices. He began walking with light, sure steps over the grass—their ugly, old voices. In the driveway, his car, bright and new and luxurious, was waiting for him.

"I s it God knocking?"
"No, no. That isn't God. That isn't God."

"Then it's the hanging baskets. The wind is blowing the vine-baskets against the house."

"After the wind has died, you may go out on the porch and look at the wall of the house, at the places where the wire baskets have chipped more paint off the boarding."

"They are Grandmother's baskets."

Then his little humpbacked grandmother is found dead in her bed one morning, and he must play in his room upstairs for two days. Out his window he watches automobiles coming from far off. They turn on streets which wind for no reason through a field, wide streets with sidewalks but with few houses and no trees along their borders. Down his street there is only the house on the corner and the speckled stucco next door where the little girl comes and leans against one of the porch pillars.

Everywhere in the fields are white signs with blue and red lettering that hurts the eye.

During the second day the Negro cook Cleo comes up and plays parcheesi with him while downstairs the music and the preaching go on. From his window he watches the hearse drive away with the long line of cars following it. On the winding street through the fields the long line moves like a black snake. Cleo says, "She wuz lyin' 'ere in bed when we find 'er—just like she be asleep."

Cleo leads him down the stairs by his hand, and they watch the Negro men loading stacks of folding chairs on a truck.

After the funeral some big wicker baskets are left sitting about in the front hall and on the porch. Just at twilight one day everything outside the living room window looks yellowish. Then the rain comes like a burst of tears; and the wind blows the wicker baskets over, and the tin cans from inside them roll about the porch floor. The tin cans and the wicker stands and the swinging baskets make a clatter like a jazz band.

Even his mother goes to the window and looks out. And he says to her, "The wood will look pinkish in the spots where the paint is gone."

All the wicker baskets are at last stacked behind the garage and burned like old boxes. The tin cans serve in turn, as one after another rusts, for watering troughs to the white pointer which runs on a wire in the back yard. And the swinging baskets ("your poor grandmother's last efforts at gardening") are missing from the porch. After dinner on Sunday Cleo wraps them in newspaper and goes off toward the trolley with one under each arm.

The painters arrive that spring with ladders and spotted canvas, and paint his house a fresh white. Ever after he can see only sunken places on the white clapboard where the baskets knocked for years.

His father and the father of the little girl next door like to play "catch." They play on Sunday afternoons through every spring. Then his father wears a black sweater with yellow stripes that go around him like tiger stripes; and her father, whose hair is gray, wears a sweater that buttons down the front. Each of the men has a big five-fingered glove, and they sit on the porch the first spring-like Sunday and oil their gloves. Sometimes Joseph, the Negro who works next door, plays with them, and then the three men will yell such things as, "Out on first!"

Once the little girl's mother calls Joseph into the house, and Joseph throws his glove to the boy as he runs toward the kitchen. His father whistles through his fingers and shouts, "Replacement on third!" Joseph's glove smells sweatier than his father's. It has more stuffing and no fingers outside; and it's wet inside. But the boy soon forgets, for he has caught the first baseball ever thrown to him.

In a few weeks he is thinking, "I can catch about as well as either of them." And after his own yellow mitt comes and a ball and a bat with black taping, he plays catch with other boys during school recess. There he sometimes recalls Joseph and his smelly mitt and wonders what ever has become of the two, for the little girl's mother now has a Negro who doesn't like to play catch.

After two years of baseball he is certain that he can catch as well as the men, though he can't throw as hard as they might. He plays with them often.

A ball comes so straight and hard from the little girl's father that the boy throws off his glove and rubs his palm on his pants leg.

His father, without a word, speeds toward him and picks up the ball.

The boy did not have to take off his glove. He just feels disgraced because he cannot throw one back as hard.

His father hurls the ball at the neighbor, who sees it barely in time to shield his glasses with his forearm. But the ball strikes the man's elbow and falls to the ground. As he straightens his arm, he winces. But he makes a sudden lurch and sweeps the ball from the ground with his right hand. His upper lip shortens under his nose, showing his purplish gums. He squints and sends the ball back to the younger man.

The boy watches the ball as it flies. With a quick wave of his hand his father motions him to go. He feels his way backward toward his house, his eyes on the two men who have never before thrown much harder than he.

The ball bounces from his father's glove, but he catches it in the air and shoots it back.

The older man is smiling. His face is red and moist.

The ball goes straight back and forth.

They stand about sixty feet apart with the big round bed of zinnias and petunias between them.

Again the ball bounces from the younger man's glove. It falls on the grass. He stoops slowly to pick it up, his gaze on his neighbor. The sod is a fresh green and his body makes no shadow on it, for dark clouds have been gathering in the sky of the March afternoon. The father takes a slow, deliberate wind-up which seems so professional to the boy that his mouth falls open.

But the neighbor laughs aloud and sends a ball back that jolts the boy's father. The boy blushes.

The speed of the ball is slow for a few throws, then gathers speed, then slows, and suddenly speeds again.

The boy's back is to the white clapboard of his house. He is breathing heavily, his little chest rising and falling. Across the lawns he sees the little girl leaning against a pillar on her own porch. She is bouncing a red rubber ball, and he thinks, "Why, the dumb thing doesn't see it at all." He is sweating as hard as the men when the rain begins to fall; but he feels only an occasional drop, for he is under the eaves of the house. As the rain comes harder and the two men pay no heed, he sees the little girl give closer attention to the game of catch. He smiles in his scorn for her as she steps to the edge of the porch and stands in the afternoon light which is yellow now.

The rain streams now like a waterfall.

It pours off the eaves of the house as from a pitcher and runs about his feet.

Either man can hardly hold the ball. It will slip from his fingers, and he will pick it up and hurl it toward the other. The striped sweater and the buttoned sweater both are heavy and are dripping water.

The older man takes off his fogged glasses and puts them in the pocket of his sweater, and then he throws the ball straight again.

The boy's father shoots it back quickly, with an oath.

His neighbor stops the ball high above his head and laughs. He dries the ball on the underside of his sweater before he throws it this time.

Now the little girl has begun to cry. She lets her red rubber ball go, and it rolls off the porch and into the rain.

The boy's father slips and falls on the grass when he stops the baseball in his wet glove, but he jumps up, dries his hand and the ball, and throws the ball again. It smacks the wet leather of the older man's glove, and he stands shaking a stinging hand, and he has begun to cough now. As he draws back his arm to throw, the little girl begins bouncing herself up and down on the porch and calling to him. And the baseball crashes through his neighbor's garage window.

The two men stand in the rain, each with his gaze fixed on the blurred figure of the other. Then the boy's father turns his back and starts slowly through the rain toward his own house. The little girl runs to meet her father, but he pushes her and looks back once more toward the little boy and his father.

The boy and the little girl walk on opposite sides of the street

from that time, but, anyway, he is now too old for girls. There
are little boys who live in new houses which are now scattered
along the winding streets and along his own block, and he is
learning to fight with his fists. One day he tears the scab off a
sore on his deskmate's wrist. After school they fight behind a
white and red and blue For Sale sign in the lot where the Catholic church is going to be built. During his bath after the fight
he finds that the deskmate has given him a bruise on his thigh,
and the bruise is still there the next Friday when the deskmate's
sore has gotten a new scab; so he, all of a sudden, tears off the
second scab with his fingernail. This time the deskmate goes to
the teacher and shows her his sore. The teacher changes their
seats. And the last he remembers of the matter is his former
deskmate's writing on the blackboard with a white bandage
on his wrist.

The new Catholic church is hardly finished in August when
the new school building is started in the next block. The
church is of yellow brick with a great round window above
the main doorway. And for the new school the workmen are
digging in the ground all through August. The lot they work
in has always been covered with waist-high yellow grass, and
every day the boy looks at the grass which the workmen have
trampled down until it lies flat like the hair on a boy's head.
He has never played in that lot with its high grass as he once
used to do in the church lot, and has felt that it looked like
"the central plains of Africa." But the workmen dig deep, and
now the heaps of red dirt look like the "forbidding Caucasian
mountains."

By Christmas the workmen have only laid the concrete in the
long, narrow basement and put up a few concrete shafts, and
the thing stands like that until spring. Finally he gets used to
the lot looking that way.

Some of the children, especially the new children, like to
climb down into the long basement, and they build a snow
man there during the last snow in March. But a feeling that the
lot isn't completely changed and yet isn't as it has been keeps
the boy away. Things have changed in the suburb; repeatedly
he has told the new children how things once were, he is that

conscious of it; but something forever keeps him from trying to observe too closely just how the new buildings go up.

One day the little girl's father is dead. The boy's own mother and father talk for a long while in their bedroom with the door closed. Afterward his father goes next door, and still later the Negro man comes and asks his mother to come. The boy sits at the window of his little room upstairs all afternoon and watches the other neighbors come and go across the lawns.

Two young neighbor women stand on a lawn across the street and talk, gesticulating; and one keeps shrugging her shoulders. The little girl appears outside the back door of her house with a pair of scissors which glisten in the sunlight. Her dress is white and it's so plain and long that her legs look short and her body very long. She goes to the round zinnia bed and looks ponderously at the flowers.

The window is up, and the boy sits on the sill, his head leaning against the screen. The girl bobs up and down among dull-colored flowers, very soon holding an armful of zinnias.

The boy begins to whistle a doleful cowboy tune.

She looks up from the center of the zinnia bed. He stops short. She scans the windows of the house, but she cannot make out his figure through the black wire screen. She stoops again, and he whistles one high note. She peers suddenly up at his window, opens her mouth and, sobbing, scampers on her short legs into her house.

And he stays at the window, looking out over the tile and shingled rooftops of the new houses and at the yellow tower of the new Catholic church.

Soon after school starts that fall the house next door is sold, and the little girl and her mother are moved into his own mother's guest room, the room which was once his grandmother's.

"I'll miss having a guest room," his mother says, "but it's not permanent."

One afternoon people come in automobiles and on foot from the neighborhood, and the furniture is moved out of the stucco house into the yard and sold. The boy sits on the edge of the porch and thinks, This is a sight I won't forget—beds and tables and easy chairs on the lawn, especially with men and women dropping down into the chairs and then getting up and looking at them with their heads cocked to one side.

What didn't sell is brought into his house, and the sitting room seems a different place with the new green chair and footstool which doesn't match the set.

The little girl is a grade ahead of him and so goes to the new school which is called "Junior High." She has to go to school earlier than he, and he is grateful for this. For she is now an inch taller than himself, and it makes him uncomfortable to walk with her.

One Saturday at noon, as he comes in from baseball, she meets him at the front door.

"Something's happened," she says.

He is putting his mitt and ball into the closet under the stairs. He looks at her and feels that she is somehow too tall to be wearing the plaid knee socks.

"Your daddy's lost his job," she says.

The boy answers resentfully that his father will get another as quickly as he has lost this one, and he goes upstairs. But as he passes his father's room he sees him stretched across the bed and sees the two women seated in rocking chairs, looking at one another. He tiptoes back downstairs and goes into the sitting room where the little girl is reading a magazine. He sits down and looks at her—lounging in the green chair with her round, bare knees over the green stool. She puts the magazine aside.

"Mama's going to work," she says. "And I guess I will, some way."

The changes that will come flood his imagination. The past seems absolutely static in the light of what he feels is to come.

"So will I," he says.

Soon he is able to get a paper route, and now his mother rouses him at three every morning and gives him coffee before he goes out. Through the winter he wears a pair of his father's hunting boots with several pairs of socks to make them fit. One morning his mother runs barefooted through the snow on the lawn, shining the flashlight that he has forgotten. She calls to him:

"Your light! Your light! You forgot your light!"

The sight of her there in the dark and cold, barefooted and in her kimono, is so literally dreadful to him that he turns and runs from the sight. And he can hear her calling, "Your light! Your light! Your light!" until he is almost to the trolley line where he picks up his papers.

The boy's imagination is soon conjuring pictures of the two families on the fourth floor of a downtown tenement house. Several families on his block have had to move from their houses during this fall, and other houses on his route have been found empty on collection day. But his mother will say to him over his cup of coffee, "The house is mine. I'll work my fingers to the bone to keep it." She finally has to give up Cleo, the cook; and they only feed the Negro man who has worked for the little girl's mother, until he can pick up another job.

The little girl's mother has started to business school. She and his father leave in the automobile each morning. He can see them pass from the schoolhouse window and realizes that the automobile is getting to be an old number. When he comes home in the afternoons, his mother will sometimes be washing or ironing the clothes in the kitchen. It's when he comes in one day and sees her on her knees waxing the dining room floor that he first observes how narrow her hips have got; and he turns from her and goes up the stair, two steps at a time, to his room. He looks at the school pennants about the walls, and his tears blur the scene. He looks out his window over the rooftops of the suburb and hears the boys yelling down behind the new school. And he takes off his leather jacket and slips his black football jersey on over his head.

But it seems that even his father's loss of his job hasn't been as simple and as quick as he had supposed. His father's whole company is going out of business, and there are articles about it in the newspaper every few days, his father's testimony in the courtroom being quoted once. During the weeks that his father is at home, before he has found the new job "on commission," he will sometimes walk up and down the front porch with his hat and coat on; and the boy's mother will look out the window at him and say to her son or to the little girl, "Through the whole litigation his innocence, honesty, and integrity were not once questioned."

By spring the little girl's mother has an office job at the same place his father sells from. They have not renewed the automobile license this year, and every morning the two breadwinners walk three blocks, by the little hedges and young Lombardy poplars, to the trolley.

One Saturday morning the boy comes back from his paper route late and passes the pair on the sidewalk. The little girl's mother says something to his father, who calls out to him, "Hold yourself up straight!" and calls him, "Longlegs." So he throws his shoulders back and begins to run. He hears them laughing until he turns the corner, and then he feels shaken up inside and hot about the forehead.

His mother is at her sewing machine by her bedroom window. He comes and stands beside her and with a half smile on his face says, "I'm catching lockjaw, I guess. I feel stiff in my jaw, under here, and everybody says that's the first symptom." His mother slips two fingers down his shirt collar, feeling the nape of his neck.

"Why, you're cooked with fever," she says. And she hasn't got him into bed in his little room before he begins to cough from his chest. It had poured rain through the first half of his route that morning; and she had tried to persuade him to wear his "rain things." "You've caught your death of cold in that rain," she says.

By the next afternoon he is considered "a very sick boy." His temperature is 103½. The doctor comes and says that it may turn into pneumonia.

"Now, if this does take a turn for the worst, it will be best to have him in a hospital."

"No, I want him at home."

"*They* can take better care of him."

"I think not, Doctor."

"You'll need a nurse."

"I must take care of him, Doctor."

The voices sound like echoes, and the human figures seem far away. Later he can hear the murmur of voices in his mother's room. His father and the little girl's mother are arguing with her, and they sound as though they may be away in some valley.

The next day, Monday, his mother tiptoes about his room, and the doctor comes twice. He can hear the doctor's voice more distinctly in the front hall downstairs than when he is by his bed talking to him.

Sometimes the little girl will sit in the room with him and read her magazine. He lies there during the afternoon with flannel and plasters about him, content to look at the walls and think of the other wallpapers that he remembers there. One can hardly see the wallpaper, for it is decorated with pennants and calendars.

In the middle of the night he wakes and sees that the light is wrapped in a piece of blue tissue paper. His mother says, "You've been out of your head for five hours."

"How sick am I, Mother?"

"You haven't pneumonia."

The doctor comes in a while and tells him he'll begin to get better now.

His father comes too and pats him on the back of his warm, limp hand, but says nothing. And when he leaves the room, the boy remembers the dreams of his delirium: His father and the mother of the little girl lay dead on the streetcar tracks. Cleo, the cook, was back in the kitchen, and his mother was telling her, "You can't really call the accident a tragedy." And he and his mother broke into gales of laughter.

The next fall the boy himself goes to Junior High. But the little girl dresses and acts so much older than he does now that he doesn't mind walking with her. She has gotten very fat, and he teases her about that and about the boys that talk to her at recess. Occasionally she will lend him money, but it is only to keep him from teasing her about the boys during dinner at night. She is so fat and so polite in public now that she seems a different person from "the little girl," as different as his mother is from her former self, as different as the corner on the trolley line is with the new drugstore on it.

He works in the drugstore after school. He serves sodas to the high-schoolers in automobiles and wears a white apron and a white fatigue cap on the side of his head. One afternoon he sees, through the drugstore window, a tall, thin woman approaching the store. It is a familiar figure, yet he can't identify it as his mother for several seconds. She rarely leaves their street now that the automobile is shut up in the garage without any license, and she has lost even more weight in the past months. He thinks, I have a right to resent her coming to the store if it is not on business. He steps away from the window and waits.

When she doesn't come through the door, he looks out again; and it is just in time to see her step up into the trolley car that rumbles off toward town.

And yet it is not many days after this that he hears her tell his father over the telephone that she won't meet him in town for dinner because she dislikes to ride the trolley.

The little girl's mother and his father stay in town to work two, sometimes three, nights a week, and they never come out on Saturday afternoons now. They usually call and try to get his mother to meet them somewhere. When they come to dinner on Saturday nights his father invariably smells of whisky, and the boy sometimes feels certain that a part of the odor comes from the little girl's mother. His father will say at the dinner table, "I'll tell you this selling game is different. Sociability counts for everything."

Again and again he sees his mother take the trolley for town in the afternoons. He suspects her of going in the mornings some days, for twice he has found her making the beds when he comes by home to leave his books after school. He wonders, sitting in the glare of the many-windowed schoolroom, if his mother is this very minute on one of her mysterious missions and if his father and the little girl's mother are drinking with someone over a sale downtown. If so, his house, a few blocks away, is empty. Not even the white pointer runs in the yard, for his father never hunts any more and has said that he's not mean enough to keep a dog and not hunt him. It pleases the boy to think of the house totally empty and to reflect that under the paint the marks that the vine-baskets made are actually still there.

At home he listens. He pretends to sleep on the couch after dinner at night. Spring comes, and he sits on the porch—under the window. He never closes the door to his room. He listens, and at last he hears.

He stands in the upstairs hall one night, poised, ready to move to the bathroom if the parents' door opens. His mother has made some sort of confession, and his father is saying, "Why didn't you tell me?" Those are the only audible words. But in a few days his father tells him that his mother is going to the hospital. She is going to have a mighty serious operation.

And she packs a little Gladstone bag at bedtime one night. He watches her from the hall, putting in the pink silk night-gowns, the quilted bathrobe, and her hair brush. In the morning his father and the little girl's mother and his mother go into town on the trolley together.

He is called to the principal's office from his geometry class. The principal, Miss Cartright, is an unpredictable, white-haired woman behind a pair of horn-rimmed glasses. The expression on her face is an absolutely new one this time.

"My child . . ."

"Yes, ma'am, Miss Cartright."

"You are a young man now. Do you understand?"

"Yes'm."

"I feel that you are unprepared for what I have to tell you, but you must accept it bravely."

"Yes'm."

"You are aware that your mother has not been well?"

"She's in the hospital. She's not dead, is she?"

"She died this morning . . . under the knife."

"May I get my books?"

"Yes, but wait a moment, child."

"Hadn't I better hurry home?"

"Wait, child. We must be sure that you know what this means."

"I know."

"You'll not see your mother alive again. You'll not have her careful, guiding hand to help you."

"Yes'm, I know, Miss Cartright."

"There will be hours of loneliness. And your father's not your mother. He can't take her place, however hard he try. . . .

There, there. None of this in a big boy like you. Come to me.
I want to be some comfort to you, not just a teacher."

The funeral is held in the undertaker's parlor, and the boy looks
in the coffin at his mother's powdered face. At the cemetery,
when they are arranging the flowers over the grave, he recalls
how the wicker baskets blew about the porch after his grandmother's funeral and how his mother went to the window and
looked out.

For several weeks he waits to hear of his father's plans to sell
the house. The other two argued with his mother over that
the night before she went to the hospital, and he heard his
father say after the funeral that it would have added ten years
to her life if she had sold the house. "This house," he said,
"was the biggest tumor she had." But nothing was said of a
sale after that.

All that summer the boy keeps the yard as though his
mother were alive and nagging him about it. The girl does the
housekeeping with the help of a Negro woman named Jessie.
Their parents take them to a downtown picture show at least
one night a week now. Coming back one night on the trolley
he says to the little girl's mother, "Why doesn't Daddy sell the
place and move to town?" But she changes to another topic for
conversation as though she had not heard him.

When he and the girl are at the top of the stairs that night,
she whispers, "Don't you know, Foolish, that you own the
house and can't sell it till you're twenty-one?"

This year the girl has begun at the high school; so she has to
take the trolley into town with her mother and his father. She
wears silk stockings all of the time and she fixes her black hair
in a knot on the back of her fat, white neck. She has a friend
named Susie who uses quantities of lipstick and cheek rouge
and who comes home with her many afternoons. The boy pays
little attention to them until one night Susie stays for dinner, a
night when the grown people don't come home. During dinner
the girls tell long stories with elements in them which he thinks
are very funny but which he thinks they don't understand,
being girls. After this he likes to talk with them and to try to
find out how much they do understand. He will sit sometimes

and just watch them file their fingernails. But when Susie offers him her picture once, he says he doesn't want it.

Then his father calls him into the living room one Sunday and tells him that the girl is a young lady now; and tells him that he must let her have his room and that he must move his belongings into his father's room. The boy hangs his head in protest. Finally he looks up and says, "I don't want to, Daddy."

The girl's mother is sitting across the room, and she looks at him soberly and says nothing. He sees, as if for the first time, that she wears as much lipstick and cheek rouge as Susie, and that her hair, gray on top, is bobbed and combed close to her head like a man's. His father stands up; he goes and sits on the arm of her chair. "You'll move your things after dinner tonight," he says. As the boy leaves the room, the father calls, "I'll help you, old man." And the girl's mother says something in too hushed a tone for him to hear her words.

But he likes rooming with his father. He is allowed to put his pennants on the walls of the big room and is told that he can arrange the furniture any way he likes. Often the two will go to bed at the same time and will lie in the dark talking of baseball. He sees the whole household with a different perspective. And now it is his father who is a different person.

There are times when he hears his father come into the room long after he has been in bed. And when the heavy body slips under the cover beside him, he can smell the alcohol and feel and hear the heavy breathing. Then he dreams of a day, certainly not more than a year or two hence, when he will be able to ask his father for a cigarette.

One night the boy and his father are in bed in their dark room when the clock thumps past ten.

"Are you awake still, son?"

"Wide awake."

"Tell me how much you are saving of what you earn."

"All right, s'r. Half of it."

"You must learn just how much it means to save money. If you don't save, then you will have to work when you are tired."

"When I'm old?"

"You may get tired before you get old. And if you're tired and know you'll never be able to rest, you'll get desperate."

"Oh, I suppose that *would* make you turn crooked."

"It might, if you could let yourself. If you can't let yourself turn crooked, despair will make things bad in a hundred other ways, anyhow."

"How much money do you make, Daddy?"

"In a good month?"

"Yes, that'll do."

"Enough to pay back what I borrow in a bad month."

"You aren't mentioning figures, I guess?"

"I didn't press *you*, did I?—for how much you save."

"I'll tell you."

"No. No, don't."

"It's a good deal."

"Yes. I'm afraid of how much it might sound like to me."

One night the boy is awakened by the sound of heavy rain. "I must put down the window," he thinks. But presently someone, barefooted, tiptoes through the bedroom door, across the room, toward the window. It is his father; and he removes the prop and lowers the window noiselessly but for the squeak of the sash, and he leaves the room again. Then quite distinctly his voice comes from the hallway: "Both of them." And presently the door to Grandmother's former bedroom scrapes the floor as it closes, and the boy tries to visualize the dark scene on his mother's guest room bed.

It is a day when the wind rustles the treetops, even the tops of slender poplars; and yet the wind is so soft, nearer to the earth, that it barely stirs the flaps of the boy's shirt collar. The sky is turquoise, and the hurried clouds look pink in their centers. The boy stands in the middle of the circular flower bed, surveying his work. His shirt is khaki and his trousers are faded blue jeans. His height measures somewhat over five feet, and atop his head his straight, brown hair stirs gently with the flaps of his shirt collar. His shirt sleeves are rolled above the elbows of his long, thin, white arms. In his right hand he holds a rusty trowel.

One third done, he says. From his feet, in the center of the flower bed, a section of broken earth, cleared of all the green spring shoots but the little zinnia and petunia plants, stretches out to the rock border. One hundred and twenty degrees, he says; and he turns to the other two thirds of the bed, which are green with clover and grass and dandelion. His long shadow falls across those two thirds to the border and divides them evenly. He points with the trowel to the section on his left and pronounces: "Four-thirty." Then he points to that at his right hand and says: "Five o'clock." He stoops, drives the trowel around the roots of a dandelion plant, and shaking the dirt from the root throws the weed beyond the stone border of the bed.

Inside the house the telephone is ringing. It rings for so long a time that he stands up and looks over his shoulder toward the house. The ringing ceases, and he stoops again and digs. It is not long before the girl is walking along the wall of the white clapboard house. The boy is on his knees working carefully between two tiny zinnia shoots. He watches her approach from the corner of his eye. She wears high-heeled brown and white shoes and no stockings on her legs, which are fat and at the same time muscular. Her skirt, a plaid material with a predominance of green and orange, is stretched around her big hips. And her tan sweater fits too closely under the arms and is drawn across her matronly breasts too tight to be less than obscene.

She stands close to him with her shaven legs far apart. He looks up at her; she is standing with her hands on her hips, and he thinks that her clothes fit her as the shrunken summer covers do the big living room chairs. Her brown, bobbed hair blows in the wind, and one strand plays over her unpowdered face.

"Jim, darling," she says, "they're married."

"Who's married?" he says as though to deny the possibility.

"Mother and . . . Mommy and your father."

"And you're glad?" he asks.

She weighs the question for a moment. "I don't think I care a snap, Jim."

He looks at his trowel and then inquires with indifference in his voice: "Did you know they would?"

"Only by conjecture. But Mommy just called on the phone, and I talked to both of them."

With some deliberation he digs his trowel into the ground and pulls up a clod of dirt with grass on it; but she remains before him. Then he asks, "Will they be out to dinner tonight?"

"No," she says, brushing the strand of hair from her face with her pink hand, "they've gone to Chicago for the weekend. I think they'll stay even longer. It's a long way up to Chicago."

The girl has turned and is walking toward the house. She walks over the grass on the balls of her feet. And he gazes after her heavy figure.

He is digging in the last green third. Of a sudden his breath seems to catch in his chest and his temples grow hot. He is squatted, resting his haunches on his heels. He raises his head in surprise at his own sensation, and he speaks out loud to himself: "I'm not sorry about *them*." But he cannot say what it is.

The light of the afternoon has a yellow tint in it. He looks at the sky. The whole western sky is a black mass, one that is advancing rapidly to meet the puffy gray clouds which clutter the eastern horizon and the sky overhead. He digs his trowel into the earth, uproots, tears, and digs again.

The shrill whistles in the distance have blown for five o'clock, and he is working assiduously at the blades of grass that grow from between the rocks of the border. He has finished the last third of the bed, but he works on. He does not raise his head; his eyes follow his fingers plucking grass from between the rocks. Something has filled him with a dread of quitting. It isn't, he tells himself, the thought that he must realize the marriage of his father to the mother of the girl, that he must go into the house with only that to occupy his mind. And yet he can't assure himself that it is only a dread of the memories that the yellow light will bring when he looks up into it. He feels the first drop of water on the back of his neck at exactly the moment that he hears the voice of the girl:

"Jim, darling, do come in out of the rain."

He stares up at the white clapboard house through the bilious light and discerns the figure of the girl at the window of her bedroom, the room which once was his own.

He drops his trowel on the grass and walks, with his heart beating under his tongue. The electric light burns in the girl's room, and he can see her in the window through the black screen. He walks with his arms hanging straight at his sides as though he carries two heavy pails of water in his hands. In that strange light his eyes meet the girl's eyes through the fine mesh of the screen. Her eyes are darker than her hair.

A clap of thunder jerks the eyes of both toward the sky, and the rain bursts upon him. He runs three steps and leaps over the shrubbery onto the end of the porch. There he turns his face toward the yard and stands rigid, and his pulse throbs in his wrists. He senses that the girl is still at the window.

His hand turns the cold brass knob of the front door, and he flings open the door. The furniture of the hall is a group of strange objects to him. How weird are the roosters in the design of the floor rug, the crack on the table top mended with yellow plastic wood, and the crazy angle of the mirror. He is unbuttoning his wet shirt as he runs up the stair and he tears it off as he shoves open the door to the room in which he once used to sleep.

The bed is between him and the girl, who is wearing a crepe de Chine negligee. She sits down on the other side of the bed, puts one hand softly on the pillow, and says, "What do you want, Jimmy?" He crosses the room. She twists her body and throws herself face downward on the bed. The boy stands over her, his wet shirt in his hand, looking at the back of her head. The girl rolls over on her back and smiles up at him.

He looks into her brown eyes under her heavy low brow and sees, he feels, the innocence of someone years younger than himself, the innocence of a very little girl. Her head is sunk in the fat, white pillow. She crooks her elbow behind her head and smiles up at him. She shifts the position of her body and rubs her bare feet together. Her eyes, he thinks, are like the brown eyes of a young dog. His temples are ablaze and presently he knows that his whole face and perhaps his whole bare chest is the color of the girl's rouged cheeks. He quickly turns his back to her and finds himself looking out the window through falling rain at the rooftops of the suburb. While his eyes are fixed on the yellow tower of the Catholic church and he stands braced by his hands on the window sill, the sudden loud laughter of the girl on the bed slaps his ears.

He doesn't know how long the laughter lasts. The rain falls outside the open window, and now and again a raindrop splashes through the screen onto his face. At last it is almost night when the rain stops, and if there is any unnatural hue in the light, it is green. His heart has stopped pounding now, and all the heat has gone from his face. He has heard the hanging baskets beat against the house and felt the silence after their removal. He has heard the baseball smacking in the wet gloves of the men and seen the furniture auctioned on the lawn. The end of his grandmother, the defeat of his mother, the despair of his father, and the resignation of his new stepmother are all in his mind. The remarkable thing in the changed view from the window which had once been his lies in the tall apartment houses which punctuate the horizon and in the boxlike, flat-roofed ones in his own neighborhood. Through this window the girl too, he knows, must have beheld changes. He takes his hand from the sill and massages his taut face on which the raindrops have dried.

When he faces her again, he says that they must prepare some sort of welcome, that they must get busy.

The Fancy Woman

H E WANTED no more of her drunken palaver. Well, sure enough. Sure enough. And he had sent her from the table like she were one of his half-grown brats. *He,* who couldn't have walked straight around to her place if she *hadn't* been lady enough to leave, sent *her* from the table like either of the half-grown kids he was so mortally fond of. At least she hadn't turned over three glasses of perfectly good stuff during one meal. Talk about vulgar. She fell across the counterpane and slept.

She awoke in the dark room with his big hands busying with her clothes, and she flung her arms about his neck. And she said, "You marvelous, fattish thing."

His hoarse voice was in her ear. He chuckled deep in his throat. And she whispered: "You're an old thingamajig, George."

Her eyes opened in the midday sunlight, and she felt the back of her neck soaking in her own sweat on the counterpane. She saw the unfamiliar cracks in the ceiling and said, "Whose room's this?" She looked at the walnut dresser and the wardrobe and said, "Oh, the kids' room"; and as she laughed, saliva bubbled up and fell back on her upper lip. She shoved herself up with her elbows and was sitting in the middle of the bed. Damn him! Her blue silk dress was twisted about her body; a thin army blanket covered her lower half. "He didn't put that over me, I know damn well. One of those tight-mouth niggers sneaking around!" She sprang from the bed, slipped her bare feet into her white pumps, and stepped toward the door. Oh, God! She beheld herself in the dresser mirror.

She marched to the dresser with her eyes closed and felt about for a brush. There was nothing but a tray of collar buttons there. She seized a handful of them and screamed as she threw them to bounce off the mirror, "This ain't my room!" She ran her fingers through her hair and went out into the hall and into her room next door. She rushed to her little dressing table. There was the bottle half full. She poured out a jigger and drank it. Clearing her throat as she sat down, she said, "Oh, what's the matter with me?" She combed her hair back quite carefully, then pulled the yellow strands out of the amber comb; and when she had greased and wiped her face and had rouged her lips and the upper portions of her cheeks, she smiled at herself in the mirror. She looked flirtatiously at the bottle but shook her head and stood up and looked about her. It was a long, narrow room with two windows at the end. A cubbyhole beside the kids' room! But it *was* a canopied bed with yellow ruffles that matched the ruffles on the dressing table and on the window curtains, as he had promised. She went over and turned back the covers and mussed the pillow. It might not have been the niggers! She poured another drink and went down to get some nice, hot lunch.

The breakfast room was one step lower than the rest of the house; and though it was mostly windows the venetian blinds were lowered all round. She sat at a big circular table. "I can't make out about this room," she said to the Negress who was refilling her coffee cup. She lit a cigarette and questioned the servant, "What's the crazy table made out of, Amelia?"

"It makes a good table, 'spite all."

"It sure enough does make a strong table, Amelia." She kicked the toe of her shoe against the brick column which supported the table top. "But what *was* it, old dearie?" She smiled invitingly at the servant and pushed her plate away and pulled her coffee in front of her. She stared at the straight scar on Amelia's wrist as Amelia reached for the plate. What big black buck had put it there? A lot these niggers had to complain of in her when every one of them was all dosed up.

Amelia said that the base of the table was the old cistern. "He brung that top out f'om Memphis when he done the po'ch up this way for breakfas' and lunch."

The woman looked about the room, thinking, "I'll get some confab out of this one yet." And she exclaimed, "Oh, and that's the old bucket to it over there, then, with the vines on it, Amelia!"

"No'm," Amelia said. Then after a few seconds she added, "They brung that out f'om Memphis and put it there like it was it."

"Yeah . . . yeah . . . go on, Amelia. I'm odd about old-fash-ioned things. I've got a lot of interest in any antiques."

"That's all."

The little Negro woman started away with the coffee pot and the plate, dragging the soft soles of her carpet slippers over the brick floor. At the door she lingered, and, too cunning to leave room for a charge of impudence, she added to the hateful "That's all" a mutter, "Miss Josephine."

And when the door closed, Miss Josephine said under her breath, "If that black bitch hadn't stuck that on, there wouldn't be another chance for her to sneak around with any army blankets."

George, mounted on a big sorrel and leading a small dapple-gray horse, rode onto the lawn outside the breakfast room. Josephine saw him through the chinks of the blinds looking up toward her bedroom window. "Not for me," she said to herself. "He'll not get *me* on one of those animals." She swallowed the last of her coffee on her feet and then turned and stomped across the bricks to the step-up into the hallway. There she heard him calling:

"Josie! Josie! Get out-a that bed!"

Josephine ran through the long hall cursing the rugs that slipped under her feet. She ran the length of the hall looking back now and again as though the voice were a beast at her heels. In the front parlor she pulled up the glass and took a book from the bookcase nearest the door. It was a red book, and she hurled herself into George's chair and opened to page sixty-five:

nity, with anxiety, and with pity. Hamilcar was rubbing himself against my legs, wild with delight.

She closed the book on her thumb and listened to George's bellowing: "I'm coming after you!"

She could hear the sound of the hoofs as George led the horses around the side of the house. George's figure moved outside the front windows. Through the heavy lace curtains she could see him tying the horses to the branch of a tree. She heard him on the veranda and then in the hall. Damn him! God damn him, he couldn't make her ride! She opened to page sixty-five again as George passed the doorway. But he saw her, and he stopped. He stared at her for a moment, and she looked at him over the book. She rested her head on the back of the chair and put a pouty look on her face. Her eyes were fixed on his hairy arms, on the little bulk in his rolled sleeves, then on the white shirt over his chest, on the brown jodhpurs, and finally on the blackened leather of his shoes set well apart on the polished hall floor. Her eyelids were heavy, and she longed for a drink of the three-dollar whiskey that was on her dressing table.

He crossed the carpet with a smile, showing, she guessed, his delight at finding her. She smiled. He snatched the book from her hands and read the title on the red cover. His head went back, and as he laughed she watched through the open collar the tendons of his throat tighten and take on a purplish hue.

At Josephine's feet was a needlepoint footstool on which was worked a rust-colored American eagle against a background of green. George tossed the red book onto the stool and pulled Josephine from her chair. He was still laughing, and she wishing for a drink.

"Come along, come along," he said. "We've only four days left, and you'll want to tell your friend-girls you learned to ride."

She jerked one hand loose from his hold and slapped his hard cheek. She screamed, "Friend-girl? You never heard me say friend-girl. What black nigger do you think you're talking down to?" She was looking at him now through a mist of tears and presently she broke out into furious weeping.

His laughter went on as he pushed her across the room and into the hall, but he was saying: "Boochie, Boochie. Wotsa matter? Now, old girl, old girl. Listen: You'll want to tell your girl friends, your *girl friends*, that you learned to ride."

That was how George was! He would never try to persuade her. He would never pay any attention to what she said. He wouldn't argue with her. He wouldn't mince words! The few times she had seen him before this week there had been no chance to talk much. When they were driving down from Memphis, Saturday, she had gone through the story about how she was tricked by Jackie Briton and married Lon and how he had left her right away and the pathetic part about the baby she never even saw in the hospital. And at the end of it, she realized that George had been smiling at her as he probably would at one of his half-grown kids. When she stopped the story quickly, he had reached over and patted her hand (but still smiling) and right away had started talking about the sickly-looking tomato crops along the highway. After lunch on Saturday when she'd tried to talk to him again and he had deliberately commenced to play the victrola, she said, "Why won't you take me seriously?" But he had, of course, just laughed at her and kissed her; and they had already begun drinking then. She couldn't resist him (more than other men, he could just drive her wild), and he would hardly look at her, never had. He either laughed at her or cursed her or, of course, at night would pet her. He hadn't hit her.

He was shoving her along the hall, and she had to make herself stop crying.

"Please, George."

"Come on, now! That-a girl!"

"Honest to God, George. I tell you to let up, stop it."

"Come on. *Up* the steps. *Up! Up!*"

She let herself become limp in his arms but held with one hand to the banister. Then he grabbed her. He swung her up into his arms and carried her up the stairs which curved around the back end of the hall, over the doorway to the breakfast room. Once in his arms, she didn't move a muscle, for she thought, "I'm no featherweight, and we'll both go tumbling down these steps and break our skulls." At the top he fairly slammed her to her feet and, panting for breath, he said without a trace of softness: "Now, put on those pants, Josie, and I'll wait for you in the yard." He turned to the stair, and she heard what he said to himself: "I'll sober her. I'll sober her up."

As he pushed Josephine onto the white, jumpy beast he must have caught a whiff of her breath. She knew that he must have! He was holding the reins close to the bit while she tried to arrange herself in the flat saddle. Then he grasped her ankle and asked her, "Did you take a drink upstairs?" She laughed, leaned forward in her saddle, and whispered: "Two. Two jiggers."

She wasn't afraid of the horse now, but she was dizzy. "George, let me down," she said faintly. She felt the horse's flesh quiver under her leg and looked over her shoulder when it stomped one rear hoof.

George said, "Confound it, I'll sober you." He handed her the reins, stepped back, and slapped the horse on the flank. "Hold on!" he called, and her horse cantered across the lawn.

Josie was clutching the leather straps tightly, and her face was almost in the horse's mane. "I could kill him for this," she said, slicing out the words with a sharp breath. God damn it! The horse was galloping along a dirt road. She saw nothing but the yellow dirt. The hoofs rumbled over a three-plank wooden bridge, and she heard George's horse on the other side of her. She turned her face that way and saw George through the hair that hung over her eyes. He was smiling. "You dirty bastard," she said.

He said, "You're doin' all right. Sit up, and I'll give you some pointers." She turned her face to the other side. Now she wished to God she hadn't taken those two jiggers. George's horse quickened his speed and hers followed. George's slowed and hers did likewise. She could feel George's grin in the back of her neck. She had no control over her horse.

They were galloping in the hot sunlight, and Josie stole glances at the flat fields of strawberries. "If you weren't drunk, you'd fall off," George shouted. Now they were passing a cotton field. ("The back of my neck'll be blistered," she thought. "Where was it I picked strawberries once? At Dyersburg when I was ten, visiting some Godforsaken relations.") The horses turned off the road into wooded bottom land. The way now was shaded by giant trees, but here and there the sun shone between foliage. Once after riding thirty feet in shadow, watching dumbly the cool blue-green underbrush, Josie felt the sun suddenly on her neck. Her stomach churned, and the eggs and coffee from breakfast burned her throat as it all gushed forth, splattering her pants leg and the brown saddle and the horse's side. She looked over the horse at George.

But there was no remorse, no compassion, and no humor in George's face. He gazed straight ahead and urged on his horse.

All at once the horses turned to the right. Josie howled. She saw her right foot flying through the air, and after the thud of the fall and the flashes of light and darkness she lay on her back in the dirt and watched George as he approached on foot, leading the two horses.

"Old girl . . ." he said.

"You get the hell away from me!"

"Are you hurt?" He kneeled beside her, so close to her that she could smell his sweaty shirt.

Josie jumped to her feet and walked in the direction from which they had ridden. In a moment George galloped past her, leading the gray horse and laughing like the son-of-a-bitch he was.

"Last night he sent me upstairs! But this is more! I'm not gonna have it." She walked through the woods, her lips moving as she talked to herself. "He wants no more of my drunken palaver!" Well, he was going to get no more of her drunken anything now. She had had her fill of him and everybody else and was going to look out for her own little sweet self from now on.

That was her trouble, she knew. She'd never made a good thing of people. "That's why things are like they are now," she said. "I've never made a good thing out of anybody." But it was real lucky that she realized it now, just exactly when she had, for it was certain that there had never been one whom more could be made out of than George. "God damn him," she said, thinking still of his riding by her like that. "Whatever it was I liked about him is gone now."

She gazed up into the foliage and branches of the trees, and the great size of the trees made her feel real small, and real young. If Jackie or Lon had been different she might have learned things when she was young. "But they were both of 'em easygoin' and just slipped out on me." They *were* sweet. She'd never forget how sweet Jackie always was. "Just plain sweet." She made a quick gesture with her right hand: "If only they didn't all get such a hold on me!"

But she was through with George. This time *she* got through first. He was no different from a floorwalker. He had more sense. "He's educated, and the money he must have!" George had more sense than a floorwalker, but he didn't have any manners. He treated her just like the floorwalker at Jobe's had that last week she was there. But George was worth getting around. She would find out what it was. She wouldn't take another drink. She'd find out what was wrong inside him, for there's something wrong inside everybody, and somehow she'd get a hold of him. Little Josephine would make a place for herself at last. She just wouldn't think about him as a man.

At the edge of the wood she turned onto the road, and across the fields she could see his house. That house was just simply as old and big as they come, and wasn't a cheap house. "I wonder if he looked after getting it fixed over and remodeled." Not likely. She kept looking at the whitewashed brick and shaking her head. "No, by Jesus," she exclaimed. "*She* did it!" George's wife. All of her questions seemed to have been answered. The wife had left him for his meanness, and he was lonesome. There was, then, a place to be filled. She began to run along the road. "God, I feel like somebody might step in before I get there." She laughed, but then the heat seemed to strike her all at once. Her stomach drew in. She vomited in the ditch, and, by God, it was as dry as cornflakes!

She sat still in the grass under a little maple tree beside the road, resting her forehead on her drawn-up knees. All between Josie and her new life seemed to be the walk through the sun in these smelly, dirty clothes. Across the fields and in the house was a canopied bed and a glorious new life, but she daren't go into the sun. She would pass out cold. "People kick off in weather like this!"

Presently Josie heard the voices of niggers up the road. She wouldn't look up, she decided. She'd let them pass, without looking up. They drew near to her and she made out the voices of a man and a child. The man said, "Hursh!" and the voices ceased. There was only the sound of their feet padding along the dusty road.

The noise of the padding grew fainter. Josie looked up and saw that the two had cut across the fields toward George's house. Already she could hear the niggers mouthing it about the kitchen. That little yellow Henry would look at her over his shoulder as he went through the swinging door at dinner tonight. If she heard them grumbling once more, as she did Monday, calling her "she," Josie decided that she was going to come right out and ask Amelia about the scar. Right before George. But the niggers were the least of her worries now.

All afternoon she lay on the bed, waking now and then to look at the bottle of whiskey on the dressing table and to wonder where George had gone. She didn't know whether it had been George or the field nigger who sent Henry after her in the truck. Once she dreamed that she saw George at the head of the stairs telling Amelia how he had sobered Miss Josephine up. When she awoke that time she said, "I ought to get up and get myself good and plastered before George comes back from wherever he is." But she slept again and dreamed this time that she was working at the hat sale at Jobe's and that she had to wait on Amelia who picked up a white turban and asked Josie to model it for her. And the dream ended with Amelia telling Josie how pretty she was and how much she liked her.

Josie had taken another hot bath (to ward off soreness from the horseback ride) and was in the sitting room, which everybody called the back parlor, playing the electric victrola and feeling just prime when George came in. She let him go through the hall and upstairs to dress up for dinner without calling to him. She chuckled to herself and rocked to the time of the music.

George came with a real mint julep in each hand. His hair was wet and slicked down over his head; the part, low on the left side, was straight and white. His cheeks were shaven and were pink with new sunburn. He said, "I had myself the time of my life this afternoon."

Josie smiled and said that she was glad he had enjoyed himself. George raised his eyebrows and cocked his head to one side. She kept on smiling at him, and made no movement toward taking the drink that he held out to her.

George set the glass on the little candle stand near her chair and switched off the victrola.

"George, I was listening . . ."

"Ah, now," he said, "I want to tell you about the cockfight."

"Let me finish listening to that piece, George."

George dropped down into an armchair and put his feet on a stool. His pants and shirt were white, and he wore a blue polka dot tie.

"You're nice and clean," she said, as though she had forgotten the victrola.

"Immaculate!" There was a mischievous grin on his face, and he leaned over one arm of the chair and pulled the victrola plug from the floor socket. Josie reached out and took the glass from the candle stand, stirred it slightly with a shoot of mint, and began to sip it. She thought, "I *have* to take it when he acts this way."

At the dinner table George said, "You're in better shape tonight. You look better. Why don't you go easy on the bottle tonight?"

She looked at him between the two candles burning in the center of the round table. "I didn't ask you for that mint julep, I don't think."

"And you ain't gettin' any more," he said, winking at her as he lifted his fork to his lips with his left hand. This, she felt, was a gesture to show his contempt for her. Perhaps he thought she didn't know the difference, which, of course, was even more contemptuous.

"Nice manners," she said. He made no answer, but at least he could be sure that she had recognized the insult. She took a drink of water, her little finger extended slightly from the glass, and over the glass she said, "You didn't finish about the niggers having a fight after the chickens did."

"Oh, yes." He arranged his knife and fork neatly on his plate. "The two nigs commenced to watch each other before their chickens had done scrapping. And when the big rooster gave his last hop and keeled over, Ira Blakemoor jumped over the two birds onto Jimmy's shoulders. Jimmy just whirled round and round till he threw Ira the way the little mare did you this morning." George looked directly into Josie's eyes between the candles, defiantly unashamed to mention that event, and he smiled with defiance and yet with weariness. "Ira got up and the two walked around looking at each other like two black games before a fight." Josie kept her eyes on George while the story, she felt, went on and on and on.

That yellow nigger Henry was paused at the swinging door, looking over his shoulder toward her. She turned her head and glared at him. He was not even hiding this action from George, who was going on and on about the niggers' fighting.

This Henry was the worst hypocrite of all. He who had slashed Amelia's wrist (it was surely Henry who had done it), and probably had raped his own children, the way niggers do, was denouncing her right out like this. Her heart pounded when he kept looking, and then George's story stopped.

A bright light flashed across Henry's face and about the room which was lit by only the two candles. Josie swung her head around, and through the front window she saw the lights of automobiles that were moving through the yard. She looked at George, and his face said absolutely nothing for itself. He moistened his lips with his tongue.

"Guests," he said, raising his eyebrows. And Josie felt that in that moment she had seen the strongest floorwalker weaken. George had scorned and laughed at everybody and every situation. But now he was ashamed. He was ashamed of her. On her behavior would depend his comfort. She was cold sober and would be *up* to whatever showed itself. It was her real opportunity.

From the back of the house a horn sounded, and above other voices a woman's voice rose, calling "Whoohoo!" George stood up and bowed to her beautifully, like something she had never seen, and said, "You'll excuse me?" Then he went out through the kitchen without saying "scat" about what she should do.

She drummed on the table with her fingers and listened to George's greetings to his friends. She heard him say, "Welcome, Billy, and welcome, Mrs. Billy!" They were the only names she recognized. It was likely the Billy Colton she'd met with George one night.

Then these *were* Memphis society people. Here for the night, at least! She looked down at her yellow linen dress and straightened the lapels at the neck. She thought of the women with their lovely profiles and soft skin and natural-colored hair. What if she had waited on one of them once at Jobe's or, worse still, in the old days at Burnstein's? But they had probably never been to one of those cheap stores. What if they stayed but refused to talk to her, or even to meet her? They could be mean bitches, all of them, for all their soft hands and shaved legs. Her hand trembled as she rang the little glass bell for coffee.

She rang it, and no one answered. She rang it again, hard, but now she could hear Henry coming through the breakfast room to the hall, bumping the guests' baggage against the doorway. Neither Amelia nor Mammy, who cooked the evening meal, would leave the kitchen during dinner, Josie knew. "I'd honestly like to go out in the kitchen and ask 'em for a cup of coffee and tell 'em just how scared I am." But too well she could imagine their contemptuous, accusing gaze. "If only I could get something on them! Even catch 'em toting food just once! That Mammy's likely killed enough niggers in her time to fill Jobe's basement."

Josie was even afraid to light a cigarette. She went over to the side window and looked out into the yard; she could see the lights from the automobiles shining on the green leaves and on the white fence around the house lot.

And she was standing thus when she heard the voices and the footsteps in the long hall. She had only just turned around when George stood in the wide doorway with the men and women from Memphis. He was pronouncing her name first: "Miss Carlson, this is Mr. Roberts, Mrs. Roberts, Mr. Jackson, Mrs. Jackson, and Mr. and Mrs. Colton."

Josie stared at the group, not trying to catch the names. She could think only, "They're old. The women are old and plump. George's wife is old!" She stared at them, and when the name Colton struck her ear, she said automatically and without placing his face, "I know Billy."

George said in the same tone in which he had said, "You'll excuse me?" "Josie, will you take the ladies upstairs to freshen up while the men and I get some drinks started? We'll settle the rooming question later." George was the great floorwalker whose wife was old and who had now shown his pride to Josie Carlson. He had shown his shame. Finally he had decided on a course and was following it, but he had given 'way his sore spots. Only God knew what he had told his friends. Josie said to herself, "It's plain he don't want 'em to know who I am."

As Josie ascended the stairs, followed by those she had already privately termed the "three matrons," she watched George and the three other men go down the hall to the breakfast room. The sight of their white linen suits and brown and white shoes in the bright hall seemed to make the climb a soaring. At the top of the stairs she stopped and let the three women pass ahead of her. She eyed the costume of each as they passed.

One wore a tailored seersucker dress. Another wore a navy-blue
linen dress with white collar and cuffs, and the third wore a
striped linen skirt and silk blouse. On the wrist of this last was a
bracelet from which hung a tiny silver dog, a lock, a gold heart.

Josie observed their grooming: their fingernails, their lipstick, their hair in tight curls. There was gray in the hair of one,
but not one, Josie decided now, was much past forty. Their figures were neatly corseted, and Josie felt that the little saggings
under their chins and under the eyes of the one in the navy
blue made them more charming; were, indeed, almost a part
of their smartness. She wanted to think of herself as like them.
They were, she realized, at least ten years older than she, but in
ten years, beginning tonight, she might become one of them.

"Just go in my room there," she said. She pointed to the
open door and started down the steps, thinking that this was
the beginning of the new life and thinking of the men downstairs fixing the drinks. And then she thought of the bottle of
whiskey on her dressing table in the room where the matrons
had gone!

"Oh, hell," she cursed under her breath. She had turned
to go up the two steps again when she heard the men's voices
below. She heard her own name being pronounced carefully:
"Josie Carlson." She went down five or six steps on tiptoe and
stood still to listen to the voices that came from the breakfast room.

"You said to come any time, George, and never mentioned
having this thing down here."

George laughed. "Afraid of what the girls will say when you
get home? I can hear them. 'In Beatrice's own lovely house,'"
he mocked.

"Well, fellow, you've a shock coming, too," one of them said.
"Beatrice has sent your boys down to Memphis for a month
with you. They say she has a beau."

"And in the morning," one said, "your sister Kate's sending
them down here. She asked us to bring them, and then decided
to keep them one night herself."

"You'd better get *her* out, George."

George laughed. Josie could hear them dropping ice into
glasses.

"We'll take her back at dawn if you say."

"What would the girls say to that?" He laughed at them as he laughed at Josie.

"The girls are gonna be decent to her. They agreed in the yard."

"Female curiosity?" George said.

"Your boys'll have curiosity, too. Jock's seventeen."

Even the clank of the ice stopped. "You'll every one of you please to remember," George said slowly, "that Josie's a friend of yours and that she met the girls here by appointment."

Josie tiptoed down the stairs, descending, she felt, once more into her old world. "He'll slick me some way if he has to for his kids, I think." She turned into the dining room at the foot of the stairs. The candles were burning low, and she went and stood by the open window and listened to the counterpoint of the crickets and the frogs while Henry, who had looked over his shoulder at the car lights, rattled the silver and china and went about clearing the table.

Presently, George had come and put his hand on her shoulder. When she turned around she saw him smiling and holding two drinks in his left hand. He leaned his face close to hers and said, "I'm looking for the tears."

Josie said, "There aren't any to find, fellow"; and she thought it odd, really odd, that he had expected her to cry. But he was probably poking fun at her again.

She took one of the drinks and clinked glasses with George. To herself she said, "I bet they don't act any better than I do after they've got a few under their belts." At least she showed her true colors! "I'll keep my eyes open for their true ones."

If only they'd play the victrola instead of the radio. She liked the victrola so much better. She could play "Louisville Lady" over and over. But, *no*. They all wanted to switch the radio about. To get Cincinnati and Los Angeles and Bennie this and Johnny that. If they liked a piece, why did they care who played it? For God's sake! They wouldn't dance at first, either, and when she first got George to dance with her, they sat smiling at each other, grinning. They had played cards, too, but poker didn't go so well after George slugged them all with that third round of his three-dollar-whiskey drinks. Right then she had begun to watch out to see who slapped whose knee.

She asked George to dance because she so liked to dance with him, and she wasn't going to care about what the others did any more, she decided. But finally when two of them had started dancing off in the corner of the room, she looked about the sitting room for the other four and saw that Billy Colton had disappeared not with his own wife but with that guy Jackson's. And Josie threw herself down into the armchair and laughed aloud, so hard and loud that everybody begged her to tell what was funny. But she stopped suddenly and gave them as mean a look as she could manage and said, "Nothin'. Let's dance some more, George."

But George said that he must tell Henry to fix more drinks, and he went out and left her by the radio with Roberts and Mrs. Colton. She looked at Mrs. Colton and thought, "Honey, you don't seem to be grieving about Billy."

Then Roberts said to Josie, "George says you're from Vicksburg."

"I was raised there," she said, wondering why George hadn't told her whatever he'd told them.

"He says you live there now."

Mrs. Colton, who wore the navy blue and was the fattest of the three matrons, stood up and said to Roberts, "Let's dance in the hall where there are fewer rugs." And she gave a kindly smile to Josie, and Josie spit out a "Thanks." The couple skipped into the hall, laughing, and Josie sat alone by the radio wishing she could play the victrola and wishing that George would come and kiss her on the back of her neck. "And I'd slap him if he did," she said. Now and again she would cut her eye around to watch Jackson and Mrs. Roberts dancing. They were at the far end of the room and were dancing slowly. They kept rubbing against the heavy blue drapery at the window and they were talking into each other's ears.

But the next piece that came over the radio was a hot one, and Jackson led Mrs. Roberts to the center of the room and whirled her round and round, and the trinkets at her wrist tinkled like little bells. Josie lit a cigarette and watched them dance. She realized then that Jackson was showing off for her sake.

When George came with a tray of drinks he said, "Josie, move the victrola," but Josie sat still and glared at him as if to say, "What on earth are you talking about? Are you nuts?" He set the tray across her lap and turned and picked up the little victrola and set it on the floor.

"Oh, good God!" cried Josie in surprise and delight. "It's a portable."

George, taking the tray from her, said, "It's not for you to port off, old girl."

The couple in the center of the room had stopped their whirling and had followed George. "We like to dance, but there are better things," Jackson was saying.

Mrs. Roberts flopped down on the broad arm of Josie's chair and took a drink from George. Josie could only watch the trinkets on the bracelet, one of which she saw was a little gold book. George was telling Jackson about the cockfight again, and Mrs. Roberts leaned over and talked to Josie. She tried to tell her how the room seemed to be whirling around. They both giggled, and Josie thought, "Maybe we'll get to be good friends, and she'll stop pretending to be so swell." But she couldn't think of anything to say to her, partly because she just never did have anything to say to women and partly because Jackson, who was not at all a bad-looking little man, was sending glances her way.

It didn't seem like more than twenty minutes or half an hour more before George had got to that point where he ordered her around and couldn't keep on his own feet. He finally lay down on the couch in the front parlor, and as she and Mrs. Roberts went up the stairs with their arms about each other's waists, he called out something that made Mrs. Roberts giggle. But Josie knew that little Josephine was at the point where she could say nothing straight, so she didn't even ask to get the portable victrola. She just cursed under her breath.

The daylight was beginning to appear at the windows of Josie's narrow little room when waking suddenly she sat up in bed and then flopped down again and jerked the sheet about her. "That little sucker come up here," she grumbled, "and cleared out, but where was the little sucker's wife?" Who was with George, by damn, all night? After a while she said, "They're none of 'em any better than the niggers. I knew they couldn't be. Nobody is. By God, nobody's better than I am. Nobody can say anything to me." Everyone would like to live as free as she did! There was no such thing as . . . There was no such thing as what the niggers and the whites liked to pretend they were. She was going to let up, and do things in secret. Try to look like an angel. It wouldn't be as hard since there was no such thing.

It was all like a scene from a color movie, like one of the musicals. It was the prettiest scene ever. And they were like two of those lovely wax models in the boys' department at Jobe's. Like two of those models, with the tan skin and blond hair, come to life! And to see them in their white shorts spring about the green grass under the blue, blue sky, hitting the little feather thing over the high net, made Josie go weak all over. She went down on her knees and rested her elbows on the window sill and watched them springing about before the people from Memphis; these were grouped under a tree, sitting in deck chairs and on the grass. George stood at the net like a floor-walker charmed by his wax manikins which had come to life.

It had been George's cries of "Outside, outside!" and the jeers and applause of the six spectators that awakened Josie. She ran to the window in her pajamas, and when she saw the white markings on the grass and the net that had sprung up there overnight, she thought that this might be a dream. But the voices of George and Mrs. Roberts and Phil Jackson were completely real, and the movements of the boys' bodies were too marvelous to be doubted.

She sank to her knees, conscious of the soreness which her horseback ride had left. She thought of her clumsy self in the dusty road as she gazed down at the graceful boys on the lawn and said, "Why, they're actually pretty. Too pretty." She was certain of one thing: she didn't want any of their snobbishness. She wouldn't have it from his two kids.

One boy's racket missed the feather thing. George shouted, "Game!" The group under the tree applauded, and the men pushed themselves up from their seats to come out into the sunlight and pat the naked backs of the boys.

When the boys came close together, Josie saw that one was six inches taller than the other. "Why, that one's grown!" she thought. The two of them walked toward the house, the taller one walking with the shorter's neck in the crook of his elbow. George called to them, "You boys get dressed for lunch." He ordered them about just as he did her, but they went off smiling.

Josie walked in her bare feet into the little closet-like bathroom which adjoined her room. She looked at herself in the mirror there and said, "I've never dreaded anything so much in all my life before. You can't depend on what kids'll say." But were they kids? For all their prettiness, they were too big to be called kids. And nobody's as damn smutty as a smart-alecky shaver.

Josephine bathed in the little, square, maroon bathtub. There were maroon and white checkered tile steps built up around the tub, so that it gave the effect of being sunken. After her bath, she stood on the steps and powdered her whole soft body. Every garment which she put on was absolutely fresh. She went to her closet and took out her new white silk dress and slipped it over her head. She put on white shoes first, but, deciding she looked too much like a trained nurse, she changed to her tan pumps. Josie knew what young shavers thought about nurses.

She combed her yellow hair till it lay close to her head, and put on rouge and lipstick. Someone knocked at the bedroom door. "Yeah," she called. No answer came, so she went to the door and opened it. In the hall stood one of the boys. It was the little one.

He didn't look at her; he looked past her. And his eyes *were* as shiny and cold as those on a wax dummy!

"Miss Carlson, my dad says to tell you that lunch is ready. And I'm Buddy."

"Thanks." She didn't know what the hell else she should say. "Tell him, all right," she said. She stepped back into her room and shut the door.

Josie paced the room for several minutes. "He didn't so much as look at me." She was getting hot, and she went and put her face to the window. The people from Memphis had come indoors, and the sun shone on the brownish green grass and on the still trees. "It's a scorcher," she said. She walked the length of the room again and opened the door. Buddy was still there. Standing there in white, his shirt open at the collar, and his white pants, long pants. He was leaning against the banister.

"Ready?" he said, smiling.

As they went down the steps together, he said, "It's nice that you're here. We didn't know it till just a few minutes ago." He was a Yankee kid, lived with his mother somewhere, and rolled his *r*'s, and spoke as though there was a lot of meaning behind what he said. She gave him a quick glance to see what he meant by that last remark. He smiled, and this time looked right into her eyes.

After lunch, which Josie felt had been awful embarrassing, they traipsed into the back parlor, and George showed off the kids again. She had had a good look at the older one during lunch and could tell by the way the corners of his mouth drooped down that he was a surly one, unless maybe he was only trying to keep from looking so pretty. And all he said to the questions which George asked him about girls and his high school was "Yeah" or "Aw, naw." When Henry brought in the first round of drinks, and he took one, his daddy looked at him hard and said, "Jock?" And the boy looked his daddy square in the eye.

Buddy only shook his head and smiled when Henry offered him a drink, but he was the one that had started all the embarrassment for her at lunch. When they came into the dining room he pulled her chair out, and she looked back at him—knowing how kids like to jerk chairs. Everybody laughed, but she kept on looking at him. And then she knew that she blushed, for she thought how big her behind must look to him with her bent over like she was.

The other thing that was awful was the question that Mrs. Jackson, the smallest matron and the one with the gray streak in her hair, asked her, "And how do *you* feel this morning, Miss Carlson?" It was the fact that it was Jackson's wife which got her most. But then the fool woman said, "Like the rest of us?" And Josie supposed that she meant no meanness by her remark, but she had already blushed; and Jackson, across the table, looked into his plate. Had this old woman and George been messing around? she wondered. Probably Mrs. Jackson hadn't meant anything.

As they all lounged about the sitting room after lunch, she even felt that she was beginning to catch on to these people and that she was going to start a little pretense of her own and make a good thing out of old Georgie. It was funny the way her interest in him, any real painful interest, was sort of fading. "I've never had so much happen to me at one time," she said to herself. She sat on the floor beside George's chair and put her hand on the toe of his brown and white shoe.

Then George said, "Buddy, you've got to give us just one recitation." And Buddy's face turned as red as a traffic light. He was sitting on a footstool and looking down at his hands.

Jock reached over and touched him on the shoulder and said, "Come on, Buddy, the one about 'If love were like a rose.'" Buddy shook his head and kept his eyes on his hands.

Josie said to herself, "The kid's honestly kind-a shy." It gave her the shivers to see anybody so shy and ignorant of things. But then he began to say the poetry without looking up. It was something about a rose and a rose leaf, but nobody could hear him very good.

George said, "Louder! Louder!" The boy looked at him and said a verse about "sweet rain at noon." Next he stood up and moved his hands about as he spoke, and the blushing was all gone. He said the next one to Mrs. Roberts, and it began:

> If you were life, my darling,
> And I, your love, were death . . .

That verse ended with something silly about "fruitful breath." He went then to Billy Colton's wife, and the verse he said to her was sad. The boy *did* have a way with him! His eyes were big and he could look sad and happy at the same time. "And I were page to joy," he said. He actually looked like one of the pages they have in stores at Christmas.

But now the kid was perfectly sure of himself, and he had acted timid at first. It was probably all a show. She could just hear him saying dirty limericks. She realized that he was bound to say a verse to her if he knew that many, and she listened carefully to the one he said to Mrs. Jackson:

> If you were April's lady,
> And I were lord in May,
> We'd throw with leaves for hours
> And draw for days with flowers,
> Till day like night were shady
> And night were bright like day;

> If you were April's lady,
> And I were lord in May.

He turned on Josie in his grandest manner:

> If you were queen of pleasure,
> And I were king of pain,
> We'd hunt down love together,
> Pluck out his flying-feather
> And teach his feet a measure,
> And find his mouth a rein;
> If you were queen of pleasure,
> And I were king of pain.

And Josie sat up straight and gave the brat the hardest look she knew how. It was too plain. "Queen of pleasure" sounded just as bad as whore! Especially coming right after the verse about "April's lady." The boy blushed again when she glared at him. No one made a noise for a minute. Josie looked at George, and he smiled and began clapping his hands, and everybody clapped. Buddy bowed and ran from the room.

"He's good, George. He's good," Jackson said, squinting his beady little eyes. Jackson was really a puny-looking little guy in the light of day! And he hadn't thought the boy was any better than anybody else did. It was just that he wanted to be the first to say something.

"He's really very good," Mrs. Jackson said.

George laughed. "He's a regular little actor," he said. "Gets it from Beatrice, I guess." Everybody laughed.

George's wife was an actress, then! She'd probably been the worst of the whole lot. There was no telling what this child was really like.

"How old is he, Jock?" Jackson asked. How that man liked to hear his own voice!

"Fourteen and a half," Jock said. "Have you seen him draw?" He talked about his kid brother like he was his own child. Josie watched him. He was talking about Buddy's drawings, about the likenesses. She watched him, and then he saw her watching. He dropped his eyes to his hands as Buddy had done. But in a minute he looked up; and as the talking and drinking went on he kept his eyes on Josephine.

It wasn't any of George's business. It wasn't any of his or anybody's how much she drank, and she knew very well that *he* didn't really give a damn! But it *was* smarter'n hell of him to take her upstairs, because the boys had stared at her all after- noon and all through supper. That was really why she had kept on taking the drinks when she had made up her mind to let up. She had said, "You're jealous. You're jealous, George." And he had put his hand over her mouth, saying, "Careful, Josie." But she was sort of celebrating so much's happening to her, and she felt good, and she was plain infuriated when George kissed her and went back downstairs. "He was like his real self comin' up the steps," she said. He had told her that she didn't have the gumption God gave a crab apple.

Josie went off to sleep with her lips moving and awoke in the middle of the night with them moving again. She was feeling just prime and yet rotten at the same time. She had a headache and yet she had a happy feeling. She woke up saying, "Thank your stars you're white!" It was something they used to say around home when she was a kid. She had been dreaming about Jock. He was all right. She had dreamed that together she and Jock had watched a giant bear devouring a bull, and Jock had laughed and for some reason she had said, "Thank your stars you're white!" He was all right. She was practically sure. His eyes were like George's, and he was as stubborn.

It would have been perfectly plain to everybody if supper hadn't been such an all-round mess. What with Jackson's smutty jokes and his showing off (trying to get her to look at him), and Mrs. Colton's flirting with her husband (holding his hand on the table), nobody but George paid any attention to Jock. And she was glad that she had smacked Jackson when he tried to carry her up the stairs, for it made Jock smile his crooked smile.

"They all must be in bed," she thought. The house was so quiet that she could hear a screech owl, or something, down in the woods.

She thought she heard a noise in her bathroom. She lay still, and she was pretty sure she had heard it again. She supposed it was a mouse, but it might be something else; she had never before thought about where that door beside the bathtub might lead. There was only one place it could go. She got up and went in her stocking feet to the bathroom. She switched on the light and watched the knob. She glanced at herself in the mirror. Her new white silk dress was twisted and wrinkled. "Damn him," she whispered to herself. "He *could* have made me take off this dress." Then she thought she had seen the knob move, move as though someone had released it. She stood still, but there wasn't another sound that night.

In the morning when she turned off the bathroom light, she was still wondering. She looked out of the window; the high net was down. No one was in sight.

What they all did was to slip out on her before she woke up! And in the breakfast room that morning Amelia wanted to talk, but Josephine wasn't going to give the nigger the chance. There was no telling what they had let the niggers hear at breakfast. Amelia kept coming to the breakfast room door and asking if everything was all right, if Miss Josephine wanted this or wanted that, but Miss Josephine would only shake her head and say not a word after Amelia had once answered, "They've went back to Memphis." For all she knew, George and the kids had gone too. It would have been like him to leave her and send after her, just because he had promised her she could stay a week. (He talked like it was such a great treat for her. She hadn't given a copper about the place at first. It had been *him*.) But he'd damned well better not have left her. She'd got a taste of this sort of thing for its own sake now, and she'd stay for good!

Buddy opened the outside door of the breakfast room.

"Good morning, Miss Carlson," he said.

"Hello," Josie said. She did wonder what Jock had told Buddy, what he had guessed to tell him. Buddy wasn't at dinner last night, or she couldn't remember him there.

He was wearing khaki riding pants and a short-sleeved shirt. He sat down across the table from her. "I guess we're all that's left," he said. He picked up the sugar bowl and smiled as he examined it. The corners of his mouth turned up like in a picture kids draw on a blackboard.

"Did Jock and George go to Memphis? Did they?"

"Jock did."

"He did?"

"Yes, he did. And Henry told me he didn't much want to go. I was off riding when they all got up this morning. Daddy wanted me to go too, but I wasn't here." He smiled again, and Josie supposed he meant that he'd been hiding from them.

"Where's your dad?"

"He? Oh, he went to the village to see about some hams. What are you going to do now?"

Josie shrugged her shoulders and began to drink her coffee. Jock was gone. He might have just been scorning her with those looks all the time. She should have got that door open somehow and found out what was what. "Why didn't Jock want to go?" she asked Buddy.

"Our pleasant company, I suppose," he said. "Or yours."

She looked at him, and he laughed. She wondered could this brat be poking fun at her? "Queen of pleasure!" she said out loud, not meaning to at all.

"Did you like that poem?" he asked. It was certain that he wasn't timid when he was alone with somebody, not at least when alone with her.

"I don't know," she said. Then she looked at him. "I don't like the one you picked for me."

"That's not one of the best, is it?"

Neither of them spoke while Josie finished her coffee. She put in another spoonful of sugar before taking the last few swallows, and Buddy reddened when she motioned for him to give up the sugar bowl. Amelia came and removed the breakfast plate and the butter plate. She returned for Josie's coffee cup, and, finding it not quite ready, she stood behind Buddy's chair and put her hands on his shoulders. The scar was right beside his cheek. Buddy smiled and beat the back of his head against her ribs playfully. Finally Josie put her cup down and said, "That's all."

She went upstairs to her room. Jock had tried to get in through her bathroom last night, or he had been so on her mind that her ears and eyes had made up the signs of it. Maybe Buddy had caught Jock trying to open the door and had told George. At any rate George had sent Jock away. If he sent him away, then Jock had definitely had notions. Josie smiled over that one. She was sitting on the side of her little canopied bed,

smoking a red-tipped cigarette. There was the noise of an automobile motor in the yard. George was back! Josie went to her
dressing table and drank the last of her whiskey.

She sat on the stool before her dressing table, with her eyes on
the hall door. She listened to George's footsteps on the stairs,
and sat with her legs crossed, twitching the left foot, which
dangled. George came in and closed the door behind him.

"I've bought you a ticket on the night train, Josie. You're
goin' back tonight."

So he wasn't such a stickler for his word, after all! Not in this
case. He was sending her home. Well, what did he expect her
to say? Did he think she would beg to stay on? She would clear
out, and she wasn't the one beaten. George was beaten. One of
his kids that he was so mortally fond of, one for sure had had
notions. "Almost for sure." George opened the door and left
Josie staring after him. In a few minutes she heard his horse
gallop past the house and out onto the dirt road.

She folded her white dress carefully and laid it on the bottom
of her traveling bag. She heard Buddy somewhere in the house,
singing. She wrapped her white shoes in toilet paper and stuck
them at the ends of the bag. Buddy seemed to be wandering
through the house, singing. His voice was high like a woman's,
never breaking as she sometimes thought it did in conversation.
It came from one part of the house and then another. Josie
stopped her packing. "There's no such thing," she said.

She went down the steps like a child, stopping both feet on
each step, then stepping to the next. One hand was on her hip,
the other she ran along the banister. She walked through the
front parlor with its bookcases and fancy chairs with the eagles
worked in the needlepoint, and through the back parlor with
the rocking chairs and the silly candle stand and the victrola.
She stepped down into the breakfast room where the sunlight
came through the blinds and put stripes on the brick wall. She
went into the kitchen for the first time. Mammy, with a white
dust cap on the back of her head, had already started supper.
She stood by the big range, and Amelia sat in the corner chopping onions. Josie wasn't interested in the face of either. She
went through the dark pantry and into the dining room. She
looked through the windows there, but no one was in the yard.
She went into the hall.

Buddy was near the top of the stairway which curved around the far end of the long hall, looking down at her. "Why don't you come up here?" He pronounced every word sharply and rolled his *r*'s. But his voice was flat, and his words seemed to remain in the hall for several minutes. His question seemed to float down from the ceiling, down through the air like a feather.

"How did he get up there without me hearing him?" Josie mumbled. She took the first two steps slowly, and Buddy hopped up to the top of the stair.

The door to the kids' room was open and Josie went in. Buddy shut the white paneled door and said, "Don't you think it's time you did something nice for me?"

Josie laughed, and she watched Buddy laugh. Queen of pleasure indeed!

"I want to draw you," he said.

"Clothes and all, Bud . . . ?"

"No. That's not what I mean!"

Josie forced a smile. She suddenly felt afraid and thought she was going to be sick again but she couldn't take her eyes off him.

"That's not what I mean," she heard the kid say again, without blinking an eye, without blushing. "I didn't know you were that sort of nasty thing here. I didn't believe you were a fancy woman. Go on out of here. Go away!" he ordered her.

As Josie went down the steps she kept puckering her lips and nodding her head. She was trying to talk to herself about how many times she had been up and down the steps, but she could still see the smooth brown color of his face and his yellow hair, and she could also see her hand trembling on the banister. It seemed like five years since she had come up the steps with the matrons from Memphis.

In the breakfast room she tore open the frail door to George's little liquor cabinet and took a quart of Bourbon from the shelf. Then she stepped up into the hall and went into the sitting room and took the portable victrola and that record. As she stomped back into the hall, Buddy came running down the steps. He opened the front door and ran out across the veranda and across the lawn. His yellow hair was like a ball of gold in the sunlight as he went through the white gate. But Josie went upstairs.

She locked her door and threw the big key across the room. She knocked the bottle of toilet water and the amber brush off her dressing table as she made room for the victrola. When she had started "Louisville Lady" playing, she sat on the stool and began to wonder. "The kid's head was like a ball of gold, but I'm not gonna think about him ever once I get back to Memphis," she told herself. "No, by damn, but I wonder just what George'll do to me." She broke the blue seal of the whiskey with her fingernail, and it didn't seem like more than twenty minutes or half an hour before George was beating and kicking on the door, and she was sitting on the stool and listening and just waiting for him to break the door, and wondering what he'd do to her.

The School Girl

ALL QUESTIONS were quite easy and pleasant to settle with so sensible a girl as Jane Ellen.

"She's never been anything but a joy to us," Rachel heard Mr. Patterson say right before the child. He held up the white report card which his daughter brought home that June. Thereon Miss Hood had penned six beautiful *E*'s (standing for excellence).

One of these *E*'s was the daughter's grade in Conduct; and Mrs. Patterson slipped an arm about Jane Ellen's waist, and she said, "But for this one, all the others would have been as nothing." She kissed the single curl which was brushed down precisely in the center of the girl's forehead, apart from her head of bobbed hair, and then sent her upstairs to dress. Rachel, who was Jane Ellen's black-mammy, lingered at the foot of the stair, listening.

"She's careful of her person," said Mrs. Patterson.

"And good students are often careless of their personal appearance," the father observed further. "Even sloppy, really."

This year there was no question of whether or not the girl might attend Festival; there had been only the supremely absorbing question of what the child could wear. How high should her heels be? How long the dresses? How severe the neckline in the evening? How stunning should her new hat be? What jewelry?

"It gave me great joy to help get her new clothes ready, for she has no notions of growniness. She consciously selected the pastel shades and the white."

"Knows what she wants," said Mr. Patterson.

"Whenever the merchant brought out the suitable piece of cloth, she would say immediately, 'That will do nicely.'"

"And invariably it was something right, was it?"

"Invariably," affirmed Mrs. Patterson. Leaning forward in her chair she saw that Rachel was still in the hall, paused at the foot of the stair. "The child will need your help, Rachel," she called impatiently. And as Rachel went noiselessly up the steps she watched the mother settle back into her seat, disappearing behind the dark portiere, and she heard her saying that she declared that she had never before seen a girl so aware of the charm of "simply *being* sixteen."

Mr. Patterson said: "She's a very pretty and a very wise young thing."

Over her black-mammy's protest they had put Jane Ellen in boarding school at fifteen, in Belmont at Nashville. This was in the year 1923 and so, of course, before the old regulations had been removed, but she *did* attend two small dances out at the University that year, and she *had* returned home virtually a young lady.

Rachel held the white taffeta tea gown before the window. "Clear as bride's tulle," she said. The girl answered with a smile in the dressing table mirror. She had brushed her hair close to her head, for she possessed a great, white, broad-brimmed hat to wear to the afternoon party. Rachel watched her move from the dressing table mirror to the full length mirror in the corner of the room. She followed her and stood behind her with the dress over one arm and the white silk petticoat over the other.

Jane Ellen was admiring her new lingerie in the mirror, turning first her one side, then the other. Her figure was plump, and she was only just tall enough to miss being called stubby. Rachel looked in the mirror at the dimples in the girl's knees and in her elbows as she turned each side to the mirror. She looked closely at the lace on the shoulder strap, and blew softly through her teeth, making a noise which was not distinctly a whistle, a laugh, or a sneer; and she said, not to the girl, but to the room or to the very house, "Nothin' lack o' lace here."

Presently the girl was seated in the platform rocker with one bare leg stuck out straight before her. Rachel squatted with her back to the girl and took the leg under her arm and over her knee. She pulled a silk stocking on over the white, round ankle, straightened it at the heel and stood up as she drew it over the knee. The girl fastened a blue ribboned garter about it. Rachel drew on the other stocking. As Jane Ellen lowered her feet toward the floor, Rachel exclaimed gruffly, "Ah! Ah! look out wid j'," and slapped the soles of her stocking feet. Then she brought her the new black shoes with the rhinestone buckles on them.

The girl stood up, and Rachel, with great care, dropped the white slip over her head. Rachel stepped back and observed her. "Girl, it's to y' knees," she said. And pointing to the dress: "This here could tolerate two or three petticoats." The girl laughed and twirled about on one foot before the full length mirror. Rachel caught her wrist and ordered her, "Stop 'at projeckin'!"

Now Rachel slipped the dress over her head and pulled it down over the round little figure. It fitted close about her hips, and both Jane Ellen and Rachel set to work with the snaps at the side plackets.

The hat box was open on the bureau. Rachel was pulling the straight pins from the tissue paper and folding the paper over the edges of the box. She came toward the girl with the big white hat over one fist and the heads of the pins protruding from her lips.

Jane Ellen threw back her head and looked at her hat critically. She took it and slowly pulled it down over her hair. It was a great, white, broad-brimmed hat with the brim turned off the face like the brim of a cavalier's hat.

She tilted the hat a little to the right. She reached for her yellow quilted purse on her dressing table. She strolled past the full length mirror, smiled at herself there, then smiled at Rachel and blushed.

Her hat and dress were solid white. She frowned into the full length mirror and went and sat down before the dressing table and frowned into that greenish speckled mirror. She adjusted her hat and tugged and pushed at her curls.

Rachel stood in the middle of the room.

Jane Ellen powdered her face and applied the tiniest bit of cheek rouge. She touched her hat again, and now began to rummage in her jewelry box. She held up a rhinestone pin to the hat, then a green buckle, an orange clasp, a gold clasp. She cast down the gold clasp, slammed the box closed, and began to open the drawer to her dressing table.

Her eye was caught by something in the mirror. Rachel saw Jane Ellen's green eyes in the mirror as they followed something about the room.

All at once Jane Ellen sprang from her seat. She halted herself a moment, then came on her toes across the floor.

Rachel, the pins still in her mouth, stood, arms akimbo, in the center of the room while the girl crept past her. Now, still standing in the middle of the room, she looked over her shoulder and saw a large, yellow butterfly hovering about the open window, trying to escape thereby.

It rested on the screen, its wings together. When it fluttered, Rachel saw the exact yellow of the new purse. Then for one silent moment it opened and closed its wings with a rhythm that would seem almost contemplative; yellow wings with black freckles near the slender body between them, with black lines which curved irregularly like the graceful shape of each wing. The yellow, the very tone of the new purse.

The butterfly flew up under the green window shade; the girl sprang at the window and held the shade close over the glass. She pulled out the shade a bit to peep under, and even Rachel could hear the flutter of the wings. But the insect escaped the hand that reached upward. It flew out across the room.

Jane Ellen gave chase, leaping wildly into the air like a Russian dancer. She jumped onto her bed just as the butterfly lit on the mahogany foot post. She stalked the length of the bed, her heels sinking deep into the comfort and mattress, a sweet smile on her lips, and her green eyes focussed precisely on the yellow thing before her. She uttered a wild whoop as she caught one powdery wing between her thumb and her forefinger.

The butterfly flapped about. The girl tiptoed toward Rachel. She reached forward and took three pins from Rachel's tight lips and carried the flapping butterfly to her dressing table. Rachel saw only the motion of the dimpled elbow as the girl ran one pin again and again through the thing's soft head and soft striated body. Then the wings were held up to the expanse of white brim, and a pin stuck through each.

Once more Jane Ellen smiled at herself in the full length mirror, and she ran past Rachel out into the hall; and Rachel heard the pitter-patter of her feet upon the stair.

A Walled Garden

No, MEMPHIS in autumn has not the moss-hung oaks of Natchez. Nor, my dear young man, have we the exotic, the really exotic orange and yellow and rust foliage of the maples at Rye or Saratoga. When our five-month summer season burns itself out, the foliage is left a cheerless brown. Observe that Catawba tree beyond the wall; and the leaves under your feet here on the terrace are mustard and khaki colored; and the air, the atmosphere (who would dare to breathe a deep breath!) is virtually a sea of dust. But we do what we can. We've walled ourselves in here with these evergreens and box and jasmine. You must know, yourself, young man, that no beauty is native to us but the verdure of early summer. And it's as though I've had to take my finger, just so, and point out to Frances the lack of sympathy that there is in the climate and in the eroded countryside of this region. I have had to build this garden and say, "See, my child, how nice and sympathetic everything can be." But now she does see it my way, you understand. You understand, my daughter has finally made her life with me in this little garden plot, and year by year she has come to realize how little else there is hereabouts to compare with it.

And you, you know nothing of flowers? A young man who doesn't know the zinnia from the aster! How curious that you and my daughter should have made friends. I don't know under what circumstances you two may have met. In her League work, no doubt. She *throws* herself so into whatever work she undertakes. Oh? Why, of course, I should have guessed. She simply *spent* herself on the Chest Drive this year. . . . But my daughter has most of her permanent friends among the flower-minded people. She makes so few friends nowadays outside of our little circle, sees so few people outside our own garden here, really, that I find it quite strange for there to be someone who doesn't know flowers.

No, nothing, we've come to feel, is ever very lovely, really lovely, I mean, in this part of the nation, nothing *but* this garden; and you can well imagine what even this little bandbox of a garden once was. I created it out of a virtual chaos of a backyard—Franny's playground, I might say. For three years

I nursed that little magnolia there, for one whole summer did nothing but water the ivy on the east wall of the house; if only you could have seen the scrubby hedge and the unsightly servants' quarters of our neighbors that are beyond my serpentine wall (I suppose, at least, they're still there). In those days it was all very different, you understand, and Frances's father was about the house, and Frances was a child. But now in the spring we have what is truly a sweet garden here, modeled on my mother's at Rye; for three weeks in March our hyacinths are an inspiration to Frances and to me and to all those who come to us regularly; the larkspur and marigold are heavenly in May over there beside the roses.

But you do not know the zinnia from the aster, young man? How curious that you two should have become friends. And now you are impatient with her, and you mustn't be; I don't mean to be too indulgent, but she'll be along presently. Only recently she's become incredibly painstaking in her toilet again. Whereas in the last few years she's not cared so much for the popular fads of dress. Gardens and floral design have occupied her—with what guidance I could give—have been pretty much her life, really. Now in the old days, I confess, before her father was taken from us—I lost Mr. Harris in the dreadfully hot summer of '48 (people don't generally realize what a dreadful year that was—the worst year for perennials and annuals, alike, since Terrible '30. Things died that year that I didn't think would *ever* die. A dreadful summer)—why, she used then to run here and there with people of every sort, it seemed. I put no restraint upon her, understand. How many times I've said to my Franny, "You must make your own life, my child, as you would have it." Yes, in those days she used to run here and there with people of every sort and variety, it seemed to me. Where was it you say you met, for she goes so few places that are really *out* anymore? But Mr. Harris would let me put no restraint upon her. I still remember the strongheadedness of her teens that had to be overcome and the testiness in her character when she was nearer to twenty than thirty. And you should have seen her as a tot of twelve when she would be somersaulting and rolling about on this very spot. Honestly, I see that child now, the mud on her middy blouse and her straight yellow hair in her eyes.

When I used to come back from visiting my people at Rye, she would grit her teeth at me and give her confidence to the black cook. I would find my own child become a mad little animal. It was through this door here from the sun-room that I came one September afternoon—just such an afternoon as this, young man—still wearing my traveling suit, and called to my child across the yard for her to come and greet me. I had been away for the two miserable summer months, caring for my sick mother, but at the sight of me the little Indian turned and with a whoop she ran to hide in the scraggly privet hedge which was at the far end of the yard. I called her twice to come from out that filthiest of shrubs. "Frances Ann!" We used to call her by her full name when her father was alive. But she didn't stir. She crouched at the roots of the hedge and spied at her travel-worn mother between the leaves.

I pleaded with her at first quite indulgently and good-naturedly and described the new ruffled dress and the paper cutouts I had brought from her grandmother at Rye. (I wasn't to have Mother much longer, and I knew it, and it was hard to come home to this kind of scene.) At last I threatened to withhold my presents until Thanksgiving or Christmas. The cook in the kitchen may have heard some change in my tone, for she came to the kitchen door over beyond the latticework which we've since put up, and looked out first at me and then at the child. While I was threatening, my daughter crouched in the dirt and began to mumble things to herself which I could not hear, and the noises she made were like those of an angry little cat. It seems that it was a warmer afternoon than this one—but my garden does deceive—and I had been moving about in my heavy traveling suit. In my exasperation I stepped out into the rays of the sweltering sun, and into the yard which I so detested; and I uttered in a scream the child's full name, "Frances Ann Harris!" Just then the black cook stepped out onto the back porch, but I ordered her to return to the kitchen. I began to cross the yard toward Frances Ann—that scowling little creature who was *incredibly* the same Frances you've met—and simultaneously she began to crawl along the hedge-row toward the wire fence that divided my property from the neighbor's.

I believe it was the extreme heat that made me speak so very harshly and with such swiftness as to make my words incomprehensible. When I saw that the child had reached the fence and intended climbing it, I pulled off my hat, tearing my veil to pieces as I hurried my pace. I don't actually know what I was saying—I probably couldn't have told you even a moment later—and I didn't even feel any pain from the turn which I gave my ankle in the gully across the middle of the yard. But the child kept her nervous little eyes on me and her lips continued to move now and again. Each time her lips moved I believe I must have raised my voice in more intense rage and greater horror at her ugliness. And so, young man, striding straight through the hedge I reached her before she had climbed to the top of the wire fencing. I think I took her by the arm above the elbow, about here, and I said something like, "I shall have to punish you, Frances Ann." I did not jerk her. I didn't jerk her one bit, as she wished to make it appear, but rather, as soon as I touched her, she relaxed her hold on the wire and fell to the ground. But she lay there—in her canniness—only the briefest moment looking up and past me through the straight hair that hung over her face like an untrimmed mane. I had barely ordered her to rise when she sprang up and moved with such celerity that she soon was out of my reach again. I followed—running in those high heels—and this time I turned my other ankle in the gully, and I fell there on the ground in that yard, this garden. You won't believe it—pardon, I must sit down. . . . I hope you don't think it too odd, me telling you all this. . . . You won't believe it: I lay there in the ditch and she didn't come to aid me with childish apologies and such, but instead she deliberately climbed into her swing that hung from the dirty old poplar that was here formerly (I have had it cut down and the roots dug up) and she began to swing, not high and low, but only gently, and stared straight down at her mother through her long hair—which, you may be sure, young man, I had cut the very next day at my own beautician's and curled into a hundred ringlets.

Attendant Evils

I DROVE all over Orange Mound yesterday; I literally scoured the place. This Willie Belle is what I found. She's as good and as bad as another, and we'll have to make her *do*, impudence and all, for I believe she can be relied upon to put in an appearance every day, which is more than can be said for the lot as a whole now-a-days. It's one of the attendant evils of war, my dear daughter, one of the things which women must endure. And you'll have to learn to bear all sorts of insolence and sass throughout this duration business. I declare I spent two weeks before you came looking for a nurse who *would do*, and when I found this one yesterday, when I came upon one that I could take home with me and instruct and feel some certainty about her being here this morning when you arrived, I was ready to take any black thing I could lay my hands on at any wage. It's one of the attendant evils of war, and there'll be no cessation till the thing is over.

I went in the rain yesterday out into that section they call Possum Trot, though I knew there were no good servants there, and I drove through the Garrett Hill section and Poesy. But the niggers in Memphis simply don't want work, not even those in Orange Mound where one used always to find a pretty good nigger of some sort. A war plays havoc with things, my child. I know the signs. You won't remember how Aunt Lacey behaved during the last one, how she wouldn't use butter plates (There was "no need in nastyin' up all them dishes"), and I shan't tell you about it, for you have only kind memories of her. Well, I got my clue to this stupid, sullen Willie Belle from your Aunt Mary Gordon's new cook (who is a peach considering the times). She gave me the street number of a certain Marcella who would tell me how to get to Willie Belle's sister's house, and so I had Vergil drive me there about eleven o'clock in the morning through the pouring rain. There was a young negro man sitting in the porch swing, but he paid us no attention when we stopped before the house. I said, "Vergil, sound your horn." Vergil pressed down on the horn for several seconds, but the boy didn't even look up at us. I was determined that he should come out and talk to me, and not to have Vergil get out in the rain in his new cap

and fresh uniform and come back to my upholstery drenching
wet. "Sound it again, Vergil," I said. The boy still didn't move.
My idea was that he was too proud and fine to come out and
stand in the rain. "Throw open your door, Vergil," I said, "so
he can see we'll let him get shelter. He's too proud and fine to
come out and stand in the rain." Vergil threw open the door
and continued to press the horn. But he said with a grin:

"He's slumberin'."

I hadn't realized that at all. But he *was* asleep. That, you see,
was his contribution to the war effort—sleeping in the middle
of the morning on the porch swing. Why, they don't want to
work as long as they have one crumb of bread and a roof over
their heads.

We were about to pull away. I told Vergil to close his door,
and it was the closing of that automobile door which suddenly
brought a face to the entrance of the little shotgun house. A
fat, brown negro woman opened the screen and called, "'At
blowin' for us?"

Think of it.

The boy on the swing roused himself and, opening two sau-
cer-like eyes, he looked out at us through the rain like a drowsy
cow. Then he looked at the woman in the doorway. I leaned
forward quickly, rolled down my window, and made myself
heard: "Marcella, will you step out here, please."

"Get some'n' on my hade," she called hatefully as though I
were putting her to the most unconscionable inconvenience. A
second later she appeared with a newspaper over her head. The
nigger on the swing sat staring at us, and the woman ran out
to the car in her bare feet. She leaped over the little ditch and
just barely held herself up by slapping her big brown left hand
down on the door beside me.

"Where does Willie Belle live, Marcella?" I said.

"Willie Belle?" she said, as though she were repeating words
in some foreign tongue which she didn't understand. "Willie
Belle," she said again, now as though trying to recall a face
out of the past.

"Aren't you the Marcella who's a friend of Mrs. Gordon's
Laura?"

Then she repeated "Laura" twice with just those intonations
which she had put upon "Willie Belle." Finally she looked at

me and said with an airy smile: "Oh, aren't Laura a tall dark-complected girl?"

"Yes, yes," I said perhaps too eagerly.

"No'm," she said, "I don't know no Willie Belle. I don't know what could have made Laura tell you that I do." She turned and called to the man on the porch who was now staring off toward the blank wall of a house next door, "You know a Willie Belle?" Without even looking at us he shook his head. But I sat there in silence and looked her directly in the eye for a minute, because I knew very well that she could tell me if she but would.

Presently Vergil said, "You know anybody wants to nurse?" I looked back and forth from one of their brown faces to the other, for they do seem to have some secret language which they speak with their eyes which no white person can possibly translate.

"Just a minute," she said. "Let me ask my husband." She went back through the rain between the forsythia and the jonquils to the porch, all the while holding the wet paper over her head. She sat down beside the man on the swing. Meanwhile I rolled up the window beside me, for the rain was blowing in on the upholstery. I could see through the rain that now fell on the glass and ran in long streams down to the sill the two of them sitting there talking the whole thing over casually, slowly, as though there were no war and as though you and the baby weren't arriving for another month. I really felt as though they weren't even discussing my errand but rather all those yellow flowers in the yard. At last she got up, however, and went into the house and put a dry piece of newspaper over her head. When she was at my window once again, I rolled down the glass, and she said, "My husband says he don't know no Willie Belle." But I could tell that she had something more to say by the way she looked about the inside of my automobile, noticing the upholstery and scrutinizing every article of clothing I wore. She looked at my hat an eternity (I was wearing the black velvet one with the two blue feathers in front), my choker, my beads, and of course my fur piece. You see, she knew that I was desperate and would take almost any amount of impertinence from her. That's the way the war affects them. Whatever they can get by with they'll do, just for the sake of getting by. Finally she said with that same airy smile, "I don't suppose you mean Willie B., do you, instead of Willie Belle? Nell Ruth's sister Willie B.? Nell Ruth who lives just up here in back of me on the next street. You'll see a yellow house with a big water oak in the yard just around the corner and back two houses." Then she smiled that airy smile at me still again, standing there in the rain barefooted, with a wet newspaper over her head like a poke bonnet, but with the airiest smile you've ever seen, proud, don't you know, of her mouth full of yellow gold teeth.

I said, "Drive on, Vergil." And when we had driven up the street a way I glanced backward through the rear glass. But do you know they weren't looking after us at all, as you'd naturally expect, but the woman was still in the rain holding onto that newspaper with both hands and loosening the earth about the roots of her flowers with her bare toes. The man she called her husband, who was twenty years younger than she, was already asleep in the swing again. And mind you, my child, this Willie Belle's sister's house was virtually in a stone's throw of Marcella's.

But it was quite a different sort of looking place. It was painted, as Marcella had said, a bright yellow, and there was a tree in the yard. It sat high up above the street on a clay bank, and the house next to it was painted a pale blue. In the rain both houses seemed bright and fresh against the grey sky. Vergil sounded the horn, and I was filled with hope. I had the feeling that here I'd find the sort of girl I wanted. I felt it, even before the negro woman showed herself at the door. When she did appear. I could tell from the automobile that it was an extremely fine looking colored girl. She wore a green sweater and brown skirt, and when I motioned to her to come out to me, she nodded right intelligently and stepped back inside the house a second. She reappeared with an umbrella and wearing galoshes. She ran through the yard avoiding mud puddles, and she smiled as she moved cautiously down the slick wooden steps over the clay bank. She put her head through the window and said very nicely, "Yes, Ma'am."

"You're Willie Belle, aren't you?" I said. But of course it wasn't Willie Belle, and she said no, that it was Nell Ruth. "I'm Willie Belle's baby sister," she said, "but Willie Belle stay here with I and my husband."

She was such a clean, neat, nice looking girl that I thought I'd say no more about Willie Belle. "Nell Ruth," I said, and I cleared my throat, for the girl looked at me so intelligently and even perceptively that I felt she observed my change of plans, "have you ever done any nursing?"

"Oh, yes," she said with a serious nod, "quite a lot." Her hair, which had been very thoroughly pressed out, lay flat on her head and was brought to a neat roll behind her ears, around the back of her neck.

"Well, I'd like to give you a try," I said. "What do you get?"

"Oh, I don't nurse now a lot," she answered quickly. "My husband don't usually like me to work out. He's night watchman for Barne's Supply Company and likes me here in day time."

I glanced down at my purse on my lap and said, "I pay well, Nell Ruth. Where did you work last?"

"Ah, I nursed last for Mrs. Norris in Morningside Park. She gives eight dollars a week."

Mind you, she said eight dollars a week, my child, in which of course there was not a word of truth. But that's the war for you. And now prepare yourself for this, my daughter. I said, "I'll give you nine dollars, Nell Ruth."

For a minute she ran her forefinger back and forth behind her ear pressing her hair down tight. She pursed her lips a second and then said, "I'll ask my husband." She went cautiously up the wooden steps again. Her galoshes were unfastened and the zippers tinkled at every step. It was still raining and she drew her shoulders in tight to make sure she kept within the circumference of the silk umbrella.

She was in the house for five or ten minutes, and Vergil and I sat in silence. Presently he switched off the engine and settled in his seat, as though he knew precisely what the procedure would be and just exactly how long it would take. I was so preoccupied with the business that I didn't even roll up the window, but sat watching the rain splash off the sill onto the upholstery and about my feet. When Nell Ruth opened her front door again, I peered up over the brown clay bank and saw two other persons in the shadow behind her. As she stepped down from the porch, I had my first glimpse of this Willie Belle, for she came out onto the porch and sat down in a high-backed rocking chair. She was wearing some sort of gingham wrapper and those carpet slippers she has on upstairs now.

Nell Ruth stuck her head inside my window and said, "No'm.
He just don't like me to work out a bit." She shook her head,
saying, "You know the men folks."

"Hop in out of the rain, Nell Ruth," I said, pointing to the
front seat. And Vergil opened the door. While she was letting
down her umbrella and very deliberately closing the car door,
I said, "Nell Ruth, I'll give you ten dollars a week to nurse my
daughter's baby for the two weeks they're visiting me. It's a
four-year-old girl who's a perfect angel."

And she looked at me ever so engagingly with her head
cocked to one side and a tender smile which seemed to say
that one more word about the darling child would leave her
in tears. Then quite mechanically, with her head still slightly
cocked, her expression grew solemn and she rolled her eyes off
in the direction in which Willie Belle sat rocking away on the
porch. My eyes followed hers. And before I had time to bring
my eyes back from that figure in the faded gingham wrapper,
Nell Ruth had said, "Willie Belle might do it for nine, with
car fare." By the time I looked at her again she had begun to
loosen her umbrella.

"Do you mean you won't work at any wage?" I said. She put
her hand on the door handle and began to open it. She had
fastened her eyes on the figure who sat rocking on the porch
of the yellow house and staring off into the rain. Nell Ruth
stepped onto the running board, and I said, "If Willie Belle
comes with me now, I'll give her eight dollars." She stepped
firmly down onto the ground from the running board, and my
heart sank with the thought of your arriving, my dear, today,
and I added, "Plus car fare when I don't send her home." As
that black creature in the green sweater was prissing herself up
the slick steps, still cautiously, undisturbed by what I had said
to her, I didn't know whether she was going to send Willie Belle
or not. I watched her movements as though I might be able to
discern the answer in them, and I listened to the tinkle of the
zipper fasteners on her galoshes. Beyond her I could see Willie
Belle still rocking with a cud-chewing motion. She seemed to
have no interest in what price, if any, she had brought. The
truth is, my dear, they absolutely *have* us for this duration, and

we'll have to bear it—for that long. While I watched Nell Ruth go across the yard, carefully avoiding the puddles of water, I said to Vergil, "Vergil, some people will better themselves just so much and no more. Because her husband has a job, that girl won't work." I rolled up my window and resting my head on the back of my seat in exhaustion I said, "We'll wait a minute and see whether or not Willie Belle's coming with us." And Vergil said confidently:

"She'll be along in a minute or so."

Rain in the Heart

WHEN THE drilling was over they stopped at the edge of the field and the drill sergeant looked across the flat valley toward the woods on Peavine Ridge. Among the shifting lights on the treetops there in the late afternoon the drill sergeant visualized pointed roofs of houses that were on another, more thickly populated ridge seven miles to the west.

Lazily the sergeant rested the butt end of his rifle in the mud and turned to tell the squad of rookies to return to their own barracks. But they had already gone on without him and he stood a moment watching them drift back toward the rows of squat buildings, some with their rifles thrown over their shoulders, others toting them by the leather slings in suitcase fashion.

On the field behind the sergeant were the tracks which he and the twelve men had made during an hour's drilling. He turned and studied the tracks for a moment, wondering whether or not he could have told how many men had been tramping there if that had been necessary for telling the strength of an enemy. Then with a shrug of his shoulders he turned his face toward Peavine Ridge again, thinking once more of that other ridge in the suburban area where his bride had found furnished rooms. And seeing how the ridge before him stretched out endlessly north and south he was reminded of a long bus and streetcar ride that was before him on his journey to their rooms this night. Suddenly throwing the rifle over his shoulder, he began to make his way back toward his own barrack.

The immediate approach to the barrack of the noncommissioned officers was over a wide asphalt area where all formations were held. As the sergeant crossed the asphalt, it required a special effort for him to raise his foot each time. Since his furlough and wedding trip to the mountains, this was the first night the sergeant had been granted leave to go in to see his wife. When he reached the stoop before the entrance to the barrack he lingered by the bulletin board. He stood aimlessly examining the notices posted there. But finally drawing himself up straight he turned and walked erectly and swiftly inside.

He knew that the barrack would be filled with men ready with stale, friendly, evil jokes.

As he hurried down the aisle of the barrack he removed his blue denim jacket, indicating his haste. It seemed at first that no one had noticed him. Yet he was still filled with a dread of the jokes which must inevitably be directed at him today. At last a copper-headed corporal who sat on the bunk next to his own, whittling his toenails with his knife, had begun to sing:

> "Yes, she jumped in bed
>   And she covered up her head—"

Another voice across the aisle took up the song here:

> "And she vowed he couldn't find her."

Then other voices, some faking soprano, others simulating the deepest choir bass, from all points of the long room joined in:

> "But she knew damned well
>   That she lied like hell
>   When he jumped right in beside her."

The sergeant blushed a little, pretended to be very angry, and began to undress for his shower. Silently he reminded himself that when he started for town he must take with him the big volume of Civil War history, for it was past due at the city library. *She* could have it renewed for him tomorrow.

In the shower too the soldiers pretended at first to take no notice of him. They were talking of their own plans for the evening in town. One tall and bony sergeant with a head of wiry black hair was saying, "I've got a strong deal on tonight with a WAC from Vermont. But of course we'll have to be in by midnight."

Now the copper-headed corporal had come into the shower. He was smaller than most of the other soldiers, and beneath his straight copper-colored hair were a pair of bright gray-green eyes. He had a hairy potbelly that looked like a football. "My deal's pretty strong tonight, too," he said, addressing the tall soldier beside him. "She lives down the road a way with her family, so I'll have to be in early too. But then you and me won't be all fagged out tomorrow, eh, Slim!"

"No," the tall and angular soldier said, "we'll be able to hold our backs up straight and sort of carry ourselves like soldiers, as some won't feel like doing."

The lukewarm shower poured down over the chest and back of the drill sergeant. This was his second year in the Army and now he found himself continually surprised at the small effect that the stream of words of the soldiers had upon him.

Standing in the narrow aisle between his own bunk and that of the copper-headed corporal, he pulled on his clean khaki clothes before an audience of naked soldiers who lounged on the two bunks.

"When I marry," the wiry-headed sergeant was saying, "I'll marry me a WAC who I can take right to the front with me."

"You shouldn't do that," the corporal said, "she might be wounded in action." He and the angular, wiry-headed sergeant laughed so bawdily and merrily that the drill sergeant joined in, hardly knowing what were the jokes they'd been making. But the other naked soldiers, of more regular shapes, found the jokes not plain enough, and they began to ask literally:

"Can a WAC and a soldier overseas get married?"

"If a married WAC gets pregnant, what happens?"

"When I get married," said one soldier who was stretched out straight on his back with his eyes closed and a towel thrown across his loins, "it'll be to a nice girl like the sergeant here's married."

The sergeant looked at him silently.

"But wherever," asked Slim, "are *you* going to meet such a girl like that in such company as you keep?"

The soldier lying on his back opened one eye: "I wouldn't talk about my company if I was you. I've saw you and the corporal here with them biddy-dolls at Midway twiest."

The corporal's eyes shone. He laughed aloud and fairly shouted. "And *he* got *me* the date both times, Buck."

"Well," said Buck, with his eyes still closed and his hands folded over his bare chest, "when I marry it won't be to one of them sort. Nor not to one of your WACs neither, Slim."

Slim said, "Blow it out your barracks bag."

One of those more regularly shaped soldiers seemed to rouse himself as from sleep to say, "That's why y'like 'em, ain't it, Slim? Y'like 'em because they know how?" His joke was sufficiently plain to bring laughter from all. They all looked toward Slim. Even the soldier who was lying down opened one eye and looked at him. And Slim, who was rubbing his wiry mop of black hair with a white towel, muttered, "At least I don't pollute little kids from the roller rink like some present."

The naked soldier named Buck who was stretched out on the cot opened his eyes and rolled them in the direction of Slim. Then he closed his eyes meditatively and suddenly opened them again. He sat up and swung his feet around to the floor. "Well, I did meet an odd number the other night," he said. "She was drinking beer alone in Connor's Café when I comes in and sits on her right, like this." He patted his hand on the olive-drab blanket, and all the while he talked he was not looking at the other soldiers. Rather his face was turned toward the window at the end of his cot, and with his lantern jaw raised and his small, round eyes squinting, he peered into the rays of sunlight. "She was an odd one and wouldn't give me any sort of talk as long as I sit there. Then I begun to push off and she says out of the clear, 'Soldier, what did the rat say to the cat?' I said that I don't know and she says, 'This pussy's killin' me.'" Now all the other soldiers began to laugh and hollo. But Buck didn't even smile. He continued to squint up into the light and to speak in the same monotone. "So I said, 'Come on,' and jerked her up by the arm. But, you know, she was odd. She never did say much but tell a nasty joke now and then. She didn't have a bunch of small talk, but she come along and did all right. But I do hate to hear a woman talk nasty."

The potbellied corporal winked at the drill sergeant and said, "Listen to him. He says he's going to marry a nice girl like yours, but I bet you didn't run up on yours in Connor's Café or the roller rink."

Buck whisked the towel from across his lap and drawing it back he quickly snapped it at the corporal's little, hairy potbelly. The drill sergeant laughed with the rest and watched for a moment the patch of white that the towel made on the belly which was otherwise still red from the hot shower.

Now the drill sergeant was dressed. He combed his sandy-colored hair before a square hand mirror which he had set on the windowsill. The sight of himself reminded him of her who would already be waiting for him on that other ridge. She with her soft, Southern voice, her small hands forever clasping a handkerchief. This was what his own face in the tiny mirror brought to mind. How unreal to him were these soldiers and their hairy bodies and all their talk and their rough ways. How temporary. How different from his own life, from his real life with her.

He opened his metal footlocker and took out the history book in which he had been reading of battles that once took place on this campsite and along the ridge where he would ride the bus tonight. He pulled his khaki overseas cap onto the right side of his head and slipped away, apparently unnoticed, from the soldiers gathered there. They were all listening now to Slim who was saying, "Me and Pat McKenzie picked up a pretty little broad one night who was deaf and dumb. But when me and her finally got around to shacking up she made the damnedest noises you ever heard."

With the book clasped under his arm the drill sergeant passed down the aisle between the rows of cots, observing here a half-dressed soldier picking up a pair of dirty socks, there another soldier shining a pair of prized garrison shoes or tying a khaki tie with meticulous care. The drill sergeant's thoughts were still on her whose brown curls fell over the white collar of her summer dress. And he could dismiss the soldiers as he passed them as good fellows each, saying, "So long, Smoky Joe," to one who seemed to be retiring even before sundown, and "So long, Happy Jack," to another who scowled at him. They were good rough-and-ready fellows all, Smoky Joe, Happy Jack, Slim, Buck, and the copper-headed one. But one of them called to him as he went out the door, "I wouldn't take no book along. What you think you want with a book this night?" And the laughter came through the open windows after he was outside on the asphalt.

The bus jostled him and rubbed him against the civilian workers from the camp and the mill workers who climbed aboard with their dinner pails at the first stop. He could feel the fat thighs of middle-aged women rubbing against the sensitive places of his body, and they—unaware of such personal feelings—leaned toward one another and swapped stories about their outrageous bosses. One of the women said that for a little she'd quit this very week. The men, also mostly middle-aged and dressed in overalls and shirt-sleeves, seemed sensible of nothing but that this suburban bus somewhere crossed Lake Road, Pidgeon Street, Jackson Boulevard, and that at some such intersection they must be ready to jerk the stop cord and alight. "The days are getting a little shorter," one of them said.

The sergeant himself alighted at John Ross Road and transferred to the McFarland Gap bus. The passengers on this bus were not as crowded as on the first. The men were dressed in linen and seersucker business suits, and the women carried purses and wore little tailored dresses and straw hats. Those who were crowded together did not make any conversation among themselves. Even those who seemed to know one another talked in whispers. The sergeant was standing in the aisle but he bent over now and again and looked out the windows at the neat bungalows and larger dwelling houses along the roadside. He would one day have a house such as one of those for his own. His own father's house was the like of these, with a screened porch on the side and a fine tile roof. He could hear his father saying, "A house is only as good as the roof over it." But weren't these the things that had once seemed prosaic and too binding for his notions? Before he went into the Army had there not been moments when the thought of limiting himself to a genteel suburban life seemed intolerable by its restrictions and confinement? Even by the confinement to the company of such people as those here on the bus with him? And yet now when he sometimes lay wakeful and lonesome at night in the long dark barrack among the carefree and garrulous soldiers or when he was kneed and elbowed by the worried and weary mill hands on a bus, he dreamed longingly of the warm companionship he would find with her and their sober neighbors in a house with a fine roof.

The rattling, bumping bus pulled along for several miles over the road atop the steep ridge which it had barely managed to climb in first gear. At the end of the bus line he stepped out to the roadside and waited for his streetcar. The handful of passengers that were still on the bus climbed out too and scattered to all parts of the neighborhood, disappearing into doorways of brick bungalows or clapboard two-storiers that were perched among evergreens and oak trees and maple and wild sumac on the crest and on the slopes of the ridge. *This* would be a good neighborhood to settle down in. The view was surely a prize—any way you chose to look.

But the sergeant had hardly more than taken his stand in the grass to wait for the streetcar, actually leaning a little against a low wall that bordered a sloping lawn, when he observed the figure of a woman standing in the shadow of a small chinaberry tree which grew beside the wall.

The woman came from behind the tree and stood by the wall. She was within three or four steps of the sergeant. He looked at her candidly, and her plainness from the very first made him want to turn his face away toward the skyline of the city in the valley. Her flat-chested and generally ill-shaped figure was clothed with a baglike gingham dress that hung at an uneven knee length. On her feet was a pair of flat-heeled brown oxfords. She wore white, ankle-length socks that emphasized the hairiness of her muscular legs. On her head a dark felt hat was drawn down almost to her eyebrows. Her hair was straight and of a dark color less rich than brown and yet more brown than black, and it was cut so that a straight not wholly grease-less strand hung over each cheek and turned upward just the slightest bit at the ends.

And in her hands before her the woman held a large bouquet of white and lavender sweet peas. She held them, however, as though they were a bunch of mustard greens. Or perhaps she held them more as a small boy holds flowers, half ashamed to be seen holding anything so delicate. Her eyes did not rest on them. Rather her eyes roved nervously up and down the car tracks. At last she turned her colorless, long face to the sergeant and asked with an artificial smile that showed her broad gums and small teeth, "Is this where the car stops?"

"I think so," he said. Then he did look away toward the city.

"I saw the yellow mark up there on the post, but I wasn't real sure," she pursued. He had to look back at her, and as he did so she said, "Don't that uniform get awful hot?"

"Oh yes," he said. He didn't want to say more. But finally a thought of his own good fortune and an innate kindness urged him to speak again. "I sometimes change it two or three times a day."

"I'd sure say it would get hot."

After a moment's silence the sergeant observed, "This is mighty hot weather."

"It's awful hot here in the summer," she said. "But it's always awful here in some way. Where are you from?"

He still wanted to say no more. "I'm from West Tennessee."

"What part?" she almost demanded.

"I'm from Memphis. It gets mighty hot there."

"I oncet know somebody from there."

"Memphis gets awfully hot in the summer too."

"Well," she said, drawing in a long breath, "you picked an awful hot place to come to. I don't mind heat so much. It's just an awful place to be. I've lived here all my life and I hate it here."

The sergeant walked away up the road and leaned forward looking for the streetcar. Then he walked back to the wall because he felt that she would think him a snob. Unable to invent other conversation, he looked at the flowers and said, "They're very pretty."

"Well, if you like 'em at all," she said, "you like 'em a great lot more than I do. I hate flowers. Only the other day I say to Mother that if I get sick and go the hospital don't bring any flowers around me. I don't want any. I don't like 'em."

"Why, those are pretty," he said. He felt for some reason that he must defend their worth. "I like all flowers. Those are especially hard to grow in West Tennessee."

"If you like 'em you like 'em more than I do. Only the other day I say to my Sunday School teacher that if I would die it'd save her a lot of money because I don't want anybody to send no flowers. I hate 'em. And it ain't just these. I hate all flowers."

"I think they're pretty," he insisted. "Did you pick 'em down there in the valley?"

"They was growing wild in a field and I picked them because I didn't have nothin' else to do. Here," she said, pushing the flowers into his hands, "you take 'em. I hate 'em."

"No, no, I wouldn't think of taking your flowers. Here, you must take them back."

"I don't want 'em. I'll just throw 'em away."

"Why, I can't take your flowers."

"You have 'em, and I ain't going to take 'em back. They'll just lay there and die if you put them on the wall."

"I feel bad accepting them. You must have gone to a lot of trouble to pick them."

"They was just growing wild at the edge of a field, and the lady said they was about to take her garden. I don't like flowers. I did her a favor, and you can do me one."

"There's nothing I like better," he said, feeling that he had been ungracious. "I guess I would like to raise flowers, and I used to work in the garden some." He leaned forward, listening for the sound of the streetcar.

For a minute or two neither of them spoke. She shifted from foot to foot and seemed to be talking to herself. From the corner of his eye he watched her lips moving. Finally she said aloud, "Some people act like they're doing you a favor to pay you a dollar a day."

"That's not much in these times," he observed.

"It's just like I was saying to a certain person the other day, 'If you are not willing to pay a dollar and a half a day you don't want nobody to work for you very bad.' But I work for a dollar just the same. This is half of it right here." She held up a half dollar between her thumb and forefinger. "But last week I pay for all my insurance for next year. I put my money away instead of buying things I really want. You can't say that for many girls."

"You certainly can't."

"Not many girls do that."

"I don't know many that do."

"No sirree," she said, snapping the fingers of her right hand, "the girls in this place are awful. I hate the way they act with soldiers downtown. They go to the honky-tonks and drink beer. I don't waste anybody's money drinking beer. I put my own money away instead of buying things I might really want."

The sergeant stepped out into the middle of the road and listened for the streetcar. As he returned to the wall, a Negro man and woman rode by in a large blue sedan. The woman standing by the wall watched the automobile go over the streetcar tracks and down the hill. "There's no Negro in this town that will do housework for less than two and a half a day, and they pay us whites only a dollar."

"Why will they pay Negroes more?" he asked.

"Because they can boss 'em," she said hastily. "Just because they can boss 'em around. I say to a certain person the other day, 'You can't boss me around like a nigger, no ma'am.'"

"I suppose that's it." He now began to walk up and down in front of her, listening and looking for the streetcar and occasionally raising the flowers to his nose to smell them. She continued to lean against the wall, motionless and with her humorless face turned upward toward the car wire where were hanging six or eight rolled newspapers tied in pairs by long dirty strings. "How y'reckon them papers come to be up there?" she asked.

"Some of the neighborhood kids or paperboys did it, I guess."

"Yea. That's it. Rich people's kids's just as bad as anybody's."

"Well, the paperboys probably did it whenever they had papers left over. I've done it myself when I was a kid."

"Yea," she said through her nose. "But kids just make me nervous. And I didn't much like bein' a kid neither."

The sergeant looked along one of the steel rails that still glimmered a little in the late sunlight and remembered good times he had had walking along the railroad tracks as a child. Suddenly he hoped his first child would be a boy.

"I'll tell you one thing, soldier," the woman beside him was saying, "I don't spend my money on lipstick and a lot of silly clothes. I don't paint myself with a lot of lipstick and push my hair up on top of my head and walk around downtown so soldiers will look at me. You don't find many girls that don't do that in this awful place, do ya?"

"You certainly don't find many." The sergeant felt himself blushing.

"You better be careful, for you're going to drop some of them awful flowers. I don't know what you want with 'em."

"Why, they're pretty," he said as though he had not said it before.

Now the blue sedan came up the hill again and rolled quietly over the car tracks. Only the Negro man was in the sedan, and he was driving quite fast.

"How can a nigger like that own a car like that?"

"He probably only drives for some of the people who live along here."

"Yea. That's it. That's it. Niggers can get away with anything. I guess you've heard about 'em attacking that white girl down yonder."

"Yes . . . Yes."

"They ought to kill 'em all or send 'em all back to Africa."

"It's a real problem, I think."

"I don't care if no man black or white never looks at me if I have to put on a lot of lipstick and push my hair up and walk around without a hat."

The sergeant leaned forward, craning his neck.

"I'm just going to tell you what happened to me downtown the other day," she persisted. "I was standing looking in a store window on Broad when a soldier comes up behind me, and I'm just going to tell you what he said. He said he had a hotel room, and he asked me if I didn't want to go up to the room with him and later go somewhere to eat and that he'd give me some money too."

"I know," the sergeant said. "There's a mighty rough crowd in town now."

"But I just told him, 'No thanks. If I can't make money honest I don't want it,' is what I told him. I says, 'There's a girl on that corner yonder at Main that wants ya. Just go down there.'"

The sergeant stood looking down the track, shaking his head.

"He comes right up behind me, you understand, and tells me that he has a room in a hotel and that we can go there and do what we want to do and then go get something to eat and he will give me some money besides. And I just told him, 'No thanks. There's a girl on that corner yonder at Main that wants ya. Just go down there.' So I went off up the street a way and then I come back to where I was looking at a lot of silly clothes, and a man in a blue shirt who was standing there all the time says that the soldier had come back looking for me."

The sergeant stretched out his left arm so that his wristwatch appeared from under his sleeve. Then he crooked his elbow and looked at the watch.

"Oh, you have *some* wait yet," she said.

"How often do they run?"

"I don't know," she said without interest, "just every so often. I told him, y'see, if I can't make money honest I don't want it. You can't say that for many girls." Whenever his attention seemed to lag, her speech grew louder.

"No, you can't," he agreed.

"I save my money. Soldier, I've got two hundred and seven dollars in the bank, besides my insurance paid up for next year." She said nothing during what seemed to be several minutes. Then she asked, "Where do your mother and daddy live?"

"In West Tennessee."

"Where do you stay? Out at the camp?" She hardly gave him time to answer her questions now.

"Well, I stay out at camp some nights."

"*Some* nights? Where do you stay other nights?" She was grinning.

"I'm married and stay with my wife. I've just been married a little while but we have rooms up the way here."

"Oh, are you a married man? Where is she from? I hope she ain't from here."

"She's from Memphis. She's just finished school."

The woman frowned, blushed deeply, then she grinned again showing her wide gums. "I'd say you are goin' to take her the flowers. You won't have to buy her any."

"I do wish you'd take some of them back."

The woman didn't answer him for a long time. Finally, when he had almost forgotten what he had said last, she said without a sign of a grin, "I don't want 'em. The sight of 'em makes me sick."

And at last the streetcar came.

It was but a short ride now to the sergeant's stop. The car stopped just opposite the white two-story house. The sergeant alighted and had to stand on the other side of the track until the long yellow streetcar had rumbled away. It was as though an ugly, noisy curtain had at last been drawn back. He saw her face through an upstairs window of the white house with its precise cupola rising ever higher than the tall brick chimneys and with fantastic lacy woodwork ornamenting the tiny porches and the cornices. He saw her through the only second-story window that was clearly visible between the foliage of trees that grew in the yard.

The house was older than most of the houses in the suburban neighborhood along this ridgetop, and an old-fashioned iron fence enclosed its yard. He had to stop a moment to unlatch the iron gate, and there he looked directly up into the smiling countenance at the open window. She spoke to him in a voice even softer than he remembered.

Now he had to pass through his landlady's front hall and climb a crooked flight of stairs before reaching his rooms, and an old-fashioned bell had tinkled when he opened the front door. At this tinkling sound an old lady's voice called from somewhere in the back of the house, "Yes?" But he made no answer. He hurried up the steps and was at last in the room with his wife.

They sat on the couch with their knees touching and her hand in his.

Just as her voice was softer, her appearance was fairer even than he had remembered. He told her that he had been rehearsing this moment during every second of the past two hours, and simultaneously he realized that what he was saying was true, that during all other conversations and actions his imagination had been going over and over the present scene.

She glanced at the sweet peas lying beside his cap on the table and said that when she had seen him in the gateway with the flowers she had felt that perhaps during the time they were separated she had not remembered him even as gentle and fine as he was. Yet she had been afraid until that moment by the window that in her heart she had exaggerated these virtues of his.

The sergeant did not tell her then how he had come into possession of the flowers. He knew that the incident of the cleaning woman would depress her good spirits as it had his own. And while he was thinking of the complete understanding and sympathy between them he heard her saying, "I know you are tired. You're probably not so tired from soldiering as from dealing with people of various sorts all day. I went to the grocery myself this morning and coming home on the bus I thought of how tiresome and boring the long ride home would

be for you this evening when the buses are so crowded." He
leaned toward her and kissed her, holding her until he realized
that she was smiling. He released her, and she drew away with
a laugh and said that she had supper to tend to and that she
must put the sweet peas in water.

While she was stirring about the clean, closet-like kitchen,
he surveyed in the late twilight the living room that was still
a strange room to him, and without lighting the table or floor
lamps he wandered into the bedroom, which was the largest
room and from which an old-fashioned bay window overlooked
the valley. He paused at the window and raised the shade. And
he was startled by a magnificent view of the mountains that
rose up on the other side of the city. And there he witnessed
the last few seconds of a sunset—brilliant orange and brick
red—beyond the blue mountains.

They ate at a little table that she drew out from the wall in
the living room. "How have I merited such a good cook for
a wife?" he said and smiled when the meal was finished. They
stacked the dishes unwashed in the sink, for she had put her
arms about his neck and whispered, "Why should I waste one
moment of the time I have you here when the days are so lonesome and endless."

They sat in the living room and read aloud the letters that
had come during the past few days.

For a little while she worked on the hem of a tablecloth, and
they talked. They spoke of their friends at home. She showed
him a few of their wedding presents that had arrived late. And
they kept saying how fortunate they were to have found an
apartment so comfortable as this. Here on the ridge it was cool
almost every night.

Afterward he took out his pen and wrote a letter to his father.
He read the letter aloud to her.

Still later it rained. The two of them hurried about putting down windows. Then they sat and heard it whipping and
splashing against the window glass when the wind blew.

By the time they were both in their nightclothes the rain
had stopped. He sat on a footstool by the bed reading in the
heavy, dark history book. Once he read aloud a sentence which
he thought impressive: "I have never seen the Federal dead lie
so thickly on the ground save in front of the sunken wall at

Fredericksburg." This was a Southern general writing of the battle fought along this ridgetop.

"What a very sad-sounding sentence," she said. She was brushing her hair in long, even strokes.

Finally he put down the book but remained sitting on the stool to polish his low-quartered military shoes. She at her dressing table looked at his reflection in the mirror before her, and said, "It's stopped raining."

"It stopped a good while ago," he said. And he looked up attentively, for there had seemed to be some regret in her voice.

"I'm sorry it stopped," she said, returning his gaze.

"You should be glad," he said. "I'd have to drill in all that mud tomorrow."

"Of course I'm glad," she said. "But hasn't the rain made us seem even more alone up here?"

The sergeant stood up. The room was very still and close. There was not even the sound of a clock. A light was burning on her dressing table, and through the open doorway he could see the table lamp that was still burning in the living room. The table there was a regular part of the furnishing of the apartment. But it was a piece of furniture they might have chosen themselves. He went to the door and stood a moment studying the effect she had achieved in her arrangement of objects on the table. On the dark octagonal top was the white lamp with the urn-shaped base. The light the lamp shed contrasted the shape of the urn with the global shape of a crystal vase from which sprigs of ivy mixed with periwinkle sprang in their individual wiriness. And a square, crystal ashtray reflecting its exotic lights was placed at an angle to a small round silver dish.

He went to the living room to put out the light. Yet with his hand on the switch he hesitated because it was such a pleasing isolated arrangement of objects.

Once the light was out he turned immediately to go back into the bedroom. And now he halted in the doorway again, for as he entered the bedroom his eye fell on the vase of sweet peas she had arranged. It was placed on top of a high bureau and he had not previously noticed it. Up there the flowers looked somehow curiously artificial and not like the real sweet peas he had seen in the rough hands of the woman this afternoon. While he was gazing thus he felt his wife's eyes upon him. Yet without turning to her he went to the window, for he was utterly preoccupied with the impression he had just received and he had a strange desire to sustain the impression long enough to examine it. He kept thinking of that woman's hands.

Now he raised the shade and threw open the big window in the bay, and standing there barefoot on a small hooked rug he looked out at the dark mountains and at the lines and splotches of lights in the city below. He heard her switching off the two small lamps at her dressing table. He knew that it had disturbed her to see him so suddenly preoccupied, and it was as though he tried to cram all of a whole day's reflections into a few seconds. Had it really been the pale flowers that had impressed him so? Or had it been the setting of his alarm clock a few minutes before and the realization that after a few more hours here with her he must take up again that other life that the yellow streetcar had carried away with it this afternoon? He could hear the voices of the boys in the barrack, and he saw the figure of the woman by the stone wall under the chinaberry tree.

Now he could hear his wife moving to switch off the overhead light. There was a click. The room being dark, things outside seemed much brighter. On the slope of the ridge that dropped off steeply behind the house the dark treetops became visible. And again there were the voices of the boys in the barrack. Their crudeness, their hardness, even their baseness— qualities that seemed to be taking root in the very hearts of those men—kept passing like objects through his mind. And the bitterness of the woman waiting by the streetcar tracks pressed upon him.

His wife had come up beside him in the dark and slipped her arm about his waist. He folded his arms tightly about her. She spoke his name. Then she said, "These hours we have together are so isolated and few that they must sometimes not seem quite real to you when you are away." She too, he realized, felt a terrible unrelated diversity in things. In the warmth of her companionship, he felt a sudden contrast with the cold fighting he might take part in on a battlefield that was now distant and almost abstract.

The sergeant's eyes had now grown so accustomed to the darkness inside and outside that he could look down between the trees on the slope of the ridge. He imagined there the line after line of Union soldiers that had once been thrown into the battle to take this ridge at all cost. The Confederate general's headquarters were not more than two blocks away. If he and she had been living in those days he would have seen ever so clearly the Cause for that fighting. And *this* battlefield would not be abstract. He would have stood here holding back the enemy from the very land which was his own, from the house in which she awaited him.

But here the sergeant stopped and smiled at himself. He examined the sergeant he had just imagined in the Confederate ranks and it was not himself at all. He compared the Confederate sergeant to the sergeant on the field this afternoon who had stood a moment puzzling over the tracks that twelve rookies had made. *The sergeant is I*, he said to himself desperately, *but it is not that morning in September of '63 when the Federal dead were lying so thick on the ground.* He leaned down and kissed his wife's forehead, and taking her up in his arms he carried her to their bed. *It is only a vase of flowers*, he remarked silently, rhetorically to himself as his wife drew her arms tighter about his neck. *Three bunches from a stand of sweet peas that had taken the lady's garden.* As he let her down gently on the bed she asked, "Why did you look so strangely at the vase of flowers? What did they make you think about so long by the window?"

For a moment the sergeant was again overwhelmed by his wife's perception and understanding. He would tell her everything he had in his mind. What great fortune it was to have a wife who could understand and to have her here beside him to hear and to comprehend everything that was in his heart and mind. But as he lay in the dark trying to make out the line of her profile against the dim light of the window, there came through the rainwashed air outside the rumbling of a streetcar. And before he could even speak the thoughts which he had been thinking, all those things no longer seemed to matter. The noise of the streetcar, the irregular rumble and uncertain clanging, brought back to him once more all the incidents of the day. He and his wife were here beside each other, but suddenly he was hopelessly distracted by this new sensation. The streetcar had moved away now beyond his hearing, and he could visualize it casting its diffused light among the dark foliage and over the white gravel between the tracks. He was left with the sense that no moment in his life had any relation to another. It was as though he were living a thousand lives. And the happiness and completeness of his marriage could not seem so large a thing.

Impulsively, almost without realizing what he was doing, he sat up on the other side of the bed. "I wasn't really thinking about the flowers," he said. "I guess I was thinking of how nicely you had arranged things on the living-room table."

"Oh," she said, for by his very words *I guess* it was apparent that she felt him minimizing the importance of his own impressions this evening and of their own closeness. In the dark he went to the small rocking chair on which his clothes were hanging and drew a cigarette from his shirt pocket. He lit it and sat on the edge of the little rocker, facing the open window, and he sat smoking his cigarette until quite suddenly the rain began to fall again. At the very first sound of the rain he stood up. He moved quickly to the window and put out his cigarette on the sill near the wire screen. The last bit of smoke sifted through the wire mesh. The rain was very noisy among the leaves. He stumbled hurriedly back through the dark and into the bed where he clasped his wife in his arms.

"It's begun to rain again," she said.

"Yes," the sergeant said. "It's much better now."

The Scoutmaster

THAT YEAR all the young people in Nashville were saying, "Don't tell me that, old dear, because it makes me *too* unhappy." It was *the* answer to almost anything that could be said.

You could hear Virginia Ann saying it to her beaux in the parlor up in front. She had her own special way of saying it and would sometimes give new emphasis to the irony by saying "too, too, too unhappy" or by beginning with "Please, please don't tell me that." Whenever she said it loud enough for Father to hear her all the way back in the sitting room, he would say that he could not bear to hear her using that expression, though he said he didn't know why he could not. "I can't abide it," he would say. "That's all there is to it."

In the hall there was a picture of Father at the age of six, still wearing what he called his kilts but large enough to be holding the reins of a big walking horse on the back of which was seated Uncle Jake. My Uncle Louis, too, in his first pants, was in the picture. He was seated on the grass underneath the horse's belly with his arms about the neck of a big airedale. (But Uncle Louis had died of parrot fever when he was only twelve.) Virginia Ann would show the picture to her beaux as they were leaving at night. It was always good for a laugh, especially if it was a new beau that had just met Father or Uncle Jake, who was living at our house then. "Really," she would say, harking back to the thing that all the young people had said last year, "I think that picture is *truly* a sugar." And she would point out Father's long curls and the lace on the hem of Uncle Jake's dress. Father would say that he could not abide that expression either.

I used to hear Uncle Jake asking Father very gently why he was so "hard on" Virginia Ann and asking if he didn't know that all "modern girls" were like that. And I would sit and wonder why he was so hard on her. Father would say sometimes that he couldn't explain it even to himself.

Mother found just as much fault with Virginia Ann, but she never worried about explaining what it was that was wrong.

She would tell Uncle Jake and Aunt Grace (who was not Uncle Jake's wife but Mother's own sister, staying with us then after her divorce from Uncle Basil)—she would tell them that as each of her children passed seventeen she intended either to give them up as a bad job or, if they didn't all turn out as Virginia Ann had, to sit back and rest on her laurels. Yet Mother's groans were as loud as Father's when they heard Virginia Ann greeting her date at the front door with "Well, well, well, if it isn't my country cousin!" I would turn my eyes to her and Father as soon as I heard Virginia Ann say this, for I knew it was one of the things they could not abide.

Aunt Grace was never gentle with people the way Uncle Jake was. She would tell Mother and Father that they were real fools to be so critical of Virginia Ann, who she said was one of the brightest, cleanest girls she had ever known. Hadn't this daughter of theirs had the finest average in her junior class? And wasn't she studying practical things even in high school (business administration, accounting, shorthand!)? Father and Mother would nod and smile. Father would be put in such a grand good humor by Aunt Grace's admiration of his daughter that he would begin to tease her about some unmarried man or other in their acquaintance. Or he would take off his spectacles and smile benevolently at her as she ranted, she now making a show of her outspokenness: Wasn't Virginia Ann's behavior with her beaux above all suspicion? she would ask. Certainly she was one of the few young girls who never— Never once! Aunt Grace could vouch for it. *She* had the girl's confidence— never stepped outside the front door to say good night to her date.

"Poor Grace!" Father and Mother would sit for a long while after one of these outbursts and lament the hard lot that had been Aunt Grace's. Uncle Basil was such a hopeless ne'er-do-well, really a drunken scoundrel whose vanity and social ambitions had been his ruination; and yet they believed that deep in her heart Grace loved him still. And that was going to make it hard for her ever to marry again. How sad it was. She was still a comparatively young woman. "Today women of thirty-eight are looked upon as quite young, you know," one of them would say.

And, for all she had been through, they agreed, Aunt Grace showed her years remarkably little. Who would ever have guessed that she was actually only five years younger than dear, sweet Jake? She had a certain girlish prettiness about her that would always deny her age.

Yet it wasn't that Uncle Jake's own sad life told on him ("No one has ever borne such sadness as his with so fine a spirit"), but, Father explained, Jake had had a motherless daughter to raise and to nurse through a fatal illness at the age of nineteen, and that had kept him old-fashioned. Even if this motherless daughter of his had not been a prig and a fanatic— His daughter had died at nineteen from a skin disease she had caught in her social work. Her name had been Margaret, but he had always called her "Presh" for "precious"—even if she had not been such a one, Uncle Jake would have remained old-fashioned, Father explained, because just raising a child did that for one.

Aunt Grace stayed with us for six weeks after she had gotten her divorce. The morning that she left for her job in Birmingham I came and sat beside her on the porch swing. She pulled me up close to her and beckoned to Brother to come and sit at her other side. "I've stayed here on you forever," she said to Mother and Father who were seated about the porch with Virginia Ann and Uncle Jake, "and these two rascals are not the least of my reasons for it." Simultaneously she pressed Brother and myself so tightly to her that we found ourselves face to face, each with a cheek lying against the blue linen cloth of the suit she and Virginia Ann had been sewing on for a week. Brother had just reached the age to join Uncle Jake's Boy Scout troop, and it occurred to me that if Aunt Grace was so very young Brother would soon be old enough to marry her himself. I looked into his eyes to see if he were going to cry about her going away. But he was looking back at me with a grin on his face. Presently he stuck out his tongue, curled it up on each side till it looked like a tulip, and before I could pull away from Aunt Grace's embrace he had blown a spit bubble in my face.

A fight ensued right across Aunt Grace's lap. It was a furious, noisy scuffle and it left the new linen skirt in a hundred creases and wrinkles. Yet Aunt Grace's good humor remained unruffled. And as Uncle Jake's large and gentle hands pulled us apart I caught a quick glimpse of my aunt's face. Her head was thrown back, as to avoid the blows. Her soft creamlike complexion seemed to have just a little more color than usual. Her big blue eyes, matching her blue hat and her blue suit, were squinted as they always were when she laughed. Between her bursts of laughter she was saying, "Look! Look! Look at the little demons. See them! I wish you could see their eyes flashing."

It was Brother and I that Aunt Grace took with her in the taxi. All of the grown-ups had, of course, wanted to go with her to the station. Uncle Jake had even brought his car from the garage, and Father's car always stayed in front of the house. But she would let neither of them drive her to the depot. She would not even let Virginia Ann—who tried with Aunt Grace to make a joke about the parting though there were certainly tears caught in the long lashes of her small brown eyes—Aunt Grace would not even let her go along. They were both very gay, but Aunt Grace's gaiety had so much more unity and was so much more convincing and contagious that you hardly noticed Virginia Ann's.

When the taxi came she made everyone but the children say good-bye to her on the porch. Brother and I helped the driver take her luggage to the cab, and we waited in the backseat while she walked down the front walk with her arm about our sister's waist. Just before they reached the cab they even skipped for a few steps and sang without any special tune, "Look out, Birmingham, here comes the widow from Nashville, Tenn-tenn-tennessee."

They stopped a minute at the car door and we heard Virginia Ann saying, "I'll keep you posted on my progress with you-know-who and such stuff. It'll be, 'Dear Miss Dix, I care deeply for someone who . . .'"

"Oh, he'll come around," Aunt Grace said. "I know the type—silent, serious, indifferent."

"I'll write you all about it."

"You write me, Virginia Ann. But, Virginia Ann, here's one parting piece from your Aunt Grace before she goes: Let the boys be fools about you. Don't you ever be the fool. *Don't* be a little fool for any boy."

Virginia Ann blushed and then laughed in a high, excited voice. Aunt Grace laughed too, and they kissed each other good-bye.

It was my and Brother's first ride in a taxicab, and we were going to ride the streetcar home, a thing which we had not done many times unless accompanied by Father. I sat gazing first at the noisy meter, then at the picture of the driver on his license that hung beside the rearview mirror. We rode for several blocks through the streets lined with the two-story residences, each approximating a square or oblong shape, each roofed with tile or slate or painted shingle, each having a porch built of the same solid materials appended to the front or the side of the house, each with a yard big enough for perhaps one, two, or three trees, every last one of these houses with features so like those of my father's house that they failed to rouse any curiosity in me. And so finally I turned and simply looked at Aunt Grace.

She was just then peering over the cardboard hatbox that she held most carefully on her lap, trying to see the time by her tiny wristwatch. Her white-gloved forefinger and thumb pushed the glove of the other hand from a white silk cuff (a dainty yet full cuff extending below the blue sleeve of her suit coat) and she was bending cautiously over the big round box to get a view of the dial. I climbed to my knees and myself peered over to the face of that little white gold ornament. When I saw that the tiny black hands actually told the correct time of day I experienced a breathtaking amazement.

But I raised my eyes to Aunt Grace's face, and no longer did it seem that the watch was the cause of my amazement. I felt myself growing timid in her presence, for she had become a stranger to me. The hatbox, the watch, the white gloves, the absurdly full silk cuffs, the blue linen suit on which she had labored so long and so painstakingly, and even the tiny brown bows on her white shoes all took on a significance. The watch seemed to have been but a key. And all of those things that once indicated that Aunt Grace was one sort of person now indicated that she was quite another sort. She was not the utterly useless if wonderfully ornamental member of the family. In the solid blueness of her eyes I was surely on the verge of finding some marvelous function for her personality. (I would have said my mother's function was Motherhood and my father's, Fatherhood.) I was about to find the reason why there should be one member of a boy's family who was wise or old-fashioned enough to sit with Mother and Father and discuss the things they could not abide in Virginia Ann and yet who was foolish or newfangled enough to enjoy the very things that Virginia Ann called "the last word." But it was precisely then that the cab stopped before the entrance to the dirty limestone railroad depot, and Uncle Basil stepped up and opened the automobile door.

I hopped out onto the sidewalk and Brother after me, he taking the small suitcase and I the cardboard hatbox which I held by a heavy black ribbon that was tied in a bow knot above the side of the box. Aunt Grace followed us straightening her straw hat with her left hand, clasping her white purse under her right arm. She and Uncle Basil began to talk as though they were strangers making pleasant conversation. It seemed that Aunt Grace did not cease her chatter and her excited laughter from the time she left the taxi until we saw her on the train.

Uncle Basil's very presence was itself shocking, but I was even more astonished to find him unchanged in appearance. Actually I must have recognized him by his smart attire—his plaid coat and white trousers—for it had been fully a year since he had been to our house. I had expected dissipation to show not only in his face but in his dress as well. He paid the taxi driver over Aunt Grace's protests and summoned a Negro redcap to take all the luggage. Brother and I followed them into the station.

We followed them under the high, vaulted ceiling of the lobby and into the station yard. All the while Aunt Grace's laughter could be heard above the hum of people whom, one and all, I imagined to be taking their final farewell of one another. When we were in the station yard her laughter seemed to reach even a higher pitch.

Finally we were waiting beside the sleeping car into which the redcap had taken Aunt Grace's luggage. Brother and I studied the black wheels and the oily brakes underneath the car. The conductor in blue called, "Ullaboward." I looked up and saw Uncle Basil speaking with an expression on his face that was half serious and half playful. Aunt Grace stopped laughing just long enough to say something that made him blush. She told him not to tell her *that*, because it made her too, too unhappy. Then she turned from him to us and stooping down, she put her arms around Brother and me and kissed us again and again. "Put these two rascals on the streetcar, will you, Basil?"

When she stepped into the dark vestibule of the sleeping car I saw a bit of the lace that hemmed her "slip" showing from beneath her blue skirt. I felt that it was more like the wide lace on Mother's petticoats than the little strips on Virginia Ann's. The train began to move, and she was still in the vestibule looking over the conductor's shoulder. Presently she began to laugh as she waved to us. I suddenly turned my face so as not to see the enormous spread of her smile, but for several seconds it seemed that I could hear the sound of her strange, high laughter above the noise and commotion of the train.

Uncle Jake used afterward to repeat the witty things that Aunt Grace had said when she was staying with us. Oftentimes when the clock on the mantel of the upstairs sitting room chimed he would remind the other members of the family—sometimes only with a smile—of what Grace used to say about the quarter-hourly chiming. "Remember what Grace used to say, 'I'd as soon have someone come and knock on my door every fifteen minutes of the night and say, "Fifteen minutes have passed," as have that clock in a house of mine.'"

He would talk about what a happy nature Aunt Grace had. Whenever Mother said that she worried about how Aunt Grace was getting on in Birmingham with her new job, he would say that Aunt Grace would always be happy, that she was one of those fortunate people who have a special faculty for happiness. He would sometimes recall the songs that she and Virginia Ann had sung together when they washed dishes on Sunday night. They were the only popular songs he had ever seemed to catch on to. He would speak of her as the "Sleepy Time Gal," for she had called herself that whenever she came down to breakfast later than the rest of the family or whenever she went up to bed earlier. You could hear her on the stairs

singing in a voice that mimicked the blues singers we heard
on the radio:

> . . . you're turning night into day . . .
> My little stay at home, play at home,
> eight o'clock sleepy time gal.

At night especially her voice seemed to drift through the
whole house like a wisp of smoke. Sometimes before bed she
and Virginia Ann would don their most outlandishly faded and
ragged wrappers and with cold cream on their faces and with
their hair in a hundred metal curlers they would waltz about
the bare floor of the upstairs hall singing. They would sing
"I'd Climb the Highest Mountain" or "Three O'Clock in the
Morning." But the song that Uncle Jake said he could not help
liking best of all was called "Melancholy Baby." Mother and
Father said it was no better than other new songs. Father would
say, "I think maybe it's even a little *more* suggestive, Jake, than
the usual run." But Uncle Jake said that it had more of the old-
time feeling in it and that it put one in a mood the way music
was supposed to do. So he would sit and listen while Virginia
Ann accompanied herself and Aunt Grace on the piano:

> Every cloud must have a silver lining.
> Wait until the sun shines through.
>
> So smile, my honey dear,
> While I kiss away each tear,
> Or else I shall be melancholy too.

Yet it wasn't Aunt Grace alone that Uncle Jake remembered
kindly. He had a good word even for Uncle Basil, if it was only
to say, "Basil has a way with him that you can't help liking."

Whenever Father and Mother were out for dinner Uncle
Jake was likely to spend the whole meal talking to us about our
good fortune at having such splendid parents. "Your father,"
he'd say, "puts all of his brothers and sisters to shame, and
your mother is certainly the choice of her mother's brood. . . .
There is no finer woman in the South than your mother, and
no businessman in town is respected more than your father. . . .
I declare I don't know any other parents these days who live as

much for their children as yours do. It's always looked to me like they each learned secrets of happiness from their parents that none of the rest of us did. . . . You children are their whole life, and you ought to remember that."

After such a speech not one of us was able to speak. Virginia Ann's eyes would always fill with tears. And one evening Uncle Jake went so far as to say that Mother and Father were just the sort of parents that his and Father's own had been and that he sometimes woke in the night and wept at the realization that his parents were actually dead and that he could never, never make amends to them for the little worries he had caused them.

And that night Virginia Ann did burst right out crying. She wept in her napkin and I thought she sounded like a little kitten begging to get out of the cellar or to get in the house when it was raining. I almost cried myself to think of poor Uncle Jake in his room crying, and I vowed that I should not postpone making amends to my own mother and father even till the next morning. (I waited, in fact, all that evening in the living room for them to come in, lying on my stomach before the fire. But I dropped off to sleep with my eyes set on the orange glow of the coals, and when I awoke it was morning. I was in my bed with Brother where Uncle Jake had placed me.)

Whenever all the family were at the table Uncle Jake would often talk of the saintly nature of Uncle Louis who had died at the age of twelve from parrot fever. Neither he nor Father could remember ever having heard Uncle Louis speak an uncivil word or remember his misbehaving on any occasion. Once their father—the two of them would recall—had come through the strawberry patch behind the old house on the Nolansville Pike and found Uncle Jake and Father playing mumble-the-peg while Uncle Louis did all the berry picking. And when Uncle Louis saw his father stripping off his belt to give his brothers a whipping he ran to him and told him that he, the eldest brother, was to blame for not making them work and that he should receive the punishment. My grandfather had turned and walked to his house without another word.

Whenever Father and Uncle Jake talked about that incident Father would say that Grandfather walked away in disgust. But Uncle Jake would say that he walked away toward the house in order that they should not see how moved he was by Uncle Louis's brotherly love and spirit of self-sacrifice.

Father was not as tall as Uncle Jake when they were standing, but that was only because Uncle Jake had such long legs. When we were seated at the table they seemed to be of the same height. Each had an extremely high forehead and a pointed chin that Uncle Jake said they had got from their mother's people. Nothing could hold my interest more keenly in those days than watching them sit together at table after dinner when Mother and Virginia Ann had gone into the living room. Sometimes they would only sit and smoke in silence. Sometimes they would talk about the old times.

One night when they had talked about the Negroes who had worked their father's farm, about Cousin Lucy Grimes who turned Catholic and later went completely crazy, and about the meanness of their Uncle Bennett who lost his leg at the Battle of Stones River, they turned again to the subject of Uncle Louis's native sweetness. While they talked, I looked across the table from one to the other trying to discover why they did not really look alike since their individual features were so similar. I felt that they actually did look alike and that I was just blind to it in some way. The only differences that I could see were not ones of my own observation but differences that I had heard Mother point out now and again: Uncle Jake had lived outdoors so much with his hunting and fishing and his other activities with the Boy Scouts that his skin was considerably rougher than Father's, who had no real life but in his office and in our house. Too, Uncle Jake's hair was still a hard, young, brown color whereas Father's was full of pleasant gray streaks. Yet withal there was a softness or gentleness about Uncle Jake's eyes and about the features of his face that were not to be found in Father's kind but strong countenance.

After dinner Mother would always switch off the principal light as she left the dining room, and the men's talking was done in softer illumination from the side wall lamps.

Brother had gone one night and climbed into Father's lap, I was sitting beside Uncle Jake, and I leaned my head over on his knee. It seemed that the lights were lower than usual that night, and the Negro cook in her white serving apron seemed to take longer than ever in removing the dishes. She kept reaching over me to clear the dishes from my and Uncle Jake's places, and once she told me to sit up and quit being a bother to my Uncle Jake. But he, without turning his eyes from Father, laid his hand lightly across my chest to hold me there; and the cook went off to the sideboard shaking her head. Uncle Jake had not spoken for a long while. He had sat smoking his white-bowled pipe and listening to Father, but I could tell now by the twitching at the corner of his mouth that he was finally about to speak. When his lips parted and he simultaneously removed the pipe I remarked the long distance between the point of his chin and his eyes and noticed that the eyes themselves were set far apart and were rather popped, I thought, from this upside-down view.

Addressing Father as "Brother"—a thing he did only when they were reminiscing—he began to speak of Uncle Louis. He lifted his eyes to the ceiling, and from where I lay it seemed that he had rolled his eyeballs far back into his head, and I noticed the strange animal-like moisture of his upper lip. "Brother," he said, "I was playing with Louis one day under the mulberry tree at the end of the side porch. We had a couple of pillboxes that old Dr. Pemberton had given us and we had caught two of the caterpillars that fell from the mulberry tree. With some black thread from Mama's basket we were hitching the poor fuzzy worms to the little boxes and then filling the boxes with sand to see how heavy a load the caterpillars could manage. But Louis quite accidentally pulled the thread so tightly about the middle of one of them that he cut the little fellow half in two. Then he looked at me silently across the two pieces of worm. And, mind you, after several seconds he scrambled to his feet and ran the length of the porch to where Mama was sitting with her sewing in her lap.

"I followed hot on his heels and stood by watching him as he fell on his knees and hid his face in her sewing. Pretty soon when he began to weep and shake all over—more like a girl than a boy—Mama thought he had hurt himself on the scissors or a needle and she jerked him up from her lap. He could not speak for his sobbing, and when I had told Mama that he had only cut a little worm half in two with a piece of thread, she drew him to her, smiling and patting his head tenderly. When at last he was able to speak he said, 'I killed the little caterpillar, Mama, and he'll never, never come back to life.'"

Uncle Jake was stirring unconsciously in his chair as he spoke, and I raised up from his lap and peered across the table-cloth into Father's face. His mouth literally hung open, and he said, "Why, Jake, I've never heard you tell that before."

Uncle Jake replaced his pipe between his teeth and chewed on it. He said, "Brother, I never had much heart for telling it, because it happened the same summer he caught the fever." And in a few minutes he got up and went over and unlocked the door to the porch that nobody ever used. Before he went out Father called him in a very stern voice, but he went out anyway and sat on the porch for a long time by himself, still smoking his pipe. In the living room I asked Father if he sup-posed Uncle Jake was thinking about Uncle Louis. He said he supposed he was thinking about Aunt Margaret his wife who had died so many, many years ago and about their daughter who had been a prig and a fanatic. Mother said that Father should not talk that way before the children.

Virginia Ann had innumerable beaux. It used to seem on Sunday afternoons that all the young men in Nashville had flocked to our house, some for but a few minutes' visit, others to make an all-afternoon stay. Father called them the Arabs and the Indians. The Arabs were the timid or sulky boys who stayed a short while and then moved silently on to some other house. The Indians were those bold ones who, he said, camped or squatted on his property for the eternity of a whole Sunday afternoon.

Father really did seem to despise the Indians. But it was the Indians who were Uncle Jake's delight. He would sit and talk to them while Virginia Ann gave her attention to those whose devotion had not been proved. And when they all had finally gone, he never failed to pretend that he was worried because Virginia Ann would not choose what he called a steady from among them. He would stop Virginia Ann as she was straightening up the parlor or perhaps by the newel post at the foot of the stairs and, rolling his eyes speculatively, he would enumerate the good and bad qualities of each of those he considered potential steadies.

Virginia Ann would listen, pretending, like himself, to be in dead earnestness. I could not have told that they were not speaking their literal thoughts had it not been for the pompous gestures Uncle Jake made with his hands whenever he was making fun and for the broad smile that broke upon Virginia Ann's face whenever Uncle Jake mentioned the devotion to herself which some young Indian had confided in him.

It was at the dinner table one night in the presence of all the family that Uncle Jake began to describe a conversation he had had with Bill Evers. He began by professing to believe that Bill Evers was the beau whom Virginia Ann should choose as her steady. The things he was saying were so much of the kind he had so often said to her about other young men that I did not really listen at first. I only remarked the mock seriousness in the tone of his voice and saw him batting his eyes as he concealed a smile behind his coffee cup. Several times I watched him bring his cup up in rather a hurry to his lips and, as often before, I studied the wide gold band on the fourth finger of his left hand. Uncle Jake had large hands, and I thought, as I studied them, of how much softer to the touch they were than one could imagine from their rough appearance.

It was likely the word "revolver" that finally made me listen to what he was actually saying about that particular one of the Indians. "Yes, Bill Evers tells me," he said, "that he is never afraid anywhere on the darkest night or in the wildest country as long as he has his revolver." And Uncle Jake each time he pronounced "revolver" would roll it out magnificently.

Virginia Ann's face suddenly blossomed into a broad smile that showed her lovely white teeth and revealed perhaps here and there on her teeth little splotches of orange-red paint that Mother said she applied "so liberally" to her lips.

Then Uncle Jake reported several of the incidents wherein Bill Evers had felt himself more secure for having his revolver by his side. Once he had been camping in the Baxter Hills. Another time he had been hunting along Duck River and had met a couple of old moonshiners whom Bill had described as "very much intoxicated." Whenever Uncle Jake was quoting

Bill directly he would deepen his voice and roll his r's, and for some reason this made Virginia Ann blush. It was, of course, because Bill was the only one of her beaux that really had a man's voice. And it seemed that Uncle Jake by deepening his voice was referring to that fact rather too persistently and somehow indelicately. Possibly I was the first to feel that Virginia Ann was no longer feigning that sober expression that had settled on her face now. I was watching her when Uncle Jake said, "Bill Evers is never afraid so long as he has his revolver by his side. 'My revolver,' Bill told me, 'is my best friend and just let any fellow take care who meddles with me when I have my revolver by my side.'"

Without warning, Virginia Ann sprang from the table weeping, not like a kitten but like a wounded animal out in the woods in the Baxter Hills. She ran from the dining room crying, "Oh, you're too cruel. You're heartless."

Uncle Jake seemed unable to move or speak. He looked helplessly from Father to Mother whose faces registered nothing but half-amused surprise. Then he pushed back his chair and hurried clumsily after Virginia Ann calling, "Child . . . Child." Brother and I slipped automatically from our chairs to follow as curious witnesses to the spectacle, but Mother and Father, who were now looking at one another, smiling and shaking their heads sadly, turned quickly to us and commanded us to return to our seats.

"Poor Jake," Father said, "always has to pay for what fun he has in life."

Mother continued to take an occasional sip from her white coffee cup. Finally she sighed, "Poor Jake. I'm sure he hadn't suspected how things are."

Father raised his eyebrows. After a moment he shook his head emphatically and said that Mother was reading things into this incident. "The girl's just tired tonight," he said. "She doesn't give a snap for the boy."

Mother shook her head with equal emphasis. "No. Grace told me before she left." She replaced her cup in its saucer but continued for several seconds to hold to its handle with her thumb and forefinger. "I must say, I thought Bill Evers had long since passed out of her head. There *was* a time when young girls confided such prolonged crushes in their mothers."

From somewhere in the front part of the house we could hear Uncle Jake's voice apologizing and entreating. Eventually we began to hear Virginia Ann reassuring him. And I recalled then how in front of the church one Sunday, after services, I had been tugging at Uncle Jake's hand, trying to pull him away from a crowd of men who were talking foxhound and bird dog. My eyes, as I tugged, were on an old Negro man who was selling bags of peanuts on the street corner. I saw that the vendor was closing the lid to the primitive cart that he pushed and was preparing to move to another corner. I tugged at Uncle Jake's hand and turned to beg him to come along. But upon turning my eyes to him I saw that he had somehow managed to slip my hand into that of a strange man; and he and all the others were standing about laughing at me.

With a violent jerk I had broken loose and had run off down the street in a beastly rage. When Uncle Jake finally caught me he held me and knelt on one knee before me imploring humbly that I forgive him (instead of cajoling as most men would have done). And silently I began to blame myself for not having realized that the hand I had been pulling on had a hardness and coarseness about it that should have distinguished it from that of my gentle uncle's.

"Poor Jake." Mother used to say that Father was "an omnivorous reader," and I would say myself when I was nine or ten that she and he were both "omnivorous talkers" when they were alone together. They talked about everything and everyone under the sun. They didn't talk especially kindly or unkindly about people, but I felt that in the years of their married life they had certainly left nothing that came into their heads unsaid. I was sometimes surprised to overhear them speak with such detachment of Virginia Ann or Brother or Uncle Jake. "Poor Jake," Father would say, "he's really incapable of being very realistic about his dealing with people. His real calling, his real profession is, you know, that of the Scoutmaster. It's during those Thursday night meetings with the boys that poor Jake fulfills himself. I always knew that he'd never make a great go of it in business, and sometimes when he tells me that he should have held on to the homeplace and farmed it, I can barely keep from telling him that somebody would have gotten it away from him and that he would have ended up as the tenant, forever recollecting the good old days, y'know, when it was our own." Mother would say that she didn't understand how he had done even as good a job of raising poor Presh as he did.

"Presh's religious mania, it's always seemed to me," Mother would say, "began as very much the same sort of thing as Jake's nostalgia. It was all tied up with notions of her mother's existence in Heaven. Toward the last her social work consisted mostly of preaching to those wretched poor people in East Nashville about her mother in Heaven. She could just not be bothered with any real view of things."

Father would speculate concerning Uncle Jake's fate and what it might have been if his wife had not died when Presh was only half grown: "If only Margaret, herself, had lived to make him and Presh a home, he might not have forever been looking to the past and being so uncritical of things in the present. He might have taken hold of himself." Here Mother would disagree. Men's natures weren't changed by circumstances, she contended. And the discussion would continue thus long after my interest had lagged.

At last I would hear Mother saying, "My Love, you simply have those age-old illusions of the male about Character and Fate. You've never really been Christianized." To which Father's favorite reply was: "I think you mean I've never been Calvinized." Or he would say, "The female is the cynic of the species."

Then if it were bedtime they would go about the house together locking-up, shutting-down, turning-off, putting-out, arranging everything for the night. And I would hear them in their bedroom still talking as they undressed and went to bed.

Father would never help us celebrate the Fourth of July. He said that it was because Vicksburg had fallen to the Yankees on the Fourth. And Uncle Jake would stand behind him and say he was exactly right, though Uncle Jake would, himself, come and help us set off the firecrackers in the backyard.

But Mother, as she and Father sat playing Russian bank on the screened porch, would denounce Father as a hypocrite and remind him that he had some excuse or other for not celebrating any of the holidays in hot weather. He simply could not abide hot weather. Nothing could stir him to action from

Decoration Day till after Labor Day in September. But after that it was very different. Mother would say that a week before Thanksgiving he began to develop holiday spirits that were continuous through Easter. Yet she, in turn, could not abide the cold weather; and *that*, Father maintained, was responsible for her "scaring up" such a religious point of view about Christmas and New Year's. Except for the Thanksgiving football game they would stay home on holidays reading or playing cards or maybe receiving a few friends or kinspeople. And the next day you could hear Mother on the telephone telling the woman who took her orders at the grocery, "We had a very quiet holiday at home, which is after all a more fitting way to spend such a day. . . . The children were in and out with their friends, so it was quite gay for us. . . . I think such days, after all, should be a time for the family to be together. . . . Yes, a time for us to count our blessings."

Uncle Jake never failed to comment upon the old-fashionedness of holidays at our house. When Aunt Grace had once accused Mother and Father of being together too lazy to face any kind of weather and had said that each of them was the other's worst enemy—socially—he had come forward most earnestly in their defense. He said that their mutual sacrifice of practically all social life for the sake of the other's comfort amounted to no less than "a symbol of unity."

"Besides," he said, "it's not as though they were denying themselves the sort of social gatherings that there were in and around Nashville a generation ago."

Aunt Grace had expressed her delight at this with several seconds of laughter so violent that she finally choked. With her face still very red, her eyes watery, and her voice hoarse she said, "How perfectly wonderful, Jake!" Then she leaned toward him, narrowing her eyes till they were two dark slits in her fair complexion, and said, "But you might be surprised, Jake, at what really grand old times some of the married set do have at their 'social gatherings' today."

Uncle Jake merely nodded soberly.

Aunt Grace laughed again, but carefully now so as not to choke. "I know what you mean," she added with a wink that had a little self-consciousness about it. "Look at what it 'done done' to me."

Uncle Jake blushed and remained quite serious for a moment. But he could not long resist the persistent, infectious laughter. He smiled genially and softly repeated the phrase which he must have thought good—"A symbol of unity."

It would sometimes be irksome to Virginia Ann that Mother planned all of the meals around Father's special tastes. Rarely did an evening meal come to our table, for instance, without there appearing on the menu either turnip salad or string beans cooked in ham fat. Aunt Grace had amused Virginia Ann mightily at breakfast one morning by her response to Mother's complaint against the drudgery of planning meals. She had pulled a small daisy from the centerpiece and offered it to Mother saying, "All you have to do is pluck off the petals repeating, Turnip greens—Beans. Turnip greens—Beans.' And so on till you get the answer." Virginia Ann had already made this something of a sensitive subject with Mother who now only closed her eyes and pressed down imaginary creases in the tablecloth with her small hand.

Father seemed no more amused than Mother by the suggestion for deciding the menu and he chose that as the signal for him to down the last of his coffee, pull his napkin loosely through his napkin ring, and go into the living room to look for the morning paper.

Uncle Jake, too, rose from his chair. But he reached out and took the daisy from Aunt Grace's hand and said slyly, "It's not a bad suggestion, Grace. But you don't understand that she's just telling her fortune the way clever women have always done. She pulls the petals not saying, 'He loves me. He loves me not,' but saying, 'He loves me. He loves me.'"

Aunt Grace laughed appreciatively. "Jake, how perfectly wonderful."

But when the men had gone to work, Virginia Ann, being a little out of humor that morning, said again that she could not see why Mother had always to put Father's tastes before those of the children. Mother turned to her and spoke finally, "If you don't know why, Daughter, then let me tell you: Some fine day each of my children will have a husband or a wife or some other equally absorbing and wonderful interest in life that will take them away from me. And so some fine day I shall have only your father's tastes to cater to. I don't want there to be any doubt in his mind on that fine day that he always came first at my table. I don't like the prospect of two old souls' turning from loneliness to one another because their children have left them."

"Well spoken," said Aunt Grace soberly. But presently she began to laugh and said that she was reminded of the limerick, "There was an old lady of Romany whose husband ate nothing but hominy," and Virginia Ann and Mother began to laugh too because her laughter was so infectious.

In Nashville Thanksgiving Day might be quite warm. It might be almost a sluggishly summerlike day, and sometimes we'd find that the freakish iris in the flower bed beside the porch had a few pale, bedraggled blossoms left. But, too, there will be years when it will snow at Thanksgiving time in Nashville, and everyone will be thinking so much about the problems of Christmas ahead that they have but little heart for even the football game.

Uncle Jake always went duck hunting on the weekend before Thursday so that there'd be duck to serve with the spiced round for Thanksgiving dinner. On Thanksgiving morning he went quail hunting. Dinner was usually kept waiting on him, for Mother would say that they were, after all, his ducks. But if he was very late, the tension would sometimes become unendurable, and Mother would go through the dining room, push open the swinging door a little way, and call to the cook mournfully, "Well, we'll just have to go ahead without Mr. Jake." It seems to me now that he always came in as Father was carving the ducks. Father would go on carving the roasted fowl before him while he admired the dead partridges that Uncle Jake brought out of the large patch pockets of his khaki hunting coat. Father would stop a minute with his knife still placed in a joint of the duck and watch Uncle Jake's big fingers feeling through the soft, dark feathers over the dead bird's breast. Once I wondered momentarily whether or not I'd be able to eat my meal after seeing the poor dead partridge with the blood on its speckled neck.

But there is no aroma more affecting to the palate than that of just-carved roast duck. When the steaming slices of dark meat and drumstick were placed in front of me I had no more thoughts of the dead birds that we would eat the following Sunday. I inhaled the delicious odor of the duck, I listened to the warm, eager voices around the table, and soon I would look up to see Uncle Jake returned now in his navy blue smoking jacket and with his hands washed whiter and cleaner than I ever saw them on ordinary days.

But before Uncle Jake came there would be tension, because the Thanksgiving football game began at two o'clock. And Father and Mother, no matter the weather, did attend the Thanksgiving football game. Presumably they had long ago established this as the one really feasible outing of the year because fall weather was neither too hot nor too cold. There was also the fact that at some time in the remote past Father had been a left tackle on the University team, and Mother had come there to watch his superb tackling and blocking. Actually, too, the football game was just as necessary to Uncle Jake's happiness on that day as was his quail hunting.

All of the grown people went to the Thanksgiving game. Virginia Ann had been going almost as far back as I could remember. Finally the year arrived when even Brother was to be allowed to go with the family; and the question was naturally raised, since I was only two years younger than he, as to whether or not I too should be allowed to go.

I should certainly have been taken along that day had I not shown real indifference to it. But it was considered on the whole well enough to leave me behind since Brother would be responsibility enough for Uncle Jake on this, his favorite holiday. Further, this year Virginia Ann was planning to attend, not with the rest of the family, but with Bill Evers. And this, strangely enough, involved me.

When Brother told me that Bill Evers was her "date" for the game, I did not quite understand what he meant. For several months she had been going to movies and to dances with Bill Evers, but it just happened that I had never before noticed this use of the word "date."

Mother must have seen the puzzled expression on my countenance. She put her hand on the top of my head and explained, "Brother means that Bill Evers is going to escort Virginia Ann to the football game." It did not occur to her that "escort" meant no more to me than "date." She allowed a faint smile to play across her face that seemed to tell me that other considerations than the weight of Uncle Jake's responsibility had brought her to agreeing to leave me alone on Thanksgiving afternoon. Presently she addressed these remarks to Father and Uncle Jake: "As we used to say in the country, Bill Evers is going to carry her to the game today. And if I know Virginia Ann's beaux, he'll not come for her till after we've left for the game. Boys today don't seem to have any respect for the girls, the way they keep them waiting."

"It used to be the boys that were kept waiting," Father said. "It's really the girls' own fault. They don't require anything of them."

"It never enters Virginia Ann's head," Mother said, "whether or not promptness is a virtue in young men."

"Well, well," Uncle Jake said rather sadly yet with the obvious intention of softening the remarks being directed against his niece, "customs change. Everything changes."

Mother gazed about the room as though she were keeping most of her thoughts to herself. At last she absently put her hand on my head again and said that Uncle Jake was quite right, that everything changes. "But, in any event, my lamb here will act as chaperon when Mr. Evers does arrive today. How is the weather out, Jake?"

A cold unexpected rain fell that afternoon.

They had all observed the gray overcast sky before they left, but none of them could predict what sort of weather would result.

The rain that fell, not a downpour or a mist but a fitful and wind-driven rain, was of such an uncertain character that I could not tell whether or not it would bring the family home early.

But the wind and rain together did bring them home. The wind that sprayed the rain against the pane of the bedroom window seemed to have blown them all into the front hall at once. Or, rather, it seemed to have blown them all through the hall and into the living room where Virginia Ann and Bill Evers had for the past half hour kept a silence that I felt I could not endure another second, a silence utterly unnatural in a house where someone had always before been talking and talking.

"How dare you! You get out of here you common dog." Father's voice burst upon the quietness.

Then everyone seemed to be talking at once. Mother uttered something as near to a scream as she had ever been known to utter, "Virginia Ann, I want you to get yourself upstairs out of your father's sight."

"Get out of here and never let me catch you on my premises again."

"How could you take such an advantage?"

Uncle Jake spoke too, but what he said was inaudible from where I stood in the doorway to my and Brother's room. But the sound of their voices in the house once more had filled me with confidence, had filled me with a sense of relief now. Father's first indignant commands were the relief and the proof I'd been waiting for. All my feelings of shock and fear and resentment were gone. I could enjoy the wonderful satisfaction that Father and Mother and Uncle Jake and even Brother had been driven home by the rain to make a reality of something that I felt had been frightening because of its unreality.

I had gone to the kitchen soon after the front door had closed behind the family when they left for the game. I had waited there, watching the cook dash the pots and pans about in her great haste to get away on Thanksgiving afternoon. The doorbell finally rang, and the cook and I heard Virginia Ann in the front hall saying to Bill Evers, "Hello, Cousin." The cook ceased her noisy business long enough to listen to Virginia Ann's chatter and to smile over it. She shook her head and, using Virginia Ann's own language, she told me that that sister of mine had a dandy line with her boyfriends.

And from thereout the cook didn't seem to be making such a racket with the utensils she was cleaning. In a few minutes she reached her brown hand through the gray, soapy water and opened the drain of the sink. She stacked those dishes that she had not washed on the draining board and said that they would just have to go till tomorrow. Then she gathered her hat and her coat and umbrella and asked me to lock the backdoor behind her. "I got to make haste," she said.

When I had locked the door I gave one glance to the dirty dishes and began to move toward the dining room. But at the sound of the voices of Virginia Ann and Bill Evers I stopped in the middle of the kitchen floor. It hadn't occurred to me that those two did not leave for the football game immediately after his arrival, and I was restrained from going into the front part of the house by a sudden wave of timidity. I stood a moment studying the black and white squares of linoleum about my feet. I observed now the bread crumbs in one spot and the grease splotch in another. I saw on the long table beneath the window a crockery bowl filled with water in which pieces of cake batter floated. A large spoon lay beside it on the table, and beneath the spoon a little puddle of water had settled on the white oilcloth. I was so sensible of the general mess in which the cook had left the kitchen and of the displeasure it would cause Mother when we should come to the kitchen to fix sandwiches tonight that I could not bear to think of being confined here any longer.

Yet I waited. If they didn't leave soon they'd certainly be late for the game. It had not yet begun to rain and so there was no question in my mind as to whether or not they would go. They would go, and they would go soon. I had merely to wait.

I waited. Still there was only the sound of their voices. I listened for the noise of footsteps. But there was none. As I waited with growing impatience I remarked how strange it was to hear a man's voice that was not Father's and a woman's voice that was not Mother's sounding on and on in our living room. Finally it seemed to be only Bill Evers's voice that I heard. Whenever Virginia Ann did speak, her voice had a sweetness about it that I had never heard and that almost brought tears to my eyes.

After a while my impatience grew naturally into resentment. But as the temptation to invade their privacy increased, so did my timidity.

I decided of a sudden that I was hungry.

I went to the big white refrigerator and opened its door. It had never before been so completely stocked with edibles. And the cook in her haste to be away had apparently crammed every perishable in sight into the box without thought or care for arrangement or accessibility.

A long stalk of celery fell out on the floor at my feet. I stooped to pick it up, and as I rose I found myself looking directly in on the heap of dead quail.

At that moment I heard, or thought I heard, Virginia Ann's voice calling my name. I remained staring at the dead birds for a moment. They were stacked one upon the other in their bloody, feathery deadness in the same shelf with the respectable skeletons of the roast ducks. I resolved not to move until I had heard Virginia Ann calling again. Then I should oh so gladly shut that door on the unwelcome sight of the birds and all that food for which I knew now I felt no hunger.

But when presently she called my name again, I could not make good my resolution. I stood holding the refrigerator door half open. She had called me, there was no doubting, but there was in her voice a note of caution. There was too evident a careful gauging of her volume. She plainly did not intend to disturb me if I were safely asleep or were safely out of earshot. And now that she had called me twice without answer, how could I ever answer? It was then that I determined to creep up the little flight of steps that went up from the kitchen (and joined the front stair on the landing) and to go and wait in my room. After I reached the small square bedroom with its overlarge pieces of mahogany furniture and metal bedstead I heard not another sound, and I had waited in the silence there until I thought I could endure it not another instant.

After Father had shut the front door behind Bill Evers, I heard Virginia Ann's footsteps on the stair. I hurried to the double bed that Brother and I shared and threw myself across it, but with my face toward the doorway. Presently she passed along the hallway, her hair disheveled, her turbanlike navy blue hat in her hand. I watched her indistinct daytime shadow that followed her along the plain wall of the hallway one second after she was out of sight.

In a little while Uncle Jake and Brother came upstairs. Brother came in the room and pushed his cap back on his head as he usually did when he came in the front door downstairs. Uncle Jake stopped in the doorway. I raised myself on my elbows and pretended to yawn. Uncle Jake said to me, "Tonight's Scout meeting night and we want you to go with us as our visitor." It was more command than invitation and I said, "Yes, sir."

"You two get yourselves a nap," he said, and as he moved away he pulled the door closed behind him.

Brother went to the closet and pulled out his Scout suit. I sat up on the side of the bed. Thursday night is Scout night, I said to myself. He and Uncle Jake would be going to Scout meeting the same as on any other Thursday. This made it all quite real now. A sort of joy took possession of me. I saw that Brother, in his way, was quite as disturbed as I by what had happened. Father had already expressed his rage as he entered the house. Mother I could hear talking and weeping intermittently in Virginia Ann's bedroom. I felt somehow that I could hear Aunt Grace saying to Virginia Ann, "You're a fool. You're a real little fool."

Brother was scrutinizing his uniform, brushing his shirt, loosening the knot of his kerchief. He would not look at me. Finally, without raising his eyes, he said, "You weren't asleep. Did you or didn't you go down and spy on them?" I made no answer. Now for some reason I felt myself blushing. I had no mind to answer him, I cared not whether he thought I had crept down the steps and spied on them or had remained in our room sleeping. Though I had not done so, I felt momentarily that I had. I could hardly remember whether I had or had not. But that was no matter. Actually I seemed to have forgotten Virginia Ann and Bill Evers. I was concerned only with Brother's eagerness to get into his uniform and be gone to the Boy Scout meeting. For I saw that he was trying to interest himself in other things. He hung his khaki trousers and shirt on a chair and began to move toward the bed. When he had lain down beside me he said, "Well, they were only necking, but they sure were *at* it." It had not occurred to me to imagine what they might have been doing. I rolled over on my back and looked up at the blank ceiling. I did not know exactly how to imagine what they might have been doing. And I couldn't imagine why I had been left at home this afternoon since I was not rebuked for my failure as a chaperon. A sense of my own ignorance overshadowed all my other dark feelings. Yet it did seem that all my elders, who knew so much, were no less surprised than I by Virginia Ann.

When Uncle Jake woke us from our nap he was dressed in his khaki Scout clothes. It was dark outside, and he had turned on the light and gone back into the hall to bring in a tray of sandwiches and two glasses of milk. Brother dressed himself in his khakis, and we ate.

Brother kept trying to make Uncle Jake talk about things pertaining to the Scouts. The only thing Uncle Jake said was, "If you'll apply yourself you'll be the first Eagle in our troop."

"I'm going to," Brother said. "I'm going to if it takes every single afternoon of the week." He was still trying to think of *other things*, I reflected.

When we went downstairs we found Mother and Father back in the sitting room playing casino. Virginia Ann was looking on. Father was winning and he pretended to be very proud and boastful of his score. He called us around to look at his hand and observe how cleverly he played it. But when he had called, "Cards," and the last hand was played, Mother had much the larger stack and all but one of the spades. So now she derided him for his boasting. Father pretended to want to talk of other things. "I believe," he said with feigned formality, "I say I believe, my dear wife, that you said you had a letter from your sister Grace yesterday. What did she say? Do tell me about it."

And Mother did commence to tell him all about the "nice, fat, long, happy" letter.

So we left the house amidst a new burst of conversation between Mother and Father, and I felt a gladness that I was not going to be in the house tonight. It would have meant being there alone with Virginia Ann. For just as Mother and Father had not invited her or anyone else to join their game they would not really have allowed anyone to join their conversation.

On the way to the Scout meeting, sitting in the front seat of the automobile between my uncle and my brother, I thought of the letter from my Aunt Grace. If she had been there that afternoon I knew that she would have said, "Virginia Ann, you're a real little fool." And I did not long to see her tonight, for she would have been singing in the kitchen and in the hall, full of the sort of cheer that was in the letter, the exaggerated sort of cheer she had shown the day she left for Birmingham.

The Scout meeting was held in an unused servants' room above the garage of one of Uncle Jake's hunting friends. As we walked up the shadowy drive to the garage we could see the light already burning in the room upstairs, and several of the other Scouts were at the window. But when we came into sight just below the window I saw them leave the window hurriedly as though they were in school and the teacher was arriving.

We went into the garage and began to climb the steep, dark stairs. When we were about halfway to the top I suddenly reached forward and grasped Uncle Jake's hand. He held my hand firmly and led me to the top step. And I wondered what might have become of me tonight if it had not been for Uncle Jake.

Presently we entered the bright room and found all of the boys sitting erect on straight wooden benches that lined three walls of the bare room.

"Good evening, boys," Uncle Jake said. The sound of his voice sent a chill up my spine. I felt goose bumps on the backs of my hands. The light in the room was bare and sharp and sent a long blue-black shadow of Uncle Jake's figure against the wall.

The boys answered in a chorus of high tingly voices.

Then Uncle Jake directed me to sit down beside Brother on one of the benches, and he went to the table in the center of the room.

As my eyes moved automatically from one face to another of those boys seated on the benches I was aware that every single face was a familiar one. They were boys whom I had seen with Brother either at school or in Sunday School. Yet tonight in their Scout suits, they were total strangers. Whenever one of them met my gaze there was no communication between us. Rather, our eyes seemed to rub against each other in the cold room.

Though I was unable to follow the procedure of the meeting I did at first try to stand up and to raise my hand when the other boys did. And I even moved my lips when the oath was recited, feeling a kind of elevation by the lists of adjectives. But it was while I saw Uncle Jake's lips pronounce the words "loyal, brave, trustworthy, clean, reverent" that it seemed that he too was becoming a stranger.

After that I made no effort to understand what was being done or said. I simply watched my kind and gentle Uncle as he became more and more another stranger to me, losing himself in the role of the eternal Scoutmaster. It was later, just before the meeting was over (when the plans for Saturday's hike were completed), that I braced myself with the palms of my hands flat on the seat beside me; and while my heart pounded so that I imagined those around me would hear or feel it, I watched Uncle Jake as he stood by his table speaking to the Boy Scouts. I realized now that Father had been right. This was Uncle Jake fulfilling himself. And to fulfill one's self was to remove one's self somehow beyond the reach of my own understanding and affection. It seemed that the known Uncle Jake had moved out of his body just as Aunt Grace had moved out of hers when she sang and laughed and as the Mother and Father whose hands I liked to have placed gently on the top of my head left their bodies whenever they excluded all the world from their conversation.

To the exclusion of all the world Uncle Jake was now become a Scoutmaster. I felt myself deserted by the last human soul to whom I could turn. He, rather, had turned and hidden himself in something more serious than laughter and song and more relentless than even persistent, endless, trivial conversation with a chosen mate. He stood before us like a gigantic replica of all the little boys on the benches, half ridiculous and half frightening to me in his girlish khaki middy and with his trousers disappearing beneath heavy three-quarter woolen socks. In that cold, bare, bright room he was saying that it was our great misfortune to have been born in these latter days when the morals and manners of the country had been corrupted, born in a time when we could see upon the members of our own families—upon our own sisters and brothers and uncles and aunts—the effects of our failure to cling to the teachings and ways of our forefathers. And he was saying that it was our duty and great privilege, as Boy Scouts, to preserve those honorable things which were left from the golden days when a race of noble gentlemen and gracious ladies inhabited the land of the South. He was saying that we must preserve them until one day we might stand with young men from all over the nation to demand a return to the old ways and the old teachings everywhere.

Allegiance

"COME IN." And: "Of course I remember you and knew I should the moment your voice came drawling on the wire."

The first one, two, three steps I take across the room are taken with trepidation. And, so to speak, in midair. I am afraid that I shall yield, for even at her age the old creature is still a great beauty. And there is about her, after all, that charm which has long been discredited in my mind.

As she rings for tea I perceive that in her simplest gestures, in her smile, even in her old-lady dress there is that fascination about her which we, who knew her as children, have remembered as her "romantic quality." I discover in an instant that we have been mistaken to suppose her romantic quality was either vulgar ostentation or mere shallow vanity. And now that she is before me I know that I do not remember her, for herself, at all.

"I remember you so well, dear child, in your blue and red rompers and of course those fearful black stockings your mother would have you wear." Now I am in the air again, treading air. I can feel myself recoil at the bare reference to a woman whom she once grievously wronged, draw back at her mention of a sister she cheated in a manner so subtle and base that we have never known nor wished to know its nature, and now never shall.

Here in her little drawing room, the marble mantel lined with her famous figurines, the Japanese screen shielding her diminutive writing desk, and a lampshade dull gold stamped with fleur-de-lis, I feel myself withdraw momentarily to the bosom of a family that has been nursed on hatred of the mistress of this room. The tea is being served, but I feel that there is less reality to the moment and to the noise of the teacups than to many an hour I have sat with the others at coffee pondering a heritage of resentment against this elegant Londoner.

"I remember you better than the others, I should say. You were all of you quiet children, like your mother, but there were occasions when you alone were like my garrulous self. I used to have at my fingertips bright things you had said to me—impudent things about something I wore or something I said. . . .

But, alas, alas, I've reached an age at which the incidents of my own childhood and events of my young-ladyhood are a wee bit clearer than those of the dull years since." (I smile to hear her say "dull years," but she thinks I smile because I do not know her age.) "I suspect I'm a bit older than you guess. Your mother and I were sisters, you might say, in fact only. I was a young lady in Nashville the year she was born. I was always more aunt than sister to her. I am more of the generation of your cousin, Ellen Ballenger, who was a sort of double first cousin of ours. To be exact, Ellen was first cousin to Mama and first cousin once removed to your grandfather."

She is pouring the tea now, and this is absentminded talk. I listen but I am thinking all the while of how strange it is to hear old familiar relationships rehearsed so easily in her rather too broad English speech. She seems to have lapsed for a moment into the character of an uninteresting old Britisher recalling certain family ties of her people down in Devon or Dorset. But now she looks up to hand me my tea, saying, "Or do we still say 'first cousin once removed' in Tennessee?"

Her face colors a little as our eyes meet. Then she laughs and nervously she jingles the gold bracelets on her wrist; I observe that life has aged her more than I had at once perceived. For she has just now become utterly engrossed in the pleasurable reiteration of those old family ties.

But her laughter, which for one second has seemed as remote a sound as was the look in her eyes abstracted, is now present in the room again. Her eyes shine again with a light that is expressive and responsive. "How wicked of me to treat you so, to bore you with tedious things you know by heart. The longer you sit there the better I do remember you. It's a rather shocking transformation, you'll grant, from red rompers with a scalloped collar to the olive drab. It was not until I was addressing my note to you that I pictured you in uniform. Even with the war all about us here I had not connected events at all. I knew merely that you were in this country. (Dear old Mr. Gordon enclosed the address with my last American check.) And so, you see, it was not wartime sentiment that moved me to ask you here. Further, hadn't I put myself out on a limb, rather? I was not certain that you would bother to come." (Yet she had presumed to think I might. She has thought that one of us might have a change of heart after many years.) "I was not certain that you would bother to come, for very often young men haven't much interest in their kin. Perhaps you have given up something you would like to do this afternoon only to come here. . . . But there I go playing the old lady again."

And now I have the sense of being ignored, or of having my rudeness ignored. I feel an express shame, not of my rudeness, but of all the uncertainties of my mind as I sit in the presence of one so self-possessed. The direct and attentive gaze of her eyes is modest, even shy in a sense, yet she seems as conscious of the engaging qualities of her personality as of the pleasant effect of this little drawing room she has arranged with the light now falling from the west windows across the patterns of the carpet. While she talks I study the burgundy roosters in the patterns and once again the figurines of Louis Napoleon and Nell Gwynn and John Brown with their little china backs reflected in the mirror over the mantel. She is perceiving that I am "quiet" like my mother, and she is set now to support the conversation alone. I hear her. I raise my eyebrows. I nod agreement. I frown. Or I smile so genuinely that she is silent a moment to enjoy the satisfaction of her jest. I even remark on the irony of something, but my sentence is complete in itself and she has no illusion that I'm going to be a real talker after all. She doesn't try to draw me out. But while she speaks and while I listen I am also thinking that at some point I have betrayed, or at some point I shall betray, someone or something.

I am remembering little notes that my mother used to read aloud, notes placed unanswered on the fire in the parlor at Nashville. Now I can visualize their being penned at this little desk shielded by the Japanese screen. I can picture her counting such notes among correspondence that she must "take care of" on a day when the weather isn't fine. Mere polite inquiries they were into the health of us all with a few chatty words at the end about how early a spring London was enjoying that year or some amusing and endearing household incident— something about her ancient, now dead, but once ever-ailing English husband or about her adored stepchildren. They were notes written in an even hand and there was never any rancor or remorse in them. And there was no reference, ever, to my mother's failure to reply. Their tone presumed it to be simply a matter of temperament. She was a person who *did* write letters, my mother a "quiet" person who *didn't*. But my mother used to say, "It's beautiful, beautiful. Her selfish ends are long since accomplished. Now she develops a sort of mystical, superhuman ignorance of what has been transpiring."

My aunt's figure is thin and erect, though her clothing is draped to conceal her thinness. Presently in the midst of her portrayal of three English types that are to be avoided (if one is to admire Englishmen), I realize that she is not ignoring me or my rudeness or even my innocent silence. These are things that she is coping with. It is only that I am suffering still from the shock of the greater ignorance she pretends to. I am no longer asking how did she dare to presume that I should not return her invitation unopened (as all the other notes since my mother's lifetime have been returned). I am no longer asking how or why; for her manner, her personal appearance, even her little drawing room all bespeak her confidence in and her concern only for what is actual. What is more, they express as well her faith in the actual's being but the sum of a thousand accidents.

And that our meeting is a circumstance that she has ardently desired and wished to bring about there can be no doubt. I am certain, further, that she has known it could come about in just such a form as would allow all the privilege she is now exercising—namely, the privilege of assuming all such ignorance as should seem fitting—only by accident or by a series of accidents. In some corner of her mind there has ever been an awareness that these accidents might currently be casting themselves one upon the other. And so it must have appeared to her through the years that any little message which she could so easily scratch off might be the last, the efficient accident that the rest of the world would put down as the cause of our meeting.

"If these were normal times, nothing would please me more than to offer myself as your guide to England and the English. But how futile to speak of it even. You are in London on some terribly official business, no doubt, or on a leave so short that it will be over before you've got round to half the things you want to do. Likely you do not even want to understand this country. You want only to accomplish your mission and get yourself home again. I have been thinking as we sat here that you might be wondering how a person could bring herself to know ... I know how you silent people are. You have more thoughts than the rest of us dare suppose. I should hate to have to answer all the questions in the minds of people who have sat quietly while I talked on. And if I tried I could answer this one least well of all. My answer is, I do not know. But you must have observed that everyone has some aunt or other who has simply pulled out ... pulled out on the family with not so much as a by-your-leave. I'm just another of those aunts that people have. The world's full of them."

I think: The degree of her long anxiety for the special accidental qualities which would make up the naturalness of our meeting is patent in the pleasure she takes from its realization.

"What of my own aunts! But you never knew—perhaps never heard of—the aunts I think of, did you? Yet I remember them so much better than so many people since their time. It is incredible how long people can be dead while their voices and even the moles on their necks are remembered by someone."

I think: The degree of her long anxiety for this meeting without *conditions*, for this easy manner of meeting and her clear vision of the necessity of this ease now seem to me to have been hidden through all the years in the sensible, persistent irregularity of her notes to my mother and later to the individual children. I feel now how right were my mother's claims that this woman could endure anything to gain her ends. For it is as though in her anxiety she has known, too, how unpredictable were her chances.

But are her ends merely this in-person, this final, bold pretense at ignorance of her old wrong against my mother? If this is the depth of the interview's meaning for her, then I am tired of it already. If this is all, then I have satisfied my curiosity about her appearance and her apartments and I am ready to ask for my hat. Yet I do not even steal a glance in the direction of the small chair where my coat and cap are placed. And I ask myself, is it at this point that I betray?

Or was it when I opened her invitation (opened one of the notes our silent pact had forbidden us to do) that I betrayed?

Or will it be later when I have listened? She has settled herself now in her chair. She has accepted a cigarette from my case. She is talking of those great-aunts of mine who long ago went off to Washington and St. Louis to live with their husbands, women whom even my mother could hardly have remembered. Her speech is casual, and she appears at first to be rambling through a mixture of recent events and old memories.

Yet withal she now seems quite consciously allowing herself to become thus engrossed in things that she formerly asked my pardon for. She talks of London, and with a twinkle in her eye she speaks of the tediousness of being cut off from the Continent. Whatever are her ends I know that they are somewhere beyond a desire to play her role convincingly to the last. She seems hardly concerned with her role at all. I gasp a gasp that must be audible, because I recognize that she is still depending upon accidents, terrible accidents that are now possible within myself, in my own perceptions. She has the air of having given way to her woolgathering. *After all*, she is thinking, *the part that I can play in making him see is too small for consideration on any level.* As I read her conscious thoughts I am asking myself whether she, not subconsciously but in a consciousness too profound for such a stranger as I to read, can be attributing some magic potency to the mere actuality of this moment, to the actuality of any given moment, even to her faith in the solidness of the precious objects of her drawing room, to the sound of her own voice. If so, then, for her, each moment and indeed everything in the life and body of the world must have in itself a latent magic which might be exploited. I feel that I am in the presence of some newfangled sort of idolater and conjurer. As she speaks I become increasingly aware that she believes it is no matter now what incident or what old wives' tale she may relate, that she considers that whatever words she uses or however her conversation may turn there is but one thing she *can* say and there is no predicting what turn of her mind or speech might be the singular accident that would mean my comprehension.

But I hear only isolated sentences and snatches of sentences.

There are moments when I feel that I have dozed.

Yet I am in no sense drowsy.

Much less do I feel any boredom.

On the contrary it is a sort of literal enchantment I am caught in where all the past and all the future and all occurrences of the exterior world are of no consequence. Even the thing she has said a moment ago or the conclusion she will presently bring out are utterly lacking in any interest for me though her actual words in that split moment when they proceed from her lips consume my whole attention. Sometimes she is speaking of people who figure, or who have figured, in her life. "Mr. Williams always remembered Merle mercifully, I think." I wonder if I have smiled now when I should have frowned. She tells me that some other person she knows has always the air, with strangers, of himself being an angel entertained unawares. This gentleman will smile afterward, she says, and remark that the stranger was kind to him for no reason at all. It is, my aunt thinks, as if to say that he feels there is a perfectly good reason why the stranger should be kind to him if the stranger only knew *who* he is.

This man is probably someone here in London. But presently it seems to be of my own grandmother who has lain for forty years in a remote and neglected graveyard in Tennessee of whom she is speaking. "She was an extremely narrow and provincial woman, but this much must be said in her favor: If she never showed any originality in her housekeeping she was as well never guilty of any superficiality. Things were always easy. She knew what she was about. There was never any silly bustling when guests came, no matter how fine."

Finally her voice stops, and I wish that it had not stopped. It is as though some piece of furniture in the room had suddenly collapsed, even the chair I sit in. I come to my feet without knowing why I have risen. And immediately she rises with the same suddenness. "Perhaps, you would . . ." She hesitates. But she has regained her composure almost before I recognize her loss of it. She turns with all ease, making a gesture toward the marble mantel, and this time I do steal a glance at my things on the fragile chair.

But the cap and the dull-colored coat have lost that quality which meant the probability of my departure. They mean no more than that I am actually here. Yet I realize that it is because I have entertained no thought of leaving just now that I dared turn my eyes to them, and I only wanted to see if there would be any temptation, or rather to see if I had lost all will to go. And so I am conscious again of betrayal and still do not know whether it is a possibility or a fact. My betrayal is like some boundless fear that has really had no beginning in me and can have no end. This room and this old woman and this woman's voice constitute the only certainty. I feel strangely that I must remain until I can identify my guilt or possible guilt with some moment of the visit if not with some object in the room or some trick of her behavior. And so now I say to myself that she has been right, that all experience can be translated into the terms of any one moment of life if one believes sufficiently in the reality of that moment. "Young man, would you be good enough to admire my figurines." Her smile is full of irony. "They are said to be world famous and of inestimable value."

I have hurried to join her before the mantel. I allow her to see that she has remembered correctly my having flashes of garrulousness like her own. I chatter about John Brown and remark endlessly upon the cunningness of the little nigger who stands at his side with John Brown's pink china hand on his coal black head. I reveal my pedantry asking if it was not for Nell Gwynn that all flowers were pulled from some London park. I laugh at the face of Louis Napoleon.

I find suddenly that we are laughing together at the ridiculous sort of dignity which the artist has faithfully, if unknowingly, represented in the delicate figurine of the bourgeois emperor. Our eyes meet in the glass for an instant. Presently I see the whole room reflected there. I see the two of us looking over the heads of the world-famous figurines. I catch the sound of our commingled laughter.

Then we are facing each other again and she is saying, "What if I should ask you to leave now, should ask you to go now and come again to finish our visit some other afternoon, would you think me too insufferably odd and rude? Would you?"

And before I have thought or considered what I am saying, "But I cannot come here again."

At first her countenance seems frozen in an austerity that is totally disarming to me after so much geniality. Her glance is set for a moment on some object in a far corner of the room. It might almost be my own cap and coat, yet I know it is not with an object that she is concerned. Rather, it is the thing I have just said. She is giving its meaning her most serious consideration.

While she does so, I realize the peculiar turn our intercourse has taken. In my voice there has been almost a plea to allow me to remain since I could not come here again. But it was to say: *I have come here and glimpsed the unique sort of power and truth you have discovered or created, but now I wish to remain to disprove its worth.* Perhaps that is how she is interpreting it. Or perhaps she thinks I have been unaffected by the interview and want only to cause her all possible discomfort before I leave.

Yet of course she at last sees the thing as it is. She sees that I spoke before I thought, and laughing she shrouds herself again in her grand ignorance. "Of course you can come back, dear child, if you will. Let's say good-bye and plan on another afternoon."

Having once spoken plainly it is easy to speak plainly again. "Then I must ask you a question. I want to know why you suddenly desire me to go."

As each moment passes my departure seems to become more difficult for me. I turn with the same abruptness with which I have spoken and go to one of the long windows that overlook the quiet street and park.

There is no sound in the room, and I know that she is still standing there before the mantel. Finally her voice comes groping, yet with confidence in its effect, "Then you do think me rude."

"I don't understand, of course." But I imply that I should listen to explanation. I turn and face her. Our smiles are like smiles in photographs. "You asked your nephew to tea, my dear aunt. I suppose I am only surprised at what a very short teatime you have. I thought you English lingered over tea things."

"See here," she says coming toward me, "there is no great mystery. To be very frank, I have an engagement I had forgotten. I mixed my days. But it is one I intend keeping."

"Certainly it must be important."

"Yes, it's important as an old lady's social engagements go. But if I should describe it you would laugh."

"I should laugh. Yet it is important?"

She drops her eyes. And with her eyelids still closed—broad wrinkled, powdered lids—she says, "I promised someone I'd keep it, you see."

"Oh, it's your word and not the engagement that matters."

"You could understand that?" she asks with her eyes still closed, and I can imagine an echo to her last word "that."

I make my answer with a nod, as though not knowing that her closed eyes mean she cannot see me. But actually I do know that she has not yet my answer; and simultaneously I am filled with disgust for her and with a desire to tiptoe from her presence before she looks up again, for surely this is *it*. Once again I think I am free of the spell of this room. I can almost visualize a pure and self-righteous darkness in which I suspect she is holding herself behind those wrinkled lids. I feel that she has created a terrible war and brought me halfway round the world to prove that she, an old lady in a London apartment, can keep her word in some matter of etiquette. But the harm is not in its being only a small matter of decorum. The harm suddenly appears to be strangely in the altruism, the mere keeping of her word. It is as if her life which she has twisted and formed so willfully has been but a vast circle by which route she has returned to the simple sort of truths that my mother possessed in the beginning. I shall leave now believing what I wished to believe and what this room and this woman have for a time caused me to doubt: that my mother was good because she was simple and unworldly, that my aunt is evil because she is complicated and worldly.

Then in an instant all of my victory is swept from me by the mere opening of her large, handsome, articulate blue eyes. Her last question is now translated and spoken by her eyes. But there is also the further question, "Could you understand more?" And whatever my dull eyes may reply, her lips part and she speaks with new indirectness.

"No. It is not my word. It is something much smaller." A new earnestness has come over her countenance. It is she that has withdrawn from me now. The final accident did not occur. She is no longer hoping that I may see. I know that by "smaller" she means "larger," but beyond that I cannot conceive of what is in her mind. She gives me her hand. As we say good-bye I hear the jingling of her bracelets and observe the barely perceptible twitch at the corner of her mouth.

Now I am outside her door and on the stairs with my military coat over my arm. I wonder, with an insipid smile on my lips, at my own brutality. Have I been a soldier frightening an old lady at teatime? But as I descend the stairs, her face is before me as it was by the window when she raised the wide, wrinkled lids and exposed the brilliant blue of her eyes. I hear again the jingling of her bracelets. And it is then, suddenly recalling now the hard circles of gold rested on the ancient skin drawn over the ungainly wristbone, that I am filled with awe and with a sort of fear as of some fate I might have met at her hands. I feel that I have been in the presence of a withered savage tribeswoman, at the mercy of her absolute authority. But when finally I have passed through the vestibule and out onto the sidewalk and have inhaled gratefully the free air of the cleanswept city street there is no sense of freedom. As I wander in the half-light of evening through the wide thoroughfares and the broad squares of this foreign place, it all seems suddenly as familiar as my mother's parlor; and though my mind is troubled by a doubt of the reality of all things and I am haunted for a while by an unthinkable distrust for the logic and the rarefied judgments of my dead mother, I feel myself still a prisoner in her parlor at Nashville with the great sliding doors closed and the jagged little flames darting from the grate.

A Long Fourth

FOR OVER five years Harriet Wilson had been saying, "I'd be happier, Sweetheart, if B.T. were not even on the place." Harriet was a pretty woman just past fifty, and Sweetheart felt that she grew prettier as the years went by. He told her so, too, whenever she mentioned the business about B.T. or any other business. "I declare you get prettier by the year," he was accustomed to say. That was how the B.T. business had been allowed to run on so. Once she had pointed out to Sweetheart that he never said she grew wiser by the year, and he had replied, laughing, that it certainly did seem she would never be a judge of niggers. It was while they were dressing for breakfast one morning that he told her that, and she had quickly turned her back to him (which was the severest rebuke she was ever known to give her husband) and began to powder her neck and shoulders before the mirror. Then he had come over and put his hands on her pretty, plump shoulders and kissed her on the cheek saying, "But you're nobody's fool, darling."

Thinking of that had oftentimes been consolation to her when Sweetheart had prettied her out of some notion she had. But really she had always considered that she was nobody's fool and that she certainly was not merely a vain little woman ruled by a husband's flattery, the type her mother had so despised in her lifetime. She even found herself sometimes addressing her dead mother when she was alone. "It's not that I've become one of that sort of women in middle age, Mama. It's that when he is so sweet to me I realize what a blessing that is and how unimportant other things are." For Harriet was yet guided in some matters by well-remembered words of her mother who had been dead for thirty years. In other matters she was guided by the words of Sweetheart. In still others she was guided by what Son said. Her two daughters guided her in nothing. Rather, she was ever inclined to instruct them by quoting Mama, Sweetheart, or Son.

Their house was eight miles from downtown Nashville on the Franklin Pike, and for many years Sweetheart, who was a doctor, had had his own automobile for work and Harriet had kept a little coupe. But after the war began the doctor accepted gas rationing rather conscientiously and went to and from his office on the interurban bus. "We eye-ear-nose-and-throat men don't have to make so many professional calls," he said. Harriet usually walked down to the pike to meet him on the five-thirty bus in the evening.

It was a quarter of a mile from the pike to the house, and they would walk up the driveway hand in hand. Harriet, who said she lived in perpetual fear of turning her ankle on a piece of gravel, kept her eyes on the ground when they walked, and Sweetheart would usually be gazing upward into the foliage of the poplar trees and maples that crowded the lawn and overhung the drive or he would be peering straight ahead at the house, which was an old-fashioned, single-story clapboard building with a narrow porch across the front where wisteria bloomed in June and July. Though they rarely had their eyes on each other during this walk, they were always hand in hand and there was always talk. It was on one of these strolls, not a week before B.T. gave notice, that Harriet last uttered her old complaint, "I've always told you that I'd be happier, Sweetheart, if B.T. were not even on this place now that he's grown up."

"I know." He squeezed her hand and turned a smiling countenance to her.

"I don't think you do know," she said keeping her eyes on the white gravel. "He's grand on the outside, but all of them are grand on the outside. As long as we keep him I'm completely deprived of the services of a houseboy when I need one. When Son and his young lady come I don't know what I'll do. The girls are angels about things, but next week they should be entertaining Son and her, and not just picking up after her. It seems unreasonable, Sweetheart, to keep B.T. when we could have a nice, normal darkie that could do inside when I need him."

Sweetheart began swinging their joined hands merrily. "Ah, oh, now, B.T.'s a pretty darned good darkie, just clumsy and runs around a bit."

Harriet looked up at her husband and stopped still as though she were afraid to walk with her eyes off her feet. "Sweetheart, you know very well it's not that." And making a face she held her nose so acutely that he could feel it in the fingers of the hand he was holding.

"Well, there's nothing wrong that a little washing won't cure." He was facing her and trying now to take hold of her other hand.

"No, no, no, Sweetheart. It's constitutional with him. Last Monday I had him bathe before he came in to help old Mattie move the sideboard. Yet that room was unbearable for twenty minutes after he left. I *had* to get out, and I heard his Auntie Mattie say, 'Whew!' Mattie knows it as well as I do and is just too contrary to admit it. I'm sure that's why she moved into the attic and left him the whole shack, but she's too contrary to admit it."

The doctor threw back his head and laughed aloud. Then for a time he seemed to be studying the foliage absently and he said that he reckoned poor old Mattie loved her little nephew a good deal. "I think it's touching," he said, "and I believe Mattie would leave us in a minute if we let B.T. go."

"Not a bit of it!" said Harriet.

"Nevertheless, he's a good nigger," her husband said, "and we can't judge Negroes the way we do white people, Harriet."

"Well, I should say *not*!" Harriet exclaimed.

Harriet was not a light sleeper but she complained that she often awoke in the night when there was something on her mind. On the last night of June that summer she awoke with a start and saw by the illuminated dial of her watch that it was 3 A.M. She rolled over on her stomach with great care not to disturb Sweetheart who was snoring gently beside her. This waking, she supposed, was a result of her worries about Son's coming visit and the guest he was bringing with him. And then Son was going to the Army on the day after the Fourth. She had been worrying for weeks about Son's going into the Army and how he would fit in there. He was not like other men, more sensitive and had advanced ideas and was so intolerant of inefficiency and old-fashioned things. This was what had broken her sleep, she thought; and then there was repeated the unheard-of racket that had really awakened her.

Harriet grunted in her pillow, for she knew that it was her daughters quarreling again. A door slammed and she heard Kate's voice through the wall. "Oh, Goddy! Godamighty! Helena, won't you please shut up!" She knew at once the cause

of the quarrel: Kate had been out this evening and had turned
on the light when she came to undress. Poor thing certainly
could not pin up her hair and hang up her dress in the dark.
Yet it *was* an unreasonable hour. She wondered where the girls
ever stayed till such a late hour. They were too old now to be
quizzed about those things. But they were also too old to be
quarreling so childishly. Why, when Harriet and her sister were
their age they were married and had the responsibilities of their
own families. What a shame it is, she thought, that my girls are
not married, and it's all because of their height. Then Harriet
rebuked herself for begrudging them one minute of their time
with what few beaux they had.

For there really were so few tall men nowadays. In her own
day there had been more tall men, and tall women were then
considered graceful. Short dresses do make such a difference,
she reflected, and my girls' legs are not pretty. Harriet was not
tall herself, but Mama had been tall and Mama was known as
one of the handsomest women that ever graced the drawing
rooms of Nashville. But the girls were a little taller than even
Mama had been. And they were smart like Mama. They read all
the same books and magazines that Son did. Son said they were
quite conversant. Nevertheless they must behave themselves
while Son's friend was here. No such hours and no such quar-
rels! She did wish that Son had not planned to bring this girl
down from New York, for he had said frankly that they were
not in love, they were only friends and had the same interests.
Harriet felt certain that Son would bring no one who was not
a lady, but what real lady, she asked herself, would edit a birth-
control magazine? Just then Sweetheart rolled over and in his
sleep put his arm about her shoulders. Something reminded
her that she had not said her prayers before going to bed, and
so with his arm about her she said the Lord's Prayer and went
off to sleep.

She forgot to speak to the girls the next day about their quarreling, but on the following day she was determined to mention it. Sweetheart had left for town in his car since he was to
meet Son and Miss Prewitt's train that afternoon. Harriet was
in the front part of the house wearing a long gingham wrapper and her horn-rimmed spectacles. In one hand she clasped

the morning paper and a few of the June bills which had come in that morning's mail. The house was in good order and in perfect cleanliness, for she and the girls and Mattie had spent the past three days putting it so.

These days had been unusually cool with a little rain in the morning and again in the afternoon. Otherwise Harriet didn't know how they could have managed a general housecleaning in June. The girls had really worked like Trojans, making no complaint but indirectly. Once when it began to rain after a sultry noon hour Helena had said, "Well, thank God for small favors." Kate, when she broke her longest fingernail on the curtain rod, screamed a word that Harriet would not even repeat in her mind. But they had been perfect angels about helping. Their being so willing, so tall, and so strong is really compensation, Harriet kept telling herself, for not having the services of a houseboy. They had tied their heads up in scarfs, pulled on their garden slacks, and done all a man's work of reaching the highest ledges and light fixtures and even lifting the piano and the dining room table.

They had spent last evening on the big screened porch in the back, had eaten supper and breakfast there too, so there was not a thing to be done to the front part of the house this morning. In the living room she looked about with a pleasant, company smile for the polished floor and gave an affected little nod to the clean curtains. All she did was to disarrange some of the big chairs which Mattie had fixed in too perfect a circle. Mama used to warn Harriet against being rigid in her housekeeping. "The main thing is comfort, dearest," and Harriet knew that she had a tendency to care more for the cleanliness and order. So she even put the hearthrug at a slight angle. Then she went to the window and observed that a real July sun was rising today; so she pulled-to the draperies and went from window to window shutting out the light till the whole front part of the house was dark.

The girls slept late that morning. They had earned their rest, and Harriet went tiptoeing about the house listening for them to call for the breakfast that old Mattie had promised to serve them in bed. When ten o'clock came she had picked up in her room, given a last dusting to Son's room and to the guest room, and Mattie had swept the screened porch and was through in the kitchen. It was time to go to market. Mattie had much to do that day and it was not planned for her to go marketing with Harriet. But the girls had been such angels that Harriet and Mattie agreed they should be allowed to sleep as late as their hearts desired.

Mattie put on her straw and in Harriet's presence she was on the back porch giving B.T. some last instructions. B.T. was cleaning six frying-size chickens from their own yard. Later he must peel potatoes and gather beans, lettuce, tomatoes, and okra from what was known as the girls' victory garden. He was acknowledged a good hand at many services which could be rendered on the back porch, and his schedule there over the coming holiday weekend was a full one. "Have you cleaned up the freezer?" Harriet asked him. She too was standing with her hat on. She was looking critically at the naked chicken on which his black hands were operating with a small paring knife. Before he answered concerning the freezer she had turned to Mattie and said, "Don't serve the necks tonight, Mattie." Meanwhile B.T. had crossed the porch and brought back the big wooden bucket of the ice-cream freezer. The bucket itself had been scrubbed wonderfully clean, and with eyes directed toward her but focused for some object that would have been far behind her, B.T. exhibited the immaculate turner and metal container from within. "It does look grand, B.T.," Harriet admitted.

She was about to depart when she heard one of the girls' voices through their window across the way. (The rear of the house was of a U-shape with the big pantries and the kitchen in one wing and the bedrooms in the other.) Harriet went down through the yard and looked in the girls' window. She was astonished to find the room in complete order and the girls fully dressed and each seated on her own bed reading. Harriet's eyes were immediately filled with tears. She thought of how hard they had worked this week and with what unaccustomed deference they had treated her, calling her "Mama" sometimes instead of "Mother," sometimes even being so playful as to call her "Mammy." And this morning they had not wanted to be a bother to anyone. Further, they were reading something new so that they would be conversant with Son and Miss Prewitt. Kate jumped from the bed and said, "Why, Mammy, you're ready to go to market. I'll be right with you." Harriet turned from the window and called to Mattie to take off her straw, for Miss Kate was going to market with her.

But she didn't begin to walk toward the garage at once. The tears had left her eyes, and she stood thinking quite clearly of this change in her daughters' behavior. She was ashamed of having thought it would be necessary to mention their quarreling and their late hours to them. Perhaps they had worried as much as she about Son's getting into the Army, and probably they were as eager to make him proud of his family before Miss Prewitt.

As all of her concern for the success of the visit cleared away she began to think of what a pity it was that Son and Miss Prewitt were not in love. She would have suspected that it might really be a romance except that the girls assured her otherwise. They told her that Son did not believe in marriage and that he certainly would not subject his family and the people of Nashville to the sort of thing he did believe in. This girl was merely one of the people he knew in his publishing business. And thinking again of all Son's advanced ideas and his intolerance she could not but think of the unhappiness he was certain to know in the Army. And more than this there would be no weekly telephone calls for her and perhaps no letters and no periodic visits home. He would be going away from them all and he might just be missing and never be brought home for burial. Her imagination summoned for comfort the warmth of Sweetheart's smile and the feel of his arm about her, but there was little comfort even there.

When they returned from market they found Helena on the back porch peeling the potatoes. "What on earth is Helena doing?" Kate asked before they got out of the coupe. Harriet frowned and pressed the horn for B.T. to come and get the groceries. Then the tall daughter and the short little mother scrambled out of the car and hurried toward the porch. Almost as soon as the coupe appeared Helena had stood up. She took three long strides to the edge of the porch. When her mother and sister drew near, her eyes seemed ready to pop out of her head. Her mouth, which was large and capable of great expansions, was full open. Yet the girl was speechless.

Harriet was immediately all atremble and she felt the blood leaving her lips. To herself she said, "Something terrible has—" Then simultaneously she saw that Helena's eyes were fixed on something behind Kate and herself and she heard old Mattie's broken voice calling to her, "Miss Harriet! Oh, Missie, Missie!" She turned about quickly, dropping her eyes to her feet to make sure of her footing, and now looking up she saw the old Negro woman running toward her with her big faded kitchen apron clasped up between her clean, buff-colored hands.

The old-fashioned appellative "Missie" told Harriet a great deal. She handed Kate her purse and put out her arms to receive Mattie, for she knew that her old friend was in deep trouble. The Negress was several inches taller than Harriet but she threw herself into her little mistress's arms and by bending her knees slightly and stooping her shoulders she managed to rest her face on the bosom of the white eyelet dress while she wept. Harriet held her so for a time with her arms about her and patting her gently between the shoulder blades and just above the bow knot of her apron strings. "Now, now, Mattie," she whispered, "maybe it's not as bad as it seems. It's something about B.T., isn't it? What is it, Mattie, honey?"

"Oh, oh, oh, he gwine leave."

The voice seemed so expressive of the pain in that heart that Harriet could think only of the old woman's suffering and not at all of the cause. "My poor Mattie," she said.

But her sympathy only brought forth more tears and deeper sobs. "My little nephew is gwine leave his old auntie who raised him up when nobody else'd tetch him." Harriet did not even hear what Mattie was saying now, but she perceived that her own sympathy was encouraging self-pity and thus giving the pain a double edge. And so she tried to think of some consolation.

"Maybe he won't go after all, Mattie."

Saying this she realized the bearing of B.T.'s departure upon the holiday weekend of which this was the very eve. Then she told herself that indeed Mattie's little nephew would not go after all. "He won't go," she said; "I tell you, Mattie, he won't go if I have any power of constraining him." Her blue eyes shone thoughtfully as she watched the two girls who were now making the last of several trips to bring the groceries from the back of the coupe.

"Oh, oh, oh, yes'm he will, Missie. He's gwine Tuesday. It's the war, an' y'can't stop 'm. He gwine work at th'air fact'ry 'cause the draf membuhs don't want 'm much. But iffen he don't work at th'air fact'ry they'll have to take 'im, want 'im or not." And while his auntie was speaking B.T. appeared from the door of the unpainted cabin from which Mattie had come. He was still wearing the white coat which he always wore on the back porch, and plainly intended to continue his work through the weekend. He ran over to the car where Kate was unloading the last of the groceries and relieved her of her armful.

Harriet's relief was great. B.T. would be here through Monday! She began to caress Mattie again and to speak softly in her ear. Her eyes and her thoughts, however, were upon B.T. He was a big—neither muscular nor fat, merely big—black, lazy-looking Negro. As he came along the brick walk toward her he kept his eyes lowered to the bundle of groceries. He was what Harriet's Mama would have called a field nigger and had never learned any house manners at all. His face, to her, had ever seemed devoid of expression. He had grown up here on their suburban acreage and had been hardly more than twenty miles distant in his lifetime, but Harriet felt that she had held less converse with him than with any of the men who used to come for short intervals and do the work when B.T. was still a child. He worked hard and long and efficiently here on their small acreage, she knew, and on Saturday nights he usually got drunk down at the Negro settlement and sometimes spent the later part of that night and all day Sunday in the county jail. There had been times when he had stolen pieces of Sweetheart's and Son's clothing off the wash line, and you dare not lose any change in the porch stairs. Sometimes too they would find that he was keeping some black female thing out in the shack for a week at a time, toting food to her from the kitchen. The female things he kept were not Negro women who might have been useful about the place but were real prostitutes from Nashville (who else would have endured the smell there must be in that shack?), and Dr. Wilson was ever and anon having to take him to Nashville for the shots. But all of that sort of thing was to be expected, admitted Harriet, and it was not that which caused her antipathy—over and above his constitutional affliction— toward him. B.T. was simply wanting in those qualities which she generally found appealing in Negroes. He had neither good manners nor the affectionate nature nor the appealing humor that so many niggers have.

As he passed her there at the foot of the porch steps the odor he diffused had never seemed more repugnant and never so strong when outside the house. Mattie raised her tear-streaked brown face, knowing it was B.T. surely more from his odor than from his footstep, and as he followed the two girls to the kitchen door she called after him, "B.T., don't leave old Auntie!" Then she looked at her mistress with what Harriet acknowledged to be the sweetest expression she had ever beheld in a Negro's countenance. "Miss Harriet," she said as though stunned at her own thoughts, "it's like you losin' Mr. Son. B.T. is gwine too."

The small white woman abruptly withdrew her arms from about her servant. The movement was made in one fearful gesture which included the sudden contraction of her lips and the widening of her bright eyes. "Mattie!" she declaimed. "How dare you? That will be just exactly enough from you!" And now her eyes moved swiftly downward and to the porch steps. Without another glance at the woman she had been holding to her bosom she went up on the porch and, avoiding the kitchen where the girls were, she went along the porch up into the U of the house and entered the dark dining room. While she walked her face grew hot and cold alternately as her indignation rose and rose again. When she reached her own room in the far wing of the house she closed the door and let the knob turn to in her hand. She pulled off her hat and dropped it on her dressing table among her toilet articles and handkerchief box and stray ends of gray hair that were wrapped around a hairpin. And she went and sat down in a rocking chair near the foot of the bed and began to rock. "Like Son! Like Son!"

The very chair had violence in its rocking motion. Several times Harriet might have pushed herself over backward but for lacking the strength in her small legs. Not since she was a little child had such rage been known to her bosom, and throughout the half hour of her wildest passion she was rather aware of this. This evidence of a choleric temperament was so singular a thing for her that she could not but be taking note of herself as her feelings rose and convulsed in their paroxysm.

She wondered first that she had refrained from striking Mattie out in the yard and she remarked it humorlessly that only the approaching holiday had prevented her. The insinuation had been sufficiently plain without Mattie's putting it into words. It was her putting it into words that earned Harriet's wrath. The open comparison of Son's departure to that of the sullen, stinking, thieving, fornicating black B.T. was an injury for which Son could not avenge himself, and she felt it her bounden duty to in some way make that black woman feel the grossness of her wrong and ultimately to drive her off the premises. And it was in this vein, this very declamatory language, this elevated tone with which Harriet expressed herself in the solitude of her room. She was unconsciously trying to use the language and the rhetoric of her mother and of the only books with which she had ever had such acquaintance. Between the moments when she even pictured Mattie's being tied and flogged or thought of Mama's uncle who shot all of his niggers before he would free them, and of the Negro governor of North Carolina and the Negro senate rolling whiskey barrels up the capitol steps, of the rape and uprisings in Memphis and the riots in Chicago, between these thoughts she would actually consider the virtue of her own wrath. And recalling her Greek classes at Miss Hood's school she thought without a flicker of humor of Achilles' indignation.

Not the least of the offense was the time that Mattie had chosen. Harriet was powerless to act until this long Fourth of July was over. She meant to endure the presence of that Ethiopian woman and that ape of a man through Sunday and Monday, till her own boy had had his holiday and gone to join the Army. His last visit must not be marred, and she resolved to tell no one—not even Sweetheart—of what had occurred. The holiday would be almost intolerable to her now, and she stopped her furious rocking, and with her feet set side by side on the carpet she resolved to endure it in silence for his sake who was the best of all possible sons. Sweat was running down her forehead, and her little hands hung limp and cold.

People in Nashville had been saying for a week how Son would be missed. More than most boys, even those who had not left Nashville to work in New York or St. Louis, Son would be missed by his family when he went to the Army. People said that he had been a model son while he was growing up. And after his own talents and ability took him away to New York he had been so good about keeping in touch. He had written and telephoned and visited home regularly. That was what the older people remarked. And the young people no less admired the faithfulness and consideration he showed his parents. He had carried all the honors in his classes at school and at the University and had not grieved his parents with youthful dissipation as most Nashville boys do. What the young people thought especially fine was that, being the intellectual sort, which he certainly was, he had been careful never to offend or embarrass his family with the peculiar, radical ideas which he would naturally have. After he left Nashville he never sent home magazines in which his disturbing articles appeared, not even to his sisters who pretended to have the same kind of mind. And finally when the wild stories about his private and semipublic activities began to come back to Nashville and circulate among people, people were not so displeased with these stories as they were pleased to find on his next visit that he behaved as of old while in Nashville.

He was a tall, fair-headed young man, softly spoken, and he dressed conventionally. When he came into his mother's front hall that Saturday afternoon on the second of July he was still wearing the seersucker suit in which he had traveled. Harriet was not at the door to greet him, but as she came from her room she could hear amid the flurry of greetings his polite voice asking in his formal way if she were well. She met him at the door of the parlor and as she threw her arms about him she found herself unable to restrain her tears.

She thought, of course, that her weeping would subside in a moment and she did not even hide her face in her handkerchief. She tried to speak to him and then pushing him a little aside she tried to say something to the young woman he had brought with him. But the sight of Miss Prewitt there beside Sweetheart seemed to open new valves and it seemed that she was beginning to choke. When she had first seen Son in the doorway his very appearance had confirmed the justice of her outraged feelings this afternoon. When she saw the ladylike young woman in a black traveling dress and white gloves (as an example of his taste), it occurred to her that she had even underestimated the grossness of Mattie's reflection upon him. Her weeping became so violent now and was so entirely a physical thing that it seemed not to correspond to her feelings at all. First she tried to stifle and choke down her tears physically. This failing, she tried to shame herself into composure, thinking of what a vulgar display Mama would have called this. Presently she recognized that her state was already hysteria. Sweetheart rushed forward and supported her, and Son tried to hold one hand which she was waving about.

They walked her slowly to her room speaking to her gently. All the while she was trying at moments to think of the reason for this collapse. It was not—as they would all believe—Son's going into the Army. It could not be simply the scene she had had with her cook that afternoon. Could it be that she had always hated this black, servant race and felt them a threat to her son and her family? Such ridiculous thoughts! Then she was alternately laughing and weeping, and they put her on her bed. Sweetheart attended her and then sat holding her hand till she was absolutely quiet. Later the girls took their turns at sitting with her. All she could remember about Son that afternoon was hearing him say, out in the hall it seemed, "How unlike Mother."

It was late in the evening before they would let her move from her bed or leave her room. But by ten o'clock Sweetheart was convinced that her fretting there in bed was more harmful than a little company up in the front room would be. She declared herself to be quite recovered and after a bit of washing and powdering she presented herself to the four young people who were playing bridge in the parlor.

"Well, well, have a seat," Son said, extending his left hand to her.

His manner was casual, as was that of the others—studiedly so. For they wanted to make her comfortable. Even Miss Prewitt restrained her attentions, pretending to be absorbed in the cards although she was dummy. "The girls have given us a good trimming tonight," she said.

When Miss Prewitt spoke, Harriet observed that she had extremely crooked teeth which had been brought more or less into line probably by wearing bands as a child. Her face was rather plain but her cheeks had a natural rosiness to them and her eyes, though too small, were bright and responsive. She wore no makeup and was redolent of no detectable perfume or powder. And before she sat down in the chair which Sweetheart drew up for her, Harriet had perceived that the girl took no pains with her hair which hung in a half-long bob with some natural wave.

"We're teaching these Yankees a thing or two," Helena said, winking playfully at Kate.

"Will you listen to that?" Miss Prewitt smiled and revealed to Harriet a pleasant manner and an amiable, ladylike nature. "Your daughters keep calling their own brother and myself Yankees. But of course it's partly his fault, for I learn that he didn't write you that I'm from Little Rock, myself, and that I'm on my way home for a visit."

"Isn't that manlike?" Harriet said.

Now Son dropped his last three trumps on the table and proclaimed that that was "game." He suggested that they quit playing, but Harriet insisted that they complete the rubber. Helena began to deal the cards. For a time no one spoke. Harriet pretended to gaze about the room but she could hardly keep her eyes off Miss Prewitt. For though she found her extremely agreeable she perceived that the possibility of any romantic attachment between her and Son was out of the question. The tie between them was doubtless what the girls called an intellectual friendship. In her own girlhood people would have called it Platonic, but then they would have laughed about it. Mama had always said there could be no such relationship between young men and young women. Sweetheart always showed the smutty and cynical side to his nature when such things were discussed. Yet in some matters Son surely knew more than either Mama or Sweetheart. She had of course never, herself, known such a friendship with a man and just now she was really trying to imagine the feelings that two such friends would have for one another.

Until Miss Prewitt had spoken and thus started that train of thought in her mind Harriet had been wondering how dinner came off and whether Mattie served the chicken necks. But now her thoughts had been diverted and her nerves were somewhat relieved. It was she who finally broke the silence. "For Heaven's sake," she said, "let's not be so reserved. You're all being so careful of my feelings that Miss Prewitt will think I have a nervous ailment. My dear, that's the first time in my life I've ever carried on so. You just mustn't judge me by that scene I made. I have no sympathy with women who carry on so."

Then Sweetheart and the children did begin to tease her and make light of her carryings-on. Presently the conversation became animated and she was soon calling Miss Prewitt "Ann" as the girls did. Helena and Kate, she had never seen more cordial to a stranger than to Ann. She had never, indeed, seen them sweeter with one another. It was not until they had played their last card and had shaken hands across the table in acknowledgment of their complete victory that the strangeness of their behavior occurred to Harriet. It had been many a day since they had sat down at the same bridge table, for if they were partners they usually ended by calling each other "stupid" and if they were not partners they not infrequently accused each other of cheating.

Now Harriet felt herself trembling again and she was unable to follow the conversation. After a few minutes she said, "I think what we all need is a good night's sleep." The girls agreed at once, and so did Sweetheart. But Son suggested that he and Ann would like to sit up and talk for a while. Nobody seemed to take exception to this but Sweetheart who gave a little frown and shrugged his shoulders. Then he led Harriet off to their room, and the girls followed inquiring if there was anything they could do for Mother. As Harriet left the parlor she glanced back and observed that Ann's legs were as large and graceless as two fireplugs.

Sweetheart was in bed before her and lay there watching her own preparations at the dressing table. She felt that she was barely able to conceal from him the difficulty she had in rolling her hair and pulling on the net. But when she turned to put off the light she found him fast asleep.

She was standing in the dark for a moment and she heard the voices of Son and Ann out on the porch. Without even considering her action she stepped to the window and listened to their lowered voices.

"She's a very pretty and attractive little woman," Ann was saying, "but from things you had said I was not quite prepared to find her such a nervous woman."

"That's true. But I don't think she really is a nervous woman," Son said slowly. "I believe nobody was more surprised than herself at what happened this afternoon."

"It's not just what happened this afternoon. She was trembling most of the time in the living room tonight."

"I can't imagine what it is. Something seems to have come over her. But there's no visible change. She hasn't aged any. I looked for it in her hair and in the skin about her neck and in her figure." It hardly seemed possible to Harriet that this was Son talking about herself.

"She's certainly past her menopause, isn't she?"

"Oh, certainly. Years ago when I was still in school."

"That's rather early."

"Yes . . . Yes."

"The girls are much more conventional than I imagined, much less independent, more feminine—"

"Something," Son emphasized, "seems to have come over them, too."

"They're too young for any sort of frustration, I suppose."

This whispered but clearly audible conversation caused Harriet to feel herself alienated from all around her. It was Son's disinterested tone and objectiveness. Her mind returned to Mattie. She wondered how she and B.T. would behave through the weekend. And now looking out into the backyard where the moon was shining on the shingled roof of the cabin and through the trees to the porch steps, she considered again the words she had used to Mattie out there this afternoon.

The girls had planned a small party for Monday night, which was July Fourth. It was not to be at the Country Club, where they had always before preferred to entertain, but at the house. But on Sunday night one of Son's old friends named Harry Buchanan had invited the group to supper at the Club. Harry was married and had two small children.

At the breakfast table Sunday morning Helena said to Ann, "We didn't plan anything for last night because we knew you two would be tired from traveling. But we're having a few friends to the house tomorrow night, and tonight the Buchanans"—she hesitated and closed her eyes significantly—"have asked us to supper at the Club. I don't know why some people must entertain at clubs and hotels."

"It all sounds quite festive," Ann said.

"Yes, I'm afraid 'festive' is the word," said Kate. "When people ask you to a hotel or a club, instead of to their home, if the occasion's not 'festive' or 'gala,' what can it be? I don't take such an invitation as a great compliment."

Ann said nothing. Son looked over his pink grapefruit, perplexed. Harriet was completely mystified now by the things her daughters were saying. It sounded like pure nonsense to her although she was pleased to see them in such accord. She could not say that she disagreed with them, but it did sound like nonsense because it was the very reverse of ideas they usually expressed. Perhaps it was because they were growing older and more like herself. "One never realizes when one's children are growing up," she thought. But whether or not she agreed with them in principle she did think it ungracious and unkind of them to speak that way about Son's friend who was entertaining them tonight.

"Kate," she said, "the Buchanans have two small children and their house is so small."

The two daughters laughed. "Dear, dear Mama," Helena said, "you're such a Christian. You wouldn't say anything against *any*body on Sunday, would you?"

"Let me ask you this, Mama," said Kate. "Would your mother have liked entertaining visitors at a golf club?"

Harriet shook her head. "That was long ago when Mama entertained, and it was not the custom then."

"There you are. We're only thinking as you've taught us to think, Mama, when we think that many of the customs and ways that used to pertain in Nashville were better than what is replacing them."

Harriet asked herself if that was what she had taught them to think. She didn't know she had taught them to think anything. But her only real interest in the matter was the defense of Harry Buchanan whose wife's mother, she presently said, was a dear friend of hers and was from one of Nashville's loveliest families and certainly knew how to "do." Then Helena asked with apparent artlessness what her dear friend's maiden name had been. And the question led to a prolonged discussion between the girls and their mother and even their father of the kinship of various Nashville families. Nothing yet had amazed Harriet more than the knowledge of those kinships and connections which Helena and Kate proceeded to display.

"Why, you two girls," Sweetheart said in his innocence, "are getting to rival your mother in matters of who's kin to who." But Harriet was observing Son and Ann who remained silent and kept their eyes on their food. She herewith resolved that she would make it her special task during the remainder of the visit to avoid such talk since it seemed to cause a mysterious antagonism between the young people.

After breakfast Son and Ann left for a walk about the premises in the company of Sweetheart who wanted to show them his orchards and his four acres of oats and the old cotton patch where he had had B.T. put in lespedeza this year. They were also to see his poultry and the Jersey cow whose milk at breakfast had tasted of wild onions. He urged Helena and Kate to come along and show off the vegetable garden where they had worked and directed B.T.'s labor. But the girls declined, saying that they were through with outdoor life until the weather was cool again. Harriet said to herself, "They're perfect angels and don't want to leave the housework to me this morning."

Later Sweetheart came back to the house and settled himself on the porch with the Sunday morning paper while Son and Ann walked down the pike toward the Confederate Monument. Harriet debated the question of going to church. Sweetheart advised against it in view of her nervous agitation. Then she dismissed the idea, for she dared not reject Sweetheart's advice in such matters, though for a while there did linger the thought of how restful church service would seem. When the straightening up was done the girls went to their reading again and Harriet made a visit to the kitchen that she had been postponing all morning.

"Mattie," she said, "do you have everything?" Mattie was seated at a kitchen table with her back to the swinging door through which Harriet had entered, and she did not turn around. The table was in the center of the huge, shadowy kitchen. Directly beyond the table was the doorway to the back porch, through which opening Harriet could see B.T. also working at a table.

"I reckon," Mattie answered after a moment. There was no movement of her head when she spoke. And her head was not bent over the table. She seemed to be staring through the doorway at B.T. She was seated there on a high, unpainted wooden stool which she had long ago had B.T. make for her (though she had complained at the time of having to pay him for it out of her own stocking), and since B.T. had selfishly made the stool to accommodate his own long legs, Mattie's stocking feet drooped, rather than dangled, above her old slippers that had fallen one upon the other on the linoleum.

She was not wearing her white cap or white serving apron, so there was absolutely no relief to her black dress and her head of black hair. She was the darkest object in the whole of the dark old-fashioned kitchen—blacker even than the giant range stove whereon the vegetables were boiling and in which a fire roared that kept the kitchen so hot that Harriet looked about to see if the windows were open and found them all open but that window where the winter icebox was built on, and she knew Mattie would not open that window while there were so many tomatoes and heads of cabbage and lettuce to keep fresh.

In the kitchen there was only the sound of water boiling. Through the backdoor she could see B.T. in the bright sunlight on the porch and hear the regular thumping of his knife on the table as he chopped a coconut for the ambrosia. He seemed to be unaware of or totally indifferent to Mattie's gaze upon him. Harriet stepped back into the pantry and let the door swing shut, drawing a hot breeze across her face. The two Negroes doubtless had been sitting like that for hours without a word between them. It was a picture she was not able to forget.

Among the family friends the Wilson girls were admired no less than Son though they were considered to have more temperament. (By this it was meant that they occasionally displayed bad temper in public.) They were spoken of as devoted daughters and thoroughly capable and energetic young women. Helena, who was known generally as the blond Wilson girl though her brown hair was only a shade lighter than Kate's, sometimes taught classes at Miss Hood's school during the winter. She usually substituted, and could teach mathematics, art appreciation, or modern literature to the seniors. During the winter when there were more colds and throat trouble Kate helped with the receiving and secretarial work at Sweetheart's office.

They had large, round, pleasant faces which often seemed identical to strangers. Their voices were considered identical by everyone outside the family, even by close family friends who often remarked that they didn't speak with the vulgar drawl that so many Nashville girls have adopted. Their vocabulary and their accents were more like those of their mother. They pronounced girl as "gull" as all Nashville ladies once used to do. And so it was often shocking to a stranger after hearing their slightly metallic but very feminine and old-fashioned voices to turn and discover both girls were over six feet tall. Their ages were "in the vicinity of thirty," as was Son's, and they too never seemed to have considered matrimony.

As Harriet was returning from the kitchen her ear recognized Kate's familiar touch at the piano. It was by the bass that she could always distinguish the girls' playing; Kate's was a little the heavier but with more variations. She was playing accompaniment to the ballad "Barbara Allen," and presently Helena's straining-falsetto could be heard. Then as Harriet passed through the hall she saw through the open front door Son and Ann walking up the straight driveway from the pike. Son wore white linen trousers and a white shirt open at the collar. Ann looked very fresh and youthful in a peasantlike shirtwaist and skirt, though the flare of the skirt did seem to accentuate the heaviness of her legs. They walked over the white gravel beneath the green canopy of the trees and the picture was framed in the semicircle of lavender wisteria that blossomed round the entrance to the porch. The prettiness of it made Harriet sigh. It seemed that her sorrow over Son's going into the Army would not be so great if she could believe that he and Ann were in love. This old house and the surrounding woods and pastures had always seemed to her the very setting for romance. From the time when her girls had first begun to have a few beaux she considered what a felicitous setting the swing on the front porch or the old iron bench down by the fence stile would be for the final proposal; and during her walks with Sweetheart in the evenings she would sometimes look about the lawn trying to fix upon the best spot for a garden wedding. Now the sight of Son and Ann in this pretty frame only reminded her of their unnatural and strange relationship. They were walking far apart and Ann was speaking with deliberation and gesturing as she spoke. But apparently at the first glimpse of Harriet, Ann broke off speaking. And Harriet perceived in an instant that there was at least a trouble of some kind in their relationship. She recollected now that though Son had not been talking he had been shaking his head from side to side as though in exasperation.

Kate was still playing and Helena singing (after her fashion) when they entered the parlor. Son was not long able to restrain his laughter although he had actually pressed his hand over his mouth. When his laughter finally did explode the two girls sprang up from the piano bench. Their mother stood paralyzed, expecting a greater explosion of temper from them. But they only smiled with a shamefaced expression that was utterly artificial. Ann had turned to Son and was remonstrating with him. "I really should think you'd be ashamed," she said.

"Why, he's completely shameless and unchivalrous," Helena said with the same false expression of tolerance and good nature on her face. It was this expression which the faces of both girls were affecting that stunned and mystified Harriet beyond all bounds. She knew now that they were in league to accomplish some purpose. She could see that they were fully prepared for Son's reaction and that it was even desired.

"Hush, Son, you idiot," Kate smiled. Then turning to Ann: "That old ballad is one Mama taught us when we were children. Of course none of us have Mama's music, but we weren't expecting an audience." And finally she addressed her sister, "The only trouble is, Helena, you were not singing the right words—not the words Mama taught us."

"No," Son derided, "you were singing from *The Oxford Book of Verse*."

"I know," Helena admitted with her feigned modesty and frankness. "But, Mama," she said to Harriet, "sing us your version—the real Tennessee version."

And they all began to insist that Harriet play and sing. At first she would not, for she felt that she was being a dupe to her two daughters. It was for this that the whole scene had been arranged! If she could avoid it she would not assist them in any of their schemings. If there was to be antagonism between her children she was not going to take sides. At breakfast the girls had led her to support their criticism of country-club life and modern ways by bringing in Mama's opinions. Now her singing of an old ballad would somehow support their cause.

But Son and Ann were insisting as well. She looked at Son and he said, "Please do sing." So if her singing was what they all wanted, how could she refuse? Perhaps it would make them forget whatever was the trouble. Besides, Harriet loved so to be at the piano singing the old songs that were fixed so well in her ear and in her heart.

As she sat down before the piano Helena ran to get Sweetheart, for he would never forgive them if Mother sang without his hearing it. She would also get Mattie who loved hearing her mistress sing above all else. Then Helena returned with her father, saying that Mattie would listen from the pantry.

So as Sweetheart took his stand by the upright piano and watched her with that rare expression of alertness in his eyes and as the young people grouped themselves behind her Harriet began to play and sing. Her soprano voice came as clear and fresh as when she was nineteen. When she had finished "Barbara Allen" she followed with other ballads almost without being asked. Anyone listening could tell how well she enjoyed singing the old songs that her grandpa had taught her long ago and how well she remembered the lyrics and the melody, never faltering in the words or hesitating on the keyboard. But her lovely, natural talent was not merely of the music. She seemed actually to experience the mood of each song. And her memory and ear for the soft vowels and sharp consonants of the mountain dialect were such that what was really a precise rendition seemed effortless. All her family and their guest stood round remarking on the sweet, true quality of her voice.

At the dinner table the girls began to talk again of who was kin to whom in Nashville. "Mama," Kate said, "I didn't know till the other day that Miss Liza Parks is Mrs. Frazier Dalton's aunt. She's one of that Parks family who used to live at Cedar Hill."

Harriet could hardly resist saying that Miss Liza was also second cousin to Mr. Bob Ragsdale. But without even looking at Kate she said, "Now, what interest could that be to Ann? Tell us, Ann, how you liked Sweetheart's little farm."

"Oh, it's a beauty," Ann said. "And his methods are quite modern. He even rotates his crops and paints his barn. Dr. Wilson is certainly no backward Southern farmer. B.T. showed us the garden, and I think B.T. is a wonder."

"He's grand on outside work," Harriet said.

The two girls began to laugh, and Harriet frowned at them.

"Son has told me," Ann whispered to Harriet, for Mattie was passing in and out of the room, "about the poor fellow's peculiarity. He's going away for the Duration, I understand, but when he comes back, why doesn't he try to get a farm of his own and make a real business of it. You can tell he has a genuine love of farming, and he's quite intelligent, isn't he? He ought to—"

"Now, Ann," Son interrupted, "how on earth is a poor Negro just going to reach out and get himself a farm? How can you ask such a question with all your knowledge of conditions?"

"I was thinking that Dr. Wilson would help him. Wouldn't you, Doctor?"

"Yes, of course, if he wanted—"

The girls were laughing together again. "That's just it," Helena said, "*if* B.T. wanted to. But he's a gentleman's nigger, Ann. He worships Daddy, and Daddy couldn't live without him. It's a very old-fashioned relationship, you know what I mean? It's the same with Mother and Mattie." At this point Mattie came in. She was serving the last of the four vegetable dishes. Nobody spoke while she was in the room. The picture of Mattie and B.T. in the kitchen this morning returned to Harriet, and she found herself thinking again of what she had said to Mattie yesterday in the yard. The brooding expression in Mattie's eyes and her repeated glances at Son as she passed round the table suggested anew the hateful comparison she had drawn. But Harriet could not feel such strong resentment now. She told herself that it was because she saw now how great was the real difference between her son and Mattie's little nephew. It was too absurd even to consider. She must have been out of her head yesterday! Her nerves had been on edge. That was the answer. And Mattie had spoken to her about that foul-scented B.T. just when she was grieving most about Son's going into the Army. Today the real pain of that grief had left her. It would doubtless return. But why, she considered, had it left her now? It seemed that his putting on a uniform was as unreal and indifferent a matter to her as the mysterious life he led in New York and his intellectual friendship with Ann Prewitt and this conversation they were having at her table. Last night she had overheard Son and Ann discussing herself as objectively as they were now discussing B.T. and Negro "conditions." Then she rebuked herself and allowed that Son simply lived on a higher plane. She felt that she should be ashamed to understand so little about her son and about her daughters and the antagonism there was between the young people.

When Mattie had left the room Kate said, "Yes, it's quite the same with Mattie and Mama. Yesterday Mattie was upset by some bad news and she came and threw herself into Mama's arms and wept like a child. It seems to me that's what they really are: a race of children, a medieval peasantry. They're completely irresponsible and totally dependent upon us. I really feel that Southern white people have a great responsibility—"

"We are responsible," Ann Prewitt said, "for their being irresponsible and dependent, if that's what you mean, Kate."

"Oh, that's *not* what she means," said Helena. "Their whole race is in its childhood, Ann, with all the wonders and charm of childhood. And it needs the protection, supervision, discipline, and affection that can be given only by Southern white people who have a vital relationship and traditional ties with them. The poor nigs who I feel for are those in Chicago and New York who have no white families to turn to."

Ann was looking to Son to see if he were going to make an argument of this. But Son said only, "What do you think of that, Ann?"

With an aggrieved, shy glance at Son she said, "I think it's a lot of nonsense. But that's only my opinion."

"Well, it's my opinion too," said Son. "The people in the South cannot expect to progress with the rest of the nation until they've forgotten their color line. The whole system has got to be changed. In some strange way it hinders the whites more than the blacks. When B.T. was in the garden with us this morning I felt that this was his home more than mine and that it was because of him that I feel no real tie to this place. Even when we were children it was so. . . . The whole system has got to be changed . . . somehow . . . someway."

"Somehow!" Ann exclaimed. Then she lowered her eyes and seemed to regret having spoken.

"You have a definite idea of how, then?" Helena asked.

"Equality: economic and social."

"You can't be serious," the girls said in one voice.

"Of course, she's serious," Son rejoined. Ann was silent. She appeared to have resolved not to speak again.

"You two are speaking as New Yorkers now," Helena began, "not as Southerners. Didn't it ever occur to you that the South has its own destiny? It has an entirely different tradition from the rest of the country. It has its own social institutions and must be allowed to work out its own salvation without interference."

"Sister," Son laughed, "you're beginning to sound not merely old-fashioned but unreconstructed."

"Then unreconstructed it is," defied Kate with a gallant smile. "Who can say that the Southern states were wrong to fight for their way of life?"

"For slavery, Kate?"

"The Southern master was morally responsible, which is more than can be said for the industrial sweatshopper."

Now Son slapped his hand over his mouth and presently his vehement laughter burst forth. He pushed his chair a little way from the table and said, "Now the cat's out of the bag! I know what you girls have been reading and who you've probably been seeing—those fellows at the University in Nashville. You know what I mean, Ann! Why, Ann, I've brought you into a hotbed of Southern reactionaries. How rich! How really rich this is! Now I know what you girls have been trying to put across. You and all Southern gentlemen and gentlewomen are the heirs and protectors of the great European traditions—and agrarian tradition, I should say. That's what all of this family pride and *noblesse oblige* mean. And Ann here, my comrade, believes that come the Revolution it will all be changed overnight. How rich!"

His laughter was curiously contagious and there did seem to be a general relief among all. "And now, my wise brother," asked Kate, "what do you believe?"

Ann and the two sisters were managing to smile at one another, for Son's derision had united them temporarily. While Son was trying to get his breath Ann leaned across the table and said, "He believes nothing that's any credit to him. He's been reading *The Decline of the West*! A man his age!"

Harriet was utterly dismayed, though she did sense that the incomprehensible antagonism had reached its crisis and that the worst was over. At least the young people understood each other now. But as they were leaving the table she wished, for the first time in many years, that she could be alone for a while this afternoon. She wanted to remember how Son and Helena and Kate had been when they were children—the girls quarreling over scraps from her sewing or playing dolls on the porch and Son begging to go off swimming with B.T. when the creek was still cold in May.

Everybody slept late on the morning of the Fourth of July. Sweetheart was still snoring gently at nine-thirty. He awoke when Harriet started the electric fan. "I'm so sorry, Sweetheart," she said, "but you looked so hot there I thought the fan might help." She was already half dressed, but before she had snapped the last snap in the placket of her dress Sweetheart had put on his clothes and shaved and gone out onto the porch. She smiled as she thought of it; and then she began to hurry, for Son's voice could now be heard on the porch. Besides, there was a lot to be done in preparation for the supper party tonight. Probably the girls were already helping in the kitchen. They were being such angels this weekend!

She was smoothing the last corner of the counterpane when Kate came in.

"I feel like the devil," Kate said. She was wearing her silk negligee and her hair was uncombed and even matted in places. She was barefooted; and the girls always looked taller to Harriet in their bare feet.

"And you look like the very devil," Harriet said.

"Thanks, dear." She sat down on the bed which Harriet had just now made. She struck a match on the bottom of the bedside table and lit the cigarette which she had brought with her.

She patted the bed beside her indicating that Harriet should sit down. Harriet could always tell when the girls had been drinking a good deal the night before by the sour expression which the heavy sleep left on their features. She was long since accustomed to their drinking "socially," and to their smoking but she still did not like the smell of whiskey on them next morning. She pulled up her rocking chair and sat down.

"Mother, I do wish that Helena wouldn't drink so much. She just doesn't know how."

Harriet only shook her head, saying nothing, for Helena would have a similar report about Kate later in the morning. The truce between them was evidently over. "How was the Buchanans' party?" she asked.

"It was pretty nice." Then she shrugged her shoulders. "I want to tell you about Ann."

"What is there to tell?"

"I thought you wanted to hear about the party!" Kate said sharply.

"I do."

"Well listen, that's what I mean—how Ann behaved last night."

"She didn't misbehave?"

"I should say not. She's a perfect little lady, you know. A perfect parlor pink, as we suspected—Helena and I."

Parlor pink meant nothing to Harriet. She turned her face away toward the window to indicate that if Kate persisted in talking the kind of nonsense they talked at the table yesterday she didn't care to listen.

"She holds her liquor well, all right," Kate continued, "but after a few drinks she's not the quiet little mouse she is around here. She talks incessantly and rather brilliantly, I admit. And what I'm getting at is that when she talks Son seems to hang on her every word. He plainly thinks she's the cleverest woman alive."

"What does she talk about?"

"For one thing, she talked about birth control and its implications to Lucy Price who is a Catholic. She was really very funny about the Pope as the great papa who *doesn't* pay." Harriet had no full understanding of birth control itself, much less of its implications. And she knew that she was unreasonably prejudiced against Catholics. Why couldn't Kate talk about Ann without dragging in those things?

"She quotes Marx and Huxley and lots of young British poets. And all the while Son sits beaming with admiration as though she were Sappho or Margaret Sanger, herself."

"Is he in love with her then, Kate, if he does all that?"

"Not at all."

"And Ann herself?"

"Hardly! She's not the type. She never looks at him."

Harriet sighed.

"But there's something between them," Kate said speculatively.

"I suppose intellectual friendships can have very deep feelings."

"Pooh," said Kate.

"Then the girl is in love with him, and he—"

"No, Mother. I don't believe it." But Harriet looked at her daughter with the matted hair and the sleep-creased face and the cigarette with its smoke drifting straight upward into the breathless air. *Her* girls had never been in love. And it isn't their height, she thought, and it isn't their legs. They're like Son, she thought, and it isn't them. She got up from her chair and as she left Kate behind she met Helena at the door. Helena's face and hair and general attire were about the same as Kate's. "Kate's in there," Harriet said and brushed past the daughter who towered above her in the doorway. She went into the parlor to draw the draperies before the sun got too warm.

The day grew warm. You could almost hear the temperature rising if you stood still a minute. Harriet was so busy about the house that she thought it her activity that made her perspire. But now and then she would step out to the porch and slip on her spectacles to look at the thermometer. "What an awful day," she would say to Sweetheart who was sleeping in his chair.

The girls remained in their room until afternoon. Once or twice Harriet heard them speaking irritably to one another. When they finally appeared Helena turned on the radio in the parlor and Kate sat on the porch. They would show no interest in the coming party. They sulked about as though they had been disappointed or defeated in something.

"Quit buzzing around, Mother," Kate said. "There are only a dozen or so people coming and it's supposed to be informal."

"Oh, Goddy, I never saw so much commotion over a cold supper," Helena said.

Ann tried to help, but Harriet said, "There's nothing left to do. I just have to cut the melon balls and everything will be ready."

Later Sweetheart and Son went off to Nashville to pick up the whiskey at the hotel. Ann went along to make her Pullman reservations, for she was taking a train at one A.M. She said she had to be in Little Rock the next day.

Most of the guests parked their cars in the backyard alongside B.T.'s shack or in front of the garage. As they arrived Son went out into the yard to greet them or welcomed them on the screened porch. Supper was served buffet style, and Sweetheart brought everybody two or three drinks before they began to eat. "We want you to have an appetite," he would say.

The guests were, for the most part, Son's old school friends and their wives. There were two young men of sufficient height to escort the girls from room to room. And there was a young professor from the University and his wife who had taught at Miss Hood's School with Helena. Son was most cordial to this couple, introducing himself to them in the yard since Helena was not present when they arrived. The young professor (he explained that he was really only a teaching fellow) wore a small mustache and a dark bow tie with his linen suit. He was very timid and spoke only a few words in the course of the whole evening.

While dressing for the party Harriet observed in the mirror that her face showed the strain she had been under. She spread extra powder under her eyes and applied more rouge than was usual for her. When she had finished her toilet she removed all her personal things from the dressing table, opened a new box of powder, and brought from the closet shelf an ivory hand mirror and comb and brush. The ladies were going to use this as a powder room. From the closet shelf she also brought four small pillows with lacy slipcovers which she arranged on the bed.

She was arranging the pillows when Son knocked at her door. He entered with his own large glass in one hand and a small tumbler for her in the other. "It's mostly ginger ale," he said, "and I thought it would cool you off. It's right hot tonight."

It is this moment, she thought, that I've been waiting for through the whole weekend. And in this moment she banished all the despair that had been growing in her feelings toward Son and the girls. The insufferable insolence with which Mattie had treated her today also seemed as nothing. He has come to tell me what is in his heart. Or at least he has come so that we may have a few minutes alone before he leaves for the Army tomorrow. She glanced up at the childhood pictures of him which with pictures of the girls and a few of Mama and Papa and of Sweetheart covered one wall of her room. She pointed to a picture taken when he was thirteen wearing a skullcap on the back of his head and a sleeveless sweater. "That's my favorite," she said. "I began to notice a new look in your eyes when you were that age."

Son looked at the picture. Then his eyes roved indifferently over the other pictures there. "Well," he said, "I'd better go out and see that the girls are not sticking hat pins in Ann just to see how she reacts. Or at least not miss seeing it, myself, if they do." The guests were beginning to leave by eleven-thirty. Harriet was sitting in a straight chair on the front porch. She had been sitting there in the dark for an hour with her hands folded in her lap. Sweetheart was slumped down among the pillows on the swing nearby, asleep. The party had all been vague to Harriet, like a dream of some event she dreaded. After Son left her standing alone before the gallery of pictures in her room she was hardly able to go into the house and meet the guests. There were no tears and no signs of nervous agitation. Rather, she felt herself completely without human emotion of any sort as she lingered there in her room for a long while. When finally she did go forward and take her place by the buffet in the dining room, she pretended to be preoccupied with the food so that the guests would not notice how little concern she had for them. There were things she had planned to watch for this evening; but those things had become trivial and remote.

Early in the evening most of the party was gathered in the parlor and much of the conversation referred to things that had been said and done last night. Harry Buchanan urged Ann to express her views on something, but Ann declined. Several times Son was asking Ann what she thought about this or that, and always it seemed that Ann spoke two or three monosyllables which were followed by silence. Conversation between Son and the young professor did not materialize, and the girls did not try to draw him out as Harriet had expected. Ann and the professor were once heard talking about the "fragrance" of the wisteria. Helena took her tall, stooped young man to sit on the screened porch. Kate took hers to the chairs on the lawn. Now and then the two beaux appeared in the house on their way to the pantry with tall, empty glasses. Nothing could stir Harriet from her torpor, not even the information that in the middle of the evening B.T. had put on his hat and gone off to the settlement or to Nashville.

When she realized that the guests were beginning to go, she placed her hand on Sweetheart's knee and said, "People are leaving, Sweetheart." He followed her into the hall and the two of them stood smiling and nodding and shaking hands of guests amid the hubbub of giddy and even drunken talk about Son's going into the Army. As the last of the automobiles pulled away, backing and turning in the gravel before the garage with its headlamps flashing on B.T.'s shack and on the house and then on the trees and the white gravel of the driveway, someone called back, "Good-bye, Private Wilson!"

Harriet stood on the screened porch after the headlamps had gone round the house leaving the yard in darkness. While she was there she saw the light go off in the kitchen. The backdoor closed, and presently Mattie's dark figure moved sluggishly across the yard to the shack. There was no window on the near side of the little cabin, but when Mattie had put on the light inside, Harriet could see a square of light which a small window threw on a thick, green mint bed over by the fence. "She's going to wait up for B.T.," Harriet said. And now she went through the house and into the warm kitchen to see in what state Mattie had left things.

The dishes were not washed but they were stacked neatly on the table and in the sink. The backdoor was locked, and Harriet unlocked it so that Mattie could come in that way to go to her bed in the attic room above the kitchen. "Poor thing is so

distracted she locked herself out," she said. She stood with her
hand on the knob for a minute, for she wanted to go out and
see Mattie. She could not bring herself to go.

When she came into the parlor she found that Ann had
changed to her traveling dress. Helena and Kate were sprawled
in two of the large chairs. Sweetheart was standing by the
fireplace talking about train schedules to Little Rock. Ann was
seated on the piano bench with her feet close together and her
small delicate hands folded in her lap. Harriet had crossed the
room and was taking her seat beside Ann when Son entered
with the luggage.

"It's not quite time to go," Son said. He set the two bags
by the hall door and drew up an odd chair. Harriet had taken
one of Ann's hands between her own and was about to make a
little farewell speech when Ann spoke.

She was looking into Harriet's face but as she spoke she
turned her eyes to Son. "He thinks I have not behaved well
tonight."

"Oh, for Heaven's sake, Ann," Son said, turning in his chair
and crossing his legs. Kate and Helena visibly collected their
sprawled persons and looked attentively from Ann to Son.

"He does, indeed," said Ann. She stood up and walked to
the mantel and stood at the other end from Sweetheart. "Very
badly. He always thinks a person behaves badly who doesn't
amuse him. He cares nothing for anything I say except when
I'm talking theory of some kind. He was very willing to bring
me here before your friends to express all manner of opinion
which they and you find disagreeable while he behaves with
conventional good taste. He even discouraged me bringing the
proper clothes to make any sort of agreeable appearance. Yet
see how smartly he's turned out."

Son had now ceased to show any discomfort. He was watching Ann with the same interest that the girls showed. He was
smiling when he interrupted her, "You are really drunk, Ann.
But go on. You're priceless. You're rich. What else about me?"

"Nothing else about you," she said, undismayed. "But about
me, now . . . We have had a very beautiful and very Platonic
friendship. He has shown a marvelous respect for my intelligence and my virtue. And I, alas, have been so vulgar as to
fall in love with him." She turned to Sweetheart who stood

with his hands hanging limp at his sides and his mouth literally wide open. "It's a sad story, is it not, Doctor?" The doctor tried to smile.

Son rose from his chair saying, "Now it *is* time we go." And he and Ann left the room in such a hurry that Harriet was still seated when she heard them step out onto the porch. Then she jumped from her place on the piano bench and began to follow them.

But she had only reached the doorway to the hall when one of the girls said, "Mother, can't you see how drunk that gal really is?" As she stopped there in the hall her eyes fell on the mahogany umbrella rack where Sweetheart kept his seven walking sticks. She counted the sticks and it seemed that there were only six of them. Then she counted them again and found that all seven were in their places. She counted them several times over, and each time there were still seven sticks in the rack.

Harriet was on her knees at her bedside. She had already repeated the Lord's Prayer twice but still was unable to think of the meaning of the words as she began it the third time. Her elbows were pressing into the soft mattress, and though the room was in darkness her eyes were closed. She was repeating the prayer slowly, moving her lips as she pronounced each word, when the fierce shout of a Negro woman seemed to break not only the silence but even the darkness. Sweetheart had sprung from the bed and put on the light. Harriet remained on her knees and watched him go to the closet shelf to get his pistol. "It's Mattie," she said. "It's Mattie screaming!"

"No, it's not Mattie," she said. "I don't think it was a scream either." Sweetheart turned his eyes to her with a suddenness that struck her dumb for a moment. When she was able to speak she said, "It's one of those women B.T. has." But the doctor had understood her before she spoke again and in his white pajamas had already disappeared into the darkness of the hallway.

His hearing had been keen enough to detect that it was a Negro's voice. But his ear was not so sensitive as Harriet's. She was the only one in the house who knew that Mattie was waiting in the shack, and the shout came distinctly from that quarter; but her ear was not deceived for an instant. She raised herself from her knees and faced her two daughters who had come to her door. She knew as well now as they would know when they were told a few minutes later what scene was taking place in the low doorway of that cabin. In her mind she saw the very shadows that were then being thrown on the green mint bed.

The first shout was followed by other distinct oaths. Now Mattie's and B.T.'s voices could be heard mixing with that of the third Negro. So Harriet knew too that there had not yet been a cutting. "Hurry, Sweetheart," she called in a voice that hardly seemed her own. The girls stood watching her, and she stood motionless listening for every sound. Presently there came amid the voices the crunching sound of gravel under the wheels of her own coupe. Son was returning home from the depot. She pushed herself between the girls and went to the window in their room. From there she could see that the incident was over. Sweetheart and Son stood in the bright light from the headlamps of the automobile. They stood talking there for several minutes, and then Son came toward the house and Sweetheart went into the shack.

Son came into her room where she and the girls were waiting. His face was pale, but he was smiling. "It's not really anything," he said. "B.T. had brought one of his lady friends home, and his auntie would not receive her. I think his auntie even struck her. The lights of the car scared her off into the woods, and B.T. followed. Dad's bringing Mattie into the house."

Harriet put on her robe and went through the house to the kitchen. She waited there a long while watching the light in the shack. Finally Sweetheart appeared on the stoop. He stood there in his white pajamas for an endless time speaking into the doorway in such a quiet voice that she could not hear him. When he did turn and see her at the kitchen he left the shack and came to her at once.

"You'll have to talk to Mattie," he said. "She doesn't want to come in the house, but of course she'll have to. That pair just might come back tonight."

Harriet gazed at him blankly for a moment and then closed her eyes. "I can't go," she said.

"Harriet? You'll have to go, love. I'll go with you and wait at the door. The poor creature needs you."

"Did she ask for me?"

"No. She didn't think to. She's in a terrible state. She doesn't talk."

"Did you tell her I was coming?"

"Yes," he said, "and that's the only thing that made her even look at me."

Harriet turned away and moved toward the dining room. When he called to her she was at the swinging door and she said, "I'm going to dress."

"You've no need to dress," he said. He came round the kitchen table and stopped a few feet from her. She had never known him to speak to her in private from such a distance. "Harriet, why should this be so hard for you?"

There was no sympathy in the question, and actually he did not seem to want an answer to this precise question. He seemed to be making a larger and more general inquiry into her character than he had ever done before. She dropped her eyes to the floor and walked hurriedly by him to the backdoor. She paused there and said, "Wait here."

Mattie was seated on a squat, ladder-back chair whose short legs had the look of being worn away through long usage. Her brown hands were resting on the black dress over each knee. A dim bulb hung on a cord almost at waist level, and the gray moths that flitted around it were lighting on Mattie's head. Harriet came in and stood directly before her. When she first tried to speak she felt that she was going to be nauseated by the awful smell of B.T., a stench that seemed to be compounded of the smell of soiled and moldy clothing and the smell of condensed and concentrated human sweat. She even glanced about the room half expecting to find B.T. standing in one of the dark corners. "Mattie," she said at last, "I was unkind to you Saturday. You must not hold it against me."

Mattie raised her eyes to her mistress, and there was neither forgiveness nor resentment in them. In her protruding lower lip and in her wide nostrils there was defiance, but it was a defiance of the general nature of this world where she must pass her days, not of Harriet in particular. In her eyes there was grief and there was something beyond grief. After a moment she did speak, and she told Harriet that she was going to sit there all night and that they had all better go on to bed in the house. Later when Harriet tried to recall the exact tone and words Mattie had used—as her acute ear would normally have allowed her to do—she could not reconstruct the speech at all. It seemed as though Mattie had used a special language common to both of them but one they had never before discovered and could now never recover. Afterward they faced each other in uncommunicative silence for an indefinite time. Finally Harriet moved to the door again, but she looked back once more and she saw that besides the grief and hostility in Mattie's eyes there was an unspeakable loneliness for which she could offer no consolation.

When she told Sweetheart that Mattie still refused to leave the shack he sat down on the porch steps and said that he was going to keep watch for a while. She didn't try to dissuade him, and he said nothing more to her as she put her robe about her shoulders and went inside.

In her room she tried to resume her broken prayers. Then she lay on the bed with the light still burning and she longed to weep as she had done when she first saw Son in the doorway. Not a tear would come to her eyes. She thought of all the talking that Son and the girls had done and she felt that she was even beginning to understand what it had meant. But she sadly reflected that her children believed neither what Ann Prewitt nor what the professors at the University were offering them. To Harriet it seemed that her children no longer existed; it was as though they had all died in childhood as people's children used to do. All the while she kept remembering that Mattie was sitting out in that shack for the sole purpose of inhaling the odor in the stifling air of B.T.'s room.

When Sweetheart finally came she was on her knees again at her bedside. She heard him put out the light and let himself down easily on the other side of the bed. When she opened her eyes it was dark and there was the chill of autumn night about the room.

Porte Cochere

CLIFFORD AND Ben Jr. always came for Old Ben's birthday. Clifford came all the way from Dallas. Ben Jr. came only from Cincinnati. They usually stayed in Nashville through the following weekend, or came the weekend before and stayed through the birthday. Old Ben, who was seventy-six and nearly blind—the cataracts had been removed twice since he was seventy—could hear them now on the side porch, their voices louder than the others', Clifford's the loudest and strongest of all. "Clifford's the real man amongst them," he said to himself, hating to say it but needing to say it. There was no knowing what went on in the heads of the other children, but there were certain things Clifford did know and understand. Clifford, being a lawyer, knew something about history—about Tennessee history he knew, for instance, the difference between Chucky Jack Sevier and Judge John Overton and could debate with you the question of whether or not Andy Jackson had played the part of the coward when he and Chucky Jack met in the wilderness that time. Old Ben kept listening for Cliff's voice above the others. All of his grown-up children were down on the octagonal side porch, which was beyond the porte cochere and which, under its red tile roof, looked like a pagoda stuck out there on the side lawn. Old Ben was in his study.

His study was directly above the porte cochere, or what his wife, in her day, had called the porte cochere—he called it the drive-under and the children used to call it the portcullis—but the study was not a part of the second floor; it opened off the landing halfway up the stairs. Under his south window was the red roof of the porch. He sat by the open window, wearing his dark glasses, his watery old eyes focused vaguely on the peak of the roof. He had napped a little since dinner but had not removed his suit coat or even unbuttoned his linen vest. During most of the afternoon, he had been awake and had heard his five children talking down there on the porch—Cliff and Ben Jr. had arrived only that morning—talking on and on in such loud voices that his good right ear could catch individual words and sometimes whole sentences.

Midday dinner had been a considerable ordeal for Old Ben. Nell's interminable chatter had been particularly taxing and obnoxious. Afterward, he had hurried to his study for his pre-scribed nap and had spent a good part of the afternoon dread-ing the expedition to the Country Club for supper that had been planned for that evening. Now it was almost time to begin getting ready for that expedition, and simultaneously with the thought of it and with the movement of his hand toward his watch pocket he became aware that Clifford was taking his leave of the group on the side porch. Ah yes, at dinnertime Clifford had said he had a letter to write before supper—to his wife. Yet here it was six and he had dawdled away the afternoon palavering with the others down there on the porch. Old Ben could recognize Cliff's leave-taking and the teasing voices of the others, and then he heard Cliff's footsteps at the bottom of the stairs. In a moment he would go sailing by Old Ben's door, without a thought for anyone but himself. Old Ben's lower lip trembled. Wasn't there some business matter he could take up with Cliff? Or some personal matter? And now Cliff's footsteps on the stairs—heavy footsteps, like his own. Suddenly, though, the footsteps halted, and Clifford went downstairs again. His father heard him go across the hall and into the living room, where the carpet silenced his footsteps; he was getting writing paper from the desk there. Old Ben hastily pulled the cord that closed the draperies across the south window, leaving only the vague light from the east window in the room. No, sir, he would not advertise his presence when Cliff passed on the landing.

With the draperies drawn, the light in the room had a strange quality—strange because Old Ben seldom drew the draperies at night. For one moment, he felt that his eyes or his glasses were playing him some new trick. Then he dropped his head on the chairback, for the strange quality now seemed strangely familiar, and no longer strange—only familiar. It was like the light in the cellar where, long ago, he used to go fetch Mason jars for his great-aunt Nell Partee. Aunt Nell would send for him all the way across town to come fetch her Mason jars, and even when he was ten or twelve, she made him whistle the whole time he was down in the cellar, to make certain he didn't drink her wine. Aunt Nell, dead and gone. Was this something for Clifford's attention? Where Aunt Nell's shacky house had been, the Trust Company now stood—a near-skyscraper. Her cellar, he supposed, had been in the space now occupied by the basement barbershop—not quite so deep or so large as the shop, its area without boundaries now, suspended in the center of the barbershop, where the ceiling fan revolved. Would this be of interest to Cliff, who would soon ascend the stairs with his own train of thoughts and would pass the open door to the study without a word or a glance? And whatever Cliff was thinking about—his law, his gold, or his wife and children— would be of no real interest to Old Ben. But did not Clifford know that merely the sound of his voice gave his father hope, that his attention gave him comfort? What would old age be without children? Desolation, desolation. But what would old age be with children who chose to ignore the small demands that he would make upon them, that he had ever made upon them? A nameless torment! And with his thoughts Old Ben Brantley's white head rocked on his shoulders and his smoked glasses went so crooked on his nose that he had to frown them back into position.

But now Clifford was hurrying up the stairs again. He was on the landing outside the open study door. It was almost despite himself that the old man cleared his throat and said hoarsely, "The news will be on in five minutes, if you want to listen to it." Then as though he might have sounded too cordial (he would not be reduced to toadying to his own boy), "But if you don't want to, don't say you do." Had Cliff seen his glasses slip down his nose? Cliff, no less than the others, would be capable of laughing at him in his infirmity.

"I wouldn't be likely to, would I, Papa?" Cliff had stopped at the doorway and was stifling a yawn as he spoke, half covering his face with the envelope and the folded sheet of paper. Old Ben nodded his head to indicate that he had heard what Cliff had said, but also, to himself, he was nodding that yes, this was the way he had raised his children to talk to him.

"Just the hourly newscast," Old Ben said indifferently. "But it don't matter."

"Naw, can't make it, Papa. I got to go and write Sue Alice. The stupid woman staying with her while I'm away bores her pretty much." As he spoke, he looked directly into the dark lenses of his father's glasses, and for a brief second he rested his left hand on the doorjamb. His manner was self-possessed and casual, but Old Ben felt that he didn't need good sight to detect his poor son's ill-concealed haste to be off and away. Cliff had, in fact, turned back to the stairs when his father stopped him with a question, spoken without expression and almost under his breath.

"Why did you come at all? Why did you even bother to come if you weren't going to bring Sue Alice and the grandchildren? Did you think I wanted to see you without them?"

Clifford stopped with one foot on the first step of the second flight. "By God, Papa!" He turned on the ball of the other foot and reappeared in the doorway. "Ever travel with two small kids?" The motion of his body as he turned back from the steps had been swift and sure, calculated to put him exactly facing his father. "And in hot weather like we're having in Texas?"

Despite the undeniable thickness in Clifford's hips and the thin spot on the back of his head, his general appearance was still youthful; about this particular turning on the stairs there had been something decidedly athletic. Imperceptibly, behind the dark glasses, Old Ben lifted his eyebrows in admiration. Clifford was the only boy he had who had ever made any team at the University or done any hunting worth speaking of. For a moment, his eyes rested gently on Cliff's white summer shoes, set wide apart in the doorway. Then, jerking his head up, as though he had just heard Cliff's last words, he began, "Two small *kids*? (Why don't you use the word *brats*? It's more elegant.) I have traveled considerably with five—from here to the mountain and back every summer for fifteen years, from my thirty-first to my forty-sixth year."

"I remember," Cliff said stoically. Then, after a moment, "But now I'm going up to my room and write Sue Alice."

"Then go on up! Who's holding you?" He reached for his smoking stand and switched on the radio. It was a big cabinet radio with a dark mahogany finish, a piece from the late twenties, like all the other furniture in the room, and the mechanism was slow to warm up.

Clifford took several steps toward his father. "Papa, we're due to leave for the Club in thirty minutes—less than that now—and I intend to scratch off a note to my wife." He held up the writing paper, as though to prove his intention.

"No concern of mine! No concern of mine! To begin with, I, personally, am not going to the Club or anywhere else for supper."

Clifford came even closer. "You may go to the Club or not, as you like, Papa. But unless I misunderstand, there is not a servant on the place, and we are all going."

"That is, you are going after you scratch off a note to your wife."

"Papa, Ben Jr. and I have each come well over five hundred miles—"

"Not to see me, Clifford."

"Don't be so damned childish, Papa." Cliff was turning away again. Old Ben held his watch in his hand, and he glanced down at it quickly.

"I'm not getting childish, am I, Clifford?"

This time, Clifford's turning back was not accomplished in one graceful motion but by a sudden jerking and twisting of his shoulder and leg muscles. Behind the spectacles, Old Ben's eyes narrowed and twitched. His fingers were folded over the face of the watch. Clifford spoke very deliberately. "I didn't say *getting* childish, Papa. When ever in your life have you been anything but that? There's not a senile bone in your brain. It's your children that have got old, and you've stayed young—and not in any good sense, Papa, only in a bad one! You play sly games with us still or you quarrel with us. What the hell do you want of us, Papa? I've thought about it a lot. Why haven't you ever asked for what it is you want? Or are *we* all blind and it's really obvious? You've never given but one piece of advice to us, and that's to be direct and talk up to you like men—as equals. And we've done that, all right, and listened to your wrangling, but somehow it has never satisfied you! What is it?"

"Go on up to your letter-writing; go write your spouse," said Old Ben.

The room had been getting darker while they talked. Old Ben slipped his watch back into his vest pocket nervously, then slipped it out again, constantly running his fingers over the gold case, as though it were a piece of money.

"Thanks for your permission, sir." Clifford took a step backward. During his long speech he had advanced all the way across the room until he was directly in front of his father.

"My permission?" Old Ben said. "Let us not forget one fact, Clifford. No child of mine has ever had to ask my permission to do anything whatsoever he took a mind to do. You have all been free as the air, to come and go in this house. . . . You still are!"

Clifford smiled. "Free to come and go, with you perched here on the landing registering every footstep on the stairs and every car that passed underneath. I used to turn off the ignition and coast through the drive-under, and then think how foolish it was, since there was no back stairway. No back stairway in a house this size!" He paused a moment, running his eyes over the furniture and the other familiar objects in the shadowy room. "And how like the old times this was, Papa—your listening in here in the dark when I came up! By God, Papa, I wouldn't have thought when I was growing up that I'd ever come back and fuss with you once I was grown. But here I am, and, Papa—"

Old Ben pushed himself up from the chair. He put his watch in the vest pocket and buttoned his suit coat with an air of satisfaction. "I'm going along to the Club for supper," he said, "since there's to be no-un here to serve me." As he spoke, he heard the clock chiming the half hour downstairs. And Ben Jr. was shouting to Old Ben and Clifford from the foot of the stairs, "Get a move on up there."

Clifford went out on the landing and called down the steps. "Wait till I change my shirt. I believe Papa's all ready."

"No letter written?" Ben Jr. asked.

Clifford was hurrying up the second flight with the blank paper. "Nope, no letter this day of Our Lord."

Old Ben heard Ben Jr. say, "What did I tell you?" and heard the others laughing. He stood an instant by his chair without putting on a light. Then he reached out his hand for one of the walking canes in the umbrella stand by the radio. His hand lighting on the carved head of a certain oak stick, he felt the head with trembling fingers and quickly released it, and quickly, in three strides, without the help of any cane, he crossed the room to the south window. For several moments, he stood motionless at the window, his huge, soft hands held tensely at his sides, his long body erect, his almost freakishly large head at a slight angle, while he seemed to peer between the open draperies and through the pane of the upper sash, out into the twilight of the wide, shady park that stretched from his great yellow-brick house to the pike. Old Ben's eyes, behind the smoked lenses, were closed, and he was visualizing the ceiling fan in the barbershop. Presently, opening his eyes, he reflected, almost with a smile, that his aunt's cellar was not the only Nashville cellar that had disappeared. Many a cellar! His father's cellar, round like a dungeon; it had been a cistern in the very earliest days, before Old Ben's time, and when he was a boy, he would go around and around the brick walls and then come back with a hollow sound, as though the cistern were still half full of water. One time, ah—Old Ben drew back from the window with a grimace—one time he had been so sure there was water below! In fright at the very thought of the water, he had clasped a rung of the ladder tightly with one hand and swung the lantern out, expecting certainly to see the light reflected in the depths below. But the lantern had struck the framework that supported the circular shelves and gone whirling and flaming to the brick floor, which Ben had never before seen. Crashing on the floor, it sent up yellow flames that momentarily lit the old cistern to its very top, and when Ben looked upward, he saw the furious face of his father with the flames casting jagged shadows on the long, black beard and high, white forehead. "Come out of there before you burn out my cellar and my whole damn house to the ground!" He had climbed upward toward his father, wishing the flames might engulf him before he came within reach of those arms. But as his father jerked him up onto the back porch, he saw that the flames had already died out. The whole cellar was pitch-black dark again, and the boy Ben stood with his face against the whitewashed brick wall while his father went to the carriage house to find the old plow line. Presently, he heard his father step up on the porch again. He braced himself for the first blow, but instead there was only the deafening command from his father: "Attention!" Ben whirled about and stood erect, with his chin in the air, his eyes on the ceiling. "Where have you hidden my plow lines?" "I don't know, sir." And then the old man, with his coattails somehow clinging close to his buttocks and thighs, so that his whole powerful form was outlined—his black figure against the white brick and the door—stepped over to the doorway, reached around to the cane stand in the hall, and drew out the oak stick that had his own bearded face carved upon the head. "About face!" he commanded. The boy drew back his toe and made a quick, military turn. The old man dealt him three sharp blows across the upper part of his back. . . . Tears had run down young Ben Brantley's cheeks, even streaking down his neck under his open collar and soaking the neckline binding of his woolen underwear, but he had uttered not a sound. When his father went into the house, Ben remained for a long while standing with his face to the wall. At last, he quietly left the porch and walked through the yard beneath the big shade trees, stopping casually to watch a gray squirrel and then to listen to Aunt Sally Ann's soft nigger voice whispering to him out the kitchen window. He did not answer or turn around but walked on to the latticed summerhouse, between the house and the kitchen garden. There he had lain down on a bench, looked back at the house through the lattice-work, and said to himself that when he got to be a grown man, he would go away to another country, where there would be no maple trees and no oak trees, no elms, not even sycamores or poplars; where there would be no squirrels and no niggers, no houses that resembled this one; and, most of all, where there would be no children and no fathers.

In the hall, now, Old Ben could hear, very faintly, Ben Jr.'s voice and Laura Nell's and Katie's and Lawrence's. He stepped to the door and looked down the dark flight of steps at his four younger children. They stood in a circle directly beneath the overhead light, which one of them had just switched on. Their faces were all turned upward in the direction of the open doorway where he was standing, yet he knew in reason that they could not see him there. They were talking about him! Through his dark lenses, their figures were indistinct, their faces were blurs, and it was hard for him to distinguish their lowered voices one from another. But they were talking about him! And from upstairs he could hear Clifford's footsteps. Clifford, with his letter to Sue Alice unwritten, was thinking about him! Never once in his life had he punished or restrained them in any way! He had given them a freedom unknown to children in the land of his childhood, yet from the time they could utter a word they had despised him and denied his right to any affection or gratitude. Suddenly, stepping out onto the landing, he screamed down the stairs to them, "I've a right to some gratitude!"

They were silent and motionless for a moment. Then he could hear them speaking in lowered voices again, and moving slowly toward the stairs. At the same moment he heard Clifford's footsteps in the upstairs hall. Presently, a light went on up there, and he could dimly see Clifford at the head of the stairs. The four children were advancing up the first flight, and Clifford was coming down from upstairs. Old Ben opened his mouth to call to them, "I'm not afraid of you!" But his voice had left him, and in his momentary fright, in his fear that his wrathful, merciless children might do him harm, he suddenly pitied them. He pitied them for all they had suffered at his hands. And while he stood there, afraid, he realized, or perhaps recalled, how he had tortured and plagued them in all the ways that his resentment of their very good fortune had taught him to do. He even remembered the day when it had occurred to him to build his study above the drive-under and off the stairs, so that he could keep tab on them. He had declared that he wanted his house to be as different from his father's house as a house could be, and so it was! And now he stood in the half-darkness, afraid that he was a man about to be taken by his children and at the same time pitying them, until one of them, ascending the steps switched on the light above the landing.

In the sudden brightness, Old Ben felt that his senses had returned to him. Quickly, he stepped back into the study, closed the door, and locked it. As the lock clicked, he heard Clifford say, "Papa!" Then he heard them all talking at once, and while they talked, he stumbled through the dark study to the umbrella stand. He pulled out the stick with his father's face carved on the head, and in the darkness, while he heard his children's voices, he stumbled about the room beating the upholstered chairs with the stick and calling the names of children under his breath.

A Wife of Nashville

THE LOVELLS' old cook Sarah had quit to get married in the spring, and they didn't have anybody else for a long time—not for several months. It was during the Depression, and when a servant quit, people in Nashville (and even people out at Thornton, where the Lovells came from) tried to see how long they could go before they got another. All through the summer, there would be knocks on the Lovells' front door or on the wooden porch floor, by the steps. And when one of the children or their mother went to the door, some Negro man or woman would be standing there, smiling and holding out a piece of paper. A recommendation it was supposed to be, but the illegible note scribbled with a blunt lead pencil was something no white person could have written if he had tried. If Helen Ruth, the children's mother, went to the door, she always talked a while to whoever it was, but she hardly ever even looked at the note held out to her. She would give a piece of advice or say to meet her around at the back door for a handout. If one of the boys—there were three Lovell boys, and no girls—went to the door, he always brought the note in to Helen Ruth, unless John R., their father, was at home, sick with his back ailment. Helen Ruth would shake her head and say to tell whoever it was to go away! "Tell him to go back home," she said once to the oldest boy, who was standing in the sun-parlor doorway with a smudged scrap of paper in his hand. "Tell him if he had any sense, he never would have left the country."

"He's probably not from the country, Mother."

"They're all from the country," Helen Ruth said. "When they knock on the porch floor like that, they're bound to be from the country, and they're better off at home, where somebody cares something about them. I don't care anything about them any more than you do."

But one morning Helen Ruth hired a cheerful-looking and rather plump, light-complexioned young Negro girl named Jess McGehee, who had come knocking on the front-porch floor just as the others had. Helen Ruth talked to her at the front door for a while; then she told her to come around to the kitchen, and they talked there for nearly an hour. Jess stayed to fix lunch and supper, and after she had been there a few days, the family didn't know how they had ever got along without her.

In fact, Jess got on so well with the Lovells that Helen Ruth even decided to let her come and live on the place, a privilege she had never before allowed a servant of hers. Together, she and Jess moved all of John R.'s junk—a grass duck-hunting outfit, two mounted stags' heads, an outboard motor, and so on—from the little room above the garage into the attic of the house. John R. lent Jess the money for the down payment on a "suit" of furniture, and Jess moved in. "You would never know she was out there," Helen Ruth told her friends. "There is never any rumpus. And her room! It's as clean as yours or mine."

Jess worked for them for eight years. John R. got so one of his favorite remarks was, "The honeymoon is over, but this is the real thing this time." Then he would go on about what he called Helen Ruth's "earlier affairs." The last one before Jess was Sarah, who quit to get married and go to Chicago at the age of sixty-eight. She had been with them for six years and was famous for her pies and her banana dishes.

Before Sarah, there was Carrie. Carrie had been with them when the two younger boys were born, and it was she who had once tried to persuade Helen Ruth not to go to the hospital but to let her act as midwife. She had quit them after five years, to become an undertaker. And before Carrie there was Jane Blakemore, the very first of them all, whom John R. and Helen Ruth had brought with them from Thornton to Nashville when they married. She lasted less than three years; she quit soon after John R., Jr., was born, because, she said, the baby made her nervous.

"It's an honorable record," John R. would say. "Each of them was better than the one before, and each one stayed with us longer. It proves that experience is the best teacher."

Jess's eight years were the years when the boys were growing up; the boys were children when she came, and when she left them, the youngest, little Robbie, had learned to drive the car. In a sense, it was Jess who taught all three boys to drive. She didn't give them their first lessons, of course, because, like

Helen Ruth, she had never sat at the wheel of an automobile in her life. She had not ridden in a car more than half a dozen times when she came to the Lovells, but just by chance, one day, she was in the car when John R. let John R., Jr., take the wheel. The car would jerk and lunge forward every time the boy shifted gears, and his father said, "Keep your mind on what you're doing."

"I am," John R., Jr., said, "but it just does that. What makes it do it?"

"Think!" John R. said. "Think! . . . *Think!*"

"I *am* thinking, but what makes it do it?"

Suddenly, Jess leaned forward from the back seat and said, "You letting the clutch out too fast, honey."

Both father and son were so surprised they could not help laughing. They laughed harder, of course, because what Jess said was true. And Jess laughed with them. When they had driven another block, they reached a boulevard stop, and in the process of putting on the brake John R., Jr., killed the engine and then flooded the motor. His father shouted, "Well, let it rest! We're just stuck here for about twenty minutes!"

Jess, who was seated with one arm around a big bag of groceries, began to laugh again. "Turn off the key," she said. "Press down on the starter a spell. Then torectly you turn on the key and she'll start."

John R. looked over his shoulder at her, not smiling, but not frowning, either. Presently, he gave the order, "Try it."

"Try what *Jess said*?" John R., Jr., asked.

"Try what Jess said."

The boy tried it, and in a moment he was racing the motor and grinning at his father. When they had got safely across the boulevard, John R. turned around to Jess again. He asked in a quiet, almost humble manner—the same manner he used when describing the pains in his back to Helen Ruth—where she had learned these things about an automobile. "Law," she said, "I learnt them listening to my brother-in-law that drives a truck talk. I don't reckon I really know'm, but I can say them."

John R. was so impressed by the incident that he did not make it one of his stories. He told Helen Ruth about it, of course, and he mentioned it sometimes to his close friends when they were discussing "the good things" about Negroes.

With his sons, he used it as an example of how much you can learn by listening to other people talk, and after that day he would permit John R., Jr., to go for drives in the car without him provided Jess went along in his place. Later on, when the other boys got old enough to drive, there were periods when he turned their instruction over to Jess. Helen Ruth even talked of learning to drive, herself, with the aid of Jess.

But it never came to more than talk with Helen Ruth, though John R. encouraged her, saying he thought driving was perhaps a serious strain on his back. She talked about it for several months, but in the end she said that the time had passed when she could learn new skills. When John R. tried to encourage her in the idea, she would sometimes look out one of the sun-parlor windows toward the street and think of how much she had once wanted to learn to drive. But that had been long ago, right after they were married, in the days when John R. had owned a little Ford coupé. John R. was on the road for the Standard Candy Company then, and during most of the week she was alone in their apartment at the old Vaux Hall. While he was away John R. kept the coupé stored in a garage only two blocks east, on Broad Street; in those days traveling men still used the railroads, because Governor Peay hadn't yet paved Tennessee's highways. At that time, John R. had not believed in women driving automobiles, and Helen Ruth had felt that he must be right about it; she had even made fun of women who went *whizzing* about town, blowing horns at every intersection. Yet in her heart she had longed to drive that coupé! Jane Blakemore was working for them then, and one day Jane had put Helen Ruth's longings into words. "Wouldn't it be dandy," she said, "if me and you clomb in that car one of these weekdays and toured out to Thornton to see all the folks—white and black?"

Without a moment's hesitation, however, Helen Ruth gave the answer that she knew John R. would have given. "Now, think what you're saying, Jane!" she said. "Wouldn't we be a fool-looking pair pulling into the square at Thornton? *Think* about it. What if we should have a flat tire when we got out about as far as Nine Mile Hill? Who would change it? *You* certainly couldn't! Jane Blakemore, I don't think you use your head about anything!"

That was the way Helen Ruth had talked to Jane on more occasions than one. She was a plain-spoken woman, and she never spoke plainer to anyone than she did to Jane Blakemore during the days when they were shut up together in that apartment at the Vaux Hall. Since Jane was from Thornton and knew how plain-spoken all Helen Ruth's family were, she paid little attention to the way Helen Ruth talked to her. She would smile, or else sneer, and go on with her work of cooking and cleaning. Sometimes she would rebel and speak just as plainly as Helen Ruth did. When Helen Ruth decided to introduce butter plates to their table, Jane said, "I ain't never heard tell of no butter dishes."

Helen Ruth raised her eyebrow. "That's because you are an ignoramus from Thornton, Tennessee," she said.

"I'm ignoramus enough to know ain't no need in nastying up all them dishes for me to wash."

Helen Ruth had, however, made Jane Blakemore learn to use butter plates and had made her keep the kitchen scrubbed and the other rooms of the apartment dusted and polished and in such perfect order that even John R. had noticed it when he came on weekends. Sometimes he had said, "You drive yourself too hard, Helen Ruth."

Jess McGehee was as eager and quick to learn new things as Jane Blakemore had been unwilling and slow. She would even put finger bowls on the breakfast table when there was grapefruit. And how she did spoil the three boys about their food! There were mornings when she cooked the breakfast eggs differently for each one of them while John R. sat and shook his head in disgust at the way she was pampering his sons. John R.'s "condition" in his back kept him at home a lot of the time during the eight years Jess was with them. He had long since left off traveling for the candy company; soon after the first baby came, he had opened an insurance agency of his own.

When Jane Blakemore left them and Helen Ruth hired Carrie (after fifteen or twenty interviews with other applicants), she had had to warn Carrie that John R.'s hours might be very irregular, because he was in business for himself and wasn't able merely to punch a time clock and quit when the day ended. "He's an onsurance man, ain't he?" Carrie had asked and had showed by the light in her eyes how favorably impressed she was. "I know about him," she had said. "He's a life-onsurance man, and that's the best kind to have."

At that moment, Helen Ruth thought perhaps she had made a mistake in Carrie. "I don't like my servant to discuss my husband's business," she said.

"No'm!" Carrie said with enthusiasm. "No, *ma'am*!" Helen Ruth was satisfied, but afterward she had often to tell herself that her first suspicion had been right. Carrie was nosy and prying and morbid—and she gossiped with other people's servants. Her curiosity and her gossiping were especially trying for Helen Ruth during her and John R.'s brief separation. They actually had separated for nearly two months right after Kenneth, the middle boy, was born. Helen Ruth had gone to her father's house at Thornton, taking the two babies and Carrie with her. The boys never knew about the trouble between their parents, of course, until Kenneth pried it out of his mother after they were all grown, and, at the time, people in Nashville and Thornton were not perfectly sure that it was a real separation. Helen Ruth had tried to tell herself that possibly Carrie didn't know it was a real separation. But she was never able to deny completely the significance of Carrie's behavior while they were at Thornton. Carrie's whole disposition had seemed to change the afternoon they left Nashville. Up until then, she had been a moody, shifty, rather loud-mouthed brown woman, full of darky compliments for white folks and of gratuitous promises of extra services she seldom rendered. But at Thornton she had put the old family servants to shame with her industriousness and her respectful, unassuming manner. "You don't find them like Carrie in Thornton any more," Helen Ruth's mother said. "The good ones all go to Nashville or Memphis." But Helen Ruth, sitting by an upstairs window one afternoon, saw her mother's cook and Carrie sauntering toward the back gate to meet a caller. She saw Carrie being introduced and then she recognized the caller as Jane Blakemore. Presently the cook returned to the kitchen and Helen Ruth saw Carrie and Jane enter the servants' house in the corner of the yard. During the hour that they visited there, Helen Ruth sat quietly by the window in the room with her two babies. It seemed to her the most terrible hour of her separation from John R. When Carrie and Jane reappeared on the stoop of the servants' house and

Carrie was walking with Jane to the gate, there was no longer any doubt in Helen Ruth's mind but that she would return to her husband, and return without any complaints or stipulations. During that hour she had tried to imagine exactly what things the black Jane and the brown Carrie were talking about, or, rather, *how* and in what terms they were talking about the things they must be talking about. In her mind, she reviewed the sort of difficulties she had had with Jane and the sort she had with Carrie and tried to imagine what defense they would make for themselves—Jane for her laziness and contrariness, Carrie for her usual shiftiness and negligence. Would they blame her for these failings of theirs? Or would they blandly pass over their own failings and find fault with her for things that she was not even aware of, or that she could not help and could not begin to set right? Had she really misused these women, either the black one or the brown one? It seemed to her then that she had so little in life that she was entitled to the satisfaction of keeping an orderly house and to the luxury of efficient help. There was too much else she had not had—an "else" nameless to her, yet sorely missed—for her to be denied these small satisfactions. As she sat alone with her two babies in the old nursery and thought of the two servants gossiping about her, she became an object of pity to herself. And presently John R., wherever he might be at that moment—in his office or at the club or, more likely, on a hunting or fishing trip somewhere—became an object of pity, too. And her two babies, one in his crib and the other playing on the carpet with a string of spools, were objects of pity. Even Carrie, standing alone by the gate after Jane had gone, seemed a lone and pitiful figure.

A few days later, Helen Ruth and Carrie and the two baby boys returned to Nashville.

In Nashville, Carrie was herself again; everything was done in her old slipshod fashion. Except during that interval at Thornton, Carrie was never known to perform any task to Helen Ruth's complete satisfaction. Hardly a meal came to the table without the soup or the dessert or some important sauce having been forgotten; almost every week something important was left out of the laundry; during a general cleaning the upper sashes of two or three windows were invariably left unwashed. Yet never in her entire five years did Carrie answer back or admit an unwillingness to do the most menial or the most nonessential piece of work. In fact, one of her most exasperating pronouncements was, "You are exactly right," which was often followed by a lengthy description of how she would do the thing from then on, or an explanation of how it happened that she had forgotten to do it. Not only that, she would often undertake to explain to Helen Ruth Helen Ruth's reason for wanting it done. "You are exactly right and I know how you mean. You want them drapes shut at night so it can seem like we're living in a house out in the Belle Meade instead of this here Vox Hall flat, and some fool might be able to look in from the yard."

"Never mind the reasons, Carrie" was Helen Ruth's usual reply. But her answers were not always so gentle—not when Carrie suggested that she have the second baby at home with Carrie acting as midwife, not when Carrie spoke to her about having the third baby circumcised. And the day that Helen Ruth began packing her things to go to Thornton, she was certain that Carrie would speak out of turn with some personal advice. That would have been more than she could bear, and she was prepared to dismiss Carrie from her service and make the trip alone. But neither then nor afterward did Carrie give any real evidence of understanding the reasons for the trip to Thornton.

In fact, it was not until long afterward, when Carrie had quit them to become an undertaker, that Helen Ruth felt that Carrie's gossip with other Nashville servants had, by accident, played a part in her separation from John R. She and John R. had talked of separation and divorce more than once during the first two years they were married, in the era of Jane Blakemore. It was not that any quarreling led to this talk but that each accused the other of being dissatisfied with their marriage. When John R. came in from traveling, on a weekend or in the middle of the week—he was sometimes gone only two or three days at a time—he would find Helen Ruth sitting alone in the living room, without a book or even a deck of cards to amuse herself with, dressed perhaps in something new her mother had sent her, waiting for him. She would rise from her chair to greet him, and he would smile in frank admiration of the tall, graceful figure and of the countenance whose features seemed always composed, and softened by her hair, which was beginning to be gray even at the time of their marriage. But he had not come home many times before Helen Ruth was greeting him with tears instead of smiles. At first, he had been touched, but soon he began to complain that she was unhappy. He asked her why she did not see something of other people while he was away—the wives of his business and hunting friends, or some of the other Thornton girls who were married and living in Nashville. She replied that she did see them occasionally but that she was not the sort of woman who enjoyed having a lot of women friends. Besides, she was perfectly happy with her present life; it was only that she believed that he must be unhappy and that he no longer enjoyed her company. She understood that he had to be away most of the week, but even when he was in town, she saw very little of him. When he was not at his office, he was fishing out on Duck River or was off to a hunt up at Gallatin. And at night he either took her to parties with those hunting people, with whom she had little or nothing in common, or piled up on the bed after supper and slept. All of this indicated that he was not happy being married to her, she said, and so they talked a good deal about separating.

After the first baby came, there was no such talk for a long time—not until after the second baby. After the first baby came, Helen Ruth felt that their marriage must be made to last, regardless of hers or John R.'s happiness. Besides, it was at that time that one of John R.'s hunting friends—a rich man named Rufus Brantley—had secured the insurance agency for him; and almost before John R. opened his office, he had sold policies to other rich hunting friends that he had. For a while, he was at home more than he had ever been before. But soon, when his business was established, he began to attend more and more meets and trials, all over Tennessee and Alabama and Kentucky. He even acquired a few dogs and a horse of his own. With his friends he began to go on trips to distant parts of the country. It seemed that when he was not deer hunting in the State of Maine, he was deep-sea fishing in the Gulf. Helen Ruth did sometimes go with him to the local horse shows, but one night, at the Spring Horse Show, she had told

Mrs. Brantley that she had a new machine, and Mrs. Brantley had thought she meant an automobile instead of a sewing machine. That, somehow, had been the last straw. She would never go out with "people like the Brantleys" after that. She was pregnant again before the first baby was a year old, and this soon became her excuse for going nowhere in the evening. The women she did visit with very occasionally in the daytime were those she had known as girls in Thornton, women whose husbands were bank tellers and office managers and were barely acquainted with John R. Lovell.

After the second baby came, Helen Ruth saw these women more frequently. She began to feel a restlessness that she could not explain in herself. There were days when she could not stay at home. With Carrie and the two babies, she would traipse about town, on foot or by streetcar, to points she had not visited since she was a little girl and was in Nashville with her parents to attend the State Fair or the Centennial. She went to the Capitol, to Centennial Park and the Parthenon, even out to the Glendale Zoo. Once, with Nancy Tolliver and Lucy Parkes, two of her old Thornton friends, she made an excursion to Cousin Mamie Lovell's farm, which was several miles beyond the town of Franklin. They went by the electric interurban to Franklin, and from there they took a taxi to the farm. Cousin Mamie's husband had been a second cousin of John R.'s father, and it was a connection the Thornton Lovells had once been very proud to claim. But for a generation this branch of the family had been in decline. Major Lovell had been a prominent lawyer in Franklin and had been in politics, but when he died, he left his family "almost penniless." His boys had not gone to college; since the farm was supposed to have been exhausted, they did not try to farm it but clerked in stores in Franklin. There was said to be a prosperous son-in-law in St. Louis, but the daughter was dead and Cousin Mamie was reported to have once called her son-in-law a parvenu to his face. Helen Ruth and her friends made the excursion because they wanted to see the house, which was one of the finest old places in the county and full of antiques.

But Cousin Mamie didn't even let them inside the house. It was a hot summer day, and she had all the blinds closed and the whole L-shaped house shut up tight, so that it would be

bearable at night. She received them on the long ell porch.
Later, they moved their chairs out under a tree in the yard,
where Cousin Mamie's cook brought them a pitcher of iced tea.
While they were chatting under the tree that afternoon, they
covered all the usual topics that are dealt with when talking
to an old lady one doesn't know very well—the old times and
the new times, mutual friends and family connections, country
living and city living, and always, of course, the lot of woman
as it relates to each topic.

"Where are you and John R. living?" Cousin Mamie asked
Helen Ruth.

"We're still at the Vaux Hall, Cousin Mamie."

"I'd suppose the trains would be pretty bad for noise there,
that close to the depot."

"They're pretty bad in the summer."

"I'd suppose you had a place out from town, seeing how often
John R.'s name's in the paper with the hound and hunt set."

"That's John R.'s life," Helen Ruth said, "not mine."

"He runs with a fine pack, I must say," said Cousin Mamie.

Nancy Tolliver and Lucy Parkes nodded and smiled. Lucy
said, "The swells of Nashville, Miss Mamie."

But Cousin Mamie said, "There was a day when they weren't
the swells. Forty years ago, people like Major Lovell didn't
know people like the Brantleys. I think the Brantleys quarried limestone, to begin with. I guess it don't matter, though,
for when I was a girl in upper East Tennessee, people said the
Lovells started as land speculators hereabouts and at Memphis.
But I don't blame you for not wanting to fool with Brantleys,
Helen Ruth."

"John R. and I each live our own life, Cousin Mamie."

"Helen Ruth is a woman with a mind of her own, Miss
Mamie," Nancy Tolliver said. "It's too bad more marriages
can't be like theirs, each living their own life. Everyone admires
it as a real achievement."

And Lucy Parkes said, "Because a woman's husband hunts is
no reason for her to hunt, any more than because a man's wife
sews is any reason for him to sew."

"Indeed not," Cousin Mamie said, actually paying little
attention to what Lucy and Nancy were saying. Presently, she
continued her own train of thought. "Names like Brantley and

Partee and Hines didn't mean a thing in this state even thirty years ago."

What Lucy and Nancy said about her marriage that day left Helen Ruth in a sort of daze and at the same time made her see her situation more clearly. She had never discussed her marriage with anybody, and hearing it described so matter-of-factly by these two women made her understand for the first time what a special sort of marriage it was and how unhappy she was in it. At the time, John R. was away on a fishing trip to Tellico Plains. She did not see him again before she took the babies and Carrie to Thornton. She sent a note to his office saying that she would return when he decided to devote his time to his wife and children instead of to his hounds and horses. While she was at Thornton her letters from John R. made no mention of her note. He wrote about his business, about his hounds and horses, about the weather, and he always urged her to hurry home as soon as she had seen everybody and had a good visit. Meanwhile, he had a room at the Hermitage Club.

When Helen Ruth returned to Nashville, their life went on as before. A year later, the third boy, Robbie, was born, and John R. bought a large bungalow on Sixteenth Avenue, not too far from the Tarbox School, where they planned to send the boys. Carrie was with them for three years after the separation, and though her work did not improve, Helen Ruth found herself making excuses for her. She began to attribute Carrie's garrulity to "a certain sort of bashfulness, or the Negro equivalent to bashfulness." And with the three small boys, and the yard to keep, too, there was so much more for Carrie to do than there had been before! Despite the excuses she made for her, Helen Ruth could see that Carrie was plainly getting worse about everything and that she now seemed to take pleasure in lying about the smallest, most unimportant things. But Helen Ruth found it harder to confront Carrie with her lies or to reprimand her in any way.

During the last months before Carrie quit, she would talk sometimes about the night work she did for a Negro under-taker. To make Helen Ruth smile, she would report things she had heard about the mourners. Her job, Carrie always said, was to sweep the parlors after the funeral and to fold up the chairs. It was only when she finally gave notice to Helen Ruth that she told her what she professed was the truth. She explained that during all those months she had been learning to embalm. "Before you can get a certificate," she said, "you has to handle a bad accident, a sickness, a case of old age, a drowning, a burning, and a half-grown child or less. I been waiting on the child till last night, but now I'll be getting my certificate."

Helen Ruth would not even let Carrie go to the basement to get her hat and coat. "You send somebody for them," she said. "But *you*, you get off these premises, Carrie!" She was sincerely outraged by what Carrie had told her, and when she looked at Carrie's hands she was filled with new horror. Yet something kept her from saying all the things that one normally said to a worthless, lying servant who had been guilty of one final outrage. "*Leave*, Carrie!" she said, consciously restraining herself. "*Leave* this place!" Carrie went out the kitchen door and down the driveway to the street, bareheaded, coatless, and wearing her kitchen slippers.

After Carrie, there was old Sarah, who stayed with them for six years and then quit them to get married and go to Chicago. Sarah was too old to do heavy work even when she first came, and before she had been there a week, John R. had been asked to help move the sideboard and to bring the ladder up from the basement. He said it seemed that every minute he was in the house, he was lifting or moving something that was too much for Sarah. Helen Ruth replied that perhaps she should hire a Negro man to help in the house and look after the yard. But John R. said no, he was only joking, he thought Sarah far and away the best cook they had ever had, and besides business conditions didn't look too good and it was no time to be taking on more help. But he would always add he did not understand why Helen Ruth babied Sarah so. "From the first moment old Sarah set foot in this house, Helen Ruth has babied her," he would say to people in Helen Ruth's presence.

Sarah could neither read nor write. Even so, it took her only a short while to learn all Helen Ruth's special recipes and how to cook everything the way the Lovells liked it. For two weeks, Helen Ruth stayed in the kitchen with Sarah, reading to her from *How We Cook in Tennessee* and giving detailed instructions for every meal. It was during that time that her great sympathy for Sarah developed. Sarah was completely unashamed of her illiteracy, and it was this that first impressed Helen Ruth. She admired Sarah for having no false pride and for showing no resentment of her mistress's impatience. She observed Sarah's kindness with the children. And she learned from Sarah about Sarah's religious convictions and about her long, unhappy marriage to a Negro named Morse Wilkins, who had finally left her and gone up North.

While Sarah was working for them, John R. and Helen Ruth lived the life that Helen Ruth had heard her friends describe to John R.'s Cousin Mamie. It was not until after Sarah had come that Helen Ruth, recalling the afternoon at Cousin Mamie's, identified Lucy Parkes's words about a wife's sewing and a husband's hunting as the very answer she had once given to some of Carrie's impertinent prying. That afternoon, the remark had certainly sounded familiar, but she had been too concerned with her own decision to leave her husband to concentrate upon anything so trivial. And after their reconciliation, she tried not to dwell on things that had led her to leave John R. Their reconciliation, whatever it meant to John R., meant to her the acceptance of certain mysteries—the mystery of his love of hunting, of his choice of friends, of his desire to maintain a family and home of which he saw so little, of his attachment to her, and of her own devotion to him. Her babies were now growing into little boys. She felt that there was much to be thankful for, not the least of which was a servant as fond of her and of her children as Sarah was. Sarah's affection for the three little boys often reminded Helen Ruth how lonely Sarah's life must be.

One day, when she had watched Sarah carefully wrapping up little Robbie in his winter play clothes before he went out to play in the snow, she said, "You love children so much, Sarah, didn't you ever have any of your own?"

Sarah, who was a yellow-skinned woman with face and arms covered with brown freckles, turned her gray eyes and fixed them solemnly on Helen Ruth. "Why, I had the cutest little baby you ever did see," she said, "and Morse went and killed it."

"Morse *killed* your baby?"

"He rolled over on it in his drunk sleep and smothered it in the bed."

After that, Helen Ruth would never even listen to Sarah when she talked about Morse, and she began to feel a hatred toward any and all of the men who came to take Sarah home at night. Generally, these men were the one subject Sarah did not discuss with Helen Ruth, and their presence in Sarah's life was the only serious complaint Helen Ruth made against her. They would come sometimes as early as four in the afternoon and wait on the back porch for Sarah to get through. She knew that Sarah was usually feeding one of them out of her kitchen, and she knew that Sarah was living with first one and then another of them, but when she told John R. she was going to put her foot down on it, he forbade her to do so. And so through nearly six years she tolerated this weakness of Sarah's. But one morning in the late spring Sarah told her that Morse Wilkins had returned from up North and that she had taken him back as her husband. Helen Ruth could not find anything to say for a moment, but after studying the large diamond on her engagement ring for awhile she said, "My servant's private life is her own affair, but I give you fair warning now, Sarah, I want to see no more of your men friends—Morse or *any other*—on this place again."

From that time, she saw no more men on the place until Morse himself came, in a drunken rage, in the middle of a summer's day. Helen Ruth had been expecting something of the sort to happen. Sarah had been late to work several times during the preceding three weeks. She had come one morning with a dark bruise on her cheek and said she had fallen getting off the streetcar. Twice, Helen Ruth had found Sarah on her knees, praying, in the kitchen. The day Helen Ruth heard the racket at the back-porch door, she knew at once that it was Morse. She got up from her sewing machine and went directly to the kitchen. Sarah was on the back porch, and Morse was outside the screen door of the porch, which was hooked on the inside. He was a little man, shriveled up, bald-headed, not more than five feet tall, and of a complexion very much like Sarah's. Over his white shirt he wore a dark sleeveless sweater. "You come on home," he was saying as he shook the screen door.

Helen Ruth stepped to the kitchen door. "Is that her?" Morse asked Sarah, motioning his head toward Helen Ruth.

When Sarah turned her face around, her complexion seemed several shades lighter than Morse's. "I got to go," she said to Helen Ruth.

"No, Sarah, *he's* got to go. But *you* don't."

"He's gonna leave me again."

"That's the best thing that could happen to you, Sarah."

Sarah said nothing, and Morse began shaking the door again.

"Is he drunk, Sarah?" Helen Ruth asked.

"He's so drunk I don't know how he find his way here."

Helen Ruth went out onto the porch. "Now, you get off this place, and quick about it," she said to Morse.

He shook the screen door again. "You didn't make me come here, Mrs. Lovellel, and you can't make me leave, Mrs. Lovellel."

"I can't make you leave," Helen Ruth said at once, "but there's a bluecoat down on the corner who can."

Suddenly Sarah dropped to her knees and began praying. Her lips moved silently, and gradually she let her forehead come to rest on the top of the rickety vegetable bin. Morse looked at her through the screen, putting his face right against the wire. "Sarah," he said, "you come on home. You better come on now if you think I be there."

Sarah got up off her knees.

"I'm going to phone the police," Helen Ruth said, pretending to move toward the kitchen.

Morse left the door and staggered backward toward the driveway. "Come on, Sarah," he shouted.

"I got to go," Sarah said.

"I won't let you go, Sarah!"

"She can't make you stay!" Morse shouted. "You better come on if you coming!"

"It will be the worst thing you ever did in your life, Sarah," said Helen Ruth. "And if you go with him, you can't ever come back here. He'll kill you someday, too—the way he did your baby."

Sarah was on her knees again, and Morse was out of sight but still shouting as he went down the driveway. Suddenly, Sarah was on her feet. She ran into the kitchen and on through the house to the front porch.

Helen Ruth followed, calling her back. She found Sarah on the front porch waving to Morse, who was halfway down the block, running in a zigzag down the middle of the street, still shouting at the top of his voice. Sarah cried out to him, "Morse! Morse!"

"Sarah!" Helen Ruth said.

"Morse!" Sarah cried again, and then she began mumbling words that Helen Ruth could not quite understand at the time. Afterward, going over it in her mind, Helen Ruth realized that what Sarah had been mumbling was, "If I don't see you no more on this earth, Morse, I'll see you in Glory."

Sarah was with the Lovells for four more months, and then one night she called up on the telephone and asked John R., Jr., to tell his mother that she was going to get married to a man named Racecar and they were leaving for Chicago in the morning.

Jess McGehee came to them during the Depression. Even before Sarah left the Lovells, John R. had had to give up all of his "activities" and devote his entire time to selling insurance. Rufus Brantley had shot himself through the head while cleaning a gun at his hunting lodge, and most of John R.'s other hunting friends had suffered the same financial reverses that John R. had. The changes in the Lovells' life had come so swiftly that Helen Ruth did not realize for awhile what the changes meant in her relationship with John R. It seemed as though she woke up one day and discovered that she was not married to the same man. She found herself spending all her evenings playing Russian bank with a man who had no interest in anything but his home, his wife, and his three boys. Every night, he would give a brief summary of the things that had happened at his office or on his calls, and then he would ask her and the boys for an account of everything they had done that day. He took an interest in the house and the yard, and he and the boys made a lily pool in the back yard, and singlehanded he screened in the entire front porch. Sometimes he took the whole family to Thornton for a weekend, and he and Helen Ruth never missed the family reunions there in September.

In a sense, these were the happiest years of their married life. John R.'s business got worse and worse, of course, but since part of their savings was in the bank at Thornton that did not fail, they never had any serious money worries. Regardless of their savings, however, John R.'s loss of income and his having to give up his friends and his hunting wrought very real, if only temporary, changes in him. There were occasions when he would sit quietly and listen to his family's talk without correcting them or pointing out how foolish they were. He gave up saying "Think!" to the boys, and instead would say, "Now, let's see if we can't reason this thing out." He could never bring himself to ask for any sympathy from Helen Ruth for his various losses, but as it was during this time that he suffered so from the ailment in his back (he and Helen Ruth slept with boards under their mattress for ten years), the sympathy he got for his physical pain was more than sufficient. All in all, it was a happy period in their life, and in addition to their general family happiness they had Jess.

Jess not only cooked and cleaned, she planned the meals, did the marketing, and washed everything, from handkerchiefs and socks to heavy woolen blankets. When the boys began to go to dances, she even learned to launder their dress shirts. There was nothing she would not do for the boys or for John R. or for Helen Ruth. The way she idealized the family became the basis for most of the "Negro jokes" told by the Lovells during those years. In her room she had a picture of the family, in a group beside the lily pool, taken with her own box Brownie; she had tacked it and also a picture of each of them on the wall above her washstand. In her scrapbook she had pasted every old snapshot and photograph that Helen Ruth would part with, as well as old newspaper pictures of John R. on horseback or with a record-breaking fish he had caught. She had even begged from Helen Ruth an extra copy of the newspaper notice of their wedding.

Jess talked to the family a good deal at mealtime, but only when they had addressed her first and had shown that they wanted her to talk. Her remarks were mostly about things that related to the Lovells. She told a sad story about a "very loving white couple" from Brownsville, her home town, who had been drowned in each other's arms when their car rolled off the end of a river ferry. The point of the story was that those two people were the same, fine, loving sort of couple that John R.

and Helen Ruth were. All three of the boys made good grades in school, and every month Jess would copy their grades in her scrapbook, which she periodically passed around for the family to appreciate. When Kenneth began to write stories and articles for his high-school paper, she would always borrow the paper overnight; soon it came out that she was copying everything he wrote onto the big yellow pages of her scrapbook.

After three or four years, John R. began to say that he thought Jess would be with them always and that they would see the day when the boys' children would call her "Mammy." Helen Ruth said that she would like to agree with him about that, but actually she worried, because Jess seemed to have no life of her own, which wasn't at all natural. John R. agreed that they should make her take a holiday now and then. Every summer, they would pack Jess off to Brownsville for a week's visit with her kinfolks, but she was always back in her room over the garage within two or three days; she said that her people fought and quarreled so much that she didn't care for them. Outside her life with the Lovells, she had only one friend. Her interest was the movies, and her friend was "the Mary who works for Mrs. Dunbar." Jess and Mary went to the movies together as often as three or four times a week, and on Sunday afternoons Mary came to see Jess or Jess went to see Mary, who lived over the Dunbars' garage. Jess always took along her scrapbook and her most recent movie magazines. She and Mary swapped movie magazines, and it was apparent from Jess's talk on Monday mornings that they also swapped eulogies of their white families.

Sometimes Helen Ruth would see Mrs. Dunbar downtown or at a P.T.A. meeting; they would discuss their cooks and smile over the reports that each had received of the other's family. "I understand that your boys are all growing into very handsome men," Mrs. Dunbar said once, and she told Helen Ruth that Jess was currently comparing one of the boys—Mrs. Dunbar didn't know which one—to Neil Hamilton, and that she was comparing Helen Ruth to Irene Rich, and John R. to Edmund Lowe. As the boys got older, they began to resent the amount of authority over them—though it was small—that Jess had been allowed by their parents and were embarrassed if anyone said Jess had taught them to drive the car. When John R., Jr., began at the university, he made his mother promise not to let Jess know what grades he received, and none of the boys would let Jess take snapshots of them any more. Their mother tried to comfort Jess by saying that the boys were only going through a phase and that it would pass in time. One day, she even said this in the presence of Robbie, who promptly reported it to the older boys, and it ended with John R., Jr.'s, complaining to his father that their mother ought not to make fun of them to Jess. His father laughed at him but later told Helen Ruth that he thought she was making a mistake, that the boys were getting big enough to think about their manly dignity, and that she would have to take that into consideration.

She didn't make the same mistake again, but although Jess never gave any real sign of her feelings being hurt, Helen Ruth was always conscious of how the boys were growing away from their good-natured servant. By the time Robbie was sixteen, they had long since ceased to have any personal conversation with Jess, and nothing would have induced Robbie to submit to taking drives with her but the knowledge that his father would not allow him to use the car on dates until he had had months of driving practice. Once, when Robbie and Jess returned from a drive, Jess reported, with a grin, that not a word had passed between them during the entire hour and a half. Helen Ruth only shook her head sadly. The next day she bought Jess a new bedside radio.

The radio was the subject of much banter among the boys and their father. John R. said Helen Ruth had chosen the period of hard times and the Depression to become more generous with her servant than she had ever been before in her life. They recalled other presents she had given Jess recently, and from that time on they teased her regularly about how she spoiled Jess. John R. said that if Jess had had his back trouble, Helen Ruth would have retired her at double pay and nursed her with twice the care that he received. The boys teased her by saying that at Christmas time she reversed the custom of shopping for the servant at the ten-cent stores and for the family at the department stores.

Yet as long as Jess was with them, they all agreed that she was the best help they had ever had. In fact, even afterward, during the war years, when John R.'s business prospered again and his back trouble left him entirely and the boys were lucky enough to be stationed near home and, later, continue their education at government expense, even then John R. and the boys would say that the years when Jess was with them were the happiest time of their life and that Jess was the best servant Helen Ruth had ever had. They said that, and then there would be a silence, during which they were probably thinking about the summer morning just before the war when Jess received a telephone call.

When the telephone rang that morning, Helen Ruth and John R. and the boys had just sat down to breakfast. As was usual in the summertime, they were eating at the big drop-leaf table in the sun parlor. Jess had set the coffee urn by Helen Ruth's place and was starting from the room when the telephone rang. Helen Ruth, supposing the call was for a member of the family, and seeing that Jess lingered in the doorway, said for her to answer it there in the sun parlor instead of running to the telephone in the back hall.

Jess answered it, announcing whose residence it was in a voice so like Helen Ruth's that it made the boys grin. For a moment, everyone at the table kept silent. They waited for Jess's eyes to single out one of them. John R., Jr., and Kenneth even put down their grapefruit spoons. But the moment Jess picked up the instrument, she fixed her eyes on the potted fern on the window seat across the room. At once her nostrils began to twitch, her lower lip fell down, and it seemed only an act of will that she was twice able to say, "Yes, ma'am," in answer to the small, unreal, metallic voice.

When she had replaced the telephone on its cradle, she turned quickly away and started into the dining room. But Helen Ruth stopped her. "Jess," she asked, her voice full of courtesy, "was the call for you?"

Jess stopped, and they all watched her hands go up to her face. Without turning around, she leaned against the door jamb and began sobbing aloud. Helen Ruth sprang up from the table, saying, "Jess, honey, what *is* the matter?" John R. and the boys stood up, too.

"It was a telegram for me—from Brownsville."

Helen Ruth took her in her arms. "Is someone dead?"

Between sobs, Jess answered, "My little brother—our baby brother—the only one of 'em I cared for." Then her sobs became more violent.

Helen Ruth motioned for John R. to move the morning paper from the big wicker chair, and she led Jess in that direction. But Jess would not sit down, and she could not be pulled away from Helen Ruth. She held fast to her, and Helen Ruth continued to pat her gently on the back and to try to console her with gentle words. Finally, she said, "Jess, you must go to Brownsville. Maybe there's been some mistake. Maybe he's not dead. But you must go, anyway."

Presently, Jess did sit in the chair, and dried her eyes on Helen Ruth's napkin. The boys shook their heads sympathetically and John R. said she certainly must go to Brownsville. She agreed, and said she believed there was a bus at ten that she would try to catch. Helen Ruth patted her hand, telling her to go along to her room when she felt like it, and said that *she* would finish getting breakfast.

"I want to go by to see Mary first," Jess said, "so I better make haste." She stood up, forcing a grateful smile. Then she burst into tears again and threw her arms about Helen Ruth, mumbling, "Oh, God! Oh, God!" The three boys and their father saw tears come into Helen Ruth's eyes, and through her tears Helen Ruth saw a change come over their faces. It was not exactly a change of expression. It couldn't be that, she felt, because it was exactly the same on each of the four faces. It hardly seemed possible that so similar a change could reflect four men's individual feelings. She concluded that her own emotion, and probably the actual tears in her eyes, had made her imagine the change, and when Jess now pulled away and hurried off to her room, Helen Ruth's tears had dried and she could see no evidence of the change she had imagined in her husband's and her sons' faces.

While Jess was in her room preparing to leave, they finished breakfast. Then Helen Ruth began clearing the table, putting the dishes on the teacart. She had said little while they were eating, but in her mind she was all the while going over something that she knew she must tell her family. As she absentmindedly stacked the dishes, her lips moved silently over the simple words she would use in telling them. She knew that they were watching her, and when Robbie offered to take Jess to the bus station, she knew that the change she had seen in all their faces had been an expression of sympathy for *her* as well as of an eagerness to put this whole episode behind them. "I'll take Jess to her bus," he said.

But Helen Ruth answered, in the casual tone she had been preparing to use, that she thought it probably wouldn't be the thing to do.

"Why, what do you mean, Helen Ruth?" John R. asked her.

"It was very touching, Mother," Kenneth said in his new, manly voice, "the way she clung to you." He, too, wanted to express sympathy, but he also seemed to want to distract his mother from answering his father's question.

At that moment, Jess passed under the sun-parlor windows, walking down the driveway, carrying two large suitcases. Helen Ruth watched her until she reached the sidewalk. Then, very quietly, she told her family that Jess McGehee had no baby brother and had never had one. "Jess and Mary are leaving for California. They think they're going to find themselves jobs out there."

"You knew that right along?" John R. asked.

"I knew it right along."

"Did she know you did, Helen Ruth?" he asked. His voice had in it the sternness he used when questioning the boys about something. "No, John R., she did not. I didn't learn it from her."

"Well, I don't believe it's so," he said. "Why, I don't believe that for a minute. Her carrying on was too real."

"They're going to California. They've already got their two tickets. Mrs. Dunbar got wind of it somehow, by accident, from Mrs. Lon Thompson's cook, and she called me on Monday. They've saved their money and they're going."

"And you let Jess get away with all that crying stuff just now?" John R. said.

Helen Ruth put her hands on the handlebar of the teacart. She pushed the cart a little way over the tile floor but stopped when he repeated his question. It wasn't to answer his question that she stopped, however. "Oh, my dears!" she said, addressing her whole family. Then it was a long time before she said anything more. John R. and the three boys remained seated at the table, and while Helen Ruth gazed past them and toward the front window of the sun parlor, they sat silent and still, as though they were in a picture. What could she say to them, she kept asking herself. And each time she asked the question, she received for answer some different memory of seemingly unrelated things out of the past twenty years of her life. These things presented themselves as answers to her question, and each of them seemed satisfactory to her. But how little sense it would make to her husband and her grown sons, she reflected, if she should suddenly begin telling them about the long hours she had spent waiting in that apartment at the Vaux Hall while John R. was on the road for the Standard Candy Company, and in the same breath should tell them about how plainly she used to talk to Jane Blakemore and how Jane pretended that the baby made her nervous and went back to Thornton. Or suppose she should abruptly remind John R. of how ill at ease the wives of his hunting friends used to make her feel and how she had later driven Sarah's worthless husband out of the yard, threatening to call a bluecoat. What if she should suddenly say that because a woman's husband hunts, there is no reason for *her* to hunt, any more than because a man's wife sews, there is reason for him to sew. She felt that she would be willing to say anything at all, no matter how cruel or absurd it was, if it would make them understand that everything that happened in life only demonstrated in some way the lonesomeness that people felt. She was ready to tell them about sitting in the old nursery at Thornton and waiting for Carrie and Jane Blakemore to come out of the cabin in the yard. If it would make them see what she had been so long in learning to see, she would even talk at last about the "so much else" that had been missing from her life and that she had not been able to name, and about the foolish mysteries she had so nobly accepted upon her reconciliation with John R. To her, these things were all one now; they were her loneliness, the loneliness from which everybody, knowingly or unknowingly, suffered. But she knew that her husband and her sons did not recognize her loneliness or Jess McGehee's or their own. She turned her eyes from the window to look at their faces around the table, and it was strange to see that they were still thinking in the most personal and particular terms of how they had been deceived by a servant, the ignorant granddaughter of an ignorant slave, a Negro woman from Brownsville who was crazy about the movies and who would soon be riding a bus, mile after mile, on her way to Hollywood, where she might find the friendly faces of the real Neil Hamilton and the real Irene Rich. It was with effort that Helen Ruth thought again of Jess McGehee's departure and the problem of offering an explanation to her family. At last, she said patiently, "My dears, don't you see how it was for Jess? How else can they tell us anything when there is such a gulf?" After a moment she said, "How can I make you understand this?"

Her husband and her three sons sat staring at her, their big hands, all so alike, resting on the breakfast table, their faces stamped with identical expressions, not of wonder but of incredulity. Helen Ruth was still holding firmly to the handle of the teacart. She pushed it slowly and carefully over the doorsill and into the dining room, dark and cool as an underground cavern, and spotlessly clean, the way Jess McGehee had left it.

Their Losses

AT GRAND JUNCTION, the train slowed down for its last stop before getting into the outskirts of Memphis. Just when it had jerked to a standstill, Miss Patty Bean came out of the drawing room. She had not slept there but had hurried into the drawing room the minute she'd waked up to see how her aunt, who was gravely ill and who occupied the room with a trained nurse, had borne the last hours of the trip. Miss Patty had been in there with her aunt for nearly an hour. As she came out the nurse was whispering to her, but Miss Patty pulled the door closed with apparent indifference to what the nurse might be saying. The train had jerked to a standstill. For a moment Miss Patty, clad in a dark dressing gown and with her graying auburn hair contained in a sort of mesh cap, faced the other passengers in the Pullman car with an expression of alarm.

The other passengers, several of whom, already dressed, were standing in the aisle while the porter made up their berths, glanced at Miss Patty, then returned their attention immediately to their luggage or to their morning papers, which had been brought aboard at Corinth. They were mostly businessmen, and the scattering of women appeared to be businesswomen. In the silence and stillness of the train stop, not even those who were traveling together spoke to each other. At least half the berths had already been converted into seats, but the passengers did not look out the windows. They were fifty miles from Memphis, and they knew that nothing outside the windows would interest them until the train slowed down again, for the suburban stop of Buntyn.

After a moment Miss Patty's expression faded from one of absolute alarm to one of suspicion. Then, as though finally gathering her wits, she leaned over abruptly and peered out a window of the first section on her left. What she saw was only a deserted-looking cotton shed and, far beyond it, past winter fields of cotton stalks and dead grass, a two-story clapboard house with a sagging double gallery. The depot and the town were on the other side of the train, but Miss Patty knew this scene and she gave a sigh of relief. "Oh, uh-huh," she muttered to herself. "Grand Junction."

"Yes, sweet old Grand Junction," came a soft whisper.

For an instant Miss Patty could not locate the speaker. Then she became aware of a very tiny lady, dressed in black, seated right beside where she stood; indeed, she was leaning almost directly across the lady's lap. Miss Patty brought herself up straight, throwing her shoulders back and her heavy, square chin into the air, and said, "I was not aware that this section was occupied."

"Why, now, of course you weren't—of course you weren't, my dear," said the tiny lady. She was such an inconspicuous little soul that her presence could not alter the impression that there were only Memphis business people in the car.

"I didn't know you were there," Miss Patty explained again.

"Why, of course you didn't."

"It was very rude of me," Miss Patty said solemnly, blinking her eyes.

"Oh, no," the tiny lady protested gently.

"Oh, but indeed it was," Miss Patty assured her.

"Why, it was all right."

"I didn't see you there. I beg your pardon."

The tiny lady was smiling up at Miss Patty with eyes that seemed as green as the Pullman upholstery. "I came aboard at Sweetwater during the night," she said. She nodded toward the curtains of Miss Patty's berth, across the aisle. "I guess you were as snug as a bug in a rug when I got on."

Miss Patty lowered her chin and scowled.

"You're traveling with your sick aunt, aren't you?" the lady went on. "I saw you go in there awhile ago, and I inquired of the porter." The smile faded from her eyes but remained on her lips. "You see, I haven't been to bed. I'm bringing my mother to Brownsville for burial." She nodded in the direction of the baggage car ahead.

"I see," Miss Patty replied. She had now fixed this diminutive person with a stare of appraisal. She was someone from her own world. If she heard the name, she would undoubtedly know the family. Without the name, she already *knew* the life history of the lady, and she could almost have guessed the name, or made up one that would have done as well. Her impulse was to turn away, but the green eyes of Miss Ellen Watkins prevented her. They were too full of unmistakable sweetness and charity. Miss

Patty remained a moment, observing the telltale paraphernalia: the black gloves and purse on the seat beside Miss Ellen; the unobtrusive hat, with its wisp of a veil turned back; the fresh powder on the wrinkled neck.

"I'm Ellen Louise Watkins," the tiny lady said. "I believe you're Miss Bean, from Thornton."

Miss Patty gave a formal little bow—a Watkins from Brownsville, a daughter of the late Judge Davy Watkins. They were kin to the Crocketts. Davy Crockett's blood had come to this end: a whispering old maid in a Pullman car.

"How *is* your aunt this morning?" Miss Ellen whispered, leaning forward.

But Miss Patty had turned her back. She put her head and shoulders inside the curtains of her berth, and as Miss Ellen waited for an answer, all to be seen of Miss Patty was the dark watered silk of her dressing gown, drawn tightly about her narrow hips and falling straight to a hemline just above her very white and very thin and bony ankles.

When Miss Patty pushed herself into the aisle again and faced Miss Ellen, she held, thrown over her arms, a navy-blue dress, various white and pink particulars of underwear, and a pair of extremely long and rumpled silk stockings, and in her hands she had bunched together her black pumps, an ivory comb and brush, and other articles she would need in the dressing room. The train began to move as she spoke. "I believe," she said, as though she were taking an oath, "that there has been no change in my aunt's condition during the night."

Miss Ellen nodded. The display of clothing over Miss Patty's arms brought a smile to her lips, and she was plainly making an effort to keep her eyes off the clothing and on Miss Patty's face. This uninhibited and even unladylike display reminded her of what she had always heard about the Bean family at Thornton. They were eccentric people, and bigoted. But quickly she reproached herself for retaining such gossip in her mind. Some of the Beans used to be in politics, and unfair things are always said about people in public life. Further, Miss Ellen reminded herself, the first instant she had set eyes on Miss Patty, she had *known* the sort of person she was. Even if the porter had not been able to tell her the name, she could almost have guessed it. She knew how Miss Patty would look when she had got into those garments—as though she had dressed in the dark and were proud of it. And there would be a hat—a sort of brown fedora—that she would pull on at the last minute before she got off the train. She had known many a Miss Patty Bean in her time, and their gruffness and their mannish ways didn't frighten her. Indeed, she felt sorry for such women. "Are you going to have breakfast in the diner?" she asked.

"I am," Miss Patty replied.

"Then I'll save you a seat. I'll go ahead and get a table. There's not too much time, Miss Bean."

"As you will, Miss Watkins." Miss Patty turned toward the narrow passage that led to the ladies' dressing room. Suddenly she stopped and backed into Miss Ellen's section. She was making way for the conductor and a passenger who had evidently come aboard at Grand Junction. A porter followed, carrying a large piece of airplane luggage. The Pullman conductor came first, and the passenger, a lady, was addressing him over his shoulder. "But why could not they stop the *Pullman* at the platform, instead of the *coaches*?" It was a remarkably loud voice, and it paused after every word, obviously trying for a humorous effect.

The conductor was smiling grimly. "Here you are, ma'am," he said. "You can sit here till I find space for you—if this lady don't mind. She has the whole section." He indicated Miss Ellen's section and continued down the aisle, followed by the porter, without once looking back.

"But suppose she *does* mind?" the new passenger called after him, and she laughed heartily. Some of the other passengers looked up briefly and smiled. The lady turned to Miss Patty, who was still there holding her possessions. "*Do* you mind?" And then, "Why, Patty Bean! How very nice!"

"It is not my section." Miss Patty thrust herself into the aisle, "It is not my section, Cornelia."

"Then it must be— Why, will wonders never cease? Ellen Louise Watkins!"

Miss Ellen and Miss Patty exchanged surprised glances. "Why, of course you shall sit here with me," Miss Ellen said. "How good to see you, Cornelia!"

Cornelia Weatherby Werner had already seated herself, facing Miss Ellen. She was a large woman in all her dimensions, but a good-looking woman still. She wore a smart three-cornered hat, which drew attention to her handsome profile, and a cloth coat trimmed with Persian lamb. "I declare it's like old times," she said breathlessly. "Riding the Southern from Grand Junction to Memphis and seeing everybody you know! Nowadays it's mostly *that* sort you see on the Southern." She gestured openly toward the other passengers. "I'll bet you two have been gadding off to Washington. Are you traveling together?"

Miss Ellen and Miss Patty shook their heads.

"Ellen and I are old schoolmates, too, Patty," Cornelia continued. "We were at Ward's together after I was dismissed from Belmont. By the way," she said, smiling roguishly and digging into her purse for cigarettes, "I still have that infernal habit. It's old-fashioned now, but I still call them my coffin nails. Which reminds me—" She hesitated, a package of cigarettes in one hand, a silver lighter in the other. "Oh, do either of you smoke? Well, not before breakfast anyhow. And not on a Pullman, even when the conductor isn't looking, I'll bet. I was saying it reminds me I have just been to Grand Junction to put my old mother to her last rest." As she lit her cigarette, she watched their faces, eager for the signs of shock.

Miss Ellen gave a sympathetic "Oh." Miss Patty stared.

"You mustn't look so lugubrious," Cornelia went on. "The old dear hadn't spoken to me in thirty-one years—not since I got married and went to Memphis. I married a Jew, you know. You've both met Jake? He's a bank examiner and a good husband. Let's see, Patty, when was it I came down to Thornton with Jake? During the Depression sometime—but we saw Ellen only last May."

Miss Ellen leaned forward and stopped her, resting a tiny hand on her knee. "Cornelia, dear," she whispered, "we're all making sad trips these days. I'm taking Mother to Brownsville for burial. She died while we were visiting her invalid cousin at Sweetwater."

Cornelia said nothing. Presently she raised her eyes questioningly to Miss Patty.

"My aged aunt," Miss Patty said. "She is not dead. She is in the drawing room with an Irish nurse. I'm bringing her from Washington to spend her last days at Thornton, where she is greatly loved."

Miss Ellen looked up at Miss Patty and said, "I'm sure she is."

"She is," Miss Patty affirmed. There was a civility in her tone that had not been there when she had last addressed Miss Ellen, and the two exchanged a rather long glance.

Cornelia gazed out the window at the passing fields. Her features in repose looked tired. It was with obvious effort that she faced her two friends again. Miss Patty was still standing there, with her lips slightly parted, and Miss Ellen still rested a hand on Cornelia's knee. Cornelia shuddered visibly. She blushed and said, "A rabbit ran over my grave, I guess." Then she blushed again, but now she had regained her spirit. "Oh, just listen to me." She smiled. "I've never said the right thing once in my life. Is there a diner? Can we get any breakfast? You used to get the *best* breakfast on the Southern."

At the word "breakfast," Miss Patty did an about-face and disappeared down the passage to the ladies' room. Miss Ellen seized her purse and gloves. "Of course, my dear," she said. "Come along. We'll all have breakfast together."

There were no other passengers in the diner when Cornelia and Miss Ellen went in. The steward was eating at a small table at the rear of the car. Two Negro waiters were standing by the table talking to him, but he jumped to his feet and came toward the ladies. He stopped at the third table on the right, as though all the others might be reserved, and after wiping his mouth with a large white napkin, he asked if there would be anyone else in their party.

"Why, yes, as a matter of fact," Miss Ellen answered politely, "there will be one other."

"Do you think you can squeeze one more in?" Cornelia asked, narrowing her eyes and laughing. The steward did not reply. He helped them into chairs opposite each other and by the broad window, and darted away to get menus from his desk at the front of the car. A smiling Negro waiter set three goblets upright, filled them with water, and removed a fourth goblet and a setting of silver. "Sometime during the past thirty years,"

Cornelia remarked when the waiter had gone, "conductors and stewards lost their sense of humor. It makes you thank God for porters and waiters, doesn't it? Next thing you know— Why, merciful heavens, here's Patty already!"

Miss Ellen glanced over her shoulder. There was Miss Patty, looking as though she had dressed in the dark and were proud of it. She was hatless, her hair pulled into a loose knot on the back of her neck but apparently without benefit of the ivory comb and brush. The steward was leading her toward their table. Without smiling, Cornelia said, "He didn't have to ask her if she were the other member of this party." Miss Ellen raised her eyebrows slightly. "Most passengers don't eat in the diner any more," Cornelia clarified. "They feel they're too near to Memphis to bother." When Miss Patty sat down beside Miss Ellen, Cornelia said, "Gosh a'might, Patty, we left you only two seconds ago and here you are dressed and in your right mind. How do you do it?"

They received their menus, and when they had ordered, Miss Patty smiled airily. "I'm always in my right mind, Cornelia, and I don't reckon I've ever been 'dressed' in my life." As she said "dressed," her eyes traveled from the three-cornered hat to the brocaded bosom of Cornelia's rust-colored dress.

Cornelia looked out the window, silently vowing not to speak again during the meal, or, since speaking was for her the most irresistible of all life's temptations, at least not to let herself speak sharply to either of these crotchety old maids. She sat looking out the window, thanking her stars for the great good luck of being Mrs. Jake Werner, of Memphis, instead of an embittered old maid from Grand Junction.

Miss Ellen was also looking out the window. "Doesn't it look bleak?" she said, referring to the brown and gray fields under an overcast sky.

"Oh, doesn't it!" Cornelia agreed at once, revealing that Miss Ellen had guessed her very thoughts.

"It *is* bleak," Miss Patty said. "See how it's washed. This land along here didn't use to look like that." The two others nodded agreement, each remembering how it had used to look. "This used to be fine land," she continued, "but it seems to me that all West Tennessee is washing away. Look at those gullies! And not a piece of brush piled in them." Miss Ellen and Cornelia shook their heads vaguely; they were not really certain why there should be brush in the gullies. Cornelia discovered that a glass of tomato juice had been set before her and she began pouring salt into it. Miss Ellen was eating her oatmeal. Miss Patty took a sip from her first cup of coffee. She had specified that it be brought in a cup instead of a pot. It was black and a little cool, the way she liked it. She peered out the window again and pursued her discourse warmly. "And the towns! Look! We're going through Moscow. It's a shambles. Why, half the square's been torn away, and the rest ought to be. Mind you, we went through La Grange without even noticing it. They used to be good towns, fine towns."

"Lovely towns!" responded Miss Ellen. The thought of the vanishing towns touched her.

"There was something about them," Cornelia said, groping. "An atmosphere, I think."

Miss Patty cleared her throat and defined it: "The atmosphere of a prosperous and civilized existence."

Miss Ellen looked bewildered, and Cornelia frowned thoughtfully and pursed her lips. Presently Cornelia said profoundly, "All the business has gone to Memphis."

"Yes," Miss Patty said. "Indeed it has!"

They were being served their main course now. Cornelia looked at her trout and said to the waiter, "It looks delicious. Did you cook this, boy?"

"No, ma'am," the waiter said cheerfully.

"Well, it looks delicious. The same old Southern Railway cooking."

Miss Patty and Miss Ellen had scrambled eggs and ham. Miss Patty eyed hers critically. "The Southern Railway didn't use to cook eggs this way," she said. "And it's no improvement."

Miss Ellen leaned forward and bent her neck in order to look directly up into Miss Patty's face. "Why, now, you probably like them country style, with some white showing," she said. "*These* are what my niece calls Toddle House style. They cook them with milk, of course. They're a little like an omelet." The subject held great interest for her, and she was happy to be able to inform Miss Patty. "And you don't break them into such a hot pan. You don't really break them in the pan, that is." Miss Patty was reaching across Miss Ellen's plate for the pepper. Miss Ellen said no more about the eggs. She busied herself with a small silver box of saccharin, prying the lid open with her fingernail. She saw Cornelia looking at the box and said, "It was my grandmother's snuffbox. For years it was just a keepsake, but now I carry my tablets in it."

The old box, which Miss Patty was now examining admiringly, somehow made Cornelia return to the subject they had left off. "In my grandmother's day, there was a lot of life in this section—entertainment and social life. My own mother used to say, 'In Mama's day, there were people in the country; in my day, there were people in town; now there's nobody.'"

Miss Patty gazed at Cornelia with astonishment. "Your mother was a very wise woman, Cornelia," she said.

"That's a moot question," Cornelia answered. Now they were on a subject that she was sure she knew something about, and she threw caution to the wind. She spoke excitedly and seemed to begin every sentence without knowing how it would end. "My mother is dead now, and I don't mean to ever say another word against her, but just because she is dead, I don't intend to start deceiving myself. The fact remains that she was opinionated and narrow and mentally cruel to her children and her husband and was tied to things that were over and done with before she was born. She's dead now, but I shall make no pretense of mourning someone I did not love. We don't mourn people we don't love. It's not honest."

"No, we don't, do we?" Miss Ellen said sympathetically.

"I beg to differ with you," Miss Patty said with the merest suggestion of a smile. She, too, felt on firm ground. She had already mourned the deaths of all her immediate family and of most of her near kin. She addressed her remarks to Miss Ellen. "Mourning is an obligation. We only mourn those with whom we have some real connection, people who have represented something important and fundamental in our lives."

Miss Ellen was determined to find agreement. "Of course, of course—you are speaking of wearing black."

"I am not speaking of the symbol. I am speaking of the mourning itself. I shall mourn the loss of my aunt when she goes, because she is my aunt, because she is the last of my aunts, and particularly because she is an aunt who has maintained a worthwhile position in the world."

Miss Ellen gasped. "Oh, no, Miss Bean! Not because of her position in the world!"

"Don't mistake me, Miss Watkins."

"I beg you to reconsider. Why, why—" She fumbled, and Miss Patty waited. "Now that Mother's gone, I've lost nearly everybody, and it has always been my part and my privilege to look after the sick in our family. My two older brothers never married; they were quiet, simple, home-loving men, who made little stir in the world, content to live there in the house with Mother and Nora and me after Father was gone. And Nora, my only sister, developed melancholia. One morning, she could just not finish lacing her high shoes, and after that she seldom left the house or saw anybody. What I want to say is that we also had a younger brother, who was a distinguished professor at Knoxville, with four beautiful children. You see, I've lost them all, one by one, and it's been no different whether they were distinguished or not. I can't conceive—" She stopped suddenly, in real confusion.

"Don't mistake me," Miss Patty said calmly. "I am speaking of my aunt's moral position in the world."

"Why, of course you are," said Miss Ellen, still out of breath.

"My aunt has been an indomitable character," Miss Patty continued. "Her husband died during his first term in Congress, forty years ago, and she has felt it her duty to remain in Washington ever since. With very slight means, she has maintained herself there in the right manner through all the years, returning to Thornton every summer, enduring the heat and the inconvenience, with no definite place of abode, visiting the kin, subjecting herself to the role of the indigent relation, so that she could afford to return to Washington in the fall. Her passing will be a loss to us all, for through her wit and charm she was an influence on Capitol Hill. In a sense, she represented our district in Washington as none of our elected officials has done since the days of"—bowing her head deferentially toward Miss Ellen—"of David Crockett."

"What a marvelous woman!" exclaimed Miss Ellen.

Cornelia looked at Miss Ellen to see whether she meant Miss Patty's aunt or Miss Patty. She had been marveling privately at Miss Patty's flow of speech, and reflected that she could already see it in print in the county paper's obituary column. "If my mother had been a person of such wit and charm," she said, "I would mourn her, too."

"I never knew your mother," Miss Patty replied, "but from what you say I can easily guess the sort of woman she was. I would mourn her passing if I were in your shoes, Cornelia. She wanted to retain the standards of a past era, a better era for all of *us*. A person can't do that and be a pleasant, charming personality and the darling of a family."

"All I know," said Cornelia, taking the last bite of her trout, "is that my young ladyhood was a misery under that woman's roof and in that town." She glanced dreamily out the window. The train was speeding through the same sort of country as before, perhaps a little more hilly, a little more eroded. It sped through small towns and past solitary stations where only the tiresome afternoon local stopped—Rossville, Collierville, Bailey, Forest Hill. Cornelia saw a two-story farmhouse that was painted up only to the level of the second story. "That house has been that way as long as I can remember," she said, and smiled. "Why do you suppose they don't make them a ladder, or lean out the upstairs windows?" Then, still looking out at the dismal landscape—the uncultivated land growing up in sweet gum and old field pine, with a gutted mud road crossing and recrossing the railroad track every half mile or so—Cornelia said, "I only got away by the skin of my teeth! I came back from Ward's with a scrapbook full of names, but they were nothing but 'cute Vanderbilt boys.' I would have been stuck in Grand Junction for life, nursing Mama and all the hypochondriac kin, if I hadn't met Jake. I met him in Memphis doing Christmas shopping. He was a bank teller at Union Planters." She laughed heartily for the first time since she had come into the diner. "It was an out-and-out pickup. Jake still tells everybody it was an out-and-out pickup."

"I don't like Memphis," said Miss Patty. "I never have."

"I've never felt that Memphis liked me," said Miss Ellen.

"It's a wretched place!" Cornelia said suddenly. And now she saw that she had unwittingly shocked her two friends. The train had passed through Germantown; big suburban estates and scattered subdivisions began to appear in the countryside. There was even a bulldozer at work on the horizon, grading the land for new suburban sites. "It's the most completely snobbish place in the world," she went on. "They can't forgive you for being from the country—they hate the country so, and they can't forgive your being a Jew. They dare not. If you're either one of those, it's rough going. If you're both, you're just out! I mean *socially*, of course. Oh, Jake's done *well*, and we have our friends. But as Mama would have said—and, God knows, probably did say about us many a time—*we're* nobody." Then, for no reason at all, she added, "And we don't have any children."

"What a shame," Miss Ellen said, hastening to explain, "that you have no children, I mean. I've always thought that if—"

"Oh, no, Ellen. They might have liked me about the way I liked Mama. I'm glad that when I die, there'll be no question of to mourn or not to mourn."

"In truly happy families, Cornelia, there is no question," Miss Ellen said softly. She stole a glance at Miss Patty. "I'm just certain that Miss Bean had a very congenial and happy family, and that she loved them all dearly, in addition to being naturally proud of the things they stood for."

Miss Patty had produced a wallet from somewhere on her person and was examining her check. She slammed the wallet on the table, turned her head, and glared at the diminutive Miss Ellen. "How I regarded the members of my family as individuals is neither here nor there, Miss Watkins."

But Miss Ellen raised her rather receding chin and gazed directly up at Miss Patty. "To me, it seems of the greatest consequence." Her voice trembled, yet there was a firmness in it. "I am mourning my mother today. I spent last night remembering every endearing trait she had. Some of them were faults and some were virtues, but they were nonetheless endearing. And so I feel strongly about what you say, Miss Bean. We must love people as people, not for what they are, or were, in the world."

"My people happened to be very much *of* the world, Miss Watkins," said Miss Patty. "Not of *this* world but of *a* world that we have seen disappear. In mourning my family, I mourn that world's disappearance. How could I know whether or not I really loved them, or whether or not we were really happy? There wasn't ever time for asking that. We were all like Aunt Lottie, in yonder, and there was surely never any love or happiness in the end of it. When I went to Washington last week to fetch Aunt Lottie home, I found her living in a hateful little

hole at the Stoneleigh Court. All the furniture from larger
apartments she had once had was jammed together in two
rooms. The tables were covered with framed photographs of
the wives of Presidents, Vice-Presidents, senators, inscribed to
Lottie Hathcock. But there was not a friend in sight. During
the five days I was there, not one person called." Miss Patty
stood up and waved her check and two one-dollar bills at the
waiter.

Miss Ellen sat watching the check and the two bills with a
stunned expression. But Cornelia twisted about in her chair
excitedly. "Your aunt was Mrs. Hathcock!" she fairly screamed.
"Oh, Patty, of course! She was *famous* in her day. And don't
you remember? I met her once with you at the Maxwell House,
when we were at Belmont. You took me along, and after supper
my true love from Vandy turned up in the lobby. You were so
furious, and Mrs. Hathcock was so cute about it. She was the
cleverest talker I've ever listened to, Patty. She was interested
in spiritualism and offered to take us to a séance at Mr. Ben
Allen's house."

Miss Patty looked at Cornelia absent-mindedly. Her antagonism toward the two women seemed suddenly to have left her,
and she spoke without any restraint at all. "Aunt Lottie has
long since become a Roman Catholic. Her will leaves her little
pittance of money and her furniture to the Catholic Church,
and her religious oil paintings to me. The nurse we brought
along has turned out to be an Irish Catholic." She glanced in
the direction of their Pullman car and said, "The nurse has
conceived the notion that Aunt Lottie is worse this morning,
and she wanted to wire ahead for a Memphis priest to meet us
at the Union Station. She knows there won't be any priests at
Thornton."

Cornelia, carried away by incorrigible gregariousness, began,
"Ah, Patty, might I see her? It would be such fun to see her
again, just for old times' sake. It might even cheer her a little."

Miss Patty stared at Cornelia in silence. Finally she said,
"My aunt is a mental patient. She doesn't even remember me,
Cornelia." She snatched a piece of change from the waiter's tray
and hurried past the steward and out of the car.

Miss Ellen was almost staggering as she rose from the table.
She fumbled in her purse, trying to find the correct change

for the waiter. She was shaking her head from side to side, and opening and closing her eyes with the same rhythm.

Cornelia made no move toward rising. "Depend upon *me*," she said. "Did you *know*?"

Miss Ellen only increased the speed of her head-shaking. When she saw Cornelia still sitting there, casually lighting a cigarette, she said, "We're approaching Buntyn. I imagine you're getting off there."

"No, that's the country-club stop. I don't get off at the country-club stop."

"There's not much time," Miss Ellen said.

Presently Cornelia pulled a bill from her purse and summoned the waiter. "Well, Ellen," she said, still not getting up, "I guess there's no way I could be of help to you at the station, is there?"

"No, there's nothing, dear."

In her lethargy Cornelia seemed unable to rise and even unable to tell Miss Ellen to go ahead without her. "I suppose you'll be met by a hearse," she said, "and Patty will be met by an ambulance, and—and I'll be met by Jake." For a moment, she sat behind a cloud of cigarette smoke. There was a puzzled expression in her eyes, and she was laughing quietly at what she had said. It was one of those sentences that Cornelia began without knowing how it would end.

Uncles

I SHALL try to keep the great-uncles out of this. The plain uncles are enough. I was seventeen and had been away at college for three months. When I got off the train in St. Louis, my father and two of his brothers were there to meet me. It was Christmas time, and they were all three wearing gloves, overcoat, scarf, black shoes, and the fuzzy sort of fedora, with what Father called "the new nutria nap," that they always wore when the weather was extremely cold. My first thought upon seeing them there together was that you wouldn't have to be a member of the family to know they were manufacturers of men's hats. Had no one ever thought of calling them the mad hatters? Then, as the three of them came toward me, I remembered that there was absolutely nothing mad about the men in the hat-manufacturing Ferguson family.

My father and all four of his brothers were among the sanest men who ever lived. I say *were* not because my father or any of my uncles are dead now but because they are older, and as they get older, they become less resolutely sane. That is why my great-uncles can be kept out of this story. By the time I went away to college, they were old men. Only two of them—there had been seven altogether—were still active in the family business, and they kept irregular office hours. I did see those two great-uncles the morning I returned from college, but they had little to say to me; Great-Uncle Louis asked me what I was hoping to get for Christmas, as though I were still in knee breeches, and Great-Uncle Will, who was leaving the office as I came in, said only that Great-Aunt Marietta would want to see me.

With Father at the station were his two younger brothers, Uncle Sydney and Uncle Grover. I took hold of Father's gloved hand, gripping it firmly, and he put his other hand on my shoulder and looked me straight in the eye. Then I turned to my uncles. They didn't offer their hands.

"Hello, college boy," said Uncle Sydney.

"Hello, freshman," Uncle Grover said.

I smiled at them, though they were not smiling, and said nothing. If they had said anything at all, I could have thought of some answer to make. But I had only a few hours before left Kenyon College, which is not coeducational, and where being a freshman, in the middle thirties, seemed a most degrading experience. A few minutes later, I wished that I had thought to say, "Hello, old grads!," because it was *only* freshmen who were more despised than old grads by Kenyon upperclassmen. But I said nothing.

Presently, Father said, "Where's your hat, son?"

"I don't wear a hat," I said, and I began looking for my two pieces of luggage.

We were in the car and several blocks from the station before I had a chance to ask about my mother and my grandmother and my little sister, Nora. The thought of them and of our house, out in Parkview, filled me with sudden delight. I looked at my wristwatch and, seeing that it was nearly lunchtime, I knew that Mother would be downstairs reading the morning paper, which she always saved for that dull interval just before lunch. After breakfast, she had, I was sure, played the piano for an hour. Sometimes, forgetting time, she played right through the first two hours of her morning, and would have played all morning except that someone always called her on the telephone. But *this* morning she would not have forgotten time. I imagined that she had got up from the piano and gone for her morning's turn about the yard. (Even in winter, she went prying about the shrubbery and the bare flower beds every morning.) Then she had gone up to the sewing room and, if it was not a day when Mrs. Knox, the sewing woman, came, she had run up a few seams, which Mrs. Knox would undoubtedly have to take out and do over. After that, she had done her telephoning, and soon it had been time to go down and read the paper. "I don't know what becomes of my mornings," I had heard her say, "but I reckon it's not something I'll have to reckon for at Judgment."

"And what was the score against you in the Lansford game?" Uncle Sydney asked me. It was the last of a series of questions about Kenyon's pathetic football record that year. I had been answering their questions with the Kenyon coach's own excuses, and this one was one of the easiest to answer: "Lansford has football scholarships—Kenyon has literary scholarships."

"This freshman knows all the answers," Uncle Grover said.

There was a pause, and I turned from my uncles, who were in the back seat of the car, to my father, who was driving the car and beside whom I was sitting. "How's Mother?" I asked casually. "Grandmother and Nora all right?"

"Your mother and your grandmother are all right," he said. "Nora's failed her algebra."

"She did!" I exclaimed. "The goose!"

"Oh, well . . ." Father began. He put his hand out the window as he turned in to the Olive Street traffic, and seemed to forget what he had been going to say.

"Nora's getting to be a little beauty," Uncle Grover said. "She looks right grown-up."

"Well, she's evidently not getting any smarter," I said, still looking at Father.

"She's smart *enough*," Uncle Grover said. "She's cuter than a barrel of monkeys." He and Uncle Sydney each had two little girls of their own, younger than Nora. My other two uncles also had daughters, older than I, and I had heard my parents laugh about how sensitive all my uncles were to any reflection upon little girls. Being of a big family of boys, they had expected sons for themselves, and they could not understand why it had turned out otherwise. As it was, I was the only boy in my generation of Fergusons. It would have pleased me to hear Uncle Grover praising Nora except that I knew it had nothing to do with his feelings about her and was only an echo of his defensiveness about little girls in general.

Father had now adjusted his driving to the heavy traffic, and he said, "She *ought* to have passed her algebra, of course."

"Now, Bert," Uncle Sydney said, "what *earthly* difference can it really make?" He was the youngest brother and more inclined to argument than the others. "There's one thing I've never been able to see, and that's a *smart* woman. A *smart* woman is not actually very smart—not as a woman. They tell me that this Gracie Allen is *really* one of the smartest women alive, and look how she talks. Look what she's done, and she's not even good-looking."

"She has good-looking legs," Uncle Grover said, grinning.

"You would know," Uncle Sydney said, in parenthesis, and then continued, "And you take even this Gypsy Rose Lee, a strip-tease girl. They tell me that she's an intellectual, in reality. She reads Shakespeare and Socrates and all such serious stuff because she really likes it. But she's too smart to let anybody know about it."

"At least she doesn't bare her *soul*, eh?" Uncle Grover said. The two of them laughed, and Father smiled because he knew it was a joke.

"Your Uncle Grover's keen today," Uncle Sydney said. "But seriously, it's true. Of course, *they're* just show women, but the same principle applies. Now, for instance, who would want a Mrs. Roosevelt for a daughter, or a wife, either?"

"Who wants a Mrs. Roosevelt at *all*?" Uncle Grover said.

"Who wants a *Mr*. Roosevelt?" Father said, and they burst into laughter again.

I hadn't quite realized that Father was not taking me home until he turned in to the parking lot next to the Ferguson Building. As soon as he began pulling the steering wheel to the right, I said, "Aren't we going home?"

"No," he said, looking at me in surprise. "We have to run by the House"—"the House," to my father and his brothers, meant their place of business—"and then we thought you'd go with us to the University Club for lunch."

"I'd rather go home," I said. But the colored boy in the parking lot was already opening Father's door. As I stepped out of the car, I somehow got a cinder in my shoe, and I used getting it out as an excuse to lag behind the others. I was really very angry at their not taking me right home, and even after I had removed the cinder, I hesitated a moment to be sure I wouldn't have to walk to the side door of the building with them. When I started across the lot, they were already waiting for me at the door, standing very close together in their nearly identical hats and coats and light scarves. They looked for all the world like three big brown beavers huddling together to keep warm. Worse than walking to the door with them, I now had to traverse the distance of about thirty feet with their bright eyes watching me intently. I walked with my chin in the air, looking up toward the dirty brick building as though I were estimating its value while really I was observing a few scattered snowflakes that were falling.

When I came up to the three men, Uncle Grover took my hand and began shaking it. "Welcome to the House of Ferguson," he said.

Uncle Sydney clapped me on the back as he ushered me through the doorway ahead of them and said, "Welcome home."

I felt that those were the first friendly words I had heard since I got off the train, but as I went up the metal steps to the main-floor level, I said to myself indignantly, "Home!"

They seemed different men once we were inside "the House." They were all friendliness. At the head of the steps, Father began helping me off with my polo coat. "We keep it pretty stuffy in here," he said.

"Old fellows like us have to be careful about our rheumatism," Uncle Sydney said.

"I'll bet you haven't been in this joint more than a dozen times in your life," Uncle Grover said. "Pretty soon we'll have to begin showing you the ropes."

I waited while they removed their coats and their scarves and their gloves (they kept their hats on until we were upstairs), and then we walked toward the elevator, between the long rows of showcases where the season's hats were on display. As nearly always, the main floor was completely deserted except for the doorman at the front door and the old Negro who operated the elevator. For some reason, I couldn't remember the old Negro's name, but I shook hands with him and, on the way up, I asked him about his wife, whose name I did remember, because she had once cooked for us. He and his wife had come from my mother's home, out in Columbia. "Cora's gone back to Columbia," he said. "She left me." There was a silence. The elevator passed the floors where men and women were working, either standing over the long belts that brought out the carroted fur or tending the big blowing machine. At the sixth floor, we could hear the steam escaping from the blocking machines. All at once, the three white men in the elevator began laughing, and then the old Negro was laughing, too. Just before we got to the top floor, where the offices were, he looked at me, still smiling, and said, "I got me another wife now, Mr. Ferguson."

"He means he's got him a young wife now, about your age, *Mr. Ferguson*," Uncle Sydney said. "And a new baby on the way."

Suddenly I remembered the man's name was Rudolph, but we were already getting out of the elevator, and there was Great-Uncle Will waiting to go down in the elevator and telling me that Great-Aunt Marietta would want to see me.

We went to Great-Uncle Louis's office, and from there we went first to see Uncle John and then Great-Uncle Will's namesake, who was president of the company and whom everybody in the family called Prez. As I went into Uncle Prez's office, I was still escorted by Father, Uncle Grover, and Uncle Sydney, and, of course, now by Uncle John as well.

Uncle John had had very little to say to me while we were in his office. "Hello, my boy, it is indeed good to have you with us again," he had said when I first came in, but the rest of the time he was flustering with papers on his desk, putting away a manila folder, opening and shutting drawers. He was the oldest brother, and right after my grandfather died, there had been a period of tension in the family because Uncle John so obviously expected to be made president. That was all forgotten now, but still they took me to see Uncle John before Uncle Prez. While Uncle John was ordering his papers, or whatever he was doing, Uncle Sydney commenced pointing out to me that Uncle John's office had been redecorated that fall, calling attention to the new monk's-cloth draperies. Uncle John didn't acknowledge the admiration that I expressed rather feebly. Father and Uncle Grover were silent, but Father looked warningly at Uncle Sydney.

The moment we entered Uncle Prez's office, Uncle John began talking a blue streak. "Here is the white hope of the Ferguson firm," he said. He put his arm about my shoulders. "Here is the young fellow we are all counting on, Mr. President. Here is the young man who is going to bring us the ideas of the new generation."

Uncle Prez got up from the roll-top desk that had been my grandfather's and shook my hand. His smile and his handshake were gentler than his brothers', but there was not the warmth in the expression about his eyes that the others had. He was plainly a man who would have been satisfied to work his whole life in the sixth-floor blocking room if that had been his lot. "Sit down," he said, addressing all of us. "As soon as Miss Hauser comes back from lunch, we can all go somewhere and get a bite ourselves. Wherever we go, I'm going to have some hot black-bean soup to start with." He turned toward the window. "Just looking out that window makes me cold," he said.

"We're going to the University Club," Uncle Grover said.

Uncle John cleared his throat thoughtfully. "Let's see, let's see, now. Why go all the way out there? How about the Statler?"

"The Club's on the way home, John," Father said decisively, and added, smiling, "This boy, here, seems to be in a sort of hurry to get home and see his mammy. The table service will be quicker out there," he said for my benefit, "and we'll just have a bite."

I had a good idea of how long that "bite" would take, and, suddenly spying Uncle Prez's telephone, I picked up the receiver and called our home number. When they heard the number I called, they began to laugh.

"I believe college has made him a mother's boy," Uncle Grover said. "I don't remember he ever was before. I understood he was quite a ladies' man at John Burroughs School last year."

Then Uncle John began talking about some business matter in a deafening voice.

It took me a moment to realize that I was getting the busy signal. I put my finger on the receiver hook and looked at my watch. It was nearly twelve-thirty, long past the time when Mother did her telephoning. "The servants!" I said to myself angrily, but at once I began to wonder why I felt such a passion to get home and talk to Mother. Uncle Grover was right when he said that I had never been a mother's boy when I was growing up, and even as I got off the train that morning I had thought the person I most wanted to see was a certain girl who was a senior at John Burroughs School that year. "What has come over me?" I asked myself. My urgency somehow seemed to come from the impression that Father and my uncles had

made on me when I stepped off the train—the impression
that seeing them was only a continuation of dormitory life at
Kenyon—and, as a matter of fact, nothing had happened since
I arrived to alter that first impression.

While I sat determinedly not listening to the men's business
talk and calling the number again every two minutes, I realized that all semester I had been yearning for some relief from
what seemed the one-dimensional, exclusively masculine view
of life held by college boys and college professors, and, I found
now, by businessmen. Looking at my father and my uncles, I
thought again of how my mother's morning must have been.
While she was playing the piano, she had been making all sorts
of decisions about the housekeeping; while she was making
sure that the peony beds were covered, she had decided what
was to be done about Nora's algebra troubles; in the sewing
room, she had sung so loud that you could hardly have heard
the noise of the sewing machine (what if the seams did have
to be done over?); and while she was talking on the telephone,
sometimes screaming with laughter at her friends' foolishness,
she had been jotting down plans for meals or making her grocery list. Or perhaps she had let the decisions and the grocery
list go. If she had enjoyed her morning sufficiently, she might
have left the decisions to Grandmother and the servants, or if
she had had to put in the orders herself, a grocery list could
always be made on the spur of the moment, out of her head,
after she had called the number of the grocery store.

"Quit being so fidgety," Father said, finally. "You know how
long your mother talks on the telephone."

"She doesn't talk on the phone at this time of day."

"Well, anyhow, you must be driving that operator crazy,"
he said.

"If I were that operator," Uncle Sydney said, "I wouldn't
give you the number at all. You're a college man now, and I'd
make you wait till you got home to talk to your mother."

To myself, I said, "I know you would! You certainly would!"
Actually, I knew that he meant not if he were the operator but
if he were my father. And I could see that Father knew it, too,
because he changed the subject at once.

But it was really a worse subject that Father changed to.
"Before we leave and go to lunch, there is an important piece of

business we must attend to," he said. Only Uncle John looked at him seriously. The others knew as well as I that it was going to be something that related to me.

"What is it, Herbert?" Uncle Prez asked.

"We've got to outfit this boy with a hat, the right sort of hat, one he'll like."

"You mean he doesn't have a hat?" Uncle Prez said.

"Not with him."

"I'll bet he has a closetful at home," said Uncle Sydney.

"He does," Father said.

"But you mean he travelled without a hat?"

"He certainly did."

"He came all the way from Kenyon without a hat?"

I listened to them. They were joking. I could tell how glad they all were to see me, but I couldn't joke with them. The thought of their selecting a hat for me and forcing me to wear it to the University Club made my wrists and ankles begin to sweat.

"He got off the train bareheaded," Uncle Grover said.

I lifted the telephone receiver. "And I'm going to get back on the train bareheaded," I said. Then I called the number again. It was still busy.

"Suppose you take him down to the first floor and find him something," Uncle Prez said. "And we'll be down as soon as Miss Hauser comes in." They had been joking, but now I could see they were all becoming quite serious.

"Uncle Prez," I said, "I'm not going to get a hat."

"Oh, leave the boy alone," Uncle John said. "Every one of you knows that college boys don't wear hats."

"Of course, it's really all right for college boys not to wear hats," Uncle Sydney said. "But, you know, seriously, there's something *about* most men who don't wear hats. Women can get away with it, but not men."

"Yes, it's the old story any merchandiser knows," Uncle Prez said. "You tell a man everybody in town's wearing this particular sort of thing and he buys it. You tell a woman that and she goes away without buying. She looks for something else."

"That's right," Uncle Grover said. "There's always something phony about men who dress flamboyantly, or even about those who go to the other extreme."

"I've never seen one come to much," Uncle Prez said. "They end up clerking for some haberdasher or—"

"Or they go off to New York or Hollywood," Uncle Grover said.

"Now, there *is* that exception," Father said. "People in California do dress differently."

"Actors and artists are the only men like that who make any sort of success of themselves," Uncle Sydney said, "and they're not really men. It's more than just the way such guys dress."

"Oh, yes, yes," Uncle John agreed. "They're usually just not very intelligent."

"They're not very intelligent as *men*," Uncle Sydney said. "I understand that almost any Hollywood actor has to have his father or his brother or somebody look after his money."

At that moment, Miss Hauser and two other stenographers came in, young women wrapped in fur coats and wearing galoshes. Uncle John introduced me to them, and the other men put on their hats and began gathering up their coats and scarves.

"I'm going to try to call once more," I said to Father. "She will think it's funny if I don't call."

"Ah, your mother will understand," he said impatiently. "Come along, son." I felt that he was embarrassed by my behavior.

I had called the number but was starting to put down the receiver when suddenly I heard Mother's voice. "Central!" she was saying.

And I burst out laughing. "Hello, Mother," I said eagerly, not realizing that, though I could hear her, she could not hear me.

"Central!" she said. Then, correcting herself, she said, "Op'rator! Op'rator!" Again I laughed aloud, thinking of how I had almost forgotten that special southern-Missouri accent of hers.

"Hello, Little Dixie!" I screamed into the telephone. Now she could hear me, but I could no longer hear her very distinctly. It sounded as though she had moved away from the telephone. "Try to talk louder, Mother," I said.

"I'm screaming my lungs out, darling. How are you?"

"Couldn't be better!" I shouted.

"You're bursting my eardrums. I can't *wait* to see you."

"I can barely hear you," I said. "Grandmother and Nora all right?"

She made some answer, but I couldn't understand it.

"What?" I asked.

"Let's hang up and try to get a better connection," she said. And simultaneously Father said, "You've got a bad connection. Hang up and call again."

"No!" I shouted angrily at Father.

Mother's distant voice wailed, "Oh-oh, my ears! Please, Op'rator," she said, jiggling the telephone hook, "can't you get us a better connection?"

The operator's pleasant voice said, "There you are." And then we had a normal connection.

"Darling," Mother was saying, "I guess Nora and I won't see you till night. We've *got* to do some shopping, and you're going to have lunch with the men, aren't you?"

"I guess I am," I said, "but I could meet you downtown."

"That would be grand," she said, "but our shopping would bore you to death. Nora's having a hayride out at the farm tonight. Did your father tell you? I'll bet you've been trying to get us—she's been on the phone inviting people ever since breakfast. This is to be her one last fling. She's going to tutor through the holidays. We're all topsy-turvy—that's why I didn't come down to meet you."

"Hello," came Nora's voice from the upstairs extension.

"Hello," I said. "Flunked your algebra, eh?"

The men in the office scowled at me.

"I'm in love," Nora crooned.

Then Grandmother's voice came from the extension on the landing. "Darling boy, we can't wait to see you. I just won't go shopping. Now, you hurry along home."

Nora began to stutter excitedly, "Gr-grandmother, you've *got* to come! I want you to see the material at Vandervoort's. Mother's already seen it."

"Then, I bid to stay home!" said Mother.

Nora began giggling and saying that *she* would stay. Then they were all laughing and talking at once. It was funny hearing them and I began to laugh.

Then I stopped laughing.

"Darling," Mother said. "Darling, are you still there?"

"Yes," I said affably, "but I'll see you three silly women tonight."

"We'll be home not a minute later than four-thirty."

"See you then," I said. "Father and them are waiting on me to go to lunch." All my resistance and my anger seemed futile and absurd to me now. "They're going to fetch me a new hat."

"Something mature and very masculine, I suppose," Mother said.

"Oh, yes," I said.

As I put down the receiver, it came over me that I would never again be able to talk to Mother or to Nora or to Grandmother except in the specific role of a man. It suddenly became clear that everything clever, gentle, and light belonged to women and the world they lived in. To men belonged only the more serious things in life, the deadly practical things—constructive ideas, profitable jobs, stories with morals, jokes with points. In my innocence, I felt that I was stupid not to have understood this before, and felt, or tried to feel, a new passion to adjust myself and assimilate these things that were to be mine. Yet all that afternoon, at the University Club and, afterward, when I went back to the office with Father to pick out a hat, I was waiting only for the proper moment to come to go home. It seemed almost that the time would never come. Looking back on it, it seems that until that day I had never known what it was to wait. It was like waiting for a furlough, or even like waiting for the war to be over.

Two Ladies in Retirement

SOME NASHVILLE wit had once said, "When I look at Miss Betty Pettigru, I'm reminded of an old, old baby." Others thought she looked more like the Home-Run King himself. She was a short, plump woman, not fat but with an individual plumpness to all her limbs and to her torso, her breasts, her hands, and even to the features of her moon-shaped face. She was a lady well known in Nashville, during a period of twenty-five years, for her Sunday-night parties and for her active role in the club life of the city. Miss Betty's face and figure and her parties and her active role seemed so much a part of Nashville that hardly anyone could believe it when, in the spring of 1926, word finally got around that she was definitely going to move away and go to live in St. Louis.

At first they all said, oh, it would be merely another of her protracted visits to St. Louis, and she would come back talking of nothing but her little nephews, who, of course, weren't really her little nephews at all. She was only going for another stay with some of that Tolliver family she was kin to. Miss Betty's enemies were particularly skeptical. "Miss Betty Pettigru leave Nashville? The scene of all her victories? Nonsense! Never!" And they kept asking what on earth made her even talk of leaving. "I think I'm going to St. Louis to watch my irresistible nephews grow up," she said. "But you know me. Womanlike, I seldom know my own mind or what my reason is for doing anything."

By everyone, her talk of leaving Nashville was considered "completely and entirely absurd." But then it came out in the Sunday paper that Miss Betty Pettigru had sold her house on West End Avenue—came out not on the society page but in the real-estate section—that convinced everybody. Soon they learned that she had actually sold her lovely big limestone house, disposed of all but a few pieces of her furniture, and had left for St. Louis in the company of her cousin and close companion of many years, Mrs. Florence Blalock. In Nashville, it seemed the end of an era!

During ten years, Miss Betty and Mrs. Blalock had been paying visits together to their St. Louis relatives, the James Tollivers.

Their visits were frequent and long, yet as guests they had always had to have their stockings "rinsed out" by the maid and their breakfasts brought to their rooms, and had to be given little parties, which had been made up of mothers and aunts of the Tollivers' friends. At last, and quite unexpectedly, too, they had been told by Mr. James Tolliver himself that their visits were a bad length. Either they should come for shorter visits or they should come and live the year around as members of the household. Miss Betty had burst into tears on the spot—from pure shock, as she said afterward. James Tolliver, a very gentle and businesslike man of about forty, had tried immediately to relent. But there was no relenting once such a thing was said, and the decision had to be made.

How could anyone who had followed Miss Betty's social career imagine that she would make the choice in favor of St. Louis? The answer, of course, was that nobody but her cousin Mrs. Blalock could. Mrs. Blalock remembered the warmth with which Miss Betty had welcomed her into her house thirty years before, how she commenced calling her Flo Dear at once, how she talked of the longing she had always felt for a sister whom she could love. And, what was more, Flo Dear remembered how Miss Betty's kindness and generosity toward her continued even after she realized that her poor cousin could not supply the sort of family affection that she craved. Flo Dear knew that at the Tolliver fireside it would be a different story.

To the Tolliver boys, it seemed that Auntie Bet and Flo Dear had always lived in St. Louis and occupied those two rooms at the end of the upstairs hall. Before the two ladies had resided in the Tollivers' house six months, the boys would speak of something that had happened during last year's visit as though their "aunts" had already been living with them then, and they would have to be reminded that it was otherwise.

It wasn't long before the boys' aunts seemed to feel, with the boys, that they had always lived there. Reaching back into the days of their visits for anecdotes, they managed to vest each of the three little boys with a highly individual character. There was little Jimmy, who had a natural bent for arithmetic and knew his multiplication tables before he ever went to school a day. They stood in awe of his head for figures and wondered what it would be like to have a scientist in the family. They said proudly that they hated to think of what out-of-the-way opinions he might come to hold. Jimmy's birthday came on January 8, and when he was "just a little fellow," he had figured out that if Christmas comes on a Sunday, then so must New Year's Day, and so must the eighth day of January, and then he had calculated how many times in his life Sunday was bound to ruin those three best days of the year. His aunts marveled at him. He was the second boy and in some ways the brightest. Vance was the oldest, and about him they said, "He is a very sober child, so respectful—and beautifully mannered." As for little Landon, they felt that one could not help adoring him, because of his sweet, dreamy nature and because he was the baby.

Vance was certainly the best mannered. But not their favorite. They had no favorite. Miss Betty and Flo Dear were impartial, utterly and completely. If one of Mr. Tolliver's business friends said to them, "Tell me about your little nephews; I understand you're very fond of them," they would hardly know where to begin. Finally Flo Dear might say, "Well, Vance is the oldest."

"Yes, Vance is getting so grown up it frightens me," Miss Betty would add, as though she had been with him every minute since he was born.

All in all, the move to St. Louis gave Miss Betty Pettigru just the new start in life that it seemed to promise. She and her cousin had a small circle of acquaintances among the mothers and aunts of the Tollivers' friends, but they seldom went anywhere or saw anyone except the members of their own family. Almost at once, Flo Dear had set up her drawing board in her room (she practiced the ancient art of blazonry), and very soon had completed a Tolliver coat of arms, which was hung in the library. Before long, she was accepting commissions from various friends of the Tollivers. Miss Betty assumed just as many household duties as Amy Tolliver would allow her to. But Amy, despite her easygoing nature, was too efficient and farseeing a family manager to leave an opening for trouble in that quarter. Miss Betty, in the end, was left free during almost all her waking hours to be of service to her little nephews. It was the new start in life she hoped for, and yet, almost upon her arrival, there began an unfortunate episode that threatened to demolish all this happiness. Within a matter of weeks after the two ladies were installed a terrible competition for the boys' favor developed between Miss Betty and Vennie, the Tollivers' aging cook.

At first glance, it would seem that Miss Betty had all the advantages in the struggle with Vennie. She lived in the same part of the house as the boys did; she ate at the table with them, was treated with respect by their parents, was at their service any and every hour of the day, not excluding Saturday or Sunday, when her chaperonage and financial backing were needed for excursions to the ice-skating rink or to the amusement parks and movie houses. Plainly, she was willing to throw into the battle the entire fortune old Major Pettigru, her father, had left her. She even went so far as to replace the town car she had sold upon leaving Nashville with a sea-green touring car, whose top could be put back in pleasant weather, and she added half again to the houseboy's salary in order that he might look after the car and Flo Dear and the boys on their expeditions.

Vennie's advantages were different, but they were real ones and were early recognized by Miss Betty. Vennie lived in a basement. She had not just a room there but an apartment, complete with an outside entrance, living room, kitchen, et cetera. One reached it by descending from the back hall to a long, narrow, poorly lit passage flanked by soapy-smelling laundry rooms, a tightly locked wine cellar, and the furnace room and coal bin. Her quarters were at the end of the passage. Miss Betty was destined never to go there, but in her mind she carried a picture of it that was as clear and accurate as if she had once occupied the rooms herself. The clearness was due to her knowledge of other such quarters she had visited in years gone by, but the accuracy of detail was due to the accounts her little nephews supplied. Landon told about the pictures on Vennie's walls, pictures of Negro children in middy blouses and other absurdly old-fashioned clothes you never thought of Negroes as wearing, pictures of Negro sergeants and corporals who had actually gone to France in the Great War (they all wore spectacles and looked, somehow, very unlike Negroes), pictures of Landon's mother and father and of other white people Vennie used to work for, in Thornton, and pictures of those other white people's children. Jimmy told about the horn on Vennie's old-timey phonograph and about the player piano and how it stretched and tired your legs to pedal it. Vance never said much about how things looked down there, but he talked about Vennie's "magic stove." Nothing cooked on the gas stove upstairs ever tasted like things cooked on that little coal range in Vennie's kitchen. And not one of the boys had failed to mention the dark scariness of the passage and how safe and bright Vennie's place always seemed when you got there.

Vennie's cooking, naturally, was a big advantage, but not such a serious one in itself. Auntie Bet could treat the boys to all manner of good things to eat when they went out. And what sort of handsome presents might she not have made them if it had been permitted! But it wasn't permitted, and Miss Betty didn't have to be told but once by Mr. James Tolliver that Christmas was the time—and the only time—when boys should receive expensive presents like bicycles and motor scooters. Amy and James were quick to shake their heads accusingly at her if one of the boys came back from Forest Park Highlands with even just a toy pistol he had won in a chance game. But when a three-layer chocolate cake was discovered in the lower compartment of the sideboard, and there was every reason to think other cakes had been kept there before and partaken of at will by the boys, despite all the rules against eating between meals, no more than a teasing, jovial finger was shaken at Vennie. Miss Betty protested that it really ought to be stopped, because Vance already had hickeys all over his face from so many sweets between meals. "But what can one do?" replied James Tolliver, shrugging his shoulders. "Vennie's like somebody's granny, and since the world began, grannies have been hiding cooky jars for young 'uns."

Certainly James Tolliver would not have made that casual remark if he had known the pain it would cause Miss Betty. It came on a day when the boys had been repeating to her some of the stories they liked to hear Vennie tell, stories about the old times at Thornton and in the country along the Tennessee River where it flows north up from Mississippi. How Uncle Wash got lost in the snowy woods and slept in a hollow log for two nights, and how Mr. Ben Tolliver found him there and thought he was "dead and maybe murdered." How little

Jane Pettigru fell down the old well and Vennie's blind dwarf brother, whose name was Pettigru, too—Jules Pettigru—was the only one small enough to be let down on a rope to bring the baby out. Vennie's stories and her way of telling them were surely her greatest advantage. Or, at least, it was the thing that most unnerved Miss Betty and made her feel useless to her little nephews. Occasionally, she had heard Vennie telling some old anecdote to the whole Tolliver family. Vennie would take her stance just inside the dining-room door, arms akimbo, her head thrown back, and wearing a big smile that grew broader and broader until she finished the story in a fit of laughter. Her stories were mostly about the Tolliver family and the Tolliver Negroes, about the wondrous ways they were always rescuing each other from dangers great and small, usually ending with some fool thing a field hand Negro had said, or with Mr. Jeff Tolliver quoting the law to a pickaninny who had snatched an apple from the back porch. The really bad thing was that Miss Betty so often recognized Vennie's stories, remembered hearing other versions of them in her youth. Yet she could not tell the stories herself, or even think of them until something Vennie had told the boys reminded her. Sometimes she would recall a very different version of a story Vennie had told, but the boys were not impressed by Auntie Bet's corrections.

When the very first newness of Miss Betty's "treats" wore off, there would be times when she got all dressed and ready to take the boys somewhere and found that they were down in the basement with Vennie. Instead of sending for them, she would go to her room in a fit of depression, asking Flo Dear to tell the boys she had a headache and they would go another day.

James and Amy Tolliver were apt to say of almost anyone, "He is a genuine, intelligent, thoroughly sane person and has a fine sense of humor." They said something of the sort about Miss Betty and Flo Dear, and added that they were also "characters," which was the final term of approval. Amy especially was inclined to think everyone had a fine sense of humor. She herself saw what was funny in any situation and was wonderfully responsive to other people's humor, frequently inspiring them to say something quite beyond their ordinary wit. She would laugh heartily at things the two aunts said, though at least half the time James would say afterward that he didn't think she had been supposed to laugh. But Amy would reply, "Why, Flo Dear has a fine sense of humor," or "You don't do the boys' Auntie Bet justice, James."

No one was funnier to Amy than her own servants. She was forever laughing either at them or with them about something. But whereas many a Southern woman in a Northern city will get to be on rather intimate terms with her Southern servants, Amy never did. To some extent, she treated them with the same mixture of cordiality and formality that she used with her next-door neighbors. She nearly always liked her servants but never hesitated to "send them on their merry way" when there was reason to. "There are no second chances in Amy's service," her husband once said. "One false step and you are cast into the pit."

"Oh stuff!" said Amy. "This house serves as a sort of immigration office for Tennessee blacks in St. Louis. We bring them up here and train them, and when they leave us, they always go to something better. You *know* that's so."

James laughed and said, "Only old Vennie is a permanent fixture here, I guess."

"Ah, have no illusion about that," said Amy. "Vennie's time is bound to come. And when it does, we'll be liberated from a very subtle tyranny. When Vennie is gone, I tell you, the turnover among the others won't be nearly as fast."

It seemed too funny for words when the current maid and houseboy could not get used to the fact that Flo Dear and Miss Betty were no longer to be regarded as guests. Despite all Amy could do, Emmaline would put only company linen on their beds, and every few mornings she would slip upstairs with their breakfasts on a tray. One morning, in an effort to put a stop to that, the two ladies came marching down the stairs carrying their trays, and they proceeded, amid general hilarity, to transfer their breakfast dishes to their regular places at the table. Emmaline was called in to witness it, and Bert, the houseboy, was also present. The two Negroes laughed more heartily than even the little boys at the two aunts' clowning. Amy seemed almost hysterical. "I laughed so hard I thought I was going to have hysterics," she said afterward.

But Miss Betty said, "The only signs of hysteria I saw were in Bert and Emmaline. They seemed downright scared to me." Half an hour later, when she went upstairs, she didn't stop a second in her own room but passed right on through it and through the bathroom into Flo Dear's room. Flo Dear had preceded her upstairs by some fifteen or twenty minutes and was already at work at her drawing board. Miss Betty knew that her cousin hated being interrupted, but what she had to say could not wait. "I am now convinced," she announced, "that all this politeness is that old Vennie's doing."

Flo Dear raised her eyes and stared at Miss Betty. "It is now plain to me," said Miss Betty, "that Bert and Emmaline are taking orders from two mistresses."

Presently Flo Dear gave three quick, affirming little nods and said, "Yes, you're probably right. But you and I must not give them still two more mistresses." She and Miss Betty looked into one another's eyes for a moment, and then Miss Betty turned and retreated into the bathroom, closing the door behind her.

Yet very soon Bert and Emmaline began to have small pieces of change thrust into their hands at the oddest moments— when Bert forgot to put the pillow in Miss Betty's chair at table or when Emmaline put frayed and faded towels in the ladies' bathroom. Within a few weeks, the difficulty with the two younger servants was past.

Miss Betty's three "nephews" went to a school on Delmar Boulevard, only a few blocks from home. School was out at one o'clock on Wednesdays, and it was their privilege that day to bring home as many as four guests to lunch. Since Wednesday also happened to be Emmaline's day off, it was Vennie's privilege not only to cook but to serve the meal to the boys. It was a privilege and an advantage of which she made the most. By a ruling of Vance's, none of the white adults were allowed to be present at the meal, and Vance often directed what menu should be used. He always saw to it that Landon asked the blessing at that meal, and there was no horseplay whatsoever at the table. Vennie served in a black uniform with white cap and apron, and she never said a word until spoken to by Vance. But Vance, seated at the head of the table with his black hair slicked down on his head, the part glistening like a white scar, would faithfully begin addressing remarks to Vennie when dessert was about over. He did it in just the manner that his father did it whenever Vennie appeared at the evening meal, and Vennie responded with the same show of modesty and respect. "Oh, come on, Vennie," Vance would say. "Tell us about Uncle Wash's fight with the bear when they were laying the railroad to Texas."

Vennie would demur, saying, "Those boys don't want to hear my old-nigger talk." But finally she would be brought around by the insistence of all the boys, and never were her tales so exciting as then, and never so full of phrases like "plantation roads" and "ol' marster" and "befo' freedom." While she talked, Vance would sit winking at the other boys, just as his father would do. Vennie's favorite way of beginning was to say, "Now, every Tolliver, black or white, know this story and know it be true." It was a convincing way to begin and usually removed all doubt from the minds of her listeners. But on a Wednesday in the fall after the boys' aunts had come there to live, one long-faced little friend of Jimmy's stopped Vennie with the question "How do you mean 'black or white'? Are there black Tollivers?"

"What do you think my name is?" Vennie asked, annoyed by the interruption.

"Your name is Vennie."

"My name's Vennie Tolliver," Vennie said. Her name indeed was Tolliver, since she had once been married to one of the Negro Tollivers at Thornton. The Negro Tollivers, like the Negro Pettigrus and Blalocks, had kept the name of their former masters after emancipation, and most of them had continued in service to the Tollivers. But Vennie's husband, like Flo Dear's, had long before "disappeared off the face of the earth."

The four luncheon guests all broke into laughter because they thought Vennie was joking. Landon and Jimmy laughed, too. But Vance began to blush. His whole face turned red, even the part in his hair changed color. Vennie looked at him a moment in bewilderment, and then suddenly she began to laugh herself. "Didn't you-all know I was kin to Vance?" she said in a shrill voice, which normally was rather deep and hoarse, grew clearer and higher. "Course it ain't really the truth, 'cause I 'uz only *married*, to a sort of cousin of his. But I'm his old Auntie Vennie, all right. Ain't that so, Cousin Landon?"

Landon smiled sweetly and said he guessed it was so. Vennie never did tell her story that day. Under her breath she kept laughing so hard that she couldn't have told if she had tried. And the boys—all but Vance—kept giggling until they finished their dessert and left the table.

Worst of all for Vance was the laughter that night from the grown people. Landon told all about it at the dinner table, right where Vennie could hear every word of it. Vance at first managed to smile halfheartedly, but in the midst of all the talk and laughter he observed that there was no shade of a smile on his Auntie Bet's face. His own halfhearted smile vanished, and he and Auntie Bet exchanged a long look, which—in Vance's mind, at least—may have constituted some sort of pledge between them.

It was Vance, with his sense of what the grown-ups liked, who had invented the pet name Auntie Bet, and he would have said Auntie Flo, except that Flo Dear had discouraged it. Instead, she had asked the boys just to call her Flo Dear, the way their Auntie Bet did. She was ever considerate of Miss Betty's prerogative as a blood relation, despite all of Amy and James's impartiality. In her consideration, she went so far as to try to accept Miss Betty's views of every important thing that happened in the house. When the first complaints against Vennie were made to her by Miss Betty, she tried to admit their justice, while at the same time minimizing their importance. She imagined she saw seeds of Miss Betty's ruin in the struggle, and events pointed more and more in that direction.

By Miss Betty's "ruin" she didn't mean that Vennie would remain and Miss Betty would go, she knew that Vennie would finally be sent away, but Miss Betty's ruin would lie in her very condescension to this struggle and in the means she would use to dispose of Vennie. If only Flo Dear could delay action on Miss Betty's part, then soon enough Vennie would be discharged for reasons that wouldn't involve anyone else, because Flo Dear knew, without listening at the hot-air register in the shut-off cardroom downstairs, that if Vennie entertained and cooked on her magic stove for the boys in her basement rooms, she also entertained and cooked for a large number of those colored people, or their like, whose pictures hung on her walls, and the food, of course, all came out of Amy's kitchen. She knew there would be a last time for Amy's saying, "My grocery bills are outrageous! I don't understand where the leak is. That is, I'm not sure yet."

Miss Betty's complaints were not all of indirect thrusts through the boys and the other servants, for after Bert and Emmaline had been neutralized, Vennie began, herself, a series of personal affronts. If Miss Betty crossed the threshold of the kitchen, she put down whatever she was doing and retired to the basement. If the two were about to meet in the narrow hall or on the stairs, Vennie would turn back and manage to get out of sight before Miss Betty could call her. Miss Betty did try to call to her sometimes, or at least to speak to her—there was a period when she imagined it was not too late to make friends and join forces with her adversary—but Vennie would have none of it. At last, Miss Betty trapped her one day in the pantry and said, "Why don't you and I plan a surprise dessert for the family tonight? You make us a cake—one of your good devil's food cakes—and I'll set us up to a wonderful new sort of ice cream they're making at a place I know out on De Baliviere."

Vennie rared back and her voice became shrill: "I been making the ice cream since before you-all came here, and I'll be making it when you and her's both gone."

When Flo Dear heard about this, her heart went out to Miss Betty in a way it seldom did. But she was also frightened by the look in Miss Betty's eyes. Ruin seemed inevitable at that moment—spiritual ruin, or, more specifically, spiritual *relapse*. Flo Dear's life in Nashville had been as quiet as Miss Betty's had been active. She knew that some people in Nashville had called her "Miss Betty Pettigru's silent partner." She had overheard people speaking of her that way, but she had said to herself, "I live this way because I have *chosen* to live this way." It was true that if she had wished, she could have shared all of Miss Betty's activities, for that was what Miss Betty had once hoped she would do. But the choice had been made long before she came to live on West End Avenue. She didn't herself pretend to know when she had made the choice, but it was

made before she ever married Tolliver Blalock and became a
part of his huge family connection. In the big country family
that she was born into, they had always told her she was by
nature a mouse, to which she had replied (silently), "If I am
a mouse, at least I am a principled mouse." But when she was
twenty-two and already considered an old maid, she had been
swept off her feet by Tolliver Blalock, the black sheep of his
family and widely known as a rascal with women. He had left
her after only two months, "disappeared off the face of the
earth," leaving his hat and coat on the bank of the Tennessee
River, more as a sign that he would never return than as any
real pretense that he had drowned. As his widow, Flo Dear was
taken to the bosom of the Tolliver-Pettigru-Blalock connection
as no other in-law ever was. For years, she lived with first one
of her in-laws and then another. They quarreled over who was
to have the privilege next. Apparently there had never been a
mouse in any of those families, or at least not a *silent* mouse,
and they delighted in how she would sit and listen to what *any*
of them said. She listened, and listened especially to the old
ones, and then, one day, thinking it would help her forget for
a while the loneliness and humiliation she felt in the bosom of
her husband's fine family, she sat down and wrote out all she
had heard about their splendid history. As much as anything, it
was to clear her head of the stuff. The manuscript was discovered and she became known as the finest living authority on
the history of the Tollivers, Blalocks, and Pettigrus. After ten
years of this life in the vicinity of Thornton, there came a letter
to her from Miss Betty Pettigru, whose wealthy old father had
taken her up to Nashville in the vain hope of finding her a
suitable husband. Miss Betty was then seeking membership
in the Colonial Dames of America and she wanted Flo Dear's
help in that cause. It ended, of course, by Flo Dear's moving
up to Nashville.

    Searching through Nashville libraries for proof of Miss Bet-
ty's eligibility, Flo Dear found her true vocation, discovered the
one passion of her life. It happened in a single moment. She
was standing—tiny, plain, dish-faced creature that she was—in
the dark and towering library stacks of what is surely the musti-
est, smelliest, dirtiest, ugliest of state capitol buildings in the
Union. In her pawlike little hands she held a book whose faded

title she was trying to read on the mildewed binding. Presently, she opened the book with an impatient jerk. It came open not at the title page but at the plates of two brightly emblazoned fifteenth-century escutcheons. They were the first coats of arms Flo Dear had ever seen, and the beauty of their joyful colors seemed suddenly to illuminate her soul and give her a first taste of the pure joy of being alive. Needless to say, the joy and inspiration she received from her discovery made the matter of talent an unimportant one. In practically no time at all, she became a modern master in the art of blazonry, and by the time she left Nashville, thirty years later, there was hardly a nice house in town on whose walls a piece of her work was not hung.

Flo Dear's work became the absorbing interest of her life. Yet it wasn't entirely her fault or her work's fault that she and Miss Betty could not become "as close as sisters." At first, Flo Dear was guilty of suspecting Miss Betty of disingenuousness. She could not see why Miss Betty made over her so and she felt that she was being "cousined" to death. Outside her profession, Flo Dear soon got so she could not abide the word "cousin." She felt that if she allowed it, Miss Betty would smother her with confidences. More than her time, somehow her small supply of energy seemed to disappear when she listened to her cousin. She simply could not afford the intimacy and dependency that was being asked of her.

There was more explanation than this: When old Major Pettigru was on his deathbed, he had said to Miss Betty, who was his only child, "It's a shame and a scandal, Bet. Since I brought you to Nashville, you've expended your time making a place for yourself among strongheaded women while you ought to have been making your place in the heart of some gentle, honest man." He had said that to her in the presence of two doctors and a nurse, and so almost immediately it had become known all over town. To most people it was an amusing story, but not to Flo Dear. She felt, exactly as Major Pettigru had, that Miss Betty had expended foolishly not merely her time but her invaluable, marvelous energy as well. Perhaps, with her unprepossessing appearance and her lack of small talk, finding a husband was not feasible for Miss Betty, but something— surely *something*—better than a life of social climbing could be found. It was worse than a shame and a scandal in Flo

Dear's eyes; it was a sin. She had never told Miss Betty in so many words, but she knew that Miss Betty acknowledged in her heart that she was right. Else why had Miss Betty always made a point of matching every social victory with some act of charity? When she succeeded in having Mrs. John O'Neil Smith impeached as madam president of the Corrine Society (for having sat down to dinner with the president of a Negro college), she immediately gave a formal luncheon for the homeliest, least eligible debutante of the season. After she had blackballed every candidate for membership in the West End Book Club until the other members accepted an ambitious but illiterate satellite of her own, she paid a formal call on a notorious lady in town and went about saying that she, for one, thought that that lady's "adopted" child looked nothing in the world like its foster mother. Surely, in Nashville, Miss Betty's life had been all sin and expiation, but with never a resolution to sin no more.

"They have big get-togethers down there," Vance said.

"Big get-togethers?" said Miss Betty.

"Yes, ma'am. Sometimes there's a whole crowd and sometimes not so many. We used to always listen to them through the radiator in here, till we got tired of it. Listen! That's Vennie's cousin who works out at the Florisant Valley Club. He's from Thornton, too, and used to work for us. Listen to them! They think they're whispering now. But you can hear them just as plain."

"Yes, you can almost hear them breathing," said Auntie Bet.

"And they can't hear you at all unless you really holler."

Vance and his Auntie Bet were in the cardroom, behind the drawing room. It was a room that Amy kept shut off, because she and James were not cardplayers and it was only another room for Bert to keep clean. It was a tiny room, and the furniture had been left there by the former occupants. There was a built-in game cabinet with a dozen different size pigeonholes and compartments, and a "stationary card table," and some chairs. It all went with the house, the former occupants had said.

It was a Sunday afternoon and Vance and Auntie Bet were playing checkers. He had come back from a long walk in the park and had found her arranging some flowers in a vase on the hall table. When he invited her to go with him to the cardroom and have a game of checkers, she looked at him wonderingly, because she could tell that he had something on his mind. When they began to play, it occurred to her that perhaps the boys weren't supposed to play games like checkers on Sunday. And in the *cardroom*, too. Then she began to notice the Negro voices coming through the hot-air register in the corner of the room. She was so distracted by her thoughts and by those voices that almost before she knew it, the game was over and she was badly beaten.

"Oh, you weren't even trying, Auntie Bet," said Vance.

She smiled—or, rather turned up the corners of her mouth self-consciously. "I tried, but I got to listening to the Negroes' voices in the radiator," she said. "We must be right above Vennie's living room." And then Vance told her about the get-togethers down there.

"It's rather eerie, isn't it?" she said. "I mean how we can hear their voices and they can't hear ours."

Vance began arranging the checkers for a new game. "Sometime," he said, not looking at her, "you might just come in here—you and Flo Dear, that is—when Jimmy and Landon and I are down in Vennie's rooms." He raised his eyes and said in a grave, reflective tone of voice, "Auntie Bet, that Vennie says the darnedest things to us children. You should just hear her."

"Why *what*, Vance?" But before he could answer, Miss Betty had suddenly understood what sort of plot he was suggesting, and she abruptly got up from the table.

Vance instantly grew pale. "What's the matter, Auntie Bet?"

"Nothing's the matter, my darling," she said. "But I—I left half my flowers out of water." She was opening the door into the drawing room, but she glanced back at Vance and saw him still sitting with the checkerboard before him and with the bare light of the overhead lamp shining on his black hair, which looked rather too soft and too thick for a boy, and on the mottled complexion of his forehead, on the widespread nares of his nose. And silently Miss Betty Pettigru was saying to the oldest of her three Tolliver nephews, "Poor wounded, frightened child! What thoughts have you had of me? What thoughts?"

As she passed through the hall, she was surprised to see that she had indeed left some of her flowers lying on the big console table. She had bought them at a florist's on the way home from church that morning but had waited till Vennie left the kitchen to select her vase and arrange them. She snatched the flowers from the table and went upstairs.

In her room, she dropped the flowers in her wastebasket and, without taking off her daintily pleated dress, she lay down across the bed. This time, she was not pacing the floor after fifteen or twenty minutes. She was still lying there when Flo Dear called her to go down to supper.

As she lay on her bed this Sunday afternoon, she thought of the life she had left in Nashville. Her life there had never in her eyes been one of sin and expiation. It had just been life, plain and simple, where you did what good things you could and what bad things you must. As she looked back, it seemed that it had been hard for her to decide to leave Nashville only because it had meant facing the fact of the worthlessness of the goal she had set herself many years before—the goal set *for* her, really, by circumstances and by her personal limitations. What else could she have done with her life? She had not asked to be born in the days when Victoria was queen of England, when Southern womanhood was waited upon not by personal maids but by personal slaves. She had not asked to be born the unbeautiful, untalented heiress of a country family's fortune, or to grow up to find that the country town that gave that fortune its only meaning was decaying and disappearing, even in a physical sense. The men of her generation, and of later generations, had gone to Nashville, Memphis, Louisville, and even St. Louis, and had used their heads, their connections, and their genteel manners to make their way to the top in the new order of things. And wasn't that all *she* had done, and in the only way permissible for a Miss Pettigru from Thornton? Once the goal was defined, was it necessary that she should be any less ruthless than her male counterparts? In her generation, the ends justified the means. For men, at least, they did. Now, at last, Miss Betty saw how much like a man's life her own had been. She saw it in the eyes of the wounded, frightened child. She saw how it was that every day of her adult life had made her less a woman instead of more a woman. Or less somebody's old granny instead of more somebody's old granny. Wrong though it seemed, the things a man did to win happiness in the world—or in the only world Miss Betty knew—were of no consequence to the children he came home to at night, but every act, word, and thought of a woman was judged by and reflected in the children, in the husband, in all who loved her. "If only Flo Dear had not been so embittered before she even came to my house," Miss Betty thought miserably, "maybe my instincts would not have died so dead."

She had done nothing to bring on Vennie's dismissal, and yet Vance had seen that she was capable of doing that something and had thought she might enter into a conspiracy with little children in the house of her kinspeople. If he condemned old Vennie for saying things to "us children" that she ought not to say, what thoughts must he have of *her*? All was lost, and in the morning she would go—not back to Nashville but perhaps to Thornton itself.

Flo Dear knocked on Miss Betty's door from the hall. "It's almost supper time," she said.

"Well, I'll be along soon," Miss Betty answered, not suggesting that Flo Dear open the door and come in.

"It's Bert's Sunday on," Flo Dear reminded her, "and Amy and James are going out to dinner."

Its being Bert's Sunday on meant that Bert would prepare and serve the cold supper and that someone must check closely to see that he washed the lettuce for the salad and that the table was set properly. Amy and James's going out to dinner meant that the check on Bert would be Miss Betty and Flo Dear's responsibility.

Flo Dear inferred from Miss Betty's being alone for so long in her room that there had been another incident. She had heard Miss Betty come upstairs an hour earlier, and although she had put down her book, her mind had wandered more than once from the subject of heraldic symbolism to all the incidents of recent weeks. Miss Betty had managed to make it plain enough to her, in the way she reported the incidents, that Vennie's antagonism was directed equally at both of them. It was really Flo Dear, wasn't it, Miss Betty had asked her one day, that Vennie had made fun of to the boys and their Wednesday guests? During all their thirty years together, Flo Dear felt, this was the first deliberate unkindness Miss Betty had shown her. Yet she interpreted it as a "sign of nerves." It was so unreasonable that she could not really resent it. It was as though Miss Betty expected *her* to do something about Vennie. Even in Nashville, Miss Betty had never tried to involve *her* in her petty wars with womankind. She stood outside Miss Betty's door now, shaking her head and saying to herself, "Well, it can't go on. It can't go on. We must leave. We must leave Amy and James and their children to their peace. If we can't go back to Nashville, we—or I—can go back to Thornton." But the very thought of that prospect made Flo Blalock clasp her hands and shudder inwardly. Spending her last days among the remnants of the Tolliver-Blalock-Pettigru clan! Moving from garrulous house to garrulous house! She, the pitiable woman whom one of them had wronged. She hurried along the hall, past the room where Amy and James were dressing, down the stairs, and into the dining room to see how things were going with Bert. The light was on, but there were not even place mats on the table yet. "I declare," she whispered, "that Negro Bert is not worth his salt." She went into the pantry and into the kitchen, but one of the gas jets of the stove was burning, though no pot or pan was on the stove, or even a coffeepot.

And then, through the backdoor and vestibule, she heard Bert's footsteps on the cement driveway. She stepped to the backdoor and saw him, in his white coat, coming through the twilight from the garage—the old carriage house, where he had his room, in the coachman's loft. She could see that he saw her, and that he hesitated. "What's the matter, Bert?" she asked.

He came on up the steps. He was a tall, brown-skinned Negro and walked with a peculiar gait. Amy said he picked his feet up slewfoot and put them down pigeon-toed. As he came inside the door, he pretended to laugh. "You know what I done, Miss Flo? When I left out of here, I aimed to turn off the stove, but I turned off the light instead." He switched on the light and went to the table where the coffeepot and the open coffee can were sitting.

"And now you've left the light on in your room." She was still looking out toward the garage.

"Is I now?" He was filling the coffeepot.

Flo Dear was trembling. When she spoke, she hoped her voice would sound like Miss Betty's or Amy's or James's, or Vennie's, or *anybody's* but her own. "Somebody's out there, Bert, who hasn't any business out there. Is that so, Bert?"

Bert put the coffeepot on the stove and then looked at Miss Flo, but not in his usual simple big-eyed way. "Yes, ma'am, they is. It's Vance."

Flo Dear couldn't find the words she wanted, but she continued to stare at Bert, and she knew that even with just a stare she was taking a hand in things. And now Bert, too, knew that she was taking a hand, and when he saw that, every last bit of foolishness seemed to go out of his face.

"I'm just going to tell you about it, Miss Flo," he said. "Vance came down here in the kitchen and he was crying around and wanted to talk to me. He said he had hurt Miss Betty's feelings and wouldn't never git over it, and he was scared to talk to his daddy or Miss Amy about it. He wanted to go out yonder to my old rooms to talk with me, so I just taken him on out there, Miss Flo, and he and me had it all out. He'll be along in the house directly."

Flo Dear sat down on a chair beside the table. "Tell me how he hurt Miss Betty's feelings, Bert."

Bert, looking right into Miss Flo's eyes, stood before her and told her how Vance had got Miss Betty to go in the cardroom and all they had said there and finally how Miss Betty wouldn't really listen to Vennie and her company and wouldn't "be conniving with any little old Vance."

When he had finished, Flo Dear made no move to go. "You begin setting the table, Bert," she said. "I want to just sit here awhile."

Amy and James came downstairs in evening clothes. They were going first to a cocktail party and then to a large supper party honoring the debutante daughter of two of their friends. They knew that Miss Betty always liked to see them when they were "dressed," particularly if they were going out among people whom she considered "prominent in an important way."

Amy went to the dining-room door to see if the two ladies were in there. Bert was just beginning to set the table. "You're late getting started with that, Bert," she said.

"Yes'm, ain't I, though? I got behind." He was all big-eyed simpleness again.

"Well, have you gotten Mr. James's car out?"

"Yes'm, it's at the side."

"Hasn't Miss Betty or Miss Flo come down?"

"Miss Flo's back here," he said, and he dashed off toward the kitchen. Amy stood watching the swinging door until Flo Dear appeared.

"How lovely you look, Amy," said Flo Dear, coming into the dining room. "Nothing so becomes you as green, Amy." Compliments from her were rare but not unheard of. Such compliments on Amy's appearance were Miss Betty's prerogative, but now and then, when Miss Betty was not present, Flo Dear would say something like this.

"Why, I thank you, Flo Dear," Amy said. "A compliment from you really sets me up. You're not the wicked flatterer Aunt Betty is."

"She's just more articulate than I, Amy."

"Pooh," said Amy, turning back into the hall. "Where is she, anyway?"

"Here she comes from upstairs now," James said. He was standing near the foot of the stairs, his derby on his head, his overcoat over one arm and Amy's white *lapin* wrap over the other.

"Take off your hat in the house, James," Amy said. "What will your aunts think of you?"

"It's time we're going," James said, holding up Amy's wrap for her.

"Do wait and let me see Amy's dress," called Miss Betty from the stairs, rather spiritlessly.

The others looked up at her. "Aunt Betty, you don't sound like yourself," Amy said.

"I've been taking a nap," she said. "You look lovely, Amy. It's a stunning dress."

Amy's dress was of a dark green silk, with a long waist, a very low back, and a hemline just at her knees. Her hair was not bobbed, but tonight she had it arranged in a way that made it at first glance look so.

"She looks sixteen, doesn't she?" said Flo Dear.

Suddenly Amy called out, "Boys! Boys! We're going!"

Landon and Jimmy came racing down from upstairs, and in a moment Vance appeared in the doorway from the dining room, looking solemn and dejected. Miss Betty went to him and put an arm about his shoulders.

"If you boys behave and mind your aunts," James Tolliver said, getting into his coat, "I'll take you to East St. Louis with me next Saturday. I'm going out to see old Mr. Hendricks at the stockyards."

Jimmy was standing on the bottom step of the stairs. Partly, no doubt, because he didn't like to go to East St. Louis but mostly because he wished to satisfy his thirst for scientific truth, he asked, "Why do you say 'our aunts' when Flo Dear is not our aunt or even related to us and Auntie Bet isn't really our aunt, either?"

Jimmy's mother and father looked at him as though he had spoken an obscenity. "Jim, are you asking to be punished?" his father said. "Do you want me to take you upstairs in my dress clothes and punish you?"

Amy dropped her velvet evening bag on the console table and sat down in one of the high-backed hall chairs. This was her usual way of saying she wouldn't go somewhere until the boys stopped misbehaving. It was also a way of emphasizing her speechlessness. After a moment, she said, "Just what do you mean by that, James? What earthly power made you ask that?"

Flo Dear glanced at Miss Betty and saw that she had managed to catch Vance's eye and was shaking her head at him warningly. Jimmy was blushing and carefully avoiding the eyes of the aunts. He kept looking first at his mother and then at Landon. After a moment, Landon, who was always the one most moved by his mother's threats, said to Jimmy, "Go ahead and tell, Jimmy. It's just Vennie, and she always says she doesn't care who you tell." Then, turning to his mother, he said, "Vennie's always saying we aren't a bit of kin to Flo Dear, and not much to Auntie Bet. And she thinks they ought not to live with us unless they are close kin."

But Jimmy still had not told when his father pulled the derby off his head and was saying, "You boys—all of you—get upstairs to your rooms and get up there quick."

The three boys were upstairs and in their rooms almost before their father had taken off his overcoat. He removed the coat with great care and folded the sleeves and the collar as though he were about to pack it in a traveling bag. Then he handed it and his derby to Amy.

"Oh, James," said Miss Betty in a hoarse whisper, "don't punish the boys."

"I'm not going to punish the boys," he said. "I'm going downstairs before I leave this house and give Amy's notice to Vennie."

"No," Miss Betty said, "don't do that, James!"

But Amy said, "Tell her she needn't ever come up in the house again."

"I'll meet you at the car, Amy," he said to her, and as he went out through the dining room, he called back, "I'll tell Bert to stay in the house all evening, till we come home."

When he was gone, Amy tried to smile. "I don't know why he couldn't wear his overcoat to fire Vennie," she said. "A sign of special respect, I suppose."

Miss Betty, wearing a dazed expression, said, "This won't do, Amy. It just won't do."

"Oh, it'll do fine, Aunt Betty," said Amy. "Don't you think I know what's been going on in my own house? It was James who had to be shown. He has been Vennie's protector since long before this business. And Emmaline and Bert both gave me notice a week ago; I've been sick about it. Why, for a house-boy, you just can't beat that simpleminded Bert. No, my dears, Vennie's days of usefulness in this house are past. Her superannuation is long overdue."

Supper for Miss Betty and Flo Dear and the boys was delayed for three quarters of an hour that Sunday night. Bert was an eternity getting the food on the table, but none of them was hungry, and so it did not matter. Not long after their parents were out of the house, Vance and his brothers came downstairs and into the living room, where the two aunts were sitting together. But before the boys came down, Flo Dear and Miss Betty had exchanged a few words, and each had had a great many thoughts that were not exchanged, at least not in words.

They were seated directly opposite each other on either side of the fireplace, in two little Windsor chairs that were the only uncomfortable chairs in the room. Last embers of the usual Sunday fire were smoldering in the wood ashes between the andirons. When first they sat down, there was a long silence, with each of them staring into the embers, watching an occasional flame spring up and then die almost at once. Miss Betty's small, pudgy nose seemed swollen and her eyes were two glazed buttons. She sat with her feet placed far apart, her ankles looking swollen like her nose, and on her knees her hands rested, the ten fingers spread out like so many wrinkled little sausages. Flo Dear sat crossing and uncrossing her narrow ankles, fingering the buttons that ran from the high neck to the waist of her dress, and blinking her eyes at the fire.

At last, without changing her expression or moving a muscle of her body, Miss Betty said, "We should go on back to Nashville, I think, Flo Dear, or maybe to Thornton." She wanted to tell Flo Dear that she had had no hand in Jimmy's outburst, but it would be useless and somehow not entirely truthful to say that. Yet at the very moment she was saying that they must leave and thinking that they must, she was also thinking that if they could stay, if they could only stay, she might, with her new insight, begin to be of some use to the Tolliver boys. After all, they were rich children, just as she had been a rich child, and the world was still changing, preparing people for one thing and giving them another. And poor little Vance—what problems would be his! Not excelling in his schoolwork, certainly not good-looking, with only that one terrible talent that she, too, had—the talent for observing what things the world valued and making the most of *that*.

But she knew that she could not spend the last years of her life with Flo Dear sitting there so straight in the Windsor chair, accusing her with every crossing of her slim ankles and every blinking of her narrow eyes.

All that Flo Dear said before the boys came down was "We must do whatever seems the right thing to you and the best thing for the boys." From this, Miss Betty took hope. She detected a new softness in Flo Dear's voice. It was a softness that must have come from Flo Dear's own reassessment of things. Whether it was the thought of Thornton or her thoughts in the dark kitchen or the knowledge that Miss Betty had been truly hurt by Vance's proposal, something was making her question her old judgments of Miss Betty Pettigru. It seemed to her that perhaps to do anything at all in the world was to do wrong to *someone*. She thought of Vennie and of what would become of her now. Perhaps it was fair and just that Miss Betty should have the affection the boys gave to Vennie. Perhaps Vennie had nieces and nephews of her own. She could go and live with them or with some of her many friends. There must be many of her relatives who loved and needed old Vennie. And yet perhaps she didn't really have a family of her own. Or perhaps none of them would find her so lovable and attractive when she no longer had this good job and could make them presents and cook them meals on her little coal range. But already Flo Dear could hear Vance and Jimmy and Landon coming down the stairs into the hall.

When the boys came into the living room, with their hair combed and wearing fresh shirts, Miss Betty and Flo Dear stood up and greeted their nephews as though it were after long months of separation. And the boys seemed equally glad to see their aunts. There was even kissing and hugging, and there were some tears shed. Supper was still not on the table, and though Miss Betty complained about Bert's being "so mortally slow," Flo Dear did not say again that he wasn't worth his salt. Instead, she gathered the three boys about her chair and commenced explaining to them, as no one else in the world was so well qualified to do, just exactly what her family connection was to them, and in even greater detail she described the blood ties that existed between them and their Auntie Bet. There was a certain hollowness in her voice, and as she spoke she stared somewhat vacantly into the dying embers of the Sunday fire. The boys, however, did not notice any of this. They listened attentively to the facts she was presenting, as though they were learning life's most important lessons.

For a while, Miss Betty watched this scene with tears in her eyes. But then she went and lay down on the sofa. It would be no more protracted visit to St. Louis; she was here for life. And when, finally, Bert announced supper, Vance had to go and touch Auntie Bet's hand to wake her from a deep, dreamless slumber.

What You Hear from 'Em?

S OMETIMES PEOPLE misunderstood Aunt Munsie's question, but she wouldn't bother to clarify it. She might repeat it two or three times, in order to drown out some fool answer she was getting from some fool white woman, or man, either. "What you hear from 'em?" she would ask. And, then, louder and louder: "What you hear from 'em? *What you hear from 'em?*" She was so deaf that anyone whom she thoroughly drowned out only laughed and said Aunt Munsie had got so deaf she couldn't hear it thunder.

It was, of course, only the most utterly fool answers that ever received Aunt Munsie's drowning-out treatment. She was, for a number of years at least, willing to listen to those who mistook her "'em" to mean any and all of the Dr. Tolliver children. And for more years than that she was willing to listen to those who thought she wanted just *any* news of her two favorites among the Tolliver children—Thad and Will. But later on she stopped putting the question to all insensitive and frivolous souls who didn't understand that what she was interested in hearing—and *all* she was interested in hearing—was when Mr. Thad Tolliver and Mr. Will Tolliver were going to pack up their families and come back to Thornton for good.

They had always promised her to come back—to come back sure enough, once and for all. On separate occasions, both Thad and Will had actually given her their word. She had not seen them together for ten years, but each of them had made visits to Thornton now and then with his own family. She would see a big car stopping in front of her house on a Sunday afternoon and see either Will or Thad with his wife and children piling out into the dusty street—it was nearly always summer when they came—and then see them filing across the street, jumping the ditch, and unlatching the gate to her yard. She always met them in that pen of a yard, but long before they had jumped the ditch she was clapping her hands and calling out, "Hai-ee! Hai-ee, now! Look-a-here! Whee! Whee! Look-a-here!" She had got so blind that she was never sure whether it was Mr. Thad or Mr. Will until she had her arms around his waist. They had always looked a good deal alike, and their

274

city clothes made them look even more alike nowadays. Aunt
Munsie's eyes were so bad, besides being so full of moisture on
those occasions, that she really recognized them by their girth.
Will had grown a regular wash pot of a stomach and Thad was
still thin as a rail. They would sit on her porch for twenty or
thirty minutes—whichever one it was and his family—and then
they would be gone again.

Aunt Munsie would never try to detain them—not seriously.
Those short little old visits didn't mean a thing to her. He—
Thad or Will—would lean against the banister rail and tell
her how well his children were doing in school or college, and
she would make each child in turn come and sit beside her on
the swing for a minute and receive a hug around the waist or
shoulders. They were timid with her, not seeing her any more
than they did, but she could tell from their big Tolliver smiles
that they liked her to hug them and make over them. Usually,
she would lead them all out to her back yard and show them her
pigs and dogs and chickens. (She always had at least one frizzly
chicken to show the children.) They would traipse through her
house to the back yard and then traipse through again to the
front porch. It would be time for them to go when they came
back, and Aunt Munsie would look up at *him*—Mr. Thad or
Mr. Will (she had begun calling them "Mr." the day they married)—and say, "Now, look-a-here. When you comin' back?"

Both Thad and Will knew what she meant, of course, and
whichever it was would tell her he was making definite plans
to wind up his business and that he was going to buy a certain piece of property, "a mile north of town" or "on the old
River Road," and build a jim-dandy house there. He would
say, too, how good Aunt Munsie's own house was looking, and
his wife would say how grand the zinnias and cannas looked
in the yard. (The yard was all flowers—not a blade of grass,
and the ground packed hard in little paths between the flower
beds.) The visit was almost over then. There remained only the
exchange of presents. One of the children would hand Aunt
Munsie a paper bag containing a pint of whiskey or a carton
of cigarettes. Aunt Munsie would go to her back porch or to
the pit in the yard and get a fern or a wandering Jew, potted in
a rusty lard bucket, and make Mrs. Thad or Mrs. Will take it
along. Then the visit was over, and they would leave. From the

porch Aunt Munsie would wave goodbye with one hand and lay the other hand, trembling slightly, on the banister rail. And sometimes her departing guests, looking back from the yard, would observe that the banisters themselves were trembling under her hand—so insecurely were those knobby banisters attached to the knobby porch pillars. Often as not Thad or Will, observing this, would remind his wife that Aunt Munsie's porch banisters and pillars had come off a porch of the house where he had grown up. (Their father, Dr. Tolliver, had been one of the first to widen his porches and remove the ginger-bread from his house.) The children and their mother would wave to Aunt Munsie from the street. Their father would close the gate, resting his hand a moment on its familiar wrought-iron frame, and wave to her before he jumped the ditch. If the children had not gone too far ahead, he might even draw their attention to the iron fence which, with its iron gate, had been around the yard at the Tolliver place till Dr. Tolliver took it down and set out a hedge, just a few weeks before he died.

But such paltry little visits meant nothing to Aunt Munsie. No more did the letters that came with "her things" at Christmas. She was supposed to get her daughter, Lucrecie, who lived next door, to read the letters, but in late years she had taken to putting them away unopened, and some of the presents, too. All she wanted to hear from *them* was when they were coming back for good, and she had learned that the Christmas letters never told her that. On her daily route with her slop wagon through the square, up Jackson Street, and down Jefferson, there were only four or five houses left where she asked her question. These were houses where the amount of pig slop was not worth stopping for, houses where one old maid, or maybe two, lived, or a widow with one old bachelor son who had never amounted to anything and ate no more than a woman. And so—in the summertime, anyway—she took to calling out at the top of her lungs, when she approached the house of one of the elect, "What you hear from 'em?" Sometimes a Miss Patty or a Miss Lucille or a Mr. Ralph would get up out of a porch chair and come down the brick walk to converse with Aunt Munsie. Or sometimes one of them would just lean out over the shrubbery planted around the porch and call, "Not a thing, Munsie. Not a thing lately."

She would shake her head and call back, "Naw. Naw. Not a thing. Nobody don't hear from 'em. Too busy, they be."

Aunt Munsie's skin was the color of a faded tow sack. She was hardly four feet tall. She was generally believed to be totally bald, and on her head she always wore a white dust cap with an elastic band. She wore an apron, too, while making her rounds with her slop wagon. Even when the weather got bad and she tied a wool scarf about her head and wore an overcoat, she put on an apron over the coat. Her hands and feet were delicately small, which made the old-timers sure she was of Guinea stock that had come to Tennessee out of South Carolina. What most touched the hearts of old ladies on Jackson and Jefferson Streets were her little feet. The sight of her feet "took them back to the old days," they said, because Aunt Munsie still wore flat-heeled, high button shoes. Where ever did Munsie find such shoes any more?

She walked down the street, down the very center of the street, with a spry step, and she was continually turning her head from side to side, as though looking at the old houses and trees for the first time. If her sight was as bad as she sometimes let on it was, she probably recognized the houses only by their roof lines against the Thornton sky. Since this was nearly thirty years ago, most of the big Victorian and ante-bellum houses were still standing, though with their lovely gingerbread work beginning to go. (It went first from houses where there was someone, like Dr. Tolliver, with a special eye for style and for keeping up with the times.) The streets hadn't yet been broadened—or only Nashville Street had—and the maples and elms met above the streets. In the autumn, their leaves covered the high banks and filled the deep ditches on either side. The dark macadam surfacing itself was barely wide enough for two automobiles to pass. Aunt Munsie, pulling her slop wagon, which was a long, low, four-wheeled vehicle about the size and shape of a coffin, paraded down the center of the street without any regard for, if with any awareness of, the traffic problems she sometimes made. Seizing the wagon's heavy, sawed-off-looking tongue, she hauled it after her with a series of impatient jerks, just as though that tongue were the arm of some very stubborn, overgrown white child she had to nurse in her old age. Strangers in town or trifling high-school boys would blow their horns at her, but she was never known to so much as glance over her shoulder at the sound of a horn. Now and then a pedestrian on the sidewalk would call out to the driver of an automobile, "She's so deaf she can't hear it thunder."

It wouldn't have occurred to anyone in Thornton—not in those days—that something ought to be done about Aunt Munsie and her wagon for the sake of the public good. In those days, everyone had equal rights on the streets of Thornton. A vehicle was a vehicle, and a person was a person, each with the right to move as slowly as he pleased and to stop where and as often as he pleased. In the Thornton mind, there was no imaginary line down the middle of the street, and, indeed, no one there at that time had heard of drawing a real line on *any* street. It was merely out of politeness that you made room for others to pass. Nobody would have blown a horn at an old colored woman with her slop wagon—nobody but some Yankee stranger or a trifling high-school boy or maybe old Mr. Ralph Hadley in a special fit of temper. When citizens of Thornton were in a particular hurry and got caught behind Aunt Munsie, they leaned out their car windows and shouted: "Aunt Munsie, can you make a little room?" And Aunt Munsie didn't fail to hear *them*. She would holler, "Hai-ee, now! Whee! Look-a-here!" and jerk her wagon to one side. As they passed her, she would wave her little hand and grin a toothless, pink-gummed grin.

Yet, without any concern for the public good, Aunt Munsie's friends and connections among the white women began to worry more and more about the danger of her being run down by an automobile. They talked among themselves and they talked to her about it. They wanted her to give up collecting slop, now she had got so blind and deaf. "Pshaw," said Aunt Munsie, closing her eyes contemptuously. "Not me." She meant by that that no one would dare run into her or her wagon. Sometimes when she crossed the square on a busy Saturday morning or on a first Monday, she would hold up one hand with the palm turned outward and stop all traffic until she was safely across and in the alley beside the hotel.

Thornton wasn't even then what it had been before the Great World War. In every other house there was a stranger or a mill hand who had moved up from Factory Town. Some of the biggest old places stood empty, the way Dr. Tolliver's had until it burned. They stood empty not because nobody wanted to rent them or buy them but because the heirs who had gone off somewhere making money could never be got to part with "the home place." The story was that Thad Tolliver nearly went crazy when he heard their old house had burned, and wanted to sue the town, and even said he was going to help get the Republicans into office. Yet Thad had hardly put foot in the house since the day his daddy died. It was said the Tolliver house had caught fire from the Major Pettigru house, which had burned two nights before. And no doubt it had. Sparks could have smoldered in that roof of rotten shingles for a long time before bursting into flame. Some even said the Pettigru house might have caught from the Johnston house, which had burned earlier that same fall. But Thad knew and Will knew and everybody knew the town wasn't to blame, and knew there was no firebug. Why, those old houses stood there empty year after year, and in the fall the leaves fell from the trees and settled around the porches and stoops, and who was there to rake the leaves? Maybe it was a good thing those houses burned, and maybe it would have been as well if some of the houses that still had people in them burned, too. There were houses in Thornton the heirs had never left that looked far worse than the Tolliver or the Pettigru or the Johnston house ever had. The people who lived in them were the ones who gave Aunt Munsie the biggest fool answers to her question, the people whom she soon quit asking her question of or even passing the time of day with, except when she couldn't help it, out of politeness. For, truly, to Aunt Munsie there were things under the sun worse than going off and getting rich in Nashville or in Memphis or even in Washington, D.C. It was a subject she and her daughter Lucrecie sometimes mouthed at each other about across their back fence. Lucrecie was shiftless, and she liked shiftless white people like the ones who didn't have the ambition to leave Thornton. She thought their shiftlessness showed they were *quality*. "Quality?" Aunt Munsie would echo, her voice full of sarcasm. "Whee! Hai-ee! You talk like *you* was *my* mammy, Crecie. Well, if there be quality, there be quality *and* quality. There's quality and there's *has-been* quality, Crecie."

There was no end to that argument Aunt Munsie had with Crecie, and it wasn't at all important to Aunt Munsie. The people who still lived in those houses—the ones she called has-been quality—meant little more to her than the mill hands, or the strangers from up North who ran the Piggly Wiggly, the five-and-ten-cent store, and the roller-skating rink.

There was this to be said, though, for the has-been quality: they knew *who* Aunt Munsie was, and in a limited, literal way they understood what she said. But those *others*—why, they thought Aunt Munsie a beggar, and she knew they did. They spoke of her as Old What You Have for Mom, because that's what they thought she was saying when she called out, "What you hear from 'em?" Their ears were not attuned to that soft "r" she put in "from" or the elision that made "from 'em" sound to them like "for Mom." Many's the time Aunt Munsie had seen or sensed the presence of one of those *other* people, watching from next door, when Miss Leonora Lovell, say, came down her front walk and handed her a little parcel of scraps across the ditch. Aunt Munsie knew what they thought of her—how they laughed at her and felt sorry for her and despised her all at once. But, like the has-been quality, they didn't matter, never had, never would. Not ever.

Oh, they mattered in a way to Lucrecie. Lucrecie thought about them and talked about them a lot. She called them "white trash" and even "radical Republicans." It made Aunt Munsie grin to hear Crecie go on, because she knew Crecie got all her notions from her own has-been-quality people. And so it didn't matter, except that Aunt Munsie knew that Crecie truly had all sorts of good sense and had only been carried away and spoiled by such folks as she had worked for, such folks as had really raised Crecie from the time she was big enough to run errands for them, fifty years back. In her heart, Aunt Munsie knew that even Lucrecie didn't matter to her the way a daughter might. It was because while Aunt Munsie had been raising a family of white children, a different sort of white people from hers had been raising her own child, Crecie. Sometimes, if Aunt Munsie was in her chicken yard or out in her little patch of cotton when Mr. Thad or Mr. Will arrived, Crecie would come out to the fence and say, "Mama, some of your chillun's out front."

Miss Leonora Lovell and Miss Patty Bean, and especially Miss Lucille Satterfield, were all the time after Aunt Munsie to give up collecting slop. "You're going to get run over by one of those crazy drivers, Munsie," they said. Miss Lucille was the widow of old Judge Satterfield. "If the Judge were alive, Munsie," she said, "I'd make him find a way to stop you. But the men down at the courthouse don't listen to the women in this town any more. Not since we got the vote. And I think they'd be most too scared of you to do what I want them to do." Aunt Munsie wouldn't listen to any of that. She knew that if Miss Lucille had come out there to her gate, she must have *something* she was going to say about Mr. Thad or Mr. Will. Miss Lucille had two brothers and a son of her own who were lawyers in Memphis, and who lived in style down there and kept Miss Lucille in style here in Thornton. Memphis was where Thad Tolliver had his Ford and Lincoln agency, and so Miss Lucille always had news about Thad, and indirectly about Will, too.

"Is they doin' any good? What you hear from 'em?" Aunt Munsie asked Miss Lucille one afternoon in early spring. She had come along just when Miss Lucille was out picking some of the jonquils that grew in profusion on the steep bank between the sidewalk and the ditch in front of her house.

"Mr. Thad and his folks will be up one day in April, Munsie," Miss Lucille said in her pleasantly hoarse voice. "I understand Mr. Will and his crowd may come for Easter Sunday."

"One day, and gone again!" said Aunt Munsie.

"We always try to get them to stay at least one night, but they're busy folks, Munsie."

"When they comin' back sure enough, Miss Lucille?"

"Goodness knows, Munsie. Goodness knows. Goodness knows when any of them are coming back to stay." Miss Lucille took three quick little steps down the bank and hopped lightly across the ditch. "They're prospering so, Munsie," she said, throwing her chin up and smiling proudly. This fragile lady, this daughter, wife, sister, mother of lawyers (and, of course, the darling of all their hearts), stood there in the street with her pretty little feet and shapely ankles close together, and holding a handful of jonquils before her as if it were her bridal

bouquet. "They're *all* prospering so, Munsie. Mine *and* yours.
You ought to go down to Memphis to see them now and then,
the way I do. Or go up to Nashville to see Mr. Will. I understand he's got an even finer establishment than Thad. They've
done well, Munsie—yours *and* mine—and we can be proud
of them. You owe it to yourself to go and see how well they're
fixed. They're rich men by our standards in Thornton, and
they're going farther—*all* of them."

Aunt Munsie dropped the tongue of her wagon noisily on
the pavement. "What I want to go see 'em for?" she said angrily
and with a lowering brow. Then she stooped and, picking up
the wagon tongue again, she wheeled her vehicle toward the
middle of the street, to get by Miss Lucille, and started off
toward the square. As she turned out into the street, the brakes
of a car, as so often, screeched behind her. Presently everyone
in the neighborhood could hear Mr. Ralph Hadley tooting the
insignificant little horn on his mama's coupé and shouting at
Aunt Munsie in his own tooty voice, above the sound of the
horn. Aunt Munsie pulled over, making just enough room to
let poor old Mr. Ralph get by but without once looking back
at him. Then, before Mr. Ralph could get his car started again,
Miss Lucille was running along beside Aunt Munsie, saying,
"Munsie, you be careful! You're going to meet your death on
the streets of Thornton, Tennessee!"

"Let 'em," said Aunt Munsie.

Miss Lucille didn't know whether Munsie meant "Let 'em
run over me; I don't care" or meant "Let 'em just dare!" Miss
Lucille soon turned back, without Aunt Munsie's ever looking
at her. And when Mr. Ralph Hadley did get his motor started,
and sailed past in his mama's coupé, Aunt Munsie didn't give
him a look, either. Nor did Mr. Ralph bother to turn his face
to look at Aunt Munsie. He was on his way to the drugstore,
to pick up his mama's prescriptions, and he was too entirely put
out, peeved, and upset to endure even the briefest exchange
with that ugly, uppity old Munsie of the Tollivers.

Aunt Munsie continued to tug her slop wagon on toward
the square. There was a more animated expression on her face
than usual, and every so often her lips would move rapidly and
emphatically over a phrase or sentence. Why should she go to
Memphis and Nashville and see how rich they were? No matter

how rich they were, what difference did it make; they didn't own any land, did they? Or at least none in Cameron County. She had heard the old Doctor tell them—tell his boys and tell his girls, and tell the old lady, too, in her day—that nobody was rich who didn't own land, and nobody stayed rich who didn't see after his land firsthand. But of course Aunt Munsie had herself mocked the old Doctor to his face for going on about land so much. She knew it was only something he had heard his own daddy go on about. She would say right to his face that she hadn't ever seen *him* behind a plow. And was there ever anybody more scared of a mule than Dr. Tolliver was? Mules or horses, either? Aunt Munsie had heard him say that the happiest day of his life was the day he first learned that the horseless carriage was a reality.

No, it was not really to own land that Thad and Will ought to come back to Thornton. It was more that if they were going to be rich, they ought to come home, where their granddaddy had owned land and where their money counted for something. How could they ever be rich anywhere else? They could have a lot of money in the bank and a fine house, that was all—like that mill manager from Chi. The mill manager could have a yard full of big cars and a stucco house as big as you like, but who would ever take him for rich? Aunt Munsie would sometimes say all these things to Crecie, or something as nearly like them as she could find words for. Crecie might nod her head in agreement or she might be in a mood to say being rich wasn't any good for anybody and didn't matter, and that you could live on just being quality better than on being rich in Thornton. "Quality's better than land or better than money in the bank here," Crecie would say.

Aunt Munsie would sneer at her and say, "It never were."

Lucrecie could talk all she wanted about the old times! Aunt Munsie knew too much about what they were like, for both the richest white folks and the blackest field hands. Nothing about the old times was as good as these days, and there were going to be better times yet when Mr. Thad and Mr. Will Tolliver came back. Everybody lived easier now than they used to, and were better off. She could never be got to reminisce about her childhood in slavery, or her life with her husband, or even about those halcyon days after the old Mizziz had died and Aunt Munsie's word had become law in the Tolliver household. Without being able to book read or even to make numbers, she had finished raising the whole pack of towheaded Tollivers just as the Mizziz would have wanted it done. The Doctor told her she *had* to—he didn't ever once think about getting another wife, or taking in some cousin, not after his "Molly darling"—and Aunt Munsie *did*. But, as Crecie said, when a time was past in her mama's life, it seemed to be gone and done with in her head, too.

Lucrecie would say frankly she thought her mama was "hard about people and things in the world." She talked about her mama not only to the Blalocks, for whom she had worked all her life, but to anybody else who gave her an opening. It wasn't just about her mama, though, that she would talk to anybody. She liked to talk, and she talked about Aunt Munsie not in any ugly, resentful way but as she would about when the sheep-rains would begin or where the fire was last night. (Crecie was twice the size of her mama, and black the way her old daddy had been, and loud and good-natured the way he was—or at least the way Aunt Munsie wasn't. You wouldn't have known they were mother and daughter, and not many of the young people in town did realize it. Only by accident did they live next door to each other; Mr. Thad and Mr. Will had bought Munsie her house, and Crecie had heired hers from her second husband.) *That* was how she talked about her mama—as she would have about any lonely, eccentric, harmless neighbor. "I may be dead wrong, but I think Mama's kind of hardhearted," she would say. "Mama's a good old soul, I reckon, but when something's past, it's gone and done with for Mama. She don't think about day before yestiddy—yestiddy, either. I don't know, maybe that's the way to be. Maybe that's why the old soul's gonna outlive us all." Then, obviously thinking about what a picture of health she herself was at sixty, Crecie would toss her head about and laugh so loud you might hear her all the way out to the fair grounds.

Crecie, however, knew her mama was not honest-to-God mean and hadn't ever been mean to the Tolliver children, the way the Blalocks liked to make out she had. All the Tolliver children but Mr. Thad and Mr. Will had quarreled with her for good by the time they were grown, but they had quarreled with the old Doctor, too (and as if they were the only ones who shook off their old folks this day and time). When Crecie talked about her mama, she didn't spare her anything, but she was fair to her, too. And it was in no hateful or disloyal spirit that she took part in the conspiracy that finally got Aunt Munsie and her slop wagon off the streets of Thornton. Crecie would have done the same for any neighbor. She had small part enough, actually, in that conspiracy. Her part was merely to break the news to Aunt Munsie that there was now a law against keeping pigs within the city limits. It was a small part but one that no one else quite dared to take.

"They ain't no such law!" Aunt Munsie roared back at Crecie. She was slopping her pigs when Crecie came to the fence and told her about the law. It had seemed the most appropriate time to Lucrecie. "They ain't never been such a law, Crecie," Aunt Munsie said. "Every house on Jackson and Jefferson used to keep pigs."

"It's a brand-new law, Mama."

Aunt Munsie finished bailing out the last of the slop from her wagon. It was just before twilight. The last, weak rays of the sun colored the clouds behind the mock orange tree in Crecie's yard. When Aunt Munsie turned around from the sty, she pretended that that little bit of light in the clouds hurt her eyes, and turned away her head. And when Lucrecie said that everybody had until the first of the year to get rid of their pigs, Aunt Munsie was in a spell of deafness. She headed out toward the crib to get some corn for the chickens. She was trying to think whether anybody else inside the town still kept pigs. Herb Mallory did—two doors beyond Crecie. Then Aunt Munsie remembered Herb didn't pay town taxes. The town line ran between him and Shad Willis.

That was sometime in June, and before July came, Aunt Munsie knew all there was worth knowing about the conspiracy. Mr. Thad and Mr. Will had each been in town for a day during the spring. They and their families had been to her house and sat on the porch; the children had gone back to look at her half-grown collie dog and the two hounds, at the old sow and her farrow of new pigs, and at the frizzliest frizzly chicken Aunt

Munsie had ever had. And on those visits to Thornton, Mr. Thad and Mr. Will had also made their usual round among their distant kin and close friends. Everywhere they went, they had heard of the near-accidents Aunt Munsie was causing with her slop wagon and the real danger there was of her being run over. Miss Lucille Satterfield and Miss Patty Bean had both been to the mayor's office and also to see Judge Lawrence to try to get Aunt Munsie "ruled" off the streets, but the men in the courthouse and in the mayor's office didn't listen to the women in Thornton any more. And so either Mr. Thad or Mr. Will—how would which one of them it was matter to Munsie?—had been prevailed upon to stop by Mayor Lunt's office, and in a few seconds' time had set the wheels of conspiracy in motion. Soon a general inquiry had been made in the town as to how many citizens still kept pigs. Only two property owners besides Aunt Munsie had been found to have pigs on their premises, and they, being men, had been docile and reasonable enough to sell what they had on hand to Mr. Will or Mr. Thad Tolliver. Immediately afterward—within a matter of weeks, that is—a town ordinance had been passed forbidding the possession of swine within the corporate limits of Thornton. Aunt Munsie had got the story bit by bit from Miss Leonora and Miss Patty and Miss Lucille and others, including the constable himself, whom she did not hesitate to stop right in the middle of the square on a Saturday noon. Whether it was Mr. Thad or Mr. Will who had been prevailed upon by the ladies she never ferreted out, but that was only because she did not wish to do so.

The constable's word was the last word for her. The constable said yes, it was the law, and he admitted yes, he had sold his own pigs—for the constable was one of those two reasonable souls—to Mr. Thad or Mr. Will. He didn't say which of them it was, or if he did, Aunt Munsie didn't bother to remember it. And after her interview with the constable, Aunt Munsie never again exchanged words with any human being about the ordinance against pigs. That afternoon, she took a fishing pole from under her house and drove the old sow and the nine shoats down to Herb Mallory's, on the outside of town. They were his, she said, if he wanted them, and he could pay her at killing time.

It was literally true that Aunt Munsie never again exchanged words with anyone about the ordinance against pigs or about the conspiracy she had discovered against herself. But her daughter Lucrecie had a tale to tell about what Aunt Munsie did that afternoon after she had seen the constable and before she drove the pigs over to Herb Mallory's. It was mostly a tale of what Aunt Munsie said to her pigs and to her dogs and her chickens.

Crecie was in her own back yard washing her hair when her mama came down the rickety porch steps and into the yard next door. Crecie had her head in the pot of suds, and so she couldn't look up, but she knew by the way Mama flew down the steps that there was trouble. "She come down them steps like she was wasp-nest bit, or like some young'on who's got hisself wasp-nest bit—and her all of eighty, I reckon!" Then, as Crecie told it, her mama scurried around in the yard for a minute or so like she thought Judgment was about to catch up with her, and pretty soon she commenced slamming at something. Crecie wrapped a towel about her soapy head, squatted low, and edged over toward the plank fence. She peered between the planks and saw what her mama was up to. Since there never had been a gate to the fence around the pigsty, Mama had taken the wood ax and was knocking a hole in it. But directly, just after Crecie had taken her place by the plank fence, her mama had left off her slamming at the sty and turned about so quickly and so exactly toward Crecie that Crecie thought the poor, blind old soul had managed to spy her squatting there. Right away, though, Crecie realized it was not *her* that Mama was staring at. She saw that all Aunt Munsie's chickens and those three dogs of hers had come up behind her, and were all clucking and whining to know why she didn't stop that infernal racket and put out some feed for them.

Crecie's mama set one hand on her hip and rested the ax on the ground. "Just look at yuh!" she said, and then she let the chickens and the dogs—and the pigs, too—have it. She told them what a miserable bunch of creatures they were, and asked them what right they had to always be looking for handouts from her. She sounded like the boss-man who's caught all his

pickers laying off before sundown, and she sounded, too, like
the preacher giving his sinners Hail Columbia at camp meeting. Finally, shouting at the top of her voice and swinging the
ax wide and broad above their heads, she sent the dogs howling
under the house and the chickens scattering in every direction.
"Now, g'wine! G'wine widja!" she shouted after them. Only
the collie pup, of the three dogs, didn't scamper to the farthest
corner underneath the house. He stopped under the porch
steps, and not two seconds later he was poking his long head
out again and showing the whites of his doleful brown eyes.
Crecie's mama took a step toward him and then she halted.
"You want to know what's the commotion about? I reckoned
you would," she said with profound contempt, as though the
collie were a more reasonable soul than the other animals, and
as though there were nothing she held in such thorough disre-
spect as reason. "I tell you what the commotion's about," she
said. "They *ain't* comin' back. They ain't never comin' back.
They ain't never had no notion of comin' back." She turned her
head to one side, and the only explanation Crecie could find
for her mama's next words was that that collie pup did look so
much like Miss Lucille Satterfield.

"Why don't I go down to Memphis or up to Nashville and
see 'em sometime, like *you* does?" Aunt Munsie asked the collie.
"I tell you why. Becaze I ain't nothin' to 'em in Memphis, and
they ain't nothin' to me in Nashville. *You* can go!" she said,
advancing and shaking the big ax at the dog. "A collie dog's
a collie dog anywhar. But Aunt Munsie, she's just their Aunt
Munsie here in Thornton. I got mind enough to see *that*." The
collie slowly pulled his head back under the steps, and Aunt
Munsie watched for a minute to see if he would show himself
again. When he didn't, she went and jerked the fishing pole
out from under the house and headed toward the pigsty. Crecie
remained squatting beside the fence until her mama and the
pigs were out in the street and on their way to Herb Mallory's.

That was the end of Aunt Munsie's keeping pigs and the end
of her daily rounds with her slop wagon, but it was not the
end of Aunt Munsie. She lived on for nearly twenty years after
that, till long after Lucrecie had been put away, in fine style,

by the Blalocks. Ever afterward, though, Aunt Munsie seemed different to people. They said she softened, and everybody said it was a change for the better. She would take paper money from under her carpet, or out of the chinks in her walls, and buy things for up at the church, or buy her own whiskey when she got sick, instead of making somebody bring her a nip. On the square she would laugh and holler with the white folks the way they liked her to and the way Crecie and all the other old-timers did, and she even took to tying a bandanna about her head—took to talking old-nigger foolishness, too, about the Bell Witch, and claiming she remembered the day General N. B. Forrest rode into town and saved all the cotton from the Yankees at the depot. When Mr. Will and Mr. Thad came to see her with their families, she got so she would reminisce with them about their daddy and tease them about all the silly little things they had done when they were growing up: "Mr. Thad—him still in kilts, too—he says, 'Aunt Munsie, reach down in yo' stockin' and git me a copper cent. I want some store candy.'" She told them about how Miss Yola Ewing, the sewing woman, heard her threatening to bust Will's back wide open when he broke the lamp chimney, and how Miss Yola went to the Doctor and told him he ought to run Aunt Munsie off. Then Aunt Munsie and the Doctor had had a big laugh about it out in the kitchen, and Miss Yola must have eavesdropped on them, because she left without finishing the girls' Easter dresses.

Indeed, these visits from Mr. Thad and Mr. Will continued as long as Aunt Munsie lived, but she never asked them any more about when they were sure enough coming back. And the children, though she hugged them more than ever— and, toward the last, there were the children's children to be hugged—never again set foot in her back yard. Aunt Munsie lived on for nearly twenty years, and when they finally buried her, they put on her tombstone that she was aged one hundred years, though nobody knew how old she was. There was no record of when she was born. All anyone knew was that in her last years she had said she was a girl helping about the big house when freedom came. That would have made her probably about twelve years old in 1865, according to her statements and depictions. But all agreed that in her extreme old age Aunt Munsie, like other old darkies, was not very reliable about dates and such things. Her spirit softened, even her voice lost some of the rasping quality that it had always had, and in general she became not very reliable about facts.

Bad Dreams

THE OLD Negro man had come from somewhere in West Tennessee, though certainly not from the Tollivers' hometown. Mr. James Tolliver had simply run across him in downtown St. Louis and had become obligated or attached to him somehow. For two or three years, Mr. James had kept him as a hand around his office there, no doubt believing every day he would discover some real use for him. Then one evening, without a word to his wife or to anybody else, he brought the old fellow home with him and installed him in an empty room above the garage.

Actually, this was likely to make little difference to Mrs. James Tolliver, whom everybody called Miss Amy. It would concern Miss Amy hardly at all, since the old fellow was clearly not the house-servant type. He might do for a janitor (which was Mr. James's plan) or even a yardman (under Mr. James's close supervision), and he could undoubtedly pick up odd jobs in the neighborhood. But his tenure of the room above the garage was bound to go almost unnoticed by Miss Amy and by her three half-grown sons and two elderly female relatives. They would hardly know he was on the place. They hardly knew the room he would occupy was on the place. Yet during the first few minutes after his arrival the old Negro must have supposed that Miss Amy was a nervous and exacting fussbudget and that every member of the family had a claim on that unoccupied servant's room above the garage.

The Tollivers' garage, having been designed originally as a carriage house and stable, was of remarkable amplitude. When the Tollivers' two Lincolns were in their places at night, there was space enough for two more cars of the same wonderful length and breadth. And on the second floor, under the high mansard roof, the stairway opened onto an enormous room, or area, known as the loft room, in one end of which there was still a gaping hay chute, and from the opposite end of which opened three servant's rooms. The Tollivers' housemaid, Emmaline, and her husband, Bert, shared with their infant daughter a suite of two rooms and bath. The third room had

been unoccupied for several years and was furnished only with
an iron bedstead and a three-legged chest of drawers.

It happened that Emmaline was in her quarters on that late
afternoon in October when Mr. James arrived with the old
Negro. Her husband, who was houseboy and butler, was in
the house setting the table for dinner, and she herself had just
hurried out for one reassuring glance at their four-month-old
baby, for whom they had not yet agreed upon a name. When
the sounds of Mr. James's car reached her ears, Emmaline was
in the room with the sleeping baby. She had no idea that anything unusual was astir, but at the first sound of the Lincoln
motor she began moving away from the baby bed and toward
the door to the loft room. It was almost dark, but, craning her
neck and squinting her eyes, she gave a last loving and protec-
tive look toward the dark little object in its cagelike bed. Then
she went out, closing the door behind her. She had taken only
two steps across the rough flooring of the wide, unlighted loft
room when she saw Mr. James ascending the stairs, followed by
an old Negro man whom she had never seen before.

The Negro man halted at the top of the steps to get his
breath, and, catching the sight of Emmaline, he abruptly jerked
the tattered felt hat from his head. Emmaline, at the same
moment, commenced striding with quickened step toward him
and Mr. James.

"Is that somebody you aim to put up out here, Mr. James?"
she asked in a loud and contentious whisper as she approached
the two men.

"Is there no electric light in this room?" Mr. James said
sternly.

He had heard Emmaline's question distinctly enough, and
she knew that he was not pretending he had not. Mr. James
was, after all, Emmaline and Bert's landlord, the master of the
house where they worked, and a Tolliver of the preeminent
Tolliver family of Thornton, Tennessee, where she and Bert
were born, and this was merely his way of saying that he did not
desire to have any conversation with her about the old fellow.
But why didn't he? What could it be, Emmaline asked herself.
Then the truth about the whole situation came to her, and as
she recognized the true picture of what was happening now
and of what, indeed, had been happening for several months

past, she began uttering a volley of objections that had no relation to any truth: Why, now, Mr. James ought to have given Miss Amy some warning of this, oughtn't he? Miss Amy was going to be right upset, wasn't she, being taken by surprise, with Mr. James's moving somebody or other into her good storeroom where she was planning to put the porch furniture any week now? And besides, weren't the two old aunts expecting some of their antiques sent up from Tennessee? And where else *could* the aunts store their antiques? And wasn't it a shame, too, how crazy about playing in that room James, Jr., and little Landon always had been? Why, the room was half full of basketballs and bows and arrows and bowie knives this minute unless the boys had moved them this very day!

She was addressing this collection of untruths not to Mr. James but frankly to the old Negro, who stood with his hat in one hand and a knotty bundle of clothes under the other arm. The old man gave no sign either that he recognized Emmaline's hostility or that he really believed his moving in would cause a great stir in the family. He stood at the top of the steps gazing with respect at the great, dark, unceiled loft room, as though it might be a chapel of some kind. So little, his manner seemed to say, such a one as he knew about even the loft rooms of the rich.

Mr. James, in the meantime, was walking heavily across the floor in the direction of the empty servant's room. Suddenly Emmaline turned and ran on tiptoe after him. "Mr. James!" she whispered rather frantically.

Mr. James stopped and did a soldierly about-face. "Emmaline," he said, "I want some light in this place."

In a single moment, total darkness seemed to have overcome the loft room. And at that same moment came the waking cry of Bert and Emmaline's baby. With her next step Emmaline abandoned her tiptoeing and began stabbing the floor with her high heels. As she passed Mr. James, she reached one arm into the empty room to switch on a light and said, "Now that's what I been afraid of—that we would go and wake that baby of mine before I help Bert serve supper."

"In here," Mr. James said to the old Negro, and gestured toward the room. "And we'll have you a stove of some sort before winter sets in."

The weak light from inside the bedroom doorway only made the wide loft room seem darker. Mr. James remained completely beyond the reach of the light. "Is there no electrical outlet in this loft room, Emmaline?" he said.

The baby had set up a steady, angry wailing now. "No, sir," Emmaline replied softly.

"In here," Mr. James's voice repeated. This time the words came plainly as an order for the old man to advance. At once there was the sound of the old man's shambling across the rough flooring, and presently there was the sound of Mr. James's heavy footsteps as he went off toward the stairs. Somewhere in the darkness the two men passed each other, but Emmaline knew they made no communication as they passed. She heard Mr. James's firm footsteps as he descended the dark stairs, but still she didn't go to the baby, who was crying now in a less resentful manner. She waited by the open door until the old man came into the light.

"Who are you, old fellow?" she asked when he shuffled past her into the room. "Who are you?" As though who he was were not the thing Emmaline knew best in the world at this moment. As though guessing who the old fellow was hadn't been what gave her, a few minutes before, the full, true picture of what was now happening and what had been happening for several months past. Ever since the baby came, and before too, she had been trying to guess how the Tollivers felt about her and Bert's living here on the place with a baby. Did they want them to get rooms somewhere else? Did they want her to take the baby down to her mama's, in Tennessee, and leave her there? She had talked to Miss Amy about the first plan and then the second, hoping thus to find out just what the Tollivers thought. But Miss Amy had always put her off. "We'll talk about it later, Emmaline, after Mr. James decides what he thinks is best," she would say, or, "I'll have to discuss it with Mr. James some more." Day after day Emmaline had wondered how much talk there had already been about it and what had been said. For some reason it had all seemed to depend on Mr. James.

And now she knew why. Mr. James had been waiting to spring *this* on them. It would be all right about the baby if she and Bert would take on this old granddaddy to look after for as long as they lived. Ah, she and Bert hadn't thought of that! They had known about the old fellow ever since Mr. James first found him, and Bert had seen him a good many times, had even talked to him on various occasions at Mr. James's office. But he was such a dirty, ignorant old fellow that Bert had sheered away from much conversation or friendliness with him. Both Bert and Emmaline had even sheered away from any talk with Mr. James *about* him. They didn't like to have Mr. James connecting them in his mind with such a dirty old ignoramus just because they happened to be colored people.

But here the dirty, ignorant old fellow was, standing in the very room that Emmaline had come to think of as her baby's future nursery. Here he had come—himself to be nursed and someday, no doubt, to die on her hands. She studied the room for a moment, mocking her earlier appraisals of it as a possible nursery. What mere trash all her thoughts had been. When she had not even *known* that she could keep the two rooms she had, she had been counting on a third. She had been going to make the room that the baby slept in now into a sort of living room. Oh, the window-shopping she had already done for living-room furniture! For some reason, the piece she had set her heart on pictured the baby's room, as it would have been—painted the same pink as the old nursery in the Tollivers' house!

Emmaline looked at the room more realistically now than she ever had done before. There was no door connecting it with her and Bert's room, as there was between their room and the baby's. There was but the one door and one small window, and it really wasn't finished nearly so well as the two other servant's rooms. The walls were of rough sheathing, not plaster, and it would be harder to heat. In the neighborhood, there was a German washwoman who had been washing for people hereabouts since long before the Tollivers bought their place, and she had told Emmaline how the coachman used to sleep in this room and how the very finest carriage harness had always hung on the walls there under his protection. The massive hooks, which evidently had held the harness, were still on the walls and they caught Emmaline's eye momentarily. They were the hardware of a barn.

She and Bert were still living, after all, in a barn. And yet she had named this room a nursery. It was the plaster on the walls of her own two rooms that had deceived her. She realized that now, and realized that those rooms might never look the same to her again, just as her life here with Bert and the baby would hardly be the same while this old Tennessee hobo was present to be a part of it—to eat with them in the house (it was bad enough eating with the grouchy, complaining, overpaid cook, Nora Belle) and to share their bathroom (he would have to pass through her very own bedroom to reach the bathroom; she resolved that instant to make him use a chamber and to permit him to empty it only once a day). The ill-furnished bedroom and the old man standing in the center of it, now dropping his bundle on the lumpy mattress, brought back to her all the poverty and nigger life she had known as a girl in Tennessee, before the Tollivers had sent back for her. And this unwashed and ragged old man was like the old uncles and cousins whom she had been taught to respect as a little girl but whom she had learned to despise before she ever left home. While she stared at him, the old man replaced and then removed his hat at least three or four times. Finally, he hung the hat over one of the big harness hooks.

The hat hanging on the wall there seemed an all too familiar sight to Emmaline, and the uncovered head and the whole figure of the man seemed just as infuriatingly familiar. Perhaps she had thought she would never set eyes again on such a shiftless and lousy-looking creature. Certainly she had thought she would never again have to associate such a one with herself and with the place she lived in. His uncut and unkempt white hair was precisely like a filthy dust mop that ought to be thrown out. Even the whites of his eyes looked soiled. His skin was neither brown nor black but, rather (in this light, at least), the same worn-out gray as his overcoat. Though the evening was one in early autumn, and warm for the season, the old fellow wore a heavy overcoat that reached almost to his ankles. One of the coat's patch pockets was gone; the other was torn but was held in place with safety pins and was crammed full of something—probably his spare socks, and maybe his razor wrapped in a newspaper, or a piece of a filthy old towel. God knew what all. The coat was buttonless and hung open, showing the even more disreputable rags he wore underneath. For a moment Emmaline wondered if it was really likely that Mr. James had let the old fellow hang around his office for two or three years looking like that. And then she reflected that it was a fact, and characteristic of Mr. James.

But now the old Negro was hers, hers and Bert's. Miss Amy wouldn't so much as know he was on the place. It was Miss Amy's policy not to know janitors and yardmen existed. And Mr. James—he, too, was out of it now. The final sound of Mr. James's footsteps on the stairs seemed to echo in her ears. The old fellow was nobody's but hers and Bert's.

The baby continued to wail monotonously, and rather dispassionately now, as though only to exercise her lungs. Suddenly, Emmaline said to the old man, "That's *my* baby you hear crying in there." The old man still had not spoken a word. Emmaline turned away from him abruptly. She went first to the door of the room where she and Bert slept, and then to that of the baby's room. She opened each door slightly, fumblingly took the key from the inside, and then closed and locked the door from the loft side. When she had locked both doors and tried them noisily and removed the keys, and while the baby cried on, Emmaline took her leave. She went down the steps, through the garage, and across the yard toward the house. Just before she reached the back porch, she began hurrying her steps. Bert would be wondering what had kept her so long, and she could hardly wait to tell him.

It was nine o'clock. Emmaline had made a half-dozen trips back to see about the baby. At seven-thirty she had offered her breast, and the baby had fed eagerly for several minutes and then dozed off. It was not unusual that Emmaline should make so many trips when the baby was fretful, except that she could usually persuade Bert to go for her at least once or twice to the foot of the steps and listen. Tonight, however, Bert had seemed incapable of even listening to her reports on how the baby was crying—whether "whining sort of puppy-like" or "bawling its lungs out." When she first came in from the garage, he had asked her in his usual carefree, good-natured way if "that little old sweet baby was cutting up." But when she told him about the old fellow's being out there, all the good cheer and animation habitual to Bert seemed to go out of him for a while. In the dining room, he was as lively and foolish-talking as ever when one of the boys said something to him, but in the pantry he listened only absent-mindedly to what she said about the old fellow and not at all to her reports on the baby. Then, as soon as dinner was over and the dishes were brought out, he took off his white coat and, without stopping to eat any supper, lit into the washing of the table dishes in the pantry sink.

At nine o'clock, the two of them went up the steps into the loft room. There was no sound from the baby. They crossed in the darkness to the door of the room where they slept. Emmaline was turning the key in the lock when the door to the old man's room opened. In his undershirt and galluses, and bare-foot, he showed himself in the doorway. Presently, he made a noise like "psst" and beckoned with one hand. Bert went over to him. There was a brief, whispered exchange between them, and Bert returned to where Emmaline was waiting. He told her that the old fellow wanted to use the toilet. Emmaline stepped inside the room and switched on the light. With her finger still on the switch she looked searchingly into Bert's eyes. But his eyes told her nothing. She would have to wait a little longer to learn exactly what was going on in his head.

Then, upon hearing the old man's bare feet padding over the floor of the loft, Emmaline stepped to the door that joined her room to the baby's room, opened it softly, and went in there and waited in the dark, listening to the baby's breathing. She did this not out of any delicacy of feeling but because she felt she could not bear another sight of the dirty old man tonight. When he had been to the toilet and she had heard him go away again, Emmaline went back into their bedroom. She found Bert seated on the bed with one shoe already removed and his fingers casually unlacing the string of the other.

"Is *that* all you care?" she said belligerently. He seemed to be preparing for bed as though nothing extraordinary had happened.

"Just what you mean 'care'?" Bert answered in a whisper.

Emmaline's eyes widened. When Bert whispered, it wasn't for the baby's sake or for anybody else's but because he was resent-ing something some white person had said or done. It was a satisfaction to her to know he was mad, yet at the same time it always roiled her that he whispered at times when her impulse would be to shout. Bert would whisper even if the nearest white person was ten blocks away, and in his mind he always set about trying to weasel out of being mad. She regarded him thoughtfully for a moment. Then she pretended to shift the subject. "Didn't the old fellow ask you for nothing to eat?" she asked. "I thought he would be looking for you to bring him something." She had made herself sound quite casual. Now she moved to the door to the loft room, opened it, took the key from outside, and fitted it into the lock from the inside.

"No use locking that door," Bert said, still in a whisper. "The old fellow says he's got to go to the toilet two or three times before morning, and he don't have any chamber."

Emmaline turned around slowly. "You sound right mad about things, Bert," she said with affected calm.

"What you mean 'mad'?" Bert said, clearing his throat.

He began to smile, but well before he smiled, Emmaline could see that he was no longer mad, that he really hadn't been mad since before they left the house, that his whispering was only a sort of leftover frog in his throat from his having been mad when she first told him.

He proceeded now to pull off his other shoe. He arranged the two highly polished black shoes side by side and then, with the heel of his right foot, pushed them carefully under the bed. And now, since Bert was pigeon-toed, he sat there with the heels of his sock feet nearly a foot apart and his big toes almost touching. Before leaving the house, he had slipped on his white coat again, as protection against the mildly cool night air, because Bert was ever mindful of dangers to his health from the cold. He was perhaps even more mindful of dangers from uncleanliness. The socks on his feet, the sharply creased whipcord trousers, the starched shirt underneath the white coat, all bespoke a personal cleanliness that the symbolic whiteness of the butler's coat could never suggest. "Well, I'll tell you," he said presently, in his naturally loud and cheerful voice. "I *was* mad about it, Emmaline, but I'm not no more."

"*Was* mad about it?" she said, taking a step toward him. The emphasis of his "no more" was somehow irksome to her. "I tell you I *am* mad about it," she said. "And I aim to stay mad about it, Bert. I'm not going to have it."

"Why, no use being mad about it," Bert said. He dropped his eyes to his feet and then looked up again. "No use my being mad about it and no use your getting that crazy-woman look in your eyes about it. Ever since you came over in the house for supper, Emmaline, you been acting your crazy-woman worst." He began laughing deep in his throat. Then he got up from the bed. "Like this," he said. He trotted clownishly about the room, bent forward at the waist, with his eyes sort of popped out. "You been walking around like this." He could nearly always make Emmaline laugh by mimicking her and saying she was a crazy woman. "You been walking around like 'Stracted Mag."

But Emmaline refused to laugh. "It's not so, Bert," she said. "You know it ain't." She didn't want to give in to his resolute cheerfulness. At a time like this, she found his cheerfulness a trial to her soul.

"Why, you been your 'Stracted Mag worst tonight," he said. He went up to her and pretended to jabber wildly in her face. The 'Stracted Mag to whom he referred had been a poor, demented old Negro woman wandering the streets of their hometown when Bert and Emmaline were children, jabbering to everyone, understood by no one, but credited by all with a fierce hatred of the white race.

"Not me," Emmaline said very seriously, backing away from him. "You're the 'Stracted Mag here." It seemed downright perverse of him to be making jokes at such a time, but it was like him. Whenever he was put out of humor, whenever he quarreled with her—usually about the occasional failure to keep their rooms in order, or to keep his clothes in order and clean—or when he complained about some particularly dirty piece of work Miss Amy had set him to, he was always bound and compelled to get around at last to some happy, self-molli-fying view of the matter. He could no more tolerate protracted gloom on any subject, from himself or from anyone else, than he could go for more than an hour without washing his hands. Not, that is, except when he was awakened in the middle of the night. Then Bert wasn't himself. Right now, Emmaline could tell from the way he was acting that he either considered the situation too hopeless to be taken seriously or had already decided what was to be done. Anyhow, he had cooked up some way of looking at it cheerfully.

But Emmaline was not yet ready to accept a cheerful view. She pretended to resent his calling her 'Stracted Mag. "Who *you* to be calling anybody 'Stracted Mag. In *my* day she was giddy and foolish like you, not pop-eyed wild." Emmaline was nearly six years older than Bert and actually they had known each other only slightly in Thornton, their courtship and marriage having taken place after they had come here to work for the Tollivers. "In *my* day," Emmaline said, "she was simple foolish, not wile-eyed crazy."

"Naw! Naw!" Bert said in utter astonishment. "How can you say so?" Her contradiction of the picture he carried of that old Negro woman left Bert absurdly shaken. "How can you say so, Emmaline, when I seen her one time fighting a dog in the street?"

"Oh, I don't reckon you did, sure enough," Emmaline said in a tone she would have used with a child.

"You know I did!" Bert said. "Down on her all fours, in the horse manure, fighting and scrapping with that old spotted dog of Miss Patty Bean's. And it was just because she hated Miss Patty and all them Beans so."

"Well, not in my day," Emmaline insisted, stubbornly and purposefully. She stared straight into Bert's eyes. "In my day, she didn't mix with man nor dog. She muttered and mumbled and kept all to herself." Emmaline evidently knew the exact effect her contradiction was having upon Bert. Like the names of other characters in Thornton, 'Stracted Mag's name was on their lips almost daily and had ceased to be a mere proper noun for her and Bert. It had become a word whose meaning neither of them could have defined, though it was well established between them—a meaning that no other words in their vocabulary could express.

Bert looked at Emmaline reproachfully. He could hardly believe that she would thus tamper with the meaning of a single one of their stock of Thornton words, or even pretend to do so. He felt as he would have felt if she had threatened to deprive him of his sight or hearing by some sort of magic. She could so easily snatch this word from his vocabulary and render him even less able than he was to express his feelings about things in the world. He saw that in order to stop her, he must tell her at once how easy it was going to be to get rid of the old man. Still sitting on the bed, he reached forth and took Emmaline by the arm, just above the wrist. "Come sit down on the bed," he said urgently. "I aim to tell you about the old fellow."

Emmaline took two steps and sat down beside him. With his hand still on her forearm, he felt the tension of her muscles. She *was* her 'Stracted Mag worst tonight! He often told her in a joking way that she was like old Mag, but it was really no joke at all. He knew that many a time Emmaline would have left the Tollivers' service or said something out of the way to one of the old aunts if it had not been for him. Emmaline was a good, hardworking, smart sort of a woman—smarter than most anyone gave her credit for, but at a moment's notice she could get a look so bughouse-wild in her face that you felt you had to talk fast if you were going to keep her calm. Bert's mother had been that sort of woman, too. In fact he felt that most of the women he had ever had much to do with had been that sort; he felt that he had spent no small part of his life keeping Negro women from blurting out their resentment at white people. Emmaline was more easily handled than some, but it was because, after all, she used more sense about what she expected to get out of life than most of her sort did. Like him, she had no illusions about someday leaving domestic service. She accepted as good enough for her the prospect of spending her life in the service of such a family as the Tollivers, provided she did not have to live in the leaking, lean-to-kind of shack she had been brought up in, and provided that in her comfortable quarters she might at the same time be raising a family of her own. She and Bert saw eye to eye on that. Emmaline was smart and she was not an unhandsome woman. She was tall and, though she was a little stooped, her figure was slender and well formed, and proportions of her head and her rather long neck were decidedly graceful. Yet when excited, as she had been tonight, her eyes seemed actually to swell from their sockets, her nostrils would spread until her nose seemed completely flattened, and her heavy lower lip would protrude above her upper lip; at those times her shoulders appeared more stooped than usual, her arms longer, her brown skin darker.

"Look here," Bert was saying. "We going to get shed of that old man. You know that, don't you?"

"What you mean get shed of him?" she asked. There was contention in her voice, but already her eyes showed her satisfaction with what he said.

"I mean he can't stay here with us."

"Who says he can't, Bert?"

"You and me won't let him."

"What we got to do with it, Bert? All I know is we ain't going to stay if he does. Is that what you mean?"

"No!" Bert exclaimed—so loud that the baby stirred in her bed in the next room. "That ain't what I mean. You think we going to vacate here for *him*? Quit the best me or you either has ever had or is like to have?"

Emmaline said, "There's other people in this here very block we could work for—mighty good places, Bert."

"And bring Baby with us?" Because they had not given the baby a name, Bert used "Baby" as a name. "And you know it wouldn't be like working with folks from Thornton."

Emmaline's eyes seemed to swell again. She asked, almost begged, him to tell her. "What we going to do, Bert? He's nasty and ignorant, and living so close. I tell you this—just as sure as Mr. James is a Thornton white man, that old fellow is a Thornton sort of nigger. Maybe where one is there's got to be the other."

"We going to run him off!" Bert said. He had released her arm, but he took it again, and at the same time he began grinning at her. "We going to run him off." He said it with a carefree kind of enthusiasm, as though he were playing a game, said it in a loud voice, as though he were trying to make the old man hear. "Why, we going to run him off just by telling him we don't want him. He'll know what we mean. He'll think we mean worser than we do, and he'll git. And nobody will care."

"Mr. James will care," Emmaline warned.

"Nobody will care enough to stop us. I studied it out while I was washing dishes," he said. "Mr. James has done done all he's about to do for that old man. He allows he's fixed things so we'll be afraid *not* to look after the old man and keep him. But Mr. James's not going to do no more than that. I can tell by the way you said he walked off across the floor of the loft room. Mr. James is through and done with the old fellow. He can say to himself now that he done what he could. But both him and Miss Amy thinks heaps more of us and having us wait on them than to be letting us go because we run off such as him. Oh, Lord, we'll run him off all right."

Emmaline felt fully reassured, and her eyes seemed to have sunk back into their sockets. But she asked quietly, "How?" She could hear the old man snoring in his room and she could hear the baby beginning to whimper. But before she got up to go to the baby, she repeated, "How?"

Bert laughed under his breath. "We'll just tell him to git, and he'll git."

"When, Bert?"

"Well, tomorrow," Bert said thoughtfully. "And not the day after, either. We'll scare him off while we're new to him, and he'll think we're worser than we know how to be. He's lived hard, and with harder folks than you and me, Emmaline."

When Emmaline brought the baby in on her shoulder a few minutes later, her features were composed again, and Bert was humming softly to himself. He had removed his white coat and his shirt and had hung them on hangers in the big ward-robe beside the bed. At the sight of the baby, he commenced talking a baby talk that was incomprehensible even to Emmaline. But Emmaline beamed and let him snatch the baby from her in mock roughness. Uttering a steady stream of almost consonantless baby talk, he first threw the baby a few inches in the air, and then danced about the room with her—in his sock feet, whipcord trousers, and gleaming-white undershirt. Finally, the baby's dark, screwed-up little face relaxed into the sweetest of smiles.

"Don't wake her up no more than need be, Bert," Emmaline protested feebly. "She ain't slept half her due all day."

Bert let himself fall across the bed on his back, holding the baby at arm's length above him. Now with his muscular brown arms he was bringing the baby down to his face and then raising her again like a weight. Each time her laughing little face touched his own, Bert would say, "Timmy-wye-ea! Timmy-wye-ea!" And the meaning of this Emmaline, for sufficient reason, did understand. It was Bert's baby talk for "Kiss me right here."

Later on, after the baby had fed at Emmaline's breast and had been sung to sleep on her shoulder, she was put down in her own bed in the dark room. Then Bert and Emmaline were not long in retiring. After their light was out, they lay in bed talking for a while, though not once mentioning the old man, whose intermittent snoring they heard from the next room. As they so often did, they went to sleep debating what name they should give the baby. They could never agree (probably the baby would be called Baby all her life), but neither did they ever fully disagree about the appropriateness of the various possible names. They went off to sleep pronouncing softly to one another some of the possibilities: Amy Amelia, Shirley Elizabeth, Easter May, Rebecca Jane.

They were awakened by a terrible shrieking—a noise wild enough to be inhuman, and yet unmistakably human. Emmaline sprang from her bed and ran through the darkness to the baby's crib. So swift and unfaltering were her steps that as she reached her hands into the crib, she imagined that Bert mightn't yet be fully awake. She even muttered to herself, "I pray God he ain't." Yet in the next awful moment, when she would have caught up the baby—except that she found no baby there—the thought that Bert might be still asleep seemed the worst, last terror her heart could ever know. Searching the empty crib with her hands, she screamed Bert's name. Her voice came so shrill and loud it caused a painful sensation in her own ears.

And Bert, who all the while stood in the darkness only a few inches from her, and with the baby in his arms, raged forth at her out of the darkness, "God, woman! Goddamn, woman! You want to make your baby deaf? You yell at me like that again, woman, and I'll knock you flat on the floor." It was Bert in his worst midnight temper.

His own movements had been swifter than Emmaline's. He had even had to open the door between the rooms, yet had arrived so far ahead of Emmaline that he was holding the baby in his arms by the time her hands began searching the crib.

Perhaps he had awakened a moment before she had. It seemed
to both of them that they were already awake when the baby
cried out, and at first neither had believed it could be *their* baby
making such a noise. The two of them had come, as on one
impulse, simply to make sure about the baby. All of this, of
course, they revealed to each other much later; at the moment
they stood in the dark cursing each other.

"You'll knock *who* flat on the floor?" Emmaline cried in a
voice only a trifle less shrill and less loud than that in which
she had called Bert's name. "Give me that baby of mine!" she
demanded. She felt about for the light switch. When she found
it, she was asking, "You'll knock who flat on the floor, you
bastardy, black son of Ham?" But when the light came on, her
voice and her words changed, and so, no doubt, did her whole
face. She saw Bert, clad in his immaculately white pajamas,
holding on his shoulder the tiny, woolly-headed baby, clad in
its white cotton nightgown. Beads of sweat shone on the brown
skin of Bert's forehead. His wide, brown hands held firmly to
the little body that was squirming incessantly on his shoulder.
And in the first moment of light, Emmaline saw Bert throwing
his head back in order to look into the baby's face.

Emmaline moved toward Bert with outstretched arms.
"Honey," she said in a new voice, "hand me m'baby. Let me
have her, Bert."

Bert let her take the baby from him. He, too, seemed to have
been changed by the light. "Something's wrong with her," he
said. "She ain't made a sound since I picked her up." His eyes
were now fixed on the little face. "Look at her eyes, Emmaline!" The baby's dark eyes were fairly bulging from her head,
and she was gasping tearfully for breath. "I think your baby's
dying, Emmaline," Bert said.

Emmaline seized the baby and began patting her gently
up and down the spine. This soon restored the baby's breath
somewhat and allowed her to begin shrieking again. Emmaline walked from one room to the other, and then back again.
Back and forth she walked, talking quietly to the baby, patting
her between the shoulder blades or sometimes gently stroking
her little body. Meanwhile, Bert followed at Emmaline's heels,
trying to peer over her shoulder into the baby's face. At last the
baby left off shrieking, and began crying in a more normal way.

At this change, Bert went to the bathroom and washed his face and hands in cold water. When he returned, he said impatiently, "What's got in her?"

"She's sick somehow, Bert," Emmaline said. Though the baby had stopped shrieking, still she was crying passionately and with no hint of abatement.

"Maybe she's hungry," Bert suggested in a voice of growing impatience.

"I just tried her while you was in the bathroom and she wouldn't take it," Emmaline said. Then she said, "Oh, Lord," and by this she meant to say it was bad enough worrying over the baby without Bert's having one of his real fits of midnight anger. She thought of stories she had heard, as a girl, of men whipping their babies when they cried at night, whipping them to death sometimes. "Let him try!" she said to herself, but it didn't quiet her fears. Also, she now thought she heard sounds coming from the old man's room. She had forgotten his presence there until now. What if he should take this time to go to the toilet? . . . Bert would kill him.

All at once she knew for a certainty that the old man *would* come in. Oh, Bert would kill him when he came! Or there would be such an awful fight somebody would hear them in the house and Mr. James would come out and maybe shoot Bert with that little pistol he kept on his closet shelf. All she could see before her eyes was blood. And all the time she was pacing the floor, from the baby's room, where the light was on, to her and Bert's room, where there was no light except that which came through the open doorway.

"Someway you've got to stop her," Bert said, putting his hands over his ears. He nearly always woke when the baby cried at night, but the crying had never been like this before, had never begun so suddenly or with such piercing shrieks.

"I *is* trying to stop her, Bert, but I can't," Emmaline said excitedly. "You go on back to bed, Bert."

He sat down on the side of the bed and watched Emmaline walking and listened to the baby's crying. Once he got up and went to the dresser to peer at the face of the alarm clock. It was a quarter to one. "Aw, she's hungry and don't know it," he said after a while. "You *make* her take something. It's time she's fed."

Emmaline sat down in the big wicker rocking chair in the baby's room, slipped off the strap of her nightgown, and tried to settle the baby to her breast. But the baby pushed away and commenced thrashing about, throwing her head back and rolling her eyes in a frightening way. Now Emmaline began to sob. "The baby's sick, Bert," she said. "She's afire with fever, she is."

"Let me walk her some," Bert said, coming into the lighted room.

"Oh, don't hurt her, Bert," Emmaline pleaded. "Don't hurt her."

"Why, I ain't going to hurt no little baby," Bert said, frowning. "I ain't going to hurt Baby. You know that, Emmaline." As he took the baby, his wife saw the look of concern in his eyes. He was no longer in his midnight temper—not for the time being at least. Or, anyway, he was out of the depths of it.

But Emmaline sat in the rocking chair sobbing while Bert walked with the baby from one room to the other. Finally, he stopped before her and said, "You cut out your crying—she ain't got much fever I can feel. Something's ailing her, and she's sick all right, but your carrying on don't help none."

In the far room Emmaline could hear the old man knocking about, as though he were in the dark. He was looking for the light, she thought. And she thought, Bert can hear him too. Suddenly she wailed, "If the baby's sick, Bert, then why ain't you gone to the house to get somebody to—"

"To get somebody?" Bert shouted back at her. "What in hell do you mean?"

"To get some of them to call a doctor, Bert."

"Go wake Mr. James to call a doctor?" Now the baby began shrieking as at the outset, but Bert shouted above the shrieking. "On top of him sending that old fellow—"

"Then go out and find a doctor. Get dressed and go out and find us a doctor somewheres." She was on her feet and wresting the baby from Bert.

Bert stood nodding his head, almost smiling, in a sudden bewilderment. Then he went into the other room and took his shirt off the coat hanger. He was leaning over the dresser drawer to get out clean underwear when Emmaline heard the unmistakable sound of their door from the loft room opening. The sound came at a moment when the baby had completely lost her breath again. Emmaline commenced shaking the baby violently. "Oh, Lord! Oh, Lord God!" she cried out. She was standing in the doorway between the two rooms. Bert looked over his shoulder. She thought at first he was looking at her, but then she saw he was looking at the shadowy figure in the other doorway.

Now the baby's gasping for breath claimed Emmaline's attention again. But even so, the shadow of a question fell across her mind: Did Bert keep his knife in the drawer with his underwear? It was a needless question she asked herself, however.

She could see that Bert was smiling at the old man. "Our baby's sick." But at the moment the words meant nothing to her. There, in her arms, the baby seemed to be gagging. And then Emmaline felt her baby being jerked away from her. It happened so quickly that she could not even try to resist. She saw Bert springing to his feet. Then she beheld the dirty old man holding the baby upside down by her feet, as he would have held a chicken. Among the shadows of the room he was somehow like another shadow. Barefoot and shirtless, he gave the effect of being totally naked except for some rather new-looking galluses that held up his dark trousers. A naked-looking, gray figure, he stood holding the baby upside down and shaking her until her nightgown fell almost over her head, exposing her white diaper and her black, heaving little stomach.

Emmaline felt all the strength go out of her body, and it seemed to her that she was staggering blindly about, or falling. Indistinctly, as though from a great distance, she heard the voices of the two men. The old man's voice was very deep and—she resisted such a thought—was a voice fraught with kindliness. Presently, Emmaline realized that Bert was standing by her with his arm about her waist, and the baby was crying softly in the old man's arms.

"But something *sure* must be ailing her," Bert was saying quietly. He was talking about the baby and didn't seem to realize that though Emmaline had remained on her feet, she had lost consciousness for a moment. "She don't yell like that, and she *woke up* yelling bloody murder," Bert said.

The old man smiled. He was gap-toothed, and the few teeth he had were yellow-brown. "Bad dreams," he said. "Bad dreams is all. I reckon he thought the boogeyman after him."

Bert laughed good-naturedly. "I reckon so," he said, looking at Emmaline. He asked her if she was all right, and she nodded. "How come we didn't suppose it was bad dreams?" he asked, smiling. "It just didn't come to us, I reckon. But what could that little baby have to dream about?" He laughed again, trying to imagine what the baby could have to dream about.

Emmaline stared at Bert. At some point, he had woken up all the way and had become himself as he was in the daytime. She had a feeling of terrible loss for a moment, and the next moment was one of fear.

What if Bert *had* straightened up and turned away from the dresser drawer with his knife in his hand? Yet it wasn't that question that frightened her. It was another. Why had she tried to start Bert on his way to get a doctor? She wasn't sure, and she knew she would never be sure, whether it was really to get a doctor, or to get him away before the old man came into the room, or to get him to that drawer where he kept his knife before the old man came in. Now, in a trembling voice, she said, "Let me have the baby."

The baby had stopped crying altogether. All signs of hysteria were gone. She sniffled now and then and caught her breath, but she had forgotten her nightmare and forgotten how frightened and quarrelsome her parents' voices had sounded a short while before. In the half-darkness of the room, her eyes were focused on the buckle of one of the old man's galluses.

Emmaline came forward and took the baby, who, though she seemed sorry to leave the old man, was now in such a happy frame of mind that she made not a whimper of objection. On Emmaline's shoulder, she even made soft little pigeonlike speeches.

It was during this time, while the baby cooed in her mother's arms, that Bert and Emmaline and the old man stood staring at one another in silence, all three of them plainly absorbed in thoughts of their own. It was only for a moment, for soon the old man asked to be allowed to hold the baby again. Emmaline felt that she could not refuse him. She told him that the baby was not a boy but a girl, that they had not yet named her, but that Bert usually just called her plain Baby; and then she let the baby go to the old man. Whatever other thoughts she and

Bert were having, they both were so happy to have found the baby wasn't the least bit sick, after all, that they were content to stand there awhile contemplating the good spirits the old man had put her in. The baby changed hands several times, being passed to Bert, then to Emmaline, and then back to the old man. Finally, she began to fret.

"Now she's hungry," the old man said with authority.

There could be no doubt that that was what this sort of fretting meant. Emmaline automatically stepped up and took the baby from him. She went into the lighted room where the crib was and closed the door. As she sat down in the wicker rocking chair and gave the baby her breast, she could hear the old fellow still talking to Bert in the next room. It occurred to her then that all the while they had stood there passing the baby back and forth and delighting in the baby's good spirits, the old man had been talking on and on, as though he didn't know how to stop once he had begun. Emmaline hadn't listened to him, but as she now heard his bass voice droning on beyond the closed door, she began to recollect the sort of thing he had been saying. Off his tongue had rolled all the obvious things, all the unnecessary things, all the dull things—every last thing that might have been left unsaid: He guessed he had a way with children, they flocked to him in the neighborhood where he lived, and he looked after them and did for them. Along with the quality of kindliness in his voice was a quality that could finally make you forget kindliness, no matter how genuine. Why, he didn't mind doing for children when their folks ought to go out and have their good time of it before they got like him, "a decrepited and lonesome old wreck on time's beach." What Bert and Emmaline needed was some of their old folks from Tennessee—or the likes of them—to show them something about raising children, so they wouldn't go scaring themselves to death and worrying where they needn't. Tears of pity came into Emmaline's eyes—pity for herself. It would be like that from now on. She heard the old man's voice going on and on in the next room even after she had heard Bert letting himself down on the bed. She even thought she heard the old man saying that if they didn't want him to stay, he would leave tomorrow. That's what he *would* say, anyhow. He would be

saying it again and again for years and years because he knew
that Bert would not have the heart, any more than she would,
to run him off after tonight.

She got up and turned off the light, and then, with the baby
in her arms, found her way to the rocking chair. She continued
to sit there rocking long after the old man had talked himself out for this time and had, without shutting the bathroom
door, used the toilet and finally gone off to his own room. She
went on rocking even long after she knew the baby was asleep
and would be dead to the world until morning. During the
time she and Bert and the old man had stood in the shadowy
room in silence, each absorbed in his own thoughts, she had
been remembering that the baby's shrieking had awakened her
from a nightmare of her own. She had not been able to remember at the time what the nightmare was, but now she did. There
wasn't much to the dream. She was on the Square in Thornton. Across the courthouse yard she spied old 'Stracted Mag
coming toward her. The old woman had three or four cur dogs
on leash, and she was walking between two Thornton white
ladies whom Emmaline recognized. As the group drew near to
Emmaline, she had the impulse to run forward and throw her
arms about old Mag and tell her how she admired her serene
and calm manner. But when she began to run she saw old Mag
unleash the dogs, and the dogs rushed upon her growling and
turning back their lips to show their yellow, tobacco-stained
teeth. Emmaline tried to scream and could not. And then she
did manage to scream. But it was the baby shrieking, of course,
and she had woken from her nightmare.

As she rocked in the dark with her sleeping baby, she shook
her head, trying to forget the dream she had just remembered.
Life seemed bad enough without fool dreams to make it worse.
She would think, instead, about the old man and how she
would have to make him clean himself up and how she would
have to train him to do for the baby when the baby got older.
She even tried to think kindly of him and managed to recall
moments of tenderness with her old granddaddy and her uncles
in Thornton, but as she did so, tears of bitterness stung her
eyes—bitterness that out of the past, as it seemed, this old
fellow had come to disrupt and spoil her happy life in St. Louis.

In the next room, Bert, in his white pajamas, lay on their bed listening to the noise that the rocking chair made. It went "quat-plat, quat-plat," like any old country rocking chair. He knew the baby must be asleep by now, but he didn't want Emmaline to come back to bed yet. For while he and Emmaline and the old man had stood together in the brief silence, Bert, too, had realized that the baby had awakened *him* from a nightmare. He had thought he was a little boy in school again, in the old one-room Negro grade school at Thornton. He was seated at the back of the room, far away from the stove, and he was cold. It seemed he had forgotten to go to the privy before he left home, as he so often used to forget, but he could not bring himself to raise his hand and ask to go now. On top of all this, the teacher was asking him to read, and he could not find the place on the page. This was a dream that Bert often had. It could take one of several endings—all of them equally terrible to him. Sometimes the teacher said, "Why can't you learn, boy?" and commenced beating him. Sometimes he ran past the teacher (who sometimes was a white man) to the door and found the door locked. Sometimes he got away and ran down to the school privy, to find indescribable horrors awaiting him there.

As he lay in bed tonight, he could not or would not remember how the dream had ended this time. And he would not let himself go back to sleep, for fear of having the dream again. There had been nights when he had had the dream over and over in all its variations. Why should he go back to sleep now and have that dreadful dream when he could stay awake and think of pleasant things?—or the pleasanter duties ahead of him tomorrow, of polishing the silver, of scouring the tile floor in the pantry, perhaps of washing Miss Amy's car if she didn't go out in the afternoon. He stayed awake for a long time, but without thinking of the old man at all, without even thinking of what could be keeping Emmaline in the next room.

And while Bert lay there carefully not thinking of his bad dream and not thinking of the old man and wept bitterly because of him, wasn't it likely that the old man himself was still awake—in the dark room with the three-legged chest of drawers, the unplastered walls, and the old harness hooks? If so, was it possible that he, too, had been awakened from a bad dream tonight? Who would ever know? Bert and Emmaline would tell each other in the morning about their dreams—their loneliness was only of the moment—and when Baby grew up, they would tell her about themselves and about their bad dreams. But who was there to know about *his*? Who is there that can imagine the things that such a dirty, ignorant, old tramp of a Negro thinks about when he is alone at night, or dreams about while he sleeps? Such pathetic old tramps seem, somehow, to have moved beyond the reach of human imagination. They are too unlike us, in their loneliness and ignorance and age and dirt, for us even to guess about them as people. It may be necessary for us, when we meet them in life or when we encounter them in a story, to treat them not as people but as symbols of something we like or dislike. Or is it possible to suppose, for instance, that their bad dreams, after all—to the very end of life, and in the most hopeless circumstances—are only like Bert's and Emmaline's. Is it possible that this old fellow had been awakened tonight from a miserable dream of his own childhood in some little town or on some farm in that vague region which the Tollivers called West Tennessee? Perhaps, when he returned from the toilet, he sat up in bed, knowing that at his age he wasn't likely to get back to sleep soon, and thought about a nightmare he had remembered while standing in that shadowy room with Bert and Emmaline. It might even be that the old fellow smiled to himself and took comfort from the thought that anyway there were not for him so many nightmares ahead as there were for Bert and for Emmaline, and certainly not so many as for their little woolly-headed baby who didn't yet have a name.

The Dark Walk

I T WAS a rather old-fashioned sort of place with no entertainment except expeditions to Pikes Peak to see the sunrise, horseback riding on Tuesday and Thursday, and a depressing dance ("For Young and Old") in the dining room every Saturday night. The first thing Sylvia Harrison's children said upon arriving was: "Why, there's not even a swimming pool!" To the two older children, Margaret and Wallace, it seemed an impossible place. They were aged fifteen and sixteen at the time, and they would have much preferred being back in the heat of Chicago. To them the depressing Saturday night dances in Mountain Springs were an anathema. Wallace said the notice on the bulletin board should read: "For the *very* young and the *very* old." Twelve-year-old girls, still wearing sashes and patent-leather pumps, danced with their grandfathers. Worse still, old ladies danced together and "broke" on each other. The music was unspeakable: a drum, a piano, and a saxophone. Margaret and Wallace soon got in touch with school friends whose sensible parents were staying in Colorado Springs. The two of them were forever dashing over to the Antlers and the Broadmoor in a rented automobile; but even that was not much fun, because Sylvia always made them get back to Mountain Springs before midnight. And on Saturday night, for at least a few minutes, they had to appear at the Mountain Springs dance.

Those Saturday nights in Colorado were even more painful to Sylvia's two younger children, Charley and Nora. *They* had to stay at the dance until 10:30 and *they*, as well as their mother, had to dance time and again with old Miss Katty Moore, who owned and managed Mountain Springs Hotel. The three of them—Sylvia and the two younger children—took turns dancing with Miss Katty. When she approached their table they would whisper among themselves whose turn it was; and soon, off one of them would go in the arms of the muscular little old lady. It was a humiliating experience—the dancing was. But somehow it wasn't itself so bad as those awful moments when Miss Katty was approaching. It was that that the children dreaded all week long. The old lady would come toward them with a bouncing step, sometimes with her incredibly muscular arms outstretched as she snapped her fingers to the rhythm of the music. Her snow-white hair was bobbed, and shingled in the back. She wore a white satin evening dress, and, for dancing, a pair of low-quarter, white tennis shoes. As she stopped at their table she would roll her eyes back into her head until only the whites were showing. This was her facetious way of issuing an invitation to the dance. . . . An unbelievable sight the old woman was. And a dreadful reality she presently became for him or her whose turn it happened to be.

But why need this macabre invitation be accepted? Because old Miss Katty Moore was a native of Tennessee. Because she had taught gymnastics at Ward-Belmont School in Nashville when Sylvia was a student there and had taught Sylvia and all Sylvia's contemporaries there the art of swinging Indian clubs. It was, in fact, because of this old association that Sylvia took her family to Mountain Springs instead of to the Broadmoor that summer. She told herself it would be fun to see her old teacher again and she enjoyed thinking of the pleasure her old schoolmates would receive from the letters she would write them about Miss Katty. She pictured those old schoolmates— the half-dozen or so with whom she had kept up a regular correspondence through the years, pictured them opening her letters about Miss Katty as they stood on the front porches of their white clapboard houses in Tennessee. Four of them lived in the very town where Sylvia had grown up, and rarely did a month pass without her writing to and receiving a letter from one of them. Her life and theirs had followed such different courses in recent years that there was always something newsworthy to write. She knew how her "western trip" would interest them and could hear them exclaiming, "Good heavens! Miss Katty Moore in Colorado!"

But Sylvia Harrison would never have thought of going West at all except that Nate Harrison's business had taken him for several weeks to Denver and to Salt Lake City. She and the children had accompanied Nate to those places, and he had afterward gone with them through Yellowstone Park. After Yellowstone he had had to return to Chicago. Originally he had had his secretary make reservations for Sylvia and the children at the Broadmoor, and it was Sylvia herself, of course, who

remembered about Miss Katty and changed the plans. Nate
had laughed at her for it and had been especially *tickled* by
the fact that she was going to keep in touch with her Tennessee friends during the summer and probably wouldn't write a
line to anybody in Chicago. But he said it was all right if that
was what she wanted and said there was no use in his trying
to change her about such things. One thing he would never
attempt, so he said, was to change Sylvia about such things
as that. He, of course, never set eyes on Mountain Springs
and never danced a step with Miss Katty Moore. During the
summer Sylvia carried through her plan to write notes to her
old schoolmates (all of whom replied with messages for Miss
Katty) and when she was back in Chicago she wrote a long
letter to be passed among them, in which she depicted the
trip as "an awful failure" for the whole family. "The hotel was
really a mess," she wrote. "The long train ride was ghastly. Miss
Katty, despite her foxtrotting and two-stepping on Saturday
nights, was the only bright spot for me."

Afterward Sylvia would refer to that summer in Colorado
whenever people tried to sympathize with her for having had
to move about the country so many times. For more than ten
years Nate's business had kept the family almost constantly on
the move, but Sylvia said she would rather pack and move her
possessions a hundred times than take one such trip as that.
The children were always so keyed up on a vacation trip, and
they were always so disappointed over the way things worked
out. Whereas a move was a very different matter. It was like
ordering the groceries. The only bad thing about a move, said
Sylvia, was the respect in which it was like taking a trip—a
certain inescapable human element. For instance, on moving
day somebody in the family would burst into tears at the sight
of some particular piece of furniture's being shouldered out of
the house by the moving men. Or somebody would decide—
"somebody" being always one of the children, of course—that
he or she would never be as happy in another house or neighborhood as in the one they were leaving. It was nearly always
Sylvia's lot to combat the bursts of tears, to remind someone
that none of these houses was really home for them, to say
again that home for them would always be Tennessee. Home

was not Chicago or Detroit, or any of the other places they had lived. Home was the old Harrison place at Cedar Springs, or perhaps Sylvia's own family house at Thornton.

Yet there had been one occasion on which Sylvia herself had shed tears. It was in the year 1922, in the late spring of the year—toward the end of May. The Harrisons were then setting out from Cedar Springs for Memphis, where Nate was going to act as a sort of "efficiency vice-president" of a concern that had been badly mismanaged. On the day of that first move the sycamores and the oak trees which shaded the streets of the country town still had the first greenness of spring, and so did the grass in the big yards about the houses and in the cow pastures that came up to the edge of town. In some of the ditches along the streets day lilies were already in bloom. Nate and Sylvia had planned to be up and on their way before sunrise while it was still cool and before the roads became dusty. But they didn't get away that early, of course. Even though they had only the two children then, it was all they could do to have everything and everybody ready to set out by 7:30. The moving vans from Memphis had waited there overnight to pack the last beds, and it was seven o'clock before even the vans could get under way.

At 7:30 on that spring morning the Harrisons drove west through the old town. All the family were in the new Nash touring car. Following them in the Ford sedan were the two servants and the family pets. As they drove the length of the one long block between their house and the town square they passed a number of their fellow townsmen hurrying along their way to work. It was the sight of one of these men waving good-by to them—a man whom Sylvia Harrison hardly knew—that made her forget herself that morning and look over her shoulder in the direction of the empty house they had left behind. And the one glance was fatal.

At the first little choking sound in her throat, Nate began to slow down the car and commenced speaking comforting words to her. But Sylvia only sobbed: "Go on. Go on, Nate. Don't stop the car. If only we could have left while it was still dark! I wouldn't have minded so much if we could have left before sunup. And why couldn't we have left before the spring was so far advanced? Oh, everything is at its peak, Nate!"

Nate tried to reason with her, saying that this was the normal time of year to move. He had to keep his eyes on the road but there was a smile of infinite tenderness on his face and he even reached out his right hand and pressed the back of it gently against her cheek.

But Sylvia continued as before: "We ought to have left last year, somehow. Or we ought to have left Cedar Springs before we ever had any children."

At this slight reference to themselves, the two children in the back seat also began to cry. Nate brought the car to an abrupt stop. Behind them, the brakes of the Ford sedan screeched. And Sylvia, turning just then to comfort the children, saw over the children's heads and through the isinglass rear window of the car the astonished faces of the Negro man and woman in the sedan. She saw the Negro woman, just after the sudden stop, trying to comfort the canary bird in the cage which she held on her lap, and saw the man reaching back with his long arm to pet Toto, the fox terrier, who was riding between the bundles in the back seat of the sedan. This picture of the servants and the pets seen over the heads of her weeping children immediately revived Sylvia's spirits. With tears still in her eyes she had begun smiling and even chuckling to herself; for here in these two cars were all the members of her household. A few miles ahead of them on the road to Memphis were the four vans of furniture—almost everything in the way of furniture that her family or Nate's had ever owned.

Never in all her years of moving would Sylvia Harrison allow her friends to assist her or to sympathize with her about her moving. Nate's rise in the business world of the Midsouth and Midwest was so continuous and so prodigious that it kept the family shuttling about the country for more than ten years. Yet Sylvia never complained and never willingly accepted sympathy. On the contrary, instead of ever permitting them to commiserate with her, the letters she wrote to her friends in Tennessee were likely to contain expressions of sympathy for them—not because life had kept them in Thornton and Cedar Springs or had taken them only as far as Nashville, but for a thousand disappointments and injustices they had suffered. The same kind of thing was true in her relationship with the new friends she made and with the old friends whose paths crossed hers at one time and another. And as long as Nate lived, not even he felt free to offer Sylvia advice on the subject of moving or even to lend a hand or express any sympathy when the time for packing arrived.

After Nate died in 1939 and when Sylvia was preparing to take her family from Chicago back to Tennessee, those in her Chicago circle of friends dared not allude to the troublesomeness of moving. It had been that way, in some degree, when she left Cedar Springs, when she left Memphis, St. Louis, Detroit—everywhere. For a number of years she tried to conceal just how much furniture she did carry about the country with her, but someone—her husband, or one of the children, or even one of the servants—always let the cat out of the bag about the things she had to keep in the attic and the stuff she had to put in storage.

Wherever the Harrisons had lived they had gone out among society people, mostly among society people with a Southern background (of which they found no scarcity anywhere in the Midwest). They were admired everywhere for their geniality, their good breeding, and simply for their attractive appearances. Sylvia, even at the time of Nate's death when she was a woman of forty-four, was known in Chicago for her unusual prettiness, her charming manner, and for her very youthful figure. But she was also known—much to her distaste—as the poor, dear Southern woman who had had to move so often and who insisted on taking such a quantity of furniture everywhere. Such an attitude seemed uncalled-for and absurd to her. If there had ever been any scarcity of money, then it would have been a different matter. Her heart went out to people who had to move on a shoestring. The sight of an old rattletrap truck piled high with bare bedsprings and odd pieces of oak furniture could bring tears to her eyes. But in her case there had never been any risk or uncertainty about moving. There had always been more than enough money—both she and Nate had their own comfortable incomes from property back home—and there had always been the understanding that some day they would go back to Tennessee.

Most of the women with whom Sylvia had gone to boarding school in Nashville were women who had been, no less than she, well provided for. Their misfortunes were seldom of a money kind, although there *was* the case of Mildred Pettigru whose husband, after he had run through her small inheritance, deserted her in Shreveport, Louisiana, without even train fare back to her home at Gallatin. (Luckily, though, another schoolmate's husband who had done well in politics was able to procure the appointment of Gallatin postmistress for Mildred.) Except for Mildred's husband, however, and one other rascal, who actually ended in the penitentiary, the men whom Sylvia's friends married were responsible, energetic men who commanded the respect of everyone who knew them. Yet in the life of each of her friends there was some element or condition to touch Sylvia's loyal and compassionate heart. "I feel sorry for Letty Russell," she would say to Nate. "She and Harry have never had any children and while he's away on his contracting jobs she's stuck in the house with Harry's mother who's stone deaf and almost blind." Nate might shake his head sympathetically. Or another time he might point out to Sylvia that she was always looking for reasons to feel sorry for her friends, and then he would remind her that some people were inclined to pity *her* for all her labors in moving. "*That*," Sylvia would reply, "is something I have imposed upon myself. It is of *my* choosing that we travel with so much furniture, Nate."

Needless to say, not all of Sylvia's girlhood friends remained in the section of the country where they were born, but it was with those who did that she corresponded most faithfully and it was the signs of unhappiness in *their* lives that disturbed her most deeply. At least once a year she went back to Tennessee for a visit, to see after her property there; and in that way she continually renewed her acquaintance with her friends' manner of life. She always visited in the home of one of them, making that her headquarters, and accepted invitations to meals in the houses of innumerable others within a radius of thirty miles of Thornton. She went to their bridge parties, their church guild meetings, their sit-down teas, their Coca-Cola luncheons. She sat with them individually on their porches and in their upstairs sitting rooms talking about old times and about present times.

The fact that impressed itself upon her always was that in no household did she find the kind of harmonious relationship which she and Nate enjoyed. It wasn't that she found discord in the place of harmony. Rather, she found in place of either a vacuum. The husbands and fathers in these houses were not the tyrants of another day; they were instead . . . what *were* they instead? Sometimes, after such a visit, it seemed to Sylvia that the husbands had not been there at all.

And yet she observed that these same husbands exercised a kind of inhuman control over their families that their forebears had never done. The literal picture she carried in her mind of a typical, latter-day husband in Tennessee was one of a man in shirt sleeves, his tie removed, perhaps even his shoes off. He is seated in a canvas chair in the yard or in a wicker porch chair at the very end of the porch, reading *The Evening Tennessean* or the biweekly *Cameron County Democrat*. It is late afternoon and he is tired. At the other end of the porch is his wife with a group of friends. They are dressed fashionably, even elegantly. There has been an afternoon party here or at some other house on High Street or Church Street or College Street. But he, the husband, is a being who has retired from the social scene in Thornton. He is a working man—not a laborer but a lawyer or a dealer in electrical and plumbing fixtures or the manager of a chain store or even a doctor or a congressman. It doesn't matter. He insists on his right, his necessity to be like other men. But he insists also that his wife, Sylvia's girlhood friend, must continue to live as she always has, and he will insist upon sending his daughter to Ward-Belmont (this being before the Baptists finally took over Ward-Belmont). He is not to blame for things being the way they are, but probably he doesn't care that they are. It was he who said to his wife before she came to Chicago to visit Sylvia: "Buy yourself some really good clothes while you're there, but when you get back, for God's sake don't come near my place of business in them."

Nate, of course, said that Sylvia exaggerated this whole matter. But she once pointed out to him that even Isabel Sternberg, her old maid Jewish friend in Cedar Springs, shared the experience. Isabel's old-bachelor brothers insisted that all the rituals of the table be observed at their house, yet the brothers rarely ate at home. They ate lunch and often dinner too at the

Cardinal Café, which was next to the bank, and left Isabel to eat with the three old aunts and the little girl she had adopted.

"The Jews," Nate had said, forgetting the real topic under discussion, "are wonderful people. Especially Southern Jews. Someone ought to write a history of Southern Jews."

"It's no joke to be a Jew," Sylvia replied, thinking affectionately and sympathetically of Isabel. "Not even in the South."

During Nate's lifetime there were, on some occasions, mild disagreements between Sylvia and him about the necessity for moving from one house to another in the same city. Sylvia complained that he never bothered to get a sufficiently long lease on a house. Nate said that the truth was it was not easy (especially during the '20's) to get more than a year's lease on the kind of house they required. Owners were always coming back from Europe or deciding to sell the house. Sometimes Nate would shake his head and smile indulgently at Sylvia, which was supposed to remind her of the folly of carrying so much furniture about the country. Sometimes he would flare up as though he were about to lose his temper and threaten to buy a place, one that would hold her furniture. Then Sylvia would give in. For that always seemed to her the most impractical idea of all. When Nate made that threat, she would go to the telephone and call the transfer company.

Any decision to move was Nate's, but the activity itself was all hers. After their first move from Cedar Springs, Sylvia took more and more responsibility until at last she would ask Nate to make-himself-scarce during the actual operation and not meddle in a woman's work.

There was hardly a picture or a piece of furniture for which she did not have some special provision in time of moving. She saved all her old faded and worn-out slipcovers to protect the upholstered chairs from the danger of snags and scars. Her mother's mahogany teacart and a certain little Chippendale night stand were always packed inside the cedar chest with the blankets and bed pillows. Somewhere she had obtained an old coffin crate into which the grandfather clock would just exactly fit. For her favorite Chinese-lacquer piece and for all the portraits and the painted tapestries there were special crates which she had had constructed before she ever left Cedar Springs.

There were even a few things in the attic (or sometimes in a warehouse) which had been crated in Cedar Springs and had not been uncrated during all the years of moving.

One of the miracles of her moving technique was the way she could get the furniture set up and arranged in a new house so that any individuality in the house itself was completely obscured. If she had papering or painting done, it was in an effort to subdue obtrusive architectural design. Long before it became fashionable, she was fond of painting doors, walls and all the wood trim in a room the same color—a dusty green, a flat gray, or an off white. By some means or other her furnishings were made to dominate whatever interior they were taken into. Within two days after the Harrisons had moved—whether into a modern suburban house or a Victorian city house—it was hard for any of them to realize how recently they had moved or actually that they had moved at all. Upstairs there would be the rosewood bed, six feet wide and nearly eight feet long, whose canopy had inevitably to be stored in the attic or in a warehouse. (Even the house on Ritchie Court in Chicago did not have ceilings high enough for the canopy.) Downstairs were the family portraits and the enormous painted tapestries representing scenes and characters from Tennessee history. (The pictures, like everything else in the house, seemed always to suggest a bigger house.) And downstairs, of course, were the heavy living-room and library pieces, and the innumerable china cabinets, chests, and sideboards overflowing from the dining room into the front and back halls. No matter if a house had all manner of built-in storage space Sylvia still preferred to keep her linens and china in the storage pieces that she brought along and to keep the family books in her own glass-fronted bookcases. This made it easier, so she said, to put her hands on things. It kept her from having to stop twenty times a day to think where she had put something the last time they moved.

Despite Sylvia's express wishes to be left alone, her neighbors had been known to send over whole meals for her and her family on the day of a move. "It's as though one of us were dead," she said on one occasion. "The wonder is somebody doesn't send flowers."

One time she gave a dinner party only two days before she moved, just to prove to herself—and to everyone else, of course—that she could. It was an elaborate party, far more elaborate than she usually went in for. But in the rooms where she entertained her company all sorts of barrels and packing cases were in evidence. Guests had to talk to each other leaning over and around crates which were apparently packed and ready to be loaded. Sylvia, during most of the evening, refused to recognize the presence of the boxes and barrels. If anyone made reference to them she pretended either not to hear or to be offended by the reference.

Then, just as the party was breaking up, she called for everyone's attention, and she proceeded to go about opening barrels, crates, packing cases—revealing that all but one of them were empty and that she had not really even begun her packing. The one box that was not empty was filled with presents for the guests, presents prettily wrapped in tissue paper and tied with colored ribbons but which when opened turned out to be only absurd white elephants that Sylvia had not cared to move. . . . She had done this, of course, in a spirit of fun and gaiety. And whenever mention was made of it in later years, she would point out that it had happened in the Era of Practical Jokes, back in the '20's when she was young and energetic and full of all kinds of foolishness. It had happened when she and Nate lived down in Memphis and at a time when they were only moving from one house to another, not from one city to another. Fifteen years later, after Nate was dead and when Sylvia was making the last of all her many moves, she could hardly consider that move from one Memphis address to another a move at all.

Nate always professed to be as baffled as everyone else by Sylvia's untroubled and independent spirit at moving time. He would tell about that party she gave in Memphis and how astonished and perplexed he had been by her behavior. Or he would tell about their first move from Cedar Springs to Memphis, not about Sylvia's crying that morning but about how well she had borne the hardships of that awful trip. When they left the town square they had two hundred and eight miles of bad roads between them and the city limits of Memphis. Here and there was a ten-mile stretch of blacktop, but most of the roads were gravel and there were frequent stretches of unimproved dirt roads. All day long they had pushed toward Memphis. But at sundown they were still forty miles northeast of the city. They had had every conceivable kind of delay. One part of the road was so rough that little Wallace became car sick, necessitating a long wait by the side of the road. Twice Nate took a wrong turn, and once when he got too far ahead of the other car the Negro man, whose name was Leander, took a wrong turn. . . . Once they had to travel for two miles over a new levee road that was still wet from a rain the previous night; and because Nate was afraid the car might slide off into the swamp water he made Sylvia and the children get out and walk for at least half the length of the levee, Leander's wife getting out with them to carry little Margaret who was only a toddler at the time. In addition to these delays they had, between the two cars, nine flat tires.

Nate said they would certainly have sought shelter at night-fall except that Sylvia wouldn't hear of it. She spent half the day leaning over the back of the front seat administering to the children who alternately fought each other, cried for something to eat, bumped their heads on the arm rest, and even vomited. Yet it was Sylvia who urged the party on. When they stopped for supper she insisted that she felt as fresh as she had at break-fast. And she reminded Nate that every piece of trouble had been made easier by the kindness of friendly people who happened along just at the right moment. . . . An old Negro farm woman had brought Wallace a glass of lemonade when he was car sick. When they waited at the fork of the roads for Leander to discover his mistake and rejoin them, the people from the nearest house came out and invited them into the house to rest themselves. Sylvia even caught a cat nap lying across the feather bed in one of the big downstairs rooms of that unpainted farm-house; and Wallace joined in a game of kick-the-can which he had to be torn away from when Leander reappeared. Sylvia pointed out that during the entire day Nate and Leander had not changed a single tire or patched one inner tube without practical assistance from farmers—white and colored—who left their work in the fields to help them.

After supper in the hotel at Brownsville, Sylvia would not hear to stopping for the night. "The way people have treated us," she said, "I don't feel we've really left home yet."

Ever afterward Nate described Sylvia as a real trouper that day. He exaggerated the hardships of the trip and pictured her as a sort of pioneer heroine. But he always concluded by saying, with a broad smile on his face, that Sylvia's courage and endurance had had special inspiration on that occasion. Never until that day, he said, had she imagined that human kindness and friendliness might exist beyond a fifty-mile radius of Middle Tennessee. And, besides, to urge her on she had always before her the image of her precious furniture in the hands of those rough moving men from Memphis.

Once in 1934 when they had been living in Chicago for nearly a year Sylvia and Nate came home from a party on a snowy winter evening and stayed downstairs to talk for a while. They began by discussing the party they had been to, but they ended, as they often did at such times by talking about . . . the furniture.

Sylvia had actually started up the stairs. Nate had put out all the lights except those in the chandelier that hung above the stairs from the ceiling of the second floor. On the third step Sylvia looked over her shoulder and said, "Wasn't that Mr. Jackson witty tonight. And weren't Nellie's stories about the Gold Coast charming? It was a delightful party. Everybody responded so well to everybody else's stories." By the time she had finished speaking she had turned all the way round on the steps. Nate, from the foot of the stairs, was offering her a cigarette. She wasn't a habitual smoker, but she accepted the cigarette, bringing one bare arm out from under her velvet cape to do so. Then, throwing back her dark cape, she reached for the banister rail with her other hand and let herself down onto the carpeted step. Nate lit her cigarette and his own. He stood with one foot on the first step and leaned against the heavy newel post. "People did listen to other people's stories more than usual tonight," he said. "It was a good evening."

They talked about the party for five minutes or so. They commented on how unchanged certain of their old friends from Tennessee, who had been at the party, were, how young the two Tennessee women looked—like young girls still, compared to Chicago women of the same age. Nate leaned against the newel post and blew cigarette smoke upward in the direction of the chandelier. In the bare, dim light from above, his blond wiry hair looked lighter than it usually did during this time of his life. The fullness of his tuxedo jacket concealed the paunch which he had acquired during just the last year or two. He leaned against the post in a casual, loose-jointed way that denied any of the stiffness of forty. Sylvia watched him from the third step. Her own hair was much lighter than his, though when they had married it had been a shade darker. When she threw back her cape, it fell over a wide area of the steps; and its white silk lining all about her was like an extension of her white evening dress. Her figure was not so slight as it had once been but that was, at least in part, because fashions no longer favored slightness. Her shoulders and her prettily rounded arms were bare and their skin could not have appeared softer or clearer. She was sitting now with her arms about her knees, her cigarette between the fingers of her right hand.

Presently she heard (and she saw in Nate's face that he heard) their oldest son, Wallace, calling out something in his sleep from his room upstairs. The two of them listened attentively for a moment. Then when they heard nothing more, Nate suddenly straightened and moved away from the post he had been leaning against. He went to a table in the hall, picked up a small metal ashtray and brought it back with him to the stairs, where he sat down on the bottom step. When he spoke again his voice sounded hoarse the way it did in the morning or at any time when he had not spoken for a long while.

"Wallace has always talked in his sleep," he said.

"Not always," Sylvia said, smiling a little. "Not during the time he wasn't sleeping in the sleigh bed. That sleigh bed is uncomfortable, but he likes it."

Nate was silent a moment. "Well, regardless of what he likes, if he doesn't get his rest . . ." He broke off there and was silent another moment. Finally he said: "I suddenly have a mental picture of all the stacks of beds we have, Sylvia, and bedsprings—in the attic, in the basement, and God-knows-where."

"Well," Sylvia said, "this is where we always end when we stop down here to talk."

"I think of it as the way we *begin* to talk," Nate said. "When we get on the subject of your furniture I feel that I am mighty near to understanding the difference between the mind of man and woman. There's hardly anything I like better than hearing you chatter about your 'things.'"

Sylvia smiled affably, as she shrugged her shoulders. "I have little or nothing to say on the subject," she said softly. "Nothing you haven't already heard me say." She wanted to humor him in his mood, but the words would not come.

But Nate pursued the subject energetically, repeating things that she had said to him at one time or another in her own defense. She liked being able to put her hands on her things. She liked having the children grow up with the things she had grown up with. It wasn't important but she liked the idea of taking the furniture everywhere they went, since they could afford it, and of then some day taking it back to Tennessee with them. Why, he said to her, it would be as though she had never left Cedar Springs. Wasn't it that? he said, laughing. Wasn't it?

Sylvia nodded her head solemnly.

And now he began pointing out, with the same good nature, the tremendous expense which the moves had been to them. But he did this for the sole purpose of getting Sylvia to affirm that the moving, to her, had been worth every penny it had cost.

When at last they went upstairs Nate was still talking to her about her "things." At the top of the steps he put his arm about her waist, and suddenly, as though at the sensation of having his arm about her, Sylvia remembered something he had said to her long ago when they were first engaged. They had been sitting out in the yard at her father's house after supper at night and Nate had been talking about the various avenues that might be open to him in business. As he talked there, hidden in the dense shadows of a huge willow-oak tree, she had been thinking how very boyish his voice sounded and once when he had leaned forward for a moment she saw the faint light from the porch outline his handsomely shaped head and for one instant catch in its faintly glimmering rays the cowlick on the back of his head. "What one has to remember," she recalled his saying finally, "is that everything changes so fast in our country that a smart person can't hold on to the past—not to any part of it if he wants to be a success. It's as though we lived in a country where the currency changed every week, and you had to go every Monday morning and convert your old money into new." When he said that in the dark that night it had given Sylvia a scare, had made her feel afraid of him. Recalling it now it only impressed upon her the gentle indulgence he had shown her during the years of their marriage, but that night it had meant to her, somehow, that she would never be able to think of Nate as a mere boy again, and never of herself as a girl. Presently her sense of fright and dismay had left her. But after Nate had taken the 10:30 train back to Cedar Springs and she had returned from the depot and gone upstairs to her room, she imagined that she could now see all her childhood and young ladyhood in a new perspective. She imagined that she was seeing it as she would see it when she was a woman of forty. How fine it would seem then to have grown up the way she had, in such pleasant, prosperous, pastoral surroundings, at just the time she had, and with just the friends she had had. How she would then cherish the bittersweet tone of things as they were in Middle Tennessee in 1915. For everyone said it would all be different in twenty years. There would be no Confederate veterans left then, no old ladies who had once danced with Jeff Davis, and none of the old-time Negroes. The white people and the colored people would be more alike and yet farther apart in their independence of each other. There would be none of the bitter memories of the Civil War to make anything that bespoke the past sound sweet to the ear. Life in a Tennessee country town then would be indistinguishable from that in any other place in the land. But in *her* time and in *her* town she had seen everything that was good in the noble past of her country meeting head on with everything that was exciting and marvelous about the twentieth century. *Her* generation, she was sure, had found growing up more exciting than any generation had in a thousand years. It seemed to her that the boys of her time were as different from their fathers as motorcars from oxcarts. And the girls . . . they were not so different from their mothers, not yet; but there was a feeling of exhilaration and anticipation in the air that made the joy of being young seem almost unendurable to them and made it imperative, if they were to endure, that they bind themselves together in close friendships. Being young could not always have been like that, Sylvia told herself. Oh, surely not! And that night in her father's house, after she had put out the light in her room, she lay awake thinking of her friends and thinking of what it was like to have been young with them in that place and that time. She saw them in their summer dresses walking through the cemetery on their way to a picnic at the sand banks, saw them in the old clapboard grade school at Thornton writing Latin sentences on the huge blackboards, all of them wearing middy blouses and pleated skirts, and later a few of them at Ward-Belmont, in Nashville, swinging Indian clubs in Miss Katty Moore's gym class. She saw them dancing at the Christmas cotillion in Germania Hall, and dancing again at the old Thornton Wells Hotel on the Fourth of July, and saw them finally not as a group but each with the man she would marry walking down beside the river, under the shade of the giant trees there, following the half overgrown path known among them as the Dark Walk.

When this series of pictures had passed before her mind and she was about to drift off to sleep she found the same series beginning all over again. But this time the pictures were more in detail and in each there was a definite incident or character that revealed to her why her mind had photographed that scene. When they were picnicking at the sand banks that hot summer day they had climbed one high embankment and peered down into the next ravine to see a Negro couple there, copulating in the sand. The man was shirtless and his trousers had fallen down about his ankles. The sweat on the black skin on his buttocks and his back glistened in the blazing sunshine. The woman still wore most of her clothes. Her brown head lay back on the sand and her eyes were closed. The girls watched in silence for a few seconds, and then they hurried back to their picnic to talk, not of how the sweat had glistened on the man's skin, but of the rapturous expression they had all observed on the face of the woman. . . . Once as they sat at dusk on the porch at Thornton Wells an old woman from back in the hills had told fortunes with tea leaves all round. When the girls wearied of the fortunetelling, she proceeded to entertain them with more practical talk. She said that if they would notice how their true-loves held them when they danced that night they could judge what manner of men they were, what sort of husbands they'd make. "A man who don't hold you firm when he waltzes you," she warned them, "it's a poor bed partner he'll make." In the rooms which the girls shared in the hotel that night only Mildred Pettigru would not report what promise her true-love had shown. . . . Sylvia and Nate, strolling in the verdurous Dark Walk on a Sunday afternoon in May, had stopped near the ruins of an old lattice summerhouse, and there Nate had asked her to marry him. His face bending over her and his voice, suddenly gone a little hoarse, had seemed to fill the whole world.

Nate Harrison died of a heart attack soon after his forty-eighth birthday, in January of 1939. By the standards of Chicago bankers and board chairmen he had still been a young man. At the time of his death he was president of the American Wire and Steel Mesh Corporation, a concern which he had been brought to Chicago to reorganize in the darkest days of the Depression. His death came entirely without warning. He had played handball at the Athletic Club in the early afternoon and returned to his office at three o'clock. He was found less than twenty minutes later lying on the floor beside his desk. Sylvia had to be summoned from an afternoon party at Indian Hills, up in Winnetka. She did not see him alive again.

Two months later she made her final decision about leaving Chicago. She decided that in June she would give up the big house they had been renting on Ritchie Court and move all her possessions, including her four near-grown children, back to Tennessee. Everyone told her that the move would be too great an ordeal for her just yet and that she ought to put it off another six months, but Sylvia wouldn't listen. "Moving has practically been my life's work," she said to them. "It doesn't upset me the way it does other women."

II

There was an interval of nearly three months between the time that Sylvia announced her decision to leave Chicago and the day of the actual move from Ritchie Court. Sometime during the first weeks of this interval she began speaking of herself, to her children and to all her acquaintances, as "one of the newly poor." No one—probably not even she—could remember when she first used the phrase, but everyone was soon aware of how much she seemed to enjoy thinking of herself as a widow in straitened circumstances. Her friends in Chicago accused her of taking pleasure in the role, and so did her children. Sometimes she would admit that there was some truth in their charge and would even laughingly suggest that it was a play for sympathy on her part. But she always returned to the position that Nate's death had left the family in "straitened circumstances" which necessitated the move back to Tennessee.

From time to time she practiced little household economies, like shutting off the heat in rooms that were seldom used. She bought an electric sewing machine and attended the free classes in tailoring to which the purchase entitled her. The economy of which she tried to make the most was the dismissal of her part-time chauffeur and yard man. But even this did not represent any appreciable saving or the loss of great services. The Negro man who had done that work was the same Leander who had set out from Cedar Springs with the Harrisons seventeen years before. For several years now he had been employed by them only on a part-time basis, and had found other employment with another family in the neighborhood. Sylvia's economy in that quarter was as negligible as in any other.

Everybody recognized her pretensions to poverty as mere pretensions. Her daughter Margaret, who had had a course in psychology at her finishing school in New York that very year, suggested that she was "suffering from certain deep psychic disturbances." Fortunately, however, neither Margaret nor anyone else made the mistake of thinking Sylvia was subject to any real delusions. After Nate's death in January, Margaret had remained at home with her mother, instead of returning to school. Wallace, who was a student at the University of Virginia, had, of course, returned to Charlottesville after the funeral. By the time he came home for a few days at Easter, Sylvia had made her plans to move the family back to Cedar Springs and had invented the fiction of their financial reverses.

Wallace lost no time in expounding his theory about this fiction of his mother's. She had made it up, he said (at the dinner table on Easter day), to prevent the usual brand of sympathy she received whenever she moved. Whether or not he really believed this to be Sylvia's motive he insisted upon it in a teasing, good-humored way throughout his Easter visit and even afterward in letters he wrote home. The other children followed his lead, and as far as they were concerned there was never any further effort to interpret Sylvia's talk of financial reverses. No doubt they all knew that their father's life insurance did not entirely countervail the income from his business activities and knew that the family's income from investments and from the Tennessee property had diminished during the Depression; but they knew also that their losses were not commensurate with Sylvia's representations of them. They humored their mother in her economizing, teased her about it sometimes, and on the whole gave about as much thought to it as they might have to any other irksome little habit she might have had. Certainly it never occurred to them once that their mother was concerned, consciously or unconsciously, with justifying in their eyes her plans to return to Tennessee.

There were two people in Sylvia's acquaintance, however, to whom this possibility may have occurred. One was a man who, by Sylvia's standards, had had no vital connection with the Harrison family. His name was Mr. Peter Paul Canada and he was the owner of the house on Ritchie Court. He was a very kind and very rich old widower, and he had held on to this house, instead of selling it, because it was here that his wife had spent her happiest years. . . . The other person was Sylvia's former chauffeur, Leander Thompson.

Soon after Easter, Sylvia had gone by appointment to Mr. Canada's office in the Loop district. To him she had described herself as a widow in straitened circumstances and had made known her intention of giving up the house. Mr. Canada at once said that he would not hear of such a thing. He insisted that she and the children must continue to occupy the house without paying rent. There would be the greatest difficulty, he insisted, in finding a renter for a big house like that in these times, and it would be enormously to his advantage to have it occupied. Sylvia, as though she had not heard him, then repeated that she and the children were returning to Tennessee because there would be no problem of a place to live there. Presently, however, she seemed to realize what *he* and what *she* had said, and she smiled self-consciously. "It isn't really just a matter of rent or a place to live," she said with a worried expression about her eyes which indicated that for the moment she could not remember what it *was* a matter of. "It is a matter also," she said uncertainly and after a pause, "of other property we have in Tennessee. There is a good deal of farm land and some downtown real estate in Nashville to be looked after. And then, too, I still have my own family place at Thornton, which is a little town not too far from Cedar Springs."

Now she smiled self-consciously again and blushed a deep red. She had not only divulged the considerable extent of her property but had possibly made it, by her rambling speech, seem larger than it was. She did not try to correct this impression; the person to whom she was speaking was, after all, only her landlord. She sat blinking her eyes while Mr. Canada said: "What about your children, Mrs. Harrison? They have so many educational and social advantages in a place the size of Chicago, I should think."

"Oh, it's just the children I am thinking of," Sylvia said with enthusiasm, reminded at last of what the matter was. "It is very much to the interest of the children to go back to Tennessee where their property is and where . . . where their name will mean something to them."

"I see," said Mr. Canada, putting a freckled, wrinkled old hand up to his forehead and rubbing his brow. On one freckled finger was a wide, gold band and on his starched white cuff shone a monogrammed gold cuff link. "I had thought probably," he said sweetly, "that your children, having—to some extent—grown up here in Chicago considered themselves real Chicagoans."

Lowering his hand from his forehead Mr. Canada now turned his face away from Sylvia and toward a window that opened above the tops of other office buildings. Under different circumstances Sylvia might have attached significance to what Mr. Canada said and to his glance out his office window. But as things were—that is, he being only her landlord, she accepted the old gentleman's words that day as mere gestures, as marks of half-absentminded civility, and she replied by drawing from her purse a list of articles of furniture that had been in the house when she moved there. It was really to present this list and to have it verified that she had called in person instead of giving notice to Mr. Canada by telephone or mail. Mr. Canada looked over the list hastily and said that so far as he could recall the list seemed complete.

Only a few days after this interview with Mr. Canada, Sylvia's former chauffeur came to her house. He arrived shortly before dinnertime, and when he and Sylvia had dealt with the matter that had brought him there, Leander asked to be allowed to stay and serve the evening meal. But Sylvia very politely refused his request. Having always preferred women servants in the house, she had never let Leander serve meals unless they had just moved and hadn't yet found a downstairs maid. As chauffeur and sometimes as gardener he had served the family long and well and had been a willing worker when called upon to lend a hand in spring cleaning or at moving time. Nate had been genuinely attached to Leander, and so indeed had Sylvia. But for several years now—since the children had begun to drive—the family had required little chauffeuring. Leander had, with the consent of all, taken another job in the neighborhood but had continued, in his spare time, to care for the minuscule bit of lawn between the house and the sidewalk and to come once or twice a week to wash the cars or perhaps to drive Sylvia or one of the girls to a party. The little work he had done for them before Sylvia dismissed him altogether could hardly have been worth his while, and no doubt he had continued to do it only out of old-fashioned attachment for the family.

The purpose of his coming to see Sylvia that day had been to request that she take him back to Tennessee with her and the children. Sylvia had tried to deal with the matter as quickly as possible. "Ah, no, Leander," she said, "times are not what they were with us. It's out of the question. But you're looking well, Leander."

"No'm," said Leander, "times aren't what they was. That's why I'd be thankful to go back to Cedar Springs with you."

They were standing in the servants' dining room, behind the kitchen. In the kitchen, dinner was being prepared, but as soon as Leander and Sylvia began to speak there were no more sounds of running water from that quarter and no conversation between the cook and the maid. The awareness of an audience seemed to inspire Sylvia.

"Listen here, Leander," she said, raising her voice, "the good Lord hath dealt heavily with us Harrisons. We're having to leave all this opulence behind us. There's not the remotest possibility of my taking on the services of a chauffeur at a time when I'm having to drag my family back to the country in order to make ends meet."

As Sylvia spoke Leander stood nodding his head understandingly. He was a tall man with skin the color of wet sand, and he wore a small mustache. In his two hands he held his chauffeur's cap and as he nodded his head or when he spoke he would occasionally lean forward as though under his cap his hands were resting on a walking cane. "Times *are* bad, Miss Sylvia," he said, "and there's no place like the country when hard times come."

"No place on earth, Leander," Sylvia said, despite herself.

Leander nodded and raised one hand to stroke his chin. "But I suppose you'd go back anyway, wouldn't you, Miss Sylvia?" he asked. "Or maybe would you think the children wouldn't like it there? As for me, I don't think that's so." Sylvia looked at him blankly, as though she had heard a noise somewhere off in the house that had distracted her. "They say there's nothing so green as a city boy in the country," Leander continued, "but Wallace and them will take to it after a while. That's sure, and I wouldn't give it a thought if I was you. And for folks like you and me there's no place like the place we was born. It's only the ride back I'm asking, Miss Sylvia."

Sylvia suddenly sat down in one of the straight chairs by the table, as if thereby to express her dismay. "I don't know why you're bothering to say all this, Leander. If Mr. Nate felt times were so hard that he could only keep you part time two years before he died, how do you imagine I can re-hire you now?"

"I don't reckon you understood me," Leander began.

But Sylvia interrupted: "Yes, I did, Leander. But with all the luggage the children will have there won't be a spare inch of room in either car."

Leander bit his lower lip, thoughtfully, and nodded his head again. A few minutes later, after Sylvia had declined his offer to serve dinner, he took his leave for that day.

The children had laughed openly at Sylvia's efforts at economy. Charley, who had a head for figures, made an estimate of how much more it had cost her getting the cars washed at the service station and taking taxis in bad weather than it would have cost had she kept Leander on. His mother took such teasing in good spirits. But once when Margaret implied that having a chauffeur had always been an extravagance for them and that through the years Leander had made a good thing of them, Sylvia declared that not one of her children had an ounce of practical sense. Presently she rose and left the family circle, remarking as she did so that it was just as well Margaret had stayed home from "that finishing school" where they filled her with nothing but nonsense. A day or two later Margaret tried to apologize for whatever her offense had been, but Sylvia only fixed her with an icy stare and forbade any further talk on the subject.

This incident with Margaret was the last, not the first, of its kind. Others like it had occurred earlier, during the two months just after Nate's death. The children had, at that time, found Sylvia particularly sensitive to any criticism of any aspect of the life she and Nate had made. They found she could not tolerate their accustomed jokes about her furniture, about her long, unbroken correspondence with relatives and girlhood friends in Tennessee, about her clinging to every Southerner she met in Chicago, or about the annual trips back home to see after the two family houses. None of her efforts to maintain a continuity with the world she had grown up in was a permissible subject for their levity. Much less could she countenance any levity about the number of times the family had moved, for this she interpreted as a reflection upon Nate's career. A casual remark about the steel mesh industry could be the cue for a lecture to the children on Nate's capabilities and attainments. She talked about his great "drive" and his "genius for efficiency" and how these qualities had destined him to a place of leadership in the business world. She told them that when he was a boy in Cedar Springs everyone had supposed he would take over management of the Harrison farm land and become a member of his father's law firm, but that almost from boyhood he had had an insatiable curiosity about the "theory and management" of the nation's big business and industry. "Nate never felt any attraction toward a country law practice," she would say, "or toward managing and developing the land he and I inherited. He felt drawn toward things that were in a sense foreign to our Southern, country sort of upbringing. And with his energetic mind it was inevitable that he should find his opportunities and make good in them."

Sometimes during this period, Nate's business associates would drop by. She would talk to them, in the presence of the children, about Nate's business career. In these accounts she seldom made any reference to herself, and those she did make were only parenthetical. She would say: "After Nate finished college in Nashville (where he and I met and first went-together) he took a master's degree in economics at Yale." Or another time: "Probably a man of Nate's abilities could not have hidden himself so far in the country that the world would not have found him. After his year at Yale (when he and I had married and settled at Cedar Springs) it did seem for a while that his interest in finance and industry might turn out to be just a hobby, like his father's concern with Roman history; but actually Nate was only waiting for the right opportunity. He had turned down other things, but when the right thing came along he didn't hesitate. Part of his success, I guess, was his being able to make the right decisions."

She would talk of Nate's having gone first to Memphis, then for a short time to Cincinnati, then to Detroit, and so on. But in this connection she never referred to the actual moves which Nate's career had entailed for her. It was as though Nate had gone to all those places alone.

The Harrison children tried very hard not to say things that their mother could construe as criticism. They were ever gentle and considerate with her during this time and wanted to be whatever help and comfort to her they could. With their father all four of them had had a happy and affectionate relationship, and his death was a shock and grief to them individually. Yet being—each of them—of a normally happy and adjustable temperament they soon became absorbed again in the interests and excitements of their daily lives. Wallace returned to college in Virginia. The two younger children missed less than a week of school. Margaret did not go back to New York, but she began seeing her friends quietly and played in a tennis tournament at the Saddle and Cycle that spring. Their years of moving from city to city had not had the effect upon them that one might have supposed it would. Instead of giving them a sense of not belonging it had defined for them, to a degree beyond that enjoyed by most children, the kind of world they felt they did belong in. Wherever they had lived they had attended private schools, had gone to fortnightly dancing classes, had spent their leisure hours at the Country Club or in other houses like their own. Though they sometimes had shed tears at leaving a neighborhood or a city, they were never in much doubt about what life would be like in the next place. Unlike many of their friends they had no illusions about their school or their club's being the only one of its kind in the world. And somehow, as a result, they had in common among them an appreciation and enjoyment of life as they knew it which was more binding than any mere bond of kinship.

It was just exactly a week after Sylvia had gone to her landlord's office that she received a telephone call from him. At the time of her visit to him he had hardly been willing even to glance over the list of articles that had been in the house when Sylvia came there. But now he wished to come to the house and have a look at a few of his things. He had decided that since she was moving he should take the opportunity of disposing of the odds and ends of furniture he had left there. He wondered would it be convenient for him to come by that very afternoon. Sylvia, after a moment's hesitation, said, yes, she supposed it would be.

In order to make sure that Mr. Canada found his things Sylvia stayed home from a piano recital in which her younger daughter, Nora, was playing that afternoon. It was half past three when Mr. Canada arrived. She was waiting with the list in her hand when her maid showed the old gentleman through the broad doorway at the end of the living room. She was standing by the fireplace at the other end of the long room and she began at once to walk toward him. She greeted him in a polite, businesslike manner but without asking him to sit down. Her thought was that they would begin their inspection at once.

"The first thing," she said, "is the great console table in the hall. We left it where it was and have used it mainly because it was too heavy to move."

But before she had finished speaking she recognized an expression of confusion on Mr. Canada's face. Presently he said, "The console table? Yes. Oh, yes." Sylvia was a moment trying to account for his sudden confusion and abstraction. Then she did—to her own satisfaction at least—account for it. He had been suddenly moved, she reasoned, by the sight of this room where he once had been so happy but which he had not entered for several years now.

"Oh, won't you sit down, Mr. Canada," she said quickly, with apology in her voice. He was only her landlord, but his age and the circumstances, she reflected, did entitle him to more than mere civility from her. "My mind was so on this list," she began, "that I . . ."

He interrupted, saying, "It's more than kind of you to have let me come at all. I sincerely hope I didn't interfere with any plans."

"Indeed not," she said. "I seldom go anywhere these days."

Together they walked out of the living room and into the main hall of the house. As they entered the hall they faced a wall which was covered by three of Sylvia's painted tapestries. Sylvia guided Mr. Canada directly toward that wall. Two of the tapestries were impressive for their great size and height if for nothing more. Within their narrow, gilded frames were represented human figures of considerably more than life size and with a distinctly allegorical look (despite their nineteenth-century dress). Hung between these two was a horizontal pastoral picture, and below it stood Mr. Canada's table—a heavy Jacobean oak reproduction.

Sylvia and Mr. Canada stopped a few feet from the wall and stood there in silence for a moment, like two people before an altar. At last Mr. Canada said in a voice full of mystification: "They were here, you say, when you came? They're larger than I remember them, certainly."

Sylvia drew away from him a little and looked directly up into his eyes. "The pictures, Mr. Canada? Why, they're ours, I assure you—*mine*, that is!" Her eyes shone and her lips had already parted to pronounce the absurdity of his claim when he suddenly burst into hearty laughter.

"I'm so sorry," he said. "I thought you were pointing them out as something that was mine." He continued to laugh, and it was not too hard to see that he was laughing partly at his mistake but partly too at Sylvia's show of temper.

Sylvia didn't share his amusement. "It is the table that is yours," she said.

"Well, now," he said, checking his laughter and leaning forward to put his hand on the dark surface of the table top, "so this is a console table. To tell the truth, Mrs. Harrison, I haven't the slightest recollection of it, though I suppose it does belong to me."

"It's all yours, Mr. Canada," Sylvia said sulkily, employing the slangy phrase of her children to express both disparagement of the table and resentment against its owner for taking up her afternoon this way.

But Mr. Canada, instead of taking notice of Sylvia's tone of voice, commenced praising the tapestries, insisting that he did really have some vague recollection of pictures like them—not among his wife's possessions but in his father's old house over in the Western Reserve.

Sylvia assured him that she didn't think the pictures were works of art but said that they were of historical interest to people from Tennessee. One of them pictured Davy Crockett making his way through the wilds of West Tennessee wearing a swallow-tail coat, a black shoestring tie, and on his head a coonskin cap. Its companion picture represented Bonnie Kate Sherrill, the heroine of East Tennessee, holding hands with gallant young John Sevier, presumably just after he had rescued her from the Indians at Fort Loudon. Sylvia identified these figures and prolonged the incident further by pointing out the quaint anachronisms in their dress and by telling how her father had commissioned the painting of the pictures by a small-town house painter who, though totally illiterate, was steeped in the legends of pioneer days.

But it was not vanity that had set her to talking about the tapestries. Mr. Canada's refusal to notice her rudeness and his giving himself so to praise of her pictures had finally made her see that it was not to look at his possessions he had come there today. She understood that the sooner she ceased to treat him like an ordinary tradesman the sooner she would learn his real motive.

From the hall she led him to the far corners of the house, checking off the articles in the order in which they appeared on her list. In less than half an hour she and Mr. Canada had returned to the living room where Sylvia had invited him to join her for tea or for a Coca-Cola. In the course of their inspection her manner toward him grew more courteous, but by the time they came to the living room she was beginning to despair of discovering an ulterior motive. They sat down in two chairs about midway in the long room, and she spoke again in her business voice: "I presume it will be all right if we don't move exactly on the first of the month, Mr. Canada. My younger children's schools don't let out until the fourth or fifth of June."

Mr. Canada suddenly blossomed with smiles. He was a man whose general manner and appearance attested to his seventy years. But at a moment like this one the years seemed to fall away from him. The color rose in his face, and in his eyes shone an ardor and a naïveté that were youthfulness itself. "Your question hardly needs an answer from me," he said. "The longer you stay, the more it is to my advantage. And by the way," he said, the words now spilling out, "speaking of your children, I happened to lunch recently with Louis Norris, who is principal of your younger boy's school. He says your boy's a good student and that a scholarship could be arranged for him if you decided not to leave. He said it would be a shame . . ."

But here Sylvia interrupted. And now it was she who burst into laughter. "Mr. Canada," she said, "how very kind of you. And how transparent!"

"I don't quite follow you," he said with dignity and without appreciation of her humor.

"Let's not speak of it again," said Sylvia, suddenly looking very serious.

"I didn't mean to offend you," he said.

Sylvia didn't answer. She was content now to let him think her offended. That was the easiest way of changing the subject. Presently she began to talk to him about things that she would have talked to any other visitor about. How changeable the weather had been lately—"summer one day and winter the next." What a dreadful train wreck that was down in Englewood yesterday! . . . But as they talked and drank their Coca-Colas Sylvia kept thinking of how long Mr. Canada had waited for her to mention the children and how, after all that waiting, he had given himself away by pouncing so upon his opportunity. Like Nate, she reflected, casually, this old gentleman seemed incapable of using his intelligence for anything outside the sphere of business.

Just when Mr. Canada was leaving the house that afternoon Sylvia's daughter Nora returned from her piano recital. At the front door Sylvia introduced them to each other and then detained Nora to ask how the recital had gone. "You didn't miss a thing, Mother," Nora said. "You should be glad something came up to keep you away." She said this in Mr. Canada's presence, and when he had gone Sylvia reprimanded Nora for the rudeness. "Why do you care?" Nora asked, taking off her jacket. "Is he trying to court you, Mother?"

"Nora!" Sylvia said, with exasperation. "How absurdly you are behaving. The man is old enough to be my father."

"Oh, is he?" said Nora. "Well, it's not easy to tell the ages of grown people."

Before the day of the move from Ritchie Court arrived, Sylvia had had other visits from Mr. Canada. Usually he made some pretense of business, but of his half-dozen visits there were at least two occasions when he forgot to mention any reason for coming. After the first day Sylvia always received him hospitably and chatted with him in the living room during the hour or more that he stayed. Her children could not understand why she tolerated his attentions, and Sylvia was not at all clear about it in her own mind. She resented his clumsy gestures about the house rent and the scholarship for Charley, and she was embarrassed before her children to have to acknowledge his obvious aspirations as a suitor. But to the children she laughed both about his gestures and about his aspirations, and she continued to let him come to the house. She continued even after the children's amusement at the situation turned to disapproval and their good-natured teasing to accusing silence. Yet to the very end there was no change in hers and Mr. Canada's relationship and she was ever looking forward to the time when she would see him no more.

She looked forward to that time, she soon found, with just the same pleasure that she looked forward to the day when she would not see Leander Thompson again. For Leander, like Mr. Canada, didn't come to see Sylvia just the one time. Actually, he turned up again on the very morning after Mr. Canada's first call at the house, and he stayed even longer than Mr. Canada had done.

Sylvia was still at the breakfast table when he arrived, and she waited until she and Margaret had had their second cups of coffee before telling the maid to let him come into the dining room.

Leander began speaking before he was well into the room. "Miss Sylvia, I've been let go," he said. "Those people have accused me of taking things—over there!" As he spoke he had come forward, and he stopped within a few feet of Sylvia's chair at the table. As he said "over there" he gestured with his cap in the general direction of the house where he had been working since he left the Harrisons' service. "Miss Sylvia, you know—and you know, Miss Margaret—that I wouldn't take nothing that didn't belong to me. They say I took two pocket watches and a bottle of their whisky, and you all know how sparing I am of whisky."

He was in such an obvious state of excitement that Sylvia asked him to sit down in one of the straight chairs that were lined against the wall. At first he refused, but Sylvia said that she would not talk to him until he had sat down and calmed himself. Once he was seated, Sylvia asked, "When did all this happen, Leander?"

"It happened just this morning when I came in to work. They—he, Mr. Warren—said they found the pocket watches and half bottle of whisky on my shelf in their garage where

I generally keep my things. But, before God, somebody else had put them there." He spoke hurriedly, running his words together in a way totally unlike his usual, deliberate manner of speech. Presently he slumped in the chair and stared at the floor, all the while shaking his head. "What would I do with their watches or their sort of whisky?"

A rather dazed expression came over Sylvia's face, and it was Margaret, having observed her mother's expression, who spoke next. "Leander, we believe you," she said impatiently. "But you ought not to take on this way!" Margaret had never seen Leander cast aside his cheerfulness or his dignity before—not to this extent. And when he raised a beseeching gaze to her, she quickly dropped her eyes to her empty coffee cup.

Sylvia glanced at Margaret and for a moment watched the peculiar expression which had settled about her mouth. Then she said, "Leander, how long has it been since this happened? What time was it?"

"I've just come from over there, Miss Sylvia."

"You didn't wait long. Didn't you try to explain?"

"Not over much."

"Did Mr. Warren threaten to have you arrested?"

"No'm. He offered to pay me a month's wages, but I said, 'No, sir—nothing!'" Until now Leander had continued to look at Margaret, and now it was only out of the corner of his eye that he glanced at Sylvia. "I'm not making this up, Miss Sylvia," he said.

"I thought possibly you were," she said.

"No'm," Leander said, "it's something that happened."

"I might be able to persuade them to forget it," Sylvia said, rising from her chair.

"I don't want you to do that, Miss Sylvia," Leander said, also rising. "I'm through over there." On his feet again, he seemed more himself. But Sylvia looked into his face and was aware that there was still something different about him. She told him to go out and see if their cars didn't need a washing and to come back and talk to her again after that.

When he had gone and she and Margaret had passed from the dining room into the living room, Sylvia said: "You certainly behaved in a queer fashion, curling your lip at poor Leander."

"I couldn't help it, Mother," Margaret protested. "I honestly couldn't. I was suddenly filled with revulsion and loathing for him. He's so obviously schizophrenic! He stole those things just so he *would* be caught. You must have felt the same way I did. He's pathetic, but any real psychopath is repulsive to a normal person."

"You're mistaken, Margaret," Sylvia said with emphasis.

"You don't think he took those watches and that whisky?"

"Of course he did. But he's not crazy. He's only hell-bent upon going back to Tennessee with us."

"So hell-bent that it's made him lose contact with reality."

"Leander's not crazy, Margaret; he's only willful. I'm not a bit surprised he's done this. When we left Cedar Springs, Margaret, I let it be known among the Negroes that I wanted a married couple to take with me. Leander wasn't married, but he got married on two days' notice! You've heard me tell that. And he married the stupidest girl he could find just so he could be sure we'd send her back home pretty soon . . . *as*, of course, we had to do."

Margaret, who knew this story of Leander's marriage quite well, hardly listened to her mother now. Evidently Sylvia had convinced her of Leander's sanity, and by so doing had robbed the incident of all psychological interest. Her thoughts returned to something more substantial—that is, to the impression which Leander's physical appearance had made on her. "When he looked up at me with that dopey look in his eyes it was all I could do to keep from shuddering," she said. "And he looks like a different person with that mustache shaved off."

"Oh, *that's* what's different," Sylvia said. "His mustache is gone."

"He looked silly with it," Margaret said thoughtfully, "but even worse without it, after all." Leander had grown his mustache only since he left the Harrisons' full-time employ, and when it first appeared there had been a good deal of fun made of it by the Harrison children. He had told one of them at the time that "somehow" he always got so he looked like whomever he worked for, and his new employer wore a small black mustache.

"He looks naked without it," Margaret said with finality. "That's it—naked and perfectly ghastly."

"One thing is certain," Sylvia said with a faint smile. "He didn't stop to shave his mustache after they accused him of stealing this morning."

When Leander returned from washing the cars he gave Sylvia a second, slightly more detailed account of his dismissal. Sylvia showed little interest. She heard him out, but when he had finished she made no comment. And from that moment both she and Leander were satisfied to make no further reference to the incident. They talked together for nearly an hour that morning, and on each of Leander's subsequent visits to the house they talked for as long a time. The scene of their talks was usually the plain, square little servants' dining room behind the kitchen. They sat on opposite sides of the room, facing one another across the brown oak table, each in a straight chair against the buff-colored wall. The avowed topic of their conversations was always the problem of finding Leander another suitable job, but Leander's many digressions and parentheses— the latest news he had had from Cedar Springs or some anecdote he remembered from his years with the Harrisons—were so frequent and lengthy that only Sylvia's persistence kept the purpose of their talks before them.

The many calls which Leander and Mr. Canada paid could hardly have escaped comment from Sylvia's children. The very number of times the two men came was enough to draw comment, but it was the regularity with which the visits of the two men were alternated that inspired the children's real efforts at wit. Wallace was off in Virginia, but even his letters were filled with references to his mother's "two suitors," about whom his younger brother had kept him posted.

Margaret and Nora called Sylvia a "wicked two-timer" and warned her that sooner or later she would get her dates mixed. Sylvia entered into the fun and occasionally referred to her callers as the Black Knight and the White Knight. Yet despite all the fun and teasing, Sylvia could, almost from the beginning, detect a growing dislike on the part of the children for the two men as individuals and could detect their increasing disapproval of her continuing to let them come to the house. And their dislike and disapproval, strangely enough, seemed to increase her own unwillingness, or inability, to put an end to the visits.

Each time Leander came he appeared a little more unkempt than the time before. Patches even appeared on his coat sleeves and trousers, and he gave up his chauffeur's cap in favor of a floppy old fedora. Sylvia's two daughters said they "lived in dread" of meeting him when coming or going and of having to explain him to their friends. What difference did it make that it was only a pose and that he had a closet full of clothes wherever he lived? He looked and behaved like a tramp or something out of a book, bowing and scraping before them as he had never done in the past. And they were completely disgusted when they learned that though their mother had found him several jobs he refused them all because the employers were not up to his standards. "It's plain that he's not going to take another job," Margaret said, "and it's plain that you're going to continue to feel responsible for him, Mother. So why not just give in and agree to take him back to Tennessee with us?" In reply Sylvia had opened her mouth to make one of her hard-times speeches, but they all broke into laughter. And she only laughed with them.

Mr. Canada's presence they found harder still to explain to their friends. What could they say upon coming into the house with some friend and finding their mother, who still wore black whenever she went out, entertaining a strange old man in the living room. It would not have been so bad if he had been someone she had always known or someone that they or she knew something about. In that case they could have at least pretended he was there to express sympathy or to offer advice.

It was a busy season for the three Harrison children who were at home. It seemed to Sylvia that they were enjoying their friends more than ever before, were more than ever absorbed in the life from which she was about to take them. With her they were affectionate and considerate, as they had always been. Their criticism of her tolerance for Mr. Canada and Leander did not carry over into other things. It was clear that they felt no resentment of the move they were about to make, and she understood why they did not. They had been brought up always in the expectation of the family's some day returning to Tennessee. The possibility of not returning had hardly occurred to them. Being young, they were excited by the prospect of any change, and they had no real conception of just how great a change this would be. And, in the last weeks before the move from Ritchie Court, Sylvia became aware that she was herself no longer so sensitive to remarks the children made about her and Nate and their family background. One Saturday morning she overheard Charley and one of his fourteen-year-old friends in the living room talking about the family portraits which hung there. The friend was one of a set of new friends whom Charley had just recently begun bringing to the house, and he was seeing the portraits for the first time. From the next room Sylvia could tell that the two boys were stopping before each of the four pictures in there. The first three they came to were portraits of men, dark pictures in which only the faces and white shirt fronts were immediately distinguishable. Two of these were by a "famous" itinerant painter of the 1830's—as was also the fourth picture—and were thought remarkable for the family resemblance between the subjects. The fourth picture was much the largest and the only colorful picture of the group. It was a full-length, life-size portrait of a great-grandmother of Sylvia's, a raving beauty according to the painter's brush, standing in white voile and silk with her little twin daughters—not a day over three—on either side at her feet. One of the little girls was standing, holding a bouquet of flowers in her arms. The other was seated and held a bowl of fruit in her lap. Both of them were barefoot, yet they wore grownup-looking pastel dresses, décolleté like their mother's; and their facial expressions suggested that they were making a conscious effort to look as dour and disenchanted as all their elders in the other portraits.

The portraits of the men had brought only the briefest comment from Charley's friend. About one he said: "That old gentleman looks like he has the sour belches." About another he asked, "What is that supposed to be in his hand?" But when he came to the portrait of the great-grandmother he responded at once with warm feeling. It was the prettiest portrait he had ever seen! It looked exactly like something out of *Gone with the Wind*! That was his first reaction. A moment later, however, with astonishing abruptness he changed his tone completely. "No," he said, "I don't think I like it so much after all. Those two little girls give me the creeps!"

Charley laughed when he said this. And presently his friend laughed and said: "They *are* funny, aren't they? They are like two little dwarfs, not like real children."

"I had never thought of it, but that's so," said Charley.

"Children aren't just little grownups," his friend continued. "They're made differently. I've noticed that myself and I'm not even an artist. Why, those two little girls look like something out of the funny paper." Then for several minutes he and Charley stood before the pictures giggling.

Sylvia, in the dining room, only smiled a little and quietly continued with the inventory she was taking of her china.

III

Even if Sylvia had wanted them there the Harrison children could hardly have been kept at home on the day of the move. Nora stayed until noon, but she was there because most of her friends lived in the neighborhood. Even she was in-and-out during the morning, and at noon she was to dress herself in her most grown-up clothes and set out for a luncheon being given for her in the next block. The other children had left the house soon after breakfast on their last rounds of visits with friends. Wallace, just back from Virginia, had an all-day date with "a certain Hollins College girl who lived up in Evanston." She and he would make his rounds together. And the two other children—Margaret and Charley—each had a variety of appointments to keep.

Not one of them had left the house without apologizing for not staying to help, but Sylvia had laughed at them and said having them out of the way was good riddance. She required only that they get in touch with her in the early afternoon, by which time she expected to be able to gauge the hour the vans would be loaded. "Before nightfall," she had told them at breakfast, "we'll be on our way to Tennessee." They would spend the night somewhere along the way in Illinois. They would set out, as she and Nate and their whole tribe had set out from Cedar Springs so many years before, in two cars. But this time there would be no servants and no pets, and probably there would not be so many flat tires along the way. Wallace would be driving the Packard limousine, and she and Margaret would take turns at the wheel of the roadster.

At about ten o'clock that morning Sylvia happened to be in the sewing room, which was one of the little rooms that opened off the back hall upstairs. She had, at the last minute, discovered a tear in one of the old summer slipcovers that she always put on the living-room furniture when she moved; and now, though the movers were already putting some of the heavier pieces in the vans, she was taking time out to mend that tear.

She had just finished this job of mending and was closing the sewing machine when she heard a hurried tiptoeing on the back stairs. She knew at once it must be Nora, since all the other children were already gone. Presently Nora stood in the sewing-room doorway, all out of breath. After a moment she said, "Mother, Leander's downstairs and says he still wants to go with us. . . . And so is Mr. Canada."

"*Well*, Leander *can't*," Sylvia said almost before Nora had stopped speaking. "And I don't dream Mr. Canada wants to!"

"I didn't mean Mr. Canada did," Nora said in a whisper. "He has some sort of flower in his buttonhole, and he's brought you a dozen roses, I think."

Sylvia was gathering up the bulky slipcover that she had mended, not looking at Nora. "Mr. Canada is a very nice old man," she said.

Nora said nothing for a moment. Then she whispered, "But what shall I say to Leander? I think he's been drinking." Nora was now a girl of fifteen. She looked quite grown up and was already allowed to go to parties with boys sometimes. But her whispering and this carrying of messages between adults were things she still seemed to take a childish pleasure in.

"Why, my child," her mother answered, stuffing the electric cord into the machine and looking squarely at Nora for the first time, "say to Leander that he can't. I don't want to see him. He knows I haven't time to fool with any of his foolishness today. Tell him to go off somewhere else and sober up. It is our prerogative as one of the newly poor not to have to fool with the likes of Leander."

So saying, Sylvia gathered the slipcover under one arm, asked Nora in which room Mr. Canada was waiting, then, slipping past Nora, she walked toward the head of the staircase. Her step was light and quick. As she passed a wooden packing case in the center of the hall she stretched out her free hand and ran her fingers lightly along one side of it, barely touching its rough surface with her fingertips. It was a graceful, youthful gesture, plainly inadvertent, and plainly indicative of how absorbed she was in her thoughts of the moment. There was nothing about the way she walked or about any of her movements now to suggest the precise, deliberate, middle-aged manner in which she had dealt with her sewing machine and with her daughter. Even the matronly styled housedress she had put on this morning did not altogether conceal the still youthful lines of her figure. And suddenly, as she reached the head of the back stairway, the serious, staid expression on her face gave way to one of amusement. Waiting downstairs to see her were two persons whom she had been fully expecting to arrive at the house sometime during this day. What amused her, suddenly, was the thought of their arriving at the same moment. Each had come, she knew, because in the goodness of his heart he wanted to be of help to her in the move. They honestly imagined—it seemed incredibly funny to Sylvia—that she needed the help of a man at such a time . . . *she* to whom moving had been a life's work.

Sylvia started downstairs that morning with the intention of dismissing her two callers immediately. But, by the time she was halfway down the straight flight into the back hall, she had witnessed—in the hall below—a spectacle that would change her plans for that day and for many another after it. What she saw was actually only a little scene between Leander and Mr. Canada, but she recognized it at once as a scene from which enormous meaning for herself might be drawn. At first glance she observed only that the two men were standing in conversation with one another at the far end of the hall. Yet even that was enough to arrest her momentarily on the stairs. Somehow, even that filled her with sudden alarm—an emotion to which she was almost a total stranger. When she saw, a moment later, that their conversation was by no means a civil one, that both were talking at once and shaking their heads (if not quite their fists) at one another, the sight filled her with such consternation that she dropped the heavy slipcover on the steps.

As she stooped to gather the slipcover into her arms again, it occurred to her first to turn back up the steps. Deciding against that, her next impulse was to call out to Nora to stay upstairs out of harm's way. She did neither, however. When she presently realized that Nora had, of her own accord, lingered above, she proceeded very slowly down the steps with her eyes fixed on the two men. They were standing near the doorway that led into the front part of the house. Apparently neither of them realized that it was she who was approaching. If aware of anyone's presence they probably thought it was Nora returning with messages for them. Only when she was almost at the foot of the stairs, Sylvia saw Mr. Canada glance at her for the first time. Seeing her, he dropped his eyes to the floor and commenced backing through the doorway and into the dark center hall beyond. His face, already flushed with anger, grew even redder, and Sylvia knew that he would be overcome with embarrassment at having seemed to invade her domestic privacy. Leander, on his part, appeared to understand what Mr. Canada's withdrawal meant. Without looking at Sylvia he turned and walked directly into the kitchen, his head literally bowed down.

At the foot of the stairs Sylvia stopped again. She knew now that she was still not ready to order either Leander Thompson or Mr. Canada away from the house, even knew that she would need them there that day until the very last piece of furniture was loaded on the last van. That neither of them would be of any assistance whatsoever in the business of packing and loading she knew also, and knew, in fact, how much they would be in the way. She might even have predicted—so clear was she, in a sense, about the turn events were going to take—how Leander in the course of the day would manage to break out a window light in the library (when trying to get out of the way of the movers) and would upset a huge bottle of cleaning fluid on the parqueted floor of the hall. Or how Mr. Canada would have to be asked, time and again, to get up from a comfortable couch or chair that the movers were ready to load. But any hindrance or inconvenience which their presence would be to actual moving seemed unimportant. The important thing was the fact that Leander's and Mr. Canada's quarreling there in the doorway had filled her with consternation and alarm.

Until now Sylvia had supposed that the two men represented for her the two sides of a rather simple question, the question of whether or not it was wise of her to be taking her family back to Tennessee. On one side Mr. Canada seemed to represent everything that was against her doing so. Not since the first time he came to see her had he made any direct reference to the subject, but his talk had always been about things pertaining to Chicago. Sometimes it was about the business world in which Nate had lived, sometimes about the civic enterprises to which he nowadays devoted much of his time, sometimes about his own career and the opportunities which Chicago offered "a young man with good connections and a head for business." For a while after each of his visits Sylvia had been able to think of almost nothing but her own selfishness.

In her selfishness she had never made any effort to understand Nate's business career and thereby to share his greatest interest in life. In her selfishness she had insisted always upon the temporariness of their life away from Tennessee, had lived as though the great facts of their life were that they had come from Cedar Springs and that they would someday return there. And now in her selfishness she was about to take her children away from a place which perhaps meant the same to them that Tennessee did to her. . . . On the other side, Leander seemed to represent everything that favored the move. Although he refused any job she found for him, still he didn't go on trying to persuade her to take him with her to Cedar Springs. Instead, he talked to her about other moves he had made with the family. He recalled the number of flat tires they had had the day they left Cedar Springs and drove to Memphis, and how helpful the country people had been along the way. He recalled times when one or another of the children had cried over leaving some house and how Sylvia would always say, "I have no feeling about this house. This house isn't home to *us*." But he talked even more about Cedar Springs itself, about the colored people and the white people there. He spoke of having written his sister-in-law that the Harrisons were coming home and of her having replied that "every colored person in Logan County" was hoping to work for them. He reminisced about

members of Nate's family in Cedar Springs, asking her which
of them were still alive. And he asked about her own brother
in Thornton and her brother in Nashville. He said he supposed
they would look after her land and money for her and that that
was probably her big reason for going back. He said it was good
to have kinfolk to fall back on. He said it was good to live in
a place where they knew who you really were. There wasn't
anything in the world like living in a place where there were
no questions you didn't know the answers to.

But after Leander's visits it had been just the same as after
Mr. Canada's. Sylvia could think of nothing but her own selfishness. She had judged herself, she had condemned herself,
yet she had never considered giving up the move. She could
no more have thought of that than she could have thought
of trying to change the sequence of the seasons. It sometimes
seemed queer to her that after hearing both sides of the argument, so to speak, she experienced exactly the same sensations.
And she wondered exactly what position Leander represented
in the argument. That is, it was easy for her to associate Mr.
Canada with Nate and thus make him represent one side. But
was it possible to make Leander the symbol for what might
be called her side of the argument? While she was still paused
at the foot of the back stairs she realized that this had indeed
not been possible by any ridiculous stretch of the imagination.
And now the cause for her alarm and consternation became
clear to her.

She had no side, no voice in the argument, and had never had
one. The two voices she had been listening to for weeks past
had both been Nate's voice. They were voices she had heard
for years and years. The two men, quarreling in her back hall,
seemed to represent the two sides of Nate. He had, through all
the years, *wanted* her to *want* to go back to Tennessee. That
was what his tolerance had meant. Her own wishes had never
entered into it. That was what Nate's tolerance had meant.
It had meant his freedom from a part of himself, a part of
himself that would have bound him to a place and to a past
time otherwise inescapable. He had *wanted* her to insist upon
taking all that furniture everywhere they went. That was what
his tolerance had meant. She felt now an immense weariness,
felt as though she had been carrying all that absurd furniture

on her back these twenty years. And for what purpose? Why, so that Nate might be free to live that part of life in which there somehow must be no furniture. His selfishness, for the moment, seemed so monstrous to her that she almost smiled at the judgments she had passed upon herself.

It was not then, however, that Sylvia made her decision which so baffled everyone. Perhaps there was no actual moment of decision. But as she went about the duties which that moving day held for her she found herself imagining a life totally different from any that she would have before been capable of imagining. She envisioned herself not as a widow living alone in the City of Chicago, not even as a woman living in an American city, but merely as a Person alive in an Unnamed City. The nameless streets of the Unnamed City were populated with other Persons who were all sexless, ageless, nameless; and in some unaccountable way she seemed to excel everyone there in their very sexlessness and agelessness and namelessness. This vision kept returning to her all day long, interrupting her efforts to concentrate on the tasks she had set herself, sometimes so disconcerting her that she could not answer the questions of the moving men. Yet whenever it faded from her mind's eye her one thought was that she must recapture it. And nothing helped so to keep it before her as the presence of Leander and Mr. Canada.

Their presence was so indispensable to her that there was no promise she would not have made to keep them there that day. As for the trouble between them in the hall, she had guessed its cause before she had exchanged a word with either of them. While waiting for her they had met, and each had regarded the other as an intruder. They had met, as it turned out, in the so-called center hall, by the telephone. Mr. Canada, wishing to call his office, had had to wait several minutes while Leander finished a casual conversation with someone whom he addressed in terms of endearment. In the closeness of that little passage where the telephone was situated (actually a windowless area under the broad landing of the front stairs) the smell of whisky on Leander's breath was unmistakable to Mr. Canada. And so, in Sylvia's interest, Mr. Canada felt obliged to ask him the nature of his business in the house today. Leander, resentful of being questioned by a stranger in the Harrison house, replied that he would like to know the same of Mr. Canada. Then, by mutual consent, they had stepped into the back hall to settle the matter.

The details of the incident were revealed to Sylvia in the course of the day; but the details interested her little, and neither did the whole incident itself once she had guessed its cause. The behavior of the two men became more and more clownlike as the day progressed. Mr. Canada's manner with the movers became more imperious each time he was asked to rise from a comfortable chair, and there were moments when Sylvia feared that one of those big, burly men, sweating through their khaki coveralls, might lay hand on the old gentleman.

With the moving men Leander was humility itself, particularly with those of his own race. Yet he impeded the general progress by forever getting in the way and by the more insidious means of sharing his whisky with some of the movers themselves. After Sylvia explained Leander's history to Mr. Canada and explained how his rags and even his drinking were supposed to draw her sympathy, and after she assured Leander that Mr. Canada was not there in the role of the landlord evicting a tenant, each of them became reconciled to spending that day under the same roof with the other.

Toward the end of the afternoon, only a short while before her scattered children began to gather in, Sylvia stood just inside the front door of the house watching the last of her furniture being loaded on the last van. Behind her in the big entrance hall were her former chauffeur and her former landlord. Mr. Canada was leaning against the oak console table, which was the only piece of furniture left in the hall and on which the dozen roses he had brought Sylvia had been placed in a large watering can. At the rear of the hall Leander sat on the bottom step of the stairway, his elbows resting on his knees, his face buried in his hands. Though neither of the men had been allowed to lift a hand in the moving, both were in shirt sleeves and both appeared to be in a state of near-exhaustion.

Sylvia watched her furniture disappearing into the dark mouth of the van. As she did so there came to her again the vision of that strange, vague life in that strange, vague city—a city and a life which, being without names or attributes of any kind, could exist only as opposites of something else. And now, at the end of the day, that something else was somehow revealed to her. It was a particular moment in time, a situation, a thing she had experienced, a place. She thought at first it must be something that had happened at Cedar Springs, but almost at once she saw that it wasn't the town where she had gone to live as a bride but was that neighboring town where she had lived as a girl. It was Thornton, the old, dying town on the bluffs above the Tennessee River. It was there that she had known the name and quality of everything. It was there, more than anywhere else, that everything had had a name. Not only the streets and alleys there had had names; there had been names for the intersections of streets: Wifeworking Corner, the Blocks, the Step-down. Not only the great houses and small houses had names; on the outskirts of the town were two abandoned barns known as the Hunchback's Barn and General Forrest's Stable. Usually the houses bore the names of the families that had lived in them longest or lived in them first. But some of the houses had names like Heart's Ease and Robin's Roost and New Scuppernong, and some had more than one name; there were cases where two families in town obstinately called the same house by different names because each family had once owned and given a name to it. For every little lane or path or right-of-way through the fields surrounding the town there was a name, and down along the river underneath the giant sycamores and willow oaks and poplars, just below the bluffs on which the town stood, there was that path which had been known since Indian times as the Dark Walk. On Sunday afternoons in the early spring, and in the fall after the mosquitoes were gone, courting couples from the town strolled there. In Sylvia's grandmother's day it had been the custom for the town's best families to stroll there, dressed in their Sunday finery, after church. In those distant days the Dark Walk had been kept as a sort of town common or park, with the grass trimmed right down to the water's edge. But to Sylvia's generation it had a very different character. Vines of muscadine and fox grape reached from tree to tree, often obscuring any view of the river, and an undergrowth of pines and dogwood and Judas tree had sprung up between the walk and the steep escarpment. For the young people of that latter day there was an element of mystery and danger in the walk. It had not yet become the illicit kind of lover's lane which it was surely destined to be in another, still later time. It was protected from that fate by the townspeople's memory of what it had once been, and it was in a sense still considered the private property of the genteel and the well-to-do. Sylvia and her contemporaries went there with the consent—even the blessing—of their elders, and the danger and mystery of which they were aware existed only in the bright colored spiders which sometimes spun their webs across the path or in the fat water moccasins hurrying innocently across the path into the rank growth of creeper and poison ivy. Sylvia had gone there with Nate, and he had brushed aside glistening spiderwebs, had tossed a rock in the direction in which she had thought she saw a moccasin, and had asked her to marry him. To her on that day so long ago it had seemed an additional happiness that he had asked her while they strolled in that traditional spot. Then and during the many years since, she had cherished the image of herself as a young girl in white dimity repeating and sharing the experience of all the other girls to whom life had seemed to begin anew as they lingered by the ruins of an old lattice summerhouse or at the point where Thornton Creek joined the river.

She had cherished the image. And then the last afternoon in Ritchie Court, while she stood in the doorway of the house she was about to leave, she called up the image, and she found it had changed. She and the other young girls no longer seemed to be beginning life anew in the Dark Walk. They were all dressed in black, and it seemed that the experience they had shared there was really the beginning of widowhood. From the moment they pledged their love they were all, somehow, widows; and she herself had become a widow not the day Nate was found dead in his office but the day he asked her to marry him, in the Dark Walk. It seemed to her that in some way or other all the men of that generation in that town had been killed in the old war of her grandfather's day. Or they had been set free by it. Or their lives had been changed in a way that the women's lives were not changed. The men of Nate's time had crossed over a border, had pushed into a new country, or fled into a new country. And their brides lived as widows clinging to things the men would never come back to and from which they could not free themselves. Nate had gone literally to a new country, but Sylvia knew in her heart that it would have been the same if they had never left Cedar Springs. She could not blame him, but she could no longer blame herself either.

When the movers began tying up the gate of the last van Sylvia turned and stepped back into the hall. Without looking at him she called Leander's name. Leander lunged forward from his place on the steps. He staggered the length of the hall, dragging his coat and tie after him, and stopped directly before Sylvia, his eyes downcast, the very flesh of his face seeming to hang half molten from the bones. Is this Leander? Sylvia asked herself. And then: Is he really as drunk as this? Aloud she was saying to him: "I am going to arrange with the moving men for you to ride back home in the van." There was not kindness but disdain for him in her voice, and Leander did not lift his eyes. "The children and I are not going, after all," she said. Leander's face registered nothing. To Sylvia this seemed to mean that he had known before she had that she would make this outrageously sudden and irrational decision.

Watching his face closely, though without hope of understanding what was going on in his mind, she continued, "We're not going, but the furniture is going, as planned, and there'll be a place for you." As she spoke, it came over her that whether he was now drunk or not, the character of this man had suffered real degradation of some kind during the time since he first came begging her to take him back to Tennessee. Instead of the disdain and the contempt which his abject, groveling manner inspired in her she wanted to pity him and blame herself for his pathetic condition. Tears did come to her eyes momentarily, but they were not for Leander, and she hadn't the illusion that they were. When at last Leander looked up he seemed in no wise moved by her tears. Their eyes met for one meaningless moment and then each turned away, he in the direction of the van outside the door, she, her eyes dry again, toward Mr. Canada, who was still leaning against the console table and staring at her. "Would you happen to know of a place," she said to Mr. Canada in a tone of utmost indifference, "a temporary place . . ." Mr. Canada moved toward her mechanically. She read in his face that he was trying to decide something—some such question as whether he should exercise his authority in an apartment building that he owned or perhaps use his influence elsewhere to find a suitable place for her and the children. A certain brightness came into his eyes, as it had that day when he mentioned the scholarship for little Charley, but not the same brightness exactly. This and a sudden color in his face and a quickness in his step made him seem less an old man than she usually thought of him as being. But instead of an effect of youthful ardor and naïveté there was one of shrewdness and of a relish for this opportunity to show his powers and resources for their own sake. His eyes shone, Sylvia observed, but not with love for her.

In only a minute or two he was leaving to arrange for a place for her to take her family that night. "Anything but a hotel," she said as he turned away.

"I think I know what you want," he said, not looking back. His phrasing and the tone of his voice were precisely those she had heard from the mouths of a hundred real-estate agents, and as he went down the cement steps to the street Sylvia found herself watching him with just such indifference as she would have watched one of those agents. Yet, somehow, the way he slipped into his jacket going down the steps, his agedness, his obvious loneliness, even the very fact of his considerable wealth all seemed to Sylvia deserving of her pity—of that at least. And she was, at this moment, conscious of her guilt for having permitted him to continue coming to see her. She would no more have been capable of shedding tears for Mr. Canada, however, than she had been for Leander. And possibly nothing in the whole world except the sight which awaited her when she turned back into the hall could have evoked from her the torrent of tears, the violent, uncontrollable sobs which then, for minutes that seemed hours, wrenched and shook her physical being. . . . She had turned back from the doorway and had caught, in a mirrored panel on the opposite wall, one miserable glimpse of her own image.

As she wept, she hardly knew why she did so. Yet she did comprehend now that it was because she was too full of sympathy for herself that she had not felt sympathy for Leander or Mr. Canada. She kept thinking of the hurt she had done them both and it occurred to her that she might be about to hurt her children by remaining in Chicago, where, for them, there might conceivably be the same obstacles for understanding that there had been for her in Tennessee. But how could she *know*? One knew too pitiably little about what one did to one's self, without trying to know what one had done to others. She didn't at all understand the full meaning of the decision she had made this afternoon. But she believed that in time an understanding of it would come to her. It would come without her knowing it, perhaps while she slept. She knew, at least, that in the future she would regard the people she loved very differently from the way she had in the past. And it wasn't that she would love them less; it was that she would in some sense or other learn to love herself more.

When the children came in, one by one, and Sylvia told them of her decision that the furniture should go on but that they should stay in Chicago and move into new quarters, each of them seemed more stunned and at the same time more overjoyed than the one before. Even the knowledge that their new quarters would be in an apartment house which Mr. Canada owned did not dampen their enthusiasm. And when finally the vans pulled away from the house, they all stood in the street laughing at the sight of Leander's feet which were all that could be seen of him as he lay, already asleep, amid the furniture.

Her family slept that night in an apartment whose windows overlooked Lake Michigan. There were seven large rooms, all without furnishings of any kind except the beds which Mr. Canada had had sent up from the basement of the building. Next morning the four children woke early, and they were all still excited by the unexpected change of plans. Sylvia did not wake early, however. She slept until almost midday, and the children, knowing how exhausted she would be from the strain of yesterday, went tiptoeing and whispering about the bright, empty rooms, careful not to wake her from her sound sleep. They took their turns going out to breakfast so as not to leave her to awake alone in a strange place.

When Sylvia woke at last it was after 11:30. The door to the room where she slept was closed. Beyond it she could hear the lowered voices of the children. Upon waking there was no moment of confusion for her, as there probably had been for each of them that morning. She knew at once where she was. And she did not immediately let them know that she was awake. She got out of bed and walked barefoot to the window that opened on the Lake and for some time stood gazing upon the scene outside. She knew that the day and the hour had come when she must think of herself not as one bereaved but as a being who had been set free. Presently she would face her children in the empty rooms of this strange apartment and they would see her still as the widow of Nate Harrison, but Sylvia knew that that did not describe who she was today or who she would be in days ahead. Barefoot and clad only in her silk nightgown, her figure in the window could almost have been mistaken for that of a little girl. She looked diminutive and fragile and defenseless. And as she stared out over the tree-tops along Sheridan Road and at the vast green waters of Lake Michigan, she didn't fail to be aware of her own smallness. But she was aware too that the discovery and the decision she had made about her life in the past twenty-four hours constituted the one important discovery and the one important decision that anyone, regardless of sex or age or physical size, could make. Nothing could alter that certainty. It had no relation to one's sex or to the times in which one lived or to one's being a woman from a country town in Tennessee or to one's being the mother of four grown children established in an apartment on Lake Shore Drive. It was not diminished, either, by any thought of the boundless and depthless waters of the lake or the endless stretches of the city.

Finally Sylvia turned back to her new room and to the sound of her children's adult voices. As she walked toward the door leading to the other rooms she began thinking of the immediate need to furnish the apartment. She would go shopping today—this very afternoon. She would bring into her new quarters only what was new and useful and pleasing to the eye. She thought with new pleasure of being surrounded only by what she herself had selected. Everything would be according to her own tastes, and even of that there would be only enough to serve the real needs and comforts of the family. There must be nothing anywhere in the apartment to diminish the effect of newness and brightness or to remind her of the necessity there had been to dispense with all that was old and useless and inherited.

1939

TWENTY YEARS ago, in 1939, I was in my senior year at Kenyon College. I was restless, and wasn't sure I wanted to stay on and finish college. My roommate at Kenyon was Jim Prewitt. Jim was restless, too. That fall, he and I drove to New York City to spend our Thanksgiving holiday. Probably both of us felt restless and uneasy for the same reasons that everyone else did in 1939, or for just the obvious reasons that college seniors always do, but we imagined our reasons to be highly individual and beyond the understanding of the other students.

It was four o'clock on Wednesday afternoon when we left Gambier, the little Ohio village that gives Kenyon its post office address. We had had to wait till the four o'clock mail was put in the Gambier post office, because each of us was expecting a check from home. My check came. Jim's did not. But mine was enough to get us to New York, and Jim's would be enough to get us back. "Enough to get back, *if* we come back!" That became our motto for the trip. We had both expressed the thought in precisely the same words and at precisely the same moment as we came out of the post office. And during the short time it took us to dash back across the village street, with its wide green in the center, and climb the steps up to our room in Douglass House and then dash down again with our suitcases to the car, we found half a dozen excuses for repeating our motto.

The day was freakishly warm, and all of our housemates were gathered on the front stoop when we made our departure. In their presence, we took new pleasure in proclaiming our motto and repeating it over and over while we threw our things into the car. The other boys didn't respond, however, as we hoped they would. They leaned against the iron railing of the stoop, or sat on the stone steps leaning against one another, and refused to admit any interest in our "childish" insinuation: *if* we came back. All seven of them were there and all seven were in agreement on the "utter stupidity" of our long Thanksgiving trip as well as that of our present behavior. But they didn't know our incentive, and they couldn't be expected to understand.

For two years, Jim and I had shared a room on the second floor of old Douglass House. I say "old" because at Kenyon in those days there was still a tendency to prefix that adjective to the name of everything of any worth on the campus or in the village. Oldness had for so many years been the most respected attribute of the college that it was natural for its prestige to linger on a few years after what we considered the new dispensation and the intellectual awakening. Old Douglass House *was* an oldish house, but it had only been given over for use as a dormitory the year that Jim and I—and most of our friends—came to Kenyon. The nine of us moved into it just a few weeks after its former occupants—a retired professor and his wife, I believe—had moved out. And we were to live there during our three years at Kenyon (all of us having transferred from other colleges as sophomores)—to live there without ever caring to inquire into the age or history of the house. We were not the kind of students who cared about such things. We were hardly aware, even, of just how quaint the house was, with its steep white gables laced with gingerbread work, and its Gothic windows and their arched window blinds. Our unawareness—Jim's and mine—was probably never more profound than on that late afternoon in November, when we set out for New York. Our plan was to spend two days in Manhattan and then go on to Boston for a day with Jim's family, and our only awareness was of that plan.

During the previous summer, Jim Prewitt had become engaged to a glorious, talented girl with long flaxen hair, whom he had met at a student writers' conference somewhere out West. And I, more attached to things at home in St. Louis than Jim was to things in Boston—*I* had been "accepted" by an equally glorious dark-eyed girl in whose veins ran the Creole blood of old-time St. Louis. By a happy coincidence both of these glorious girls were now in New York City. Carol Crawford, with her flaxen hair fixed in a bun on the back of her neck and a four-hundred-page manuscript in her suitcase, had headed East from the fateful writers' conference in search of a publisher for her novel. Nancy Gibault had left St. Louis in September to study painting at the National Academy. The two girls were as yet unacquainted, and it was partly to the

correcting of this that Jim and I meant to dedicate our Thanksgiving holiday.

The other boys at Douglass House didn't know our incentive, and when we said goodbye to them there on the front
steps I really felt a little sorry for them. Altogether, they were a
sad, shabby, shaggy-looking lot. All of us who lived at Douglass
House were, I suppose. You have probably seen students who
look the way we did—especially if you have ever visited Bard
College or Black Mountain or Rollins or almost any other college nowadays. Such students seem to affect a kind of hungry,
unkempt look. And yet they don't really know what kind of
impression they want to make; they only know that there are
certain kinds they *don't* want to make.

Generally speaking, we at Douglass House were reviled by the
rest of the student body, all of whom lived in the vine-covered
dormitories facing the campus, and by a certain proportion of
the faculty. I am sure we were thought of as a group as closely
knit as any other in the college. We were even considered a sort
of fraternity. But we didn't see ourselves that way. We would
have none of that. Under that high gabled roof, we were all
independents and meant to remain so. Housing us "transfers"
together this way had been the inspiration of the dean or the
president under the necessity of solving a problem of overflow
in the dormitories. Yet we did not object to his solution, and
of our own accord we ate together in the Commons, we hiked
together about the countryside, we went together to see girls in
nearby Mount Vernon, we enrolled in the same classes, flocked
more or less after the same professors, and met every Thursday
night at the creative writing class, which we all acknowledged
as our reason for being at Kenyon. But think of ourselves as a
club, or as dependent upon each other for companionship or
for anything else, we would not. There were times when each
of us talked of leaving Kenyon and going back to the college
or university from which he had come—back to Ann Arbor or
Olivet, back to Chapel Hill, to Vanderbilt, to Southwestern,
or back to Harvard or Yale. It was a moderately polite way
each of us had of telling the others that *they* were a bunch of
Kenyon boys but that *he* knew something of a less cloistered
existence and was not to be confused with their kind. We were

so jealous of every aspect of our independence and individuality that one time, I remember, Bruce Gordon nearly fought
with Bill Anderson because Bill, for some strange reason, had
managed to tune in, with his radio, on a Hindemith sonata that
Bruce was playing on the electric phonograph in his own room.

Most of us had separate rooms. Only Jim Prewitt and I shared
a room, and ours was three or four times as big as most dormitory cubicles. It opened off the hall on the second floor, but it
was on a somewhat lower level than the hall. And so when you
entered the door, you found yourself at the head of a little flight
of steps, with the top of your head almost against the ceiling.
This made the room seem even larger than it was, as did the
scarcity and peculiar arrangement of the furniture. Our beds,
with our desks beside them, were placed in diagonally opposite
corners, and we each had a wobbly five-foot bookshelf set up
at the foot of his bed, like a hospital screen. The only thing we
shared was a little three-legged oak table in the very center of
the room, on which were a hot plate and an electric coffeepot,
and from which two long black extension cords reached up to
the light fixture overhead.

The car that Jim and I were driving to New York did not
belong to either of us. It didn't at that time belong to anybody, really, and I don't know what ever became of it. At the
end of our holiday, we left it parked on Marlborough Street in
Boston, with the ignition key lost somewhere in the gutter. I
suppose Jim's parents finally disposed of the car in some way
or other. It had come into our hands the spring before, when
its last owner had abandoned it behind the college library and
left the keys on Jim's desk up in our room. He, the last owner,
had been one of us in Douglass House for a while—though
it was, indeed, for a very short while. He was a poor boy who
had been at Harvard the year that Jim was there, before Jim
transferred to Kenyon, and he was enormously ambitious and
possessed enough creative energy to produce in a month the
quantity of writing that most of us were hoping to produce
in a lifetime. He was a very handsome fellow, with a shock
of yellow hair and the physique of a good trackman. On him
the cheapest department store clothes looked as though they
were tailor-made, and he could never have looked like the rest

of us, no matter how hard he might have tried. I am not sure that he ever actually matriculated at Kenyon, but he was there in Douglass House for about two months, clicking away on first one typewriter and then another (since he had none of his own); I shall never forget the bulk of manuscript that he turned out during his stay, most of which he left behind in the house or in the trunk of the car. The sight of it depressed me then, and it depresses me now to think of it. His neatly typed manuscripts were in every room in the house—novels, poetic dramas, drawing-room comedies, lyrics, epic poems, short stories, scenarios. He wasn't at all like the rest of us. And except for his car he has no place in this account of our trip to New York. Yet since I have digressed this far, there is something more that I somehow feel I ought to say about him.

Kenyon was to him only a convenient place to rest awhile (for writing was not work to him) on his long but certain journey from Harvard College to Hollywood. He used to say to us that he wished he could do the way we were doing and really dig in at Kenyon for a year or so and get his degree. The place appealed to him, he said, with its luxuriant countryside, and its old stone buildings sending up turrets and steeples and spires above the treetops. If he stayed, he would join a fraternity, so he said, and walk the Middle Path with the other fraternity boys on Tuesday nights, singing fraternity songs and songs of old Kenyon. He said he envied us—and yet he hadn't himself time to stay at Kenyon. He was there for two months, and while he was there he was universally admired by the boys in Douglass House. But when he had gone, we all hated him. Perhaps we were jealous. For in no time at all stories and poems of his began appearing in the quarterlies as well as in the popular magazines. Pretty soon one of his plays had a good run on Broadway, and I believe he had a novel out even before that. He didn't actually go to Hollywood till after the war, but get there at last he did, and now, I am told, he has a house in the San Fernando Valley and has the two requisite swimming pools, too.

To us at Kenyon he left his car. It was a car given to him by an elderly benefactor in Cambridge, but a car that had been finally and quite suddenly rendered worthless in his eyes by a publisher's advance, which sent him flying out of our world by the first plane he could get passage on. He left us the car without any regret, left it in the same spirit that American tourists left their cars on the docks at European ports when war broke out that same year. In effect, he tossed us his keys from the first-class deck of the giant ship he had boarded at the end of his plane trip, glad to know that he would never need the old rattletrap again and glad to be out of the mess that all of us were in for life.

I have said that I somehow felt obliged to include everything I have about our car's last real owner. And now I know why I felt so. Without that digression it would have been impossible to explain what the other boys were thinking—or what we thought they were thinking—when we left them hanging about the front stoop that afternoon. They were thinking that there was a chance Jim and I had had an "offer" of some kind, that we had "sold out" and were headed in the same direction that our repudiated brother had taken last spring. Perhaps they did not actually think that, but that was how we interpreted the sullen and brooding expressions on their faces when we were preparing to leave that afternoon.

Of course, what their brooding expressions meant made no difference to Jim or me. And we said so to each other as, with Jim at the wheel, we backed out of the little alleyway beside the house and turned into the village street. We cared not a hoot in hell for what they thought of us or of our trip to New York. Further, we cared no more—Jim and I—for each other's approval or disapproval, and we reminded each other of this then and there.

We were all independents in Douglass House. There was no spirit of camaraderie among us. We were not the kind of students who cared about such things as camaraderie. Besides, we felt that there was more than enough of that spirit abroad at Kenyon, among the students who lived in the regular dormitories and whose fraternity lodges were scattered about the wooded hillside beyond the village. In those days, the student body at Kenyon was almost as picturesque as the old vine-clad buildings and the rolling countryside itself. So it seemed to us, at least. We used to sit on the front stoop or in the upstairs windows of Douglass House and watch the fops and dandies of the campus go strolling and strutting by on their way to the post office or the bank, or to Jean Val Dean's short-order joint. Those three establishments, along with Dicky Doolittle's filling station, Jim Lynch's barber shop, Jim Hayes's grocery store, Tom Wilson's Home Market, and Mrs. Titus's lunchroom and bakery (the Kokosing Restaurant), constituted the business district of Gambier. And it was in their midst that Douglass House was situated. Actually, those places of business were strung along just one block of the village's main thoroughfare. Each was housed in its separate little store building or in a converted dwelling house, and in the spring and in the fall, while the leaves were still on the low hanging branches of the trees, a stranger in town would hardly notice that they were places of business at all.

From the windows of Douglass House, between the bakery and the barber shop, we could look down on the dormitory students who passed along the sidewalk, and could make our comment on what we considered their silly affectations—on their provincial manners and their foppish, collegiate clothing. In midwinter, when all the leaves were off the trees, we could see out into the parkway that divided the street into two lanes—and in the center of the parkway was the Middle Path. For us, the Middle Path was the epitome of everything about Kenyon that we wanted no part of. It was a broad gravel walkway extending not merely the length of the village green; it had its beginning, rather, at the far end of the campus, at the worn doorstep of the dormitory known as Old Kenyon, and ran the length of the campus, on through the village, then through the wooded area where most of the faculty houses were, and ended at the door of Bexley Hall, Kenyon's Episcopal seminary. In the late afternoon, boys on horseback rode along it as they returned from the polo field. At noon, sometimes, boys who had just come up from Kenyon's private airfield appeared on the Middle Path still wearing their helmets and goggles. And after dinner every Tuesday night the fraternity boys marched up and down the path singing their fraternity songs and singing fine old songs about early days at Kenyon and about its founder, Bishop Philander Chase:

> The first of Kenyon's goodly race
> Was that great man Philander Chase.

He climbed the hill and said a prayer
And founded Kenyon College there.

He dug up stones, he chopped down trees,
He sailed across the stormy seas,
And begged at ev'ry noble's door,
And also that of Hannah More.

He built the college, built the dam,
He milked the cow, he smoked the ham;
He taught the classes, rang the bell,
And spanked the naughty freshmen well.

At Douglass House we wanted none of that. We had all
come to Kenyon because we were bent upon becoming writers
of some kind or other and the new president of the college had
just appointed a famous and distinguished poet to the staff
of the English Department. Kenyon was, in our opinion, an
obscure little college that had for more than a hundred years
slept the sweet, sound sleep that only a small Episcopal college can ever afford to sleep. It was a quaint and pretty spot.
We recognized that, but we held that against it. That was not
what we were looking for. We even collected stories about other
people who had resisted the beauties of the campus and the
surrounding countryside. A famous English critic had stopped
here on his way home from a long stay in the Orient, and when
asked if he did not admire our landscape he replied, "No. It's
too rich for my blood." We all felt it was too rich for ours, too.
Another English visitor was asked if the college buildings did
not remind him of Oxford, and by way of reply he permitted
his mouth to fall open while he stared in blank amazement at
his questioner.

Despite our feeling that the countryside was too rich for our
blood, we came to know it a great deal better—or at least in
more detail—than did the polo players or the fliers or the members of the champion tennis team. For we were nearly all of us
walkers. We walked the country roads for miles in every direction, talking every step of the way about ourselves or about our
writing, or if we exhausted those two dearer subjects, we talked
about whatever we were reading at the time. We read W. H.
Auden and Yvor Winters and Wyndham Lewis and Joyce and

Christopher Dawson. We read *The Wings of the Dove* (aloud!) and *The Cosmological Eye* and *The Last Puritan* and *In Dreams Begin Responsibilities.* (Of course, I am speaking only of books that didn't come within the range of the formal courses we were taking in the college.) On our walks through the country—never more than two or three of us together—we talked and talked, but I think none of us ever listened to anyone's talk but his own. Our talk seemed always to come to nothing. But our walking took us past the sheep farms and orchards and past some of the old stone farmhouses that are scattered throughout that township. It brought us to the old quarry from which most of the stone for the college buildings and for the farmhouses had been taken, and brought us to Quarry Chapel, a long since deserted and "deconsecrated" chapel, standing on a hill two miles from the college and symbolizing there the failure of Episcopalianism to take root among the Ohio country people. Sometimes we walked along the railroad track through the valley at the foot of the college hill, and I remember more than once coming upon two or three tramps warming themselves by a little fire they had built or even cooking a meal over it. We would see them maybe a hundred yards ahead, and we would get close enough to hear them laughing and talking together. But as soon as they noticed us we would turn back and walk in the other direction, for we pitied them and felt that our presence was an intrusion. And yet, looking back on it, I remember how happy those tramps always seemed. And how sad and serious we were.

Jim and I headed due East from Gambier on the road to Coshocton and Pittsburgh. Darkness overtook us long before we ever reached the Pennsylvania state line. We were in Pittsburgh by about 9 P.M., and then there lay ahead of us the whole long night of driving. Nothing could have better suited our mood than the prospect of this ride through the dark, wooded countryside of Pennsylvania on that autumn night. This being before the days of the turnpike—or at least before its completion—the roads wound about the great domelike hills of that region and through the deep valleys in a way that answered some need we both felt. We spoke of it many times during the night, and Jim said he felt he knew for the first time the meaning of "verdurous glooms and winding mossy ways." The two of us were setting out on this trip not in search of the kind of quick success in the world that had so degraded our former friend in our eyes; we sought, rather, a taste—or foretaste—of "life's deeper and more real experience," the kind that dormitory life seemed to deprive us of. We expressed these yearnings in just those words that I have put in quotation marks, not feeling the need for any show of delicate restraint. We, at twenty, had no abhorrence of raw ideas or explicit statement. We didn't hesitate to say what we wanted to be and what we felt we must have in order to become that. We wanted to be writers, and we knew well enough that before we could write we had to have "mature and adult experience." And, by God, we *said* so to each other, there in the car as we sped through towns like Turtle Creek and Greensburg and Acme.

I have observed in recent years that boys the age we were then and with our inclinations tend to value ideas of this sort above all else. They are apt to find their own crude obsession with mere ideas the greatest barrier to producing the works of art they are after. I have observed this from the vantage ground of the college professor's desk, behind which the irony of fate has placed me from time to time. From there, I have also had the chance to observe something about *girls* of an artistic bent or temperament, and for that reason I am able to tell you more about the two girls we were going to see in New York than I could possibly have known then.

At the time—that is, during the dark hours of the drive East—each of us carried in his mind an image of the girl who had inspired him to make this journey. In each case, the image of the girl's face and form was more or less accurate. In my mind was the image of a brunette with dark eyes and a heart-shaped face. In Jim's was that of a blonde, somewhat above average height, with green eyes and perhaps a few freckles on her nose. That, in general, was how we pictured them, but neither of us would have been dogmatic about the accuracy of his picture. Perhaps Carol Crawford didn't have any freckles. Jim wasn't sure. And maybe her eyes were more blue than green. As for me, I wouldn't have contradicted anyone who said Nancy Gibault's face was actually slightly elongated, rather than heart-shaped, or that her hair had a decided reddish cast to it. Our impressions of this kind were only more or less accurate, and we would have been the first to admit it.

But as to the talent and the character and the original mind of the two glorious girls, we would have brooked no questioning of our concepts. Just after we passed through Acme, Pennsylvania, our talk turned from ourselves to these girls—from our inner yearnings for mature and adult experience to the particular objects toward which we were being led by these yearnings. We agreed that the quality we most valued in Nancy and Carol was their "critical" and "objective" view of life, their unwillingness to accept the standards of "the world." I remember telling Jim that Nancy Gibault could always take a genuinely "disinterested" view of any matter—"disinterested in the best sense of the word." And Jim assured me that, whatever else I might perceive about Carol, I would sense at once the originality of her mind and "the absence of anything commonplace or banal in her intellectual make-up."

It seems hard to believe now, but that was how we spoke to each other about our girls. That was what we thought we believed and felt about them then. And despite our change of opinions by the time we headed back to Kenyon, despite our complete and permanent disenchantment, despite their unkind treatment of us—as worldly and as commonplace as could be—I know now that those two girls were as near the concepts we had of them to begin with as any two girls their age might be, or should be. And I believe now that the decisions *they* made about *us* were the right decisions for *them* to make. I have only the vaguest notion of how Nancy Gibault has fared in later life. I know only that she went back to St. Louis the following spring and was married that summer to Lon Havemeyer. But as for Carol Crawford, everybody with any interest in literary matters knows what became of her. Her novels are read everywhere. They have even been translated into Javanese. She is, in her way, even more successful than the boy who made the long pull from Harvard College to Hollywood.

Probably I seem to be saying too much about things that I understood only long after the events of my story. But the need for the above digression seemed no less urgent to me than did that concerning the former owner of our car. In his

case, the digression dealt mostly with events of a slightly earlier time. Here it has dealt with a wisdom acquired at a much
later time. And now I find that I am still not quite finished
with speaking of that later time and wisdom. Before seeing me
again in the car that November night in 1939, picture me for
just a moment—much changed in appearance and looking at
you through gold-rimmed spectacles—behind the lectern in
a classroom. I stand before the class as a kind of journeyman
writer, a type of whom Trollope might have approved, but one
who has known neither the financial success of the facile Harvard boy nor the reputation of Carol Crawford. Yet this man
behind the lectern is a man who seems happy in the knowledge
that he knows—or thinks he knows—what he is about. And
from behind his lectern he is saying that any story that is written in the form of a memoir should give offense to no one,
because before a writer can make a person he has known fit into
such a story—or any story, for that matter—he must do more
than change the real name of that person. He must inevitably
do such violence to that person's character that the so-called
original is forever lost to the story.

   The last lap of Jim's and my all-night drive was the toughest.
The night had begun as an unseasonably warm one. I recall
that there were even a good many insects splattered on our
windshield in the hours just after dark. But by the time we
had got through Pittsburgh the sky was overcast and the temperature had begun to drop. Soon after 1 A.M. we noticed the
first big, soft flakes of snow. I was driving at the time, and Jim
was doing most of the talking. I raised one finger from the
steering wheel to point out the snow to Jim, and he shook his
head unhappily. But he went on talking. We had maintained
our steady stream of talk during the first hours of the night
partly to keep whoever was at the wheel from going to sleep,
but from this point on it was more for the purpose of making
us forget the threatening weather. We knew that a really heavy
snowstorm could throw our holiday schedule completely out
of gear. All night long we talked. Sometimes the snow fell
thick and fast, but there were times, too, when it stopped altogether. There was a short period just before dawn when the
snow turned to rain—a cold rain, worse than the snow, since

it began to freeze on our windshield. By this time, however, we had passed through Philadelphia and we knew that somehow or other we would make it on to New York.

We had left Kenyon at four o'clock in the afternoon, and at eight the next morning we came to the first traffic rotary outside New York, in New Jersey. Half an hour later we saw the skyline of the city, and at the sight of it we both fell silent. I think we were both conscious at that moment not so much of having arrived at our destination as of having only then put Kenyon College behind us. I remember feeling that if I glanced over my shoulder I might still see on the horizon the tower of Peirce Hall and the spires of Old Kenyon Dormitory. And in my mind's eye I saw the other Douglass House boys—all seven of them—still lingering on the stone steps of the front stoop, leaning against the iron railing and against one another, staring after us. But more than that, after the image had gone I realized suddenly that I had pictured not seven but *nine* figures there before the house, and that among the other faces I had glimpsed my own face and that of Jim Prewitt. It seemed to me that we had been staring after ourselves with the same fixed, brooding expression in our eyes that I saw in the eyes of the other boys.

Nancy Gibault was staying in a sort of girls' hotel, or rooming house, on 114th Street. Before she came down from her room that Thanksgiving morning, she kept me waiting in the lobby for nearly forty-five minutes. No doubt she had planned this as a way of preparing me for worse things to come. As I sat there, I had ample time to reflect upon various dire possibilities. I wondered if she had been out terribly late the night before and, if so, with whom. I thought of the possibility that she was angry with me for not letting her know what day I would get there. (I had had to wait on my check from home, and there had not been time to let her know exactly when we would arrive.) I reflected, even, that there was a remote chance she had not wanted me to come at all. What didn't occur to me was the possibility that *all* of these things were true. I sat in that dreary, overheated waiting room, still wearing my overcoat and holding my hat in my lap. When Nancy finally came down,

she burst into laughter at the sight of me. I rose slowly from
my chair and said angrily, "What are you laughing at? At how
long I've waited?"

"No, my dear," she said, crossing the room to where I stood.
"I was laughing at the way you were sitting there in your overcoat with your hat in your lap like a little boy."

"I'm sweating like a horse," I said, and began unbuttoning
my coat. By this time Nancy was standing directly in front of
me, and I leaned forward to kiss her. She drew back with an
expression of revulsion on her face.

"Keep your coat on!" she commanded. Then she began giggling and backing away from me. "If you expect me to be seen
with you," she said, "you'll go back to wherever you're staying
and shave that fuzz off your lip."

For three weeks I had been growing my first mustache.

I had not yet been to the hotel where Jim and I planned to
stay. It was a place that Jim knew about, only three or four
blocks from where Nancy was living, and I now set out for
it on foot, carrying my suitcase. Our car had broken down
just after we came up out of the Holland Tunnel. It had been
knocking fiercely for the last hour of the trip, and we learned
from the garage man with whom we left it that the crankcase
was broken. It seems we had burned out a bearing, because we
had forgotten to put any oil in the crankcase. I don't think we
realized at the time how lucky we were to find a garage open
on Thanksgiving morning and, more than that, one that would
have the car ready to run again by the following night.

After I had shaved, I went back to Nancy's place. She had
gone upstairs again, but this time she did not keep me waiting
so long. She came down wearing a small black hat and carrying
a chesterfield coat. Back in St. Louis, she had seldom worn a
hat when we went out together, and the sight of her in one now
made me feel uncomfortable. We sat down together near the
front bay window of that depressing room where I had waited
so long, and we talked there for an hour, until it was time to
meet Jim and Carol for lunch.

While we talked that morning, Nancy did not tell me that
Lon Havemeyer was in town from St. Louis, much less that
she had spent all her waking hours with him during the past

week. I could not have expected her to tell me at once that she was now engaged to marry him, instead of me, but I did feel afterward that she could have begun at once by telling me that she had been seeing Lon and that he was still in town. It would have kept me from feeling quite so much at sea during the first hours I was with her. Lon was at least seven or eight years older than Nancy, and for five or six years he had been escorting debutantes to parties in St. Louis. His family were of German origin and were as new to society there as members of Nancy's family were old to it. The Havemeyers were also as rich nowadays as the Gibaults were poor. Just after Nancy graduated from Mary Institute, Lon had begun paying her attentions. They went about together a good deal while I was away at college, but between Nancy and me it had always been a great joke. To us, Lon was the essence of all that we were determined to get away from there at home. I don't know what he was really like. I had heard an older cousin of Nancy's say that Lon Havemeyer managed to give the impression of not being dry behind the ears but that the truth was he was "as slick as a newborn babe." But I never exchanged two sentences with him in my life—not even during the miserable day and a half that I was to tag along with him and Nancy in New York.

It may be that Nancy had not known that she was in love with Lon or that she was going to marry him until she saw me there, with the fuzz on my upper lip, that morning. Certainly I must have been an awful sight. Even after I had shaved my mustache, I was still the seedy-looking undergraduate in search of "mature experience." It must have been a frightful embarrassment to her to have to go traipsing about the city with me on Thanksgiving Day. My hair was long, my clothes, though quite genteel, were unpressed, and even rather dirty, and for some reason I was wearing a pair of heavy brogans. Nancy had never seen me out of St. Louis before, and since she had seen me last, she had seen Manhattan. To be fair to her, though, she had seen something more important than that. She had, for better or for worse, seen herself.

We had lunch with Jim and Carol at a little joint over near Columbia, and it was only after we had left them that Nancy told me Lon Havemeyer was in town and waiting that very moment to go with us to the Metropolitan Museum. I burst out laughing when she told me, and she laughed a little, too. I don't remember when I fully realized the significance of Lon's presence in New York. It wasn't that afternoon, or that night, even. It was sometime during the next day, which was Friday. I suppose that I should have realized it earlier and that I just wouldn't. From the time we met Lon on the museum steps, he was with us almost continuously until the last half hour before I took my leave of Nancy the following night. Sometimes I would laugh to myself at the thought of this big German oaf's trailing along with us through the galleries in the afternoon and then to the ballet that night. But I was also angry at Nancy from the start for having let him horn in on our holiday together, and at various moments I pulled her aside and expressed my anger. She would only look at me helplessly, shrug, and say, "I couldn't help it. You really have got to try to see that I couldn't help it."

After the ballet, we joined a group of people who seemed to be business acquaintances of Lon's and went to a Russian night-club—on Fourteenth Street, I think. (I don't know exactly where it was, for I was lost in New York and kept asking Nancy what part of town we were in.) The next morning, about ten, Nancy and I took the subway down to the neighborhood of Fifty-seventh Street, where we met Lon for breakfast. Later we looked at pictures in some of the galleries. I don't know what became of the afternoon. We saw an awful play that night. I know it was awful, but I don't remember what it was. The events of that second day are almost entirely blotted from my memory. I only know that the mixture of anger and humiliation I felt kept me from ducking out long before the evening was over—a mixture of anger and humiliation and something else, something that I had begun to feel the day before when Nancy and I were having lunch with Jim and Carol Crawford.

Friday night, I was somehow or other permitted to take Nancy home alone from the theater. We went in a taxi, and neither of us spoke until a few blocks before we reached 114th Street. Finally I said, "Nancy." And Nancy burst into tears.

"You won't understand, and you will never forgive me," she said through her tears, "but I am so terribly in love with him."

I didn't say anything till we had gone another block. Then I said, "How have things gone at the art school?"

Nancy blew her nose and turned her face to me, as she had not done when she spoke before. "Well, I've learned that I'm not an artist. They've made me see that."

"Oh," I said. Then, "Does that make it necessary to—"

"It makes everything in the world look different. If I could only have known in time to write you."

"When did you know?"

"I don't know. I don't know when I knew."

"Well, it's a good thing you came to New York," I said. "You almost made a bad mistake."

"No," she said. "You mustn't think I feel that about you."

"Oh, not about me," I said quickly. "About being an artist. When we were at lunch yesterday, you know, with Jim and his girl, it came over me suddenly that you weren't an artist. Just by looking at you I could tell."

"What a cruel thing to say," she said quietly. All the emotion had gone out of her voice. "Only a child could be so cruel," she said.

When the taxi stopped in front of her place, I opened the door for her but didn't get out, and neither of us said goodbye. I told the driver to wait until she was inside and then gave him the address of my hotel. When, five minutes later, I was getting out and paying the driver, I didn't know how much to tip him. I gave him fifteen cents. He sat with his motor running for a moment, and then, just before he pulled away, he threw the dime and the nickel out on the sidewalk and called out to me at the top of his voice, "You brat!"

The meeting between Nancy and Carol was supposed to be one of the high points of our trip. The four of us ate lunch together that first day sitting in the front booth of a little place that was crowded with Columbia University students. Because this was at noon on Thanksgiving Day, probably not too many restaurants in that neighborhood were open. But I felt that every student in the dark little lunchroom was exulting in his freedom from a certain turkey dinner somewhere, and from some particular family gathering. We four had to sit in the very

front booth, which was actually no booth at all but a table and
two benches set right in the window. Some people happened
to be getting up from that table just as we came in and Carol,
who had brought us there, said, "Quick! We must take this
one." Nancy had raised up on her tiptoes and craned her neck,
looking for a booth not quite so exposed.

"I think there may be some people leaving back there," she
said.

"No," said Carol in a whisper. "Quick! In here." And when
we had sat down, she said, "There are some dreadful people
I know back there. I'd rather die than have to talk to them."

Nancy and I sat with our backs almost against the plate-
glass window. There was scarcely room for the two of us on
the bench we shared. I am sure the same was true for Jim and
Carol, and they faced us across a table so narrow that when
our sandwiches were brought, the four plates could only be
arranged in one straight row. There wasn't much conversation while we ate, though Jim and I tried to make a few jokes
about our drive through the snow and about how the car broke
down. Once, in the middle of something Jim was saying, Carol
suddenly ducked her head almost under the table. "Oh, God!"
she gasped. "Just my luck!" Jim sat up straighter and started
peering out into the street. Nancy and I looked over our shoulders. There was a man walking along the sidewalk on the other
side of the broad street.

"You mean that man way over there?" Nancy asked.

"Holy God, yes," hissed Carol. "Do please stop gaping
at him."

Nancy giggled. "Is he dreadful, too?" she asked.

Carol straightened and took a sip of her coffee. "No, he's
not exactly dreadful. He's the critic Melville Bland." And after
a moment: "He's a full professor at Columbia. I was supposed
to have dinner today with him and his stupid wife—she's the
playwright Dorothy Lewis and really *awfully* stupid—at some
chichi place in the East Sixties, and I told them an awful lie
about my going out to Connecticut for the day. I'd rather be
shot than talk to either of them for five minutes."

I was sitting directly across the table from Carol. While we
were there, I had ample opportunity to observe her, without
her seeming to notice that I was doing so. My opportunity

came each time anyone entered the restaurant or left it. For nobody could approach the glass-front door, either from the street or from inside, without Carol's fastening her eyes upon that person and seeming to take in every detail of his or her appearance. Here, I said to myself, is a real novelist observing people—*objectively* and *critically*. And I was favorably impressed by her obvious concern with literary personages; it showed how committed she was to a life of writing. Carol seemed to me just the girl that Jim had described. Her blond hair was not really flaxen. (It was golden, which is prettier but which doesn't sound as interesting as flaxen.) It was long and carelessly arranged. I believe Jim was right about its being fixed in a knot on the back of her neck. Her whole appearance showed that she cared as little about it as either Jim or I did about ours . . . Perhaps *this* was what one's girl really ought to look like.

When we got up to leave, Nancy lingered at the table to put on fresh lipstick. Carol wandered to the newspaper stand beside the front door. Jim and I went together to pay our bills at the counter. As we waited for our change, I said an amiable, pointless "Well?"

"Well what?" Jim said petulantly.

"Well, they've met," I said.

"Yeah," he said. "They've met." He grinned and gave his head a little shake. "But Nancy's just another society girl, old man," he said. "I had expected something more than that." He suddenly looked very unhappy, and rather angry, too. I felt the blood rising in my cheeks and knew in a moment that I had turned quite red. Jim was much heavier than I was, and I would have been no match for him in any real fight, but my impulse was to hit him squarely in the face with my open hand. He must have guessed what I had in mind, for with one movement he jerked off his horn-rimmed glasses and jammed them into the pocket of his jacket.

At that moment, the man behind the counter said, "Do you want this change or not, fellows?"

We took our change and then glared at each other again. I had now had time to wonder what had come over Jim. Out of the corner of my eye I caught a glimpse of Carol at the newsstand and took in for the first time, in that quick glance, that she was wearing huaraches and a peasant skirt and blouse, and that what she now had thrown around her shoulders was not a topcoat but a long green cape. "At least," I said aloud to Jim, "Nancy's not the usual bohemian. She's not the run-of-the-mill arty type."

I fully expected Jim to take a swing at me after that. But, instead, a peculiar expression came over his face and he stood for a moment staring at Carol over there by the newsstand. I recognized the expression as the same one I had seen on his face sometimes in the classroom when his interpretation of a line of poetry had been questioned. He was reconsidering.

When Nancy joined us, Jim spoke to her very politely. But once we were out in the street there was no more conversation between the two couples. We parted at the first street corner, and in parting there was no mention of our joining forces again. That was the last time I ever saw Carol Crawford, and I am sure that Jim and Nancy never met again. At the corner, Nancy and I turned in the direction of her place on 114th Street. We walked for nearly a block without either of us speaking. Then I said, "Since when did you take to wearing a hat everywhere?"

Nancy didn't answer. When we got to her place, she went upstairs for a few minutes, and it was when she came down again that she told me Lon Havemeyer was going to join us at the Metropolitan. Looking back on it, I feel that it may have been only when I asked that question about her hat that Nancy decided definitely about how much Lon and I were going to be seeing of each other during the next thirty-six hours. It is possible, at least, that she called him on the telephone while she was upstairs.

I didn't know about it then, of course, but the reception that Jim Prewitt found awaiting him that morning had, in a sense, been worse even than mine. I didn't know about it and Jim didn't tell me until the following spring, just a few weeks before our graduation from Kenyon. By that time, it all seemed to us like something in the remote past, and Jim made no effort to give me a complete picture of his two days with Carol. The thing he said most about was his reception upon arriving.

He must have arrived at Carol's apartment, somewhere on Morningside Heights, at almost the same moment that I arrived at Nancy's place. He was not, however, kept waiting for forty-five minutes. He was met at the door by a man whom he described as a flabby middle-aged man wearing a patch over one eye, a T shirt, and denim trousers. The man did not introduce himself or ask for Jim's name. He only jerked his head to one side, to indicate that Jim should come in. Even before the door opened, Jim had heard strains of the Brandenburg Concerto from within. Now, as he stepped into the little entryway, the music seemed almost deafening, and when he was led into the room where the phonograph was playing, he could not resist the impulse to make a wry face and clap his hands over his ears.

But although there were half a dozen people in the room, nobody saw the gesture or the face he made. The man with the patch over his eye had preceded him into the room, and everyone else was sitting with eyes cast down or actually closed. Carol sat on the floor tailor fashion, with an elbow on each knee and her face in her hands. The man with the patch went to her and touched the sole of one of her huaraches with his foot. When she looked up and saw Jim, she gave him no immediate sign of recognition. First she eyed him from head to foot with an air of disapproval. Jim's attire that day, unlike my own, was extremely conventional (though I won't say he ever looked conventional for a moment). At Kenyon, he was usually the most slovenly and ragged-looking of us all. He really went about in tatters, sometimes even with the soles hanging loose from his shoes. But in his closet, off our room, there were always to be found his "good" shoes, his "good" suit, his "good" coat, his "good" hat, all of which had been purchased for him at Brooks Brothers by his mother. Today he had on his "good" things. Probably it was that that made Carol stare at him as she did. At last she gave him a friendly but slightly casual smile, placed a silencing forefinger over her lips, and motioned for him to come sit down beside her and listen to the deafening tones of the concerto.

While the automatic phonograph was changing records, Carol introduced Jim to the other people in the room. She introduced him and everyone else—men and women alike—by their surnames only: "Prewitt, this is Carlson. Meyer, this is Prewitt." Everyone nodded, and the music began again at the same volume. After the Bach there was a Mozart symphony. Finally Jim, without warning, seized Carol by the wrist, forcibly led her from the room, and closed the door after them. He was prepared to tell her precisely what he thought of his reception, but he had no chance to. "Listen to me," Carol began at once—belligerently, threateningly, all but shaking her finger in his face. "I have sold my novel. It was definitely accepted three days ago and is going to be published in the spring. And two sections from it are going to be printed as stories in the *Partisan Review*."

From that moment, Jim and Carol were no more alone than Nancy and I were. Nearly everywhere they went, they went with the group that had been in Carol's apartment that morning. After lunch with us that first noon, they rejoined the same party at someone else's apartment, down in Greenwich Village. When Jim told me about it, he said he could never be sure whose apartment he was in, for they always behaved just as they did at Carol's. He said that once or twice he even found himself answering a knock at the door in some strange apartment and jerking his head at whoever stood outside. The man with the patch over his eye turned out to be a musicologist and composer. The others in the party were writers whose work Jim had read in New Directions anthologies and in various little magazines, but they seemed to have no interest in anything he had to say about what they had written, and he noticed that their favorite way of disparaging any piece of writing was to say "it's *so* naïve, *so* undergraduate." After Jim got our car from the garage late Friday afternoon, they all decided to drive to New Jersey to see some "established writer" over there, but when they arrived at his house the "established writer" would not receive them.

Jim said there were actually a few times when he managed to get Carol away from her friends. But her book—the book that had been accepted by a publisher—was Carol's Lon Havemeyer, and her book was always with them.

Poor Carol Crawford! How unfair it is to describe her as she was that Thanksgiving weekend in 1939. Ever since she was a little girl on a dairy farm in Wisconsin she had dreamed of becoming a writer and going to live in New York City. She had not merely dreamed of it. She had worked toward it every waking hour of her life, taking jobs after school in the wintertime, and full-time jobs in the summer, always saving the money to put herself through the state university. She had made herself the best student—the prize pupil—in every grade of grammar school and high school. At the university she had managed to win every scholarship in sight. Through all those years she had had but one ambition, and yet I could not have met her at a worse moment in her life. Poor girl, she had just learned that she *was* a writer.

Driving to Boston on Saturday, Jim and I took turns at the wheel again. But now there was no talk about ourselves or about much of anything else. One of us drove while the other slept. Before we reached Boston, in mid-afternoon, it was snowing again. By night, there was a terrible blizzard in Boston.

As soon as we arrived, Jim's father announced that he would not hear of our trying to drive back to Kenyon in such weather and in such a car. Mrs. Prewitt got on the telephone and obtained a train schedule that would start us on our way early the next morning and put us in Cleveland sometime the next night. (From Cleveland we would take a bus to Gambier.) After dinner at the Prewitts' house, I went with Jim over to Cambridge to see some of his prep-school friends who were still at Harvard. The dinner with his parents had been painful enough, since he and I were hardly speaking to each other, but the evening with him and his friends was even worse for me. In the room of one of these friends, they spent the time drinking beer and talking about the undergraduate politics at Harvard and about the Shelley Poetry Prize. One of the friends was editor of the *Crimson*, I believe, and another was editor of the *Advocate*—or perhaps he was just on the staff. I sat in the corner pretending to read old copies of the *Advocate*. It was the first time I had been to Boston or to Cambridge, and ordinarily I would have been interested in forming my own impressions of how people like the Prewitts lived and of what Harvard students were like. But, as things were, I only sat cursing the fate that had made it necessary for me to come on to Boston instead of returning directly to Kenyon. That is, my own money having been exhausted, I was dependent upon the money Jim would get from his parents to pay for the return trip.

Shortly before seven o'clock Sunday morning, I followed Jim down two flights of stairs from his room on the third floor of his family's house. A taxi was waiting for us in the street outside. We were just barely going to make the train. In the hall I shook hands with each of his parents, and he kissed them goodbye. We dashed out the front door and down the steps to the street. Just as we were about to climb into the taxi, Mrs. Prewitt came rushing out, bareheaded and without a wrap, calling to us that we had forgotten to leave the key to the car, which was parked there in front of the house. I dug down into my pocket and pulled out the key along with a pocketful of change. But as I turned back toward Mrs. Prewitt I stumbled on the curb, and the key and the change went flying in every direction and were lost from sight in the deep snow that lay on the ground that morning. Jim and Mrs. Prewitt and I began to search for the key, but Mr. Prewitt called from the doorway that we should go ahead, that we would miss our train. We hopped in the taxi, and it pulled away. When I looked back through the rear window I saw Mrs. Prewitt still searching in the snow and Mr. Prewitt moving slowly down the steps from the house, shaking his head.

On the train that morning Jim and I didn't exchange a word or a glance. We sat in the same coach but in different seats, and we did not go into the diner together for lunch. It wasn't until almost dinnertime that the coach became so crowded that I had either to share my seat with a stranger or to go and sit beside Jim. The day had been long, I had done all the thinking I wanted to do about the way things had turned out in New York. Further, toward the middle of the afternoon I had begun writing in my notebook, and I now had several pages of uncommonly fine prose fiction, which I did not feel averse to reading aloud to someone.

I sat down beside Jim and noticed at once that *his* notebook was open, too. On the white, unlined page that lay open in his lap I saw the twenty or thirty lines of verse he had been working on. It was in pencil, quite smudged from many erasures, and was set down in Jim's own vigorous brand of progressive-school printing.

"What do you have there?" I said indifferently.

"You want to hear it?" he said with equal indifference.

"I guess so," I said. I glanced over at the poem's title, which was "For the Schoolboys of Douglass House," and immediately wished I had not got myself into this. The one thing I didn't want to hear was a preachment from him on his "mature experience" over the holiday. He began reading, and what he read was very nearly this (I have copied this part of the poem down as it later appeared in *Hika*, our undergraduate magazine at Kenyon):

> Today while we are admissibly ungrown,
> Now when we are each half boy, half man,
> Let us each contrast himself with himself,
> And weighing the halves well, let us each regard
> In what manner he has not become a man.
>
> Today let us expose, and count as good,
> What is mature. And childish peccadillos
> Let us laugh out of our didactic house—
> The rident punishment one with reward
> For him bringing lack of manliness to light.

But I could take no more than the first two stanzas. And I knew how to stop him. I touched my hand to his sleeve and whispered, "Shades of W. B. Yeats." And I commenced reciting:

> Now that we're almost settled in our house
> I'll name the friends that cannot sup with us
> Beside a fire of turf in th' ancient tower . . .

Before I knew it, Jim had snatched my notebook from my hands, and began reading aloud from it:

She had told him—Janet Monet had, for some inscrutable reason which she herself could not fathom, and which, had he known—as she so positively and with such likely assurance thought he knew—that if he came on to New York in the weeks ensuing her so unbenign father's funeral, she could not entertain him alone. . . .

Then he closed my notebook and returned it to me. "I can put it into rhyme for you, Mr. Henry James," he said. "It goes like this:

> She knew that he knew that her father was dead.
> And she knew that he knew what a life he had led—

While he was reciting, with a broad grin on his face and his eyes closed, I left him and went up into the diner to eat dinner. The next time we met was in the smoking compartment, at eight o'clock, an hour before we got into Cleveland.

It was I who wandered into the smoking compartment first. I went there not to smoke, for neither Jim nor I started smoking till after we left college, but in the hope that it might be empty, which, oddly enough, it was at that moment. I sat down by the window, at the end of the long leather seat. But I had scarcely settled myself there and begun staring out into the dark when the green curtain in the doorway was drawn back. I saw the light it let in reflected in the windowpane, and I turned around. Jim was standing in the doorway with the green curtain draped back over his head and shoulders. I don't know why, but it was only then that I realized that Jim, too, had been jilted. Perhaps it was the expression on his face—an expression of disappointment at not finding the smoking compartment empty, at being deprived of his one last chance for solitude before returning to Douglass House. And now—more than I had all day—I hated the sight of him. My lips parted to speak, but he literally took the sarcastic words out of my mouth.

"Ah, you'll get over it, little friend," he said.

Suddenly I was off the leather seat and lunging toward him. And he had snatched off his glasses, with the same swift gesture he had used in the restaurant, and tossed them onto the seat. The train was moving at great speed and must have taken a sharp turn just then. I felt myself thrown forward with more force than I could possibly have mustered in the three or four steps I took. When I hit him, it was not with my fists, or even my open hands, but with my shoulder, as though I was blocking in a game of football. He staggered back through the doorway and into the narrow passage, and for a moment the green curtain separated us. Then he came back. He came at me just as

I had come at him, with his arms half folded over his chest. The blow he struck me with his shoulders sent me into the corner of the leather seat again. But I, too, came back.

Apparently neither of us felt any impulse to strike the other with his fist or to take hold and wrestle. On the contrary, I think we felt a mutual abhorrence and revulsion toward any kind of physical contact between us and if our fight had taken any other form than the one it did, I think that murder would almost certainly have been committed in the smoking compartment that night. We shoved each other about the little room for nearly half an hour, with ever-increasing violence, our purpose always seeming to be to get the other through the narrow doorway and into the passage—out of sight behind the green curtain.

From time to time, after our first exchange of shoves, various would-be smokers appeared in the doorway. But they invariably beat a quick retreat. At last one of them found the conductor and sent him in to stop us. By then it was all over, however. The conductor stood in the doorway a moment before he spoke, and we stared at him from opposite corners of the room. He was an old man with an inquiring and rather friendly look on his face. He looked like a man who might have fought game-cocks in his day, and I think he must have waited that moment in the doorway in the hope of seeing something of the spectacle that had been described to him. But by then each of us was drenched in sweat, and I know from a later examination of my arms and chest and back that I was covered with bruises.

When the old conductor was satisfied that there was not going to be another rush from either of us, he glanced about the room to see if we had done any damage. We had not even upset the spittoon. Even Jim's glasses were safe on the leather seat. "If you boys want to stay on this train," the conductor said finally, "you'll hightail it back to your places before I pull that emergency cord."

We were only thirty minutes out of Cleveland then, but when I got back to my seat in the coach I fell asleep at once. It was a blissful kind of sleep, despite the fact that I woke up every five minutes or so and peered out into the night to see if I could see the lights of Cleveland yet. Each time, as I dropped off to sleep again, I would say to myself what a fine sort of sleep it was, and each time it seemed that the wheels of the train were saying: *Not yet, not yet, not yet.*

After Cleveland there was a four-hour ride by bus to Gambier. Sitting side by side in the bus, Jim and I kept up a continuous flow of uninhibited and even confidential talk about ourselves, about our writing, and even about the possibility of going to graduate school next year if the army didn't take us. I don't think we were silent a moment until we were off the bus and, as we paced along the Middle Path, came in sight of Douglass House. It was 1 A.M., but through the bare branches of the trees we saw a light burning in the front dormer of our room. Immediately our talk was hushed, and we stopped dead still. Then, though we were as yet two hundred feet from the house and there was a blanket of snow on the ground, we began running on tiptoe and whispering our conjectures about what was going on in our room. We took the steps of the front stoop two at a time, and when we opened the front door, we were met by the odor of something cooking—bacon, or perhaps ham. We went up the long flight to the second floor on tiptoe, being careful not to bump our suitcases against the wall or the banisters. The door to our room was the first one at the top of the stairs. Jim seized the knob and threw the door open. The seven whom we had left lolling around the stoop on Wednesday were sprawled about our big room in various stages of undress, and all of them were eating. Bruce Gordon and Bill Anderson were in the center of the room, leaning over my hot plate.

Jim and I pushed through the doorway and stood on the doorstep looking down at them. I have never before or since seen seven such sober—no, such frightened-looking—people. Most eyes were directed at me, because it was my hot plate. But when Jim stepped down into the room, the two boys lounging back on his bed quickly stood up.

I remember my first feeling of outrage. The sacred privacy of that room under the eaves of Douglass House had been violated; this on top of what had happened in New York seemed for a moment more than flesh and blood could bear. Then, all of a sudden, Jim Prewitt and I began to laugh. Jim dropped his suitcase and went over to where the cooking was going on and said, "Give me something to eat. I haven't eaten all day."

I stood for a while leaning against the wall just inside the door. I was thinking of the tramps we had seen cooking down along the railroad track in the valley. Finally I said, "What a bunch of hoboes!" Everyone laughed—a little nervously, perhaps, but with a certain heartiness, too.

I continued to stand just inside the door, and presently I leaned my head against the wall and shut my eyes. My head swam for a moment. I had the sensation of being on the train again, swaying from side to side. It was hard to believe that I was really back in Douglass House and that the trip was over. I don't know how long I stood there that way. I was dead for sleep, and as I stood there with my eyes closed I could still hear the train wheels saying *Not yet, not yet, not yet.*

The Other Times

CAN ANYBODY honestly like having a high-school civics teacher for an uncle? I doubt it. Especially not a young girl who is popular and good-looking and who is going to make her debut some day at the Chatham Golf and Country Club. Nevertheless, that's who the civics teacher was at Westside High School when we were growing up in Chatham. He was the brother of Letitia Ramsey's father, and he had all the failings you would expect of a high-school civics teacher and baseball coach. In the classroom he was a laughingstock for the way he butchered the King's English, and out of school he was known to be a hard drinker and general hell-raiser. But the worst part of it was that he was a bachelor and that the Ramseys had to have him for dinner practically every Sunday.

If you had a Sunday afternoon date with Letitia, there the civics teacher would be, out on the front lawn, playing catch with one of Letitia's narrow-eyed little brothers. Somehow, what disturbed *me* about this particular spectacle when I was having Sunday dates with Letitia was the uncle's and the little brother's concentration on the ball and the kind of real fondness they seemed to feel for the thing. When either of them held it in his hand for a minute, he seemed to be wanting to make a pet of it. When it went back and forth between them, smacking their gloves, they seemed to hear it saying, yours, mine, yours, mine, as though nobody else had ever thrown or caught a baseball. But of course that's not the point. The point is that it was hard to think of Letitia's having this Lou Ramsey for an uncle. And I used to watch her face when we were leaving her house on a Sunday afternoon to see if she would show anything. But not Letitia!

It may not seem fair to dwell on this unfortunate uncle of a girl like Letitia Ramsey, but it was through him that I got a clearer idea of what she was like, and the whole Ramsey family, as well. They were very well-bred people, and just as well-to-do, even in the Depression. Mr. Ramsey, like my own father, was from the country, but, also like my father, he was from one of the finest country families in the state. And Mrs. Ramsey and my mother had gone through Farleigh Institute together,

which was an old-fashioned school where they studied Latin
so long that it made a difference in the way they spoke English
all the rest of their lives.

Anyway, though I didn't take Latin, fortunately I didn't take
civics, either (since I was hoping to go to college if the Depression eased up), and fortunately I didn't go out for the baseball
team. This made it not too hard for me to pretend not to notice
who Letitia's uncle was. Also, since Letitia didn't go to the
high school but went to Miss Jordan's, a school that has more
or less replaced Farleigh Institute in Chatham, it could have
been as easy for her to pretend not to notice as it was for me.

It could have been, except that Letitia didn't want it that
way. When she and I went across the lawn to my father's car
on those Sunday afternoons and her uncle and one of her little
brothers were carrying on with that baseball, she would call
out something like "Have fun, you two!" or "Come see us
this week, Uncle Louis!" And her voice never sounded sweeter
than it did then. After we were in the car, if I hadn't thought
of something else to talk about she would sometimes begin a
long spiel like "I always forget you don't really know my uncle.
I wish you did. You probably know how mad he is about sports.
That's why my little brothers adore him. And he's just as shy
as they are. Look at him and Charlie there. When I'm dressed
up like this to go out on a date, he and the boys won't even
look at me."

The truth is I felt that Letitia Ramsey was just as smart as
she could be—not in school, necessarily, but in the way she
handled subjects like undesirable relatives. I think she was very
unusual in this. There was one of her friends, named Nancy
O'Connor, who had a grandmother who had once run a fruit
stand at the old curb market, up on the North Side. The grandmother lived with the O'Connors and was a right funny sort
of person, if you know what I mean, and Nancy was forever
apologizing for her. Naturally, her apologizing did nothing
but make you uncomfortable. Also, there was Trudie Hauser,
whose brother Horst was a good friend of mine. The Hausers
lived out in the German section of town, where my mother
hadn't usually gone to parties in her day, and they still lived in
the kind of castle-like house that the first one of the Hausers

to get rich had built. Poor Trudie and poor Horst! They had not one but three or four peculiar relatives living with them. And they had German servants, to whom their parents were apt to speak in German, right before you, and make Trudie and Horst, who were both very blond, blush to the roots of their hair the way blonds are apt to do. Then there was also a girl named Maria Thomas. She had a much older brother who was a moron—a real one—and if he passed through the room, or even came in and sat down, she would simply pretend that he wasn't there, that he didn't even exist.

This isn't to say, of course, that all the girls in Chatham had something like that in their families. Lots of girls—and lots of the boys, too—had families like mine, with nobody in particular to be ashamed of. Nor is it to say that the girls who did have something of this kind weren't just as popular as the others and didn't have you to their houses to parties just as often. Nancy O'Connor's family, for instance, lived in a most beautiful Spanish-style house, with beamed ceilings and orange-colored tile floors downstairs, and with a huge walled-in sort of lawn out in the back, where Nancy gave a big party every June. But, I will say, at those parties you always felt that everybody was having more fun than Nancy, all because of the old grandmother. The peculiar old woman never came out into the light of the Japanese lanterns at the party, or anywhere near the tennis court, where the dancing was. She kept always in the shadows, close to the walls that enclosed the lawn. And some-one said that Nancy said this was because her grandmother was afraid we would steal the green fruit off the trees she had trained to grow like vines up the walls.

Whether or not Nancy had a good time, her June party was always one of the loveliest events of the year in Chatham. Even though it was the Depression, we had many fine and really lovely parties, and Nancy O'Connor's usually surpassed all others. It was there, at one of them, two nights after we had graduated from high school, that Horst Hauser and Bob Southard and I made up our minds to do a thing that we had been considering for some time and that a lot of boys like us must have done at one time or another. We had been seniors that year, you understand, and in Chatham boys are apt to go pretty wild during their senior year in high school. That is the time when you get to know a city as you will never have a chance to again if you come from the kind of people that I do. I have lived away from Chatham quite a long while now, mostly in places which are not too different from it but about which I never kid myself into thinking I know very much. Yet, like a lot of other men, I carry in my head, even today, a sort of detailed map of the city where I first learned to drive a car and first learned to make dates with girls who were not strictly of the kind I was brought up to date. And I don't mean nice girls like Nancy and Trudie, whose parents were different from mine but who were themselves very nice girls indeed. Chatham being only a middle-sized city—that is, without a big-league baseball team, yet with almost a quarter of a million big-league fans— and being not thoroughly Midwestern and yet not thoroughly Southern either, the most definitely complimentary thing I usually find to say about it is that it was a good place to grow up in. By which I don't mean that it is a good place to come *from*, or anything hateful like that.

For I like Chatham. And I remember everything I ever knew about it. Sometimes, when I go back there for a visit, I can direct people who didn't grow up there to a street or a section of town or even to some place out in the country nearby that they wouldn't have guessed I had any knowledge of. And whenever I am there nowadays, the only change I notice and the only thing that gives me a sad feeling is that the whole city is so much more painted up and prosperous-looking than it used to be during the Depression. And in connection with this, there is something I cannot help feeling is true and cannot help saying. My father, who came from a country town thirty-five miles east of Chatham, used to tell us how sad it made him to see the run-down condition of the house where he was born, out there in the country. But my feeling is that there is something even more depressing about going back to Chatham today and finding the house where I lived till I was grown— and the whole city, too—looking in much better shape than it did when I called it home. There are moments when I almost wish I could buy up the whole town and let it run down just a little.

Of course, that's an entirely selfish feeling, and I realize it. But it shows what wonderful times we had—decent good times, and others not so decent. And it shows that while we were having those fine times we knew exactly what everything around us was like. We didn't like money's being so tight and didn't like it that everything from the schoolhouse to the country club was a little shabby and run-down. We boys certainly *minded* wearing our fathers' cut-down dinner jackets, and the girls certainly *minded* wearing their older sisters' hand-me-down evening dresses; although we knew that our party clothes looked all right, we knew, too, that our older brothers and sisters, five years before, wouldn't have put up with them for five minutes. We didn't like any of this a bit, and yet it was *ours* and the worriers among us worried even then about how it was all bound to change.

Of course, when the change came, it wasn't at all what anyone had expected. For it never occurred to us then that a war would come along and solve all the problems of the future for us, in one way or another. Instead, we heard so much talk of the Depression that we thought that times were bound to get even worse than they had been, and that all the fun would go out of life as soon as we finished high school, or, at the latest, after college. If you were a worrier, as I was, it didn't seem possible that you would ever be able to make a living of the kind your father had always made. And I sat around some nights, when I ought to have been studying, wondering how people would treat me when I showed that I couldn't make the grade and began to go to pieces. It was on those nights that I used to think about Letitia Ramsey's uncle, whom I considered the most dismal failure of my acquaintance, and then think about how he was treated by Letitia. This became a thing of such interest to me that I was never afterward sure of my own innocence in the way matters developed the night of Nancy O'Connor's party.

I don't need to describe the kind of mischief the boys in my crowd were up to that year—that is, on nights when we weren't having movie dates or going to parties with the usual "nice girls" we had always known. Our mischief doesn't need going into here, and besides it is very old hat to anyone who grew up with the freedom boys have in places like Chatham (especially at a time like the Depression, when all the boys' private schools were closed down). Also, I suppose it goes without saying that we were pretty careful not to mix the one kind of wonderful time we were having with the other. To the girls we had known longest, we did make certain jokes and references they couldn't understand, or pretended they couldn't. We would kid each other, in front of them, about jams we had been in when they weren't along, without ever making any of it very clear. But that was as far as we went until, toward the end of the year, some of the girls got so they would beg us, or dare us, to take them with us some night to one of our "points of interest," which was how we referred to the juke joints and roadhouses we went to. We talked about the possibility of this off and on for several weeks. (Five years before, it wouldn't have taken our older brothers five minutes to decide to do such a thing.) And finally, on the night of Nancy O'Connor's party, Horst Hauser and Bob Southard and I decided that the time had come.

The three of us, with our dates, slipped away from the party just after midnight, telling Nancy that we would be back in about an hour, which we knew we wouldn't. And we didn't tell her mother we were going at all. We crossed the lawn and went out through a gate in the back wall at one of the corners, just behind a sort of tool house that Nancy called "the dovecote." She had told us how to find the gate, and she told us also to watch for her grandmother. And, sure enough, just as we were unlocking the gate, there came the old grandmother running along the side wall opposite us, and sticking close to it even when she made the turn at the other corner. She was wearing a long black dress, and at the distance from which we saw her I thought she might easily have been mistaken for a Catholic nun.

But we got the gate open and started through it and into the big vacant lot we had to cross to get to Horst Hauser's car. I held the gate for the other couples, and then for my own date. While I was doing this, I kept one eye on the old woman. But I also peered around the dovecote and saw Nancy O'Connor leave the bright lights of the tennis court and head across the grass under the Japanese lanterns, walking fast in order to catch her grandmother before she reached us. And when I shut the gate after me, I could just imagine the hell the old woman was going to catch.

It wasn't very polite, leaving Nancy's party that way and making trouble in the family—for Nancy was sure to blame the old woman for our going, somehow—but the whole point is that the girl who happened to be my date that night and for whom I had stood there holding the gate was none other than Letitia Ramsey.

Now, there is no use in my not saying right here that all through that spring Letitia's uncle, whom the high-school students generally spoke of as "the Ram," had been having the usual things said about him. And there is no use in my denying that by this time I knew those things were so. For we hadn't had our *other* wonderful times all winter long without running into the Ram at a number of our points of interest—him, along with a couple of his star athletes and his and their girl friends. In fact, I knew by this time that the rumors all of us had heard about him every year since we entered high school were true, and I knew, too, that it was the very athletes he coached and trained and disciplined from the day they first reported for practice, after junior high, that he ended by making his running mates when they were seniors.

But all that sort of thing, in my opinion, is pretty much old hat to most people everywhere. The important thing to me is that when we decided to leave Nancy's wonderful party that night and take our dates with us out to a dine-and-dance joint called Aunt Martha's Tavern, something crossed my mind. And I am not sure that it wasn't something I hoped for instead of something I dreaded, as it should have been. It was that this Aunt Martha's Tavern was exactly where we were most likely to run into the Ram on a Saturday night, which this happened to be, with, of course, one of his girl friends and a couple of his athletes with their girl friends, too.

Well, it couldn't have been worse. We all climbed into Horst Hauser's car and drove out west of town to Aunt Martha's. It was the kind of place where you had to ring several times before they would come and let you in. And when we had rung the bell the second time and were standing outside under the light, with its private flock of bugs whirling around it, waiting there for Aunt Martha to have a look at us through some crack somewhere and decide if she would let us in, a rather upsetting thing happened to me. We were all standing on the stoop together, facing the big, barnlike batten door to the place. Letitia was standing right next to me, and I just thought to myself I would steal a quick glance at her while she wasn't noticing. I turned my head only the slightest bit, but I saw at once that *she* was already looking at *me*. When our eyes met, I felt for the first second or two that she didn't realize they *had* met, because she kept right on looking without changing her expression. I couldn't at once tell what the expression meant. Then it came over me that there was something this girl was expecting me to say—or, at least, hoping I would say. I said the first thing that popped into my mind: "They always make you wait like this." And Letitia Ramsey looked grateful, even for that.

At last, the door was pulled open, though only just about six inches, and inside we saw the face of Aunt Martha's old husband. The old fellow gaped at the girls for a couple of seconds with a stupid grin on his face—he was a deaf-mute and a retired taxidermist—and then he threw the door wide open. We went inside—and, of course, there the Ram was, out on the floor dancing.

There weren't any lights on to speak of, except around the sides, in the booths, and the curtains to some of the booths were drawn. But even so, dark as it was, and with six or eight other couples swinging around on the dance floor, right off the bat I spotted the Ram. Maybe I only recognized him because he was doing the old-time snake-hips dancing that he liked to do when he was high. I can't be sure. But I have the feeling that when we walked into that place that night, I would have seen the Ram just as plainly even if he had not been there—seen the freckled hand he pumped with when he danced, seen the white sharkskin suit, seen the head of sandy hair, a little thin on top but with the sweaty curls still thick along his temples and on the back of his neck.

Once we were inside, I glanced at Letitia again. And for some reason I noticed now that either before she left the party or in the car coming out here she had moved the gardenia corsage that I had sent her from the shoulder strap of her dress to the center of its low-cut neckline. When I saw this, I suddenly turned to Bob and Horst and said, "Let's not stay here."

Letitia and the other two girls smiled at each other. "I think he thinks we'll disgrace him," Letitia said after a moment.

I don't know when she first saw her uncle. It may have been when I did, right off the bat. It being Letitia, you couldn't tell. Or I couldn't. The one clue I had was that when the old deaf-mute made signs for us to follow him across the floor to an empty booth, I saw her throw her little powder blue evening jacket, which was the same color as her dress, around her shoulders. It was a hot night, and before that she had only been carrying it over her arm.

Yet it wasn't necessarily her uncle's presence that caused Letitia to put the jacket around her bare shoulders. It could have been just the kind of place we were in. It could have been Martha's crazy-looking old husband, with his tufts of white hair sticking out in all directions. It seemed to me at the time that it might be only the sight of the old man's stuffed animal heads, which were hung all around the place. You didn't notice most of these with it so dark, but above the beer counter were the heads of three collie dogs, and as we went across the floor, the bubbly lights of the jukebox would now and again catch a gleam from the glass eyes of those collie dogs. Any other time in the world, I think the effect would have seemed irresistibly funny to me. I would have pointed it out to Horst and Bob, and afterward there would have been cryptic references made to it before girls like Letitia who normally wouldn't ever have been inside such a place.

We went into our booth, which was a big one in a corner, and almost as soon as we sat down, I saw two of the Ram's athletes come out on the dance floor with their girls. The Ram had disappeared, and I didn't see him dancing again. But every so often the two athletes would come out and dance for the length of about half a record and then go back to their booth, pushing the curtains apart just enough to let themselves slip through. None of us said a word about seeing them out there. And, of course, nobody mentioned the Ram. I guess we were all pretty uncomfortable about it, because we made a lot of uncomfortable and silly conversation. All of us except Letitia. We joked and carried on in a very foolish way, trying to cover up. But everything we said or did seemed to make my toes curl under.

For instance: Bob pretended he was going to close the curtains to our booth, and there was a great scramble between him and his date over keeping them open. And all the while, across the way, the curtains to the Ram's booth were never opened wider than it took for one person to slip in or out.

Also: "Where in the world *are* we?" one of the girls asked. That we were way out in the country, of course, they knew, but *where?* And it had to be explained that Aunt Martha's Tavern was across the line in Clark County, about twelve miles due west of Chatham, which is in Pitt County, and this meant we were only about three miles from Thompsonville. Thompsonville, I knew, if some of the others didn't, was where Letitia's uncle and her father grew up. We were in an area that Letitia's Uncle Louis must have known pretty well for a long time.

And finally: There was the business about Aunt Martha. She came herself to take our orders. None of us was hungry, and the girls wouldn't even order Cokes. But she took us boys' orders for mixers, and while she was there, Horst Hauser tried to get her to sing "Temptation" for us. Martha wasn't so very old—you could tell it by her clear, smooth skin and her bright green eyes—and nobody really called her Aunt Martha. But she must have weighed about three hundred pounds and she hadn't a tooth in her head. She wore her hair in what was almost a crew cut. And she was apt to be barefoot about half the time; she was barefoot that night. She wouldn't sing "Temptation" for us, but she talked to the girls and told them how pretty their dresses were and asked them their names—"Just your first names, I'm no good at last names," she said—so she would be sure to remember them next time they came. "You know," she said. "In case you come with some other fellows, and not these jelly beans." And she gave them a big wink.

We three boys pretended to look very hurt, and she said, "They know I'm a tease. These here boys are my honey babes." Then she looked at us awfully close to make sure that we did know. She hung around telling the girls how her old husband had built the tavern singlehanded, as a wedding present for her, and how, after practicing taxidermy "in many parts of the world and for over forty years," he had given it up and settled down in the country with her, and how generally sweet he was. "It mayn't seem likely to you girls," she said, her green eyes getting a damp look, "but they can be just as fine and just as noble without a tongue in their head as with one." Then, from fear of being misunderstood, maybe, or not wanting to depress the customers, she added, "And just as much fun, honey babes!" She gave us boys a wink and went off in a fit of laughter.

When she had gone, we all agreed that Martha was a good soul and that the old deaf-mute was a lucky man. But we couldn't help trying to take her off. And I laughed with the others till, suddenly, it occurred to me that her accent and her little turns of speech sounded, on our lips, just like things the Ram was quoted as saying in his civics class. He said "territority" and "A-rab" and "how come" and "I'm done." I knew that Letitia's own father didn't say things like that; it only showed the kind of low company Lou Ramsey had always kept, even as a boy in Clark County.

Well, when Martha went for the mixers, it was time for Bob and Horst and me to flip a coin to see who was going outside and buy us a pint of whiskey at the back door, which was where you always had to buy it. Unfortunately, I was odd man, and so I began collecting the money from the other two. Letitia didn't understand about the whiskey, and we had to explain to her about local option and Clark County's being a dry county, and about bootleg's being cheaper than the legal whiskey in Chatham. But while we explained, she didn't seem to listen. She only kept looking at me questioningly, and finally she squinted her eyes and said, "Are you sure you know how to buy it, and where?"

I went out the front door and around to the kitchen door, and bought the whiskey from Martha's husband, who had gone back there to meet me. I was glad for a breath of fresh air and to be away from the others for a few minutes. And yet I was eager to get back to them, too. I hurried toward the front, along the footpath between the parking lot and the side wall of the tavern—a dark wall of unpainted vertical planking. The night seemed even hotter and muggier now than it had earlier.

The sky, all overcast, with no stars shining through anywhere, was like an old, washed-out gray sweater. On the far side of the parking lot, a few faint streaks of light caught my eye. I knew they came from Aunt Martha's tourist cabins, which were ranged along the edge of the woods over there. The night was so dark it was hard to tell much about the cars in the parking lot, but I could tell that they were mostly broken down jalopies and that the lot looked more like a junkyard than any real parking lot. Everything I saw looked ugly and raw and unreal to me, and when I came round to the front, where the one big light bulb above the entrance still flickered brightly in its swarm of bugs, I could see a field of waist-high corn directly across the road, and somehow it looked rawer and more unreal to me than anything else.

When I rang at the front door to be let in again, the old man had already come through the place. He opened up for me, grinning as though it were a big joke between us—his having got there as soon as I did. But I didn't want any of his dumb-show joking just then. He was making all kinds of silly signs with his hands, but I passed by him and went on back to our booth. And I was struck right away by how happy Letitia looked when she saw me. She didn't seem to be concerned about her uncle at all, which, of course, was what I was watching to see. I was glad, and yet it didn't ease my mind a bit. What were you to make of such a girl? Ever since we got there, I had been watching her in a way that I felt guilty about, because I knew it was more curiosity than sympathy. And I was certain now that she had been watching me, for some kind of sign. I couldn't have been more uncomfortable. It was strange. She was such a marvelously pretty girl, really!—with her pale yellow hair and her almond eyes, with her firm little mouth that you couldn't help looking at when she opened it a little and smiled, no matter how much respect you had for her, and no matter what else you had on your mind. I kept looking at her, and I tried not to seem too self-conscious when I drew the pint of whiskey out of the pocket of my linen jacket and put it on the table.

But I did feel self-conscious about it, and even more so because she continued to sit there just as casually as though we were having a milkshake somewhere after the show and were settling down to enjoy ourselves for the rest of the evening. When I first came back, she had looked at me as though I were a hero because I had gone around to the back door to buy a pint of bootleg whiskey and had got back alive, and now she commenced puttering around with the glasses and the mixers with a happy, helpful attitude. Bob and Horst and their two dates were still jabbering away as much as before, but Letitia made me feel now that they weren't there at all. She had set the three tumblers in front of me, and so I worked away at opening the pint bottle and then began pouring drinks for us three boys. I wasn't sure how much we ought to have right at first, and I decided I had got too much in two of the glasses. I tried to pour some back into the bottle, and made such a mess of it that I cursed under my breath. During this time, the jukebox was playing away, of course, but I do think I was half aware of some other noise somewhere, though it didn't really sink in. It didn't even sink in when Letitia put her hand on my sleeve, or when I looked up at her and saw her looking at me very much as she had outside the door a while before. The others still went on talking, and after a second Letitia drew away her hand. She began fidgeting with her gardenias, and she wasn't looking at me any more. For a moment, I wondered if she hadn't really expected us to have the drinks. But it wasn't that, and now I saw that she had tilted her head to one side to get a better view of something across the floor. I cut my eyes around and saw that the curtains to the Ram's booth had been pulled apart and that there he was, in plain view, with his girl and his star pitcher and outfielder and their two girls. I thought to myself, She's just now realized that they're all here together. Then I took another look over there, wondering why in hell they hadn't kept those curtains drawn, and I saw that something very unusual was up.

This all happened in an instant, of course—much quicker than I can tell it. The Ram was getting up very slowly from his seat and seemed to be giving some kind of orders to his pitcher and his outfielder. His own girl was still sitting at the table, and she stayed there, but the two other girls were climbing on top of the table. Pretty soon, they had opened the little high window above their booth—there was one above each of the booths—and you could see that the next thing they were going to do was to try to climb out that window. I guess they did climb out, and it wasn't long before people in some of the other booths were doing the same thing.

After a minute or so, there was nobody left on the dance floor, and all of a sudden someone unplugged the jukebox. Without the music, we could hear the knocking on the doors of the tourist cabins, and I began to notice lights flashing outside the little window above our booth. I knew now there was a raid on the cabins, but I didn't want to be the first to mention the existence of those cabins to the girls. And though I was sure enough of it, I just couldn't make myself admit that the raid would be happening to the tavern, too, in about three minutes.

I saw the Ram leave his booth, and he seemed to be starting in the direction of ours. Letitia looked relieved now, and actually leaned forward across the table as though she were trying to catch his eye. Both Bob Southard and I got up and started out to meet him, but he held out a stiff arm, motioning us back, and he went off toward the beer counter without ever looking at Letitia.

When Bob and I turned back toward our booth, Horst and the girls were standing up, saying nothing. But Letitia gave me a comforting smile and she opened her mouth to say something that she never did say. I can almost believe she had been about to tell me how shy her uncle was, and to ask if I noticed how he wouldn't look at her when she was dressed up this way.

But now the Ram was headed back toward us with Martha, and Martha had slipped on some brown loafers. There was loud banging now on the front and back doors of the tavern, but apparently she and her husband weren't set to open up yet; I guessed the old man hadn't finished hiding the whiskey. By now, anybody who was going to get away had to chance it through the windows. We could hear people dropping on the ground outside those little high windows, and hear some of them grunting when they landed.

As soon as the Ram and Martha got near us, he said, "We're going to put you out of sight somewhere. They won't want to take too many in. They just want their quota."

Martha wasn't ruffled a bit. I suppose she could see we were, though. She looked at the girls and said, "Chickabiddies, I wouldn't have had this happen for nothing in this world."

The Ram glanced back at his own booth, to make sure that his athletes were still there—and maybe his girl friend. They hadn't moved a muscle. They just sat there very tense, watching the Ram. You would have thought they were in the bullpen waiting for a signal from him to come in and pitch. But they never got one. The Ram said to Martha, "Just anywhere you stick her and the rest of them is all right, but upstairs in your parlor would be mighty nice." From the way he said it, you would have thought he was speaking to one of the old lady teachers at Westside.

"You know I ain't about to hide nobody upstairs," she said firmly but politely. "Not even for you, honey baby."

"Then put them in the powder room yonder," he said.

"If they'll fit, that's fine," she said. She led the way and we followed.

It was over at the end of the counter—just a little closet, with "SHE" painted on the door and a toilet inside, and not even one of the little high windows. Martha made sure the key was in the lock, inside, and told us to turn off the light and lock ourselves in. We had to squeeze to get in, and one of us would have stood on the toilet except there wasn't a lid. While we were crowding in, the banging on the doors kept getting louder and began to sound more in earnest, and Martha's husband ambled up and stood watching us with his mouth hanging open. Martha looked around at him and burst out laughing. "He can't hear it thunder, bless his heart," she said. And the old fellow laughed, too.

The Ram said, "Get them inside, please, ma'am. They'll *have* to fit."

But Martha merely laughed at him. "You better git yourself *out*side if you expect to git," she said.

"I don't expect to git," he said.

"What'sa matter?"

He looked back over his shoulder at the room, where there were only eight or ten people left, most of them staggering around in the shadows, looking for a window that wasn't so high. "They'll have to have their quota of customers," he said, "or they might make a search."

"Well, it's your funeral you're planning, not mine," Martha said, and she winked at nobody in particular. Then her little green eyes suddenly darted another look at her husband. "O.K.," she said, "and I better take a quick gander to see he left out their quota of whiskey-take." With that, she slipped her feet out of her shoes again and padded along behind the counter and into the kitchen, with the old man following her. The banging on the doors couldn't get any louder, but they could have knocked the doors down by this time if they had really been as earnest about it as they made it sound. And we would long since have been locked inside the toilet except that while the Ram and Martha were having their final words, Letitia had put one foot over the sill again and was waiting to say something to her uncle.

"Uncle Louis," she began very solemnly. The Ram's face turned as red as a beet. Not just his face but the top of his head, too, where his sandy hair had got so thin. And, from the quick way he jerked his head around and fixed his eyes on the front door, it seemed as if he hadn't heard the banging over there till now. The truth was he *didn't* want to look at Letitia. But of course he had to, and it couldn't wait. So he sticks out that square chin, narrows his eyes under those blond eyebrows of his, and gives Letitia the hardest, impatientest look in the world. But it was nothing. The thing that was something was not the expression on *his* face but the one on hers. I won't ever forget it, though I certainly can't describe it. It made me think she was going to thank him from the bottom of her heart or else say how sorry she was about everything, or even ask him if something couldn't be done about hiding those poor athletes of his. I thought most likely it would be something about the athletes, since their being there with him was bound to make a scandal if it got into the newspapers. But in a way what she said was better than any of that. She said, "I don't have any money with me, Uncle Louis. Do you think I ought to have some money?"

"*Good* girl!" he practically shouted. And the guy actually smiled—the very best, most unselfish kind of smile. He

reached down in his pocket and pulled out a couple of crum-
pled-up bills. I saw that one of them was a five. Letitia took the
two bills and stuffed them in the pocket of her jacket. "Good
girl," he said again, not quite so loud. He was smiling, and
seemed nearly bursting with pride because Letitia had thought
of something important that he had overlooked.

"It's going to be all right, isn't it?" she said then.

"Why, sure it is," he said. It was as though the whole raid
was something that was happening just to them and concerned
nobody else. And now she gave him that look again, and what
it showed, and what it had shown before, was nothing on earth
but the beautiful confidence she had in him—all because he
was an uncle of hers, I suppose.

"Good night, darling," she said. She stepped back into the
toilet with the rest of us, and it was every bit as exciting to see
as if she had been stepping into a lifeboat and leaving him on
a sinking ship. My guess, too, is that when the Ram watched
her pulling the door to, he wished he *was* about to go down
on a real ship, instead of about to be arrested and taken off
with his girl friend and his two athletes to the jail in Thompsonville, the town where he grew up, and then to have it all
in the Chatham papers and finally lose his job as civics teacher
and baseball coach at Westside High. For that, of course, is the
way it turned out.

Somebody locked the door and we stood in there in the
dark, and then we heard Martha come back and put on her
shoes and go to open the front door. But we couldn't hear
everything, because at the first sound of the deputies' voices
the two other girls began to shake all over and whimper like
little sick animals. Bob and Horst managed to hush them up
pretty much, however, and before long I heard a man's voice
say, "Well, Lou, haven't *you* played hell?" The man sounded
surprised and pleased. "This is too bad, Lou," he said. It was
a mean, little-town voice, and you could hear the grudge in it
against anybody who had got away even as far as Chatham and
amounted to even as little as the Ram did. Or that was how I
felt it sounded. "That wouldn't be some of your champs over
there, would it, Lou?"

Letitia didn't make a sound. She just shivered once, as
though a rabbit had run over her grave, or as though, in the

awful stink and heat of that airless toilet, she was really cold. It was black as pitch in there, but I was pressed up against Letitia and I felt that shiver go over her. And then, right afterward, I could tell how easily she breathed, how relaxed she was. I wanted to put my arms around her, but I didn't dare—not in a place like that. I didn't dare even think about it twice.

Once our door was shut, we never heard the Ram's voice again.

In a very few minutes, the sheriff's men seemed to have got everybody out of the tavern except Martha and her husband. The two girls had stopped all their whimpering and teeth-chattering now, and we heard one of the men—the sheriff himself, I took it—talking to Martha while the others were carrying away whatever whiskey had been left out for them to find.

"Kind of sad about Lou Ramsey," he said, with a little snicker.

"I don't know him," Martha said, cutting things short. "I don't know any of them by their last names. That's your business, not mine."

The man didn't answer for a minute, but when he did, he sounded as though she had hurt his feelings. "You ought to be fair, Mrs. Mayberry," he said, "and not go blaming me for taking in them that just stands around waiting for it." I thought I could tell now that they were both sitting on stools at the counter.

"I don't mind, if he don't mind," she said. "It's his funeral, not mine." And now it sounded as though it was the Ram she was mad at, even more than the man she was talking to.

After a minute, he said, "I never been so hot as tonight."

"It's growing weather, honey baby," she said, and slapped her hand down on the counter.

"There's not nobody else around?" he asked her suddenly.

"What are you asking me that for, honey baby?" she said. "You got as many as your little jail will 'most hold."

We heard him laugh, and then neither of them said anything more for a minute. The other men seemed to have made their last trips to the kitchen and back now, and I heard the man with Martha get down off his stool at the counter.

"Well'm," he said, "which one of you cares to make the ride this time?"

"Whichever one you favors," she said.

"You know me," he said. "How's them kids?" For a second I was absolutely sure he meant us. But then he said, "How you manage to keep 'em quiet enough up there? You put cotton in their ears?" Martha didn't answer him, and finally he said, "What'sa matter with you tonight, Mrs. Mayberry?"

"You wouldn't kid me about something like my kids, would you, Sheriff?" she asked, in a hard voice.

"Like what?"

"Like saying nobody's never told you they was born just as deaf as their daddy, yonder."

"You don't say, Mrs. Mayberry," he said, sounding out of breath. "Nobody ever told me that, I swear to God. Why, I've seen them two towheads playing around out there in the lot, but nobody said to me they was deaf."

"Can't hear it thunder," she said, and all at once she laughed. Then she let out a long moan, and next thing she was crying.

"Mrs. Mayberry," the sheriff said, "I am sure sorry."

"No," she said, and she stopped crying just as quick as she had begun. "When somebody says they're sorry about it, I say no, it's a blessing. My kids ain't never going to hear the jukebox play all night, and no banging on doors, neither. It's a blessing, I say, all they won't hear, though it's a responsibility to me. But I won't be sitting up wondering where they are, the way you'll likely be doing with your young'uns, Sheriff. It's a blessing the good Lord sends to some people. It's wrong, but it's *something*. It's *something* I got which most people ain't. Till the day they die, they'll be just as true to me as the old man there."

Just then, one of the sheriff's men called him from outside to say they'd better get going, and I couldn't help being glad for the sheriff's sake. "Hell," he said to Martha, "it's too bad, but one of you has to come with me."

I was glad for us, too, because we were about to smother in there and be sick at our stomachs. The sheriff went on out then, taking one of the Mayberrys along. Everything was quiet after that, except for the motor of the sheriff's truck starting up. At first, we couldn't even tell for certain whether it was Martha or the old man who had gone with the sheriff. We waited a couple of minutes, and then, from the way the floor was creaking overhead, we knew it was Martha who had stayed. In the excitement, and after her outburst, she had forgotten all about us and had gone tiptoeing upstairs to see about her little deaf children.

All at once, Bob Southard said, "Let's get out of here," and he turned the key. We burst out onto the dance floor, and the first thing my eyes hit on was Martha's two brown loafers on the pine floor at the end of the counter. They were the first thing I saw, and about the only thing for a minute or so, for we stood there nearly blinded by the bright lights, which the sheriff's men had turned on everywhere and which Martha hadn't bothered to turn out.

It was awful seeing everything lit up that way—not just the mess the place was in, which wasn't so bad considering that there had been a raid, but just seeing the place at all in that light. Those stuffed animal heads of the old man's stared at you from everywhere you could turn—dogs, horses, foxes, bulls, even bobcats and some bears, and one lone zebra—leaning out from the walls, so that their glass eyes were shining right down at you. We got out of there just as quick as we could.

The front door was standing wide open. We didn't stop to pull it to after us. We went outside and around the corner toward the parking lot, and when we showed ourselves there it was the signal for about twenty or thirty people to begin coming out of the woods, where they had been hiding. Some of them came running out, and others kind of wandered out, and at least one came crawling on his hands and knees. With the sky still that nasty gray, we couldn't have seen them at first except for the broad shafts of light that came from the open doorways of the cabins. It was a creepy sight, and the sounds these people made were creepy, too. As they came out of the woods, some of them were arguing, some of them laughing and kidding in a hateful way, and here and there a woman was crying and complaining, as though maybe she had got hurt jumping down from one of those high little windows.

We knew that as soon as they climbed into their old jalopies, there would be a terrific hassle to get out of that parking lot, and so we made a dash for Horst's sedan and all piled into it without caring who sat where or who was whose date. And we were out of that lot and tearing down the road before we even heard a single other motor get started.

All the way to Chatham, and then driving around to take everybody home, we just kept quiet except to talk every now and then about Martha and her old husband's children, about how unfair and terrible it seemed for them to be born deaf, and how unfair and terrible it was to bring up children in a place like that. Even then, it seemed to me unnatural for us not to be mentioning what had happened earlier. But I suppose we were thankful at least to have the other thing to talk about. I was sitting in the back seat, and Letitia was sitting up in the front. I watched her shaking her head or nodding now and then when someone else was talking. There was certainly nothing special I could say to her from the back seat. But when we finally got to her house and I took her up to her door, I did make myself say, "We certainly owe your uncle a lot, Letitia."

"Yes, poor darling," she said. "But it's a good thing he was there, isn't it?" That's all she said. The marvelous thing, I thought, was that she didn't seem to hold anything against me.

I was away from Chatham most of that summer. The first of July, I went down to New Orleans with a friend of mine named Bickford Harris, and he and I got jobs on a freight boat and worked our way over to England and back. We got back on the fourteenth of September, which was only about a week before I had to leave for college. I had seen Letitia at several other parties before we went off to New Orleans, and had called her on the telephone to say goodbye. I sent her a postcard from New Orleans and I sent her three postcards from England. I didn't write her a letter for the same reason that I only telephoned her, instead of asking her for a date or going by to see her, before we left. I didn't want her to think I was trying to make something out of our happening to be put together that night, and didn't want her to think it meant anything special to me. But when we got back in September, I did ask her for a date, and she gave it to me.

And, of course, Letitia hadn't changed a bit—or only a very little bit. I could tell she hadn't, even when I talked with her on the telephone to make the date. She said she loved my postcards, but that's all she said about them, and it was plain they hadn't made any real impression on her. She told me that she was going to be leaving within a couple of weeks, to go to a finishing school in Washington, D.C., and the next summer she was going to Europe herself, before making her debut in the fall. She talked to me about all these plans on the telephone, and I knew that when a girl in Chatham begins talking about her plans to make her debut, she already has her mind on meeting older guys. That's the "very little bit" I mean she had changed. But she did give me the date—on a Monday night, it was. I was awfully glad about it, yet the minute I walked into her house, I began wishing I had left well enough alone.

For right off the bat I heard her uncle's voice. He was back in the dining room, where they were all still sitting around the table. And I had to go in there and tell them how I'd liked working on a freight boat and how I'd liked England. I also had to shake hands all around, even with the Ram, who was already standing up when I came in, speaking rather crossly to Letitia's three little brothers and hurrying them to get through with their dinner. When I shook his hand, I could tell from the indifferent way he looked at me that he didn't know he had ever seen me before. And suddenly I said to myself, "Why, all he knows about me is that I'm not a Ramsey and I'm not a baseball player."

Most of the time I was in the room, he was still hurrying Letitia's little brothers, under his breath, to finish their dinner. Everyone else had finished, and he was waiting to take her brothers somewhere afterward. I knew what he had been doing since June, when he found out he wouldn't be teaching at the high school in the fall. He had landed a soft daytime job with one of the lumber companies in Chatham, which had hired him so it would have him to manage the company's baseball team. As we were going out through the living room, I heard his voice getting louder and very cross again with the boys, the way it had sounded when I came in. Letitia heard it, too, and only laughed to herself. Outside, when we were walking across the lawn toward my car, she explained that her uncle was taking her little brothers to a night baseball game, in the commercial league, and that there was nothing in the world they loved better.

Letitia and I had a nice time that night, I suppose. It was just like other dates we'd had. We ran into some people at the movie, and we all went for a snack somewhere afterward. The

thing is I don't pretend that I ever did get to know Letitia
Ramsey awfully well. As I have said, it was only by chance that
she and I were put together for Nancy O'Connor's dance that
year. We simply ran with the same crowd, and in our crowd the
boys all knew that they would be going to college (or hoped
so), and the girls that they would be going off to finishing
school, up East or in Virginia, for a year or two and then be
making their debuts, and so we tended not to get too serious
about each other. It wasn't a good idea, that's all, because it
could break up your plans and your family's. The most that
usually happened was some terrific crushes and, naturally, some
pretty heavy necking that went along with the crushes. But
there was never even anything like that between Letitia and
me. I never felt that I knew her half as well as I did several of
her friends that I had even fewer dates with.

Still, I do know certain things from that evening at Aunt
Martha's Tavern. I know how Letitia looked at an uncle who
never had—and never has yet—amounted to anything. And
I know now that while I watched her looking at him, I was
really wishing that I knew how to make a girl like her look at
me that trusting way, instead of the way she had been looking
at me earlier. It almost made me wish that I was one of the
big, common fellows at Westside High who slipped off and got
married to one of the public-school girls in their class and then
told the teachers and the principal about it, like a big joke, after
they'd got their diplomas on graduation night. But the point is
I *didn't* know how to make a girl like her look at me that way.
And the question is why *didn't* I know how?

Usually, I tell myself that I didn't because I was such a worrier and that I wouldn't have been such a worrier if there hadn't
been a Depression, or if I had known a war was going to come
along and solve everything. But I'm not sure. Once, during
the war, I told this to a guy who didn't come from the kind of
people that I do. He only laughed at me and said he wanted to
hear more about those other times we were having that year.
I pointed out that those other good times weren't the point
and that a girl like Letitia Ramsey was something else again.
"Yea," he said, looking rather unfriendly. "That's how all you
guys like to talk."

But the worst part, really, is what it's like when you see someone like Letitia nowadays. She may be married to a guy whose
family money is in downtown real estate and who has never
had a doubt in his life, or maybe to some guy working on
commission and drinking himself to death. It doesn't matter
which. If it is a girl like Letitia who's married to him, he's part
of her family now, and all men outside her family are jokes to
her. And she and this fellow will have three or four half-grown
children, whom nobody can believe she is really the mother
of, since she looks so young. Well, the worst part is when you
are back home visiting and meet her at a dinner party, and she
tells you before the whole table how she was once on the verge
of being head over heels in love with you and you wouldn't
give her a tumble. It's always said as a big joke, of course, and
everyone laughs. But she goes on and on about it, as though
it was really something that had been worrying her. And the
more everybody laughs, the more she makes of it and strings it
out. And what it shows, more than any number of half-grown
children could ever do, is how old she is getting to be. She says
that you always seemed to have your mind on other things and
that she doesn't know yet whether it was higher things or lower
things. Everyone keeps on laughing until, finally, she pretends
to look very serious and says that it is all right for them to laugh
but that it wasn't funny at the time. Her kidding, of course, is
a big success, and nobody really minds it. But all I ever want
to say—and don't ever say—is that as far as I am concerned, it
isn't one bit funnier now than it was then.

Venus, Cupid, Folly and Time

THEIR HOUSE alone would not have made you think there was anything so awfully wrong with Mr. Dorset or his old-maid sister. But certain things about the way both of them dressed had, for a long time, annoyed and disturbed everyone. We used to see them together at the grocery store, for instance, or even in one of the big department stores downtown, wearing their bedroom slippers. Looking more closely, we would sometimes see the cuff of a pajama top or the hem of a hitched-up nightgown showing from underneath their ordinary daytime clothes. Such slovenliness in one's neighbors is so unpleasant that even husbands and wives in West Vesey Place, which was the street where the Dorsets lived, had got so they didn't like to joke about it with each other. Were the Dorsets, poor old things, losing their minds? If so, what was to be done about it? Some neighbors got so they would not even admit to themselves what they saw. And a child coming home with an ugly report on the Dorsets was apt to be told that it was time he learned to curb his imagination.

Mr. Dorset wore tweed caps and sleeveless sweaters. Usually he had his sweater stuffed down inside his trousers with his shirt tails. To the women and young girls in West Vesey Place this was extremely distasteful. It made them feel as though Mr. Dorset had just come from the bathroom and had got his sweater inside his trousers by mistake. There was, in fact, nothing about Mr. Dorset that was not offensive to the women. Even the old touring car he drove was regarded by most of them as a disgrace to the neighborhood. Parked out in front of his house, as it usually was, it seemed a worse violation of West Vesey's zoning than the house itself. And worst of all was seeing Mr. Dorset wash the car.

Mr. Dorset washed his own car! He washed it not back in the alley or in his driveway but out there in the street of West Vesey Place. This would usually be on the day of one of the parties which he and his sister liked to give for young people or on a day when they were going to make deliveries of the paper flowers or the home-grown figs which they sold to their friends. Mr. Dorset would appear in the street carrying two buckets

418

of warm water and wearing a pair of skin-tight coveralls. The skin-tight coveralls, of khaki material but faded almost to flesh color, were still more offensive to the women and young girls than his way of wearing his sweaters. With sponges and chamois cloths and a large scrub brush (for use on the canvas top) the old fellow would fall to and scrub away, gently at first on the canvas top and more vigorously as he progressed to the hood and body, just as though the car were something alive. Neighbor children felt that he went after the headlights exactly as if he were scrubbing the poor car's ears. There was an element of brutality in the way he did it and yet an element of tenderness too. An old lady visiting in the neighborhood once said that it was like the cleansing of a sacrificial animal. I suppose it was some such feeling as this that made all women want to turn away their eyes whenever the spectacle of Mr. Dorset washing his car presented itself.

As for Mr. Dorset's sister, her behavior was in its way just as offensive as his. To the men and boys in the neighborhood it was she who seemed quite beyond the pale. She would come out on her front terrace at midday clad in a faded flannel bathrobe and with her dyed black hair all undone and hanging down her back like the hair of an Indian squaw. To us whose wives and mothers did not even come downstairs in their negligees, this was very unsettling. It was hard to excuse it even on the grounds that the Dorsets were too old and lonely and hard-pressed to care about appearances any more.

Moreover, there was a boy who had gone to Miss Dorset's house one morning in the early fall to collect for his paper route and saw this very Miss Louisa Dorset pushing a carpet sweeper about one of the downstairs rooms without a stitch of clothes on. He saw her through one of the little lancet windows that opened on the front loggia of the house, and he watched her for quite a long while. She was cleaning the house in preparation for a party they were giving for young people that night, and the boy said that when she finally got hot and tired she dropped down in an easy chair and crossed her spindly, blue-veined, old legs and sat there completely naked, with her legs crossed and shaking one scrawny little foot, just as unconcerned as if she didn't care that somebody was likely to walk in on her at any moment. After a little bit the boy saw her get

up again and go and lean across a table to arrange some paper
flowers in a vase. Fortunately he was a nice boy, though he lived
only on the edge of the West Vesey Place neighborhood, and
he went away without ringing the doorbell or collecting for
his paper that week. But he could not resist telling his friends
about what he had seen. He said it was a sight he would never
forget! And she an old lady more than sixty years old who, had
she not been so foolish and self-willed, might have had a house
full of servants to push that carpet sweeper for her!

This foolish pair of old people had given up almost everything in life for each other's sake. And it was not at all necessary. When they were young they could have come into a
decent inheritance, or now that they were old they might
have been provided for by a host of rich relatives. It was only
a matter of their being a little tolerant—or even civil—toward
their kinspeople. But this was something that old Mr. Dorset
and his sister could never consent to do. Almost all their lives
they had spoken of their father's kin as "Mama's in-laws" and of
their mother's kin as "Papa's in-laws." Their family name was
Dorset, not on one side but on both sides. Their parents had
been distant cousins. As a matter of fact, the Dorset family in
the city of Chatham had once been so large and was so long
established there that it would have been hard to estimate how
distant the kinship might be. But still it was something that the
old couple never liked to have mentioned. Most of their mother's close kin had, by the time I am speaking of, moved off to
California, and most of their father's people lived somewhere
up East. But Miss Dorset and her old bachelor brother found
any contact, correspondence, even an exchange of Christmas
cards with these in-laws intolerable. It was a case, so they said,
of the in-laws respecting the value of the dollar above all else,
whereas they, Miss Louisa and Mr. Alfred Dorset, placed
importance on other things.

They lived in a dilapidated and curiously mutilated house
on a street which, except for their own house, was the most
splendid street in the entire city. Their house was one that you
or I would have been ashamed to live in—even in the lean years
of the early thirties. In order to reduce taxes the Dorsets had
had the third story of the house torn away, leaving an ugly, flat-
topped effect without any trim or ornamentation. Also, they

had had the south wing pulled down and had sealed the scars not with matching brick but with a speckled stucco that looked raw and naked. All this the old couple did in violation of the strict zoning laws of West Vesey Place, and for doing so they would most certainly have been prosecuted except that they were the Dorsets and except that this was during the Depression when zoning laws weren't easy to enforce in a city like Chatham.

To the young people whom she and her brother entertained at their house once each year Miss Louisa Dorset liked to say: "We have given up everything for each other. Our only income is from our paper flowers and our figs." The old lady, though without showing any great skill or talent for it, made paper flowers. During the winter months, her brother took her in that fifteen-year-old touring car of theirs, with its steering wheel on the wrong side and with isinglass side curtains that were never taken down, to deliver these flowers to her customers. The flowers looked more like sprays of tinted potato chips than like any real flowers. Nobody could possibly have wanted to buy them except that she charged next to nothing for them and except that to people with children it seemed important to be on the Dorsets' list of worthwhile people. Nobody could really have wanted Mr. Dorset's figs either. He cultivated a dozen little bushes along the back wall of their house, covering them in the wintertime with some odd-looking boxes which he had had constructed for the purpose. The bushes were very productive, but the figs they produced were dried up little things without much taste. During the summer months he and his sister went about in their car, with the side curtains still up, delivering the figs to the same customers who bought the paper flowers. The money they made could hardly have paid for the gas it took to run the car. It was a great waste and it was very foolish of them.

And yet, despite everything, this foolish pair of old people, this same Miss Louisa and Mr. Alfred Dorset, had become social arbiters of a kind in our city. They had attained this position entirely through their fondness for giving an annual dancing party for young people. To *young* people—to *very* young people—the Dorsets' hearts went out. I don't mean to suggest that their hearts went out to orphans or to the children of the poor, for they were not foolish in that way. The guests at their little dancing parties were the thirteen- and fourteen-year-olds from families like the one they had long ago set themselves against, young people from the very houses to which, in season, they delivered their figs and their paper flowers. And when the night of one of their parties came round, it was in fact the custom for Mr. Alfred to go in the same old car and fetch all the invited guests to his house. His sister might explain to reluctant parents that this saved the children the embarrassment of being taken to their first dance by Mommy or Daddy. But the parents knew well enough that for twenty years the Dorsets had permitted no adult person, besides themselves, to put foot inside their house.

At those little dancing parties which the Dorsets gave, peculiar things went on—unsettling things to the boys and girls who had been fetched round in the old car. Sensible parents wished to keep their children away. Yet what could they do? For a Chatham girl to have to explain, a few years later, why she never went to a party at the Dorsets' was like having to explain why she had never been a debutante. For a boy it was like having to explain why he had not gone up East to school or even why his father hadn't belonged to the Chatham Racquet Club. If when you were thirteen or fourteen you got invited to the Dorsets' house, you went; it was the way of letting people know from the outset who you were. In a busy, modern city like Chatham you cannot afford to let people forget who you are— not for a moment, not at any age. Even the Dorsets knew that.

Many a little girl, after one of those evenings at the Dorsets', was heard to cry out in her sleep. When waked, or half waked, her only explanation might be: "It was just the fragrance from the paper flowers." Or: "I dreamed I could really smell the paper flowers." Many a boy was observed by his parents to seem "different" afterward. He became "secretive." The parents of the generation that had to attend those parties never pretended to understand what went on at the Dorsets' house. And even to those of us who were in that unlucky generation, it seemed we were half a lifetime learning what really took place during our one evening under the Dorsets' roof. Before our turn to go ever came round, we had for years been hearing about what it was like from older boys and girls. Afterward, we continued to hear about it from those who followed us. And, looking back on it, nothing about the one evening when you were actually there ever seemed quite so real as the glimpses and snatches which you got from those people before and after you—the secondhand impressions of the Dorsets' behavior, of things they said, of looks that passed between them.

Since Miss Dorset kept no servants, she always opened her own door. I suspect that for the guests at her parties the sight of her opening her door, in her astonishing attire, came as the most violent shock of the whole evening. On these occasions, she and her brother got themselves up as we had never seen them before and never would again. The old lady invariably wore a modish white evening gown, a garment perfectly fitted to her spare and scrawny figure and cut in such high fashion that it must necessarily have been new that year. And never to be worn but that one night! Her hair, long and thick and newly dyed for the occasion, would be swept upward and forward in a billowy mass which was topped by a corsage of yellow and coral paper flowers. Her cheeks and lips would be darkly rouged. On her long bony arms and her bare shoulders she would have applied some kind of suntan powder. Whatever else you had been led to expect of the evening, no one had ever warned you sufficiently about the radical change to be noted in her appearance—or in that of her brother, either. By the end of the party Miss Louisa might look as dowdy as ever, and Mr. Alfred a little worse than usual. But at the outset, when the party was assembling in their drawing room, even Mr. Alfred appeared resplendent in a nattily tailored tuxedo, with exactly the shirt, the collar, and the tie which fashion prescribed that year. His gray hair was nicely trimmed, his puffy old face freshly shaven. He was powdered with the same dark powder that his sister used. One felt even that his cheeks had been lightly touched with rouge.

A strange perfume pervaded the atmosphere of the house. The moment you set foot inside, this awful fragrance engulfed you. It was like a mixture of spicy incense and sweet attar of roses. And always, too, there was the profusion of paper flowers. The flowers were everywhere—on every cabinet and console, every inlaid table and carved chest, on every high, marble mantelpiece, on the bookshelves. In the entrance hall special tiers must have been set up to hold the flowers, because they were there in overpowering masses. They were in such abundance that it seemed hardly possible that Miss Dorset could have made them all. She must have spent weeks and weeks preparing them, even months, perhaps even the whole year between parties. When she went about delivering them to her customers, in the months following, they were apt to be somewhat faded and dusty; but on the night of the party, the colors of the flowers seemed even more impressive and more unlikely than their number. They were fuchsia, they were chartreuse, they were coral, aquamarine, brown, they were even black.

Everywhere in the Dorsets' house too were certain curious illuminations and lighting effects. The source of the light was usually hidden and its purpose was never obvious at once. The lighting was a subtler element than either the perfume or the paper flowers, and ultimately it was more disconcerting. A shaft of lavender light would catch a young visitor's eye and lead it, seemingly without purpose, in among the flowers. Then just beyond the point where the strength of the light would begin to diminish, the eye would discover something. In a small aperture in the mass of flowers, or sometimes in a larger grotto-like opening, there would be a piece of sculpture—in the hall a plaster replica of Rodin's "The Kiss," in the library an antique plaque of Leda and the Swan. Or just above the flowers would be hung a picture, usually a black and white print but sometimes a reproduction in color. On the landing of the stairway leading down to the basement ballroom was the only picture that one was likely to learn the title of at the time. It was a tiny color print of Bronzino's "Venus, Cupid, Folly and Time." This picture was not even framed. It was simply tacked on the wall, and it had obviously been torn—rather carelessly, perhaps hurriedly—from a book or magazine. The title and the name of the painter were printed in the white margin underneath.

About these works of art most of us had been warned by older boys and girls; and we stood in painful dread of that moment when Miss Dorset or her brother might catch us staring at any one of their pictures or sculptures. We had been warned, time and again, that during the course of the evening moments would come when she or he would reach out and touch the other's elbow and indicate, with a nod or just the trace of a smile, some guest whose glance had strayed among the flowers.

To some extent the dread which all of us felt that evening at the Dorsets' cast a shadow over the whole of our childhood. Yet for nearly twenty years the Dorsets continued to give their annual party. And even the most sensible of parents were not willing to keep their children away.

But a thing happened finally which could almost have been predicted. Young people, even in West Vesey Place, will not submit forever to the prudent counsel of their parents. Or some of them won't. There was a boy named Ned Meriwether and his sister Emily Meriwether, who lived with their parents in West Vesey Place just one block away from the Dorsets' house. In November, Ned and Emily were invited to the Dorsets' party, and because they dreaded it they decided to play a trick on everyone concerned—even on themselves, as it turned out . . . They got up a plan for smuggling an uninvited guest into the Dorsets' party.

The parents of this Emily and Ned sensed that their children were concealing something from them and suspected that the two were up to mischief of some kind. But they managed to deceive themselves with the thought that it was only natural for young people—"mere children"—to be nervous about going to the Dorsets' house. And so instead of questioning them during the last hour before they left for the party, these sensible parents tried to do everything in their power to calm their two children. The boy and the girl, seeing this was the case, took advantage of it.

"You must not go down to the front door with us when we leave," the daughter insisted to her mother. And she persuaded both Mr. and Mrs. Meriwether that after she and her brother were dressed for the party they should all wait together in the upstairs sitting room until Mr. Dorset came to fetch the two young people in his car.

When, at eight o'clock, the lights of the automobile appeared in the street below, the brother and sister were still upstairs—watching from the bay window of the family sitting room. They kissed Mother and Daddy goodbye and then they flew down the stairs and across the wide, carpeted entrance hall to a certain dark recess where a boy named Tom Bascomb was hidden. This boy was the uninvited guest whom Ned and Emily were going to smuggle into the party. They had left the front door unlatched for Tom, and from the upstairs window just a few minutes ago they had watched him come across their front lawn. Now in the little recess of the hall there was a quick exchange of overcoats and hats between Ned Meriwether and Tom Bascomb; for it was a feature of the plan that Tom should attend the party as Ned and that Ned should go as the uninvited guest.

In the darkness of the recess, Ned fidgeted and dropped Tom Bascomb's coat on the floor. But the boy, Tom Bascomb, did not fidget. He stepped out into the light of the hall and began methodically getting into the overcoat which he would wear tonight. He was not a boy who lived in the West Vesey Place neighborhood (he was in fact the very boy who had once watched Miss Dorset cleaning house without any clothes on), and he did not share Emily's and Ned's nervous excitement about the evening. The sound of Mr. Dorset's footsteps outside did not disturb him. When both Ned and Emily stood frozen by that sound, he continued buttoning the unfamiliar coat and even amused himself by stretching forth one arm to observe how high the sleeve came on his wrist.

The doorbell rang, and from his dark corner Ned Meriwether whispered to his sister and to Tom: "Don't worry. I'll be at the Dorsets' in plenty of time."

Tom Bascomb only shrugged his shoulders at this reassurance. Presently when he looked at Emily's flushed face and saw her batting her eyes like a nervous monkey, a crooked smile played upon his lips. Then, at a sign from Emily, Tom followed her to the entrance door and permitted her to introduce him to old Mr. Dorset as her brother.

From the window of the upstairs sitting room the Meriwether parents watched Mr. Dorset and this boy and this girl walking across the lawn toward Mr. Dorset's peculiar-looking car. A light shone bravely and protectively from above the entrance of the house, and in its rays the parents were able to detect the strange angle at which Brother was carrying his head tonight and how his new fedora already seemed too small for him. They even noticed that he seemed a bit taller tonight.

"I hope it's all right," said the mother.

"What do you mean 'all right'?" the father asked petulantly.

"I mean—" the mother began, and then she hesitated. She did not want to mention that the boy out there did not look like their own Ned. It would have seemed to give away her feelings too much. "I mean that I wonder if I should have put Sister in that long dress at this age and let her wear my cape. I'm afraid the cape is really inappropriate. She's still young for that sort of thing."

"Oh," said the father, "I thought you meant something else."

"Whatever else did you think I meant, Edwin?" the mother said, suddenly breathless.

"I thought you meant the business we've discussed before," he said, although this was of course not what he had thought she meant. He had thought she meant that the boy out there did not look like their Ned. To him it had seemed even that the boy's step was different from Ned's. "The Dorsets' parties," he said, "are not very nice affairs to be sending your children to, Muriel. That's all I thought you meant."

"But we *can't* keep them away," the mother said defensively.

"Oh, it's just that they are growing up faster than we realize," said the father, glancing at his wife out of the corner of his eye.

By this time Mr. Dorset's car had pulled out of sight, and from downstairs Muriel Meriwether thought she heard another door closing. "What was that?" she said, putting one hand on her husband's.

"Don't be so jumpy," her husband said irritably, snatching away his hand. "It's the servants closing up in the kitchen."

Both of them knew that the servants had closed up in the kitchen long before this. Both of them had heard quite distinctly the sound of the side door closing as Ned went out. But they went on talking and deceiving themselves in this fashion during most of the evening.

Even before she opened the door to Mr. Dorset, little Emily Meriwether had known that there would be no difficulty about passing Tom Bascomb off as her brother. In the first place, she knew that without his spectacles Mr. Dorset could hardly see his hand before his face and knew that due to some silly pride he had he never put on his spectacles except when he was behind the wheel of his automobile. This much was common knowledge. In the second place, Emily knew from experience that neither he nor his sister ever made any real pretense of knowing one child in their general acquaintance from another. And so, standing in the doorway and speaking almost in a whisper, Emily had merely to introduce first herself and then her pretended brother to Mr. Dorset. After that the three of them walked in silence from her father's house to the waiting car.

Emily was wearing her mother's second-best evening wrap, a white lapin cape which, on Emily, swept the ground. As she walked between the boy and the man, the touch of the cape's soft silk lining on her bare arms and on her shoulders spoke to her silently of a strange girl she had seen in her looking glass upstairs tonight. And with her every step toward the car the skirt of her long taffeta gown whispered her own name to her: *Emily . . . Emily.* She heard it distinctly, and yet the name sounded unfamiliar. Once during this unreal walk from house to car she glanced at the mysterious boy, Tom Bascomb, longing to ask him—if only with her eyes—for some reassurance that she was really she. But Tom Bascomb was absorbed in his own irrelevant observations. With his head tilted back he was gazing upward at the nondescript winter sky where, among drifting clouds, a few pale stars were shedding their dull light alike on West Vesey Place and on the rest of the world. Emily drew her wrap tightly about her, and when presently Mr. Dorset held open the door to the back seat of his car she shut her eyes and plunged into the pitch blackness of the car's interior.

Tom Bascomb was a year older than Ned Meriwether and he was nearly two years older than Emily. He had been Ned's friend first. He and Ned had played baseball together on Saturdays before Emily ever set eyes on him. Yet according to Tom Bascomb himself, with whom several of us older boys talked just a few weeks after the night he went to the Dorsets', Emily always insisted that it was she who had known him first. On what she based this false claim Tom could not say. And on the two or three other occasions when we got Tom to talk about that night, he kept saying that he didn't understand what it was that had made Emily and Ned quarrel over which of them knew him first and knew him better.

We could have told him what it was, I think. But we didn't. It would have been too hard to say to him that at one time or another all of us in West Vesey had had our Tom Bascombs. Tom lived with his parents in an apartment house on a wide thoroughfare known as Division Boulevard, and his only real connection with West Vesey Place was that that street was included in his paper route. During the early morning hours he rode his bicycle along West Vesey and along other quiet streets like it, carefully aiming a neatly rolled paper at the dark loggia, at the colonnaded porch, or at the ornamented doorway of each of the palazzi and châteaux and manor houses that glowered at him in the dawn. He was well thought of as a paper boy. If by mistake one of his papers went astray and lit on an upstairs balcony or on the roof of a porch, Tom would always take more careful aim and throw another. Even if the paper only went into the shrubbery, Tom got off his bicycle and fished it out. He wasn't the kind of boy to whom it would have occurred that the old fogies and the rich kids in West Vesey could very well get out and scramble for their own papers.

Actually, a party at the Dorsets' house was more a grand tour of the house than a real party. There was a half hour spent over very light refreshments (fruit Jello, English tea biscuits, lime punch). There was another half hour ostensibly given to general dancing in the basement ballroom (to the accompaniment of victrola music). But mainly there was the tour. As the party passed through the house, stopping sometimes to sit down in the principal rooms, the host and hostess provided entertainment in the form of an almost continuous dialogue between themselves. This dialogue was famous and was full of interest, being all about how much the Dorsets had given up for each other's sake and about how much higher the tone of Chatham society used to be than it was nowadays. They would invariably speak of their parents, who had died within a year of each other when Miss Louisa and Mr. Alfred were still in their teens; they even spoke of their wicked in-laws. When their parents died, the wicked in-laws had first tried to make them sell the house, then had tried to separate them and send them away to boarding schools, and had ended by trying to marry them off to "just anyone." Their two grandfathers had still been alive in those days and each had had a hand in the machinations, after the failure of which each grandfather had disinherited them. Mr. Alfred and Miss Louisa spoke also of how, a few years later, a procession of "young nobodies" had come of their own accord trying to steal the two of them away from each other. Both he and she would scowl at the very recollection of those "just anybodies" and those "nobodies," those "would-be suitors" who always turned out to be misguided fortune hunters and had to be driven away.

The Dorsets' dialogue usually began in the living room the moment Mr. Dorset returned with his last collection of guests. (He sometimes had to make five or six trips in the car.) There, as in other rooms afterward, they were likely to begin with a reference to the room itself or perhaps to some piece of furniture in the room. For instance, the extraordinary length of the drawing room—or reception room, as the Dorsets called it—would lead them to speak of an even longer room which they had had torn away from the house. "It grieved us, we wept," Miss Dorset would say, "to have Mama's French drawing room torn away from us."

"But we tore it away from ourselves," her brother would add, "as we tore away our in-laws—because we could not afford them." Both of them spoke in a fine declamatory style, but they frequently interrupted themselves with a sad little laugh which expressed something quite different from what they were saying and which seemed to serve them as an aside not meant for our ears.

"That was one of our greatest sacrifices," Miss Dorset would say, referring still to her mother's French drawing room.

And her brother would say: "But we knew the day had passed in Chatham for entertainments worthy of that room."

"It was the room which Mama and Papa loved best, but we gave it up because we knew, from our upbringing, which things to give up."

From this they might go on to anecdotes about their childhood. Sometimes their parents had left them for months or even a whole year at a time with only the housekeeper or with trusted servants to see after them. "You could trust servants then," they explained. And: "In those days parents could do that sort of thing, because in those days there was a responsible body of people within which your young people could always find proper companionship."

In the library, to which the party always moved from the drawing room, Mr. Dorset was fond of exhibiting snapshots of the house taken before the south wing was pulled down. As the pictures were passed around, the dialogue continued. It was often there that they told the story of how the in-laws had tried to force them to sell the house. "For the sake of economy!" Mr. Dorset would exclaim, adding an ironic "Ha ha!"

"As though money—" he would begin.

"As though money ever took the place," his sister would come in, "of living with your own kind."

"Or of being well born," said Mr. Dorset.

After the billiard room, where everyone who wanted it was permitted one turn with the only cue that there seemed to be in the house, and after the dining room, where it was promised refreshments would be served later, the guests would be taken down to the ballroom—purportedly for dancing. Instead of everyone's being urged to dance, however, once they were assembled in the ballroom, Miss Dorset would announce that she and her brother understood the timidity which young people felt about dancing and that all that she and he intended to do was to set the party a good example . . . It was only Miss Louisa and Mr. Alfred who danced. For perhaps thirty minutes, in a room without light excepting that from a few weak bulbs concealed among the flowers, the old couple danced; and they danced with such grace and there was such perfect harmony in all their movements that the guests stood about in stunned silence, as if hypnotized. The Dorsets waltzed, they two-stepped, they even fox-trotted, stopping only long enough between dances for Mr. Dorset, amid general applause, to change the victrola record.

But it was when their dance was ended that all the effects of the Dorsets' careful grooming that night would have vanished. And, alas, they made no effort to restore themselves. During the remainder of the evening Mr. Dorset went about with his bow tie hanging limply on his damp shirtfront, a gold collar button shining above it. A strand of gray hair, which normally covered his bald spot on top, now would have fallen on the wrong side of his part and hung like fringe about his ear. On his face and neck the thick layer of powder was streaked with perspiration. Miss Dorset was usually in an even more disheveled state, depending somewhat upon the fashion of her dress that year. But always her powder was streaked, her lipstick entirely gone, her hair falling down on all sides, and her corsage dangling somewhere about the nape of her neck. In this condition they led the party upstairs again, not stopping until they had reached the second floor of the house.

On the second floor we—the guests—were shown the rooms which the Dorsets' parents had once occupied (the Dorsets' own rooms were never shown). We saw, in glass museum cases along the hallway, the dresses and suits and hats and even the shoes which Miss Louisa and Mr. Alfred had worn to parties when they were very young. And now the dialogue, which had been left off while the Dorsets danced, was resumed. "Ah, the happy time," one of them would say, "was when we were *your* age!" And then, exhorting us to be happy and gay while we were still safe in the bosom of our own kind and before the world came crowding in on us with its ugly demands, the Dorsets would recall the happiness they had known when they were very young. This was their *pièce de résistance*. With many a wink and blush and giggle and shake of the forefinger—and of course standing before the whole party—they each would remind the other of his or her naughty behavior in some old-fashioned parlor game or of certain silly little flirtations which they had long ago caught each other in.

They were on their way downstairs again now, and by the time they had finished with this favorite subject they would be downstairs. They would be in the dark, flower-bedecked downstairs hall and just before entering the dining room for the promised refreshments: the fruit Jello, the English tea biscuits, the lime punch.

And now for a moment Mr. Dorset bars the way to the dining room and prevents his sister from opening the closed door. "Now, my good friends," he says, "let us eat, drink, and be merry!"

"For the night is yet young," says his sister.

"Tonight you must be gay and carefree," Mr. Dorset enjoins.

"Because in this house we are all friends," Miss Dorset says. "We are all young, we all love one another."

"And love can make us all young forever," her brother says. "Remember!"

"Remember this evening always, sweet young people!"

"Remember!"

"Remember what our life is like here!"

And now Miss Dorset, with one hand on the knob of the great door which she is about to throw open, leans a little toward the guests and whispers hoarsely: "This is what it is like to be young forever!"

Ned Meriwether was waiting behind a big japonica shrub near the sidewalk when, about twenty minutes after he had last seen Emily, the queer old touring car drew up in front of the Dorsets' house. During the interval, the car had gone from the Meriwether house to gather a number of other guests, and so it was not only Emily and Tom who alighted on the sidewalk before the Dorsets' house. The group was just large enough to make it easy for Ned to slip out from his dark hiding place and join them without being noticed by Mr. Dorset. And now the group was escorted rather unceremoniously up to the door of the house, and Mr. Dorset departed to fetch more guests.

They were received at the door by Miss Dorset. Her eyesight was no doubt better than her brother's, but still there was really no danger of her detecting an uninvited guest. Those of us who had gone to that house in the years just before Ned and Emily came along could remember that, during a whole evening, when their house was full of young people, the Dorsets made no introductions and made no effort to distinguish which of their guests was which. They did not even make a count of heads. Perhaps they did vaguely recognize some of the faces, because sometimes when they had come delivering figs or paper flowers to a house they had of necessity encountered a young child there, and always they smiled sweetly at it, asked its age, and calculated on their old fingers how many years must pass before the child would be eligible for an invitation. Yet at those moments something in the way they had held up

their fingers and in the way they had gazed *at* the little face
instead of into it had revealed their lack of interest in the individual child. And later, when the child was finally old enough
to receive their invitation, he found it was still no different
with the Dorsets. Even in their own house it was evidently to
the young people as a group that the Dorsets' hearts went out;
while they had the boys and girls under their roof they herded
them about like so many little thoroughbred calves. Even when
Miss Dorset opened the front door she did so exactly as though
she were opening a gate. She pulled it open very slowly, standing half behind it to keep out of harm's way. And the children,
all huddled together, surged in.

How meticulously this Ned and Emily Meriwether must
have laid their plans for that evening! And the whole business
might have come out all right if only they could have foreseen
the effect which one part of their plan—rather a last-minute
embellishment of it—would produce upon Ned himself. Barely
ten minutes after they entered the house, Ned was watching
Tom as he took his seat on the piano bench beside Emily. Ned
probably watched Tom closely, because certainly he knew what
the next move was going to be. The moment Miss Louisa Dorset's back was turned Tom Bascomb slipped his arm gently
about Emily's little waist and commenced kissing her all over
her pretty face. It was almost as if he were kissing away tears.

This spectacle on the piano bench, and others like it which
followed, had been an inspiration of the last day or so before
the party. Or so Ned and Emily maintained afterward when
defending themselves to their parents. But no matter when it
was conceived, a part of their plan it was, and Ned must have
believed himself fully prepared for it. Probably he expected
to join in the round of giggling which it produced from the
other guests. But now that the time had come—it is easy to
imagine—the boy Ned Meriwether found himself not quite
able to join in the fun. He watched with the others, but he was
not quite infected by their laughter. He stood a little apart, and
possibly he was hoping that Emily and Tom would not notice
his failure to appreciate the success of their comedy. He was
no doubt baffled by his own feelings, by the failure of his own
enthusiasm, and by a growing desire to withdraw himself from
the plot and from the party itself.

It is easy to imagine Ned's uneasiness and confusion that night. And I believe the account which I have given of Emily's impressions and her delicate little sensations while on the way to the party has a ring of truth about it, though actually the account was supplied by girls who knew her only slightly, who were not at the party, who could not possibly have seen her afterward. It may, after all, represent only what other girls imagined she would have felt. As for the account of how Mr. and Mrs. Meriwether spent the evening, it is their very own. And they did not hesitate to give it to anyone who would listen.

It was a long time, though, before many of us had a clear picture of the main events of the evening. We heard very soon that the parties for young people were to be no more, that there had been a wild scramble and chase through the Dorsets' house, and that it had ended by the Dorsets locking some boy—whether Ned or Tom was not easy to determine at first—in a queer sort of bathroom in which the plumbing had been disconnected, and even the fixtures removed, I believe. (Later I learned that there was nothing literally sinister about the bathroom itself. By having the pipes disconnected to this, and perhaps other bathrooms, the Dorsets had obtained further reductions in their taxes.) But a clear picture of the whole evening wasn't to be had—not without considerable searching. For one thing, the Meriwether parents immediately, within a week after the party, packed their son and daughter off to boarding schools. Accounts from the other children were contradictory and vague—perversely so, it seemed. Parents reported to each other that the little girls had nightmares which were worse even than those which their older sisters had had. And the boys were secretive and elusive, even with us older boys when we questioned them about what had gone on.

One sketchy account of events leading up to the chase, however, did go the rounds almost at once. Ned must have written it back to some older boy in a letter, because it contained information which no one but Ned could have had. The account went like this: When Mr. Dorset returned from his last roundup of guests, he came hurrying into the drawing room where the others were waiting and said in a voice trembling with excitement: "Now, let us all be seated, my young friends, and let us warm ourselves with some good talk."

At that moment everyone who was not already seated made a dash for a place on one of the divans or love seats or even in one of the broad window seats. (There were no individual chairs in the room.) Everyone made a dash, that is, except Ned. Ned did not move. He remained standing beside a little table rubbing his fingers over its polished surface. And from this moment he was clearly an object of suspicion in the eyes of his host and hostess. Soon the party moved from the drawing room to the library, but in whatever room they stopped Ned managed to isolate himself from the rest. He would sit or stand looking down at his hands until once again an explosion of giggles filled the room. Then he would look up just in time to see Tom Bascomb's cheek against Emily's or his arm about her waist.

For nearly two hours Ned didn't speak a word to anyone. He endured the Dorsets' dialogue, the paper flowers, the perfumed air, the works of art. Whenever a burst of giggling forced him to raise his eyes, he would look up at Tom and Emily and then turn his eyes away. Before looking down at his hands again, he would let his eyes travel slowly about the room until they came to rest on the figures of the two Dorsets. That, it seems, was how he happened to discover that the Dorsets understood, or thought they understood, what the giggles meant. In the great mirror mounted over the library mantel he saw them exchanging half-suppressed smiles. Their smiles lasted precisely as long as the giggling continued, and then, in the mirror, Ned saw their faces change and grow solemn when their eyes—their identical, tiny, dull, amber-colored eyes—focused upon himself.

From the library the party continued on the regular tour of the house. At last when they had been to the ballroom and watched the Dorsets dance, had been upstairs to gaze upon the faded party clothes in the museum cases, they descended into the downstairs hall and were just before being turned into the dining room. The guests had already heard the Dorsets teasing each other about the silly little flirtations and about their naughtiness in parlor games when they were young and had listened to their exhortations to be gay and happy and carefree. Then just when Miss Dorset leaned toward them and whispered, "This is what it is like to be young forever," there rose a chorus of laughter, breathless and shrill, yet loud and intensely penetrating.

Ned Meriwether, standing on the bottom step of the stairway, lifted his eyes and looked over the heads of the party to see Tom and Emily half hidden in a bower of paper flowers and caught directly in a ray of mauve light. The two had squeezed themselves into a little niche there and stood squarely in front of the Rodin statuary. Tom had one arm placed about Emily's shoulders and he was kissing her lightly first on the lobe of one ear and then on the tip of her nose. Emily stood as rigid and pale as the plaster sculpture behind her and with just the faintest smile on her lips. Ned looked at the two of them and then turned his glance at once on the Dorsets.

He found Miss Louisa and Mr. Alfred gazing quite openly at Tom and Emily and frankly grinning at the spectacle. It was more than Ned could endure. "Don't you *know*?" he wailed, as if in great physical pain. "Can't you *tell*? Can't you see who they *are*? They're *brother* and *sister*!"

From the other guests came one concerted gasp. And then an instant later, mistaking Ned's outcry to be something he had planned all along and probably intended—as they imagined—for the very cream of the jest, the whole company burst once again into laughter—not a chorus of laughter this time but a volley of loud guffaws from the boys, and from the girls a cacophony of separately articulated shrieks and trills.

None of the guests present that night could—or would—give a satisfactory account of what happened next. Everyone insisted that he had not even looked at the Dorsets, that he, or she, didn't know how Miss Louisa and Mr. Alfred reacted at first. Yet this was precisely what those of us who had gone there in the past *had* to know. And when finally we did manage to get an account of it, we knew that it was a very truthful and accurate one. Because we got it, of course, from Tom Bascomb.

Since Ned's outburst came after the dancing exhibition, the Dorsets were in their most disheveled state. Miss Louisa's hair was fallen half over her face, and that long, limp strand of Mr. Alfred's was dangling about his left ear. Like that, they stood at the doorway to the dining room grinning at Tom Bascomb's antics. And when Tom Bascomb, hearing Ned's wail, whirled about, the grins were still on the Dorsets' faces even though the guffaws and the shrieks of laughter were now silenced. Tom said that for several moments they continued to wear their grins like masks and that you couldn't really tell how they were taking it all until presently Miss Louisa's face, still wearing the grin, began turning all the queer colors of her paper flowers. Then the grin vanished from her lips and her mouth fell open and every bit of color went out of her face. She took a step backward and leaned against the doorjamb with her mouth still open and her eyes closed. If she hadn't been on her feet, Tom said he would have thought she was dead. Her brother didn't look at her, but his own grin had vanished just as hers did, and his face, all drawn and wrinkled, momentarily turned a dull copperish green.

Presently, though, he too went white, not white in faintness but in anger. His little brown eyes now shone like resin. And he took several steps toward Ned Meriwether. "What we know is that you are not one of us," he croaked. "We have perceived that from the beginning! We don't know how you got here or who you are. But the important question is, What are you doing here among these nice children?"

The question seemed to restore life to Miss Louisa. Her amber eyes popped wide open. She stepped away from the door and began pinning up her hair which had fallen down on her shoulders, and at the same time addressing the guests who were huddled together in the center of the hall. "Who is he, children? He is an intruder, that we know. If you know who he is, you must tell us."

"Who *am* I? Why, I am Tom Bascomb!" shouted Ned, still from the bottom step of the stairway. "I am Tom Bascomb, your paper boy!"

Then he turned and fled up the stairs toward the second floor. In a moment Mr. Dorset was after him.

To the real Tom Bascomb it had seemed that Ned honestly believed what he had been saying; and his own first impulse was to shout a denial. But being a level-headed boy and seeing how bad things were, Tom went instead to Miss Dorset and whispered to her that Tom Bascomb was a pretty tough guy and that she had better let *him* call the police for her. She told him where the telephone was in the side hall, and he started away.

But Miss Dorset changed her mind. She ran after Tom telling him not to call. Some of the guests mistook this for the beginning of another chase. Before the old lady could overtake Tom, however, Ned himself had appeared in the doorway toward which she and Tom were moving. He had come down the back stairway and he was calling out to Emily, "We're going *home*, Sis!"

A cheer went up from the whole party. Maybe it was this that caused Ned to lose his head, or maybe it was simply the sight of Miss Dorset rushing at him that did it. At any rate, the next moment he was running up the front stairs again, this time with Miss Dorset in pursuit.

When Tom returned from the telephone, all was quiet in the hall. The guests—everybody except Emily—had moved to the foot of the stairs and they were looking up and listening. From upstairs Tom could hear Ned saying, "All right. All right. All right." The old couple had him cornered.

Emily was still standing in the little niche among the flowers. And it is the image of Emily Meriwether standing among the paper flowers that tantalizes me whenever I think or hear someone speak of that evening. That, more than anything else, can make me wish that I had been there. I shall never cease to wonder what kind of thoughts were in her head to make her seem so oblivious to all that was going on while she stood there, and, for that matter, what had been in her mind all evening while she endured Tom Bascomb's caresses. When, in years since, I have had reason to wonder what some girl or woman is thinking—some Emily grown older—my mind nearly always returns to the image of that girl among the paper flowers. Tom said that when he returned from the telephone she looked very solemn and pale still but that her mind didn't seem to be on any of the present excitement. Immediately he went to her and said, "Your dad is on his way over, Emily." For it was the Meriwether parents he had telephoned, of course, and not the police.

It seemed to Tom that so far as he was concerned the party was now over. There was nothing more he could do. Mr. Dorset was upstairs guarding the door to the strange little room in which Ned was locked up. Miss Dorset was serving lime punch to the other guests in the dining room, all the while listening with one ear for the arrival of the police whom Tom pretended he had called. When the doorbell finally rang and Miss Dorset hurried to answer it, Tom slipped quietly out through the pantry and through the kitchen and left the house by the back door as the Meriwether parents entered by the front.

There was no difficulty in getting Edwin and Muriel Meriwether, the children's parents, to talk about what happened after they arrived that night. Both of them were sensible and clear-headed people, and they were not so conservative as some of our other neighbors in West Vesey. Being fond of gossip of any kind and fond of reasonably funny stories on themselves, they told how their children had deceived them earlier in the evening and how they had deceived themselves later. They tended to blame themselves more than the children for what had happened. They tried to protect the children from any harm or embarrassment that might result from it by sending them off to boarding school. In their talk they never referred directly to Tom's reprehensible conduct or to the possible motives that the children might have had for getting up their plan. They tried to spare their children and they tried to spare Tom, but unfortunately it didn't occur to them to try to spare the poor old Dorsets.

When Miss Louisa opened the door, Mr. Meriwether said, "I'm Edwin Meriwether, Miss Dorset. I've come for my son Ned."

"And for your daughter Emily, I hope," his wife whispered to him.

"And for my daughter Emily."

Before Miss Dorset could answer him, Edwin Meriwether spied Mr. Dorset descending the stairs. With his wife, Muriel, sticking close to his side Edwin now strode over to the foot of the stairs. "Mr. Dorset," he began, "my son Ned—"

From behind them, Edwin and Muriel now heard Miss Dorset saying, "All the invited guests are gathered in the dining room." From where they were standing the two parents could see into the dining room. Suddenly they turned and hurried in there. Mr. Dorset and his sister of course followed them.

Muriel Meriwether went directly to Emily who was standing in a group of girls. "Emily, where is your brother?"

Emily said nothing, but one of the boys answered: "I think they've got him locked up upstairs somewhere."

"Oh, no!" said Miss Louisa, a hairpin in her mouth—for she was still rather absent-mindedly working at her hair. "It is an intruder that my brother has upstairs."

Mr. Dorset began speaking in a confidential tone to Edwin. "My dear neighbor," he said, "our paper boy saw fit to intrude himself upon our company tonight. But we recognized him as an outsider from the start."

Muriel Meriwether asked: "Where *is* the paper boy? Where is the paper boy, Emily?"

Again one of the boys volunteered: "He went out through the back door, Mrs. Meriwether."

The eyes of Mr. Alfred and Miss Louisa searched the room for Tom. Finally their eyes met and they smiled coyly. "*All* the children are being mischievous tonight," said Miss Louisa, and it was quite as though she had said, "all *we* children." Then, still smiling, she said, "Your tie has come undone, Brother. Mr. and Mrs. Meriwether will hardly know what to think."

Mr. Alfred fumbled for a moment with his tie but soon gave it up. Now with a bashful glance at the Meriwether parents, and giving a nod in the direction of the children, he actually said, "I'm afraid we've all decided to play a trick on Mr. and Mrs. Meriwether."

Miss Louisa said to Emily: "We've hidden our brother somewhere, haven't we?"

Emily's mother said firmly: "Emily, tell me where Ned is."

"He's upstairs, Mother," said Emily in a whisper.

Emily's father said: "I wish you to take me to the boy upstairs, Mr. Dorset."

The coy, bashful expressions vanished from the faces of the two Dorsets. Their eyes were little dark pools of incredulity, growing narrower by the second. And both of them were now trying to put their hair in order. "Why, *we* know nice children when we see them," Miss Louisa said peevishly. There was a pleading quality in her voice, too. "We knew from the beginning that that boy upstairs didn't belong amongst us," she said. "Dear neighbors, it isn't just the money, you know, that makes the difference." All at once she sounded like a little girl about to burst into tears.

"It isn't just the money?" Edwin Meriwether repeated.

"Miss Dorset," said Muriel with new gentleness in her tone, as though she had just recognized that it was a little girl she was talking to, "there has been some kind of mistake—a misunderstanding."

Mr. Alfred Dorset said: "Oh, we wouldn't make a mistake of that kind! People *are* different. It isn't something you can put your finger on, but it isn't the money."

"I don't know what you're talking about," Edwin said, exasperated. "But I'm going upstairs and find that boy." He left the room with Mr. Dorset following him with quick little steps—steps like those of a small boy trying to keep up with a man.

Miss Louisa now sat down in one of the high-backed dining chairs which were lined up along the oak wainscot. She was trembling, and Muriel came and stood beside her. Neither of them spoke, and in almost no time Edwin Meriwether came downstairs again with Ned. Miss Louisa looked at Ned, and tears came into her eyes. "Where is my brother?" she asked accusingly, as though she thought possibly Ned and his father had locked Mr. Dorset in the bathroom.

"I believe he has retired," said Edwin. "He left us and disappeared into one of the rooms upstairs."

"Then I must go up to him," said Miss Louisa. For a moment she seemed unable to rise. At last she pushed herself up from the chair and walked from the room with the slow, steady gait of a somnambulist. Muriel Meriwether followed her into the hall and as she watched the old woman ascending the steps, leaning heavily on the rail, her impulse was to go and offer to assist her. But something made her turn back into the dining room. Perhaps she imagined that her daughter, Emily, might need her now.

The Dorsets did not reappear that night. After Miss Louisa went upstairs, Muriel promptly got on the telephone and called the parents of some of the other boys and girls. Within a quarter of an hour, half a dozen parents had assembled. It was the first time in many years that any adult had set foot inside the Dorset house. It was the first time that any parent had ever inhaled the perfumed air or seen the masses of paper flowers and the illuminations and the statuary. In the guise of holding consultations over whether or not they should put out the lights and lock up the house, the parents lingered much longer than was necessary before taking the young people home. Some of them even tasted the lime punch. But in the presence of their children they made no comment on what had happened and gave no indication of what their own impressions were—not even their impressions of the punch. At last it was decided that two of the men should see to putting out the lights everywhere on the first floor and down in the ballroom. They were a long time in finding the switches for the indirect lighting. In most cases, they simply resorted to unscrewing the bulbs. Meanwhile the children went to the large cloak closet behind the stairway and got their wraps. When Ned and Emily Meriwether rejoined their parents at the front door to leave the house, Ned was wearing his own overcoat and held his own fedora in his hand.

Miss Louisa and Mr. Alfred Dorset lived on for nearly ten years after that night, but they gave up selling their figs and paper flowers and of course they never entertained young people again. I often wonder if growing up in Chatham can ever have seemed quite the same since. Some of the terror must have gone out of it. Half the dread of coming of age must have vanished with the dread of the Dorsets' parties.

After that night, their old car would sometimes be observed creeping about town, but it was never parked in front of their house any more. It stood usually at the side entrance where the Dorsets could climb in and out of it without being seen. They began keeping a servant too—mainly to run their errands for them, I imagine. Sometimes it would be a man, sometimes a woman, never the same one for more than a few months at a time. Both of the Dorsets died during the Second World War while many of us who had gone to their parties were away from Chatham. But the story went round—and I am inclined to believe it—that after they were dead and the house was sold, Tom Bascomb's coat and hat were found still hanging in the cloak closet behind the stairs.

Tom himself was a pilot in the war and was a considerable hero. He was such a success and made such a name for himself that he never came back to Chatham to live. He found bigger opportunities elsewhere I suppose, and I don't suppose he ever felt the ties to Chatham that people with Ned's kind of upbringing do. Ned was in the war too, of course. He was in the navy and after the war he did return to Chatham to live, though actually it was not until then that he had spent much time here since his parents bundled him off to boarding school. Emily came home and made her debut just two or three years before the war, but she was already engaged to some boy in the East; she never comes back any more except to bring her children to see their grandparents for a few days during Christmas or at Easter.

I understand that Emily and Ned are pretty indifferent to each other's existence nowadays. I have been told this by Ned Meriwether's own wife. Ned's wife maintains that the night Ned and Emily went to the Dorsets' party marked the beginning of this indifference, that it marked the end of their childhood intimacy and the beginning of a shyness, a reserve, even an animosity between them that was destined to be a sorrow forever to the two sensible parents who had sat in the upstairs sitting room that night waiting until the telephone call came from Tom Bascomb.

Ned's wife is a girl he met while he was in the navy. She was a Wave, and her background isn't the same as his. Apparently, she isn't too happy with life in what she refers to as "Chatham proper." She and Ned have recently moved out into a suburban development, which she doesn't like either and which she refers to as "greater Chatham." She asked me at a party one night how Chatham got its name (she was just making conversation and appealing to my interest in such things) and when I told her that it was named for the Earl of Chatham and pointed out that the city is located in Pitt County, she burst out laughing. "How very elegant," she said. "Why has nobody ever told me that before?" But what interests me most about Ned's wife is that after a few drinks she likes to talk about Ned and Emily and Tom Bascomb and the Dorsets. Tom Bascomb has become a kind of hero—and I don't mean a wartime hero—in her eyes, though of course not having grown up in Chatham she has never seen him in her life. But she is a clever girl, and there are times when she will say to me, "Tell me about Chatham.

Tell me about the Dorsets." And I try to tell her. I tell her to remember that Chatham looks upon itself as a rather old city. I tell her to remember that it was one of the first English-speaking settlements west of the Alleghenies and that by the end of the American Revolution, when veterans began pouring westward over the Wilderness Road or down the Ohio River, Chatham was often referred to as a thriving village. Then she tells me that I am being dull, because it is hard for her to concentrate on any aspect of the story that doesn't center around Tom Bascomb and that night at the Dorsets'.

But I make her listen. Or at least one time I did. The Dorset family, I insisted on saying, was in Chatham even in those earliest times right after the Revolution, but they had come here under somewhat different circumstances from those of the other early settlers. How could that really matter, Ned's wife asked, after a hundred and fifty years? How could distinctions between the first settlers matter after the Irish had come to Chatham, after the Germans, after the Italians? Well, in West Vesey Place it could matter. It had to. If the distinction was false, it mattered all the more and it was all the more necessary to make it.

But let me interject here that Chatham is located in a state about whose history most Chatham citizens—not newcomers like Ned's wife, but old-timers—have little interest and less knowledge. Most of us, for instance, are never even quite sure whether during the 1860's our state did secede or didn't secede. As for the city itself, some of us hold that it is geographically Northern and culturally Southern. Others say the reverse is true. We are all apt to want to feel misplaced in Chatham, and so we are not content merely to say that it is a border city. How you stand on this important question is apt to depend entirely on whether your family is one of those with a good Southern name or one that had its origin in New England, because those are the two main categories of old society families in Chatham.

But truly—I told Ned's wife—the Dorset family was never in either of those categories. The first Dorset had come, with his family and his possessions and even a little capital, direct from a city in the English Midlands to Chatham. The Dorsets came not as pioneers, but paying their way all the way. They had not bothered to stop for a generation or two to put down roots in Pennsylvania or Virginia or Massachusetts. And this was the distinction which some people wished always to make. Apparently those early Dorsets had cared no more for putting down roots in the soil of the New World than they had cared for whatever they had left behind in the Old. They were an obscure mercantile family who came to invest in a new Western city. Within two generations the business—no, the industry!—which they established made them rich beyond any dreams they could have had in the beginning. For half a century they were looked upon, if any family ever was, as our first family.

And then the Dorsets left Chatham—practically all of them except the one old bachelor and the one old maid—left it just as they had come, not caring much about what they were leaving or where they were going. They were city people, and they were Americans. They knew that what they had in Chatham they could buy more of in other places. For them Chatham was an investment that had paid off. They went to live in Santa Barbara and Laguna Beach, in Newport and on Long Island. And the truth which it was so hard for the rest of us to admit was that, despite our families of Massachusetts and Virginia, we were all more like the Dorsets—those Dorsets who left Chatham— than we were *un*like them. Their spirit was just a little closer to being the very essence of Chatham than ours was. The obvious difference was that we had to stay on here and pretend that our life had a meaning which it did not. And if it was only by a sort of chance that Miss Louisa and Mr. Alfred played the role of social arbiters among the young people for a number of years, still no one could honestly question their divine right to do so.

"It may have been their right," Ned's wife said at this point, "but just think what might have happened."

"It's not a matter of what might have happened," I said. "It is a matter of what did happen. Otherwise, what have you and I been talking about?"

"Otherwise," she said with an irrepressible shudder, "I would not be forever getting you off in a corner at these parties to talk about my husband and my husband's sister and how it is they care so little for each other's company nowadays."

And I could think of nothing to say to that except that probably we had now pretty well covered our subject.

Promise of Rain

UNDERSTAND, THERE was never anything *really* wrong with Hugh Robert. He was a well-built boy, strong and quick and bursting with vitality. That, at least, was the impression of himself he managed to give people. I guess he did it just by carrying himself well and never letting down in front of anyone. Actually, he was no better built than my other boys. And how is one really to know about a person's vitality? He had a bright look in his blue eyes, a fresh complexion, and a shock of black curly hair on a head so handsomely shaped that everybody noticed it. It was the shape of his head, I imagine, that made people feel Hugh was so much better-looking than his older brothers. All the girls were crazy about him. And even if I am his father, I have to say that he was a boy who seemed fairly crazy about himself.

When Hugh was sixteen, I kept a pretty close watch on him—closer than I ever had time to keep on the others. I observed how he seldom left for school in the mornings without stopping a moment before the long gilt-framed mirror in the front hall. Sometimes he would seem to be looking at himself with painful curiosity and sometimes with pure admiration. Either way it was unbecoming of him. But still I wasn't too critical of the morning looks he gave himself. I did mind, however, his doing the same thing again when he got home from school in the afternoons. Many a winter's afternoon I would already be home when he came in, and from where I sat in the living room, or in the library across the hall, I could tell by his footsteps that he was stopping to see himself in that great expanse of looking glass.

For Hugh's own good I used, some afternoons, to let him catch me watching him at the mirror. I thought it might break him of the habit. But his eyes would meet mine without the least shame and he would say something he didn't mean, like "I'm not much to look at, am I, Mr. Perkins?" And he continued to stop there and ogle himself in the mirror whenever it suited him to. He would often call me Mr. Perkins like that, and call his mother Mrs. Perkins. We could never be quite sure how it was meant, and I don't think he intended us to be.

447

When he was being outright playful, he was apt to call us Will and Mary.

Hugh kept his schoolbooks in a compartment of the cupboard in the downstairs hall. The cupboard I speak of was a big oak, antique thing, a very expensive piece of furniture, which Hugh's mother had bought in Europe during our 1924 trip—ten years before. Hugh's schoolbooks seldom got farther into the house than the hall cupboard. If I complained about this to Mary, she would refer me to his report card, with its wall of straight A's. If I carried my attack further and mentioned the silly kinds of subjects he was taking, she would sigh and blame it on his having to go to the public school. As though I *wanted* Hugh to go to the public school! And as though I wanted to be home those afternoons when he came in from school! It was just that Hugh Robert grew up during bad times for us, which, as I see it, was no more my fault than it was his. Those were years when it seemed that my business firm might have to close its doors almost anytime. I couldn't *afford* to keep a boy in private school. And as for myself, I just couldn't bear to hang around the office all of those long, dead winter afternoons at the bottom of the Depression.

I can see Hugh now in his corduroy jacket and sheepskin collar stooping down to slip his books always in the same corner of the same compartment of the hall cupboard. He was orderly and systematic about everything like that. His older brothers had never measured up to him in this respect. In an instant he could tell you the whereabouts of any of his possessions. He had things stashed away—ice skates, baseball gloves, and other athletic equipment, as well as sets of carpentry tools, car tools, and radio parts—had them pushed neatly away in nooks and shelves and drawers all over the house. They were all things he had been very much excited about at one time or another. Hugh would plague us to buy him something, and then when we did and he didn't get the satisfaction out of it he had expected, he would brood about it for weeks. Finally, he would put it away somewhere. If it was something expensive and we asked him what became of it, he would say it was just one of his "mistakes" and that we needn't think he had forgotten it. Sometimes when I was looking for something I had misplaced, I would come on one of those nests of "mistakes" and know at once it was Hugh's. I remember its occurring to me once that it wouldn't take Hugh Robert thirty seconds to lay his hands on anything he owned, and that he would be able in ten minutes' time to assemble *everything* he owned and be on his way, if ever that notion struck him. It wasn't a thought that would ever have occurred to me in connection with the other children.

Our daughter and two older boys were married and gone from the house by this time, but when they were home with their spouses on a Sunday they'd say we were still babying Hugh, and say that they knew what would have happened to *them* if they had ever tried calling us by our first names. I suppose you really can't help babying the youngest, in one way or another, and favoring him a little over the others, especially when he comes along as a sort of trailer after the others are already up in school. But to Hugh's mother it was very annoying to have the older children point this out, and she would deny it hotly. If on a Monday morning, after the others had been there on Sunday, Hugh came down to breakfast and began that first-name or Mr.-and-Mrs. business, Mary was likely to try to talk to him as she used to talk to the other children, and tell him that it was not very respectful of him. It never did any good, though, and she would say afterward that I never supported her in these efforts. I don't know. I do know, though, that disrespectful is hardly the word for my son Hugh Robert Perkins—not when he was sixteen, not when he was younger than that, not even nowadays, when he favors us with one of his rare visits and sits around the house for three days talking mostly about himself and about how broke I was when he was growing up. Mary says he's the only person who can remind me, nowadays, of how hard up we were then without making me mad. If that is so, it is because he seems to take such innocent pleasure in remembering it. He talks about it in a way that makes you feel he is saying, "I owe *everything* to that!"

It got to be the fashion in those days for high-school boys to wear the knee bands of their golf knickers unfastened, letting the baggy pants legs hang loose down to their ankles. They went to school that way, and it looked far worse to me than even the shirttail-out fashion that came along after the war. I had never seen Hugh wearing his own plus fours that way, but I remarked to him one day that I regarded it as the ugliest, sloppiest, most ungentlemanly habit of dress I had ever encountered. And I asked him what in the world possessed those boys to make them do it. I think he took this as a nasty slam against his classmates. "I don't know why they do it," he said, with something of a sneer, "but I could find out for you, Mr. Perkins." I told him never mind, that I didn't want to know.

Next day Hugh appeared at breakfast with his knickers hanging down about his ankles. He lunged into the room with his buckles on his knee bands jangling like spurs. Naturally, I was supposed to blow up and tell him to fasten them. But I pretended not even to notice, and I wouldn't let Mary mention it to him. He wore them that way for a couple of days, and then seeing he wasn't going to get a rise out of me, he stopped. He seemed dispirited and rather gloomy for a day or so. Then, finding me at home after school one afternoon, he said out of the clear, "I made a discovery for you, Dad."

"What's that?" I said. I really didn't know what he meant.

"I found out why those fellows wear their plus fours drooping down. I tried wearing my own that way for a couple of days, though you didn't even notice it." And he had the cheek to wink at me in the hall mirror.

"Well?" I said noncommittally. I remembered I had said I didn't want to know why. But I didn't remind him, because I knew he remembered, too.

He had already put his books away, and he was about to take his jacket to the closet behind the stair. He stood running one finger along the ribbing of the corduroy jacket, which he had thrown over his arm, and he had a dejected look on his face. "It makes them feel kind of reckless and devil-may-care and as if they don't give a darn for what anybody thinks of how they look." This he volunteered, mind you. I had only said, "Well?"

I thought he would continue, but when he didn't I asked, "You don't recommend it? You didn't like the feeling?"

"It didn't make *me* feel that way. It only made me understand how it makes *them* feel. I didn't get any kick out of it. I don't blame them too much, though. Those guys don't have much to make them feel important."

I had to bite my tongue to keep from asking the boy what he had to make him feel important. But I let it go at that, because I saw what he was getting at. I realized I was supposed to feel pretty cheap for having criticized the people he went to school with.

Hugh didn't have any duties at home. We weren't people who lived in any do-it-yourself world in those days, no matter how bad business was. I still kept me a yardman in summer and a furnaceman in winter. I can't help saying that in that respect I did as well by Hugh as by his older brothers. When he came home in the afternoon and had stuck his books in the cupboard he was *free*—free as a bird. He might have looked at himself in the mirror all afternoon if he had wanted to. Or he might have been out on the town with a bunch of the high-school roughnecks. But Hugh wasn't a ruffian, and he wasn't an idler, either; not in the worst sense. He was vain and self-centered, but you knew that while he stood before that looking glass unbuckling his corduroy jacket he was trying to make judgments and decisions about himself; he was checking something he had thought about himself during the day.

In the mirror Hugh's blue eyes would seem to study their own blueness for a time, and then, not satisfied, they would begin to explore the hall—the hall, that is, as reflected in the glass, and with himself, of course, always in the foreground. If I had purposely planted myself in the library doorway, that's when his eyes would light on me. He would look at me curiously for a split second—before he let his eyes meet mine—look at me as he did at everything else in view. The first time it happened, I thought the look meant he was curious and resentful about my being home from the office so early. Next time, I saw that this wasn't so and that he was merely fitting me into his picture of himself. I remember very well what he said to me on one of these occasions: "Mr. Perkins, even among mirrors there's a difference! Especially the big ones. They all give you different ideas of how you look." He rambled on, seemingly without any embarrassment. "I saw myself in a big one downtown one day and there was a second when I couldn't place where I'd seen that uncouth, unkempt, uncanny individual before. And at school there's a huge one in the room where we take typing—don't ask me what it's there for. It makes me look

like everybody else in the class, with all of us pecking away at
typewriters. We all look so much alike I can hardly find myself
in it." When Hugh finished that spiel, I found myself blushing—blushing for him. I hated so to think of the boy gaping
at himself in mirrors all over town the way he did in that one
in my front hall.

During the summer after Hugh turned seventeen I had the
misfortune to learn, firsthand, something about his habits
away from home—that is, when he did take a notion to use
his freedom differently and go out on the town with his cronies from the high school. I am not speaking of nightlife,
though there was beginning to be some of that, too, but of
the hours that young people have to kill in the daytime. The
city of Chatham, which is where we have always lived, is not
the biggest city in our state. Since the Second World War it has
grown substantially, and the newspapers claim that there are
now half a million people in the "municipal area," by which
they mean almost the whole county. But twenty-five years ago
people didn't speak of it as being more than half that size.
For me to encounter my son Hugh downtown or riding along
Division Boulevard couldn't really be thought a great coincidence—especially not since, almost without knowing it, I had
developed the habit of keeping an eye out for that head of his.
   I would catch a glimpse of him on the street and, with my
mind still on some problem we had at the office, wouldn't
know right away what it was I had seen. Often I had to turn
around and look to be sure. There Hugh would be, his dark
head moving along in a group of other youthful heads—frequently a girl's head for every boy's—out under the boiling
July sun, in a section of the city that they couldn't possibly
have had any reason for being in. There was at least one occasion when I was certain that Hugh saw me, too. I was in the
backseat of the car, and when I turned and looked out the rear
window, Hugh was waving. But I was crowded in between two
hefty fellows—two of my men from the office—and couldn't
have returned his wave even if I had tried. On that occasion,
we were riding through a section of town that used long ago to
be called the Irish Flats. The men with me were both of them
strictly Chatham Irish, and as we rode along I commenced

teasing them about how tough that section used to be and how when I was a boy a "white man" didn't dare put foot in that end of town.

Perkins Finance Company, which was the name of our firm before we reorganized in 1946, used to make loans on small properties all over Chatham. Since the boys took over—my two older boys and my daughter's husband—they haven't wanted to deal much in that kind of thing. We have bigger irons in the fire now, and the boys have even put a cable address on the company stationery, along with the new name: Perkins, Hodgeson Investments. (The Hodgeson's for my daughter's husband.) But our small loans were what saved us in the Depression. The boys weren't with me in the firm then, of course. When they came back from college up East, just at the time of the Crash, I wouldn't let them come in with me. I got them jobs in two Chatham banks which I *knew* weren't going to fail. They were locked up down there in their cages all day and went home to their young wives at night without ever having any notion of the kind of hide-and-seek games Hugh and I were playing in our idleness. What I would often do—when I didn't go home in the afternoon—was to ride around town with some of my men and look at the property we had an interest in. Aside from any business reason, it did something for me—more than going home did, more than a round of golf, or going to the ball game even. It did something for me to get out and look at the town, to see how it had stopped building and growing. The feeling I got from it was that Time itself had stopped and was actually waiting for me instead of passing me by and leaving me behind just when I was in my prime. At the time, I already had a son-in-law and two daughters-in-law, but I wasn't an old man. I had just turned fifty. In the hot summertime of the Depression I could sometimes look at Chatham and feel about it that it was a big, powerful, stubborn horse that wouldn't go. I was still in the saddle, it seemed—or I had just dismounted and had a tight grip on the reins near the bit and was meaning to remount. Perhaps I even had in mind beating the brute somehow, to make it go; for I was young enough then to be impatient and to feel that I just couldn't wait for the town to begin to move again. I knew I had to have my second chance. Hugh could take whatever pleasure and instruction he would from exploring the city as it was in those days and getting to know different kinds of people. It corresponded to something in his makeup. Or it answered some need of his temperament. Anyway, he seemed to be born for it. But, as for me, I could hardly wait for things to begin to move again and to be the way they had been before.

Yet I was a man old enough to take a certain reasonable satisfaction in everything's suddenly stopping still the way it did in the Depression and giving me the chance to look at the city the way I could then. It has a beauty, a town like Chatham does. Even with things getting mighty shabby, as they were in 1933, Division Boulevard was a magnificent street with handsome stone and tile-faced office buildings and store buildings downtown, with the automobile showrooms taking up beyond the overpass at the Union Station—a cathedral of a building!—and after that a half mile of old mansions from the last century, most of them long since turned into undertaking parlors, all of them so well built that no amount of abuse or remodeling seemed to alter them much; and then almost a mile of small apartment houses, and after that the clinics and the State Medical Center and the two big hospitals.

Beyond the hospitals, Division Boulevard runs right through Lawton Park. On one side you get a glimpse among the trees of the Art Gallery; farther along on that side, there is the bronze monument to the doughboy. On the other side is a mound with Lawton Park spelled out in sweet alyssum and pinks and ground myrtle; and away over on that side you can see among the treetops the glass dome of the birdhouse at the zoo. It's a handsomely kept park—was all the way through the Depression even—and when you come out at the other end, there before your eyes is the beginning of Singleton Heights!

From Singleton Heights on out past the Country Club to the Hunt and Polo Grounds it's all like a fairyland. Great stucco and stone houses, and whitewashed brick, acres upon acres of them. All of them planted round with evergreens and flowering fruit trees, with wide green lawns—the sprinklers playing like fountains all summer long—lawns that are really meadows, stretching off to low stone walls or rustic fences or even a sluggish little creek with willow trees growing along its banks in places. It's the sort of thing that when you've been off to New

York, or maybe to Europe for the summer, and come back to it, the very prettiness of it nearly breaks your heart.

But I ought to say, before speaking of Hugh again, that Singleton Heights and the Country Club area beyond are not the only fine neighborhoods in Chatham and it is not of those sections of Chatham that I think when I'm up at the lake in the summer or away on a business trip. My own house, for instance, is in one of the gated-off streets that were laid out just north of Lawton Park at the turn of the century. The houses there are mostly big three-story houses. There's a green parkway down the center of the street, and we have so many forest trees you would think you were in the middle of Lawton Park itself. But, actually, it's not even the Lawton Park area that's most typical of Chatham, any more than Singleton Heights or the Country Club area. And, in my mind, it is certainly not the new do-it-yourself ranch-house district that means Chatham to me. . . . It is the block after block of modest two-story houses, built thirty to forty years ago now, that seem most typical and give me a really comfortable feeling. It was the people in those houses who managed to keep paying something on their loans in the Depression. Whenever I think of Chatham when Mary and I go away in the summer and think of how pleasant it can be to be there despite the awful heat, I think first of those bungalows built of good wire-cut brick, with red and orange tile roofs and big screened porches, of the little privet hedges that divide their sixty-foot lots, and of the maples and oaks and sycamores whose summer shade their front yards share.

The summer Hugh was seventeen I must have seen him hoofing it along the sidewalk or standing at the curb of every block of Division Boulevard. I could never be certain that the men with me recognized him, and once I asked Joe McNary, "What were those kids doing back there on the curb?"

"They're hitchhiking, Will," he said.

"Hitchhiking?" I had never heard the term before, but I knew at once what it meant. "Where are they going?" I said.

"Nowhere. They're just doing the town. There's no harm in it, I guess."

I guess he was right. Hugh never got into any trouble that I know of, except over a car that he and his buddies made a down payment on, one time. They put down seven dollars on an old Packard touring car and drove it around town till it ran out of gas. They had bought the car in Hugh's name, and so when the police found it parked at the roadside out near the Polo Club, they gave me a ring. I told them just to take it back to the dealer and that I'd pay whatever fine it was. But they were pretty inquisitive, and I had to go down to the police station and answer a lot of questions. It was an embarrassing experience for me, because I had to confess that I hadn't known of Hugh's part in the adventure and didn't know the names of the other boys who went in on it with him. From the police station I had to get Hugh on the telephone at the high school and find out the names of the other boys. He didn't want to tell me. And we had to argue it out right then, which was the bad part, with him talking from the principal's office and with me at the sergeant's desk at the police station. Hugh ended by giving me the boys' names, and we never heard any more about it from the police, though I did have to pay the used-car dealer something to make him forget the whole business.

Hugh Robert was in the dumps for a couple of weeks afterward. Instead of excusing himself from the dinner table, as he had always done when his mother and I sat dawdling over our coffee, he would sit there pretending to listen to what we had to say, or he would just gaze despairingly up into the glass prisms of the chandelier above the table. One night when I felt I couldn't stand his black mood any longer, I gave his mother a sign to leave us alone. At first she frowned and refused to do it. Finally though, when I grew as silent as Hugh, she invented a reason to have to go to the kitchen. As soon as I heard her and the cook's voices out there, I said, "What's the matter, Hugh. What are you thinking about?"

He said, "I was thinking about how sorry I am. I really am, Dad."

"What's this?" I said.

"I'm sorry you had to pay that money on the car."

"Is that all?"

"No. Worse than that was their having you down at the station. I know you hated that worse than paying the money." Right away, you see, he was making me out as some kind of pantywaist.

"I didn't give a hoot in hell about going to the police station," I said. "But it was a damn-fool idea you boys had."

"You don't have to tell me that," he said. "It was the stupidest idea I've ever had. It was an awful mistake."

What could you say to such a boy? I wanted to ask him where they would have gone if they had had more gas, but his mother came bustling back from the kitchen then, followed by Lucy May, the cook, who began pressing Hugh to have a second helping of chocolate pie, which, if I remember correctly, he did.

One other time, when I was out with another group of men, and in another part of town, I asked, "What do you suppose those kids are doing out here?"

"*Out* here?" one of them said, and I could tell from his lack of interest that he hadn't recognized Hugh. But I think the fellow who was driving the car that day must have known that what I meant was: What was a son of mine doing so far from home?

"Oh," he said, "I can guess pretty well what they're doing. They've heard there's a drugstore in this end of town that sells milk shakes for a nickel. It's something like that; you can just count on it." We were in a perfectly decent neighborhood out on the south side, where a lot of the rich Germans used to live. It's a nice section and didn't get too awfully run-down during the Depression. I could hardly have told the difference between it and my own section if I hadn't known Chatham well.

Still another time, we had parked the car and were crossing the street toward a little Italian grocery store and lunchroom, a place just west of Court Square and near the old canal. It was a pretty rough and slummy part of town. (Not long afterward FDR had the whole area demolished and put one of his housing projects there.) But the little joint, which was called Baccalupo's Quick Lunch & Grocery, was getting to be well known for its rye and prosciutto and its three-point-two draft beer. As we headed across the street, I saw Hugh and two other boys running out of the place, with Tony Baccalupo, a swarthy little dwarf of a man, after them. I watched Tony overtake them and snatch some fruit away from them. Then the boys went off laughing together at Tony, who stood shouting something in Italian at the top of his voice. Tony was himself a sort of half-wit, I suppose. He was not the proprietor but the proprietor's younger brother—or older brother. When we got inside, I found the opportunity to ask him about the boys who had gone out just before we came in.

"They jelly beans," he said. "They just-a jelly beans. They think they plenty smart and I see 'em making the fun of me, winking in the mirror over the counter. But they got no money, got no jobs, not even know how to make-a the real trouble. They steal them grapefruit just-a to make-a me hafta run out in the street and get a sweat." He spat in the sawdust on the floor, and began taking our orders.

It got so, instead of watching for Hugh, I tried not to see him. All summer, he was wandering about town, hitchhiking from one point to another, never with any real destination, sometimes driving my old Pierce-Arrow, when his mother didn't need it. He didn't really like to take the car, however; it was an old limousine with a glass between the front and back seats, and used too much gas. He and his friends drifted about town, not ever knowing where they were, really, because to them the different parts of the city didn't mean anything. I would be riding in the backseat of a car or walking on the sidewalk, aware only of how all business and progress had bogged down, wondering if and when we could ever get it going again, searching for the first sign of a comeback. Hugh and his gang were searching for something, too, you might say. Searching for mirrors to admire themselves in. Or that's how it seemed. Every time I saw them, I would think of Tony's word: jelly beans.

One night when I got up from the dinner table, Hugh was just coming in from one of his days of wandering about town. We met in the dining-room doorway. "I hope you're making the most of your freedom, son," I said.

He looked at me for a moment, almost squinting. Then he opened his eyes wide, and turned his blue gaze on the room in general, blinking his eyelids two or three times as though they were camera shutters, his eyes registering everything, including the black cook; Mary had buzzed for her when she heard Hugh shut the front door, and Lucy May was now holding the swinging door a little way open. Finally he squinted at me again—squinted so that you couldn't have told the color of his eyes. And I repeated, "I hope you're making the most of your freedom."

"I wonder if I *am*," he said, smiling, with a tinge of contempt in his smile and in his voice, I thought.

I looked over my shoulder at his mother, and she shook her head, meaning for me not to say anything more.

It was as though Hugh and I were drifting about through two different cities that were laid out on the very same tract of land. I used to feel we were even occupying two different houses built upon one piece of ground—houses of identical dimensions and filling one and the same area of cubic space. It was just a feeling I had. It first came to me one afternoon when I watched Hugh looking at himself in the mirror. I imagined that the interior that Hugh and I saw there wasn't the same as the one I stood in. That's all there was to it. But probably even to mention that feeling of mine is carrying things too far. I don't want to be misleading about this mirror business. I don't think the mirror-gazing itself was any real fetish with Hugh. In the first place, he didn't *always* make for the mirror as soon as he came in. Sometimes he would slip his books into the hall cupboard and go straight to the telephone; he was a great one for the telephone.

And what a lot of common talk we had to listen to on the telephone: "Did he say that? . . . I saw her looking at me and I wondered what she thought. . . . 'What do you mean?' I mean what she thought about *me*. . . ."

Always himself. Often as not, one of his girls would call him.

There was a girl named Ida, who nearly drove us all crazy. In the beginning, Hugh was mightily smitten by her. Of that I am quite certain. She was the belle of the class when Hugh entered the tenth grade at the high school, and throughout most of that year it seemed as though he looked for excuses to mention Ida Thomas's name at the dinner table. We didn't get much notion of her except that she was "a gorgeous redhead" and that she had so many admirers that Hugh "couldn't get near her with a ten-foot pole." Nevertheless, he clearly liked for us to tease him about her, though he would always insist that "she didn't know he existed." But at last—and after considerable effort, I gather—he managed to make Ida aware of his existence. From that day the girl gave him no peace.

She would telephone him two or three times in one evening:
She was a brash little thing and would engage Hugh's mother
in conversation if she answered the telephone, or even me, if
I answered it: "How are *you*, Mr. Perkins? . . . How's Mrs.
Perkins? . . . And how's that good-looking son of yours—your
pride and joy, so they tell me?" Hugh had a time shaking her,
I guess. He got so he wouldn't come to the telephone if Mary
or I answered and recognized Ida's voice, and he would never
answer it himself. She took to writing him letters at home and
finally tended to embarrass the boy with his family. One card
said, "Roses are red, violets are blue. Sugar's sweet and so is
Hugh." Another said, "Someday I'll ride in your Pierce-Arrow,
Hugh Robert Perkins."

One Sunday, I got Hugh to go for a walk with me while his
mother was at church, and I asked him outright why he put up
with so much nonsense from the girl. "I feel sorry for her," he
said. As though that were any kind of an excuse.

"She's not as popular as she used to be?" I asked.

"Certainly she is!" he said.

"Oh," I said. "Then you feel sorry for her because she has all
the other fellows but *not* you?"

He laughed aloud. "I never thought of it that way, Mr. Perkins," he said, as if he thought I was only joking.

So I laughed, too, and took the opportunity to ask another
question. "Tell me, son," I said, "what turned you against her?
Was it the telephone calls?"

"No. Not exactly. You see, it wasn't even *me* she was interested in. She was impressed by your old Pierce-Arrow. And still
more by our living in West Vesey Place."

"But you didn't exactly like those telephone calls. And what
about those postcards, Hugh?"

"Why, she didn't know any better, Dad!" For a minute he
stopped there on the street on Sunday morning and looked at
me as though it was I who didn't have good sense about such
things. "That's why I had to put up with it. That's why I felt
sorry for her."

He was very cagey, and I didn't bother him any further
about Ida, since it was all over by then anyway. But judging
from the gloom he dwelt in for several months, he must have
considered Ida one of his worst mistakes.

Hugh wouldn't study, and he wasn't really too hot an athlete, although certainly for a while he thought he was going to be. He made several of his "mistakes" in the athletic line, and would, of course, fall into a black mood each time he was dropped from a team or was even kept on the sidelines. His mother said he couldn't excel in athletics because he had to compete with the big, tough fellows who went out for sports at Chatham West High. And she said that the schoolwork at the public school was too easy and didn't occupy him. Maybe she was right. I know that when his two brothers had finished at Chatham Academy they had had trigonometry and Latin and even some Greek. Both of them passed the College Board examinations with flying colors and had a summer in Europe before starting college. Hugh wouldn't even *talk* about going to college—not to any local college that I could afford to send him to. Since the war, of course, he has gotten himself some kind of degree at Columbia University on the G.I. Bill. But during high school, when we mentioned college to him, he only laughed at the idea. One Sunday in his senior year, when the other children were at the house and the subject came up, he said, "Why, I've already been to the best college in our part of the country, the College of William and Mary"—meaning his mother and me, of course. "I've been studying diplomacy, and next June I'll be ready for the foreign service."

The others took this as a joke, but it made me realize how soon he might be gone from us to wherever he had in mind going. I was only half through my meal, but involuntarily I began searching my pockets for my pipe and a match. It's hard having your youngest be the one who disappoints you. I sat there searching for my pipe, thinking that I could just imagine how the letter he would leave would look on the library table, or how he would come down to breakfast one morning and say he had written off and gotten himself a job somewhere away from us—away from Chatham! I suppose it was rather simpleminded and old-fashioned of me to think about it the way I did.

In his senior year, Hugh actually began to show an interest in his schoolwork—in a certain part of it, in a part I wouldn't have called work. You would just hardly believe the things they offered in the curriculum of that school. But anyway, the first indication I had of what was stirring was Hugh's coming to me one morning with a very odd sort of request. From some neat, dark, and no doubt carefully protected corner of the house, known only to himself, he had pulled out an old dictation machine—a Dictaphone—which I had given him as a little fellow. It was an old model that I had brought home from the office and let him use as a plaything. I had forgotten about it. It had been seven or eight years since he had asked me to take the wax cylinders downtown and have them scraped so he could use them again. But he came to me after breakfast one morning, when he was all ready to leave for school, carrying the case of cylinders that came with the Dictaphone. He looked a little shamefaced, I must say, like any big boy caught playing with one of his old toys. I was touched to see that he had hung on to something I had given him so long ago. He handed the case to me and as I examined it I remarked silently that it seemed to be in as good condition as on the day I gave it to him. "Where did you resurrect this from, Hugh?" I asked.

"I've had it put by against a rainy day," he said.

"Do you still have the machine itself?" I asked.

"Oh yes, of course," he said.

I held the case of cylinders and then I said, "You intend to sell it, I suppose—the whole outfit?"

"Why no, Mr. Perkins. I want you to have these cylinders scraped for me."

"You know it costs something to have it done?" It occurred to me that as a child he mightn't have realized that.

"Oh, certainly. I'll pay for it. I have some *money* put by, too," he said, giving me one of his quick winks, "against the same rainy day." He was no spendthrift, to be sure. I doubt that there was ever a week when he spent the whole of the small allowance his mother gave him.

I set the case of cylinders on the floor beside me and picked up the paper I had been reading when he came in. "What are you going to use them for?" I said from behind the paper.

"In connection with one of my classes," he said. "A readings course."

I looked at him over my paper. He was still standing before me and was clearly willing for me to pursue the subject. "A reading course?"

"Oral readings," he explained. "A class in oral readings, for additional speech credit." He was in dead earnest. He said they were graded according to some kind of point system and that it had been wonderful help for him to be able to hear himself on the Dictaphone, that he had already made terrific progress.

"You've already been using the Dictaphone, then?" I inquired. "The cylinders were clean when you got them out?"

"Yes," he said. "Don't you remember, I got you to have them scraped before I ever put them away?"

"No, I didn't remember," I said. "It's been a pretty long time, Hugh."

Now I found myself wondering how many nights had he already been up there in his room listening to his own voice on the Dictaphone. I went back to my paper again, because I knew I didn't want to hear any more about this business. Sooner or later, I thought, he will see it as just another of his mistakes.

But for some months to come, Hugh's concern with his voice was all we did hear about. My theory was that the boy had been trying a long while to decide what it was about himself that charmed him most. And at last he thought he knew. All that winter he was as busy as a beaver with his "speech lessons" and "exercises." I would bring home the set of cylinders freshly scraped, and they wouldn't last him much more than a week. Finally, I guess he wore them out because well before spring he quit asking me to take them. But his interest didn't stop there. He continued to engage me now and then in discussions of his current "problems" in speech, as openly and seriously as though he were talking about math or history. And first thing his mother and I knew, he was on the debating team, was trying out for a part in the class play, was even getting special instructions from the teacher in "newscasting."

It occurred to me once during this time that maybe Hugh had fallen in love with his speech teacher, Miss Arrowood. In recent months his mother had complained of a tendency in him to resent any questions about the girls he was having dates with on the weekends. If, under pressure, he mentioned the name of a particular girl, it wasn't a name that his mother knew. I couldn't explain such a business to Mary—there was no use in it—but I think I understood pretty well what Hugh was going through in that respect. And I could remember that a boy, hating himself for his own fallen and degraded state, is apt at such times to begin idealizing some attractive, sympathetic woman who is enough older than himself to seem quite beyond his aspiration—particularly if she is even vaguely the intellectual type. I didn't ask Hugh how old Miss Arrowood was or what she looked like. I just dropped by the school one afternoon in March when I knew there was to be a rehearsal of the class play.

It wasn't even necessary for me to go inside the auditorium to see what I had come to see. Through a glass panel in one of the rear doors I could see the whole stage. The play they were practicing for was one of those moronic things that they give big grown-up boys and girls to act in. (They did it even in the private schools when my older children were coming along.) This one was called *Mr. Hairbrain's Confession: A Comedy.* I read the title in a notice on the bulletin board beside the auditorium door.

After two seconds I spotted Miss Arrowood, who was giving directions from a position at the side of the stage, and I knew that my conjecture had been a false one. I say "after two seconds" because for about two seconds I mistook that lady to be one of the cast and already in costume and makeup. Her bosom was of a size and shape that one of the youngsters might have effected with a bed pillow. Her orange-colored hair may really have been a wig. On the far end of her unbelievable nose rode the inevitable pince-nez. The woman's every gesture had just the exaggeration that you could expect from any member of the cast on the night of the performance.

I realized who she was when she started giving some directions to Hugh, who was now posturing in the center of the stage. No, she wasn't directing him, after all, she was applauding something he had already done or said. Hugh, like his fellow actors, was reading his lines from the book. Every time he opened his mouth or so much as turned his dark head or struck a new position, she either nodded approval or shook with laughter. She hardly took her eyes off him. Hugh no doubt had a comic role, but I knew that nothing in that play was so funny or so interesting as Miss Arrowood's conduct would have led me to believe. I can't say exactly how long I stood watching, lost in my own damned thoughts. When finally I did leave it was because someone in the cast—not Hugh—saw me and called Miss Arrowood's attention to my presence. At once she began motioning to me to go away, waving her book in the air and shooing me with her other hand. She didn't know who I was and didn't care. Miss Arrowood knew only that she wasn't going to have any interruption of the pleasure she took from watching Hugh.

There was no more to it than that. Miss Arrowood was just another old-maid schoolteacher with a crush on one of her pupils. I doubt very much that Hugh's experience with her had any influence on his finally going into the theater the way he has. Quite naturally she must nowadays imagine herself to have been his first great influence and inspiration, but if Miss Arrowood has ever gotten to New York and found her way over to the East Side, to that little cubbyhole of a theater where my son Hugh Robert directs plays, I'll bet she doesn't understand the kind of plays he puts on any better than I do. At any rate, she didn't succeed in turning him into any radio announcer or even into an actor, thank God. I doubt that she hoped to, even; for in my opinion Hugh Robert didn't have any better voice than any of the rest of the family. Physically he is very much like the rest of us. But it is my opinion also that the lady tried to play upon Hugh's vanity for that year, for the sake of keeping him near her. And it must certainly have been she who arranged for a certain phonograph record, which he made on a machine at school, to be put on the local radio. This happened one miserable Sunday afternoon in May. It capped everything else that had happened.

Hugh rose early that Sunday morning in order to plug in the charger to the batteries of the radio. Our set was an old battery-type table model, one that I had paid a lot of money for when it was new. Hugh was fond of giving it a big thump and saying in his best smart-aleck voice, "They don't make 'em like that any-more." But he would have been the first to admit—especially on the Sunday I'm speaking of—that there are times when the electricity goes off just as you want to hear some program. I hung on to my battery set all through the Depression, just the way I did my Pierce-Arrow. And it is true, of course, that we did sometimes find, when a favorite program was due to come on, that we had forgotten to charge the batteries.

But the batteries didn't need charging at all that Sunday in May, and Hugh knew they didn't. He simply wasn't taking any chances. When I came down to breakfast, I saw the ugly little violet light burning in the charger at the end of the living room. I observed Hugh coming in there to check on them off and on all morning. Apparently when the idea of charging the batteries first struck him, he had jumped out of bed and thrown on some clothes without bothering to comb his hair or put on his shoes. He came down wearing his old run-over bedroom slippers, his everyday corduroy pants, and a wrinkled shirt that he must have pulled out of the clothes hamper. He wandered around the house like that all morning. When his mother was leaving for church at ten-thirty, I asked her if she didn't think she ought to remind him to get properly dressed before the other children came for dinner. But either she forgot to, or she decided against it, or she just "hated to" and didn't.

During the two hours his mother was gone, I could hear Hugh moving about all over the house. First he would be in the basement, then at the closet in the back hall, then upstairs somewhere, even on the third floor. Every so often he would come back to the living room to have a look at the batteries. He would sit down and try to get interested in some section of the Sunday paper. But he couldn't stay still except for short intervals. Every time he got up, the first thing he did was to go and look out one of the living-room windows. I suspect that during his wandering through the house he must now and then have stopped and looked out windows in most of the other rooms, too. To him, that day, the weather outside was the most important matter in the world.

And in spite of its being May, the weather outside was quite wintry and nasty. Rain fell during most of the morning, and there was occasional thunder, with streaks of lightning away off across town. We had been having a series of electrical storms, which generally come to us a month earlier than they did that year. This bad weather was what Hugh had pinned his hopes on. The understanding was that if the ball game—the third of the season—was called that Sunday, then Station WCM was going to fill in the first ten minutes or so of the time with a recorded reading Hugh had made of "A Message to Garcia." Though I had been unaware of it before, it seems that the station made a practice of devoting such free periods to activities of the public schools. Hugh managed that Sunday to make us all keenly aware of the fact.

I seldom missed listening to the Chatham Barons' home games. When it was a good season, I even used to go out to Runnymede Park and watch the games. The Barons, however, hadn't had such a season in almost a decade. The last time they had won their league's pennant was in 1925. But, even so, I have never been one to go running off to Cincinnati or St. Louis to see big-league games when we have a team right in Chatham to support and root for. It happened that this year the Barons had won their first two games, and I was hopeful. In particular, I hoped to be listening to the broadcast of a third game in what might turn into a winning streak. I knew why Hugh kept looking out the windows, and soon I was looking out windows, too. The rain came down pretty steady all morning and only began to let up about noon. I found I was pitting my hopes against his. I was, at least, until I saw how awfully worked up the boy was. Then I tried my best to hope with him. But I don't think I ever before had such mixed feelings about so small a thing as whether or not a ball game would be rained out.

Hugh's mother returned from church at twelve-thirty. The other children came for dinner just before one. Hugh was off upstairs when the others arrived, and had to be called to come to the table. I supposed that he had finally gone up to get himself dressed, but he came down in the same state of undress, with his hair still uncombed, and I saw at once that it offended his brothers and his sister. I saw Sister trying to signal her mother, indicating that Hugh ought at least to go and comb his hair. But her mother's eye was not to be caught that day.

Hugh was unusually silent during the meal, and his silence was contagious. From time to time I saw every member of the family taking a glance out the window to see how the weather was. After raining all morning, the skies seemed to be clearing. It was mostly bright while we sat there, with only an occasional dark interval. During those dark intervals, Hugh ate feverishly;

otherwise he only picked at his food. I'm afraid that with the rest of us the reverse was true.

Once, while Lucy May was passing around a dish, I even saw her turn her black face toward a sunlit window at Hugh's back. Just as she did so, there came from outside the clear chirping of a redbird, which brought a beautiful smile to her face. The others were making a show of keeping up the conversation while a servant was in the room, and so when she offered Hugh the dish she was able to mumble to him without their taking notice, "You hear that redbird, don't you, Hugh! He say, 'To wet! To wet!' That's a promise of rain, honey!" Hugh may or may not have heard the redbird. But he paid no more attention to Lucy May's encouraging words than he had to the encouragement and applause of Miss Arrowood.

The very instant we rose from the table, there was a flash of lightning so close to us that it brightened the windows. And there followed a deafening crack of thunder. Hugh galloped across the hall into the living room and commenced disconnecting the batteries from the charger and hooking them up to the radio. The rest of us followed, just as if there were no other room in the house we could have gone to. By the time I got in there, Hugh was tuning in on WCM. There was a roar of static, and then, as the static receded, the announcer's voice came through saying, "The next voice you hear will be that of Hugh Robert Perkins," and went on to tell who Hugh's parents were, to give his street address, and to say that he was a senior at West High and a member of Miss Arrowood's class in oral readings. Outside, a sheet of rain was falling, and there was more thunder and lightning than there had been all morning.

Through the loudspeaker the voice of Hugh Robert Perkins began with some introductory remarks, telling us how, why, when, and by whom "A Message to Garcia" had been written. It didn't sound especially like Hugh's voice, but even at the outset the static was so bad that I missed about every third word. After the first half minute of the "Message" itself, it seemed hopeless to try to listen. Yet we had to sit there, all of us—and without any assistance from Miss Arrowood or Lucy May—and suffer through the awful business with Hugh. At least, it seemed to us we had to, and we *thought* that's what we were doing.

Hugh never once looked around from the radio. His eyes were glued to the loudspeaker, which was placed on top of the set. He had pulled up a straight chair, and he sat with his legs crossed and his hands clasped over one knee. He held his neck as straight and stiff as a board and didn't move his head to left or right during the entire ten minutes. The storm and static got worse every second, and he didn't even try to improve the reception. He didn't touch the dials. Toward the very end, I saw his mother raise her eyebrows and tighten her mouth the way she does when she's about to cry, and I shook my head vigorously at her, forbidding it. I knew what she was feeling well enough; we were all feeling it: Poor boy had endured his uncertainty, had for days been pinning his hopes on the chance of rain, and now had to hear himself drowned out by the static on our old radio. I thought it might be more than flesh and blood could bear. I thought that at any moment he might spring up and begin kicking that radio set to bits. But I knew, too, that his mother's tears wouldn't help matters.

What a fortunate thing for us all that I stopped her. Because not ten seconds after I did, the reading was finished and Hugh was on his feet and facing us with a broad grin of satisfaction. I saw at once that for him there had been no static. Or, rather, that he had heard the clear, sweet, reassuring tones of his own voice calling to him through and above the static, and that his last doubts about the kind of glory he yearned for had been swept away. He ran his hand through his tangled hair self-consciously. His blue eyes shone. "There!" he said. And after a moment he said it again, "There!" And I felt as strongly then as I feel it now that that was the real moment of Hugh's departure from our midst. He tried to fix his gaze on me for a second, but it was quite beyond his powers to concentrate on any one of us present. "It's a shame . . ." he began rather vaguely, "it's a shame you had to listen to my sorry voice instead of hearing the game. But maybe the game will come on later. . . . Did you hear the place where my voice cracked? That was the worst part of all, wasn't it? I'm glad it's over with." He gave a deep sigh, and then he said, in a voice full of wonder and excitement and confidence, "Gosh!"

At once, he went upstairs and dressed himself in his Sunday clothes and left the house, saying that he had a date, or maybe it was that he was going to meet some of his cronies somewhere. I didn't bother to listen. I knew that he would be back for supper that night and that he wasn't really going to leave us for some time yet. And I knew it wouldn't be a matter of a letter on the breakfast table when he did go, because it couldn't any longer be a matter of a boy running away from home. While the other children were laughing over what had happened and were talking about what a child Hugh still was, I was thinking to myself that Hugh Robert Perkins hadn't many more of his "mistakes" ahead of him. I felt certain that this afternoon he had seen his way ahead clear, and I imagined that I could see it with him.

The other children left the house soon after lunch that Sunday. Mary went upstairs to take a nap, as she often did when we had been through something that there was no use talking about. I wandered through the downstairs rooms, feeling not myself at all. Once, I looked out a window in the library and saw that the weather had cleared, and I didn't go and turn on the radio. And I had a strange experience that afternoon. I was fifty, but suddenly I felt very young again. As I wandered through the house I kept thinking of how everything must look to Hugh, of what his life was going to be like, and of just what he would be like when he got to be my age. It all seemed very clear to me, and I understood how right it was for him. And because it seemed so clear I realized the time had come when I could forgive my son the difference there had always been between our two natures. I was fifty, but I had just discovered what it means to see the world through another man's eyes. It is a discovery you are lucky to make at any age, and one that is no less marvelous whether you make it at fifty or fifteen. Because it is only then that the world, as you have seen it through your own eyes, will begin to tell you things about yourself.

Je Suis Perdu

THE SOUND of their laughter came to him along the narrow passage that split the apartment in two. It was the laughter of his wife and his little daughter, and he could tell they were laughing at something the baby had done or had tried to say. Shutting off the water in the washbasin, he cracked the door and listened. There was simply no mistaking a certain note in the little girl's giggles. Her naturally deep little voice could never be brought to such a high pitch except by her baby brother's "being funny." And on such a day as this, the day for packing the last suitcases and for setting the furnished apartment in order, the day before the day when they would really pull up stakes in Paris and take the boat train for Cherbourg— on such a day, only the baby could evoke from its mother that resonant, relaxed, almost abandoned kind of laughter . . . *They* were in the dining room just sitting down to breakfast. *He* had eaten when he got up with the baby an hour before, and was now in the *salle de bain* preparing to shave.

The *salle de bain*, which was at one end of the long central passage, was the only room in the apartment that always went by its French name. For good reason, too: it lacked the one all-important convenience that an American expects of what he will willingly call a bathroom. It possessed a bathtub and a washbasin, and it had a bidet, which was wonderful for washing the baby in. But the missing convenience was in a closet close by the entrance to the apartment, at the very opposite end of the passage from the *salle de bain*. Altogether it was a devilish arrangement. But the separation of conveniences was not itself so devilish as the particular location of each. For instance just now, with only a towel wrapped around his middle and with his face already lathered, he hesitated to throw open the door and take part in a long-distance conversation with the rest of the family, because at any moment he expected to hear the maid's key rattling in the old-fashioned lock of the entry door down the passage. Instead, he had to remain inside the *salle de bain* with his hand on the doorknob and his gaze on the blank washbasin mirror (still misted over from the hot bath he had

471

just got out of); had to stand there and be content merely with hearing the sound of merriment in yonder, not able—no matter how hard he strained—to determine the precise cause of it.

At last, he could resist no longer. He pushed the door half open and called out to them, "What is it? What's the baby up to?"

His daughter's voice piped from the dining room, "Come see, Daddy! Come see him!" And in the next instant she had bounced out of the dining room into the passage, and she continued bouncing up and down there as if she were on a pogo stick. She was a tall little girl for her seven years, and she looked positively lanky in her straight white nightgown and with her yellow hair not yet combed this morning but drawn roughly into a ponytail high on the back of her head.

And then his wife's voice: "It's incredible, honey! You really must come! And quick, before he stops! He's a perfect little monkey!"

But already it was too late. The maid's key rattled noisily in the lock. As he quickly stepped backward into the *salle de bain* and pulled the door to, he called to them in a stage whisper, "Bring me my bathrobe."

Through the door he heard his wife's answer: "You know your bathrobe's packed. You said you wouldn't need it again. Put on your clothes."

His trousers and his shirt and underwear hung on one door hook, beside his pajamas on another. His first impulse was to slip into his clothes and go and see what it was the baby was doing. But on second thought there seemed too many arguments against this. His face was already lathered. He much, much preferred shaving as he now was, wearing only his towel. But still more compelling was the argument that it was to be a very special shave this morning. *This morning the mustache was going to go!*

Months back he had made a secret pact with himself to the effect that if the work he came over here to do was really finished when the year was up, then the mustache he had begun growing the day he arrived would *go* the day he left. From the beginning his wife had pretended to loathe it, though he knew she rather favored the idea as long as they were here, and only dreaded, as he did, the prospect of his going home with that brush on his upper lip. But he had not even mentioned the possibility of shaving the mustache. And as he wiped the mist from the mirror and then slipped a fresh blade into his razor, he smiled in anticipation of the carrying on there would be over its removal.

In the passage now there was the clacking sound of the maid's footsteps. He could hear her taking all her usual steps— putting away the milk and bread that she had picked up on her way to work, crossing to the cloak closet, and placing her worn suede jacket and her silk scarf on a hanger—just as though this were not her last day on the job; or rather, last day with *them* in the apartment, because she was coming the following day, faithful and obliging soul, to wax the floors and hang the clean curtains she herself had washed. Their blessed, hardworking Marie. According to his wife, their having had Marie constituted their greatest luck and their greatest luxury this year. He scarcely ever saw her himself, and sometimes he had passed her down on the boulevard without recognizing her until, belatedly, he realized that it had been her scarf and her jacket, and his baby in the carriage she pushed. But he had gradually assumed his wife's view that their getting hold of Marie had been the real pinnacle of all their good luck about living arrangements. Their apartment was a fourth-floor walkup, overlooking the Boulevard Saint-Michel and just two doors from the rue des Écoles; with its genuine *chauffage central* and its Swedish kitchen, and even a study for him. It was everything they could have wished for. At first they had thought they ought not to afford such an apartment as this one, but because of the children they decided it was worth the price to them. And after his work on the book got off to a good start and he saw that the first draft would almost certainly get finished this year, they decided that it would be a shame not to make the most of the year; that is, not to have some degree of freedom from housekeeping and looking after the children. And so they spoke to the concierge, who recommended Marie to them, saying that she was a mature woman who knew what it was to work but who might have to be forgiven a good deal of ignorance since she had not lived always in Paris. They had found nothing to forgive in Marie. Even her haggard appearance his wife had come to speak of as her "ascetic look." Even her reluctance to try to understand a single word of English represented, as did the noisy rattling of the door key, her extreme consideration for their privacy. Every morning at half-past eight, her key rattled in the lock to their door. She was with them all day, sometimes taking the children to the park, always going out to do more marketing, never off her feet, never idle a moment until she had prepared their evening meal and left them, to ride the Métro across Paris again—almost to Saint-Denis—and prepare another evening meal for her own husband and son.

Yet this maid of theirs was, in his mind, only a symbol of how they had been served this year. It was hard to think of anything that had not worked out in their favor. They had ended by even liking their landlady, who, although she lived but a block away up the Boulevard Saint-Michel, had been no bother to them whatever, and had just yesterday actually returned the full amount of their deposit on the furniture. Their luck had, of course, been phenomenal. After one week in the Hôtel des Saints-Pères, someone there had told them about M. Pavlushkoff, "the honest real-estate agent." They had put their problem in the hands of this splendid White Russian— this amiable, honest, intelligent, efficient man, with his office (to signalize his greatest virtue, his sensibility) in the beautiful Place des Vosges. Once M. Pavlushkoff had found them their apartment they never saw him again, but periodically he would telephone them to inquire if all went well and if he could assist them in any way. And once in a desperate hour—near midnight—they telephoned him, to ask for the name of a doctor. In less than half an hour M. Pavlushkoff had sent dear old Dr. Marceau to them.

And Dr. Marceau himself had been another of their angels. The concierge had fetched round another doctor for them the previous afternoon, and he had made the little girl's ailment out to be something very grave and mysterious. He had prescribed some kind of febrifuge and the burning of eucalyptus leaves in her room. But Dr. Marceau immediately diagnosed measles (which they had believed it to be all along, with half her class at L'École Père Castor already out of school with it). Next day, Dr. Marceau had returned to give the baby an injection that made the little fellow's case a light one; and later on he saw them through the children's siege of chicken pox.

Both the children were completely charmed by the old doctor. Even on that first visit, when the little girl had not yet taken possession of the French language, she found the doctor irresistible. He had bent over her and listened to her heart not through a stethoscope but with only a piece of Kleenex spread out between her bare chest and his big pink ear. As he listened, sticking the top of his bald head directly in her face, he quite unintentionally tickled her nose with the pretty ruffle of white hair that ringed his pate. Instantly the little girl's eyes met her mother's. From her sickbed she burst into giggles and came near to causing her mother to do the same. After that, whenever the doctor came to see her, or to see her little brother, she would insist upon his listening to her heart. It would be hard to say whether Dr. Marceau was ever aware of why the little girl giggled, but he always said in French that she had the heart of a lioness, and he always stopped and kissed her on the forehead when he was leaving.

That's what the whole year had been like. There was *that*, and there had been the project—the work on his book, which was about certain Confederate statesmen and agents who, with their families, were in Paris at the end of the Civil War, and who had to decide whether to go home and live under the new regime or remain permanently in Europe.

As far as his research was concerned, he had soon found that there was nothing to be got hold of at the Bibliothèque Nationale or anywhere else in Paris that was not available at home. And yet how stimulating to his imagination it was just to walk along the rue de l'Université in the late afternoon, or along the rue de Varenne, or over on the other side of the Seine along the rue de Rivoli and the rue Saint-Antoine, hunting out the old addresses of the people he was writing about. And of course how stimulating to his work it was just being in Paris, no matter what his subject. Certain of his cronies back home at the university had accused him of selecting his subject merely as an excuse to come to Paris . . . He couldn't be sure himself what part that had played in it. But it didn't matter. *He had had the idea, and he had done the work.*

With his face smoothly shaven, and dressed in his clean clothes, he was in such gay spirits that he was tempted to go into the dining room and announce that he was dedicating this book to M. Pavlushkoff, to Dr. Marceau, to Marie, to all his French collaborators.

He found the family in the dining room, still lingering over breakfast, the little girl still in her nightgown, his wife in her nylon housecoat. At sight of his naked upper lip his wife's face lit up. Without rising from her chair, she threw out her arms, saying, "*I* must have the first kiss! How beautiful you are!"

The little girl burst into laughter again. "Mama!" she exclaimed. "Don't *say* that! *Men* aren't beautiful, *are* they, Daddy?" She still had not noticed that the mustache was gone.

It was only a token kiss he got from his wife. She was afraid that Marie might come in at any moment to take their breakfast dishes. Keeping her eyes on the door to the passage, she began pushing him away almost before their lips met. And so he turned to his daughter, trying to give her a kiss. Still she hadn't grasped what had brought on her parents' foolishness, and she wriggled away from him and out of her chair, laughing and fairly shrieking out, "What's the matter with him, Mama?"

"Just look!" whispered his wife; and at first he thought of course she meant look at him. "Look at the baby, for heaven's sake," she said.

The baby was in his playpen in the corner of the dining room. With his hands clasped on the top of his head and his fat little legs stuck out before him, he was using his heels to turn himself round and round, pivoting on his bottom.

"How remarkable!" the baby's daddy now heard himself saying.

"Watch his eyes," said the mother. "Watch how he rolls them."

"Why, he *is* rolling them! How really remarkable!" He glanced joyfully at his wife.

"That's only the half of it," she said. "In a minute he'll begin going around the other way and rolling his eyes in the other direction."

"It's amazing," he said, speaking very earnestly and staring at the baby. "He already has better coordination than I've *ever* had or ever *hope* to have. I've noticed it in other things he's done recently. What a lucky break!"

And presently the baby, having made three complete turns to the right, did begin revolving the other way round and rolling his eyes in the other direction. The two parents and the little girl were laughing together now and exchanging intermittent glances in order to share the moment fully. The most comical aspect of it was the serious expression on the baby's face, particularly at the moment when, facing them and stopping quite still, he shifted the direction of his eye rolling. At this moment the little girl's voice moved up at least one octave. She never showed any natural jealousy of her baby brother, but at such times as this she often seemed to be determined to outdo her parents in their amusement and in their admiration of the baby. Just now she was so convulsed with laughter that she staggered back to her chair and threw herself into it and leaned against the table. As she did so, one of her flailing hands struck her milk glass, which was still half full. The milk poured out over the placemat and then traced little white rivulets over the dark surface of the table.

Both parents pounced upon the child at once: "Honey! Honey! Watch out! Watch what you're doing!"

The little girl crimsoned. Her lips trembled as she said under her breath, *"Je regrette."*

"If you had drunk your milk this wouldn't have happened," said the mother, dabbing at the milk with a paper napkin.

"Regardless of that," said the father with unusual severity in his voice, "she has no business throwing herself about so and going into such paroxysms over nothing." But he knew, really, that it was not the threshing about that irritated him so much as it was the lapse into French. And it was almost as though his wife understood this and wished to point it out. For, discovering that a few drops of milk had trickled down one table leg and onto the carpet, she turned and herself called out in French to the maid to come and bring a cloth. His own mastery of French speech, he reflected, was the thing that *hadn't* gone well this year. After all, as he was in the habit of telling himself, *he* hadn't had the opportunity to converse with Marie a large part of each day, or to attend a primary school where the teacher and the other pupils spoke no English, and he hadn't—with his responsibilities to his work and his family—been able to hang about the cafés like some student. It was a consoling thought. Righteously, he put aside his irritation.

But now his little daughter, sitting erect in her chair, repeated aloud: *"Je regrette. Je regrette."* This time it affected him differently. It was impossible to tell whether she was using the French phrase deliberately or whether she wasn't even aware of doing so. But whether deliberate or not, it had its effect on her father. For a time it caused him to stare at his daughter with the same kind of interest that he had watched his son with a few moments before. And all the while his mind was busily tying the present incident to one that had occurred several weeks before. He had taken the little girl to see an old Charlie Chaplin film one afternoon at a little movie theater around the corner from them on the rue des Écoles. They had stayed on after the feature to see the newsreel, and then after the newsreel, along with a fairly large proportion of the audience, they had risen in the dark to make their way out. The ushers at the rear of the theater were not able to restrain the crowd that was waiting for seats; and so there was the inevitable melee in the aisles. When finally he came out into the lighted lobby he assumed that his little girl was still sticking close behind him, and he began getting into his mackinaw without even looking back to see that she was there. Yes, it was thoughtless of him, all right; but it was what he had done. As he tugged at the belt of the bulky mackinaw, he became aware of a small voice crying out above the noise of the canned music back in the theater. What interested him first was merely the fact that he did understand the cry: *"Je suis perdue! Je suis perdue!"* Actually he didn't recognize it as his daughter's voice until rather casually and quite by chance he glanced behind him and saw that she was not there. He threw himself against the crowd that was still emerging from the exit, all the while mumbling apologies to them in his Tennessee French which he was sure they would not understand (though himself understanding perfectly their oaths and expletives) and still hearing from the darkness ahead her repeated cry: *"Je suis perdue!"* When he found her she was standing against the side wall of the theater, perfectly rigid. Reaching down in the darkness to take her hand he found her hand made into a tight little fist. By the time he got her out into the light of the lobby her hand in his felt quite relaxed.

Along the way she had begun to cry a little, but already she was smiling at him through her tears. "I thought I was lost, Daddy," she said to him. He had been so relieved at finding her and at seeing her smiling so soon that he had not even tried to explain how it had happened, much less describe the chilling sensations that had been his at that moment when he realized it was the voice of his own child calling out to him, in French, that she was lost.

Now, in the dining room of their apartment, he was looking into the same flushed little face and suddenly he saw that the eyelashes were wet with tears. He was overcome with shame.

His wife must have discovered the tears at the same moment. He glanced at her and saw that she, too, was now filled with pity for the child and was probably thinking, as he was, that they were all of them keyed up this morning of their last day before starting home.

"Oh, it's all right, sweetie," said his wife, putting her hand on the top of the blond little head and pointing out the milk to Marie. "Accidents will happen."

Squatting down beside his daughter, he said, "Don't you notice anything different?" And he stuck his forefinger across his upper lip.

"Oh, Mama, it's gone!" she squealed. Placing her two little hands on his shoulders, she bent forward and kissed him on the mouth. "Mama, you're right," she exclaimed. "He *is* beautiful!"

After that, the spilled milk and the baby's gyrations were events of ancient history—dismissed and utterly forgotten.

A few minutes later, the little girl and Marie were beside the playpen chattering to the baby in French. His wife had wandered off into the bedroom, where she would dress and then throw herself into a final fury of packing. She had already asked him to make himself scarce this day, to keep out of the way of women's work. *His* duties, she had said, would begin when it came time to leave for the boat train tomorrow morning. Now he followed her into the bedroom to put on a tie and a jacket before setting out on his day's expedition.

She had taken off her housecoat and was standing in her slip before the big armoire, searching there among the few dresses that hadn't already been packed for something she might wear today. He stopped in front of the mirror above the chest of drawers and began slipping a tie into his collar. He was thinking of just how he would spend his last day. Not, certainly, with any of his acquaintances. He had said goodbye to everyone he wanted to say goodbye to. No, he would enjoy the luxury of being by himself, of buying a paper and reading it over coffee somewhere, of wandering perhaps one more time through the Luxembourg Gardens—the wonderful luxury of walking in Paris on a June day without purpose or direction.

When he had finished with his tie, he discovered that his wife was now watching his face in the mirror. She was smiling, and as their eyes met she said, "I'm glad you shaved it but I shall miss it a little, along with everything else." And before she began pulling her dress over her head she blew him a kiss.

IL PENSEROSO

The feeling came over him in the Luxembourg Gardens at the very moment he was passing the Medici Grotto at the end of its little lagoon. He simply could not imagine what it was that had been able to depress his spirits so devastatingly on a day that had begun so well. Looking back at the grotto, he wanted to think that his depression had been induced by the ugliness and the triteness of the sculpture about the fountain there, but he knew that the fountain had nothing to do with it. He was so eager to dispel this sudden gloom and return to his earlier mood, however, that he turned to walk back to the spot and see what else might have struck his eye. Above all, it was important for it to be something outside himself that had crushed his fine spirits this way, and that was thus threatening to spoil his day.

He didn't actually return to the spot, but he did linger a moment by the corner of the palace, beside a flower bed where two workmen—surreptitiously, it seemed to him—were sinking little clay pots of already blooming geranium plants into the black soil, trying to make it look as though the plants honestly grew and bloomed there. From here he eyed other strollers along the path and beside the lagoon, hoping to discover in one of them something tragic or pathetic which he might hold responsible for the change he had felt come over him. He would have much preferred finding an object, something

not human, to pin it on, but, that failing, he was now willing to settle for any unhappy or unpleasant-looking person—a
stranger, of course, someone who had no claim of any kind on
him. But every child and its nurse, each shabby student with
satchel and notebooks, every old gentleman or old lady waiting for his terrier or her poodle to perform in the center of the
footpath appeared relatively happy (in their limited French way,
of course, he found himself thinking)—as happy, almost, as
he must have appeared not five minutes earlier. He even tried
looking farther back on the path toward the gate into the rue
de Vaugirard, but it availed him nothing. Then his thoughts
took him beyond the gate, and he remembered the miserable twenty minutes he had just been forced to spend trying
to read his paper and enjoy his coffee in the Café Tournon,
while a bearded fellow American explained to him what was
wrong with their country and why Americans were "universally unpopular" abroad.

But even this wouldn't do. For he was as used to the ubiqui-
tous bearded American and his café explanations of everything
as he was to the ugly Italian grotto; and he disliked them to
just the same degree and found them equally incapable of disturbing him in this way. He gave up the search now, and as
he strode out into the brightness of the big sunken garden he
quietly conceded the truth of the matter: the feeling was not
evoked by his surroundings at all but had sprung from something inside himself. Further, it was not worth all this searching; it wasn't important; it would pass soon. Why, as soon as it
had run its course with him he would not even remember the
feeling again until . . . until it would come upon him again in
the same unreasonable way, perhaps in six months, or in a few
days, or in a year. When the mood was not on him, he could
never believe in it. For instance, while he had been shaving this
morning he truly did not know or, rather, he *knew not* that
he was ever in his life subject to such fits of melancholy and
gloom . . . But still the mood *was* on him now. And actually
he understood the source well enough.

It sprang from the same thing his earlier cheerful mood had
come from—his own consciousness of how well everything
had gone for him this year, and last year, and always, really. It
was precisely this, he told himself, that depressed him. At the

present moment he could almost wish that he hadn't finished the work on his book. He was able to wish this (or almost wish it) because he knew it was so typical of him to have accomplished just precisely what he had come to accomplish—and so American of him. Generally speaking, he didn't dislike being himself or being American, but to recognize that he was so definitely the man he was, so definitely the combination he was, and that certain experiences and accomplishments were now typical of him was to recognize how he was getting along in the world and how the time was moving by. He was only thirty-eight. But the bad thought was that he was no longer *going to be* this or that. He *was*. It was a matter of *be*ing. And to *be* meant, or seemed to mean at such a moment, to *be over with*. Yet this, too, was a tiresome, recurrent thought of his—very literary, he considered it, and a platitude.

He went on with his walk. The Jardin du Luxembourg was perfection this morning, with its own special kind of sky and air and its wall of flat-topped chestnuts with their own delicate shade of green foliage, and he tried to feel guilty about his wife's being stuck back there in the apartment, packing their possessions, trying to fit everything that had not gone into the foot lockers and the duffel-bags into six small pieces of luggage. But the guiltiness he tried for wouldn't materialize. Instead, he had a nasty little feeling of envy at her packing. And so he had to return to his efforts at delighting in the singular charm of the park on a day like this. "There is nothing else like it in Paris," he said, moving his lips, "which is to say there is nothing else like it in the world." And this pleased him just as long as it took for his lips to form the words.

It wasn't yet midmorning, but the little boys—both the ragged and the absurdly over-dressed-up ones—had already formed their circle about the boat basin in the center, and, balancing themselves on the masonry there, were sending their sailboats out over the bright water. This was almost a cheering sight to him. But not quite. For it was, after all, a regular seasonal feature of the place, like the puppet shows and the potted palm trees, and it was hardly less artificial in its effect.

He was rounding the lower garden of the park now; had passed the steps that led up toward the Boulevard Saint-Michel entrance and toward that overpowering monster the Panthéon.

(There were monsters and monstrous things everywhere he turned now.) He was walking just below the clumsy balustrade of the upper garden; and now, across the boat basin, across the potted flower beds and the potted palms, above the heads of the fun-loving, freedom-loving, stiff-necked, and pallid-faced Parisians, he saw the façade of the old palace itself. It also loomed large and menacing. There was no look of fun or freedom about it. It did not smile down upon the garden. Rather, out of that pile of ponderous, dirty stone, all speckled with pigeon droppings, twenty eyes glared at him over the iron fencing, which seemed surely to have been put there to protect the people from the monster—not the monster from the people. It was those vast, terrible, blank windows, like the whitened eyes of a blind horse, that made the building hideous. How could anyone ever have found it a thing of beauty? How could . . . Then suddenly: "Oh, do stop it!" he said to himself. But he couldn't stop it. Wasn't it from one of those awful windows that the great David, as a prisoner of the Revolution, had painted his only landscape? That unpleasant man David, that future emperor of art, that personification of the final dead end to a long-dying tradition! "Oh, do stop it!" he said again to himself. "Can't you stop it?"

But still he couldn't. The palace *was* a tomb. The park was a formal cemetery. He was where everything was finished and over with. Too much had already happened here, and whatever else might come would be only anticlimactic. And nothing could be so anticlimactic as an American living on the left bank of the Seine and taking a morning walk in the Jardin du Luxembourg. He remembered two novels whose first chapters took for their setting this very spot. Nothing was so deadening to a place as literature! And wasn't it true, after all, that their year in that fourth-floor walkup had been a dismal, lonely one? Regardless of his having got his work done, of his having had his afternoons free to wander not only through the streets where his heroes had once lived but also through the Louvre and the Musée Cluny and through the old crumbling *hôtels* of the Marais? Regardless of the friends they had made and even of the occasional gay evening on the town. Wasn't it really so that he had just not been willing to admit this truth until this moment? Wasn't it so, really, that he had come to Paris too late?

That this was a city for the very young and the very rich, and
that he, being neither, might as well not have come? What was
he but a poor plodding fellow approaching middle age, doing
all right, getting along with his work well enough, providing
for his family; and the years were moving by . . .

Suddenly he turned his back on the boat basin and the palace,
and started at a brisk pace up the ramp that leads toward the
great gilded south gate. And immediately he saw his daughter
in the crowd! She was moving toward him, walking under the
trees.

He saw her before she saw him. This gave him time to gather
his wits, and to recall that his wife, as soon as she got *him* out
of the apartment, was determined to get *them* out, too, so
that there would be no one to interfere with her packing. And
now, during the moment that *she* did not see him, he managed
to find something that he could be cross with her about. She
was ambling along, absent-mindedly leaning on the baby's carriage—that *awful* habit of hers—and making it all but impossible for Marie to push the carriage. She had come out from
under the trees now, and as she skipped and danced along, her
two bouncing blond ponytails, which Marie had fixed, one
directly above each ear, were literally dazzling in the sunlight.
"Daddy," she said, as she came within his shadow on the gravel
path. Her eyes were just exactly the color of the park's own blue
heaven. His wife's mother had said it didn't seem quite normal
for a girl to have such "positive blue" eyes. And her long little
face with the chin just a tiny bit crooked, like his own!

He took her hand, and they went down the ramp toward the
row of chairs on their left. "If we sit down, you'll have to pay,"
she warned him.

"That's all right," he said.

"I'll sit on your lap if you'll give me the ten francs for the
extra chair."

"And if I won't?"

"Oh, I'll sit on your lap anyway, since you've shaved that
mustache."

The old woman who collected for chairs was hot on their
heels. He paid for the single chair and tipped her the price of
another.

"I saw how much you gave her," his daughter said reproach-fully. "But it's all right. She's one of the nice ones."

"Oh, they're all nice when you get to know them," he said, laughing.

She nodded. "And isn't it a lovely park, Daddy? I think it is."

"It's too bad we're going home so soon, isn't it?" he said.

"Daddy, we just *got* here!" she protested.

"I mean going back to America, silly," he said.

"I thought you meant to the apartment . . . But we're *not* going back to America *today*."

"No, but tomorrow."

"Well, what difference does *that* make?"

He saw Marie approaching with the carriage. "Let's give our chair to Marie, since I have to be on my way," he said.

"Then you have to leave now?" she asked forlornly.

He gave her a big squeeze with his arms and held her a moment longer on his knee. He was wondering where his dark mood had gone. It was not just gone. He felt it had never been. And why had he lied to himself about this year? It *had* been a fine year. But still he kept thinking also of how she had interrupted his mood. And as soon as she was off his knee, he began to feel resentful again of the interruption and of the mysterious power she had over him. He found that he wanted the mood of despondency to return, and he knew it wouldn't for a long while. It was something she had taken from him, something she had taken from him before and would take from him again and again—she and the little fellow in the carriage there, and their mother, too, even before they were born. They would never allow him to have it for days and days at a time, as he once did. He felt he had been cheated. But this was not a mood, it was only a thought. He felt a great loss—except he didn't really feel it, he only thought of it. And he felt, he *knew* that he had after all gotten to Paris too late . . . after he had already established steady habits of work . . . after he had acknowledged claims that others had on him . . . after there were ideas and truths and work and people that he loved better even than himself.

A Friend and Protector

FAMILY FRIENDS would always say how devoted Jesse Munroe was to my uncle. And Jesse himself would tell me sometimes what he would do to anybody who harmed a hair on "that white gentleman's head." The poor fellow was much too humorless and lived much too much in the past—or in some other kind of removal from the present—to reflect that Uncle Andrew no longer had a hair on his head to be harmed. While he was telling me the things he would do, I'd often burst out laughing at the very thought of my uncle's baldness. Or that was what I told myself I was laughing about. At any rate, my outbursts didn't bother Jesse. He always went right ahead with his description of the violence he would do Uncle Andrew's assailant. And I, watching his obscene gestures and reminding myself of all the scrapes he had been in and of the serious trouble my uncle had got him out of twenty years back, I could almost believe he would do the things he said. More than one time, in fact, his delineations became so real and convincing it took my best fit of laughter to conceal the shudders he sent through me.

He was a naturally fierce-looking little man with purplish black skin and thick wiry hair, which he wore not clipped short like most Negro men's hair but long and bushed up on his head. It was intended to give him height, I used to suppose. But it contributed instead to a general sinister effect, just as his long, narrow sideburns did; and my Uncle Andrew would always insist that it was this effect Jesse strived for. He wasn't, actually, such a little man. He was of medium height. It was because he was so stoop-shouldered and was so often seen beside my Uncle Andrew that we, my aunt and I, thought of him as little. He *was* extremely stoop-shouldered, though, and his neck was so short that the lobes of his overlarge ears seemed to reach almost to the collar of his white linen jacket. Probably it was this peculiarity along with his bushy hair and his perpetually bloodshot eyes that made me say at first he was naturally fierce-looking.

He wasn't *naturally* fierce-looking. My Uncle Andrew was right about that. It was something he had achieved. And according to my uncle, the scrapes he was always getting into didn't really amount to much. My Aunt Margaret, however—my "blood aunt," married to Uncle Andrew—used to shake her head bitterly and say that Negroes could get away with anything with Uncle Andrew and that his ideas of "much" were very different from hers. "Jesse Munroe can disappear into the bowels of Beale Street," she would say in Jesse's presence, "knowing that when he comes out all he did there will be a closed chapter for 'Mr. Andrew.'" Jesse would be clearing the table or laying a fire in the living room, and while such talk went on he would keep his eyes lowered except to steal a glance now and then at my aunt.

I was a boy of fifteen when I used to observe this. I was staying there in Memphis with my uncle and aunt just after Mother died. The things Aunt Margaret said in Jesse's presence made me feel very uncomfortable. And it seemed unlike her. I used to wish Jesse would look at Uncle Andrew instead of at her and spare himself the sight of the expression on her face at those moments.

But it was foolish of me to waste sympathy on Jesse Munroe, and even at the time I knew it was. For one thing, despite all the evenings we spent talking back in the pantry during the two years I lived there, he never seemed to be really aware of me as a person. Each time we talked it was almost as though it was the first time. There was no getting to know him. Two years later when I had finished high school and was not getting along with my uncle and aunt as well as at first, I didn't live at their house anymore. But I would sometimes see Jesse at my uncle's Front Street office where I then had a job and where Jesse soon came to work as my uncle's special flunky. Uncle Andrew was a cotton broker, and it wasn't unusual for such a successful cotton man as he was to keep a factotum like Jesse around the office. I would see Jesse there, and he wouldn't even bother to speak to me. I am certain that if nowadays he is in a condition to remember anyone he doesn't remember me. I appeared on the scene too late. By the time I came along Jesse's escapades and my uncle's and aunt's reactions to them had become a regular pattern. It was too well established, over too many years, for my presence or my sympathy one way or the other to make any difference. It was the central and perhaps the only reality in Jesse's life. It had been so since before I was born and it would continue to be so, for a while at least, after I left the house.

My uncle and aunt had brought Jesse with them to Memphis when Uncle Andrew moved his office there from out at Braxton, which is the country town our family comes from. He was the only local Negro they brought with them, and since this was right after Jesse had received a suspended sentence for an alleged part in the murder of Aunt Margaret's washwoman's husband, it was assumed in Braxton that there had been some sensible understanding arrived at between Andrew Nelson and the presiding judge. Jesse was to have a suspended sentence; Uncle Andrew was to get him out of Braxton and keep him out. . . . Be that as it may, Jesse came away with them to Memphis and during the first year he hardly set foot outside their house and yard.

He was altogether too faithful and too hardworking to be tolerated by any of the trifling servants Aunt Margaret was able to hire in Memphis. For a while she couldn't keep a cook on the place. Then one finally came along who discovered how to get Jesse's goat, and this one stayed the normal time for a Memphis cook—that is, four or five years. She was Jesse's ruin, I suppose. She discovered the secret of how to get his goat, and passed it on to the maid and the furnace boy and the part-time chauffeur that Uncle Andrew kept. And they passed it on to those who came after them. They teased him unmercifully, made life a misery for him. What they said to him was that he was a country boy in the city, scared to go out on the street. Now, there is a story, seemingly known to all Negro citizens of Memphis, of a Mississippi country boy who robs his old grandmother and comes to town prepared to enjoy life. He takes a hotel room and sits in the window looking down at the crowds. But he can't bring himself to go down and "mix with 'em." The story has several versions, but usually it ends with the boy's starving to death in his room because he is scared to go down and take his chances on Beale Street. And this was how they pictured Jesse. They went so far, even, as to ridicule him that way in front of my aunt and uncle.

As a matter of fact, Jesse couldn't have been much more than a boy in those days. And his nature may really have been a timid one. Whatever other reasons there were for his behavior, probably it was due partly to his being a timid country boy. There was always something of the puritan in him, too. I could see this when I was only fifteen. I never once heard him use any profanity, or any rough language at all except when he was indicating what he would do to my uncle's imaginary attacker—and then it was more a matter of gestures than of words. When the cook my aunt had during the time I was there would sometimes make insinuating remarks about the dates I began having and about the hours I kept toward the end of my stay, Jesse would say, "You oughtn't talk that way before this white boy." If I sometimes seemed to enjoy the cook's teasing and even egged her on a little, he would get up and leave the room. Perhaps the most old-fashioned and country thing about him was that he still wore his long underwear the year round. On Mondays, when he generally had a terrible hangover and was tapering off from the weekend, he would work all day in the garden. I would see him out there even on the hottest July day working with his shirt off but still wearing his long-sleeved undershirt. The other servants took his long underwear as another mark of his primness, and whenever they talked about the light he kept burning in his room all night they would say he never put it out except once a week when he took his bath and changed his long johns.

Yet no matter how much fun they made of him to his face, when Jesse wasn't present the other servants admitted they would hate to run into him while he was off on one of his sprees, and they assured me that *they* didn't hang around the kind of places that he did. And laugh at him though they did, they respected him for the amount of work he could turn out and for the quality of it. He was a perfectionist in his work both in the house and in the yard, and especially in my uncle's vegetable garden.

The cook who found out how to get Jesse's goat shouldn't be blamed too much. She couldn't have known the harm she was doing. And surely Jesse couldn't have gone on forever never leaving the house. The time had to come. And once that teasing had started, Jesse had to *show* them. He didn't tell anyone when he first began going out. The other servants didn't live on the place regularly, and my uncle only discovered Jesse's absence by chance late one night when he wanted him for some trifle. He went out in the backyard and called up to his room above the garage. The light was on, but there was no answer. Uncle climbed the rickety outside stairs that went up to the room and banged the door to wake him. Then he came down the stairs again and went in the house and conferred with Aunt Margaret. They were worried about Jesse, thinking something might have happened to him, and so Uncle Andrew went up and forced the lock on the door to Jesse's room.

The light was burning—a little twenty-watt bulb on a cord hanging in the middle of the room—and the room was as neat as a pin. But there was no Jesse. My aunt, who can always remember every detail of a moment like that, said that from the backdoor she could hear Uncle Andrew's footstep out there in the room above the garage. For a time that was all she heard. But then finally she heard Uncle Andrew break out into a kind of laughter that was characteristic of him. It expressed all the good nature in his being and at the same time a certain hateful spirit, too. From her description I am sure it was just like his laughter when he caught you napping at Russian bank or checkers or when he saw he had you beaten and began slapping down his cards or pushing his kings around.

Presently he came out on the stoop at the head of the stairs and, still chuckling in his throat, called down to Aunt Margaret, "Our chick has left the nest." Then, closing the door, he took out his pocketknife and managed to screw the lock in place again. When he joined Aunt Margaret at the kitchen door he told her not to say anything about the incident to Jesse, that it was none of their business if he wanted a night out now and again.

Aunt Margaret could never get Jesse to tell her when he was planning an evening out, and later when he began taking an occasional Sunday off he never gave advance warning of that either. Sunday morning would come and he would simply not be on the place. It was still the same when I came there to live. After a Sunday's absence without leave, Jesse would be working my uncle's garden all day Monday. It was a big country vegetable garden right on Belvedere Street in Memphis. I have seen my aunt stand for a long period of time at one of the upstairs windows watching Jesse at work down there on a

Monday morning, herself not moving a muscle until he looked up at her. Then she would shake her head sadly—exaggerating the shake so that he couldn't miss it—and turn her back to the window. When my uncle came home in the evening on one of those Mondays he would go straight to the garden and exclaim over the wonderful weeding and chopping the garden had had. Later, in the house, he would say it was worth having Jesse take French leave now and then in order to get that good day's work in the garden from him.

His real escapades and the scrapes he got into were in a different category from his occasional weekends. In the first place, they lasted longer. When he had already been missing for three or four days or even a week there would be a telephone call late at night or early some morning. Usually it would be an anonymous call, sometimes a man's voice, sometimes a woman's. If a name were given it was one that meant nothing to Uncle Andrew, and when Jesse had been rescued he invariably maintained he had never heard the name of the caller before. He would say he just wished he knew who it was, and always protested that he hadn't wanted Uncle Andrew to be bothered. The telephone call usually went about like this: "You Mr. Andrew Nelson at Number 212 Belvedere Street?"

"Yes."

"Yo friend Jesse's in jail and he needs yo help."

Then the informer would hang up or, if questioned in time by Uncle Andrew, would give a name like "Henry White" or "Mary Jones" along with some made-up street number and a street nobody ever heard of. One time the voice said only, "Yo friend Jesse's been pisened. He's in room Number 9 at the New Charleston Hotel." Uncle Andrew had gone down to the New Charleston with a policeman, and they found Jesse seriously ill and out of his head—probably from getting hold of bad whiskey. They took him to the John Gaston Hospital where he had to stay for nearly a week.

Usually, though, it wasn't just a matter of his being on a drunk. According to my aunt, he got into dreadful fights in which he slashed other Negroes with a knife and got cut up himself, though I never saw any of his scars. Probably they were all hidden beneath his long underwear. And besides, by the time I came along they would have been old scars since by then his scrapes had, for a long time, been of a different kind. There had been a number of years when his troubles were all with women. There were women who fought over him, women who fought *him*, women who got him put in jail for bothering them, and women who got him put in jail for not helping support their children. Then, after this phase, he was involved off and on for several years in the numbers racket and the kind of gang warfare that goes along with that. Uncle Andrew would have to get the police and go down and rescue him from some room above a pool hall where the rival gang had him cornered.

My account of all this came of course from my aunt since my uncle never revealed the nature of Jesse's troubles to anyone but Aunt Margaret. She dragged it out of him because she felt she had a right to know. She may have exaggerated it all to me. But I used to think two of the points she made about it were good ones. She pointed out that the nature of his escapades grew successively worse, so that it was harder each time for Uncle Andrew to intervene. And she suspected that that gave Jesse considerable satisfaction. She also said that from the beginning all of Jesse's degrading adventures had had one thing in common: He never was able or willing to get out of any jam on his own. He would let any situation run on until there was no way he could be saved except through Uncle Andrew's intervention. "All he seems to want," she said, "is to have something worse than the time before for his 'Mr. Andrew' to save him from and dismiss as a mere nothing."

I felt at the time that this was very true, and it tended to make me agree with Uncle Andrew that Jesse Munroe's scrapes were not very important in themselves, and, in that sense, didn't "amount to much." In fact, my aunt's observation seemed so obviously true that it was hard to think of Jesse as anything but a spoiled child, which, I suppose, is the way Uncle Andrew did think of him.

The murder that Jesse had gotten mixed up in back in Braxton was as nasty a business as you hear about. Uncle Andrew would not have had a white man living about his garage who had had any connection with such a business. When *I* finally gave up my room at his house and went to live at the "Y," it was more because of *his* disapproval of my friends (and of the hours I kept) than it was because of my aunt's. And though I couldn't have said so to a living soul that I knew when I was a boy, I used to wish my uncle could have been half as tolerant of my own father, who was a weak man and got into various kinds of trouble, as he was of Jesse. My father was killed in an automobile crash when I was only a little fellow, but, for several years before, Uncle Andrew had refused to have anything to do with him personally, though he would always help him get jobs as long as they were away from Braxton and, always, on the condition that my mother and I would continue to live in Braxton with my grandparents. I was taught to believe that Uncle Andrew was right about all of this, and I still believe that he was in a way. Jesse hadn't, after all, had the advantages that my father had, and he may have been a victim of circumstances. But my father was a victim of circumstances, too, I think—as who isn't, for that matter? Even Uncle Andrew and Aunt Margaret were, in a way.

In that murder of Aunt Margaret's washwoman's husband I believe Jesse was accused of being an accessory after the fact. I don't think anyone accused him of having anything to do with the actual killing. The washwoman and a boyfriend of hers named Cleveland Blakemore had done in her husband without help from anyone. They did it in a woods lot behind a roadhouse on the outskirts of town, where the husband found them together. At the trial I think the usual blunt instrument was produced as the murder weapon. Then they had transported the body to the washwoman's house where they dismembered it and attempted to burn the parts in the chimney. But it was a rainy night and the flue wouldn't draw. They ended by pulling out the charred remains and burying them in a cotton patch behind the washwoman's house, not in one grave but in a number of graves scattered about the cotton patch. (You may wonder why I bring in these awful details of the murder, and I wonder myself. I tell them out of some kind of compulsion and because I have known them ever since I was a small child in Braxton. I couldn't have told the story without somehow bringing them in. I find I have only been waiting for the right moment. And it seems to me now that I would never have had the interest I did in Jesse except that he was someone connected with those gory details of a crime I had heard about when I was very young and which had stuck in my mind during all the years when I was growing up in the house with my pretty, gentle mother and my aged grandparents.) At any rate, it was on a rainy winter morning just a few weeks after the murder that a Negro girl, hurrying to work, took a shortcut through that cotton patch. In her haste she stumbled and fell into a hole where the pigs had rooted up what was left of the victim's left forearm and hand.

In the trial it was proved that Jesse had provided the transportation for the corpse from the woods lot to the washwoman's house. His defense contended that he just happened to be at the roadhouse that night, driving a funeral car which he had borrowed, without permission, from the undertaker's parlor where he worked as janitor, and sometimes as driver. (You can hear the voice of the prosecution: "It was the saddest funeral that car ever went to.") He was paid in advance for the trip, and it was represented to him (according to his defense) that the washwoman's husband was only dead drunk.

It was never proved conclusively that Jesse had any part in the dismemberment or in the efforts at burning. Witnesses who testified they had seen *two* men coming and going from the house to the cotton patch (in the heavy rain on that autumn night) were not reliable ones. Yet the testimony that Jesse's borrowed car was parked in front of the house during most of the night was given by Negro men and women of the highest character. Even Jesse's defense never denied his presence in there. But to me it seems quite as likely that, as his defense maintained, he was kept there at knife's point, or at least by the fear that if he attempted to go he might meet the same fate that the washwoman's husband had, as that he willingly took part in what went on. My uncle of course felt that there was no question about it, that Jesse was an innocent country boy drawn into the business by the washwoman and her friend, Cleveland Blakemore (who no doubt guessed he had taken the undertaker's car without permission), and that he wasn't to be blamed. Uncle Andrew even served as a character witness for Jesse at the trial, because he had known him before the murder when Jesse was janitor at his office as well as at the undertaker's.

I never heard any talk about the murder from Uncle Andrew and Aunt Margaret themselves. In private Aunt Margaret would tell me about some of the other troubles Jesse had been in and about how narrowly he had escaped long jail sentences. Only Uncle Andrew's ever widening connections among influential people in Memphis had been able to prevent those sentences. She said that my uncle was such a modest man that he naturally minimized Jesse's scrapes so as not to put too much importance on the things he was able to do to get him out of them.

But my uncle knew his wife well enough to know what she would have told me. Without ever giving me his version of any of the incidents he would say to me now and then that Aunt Margaret was much too severe and that she set too high standards for Jesse. And I did find it painful to hear the way she spoke to Jesse and to see the way she looked at him even after one of his milder weekends. In those days, so soon after my mother died, Aunt Margaret was always so kind and so considerate of my feelings and of my every want that it seemed out of character for her to be harsh and severe with anyone. Before that day I packed my things and moved out of her house, however, I came to doubt that it was so entirely out of character. If I had stayed there a day longer, I might have had even greater doubts. I think it is fortunate I left when I did. Our quarrel didn't amount to a lot. It was about my staying out all night one time without ever being willing to explain where I was. As soon as I was a little older and began to settle down to work and behave myself we made it up. Nowadays I'm on the best of terms with her and Uncle Andrew. And whenever I'm over at their place for a meal things seem very much the way they used to. Even the talk about Jesse goes very much the way it did when he was on the scene and in easy earshot.

When they talked about him together in the old days, especially when there was company around, it was all about his loyalty and devotion to Uncle Andrew. I agreed with every word they said on the subject, and if someone had said to me then that it was Aunt Margaret whom Jesse was most dependent upon and whose attention he most needed I would have said that person was crazy. How could anyone have supposed such a thing? And if I should advance such a theory nowadays to my uncle and aunt or to their friends they would imagine that I was expressing some long-buried resentment against Uncle Andrew. Any new analysis made in the light of what happened to Jesse after he went to work in my uncle's Front Street office would not interest them. They wouldn't be able to reverse a view based upon the impressions of all those years when Jesse was with them, a view based upon impressions received before any of them ever knew Jesse, impressions inherited from their own uncles and aunts and parents and grandparents.

I used to watch the expression on his black face when he was waiting on Uncle Andrew at table or was helping him into his overcoat when Uncle Andrew left for his office in the morning. His careful attention to my uncle's readiness for his next sleeve or for the next helping of greens made you feel he considered it a privilege to be doing all these little favors for a man who had done so many large ones for him. His attentions to my uncle impressed everyone who came to the house. If there was a party, he couldn't pass through the room, even with a tray loaded with glasses, without stopping before Uncle Andrew to nod and mutter respectfully, "Mr. Andrew." This itself was a memorable spectacle, and often was enough to stop the party talk of those who witnessed it: Uncle Andrew, so tall and erect, so bald and clean-shaven, so proudly beak-nosed, and yet with such a benign expression in those gray eyes that focused for one quick moment upon Jesse. And Jesse, stooped and purple-black and bushy-headed and red-eyed, clad in his white vestment and all but genuflecting while he held the tray of glasses perfectly steady for my uncle. It lasted only a second, and then Jesse's eyes would dart from one to another of the men standing nearest Uncle Andrew as though looking for some Cassius among them—some Judas. (And perhaps thinking all the time only that my aunt's eyes were upon him, denouncing him not merely as a sycophant and hypocrite but as a man who would have to answer for his manifold sins before the dread seat of judgment on the Last Day.) When he had moved on with his tray, some guest who had not been to the house before was apt to comment on what a wicked-looking fellow he was. My uncle would laugh heartily and say that nothing would please Jesse more than to think this was the impression he gave. "He gets himself up to look awful mean and he likes to think of himself as a devil. But actually he's as harmless as that boy standing there," Uncle Andrew would say, pointing of course to me.

I would laugh self-consciously, not really liking to have my own harmlessness pointed out. And I wonder if Jesse, already on the other side of the room, sometimes heard my laughter then and detected a certain hollowness in it that was also there when he told me the things he would do to my uncle's imaginary assailant. Because often, when I stood looking at the guest made uncomfortable by Jesse's glance, I could not help thinking of those things. In my mind's eye I would see his gestures, see him seizing his throat, rolling his eyes about, making as if to slice off his ears and nose, and indicating an even more debilitating operation. It may seem strange that I never imagined that those threats might be directed toward me personally, since I was my father's son and might easily have been supposed to bear a grudge against my uncle. But I felt that Jesse made it graphically clear that it was some Negro man like himself he had in mind as my uncle's assailant. When he was going through his routine he would usually be in the pantry and he would have placed himself in such relation to the mirror panel beside the swinging door there that, by rolling his eyes, he could be certain to see the black visage of this man he was mutilating.

It was another coincidence, like their moving to Memphis just when Jesse had to be gotten out of Braxton, that my aunt and uncle decided to give up the house and move to an apartment at just the time when it was no longer feasible for them to have Jesse Munroe working at their house. Uncle Andrew was nearly seventy years old at the time. He was spending less time at his office, and he and Aunt Margaret wanted to be free to travel. During the two years I was with them, there were three occasions when Jesse was missing from the house for about a week and had to be rescued by my uncle. I didn't know then exactly what his current outside activities were. Even Aunt Margaret preferred not to discuss it with me. She would say only that in her estimation it was worse than anything before. Later I learned that he had become a kind of confidence man and that—as in the numbers racket—his chief troubles came from his competitors. He specialized, for a time, in preying upon green country boys who had come to Memphis with their little wads of money. After I had left the house he went to something still worse. He was delivering country girls whom he picked up on Beale Street into the hands of the Pontotoc Street madams.

It was the authorities from neighboring counties in West Tennessee and Mississippi who finally began to put pressure on the police. They threatened, so I have been told, to come in and take care of Jesse themselves. Uncle Andrew moved him to a little room on the top floor of the ramshackle old building that his cotton company was in. Jesse lived up there and acted as a kind of butler and bartender in my uncle's private office, which was a paneled, air-conditioned suite far in the rear of and very different-looking from the display rooms where the troughs of cotton samples were. The trouble was that his "Mr. Andrew" was not at the office very much anymore for Jesse to wait on. And so most of the time he stayed up in his little cubbyhole on the top floor, and of course he got to drinking up my uncle's whiskey. He never left the building, never came down below the third floor, which Uncle Andrew's offices were on, and he never talked to the other Negroes who worked there. I would pass him in the hallway sometimes and speak to him, but he wouldn't even look at me. At last, of course, he went crazy up there in my uncle's office. It may have been partly from drinking so much whiskey, but at least this time we knew it wasn't bad whiskey. . . . When the office force came and opened up that morning they found him locked up in Uncle Andrew's air-conditioned, sound-proofed suite and they could see through the glass doors the wreck he had made of everything in there. He had slashed the draperies and cut up the upholstery on the chairs. There were big spots and gashes on the walls where he had thrown things—mostly bottles of whiskey and gin, which of course had been broken and left lying all about the floor. He had pushed over the bar, the filing cabinets, the refrigerator, the electric watercooler, and even the air-conditioning unit. For a while nobody could tell where Jesse himself was. It wasn't till just before I got there that they spotted him crouched under Uncle Andrew's mahogany desk. From the beginning, though, they could hear him moaning and praying and calling out now and then for help. And even before I arrived someone had observed that it wasn't for Uncle Andrew but for Aunt Margaret he was calling.

I was parking my car down in the alley when one of the secretaries who had already been up there rushed up to me and told me what had happened. I hurried around to the street side of the building and went up the stairs so fast that I stumbled two or three times before I got to the third floor. They made a place for me at the glass door and told me that if I would stoop down I could see him back in the inner office crouched under the desk. I saw him there, and what I noticed first was that he didn't have on his white jacket or his shirt but was still wearing his long-sleeved winter underwear.

Fortunately, it happened that Uncle Andrew and Aunt Margaret were not on one of their trips at the time. Everyone at the office knew this, and they knew better than to call the police. They would have known better even if Uncle Andrew had not been in town. They waited for me to come in and telephone Uncle Andrew. I went up into the front display room and picked up the telephone. It was only eight-thirty, and I knew that Uncle Andrew would probably still be in bed. He sounded half asleep when he answered. I blurted out, "Uncle Andrew, Jesse's cracked up pretty bad down here at the office and has himself locked in your rooms."

"Yes," said Uncle Andrew, guardedly.

"He's made a mess of the place and is hiding under your desk. He has a knife, I suppose. And he keeps calling for Aunt Margaret. Do you think you'll come down, or—"

"Who is it speaking?" Uncle Andrew said, as though anyone else at the office ever called him "uncle." He did it out of habit. But it gave me an unpleasant feeling. I was tempted to give some name like "Henry White" and hang up, but I said nothing. I just waited. Uncle Andrew was silent for a moment. Then I heard him clear his throat, and he said, "Do you think he'll be all right till I can get down there?"

"I think so," I said. "I don't know."

"I'll get Fred Morley and be down there in fifteen minutes," he said.

I don't know why but I said again, "He keeps calling for Aunt Margaret."

"I heard you," Uncle Andrew said. Then he said, "We'll be down in fifteen minutes."

I didn't know whether his "we" meant himself and Fred Morley, who was the family doctor, or whether it included Aunt Margaret. I don't know yet which he meant. But when he and Dr. Morley arrived, my aunt was with them, and I don't think I was ever so glad to see anyone. I kissed her when she came in.

I came near to kissing Uncle Andrew too. I was touched by how old he had looked as he came up the stairs—he and Aunt Margaret, and Dr. Morley, too—how old and yet how much the same. And I was touched by the fact that it hadn't occurred to any of the three not to come. However right or wrong their feelings toward Jesse were they were the same as they would have been thirty years before. In a way this seemed pretty wonderful to me. It did at the moment. I thought of the phrase my aunt was so fond of using about people: "true blue."

The office force, and two of the partners by now, were still bunched around the glass door peering in at Jesse and trying to hear the things he was saying. I stood at the top of the stairs watching the three old people ascend the two straight flights of steps that I had come stumbling up half an hour earlier—two flights that came up from the ground floor without a turn or a landing between floors. I thought how absurd it was that in these Front Street buildings, where so much Memphis money was made, such a thing an elevator was unknown. Except for adding the little air-conditioned offices at the rear, nobody was allowed to do anything there that would change the old-fashioned, masculine character of the cotton man's world. This row of buildings, hardly two blocks long, with their plaster facade and unbroken line of windows looking out over the brown Mississippi River were a kind of last sanctuary—generally beyond the reach of the ladies and practically beyond the reach of the law.

When they got to the top of the stairs I kissed my aunt on her powdered cheek. She took my arm and stood a moment catching her breath before we moved out of the hallway. I thought to myself that she had put more powder on her face this morning than was usual for her. No doubt she had dressed in a great hurry, hardly looking in her glass. But I observed that underneath the powder her face was flushed from the climb, and her china blue eyes shone brightly. Instead of seeming older to me now, I felt she looked younger and prettier and more feminine than I had ever before seen her. It must have been just seeing her there in a Front Street office for the first time. . . . But I still remember the delicate pressure of her hand as she leaned on my arm.

Uncle Andrew went straight to the door of his office and shooed everyone else away. I don't know whether I saw him do this or not, but I know that's how it was. Presently I found myself in the middle display room standing beside Aunt Margaret while Dr. Morley made pleasantries to her about how the appearance of cotton offices never changed. He hadn't been inside one in more than a decade, and he wondered how long it had been for her. Uncle Andrew, meanwhile, in order to be sure that Jesse heard him through the glass door and above his moaning had to speak in a voice that resounded all over the third floor of the building. Yet he didn't seem to be shouting, and he managed to put into his voice all the reassurance and forgiveness that must have been there during their private interchanges in years past. It was like hearing a radio soap opera turned on unbearably loud in a drugstore or in some other public place. "Come open the door, Jesse. You know I'm your friend. Haven't I always done right by you? It doesn't matter about the mess you've made in there. I have insurance to cover everything, and I'm not going to let anybody harm you."

It didn't do any good, though. Even in the middle room we could hear Jesse calling out—more persistently now—for Aunt Margaret to help him. Yet Aunt Margaret still seemed to be listening to Dr. Morley. I couldn't understand it. I wanted to interrupt and ask her if she didn't hear Jesse? Why had she come if she wasn't even going in there and look at him through the glass door? Didn't she feel any compassion for the poor fellow? Surely she would suddenly turn her back on us and walk in there. That seemed how she would do it.

Then for a moment my attention was distracted from Aunt Margaret to myself—to how concerned I was about whether or not she would go to him, to how very much I cared about Jesse's suffering and his need to have my aunt come and look at him! I took my eyes off Aunt Margaret and was myself resolutely trying to observe what a Front Street cotton office was really like when I felt her hand on my arm again. Looking at her I saw that underneath the powder her color was still quite high. While Dr. Morley talked on she gazed at me with moist eyes which made her look still prettier than before. And now I perceived that she had been intending all the time to go to Jesse and give the poor brute whatever comfort she could. But I saw too that there were difficulties for her which I had not imagined. Suddenly she did as she *would* do. Without a word she turned her back on us and went back there and showed herself in the glass door.

That was all there was to it really. Or for Jesse it was. It seemed to be all the real help he needed or could accept. He didn't come out and open the door, but he was relatively quiet afterward, even after Aunt Margaret was finally led away by Uncle Andrew and Dr. Morley, and even after Dr. Morley's two men came and broke the glass in the door and went in for him. When Aunt Margaret had been led away it seemed to be my turn again, and so I went back there and stood watching him until the men came. Now and then he would start to crawl out from under the desk but each time would suddenly pull back and try to hide himself again, and then again the animal grunts and groans would begin. Obviously, he was still seeing the things he had thought were after him during the night. But though he made some feeble efforts at resistance, I think he had regained his senses sufficiently to be glad when Dr. Morley's men finally came in and took him.

That was the end of it for Jesse. And this is where I would like to leave off. It is the next part that it is hardest for me to tell. But the whole truth is that my aunt did more than just show herself to Jesse through the glass door. While she remained there her behavior was such that it made me understand for the first time that this was not merely the story of that purplish-black, kinky-headed Jesse's ruined life. It is the story of my aunt's pathetically unruined life, and my uncle's too, and even my own. I mean to say that at this moment I understood that Jesse's outside activities had been not only *his*, but *ours* too. My Uncle Andrew, with his double standard or triple standard—whichever it was—had most certainly forced Jesse's destruction upon him, and Aunt Margaret had made the complete destruction possible and desirable to him with her censorious words and looks. But they did it because they had to, because they were so dissatisfied with the pale *un*ruin of their own lives. They did it because something would not let them ruin their own lives as they wanted and felt a need to do—as I have often felt a need to do, myself. As who does not sometimes feel a need to do? Without knowing it, I think, Aunt Margaret wanted to see Jesse as he was that morning. And it occurs to me now that Dr. Morley understood this at the time.

The moment she left us to go to Jesse, the old doctor became silent. He and I stood on opposite sides of one of the troughs of cotton, each of us fumbling with samples we had picked up there. Dr. Morley carefully turned his back on the scene that was about to take place in the room beyond. I could not keep myself from watching it.

I think I had never seen my aunt hurry before. As soon as she had passed into the back display room she began running on tiptoe. Uncle Andrew heard her soft footfall. As he turned around, their eyes must have met. I saw Uncle's face and saw, or imagined I saw, the expression in his gray eyes—one of utter dismay. Yet I don't think this had anything to do with Aunt Margaret. It was Jesse who was on his mind. He could not believe that he had failed to bring Jesse to his senses. I suspect that when Aunt Margaret looked into his eyes she got the impression that her husband didn't at that moment know who in the world she was. Maybe at that moment *she* couldn't have said who *he* was. I imagine their eyes meeting like the eyes of strangers, perhaps two white people passing each other on some desolate back street in the toughest part of niggertown, each wondering what dire circumstances could have brought so nice-looking a person as the other to this unlikely neighborhood. . . . At last, when Aunt Margaret drew near the glass door, Uncle Andrew stepped aside and moved out of my view.

For a time she stood before the glass panel in silence. She was peering about the two rooms inside, looking for Jesse. At last, without ever seeing where he was, I suppose, she began speaking to him. Her words were not audible to me and almost certainly they weren't so to Jesse, who continued for some time to keep on with his moaning and praying, though seeing that she had come he didn't go on calling out for her. The voice she spoke to him in was utterly sweet and beautiful. I think she was quoting scripture to him part of the time—one of the Psalms,

I believe. Instinctively, I began moving toward the doorway that joined the room I was in and the room she was in. It was the voice of that same Aunt Margaret who had spoken to me with so much kindness and sympathy and love in the days just after my mother died. I was barely able to keep from bursting into tears—tears of joy and exaltation.

Jesse didn't, as I have already said, come out and open the door. But at some point, which I didn't mark, he became quieter. Now there were only intermittent sobs and groans. After a while my aunt stopped speaking. She was searching again for his hiding place in there. Presently, Uncle Andrew appeared again. He came over to her and indicated that if she would stoop down she could see Jesse under the desk. He watched her very intently as she squatted there awkwardly before the door.

If it had seemed strange for me to see her running, a few minutes earlier, it seemed almost unbelievable now that I was seeing her squatting there that way on the floor. I watched her and I thought how unlike her it was. I think I know the very moment when she saw her friend Jesse. I could tell her body had suddenly gone perfectly rigid. She looked not like any woman I had ever seen but like some hideously angular piece of modern sculpture. And then, throwing her hands up to her face, she lost her balance. My uncle was quick and caught her before she fell. He brought her to her feet at once and as he did so he called out for assistance—not from me but from Dr. Morley. Dr. Morley brushed past me in the doorway, answering the call.

Even after she was on her feet she couldn't take her hands down from her face for several moments. When finally she did manage to do so, all her high color and all the brightness in her eyes had vanished. As they led her away it was hard to think of her as the same woman who had rested her hand on my sleeve only a little while ago. Had she really wanted to see Jesse as he was this morning? I think she had. But I think the sight of the animal crouched underneath my uncle's desk—and probably peering out at her—had been more than she was actually prepared to look upon. As she was led off by her husband and her doctor, I felt certain that Aunt Margaret had suffered a shock from which she would never recover.

But how mistaken I was about her recovery soon became clear. I waited around until Dr. Morley's men arrived and I watched them go in and take Jesse. Then I wandered through the other display rooms up to the front office, where most of the real paperwork of the firm was done and where my own desk was. The front office was really a part of the front display room, divided from it only by a little railing with a swinging gate. I knew I would find my aunt up there and I supposed I would find her lying down on the old leather couch just inside the railing. I could even imagine how Dr. Morley and my uncle, and probably one of the office girls, would be hovering about and administering to her. Yet it was a different scene I came on. Dr. Morley was seated at my desk taking down information which he said would be necessary for him to have about Jesse. He was writing it on the back of an envelope. Aunt Margaret was seated in a chair drawn up beside him. She seemed completely herself again. Uncle, standing on the other side of the doctor, was trying to supply the required information. But Aunt Margaret kept correcting most of the facts that Uncle Andrew gave. While the doctor listened with perfect patience, the two of them disputed silly points like Jesse's probable age and the correct spelling of his surname, whether it was "Munroe" or "Monroe," and what his mother's maiden name had been. . . . It was hard to believe that either Aunt Margaret or Uncle Andrew had any idea of what was happening to Jesse at that very moment or any feeling about it.

Dr. Morley had Jesse committed to the state asylum out at Bolivar. They locked him up for a while, then they made a trusty of him. Dr. Morley says he seems very happy and that he has made himself so useful that they will almost certainly never let him go. I have never been out there to see him, of course, and neither has Aunt Margaret or Uncle Andrew. But I have dreams about Jesse sometimes—absurd, wild dreams that are not like anything that ever happened. One night recently when I was at a dinner party at my uncle and aunt's apartment and someone was recalling Jesse's devotion to my uncle, I undertook to tell one of those dreams of mine. But I broke it off in the middle and pretended that that was all, because I saw my aunt, at the far end of the table, was looking as pale as if she had seen a ghost or as if I had been telling a dream that *she* had had. As soon as I stopped, the talk resumed its usual theme, and my aunt seemed all right again. But when our eyes met a few minutes later she sent me the same quick, disapproving glance that my mother used to send me at my grandfather's table when I was relating some childish nightmare I had had. "Don't bore people with what you dream," my mother used to say after we had left the table and were alone. "If you have nothing better than that to contribute, leave the talking to someone else." Aunt Margaret's rude glance said precisely that to me. But I must add that when we were leaving the dining room my aunt rested her hand rather firmly and yet tenderly on my arm as if to console and comfort me. She was by nature such a kind and gentle person that she could not bear to think she had hurt someone she loved.

Guests

THE HOUSE was not itself. Relatives were visiting from the country. It was an old couple this time, an old couple who could not sleep after the sun was up and who began yawning as soon as dinner was over in the evening. They were silent at table, leaving the burden of conversation to their host and hostess, and they declined all outside invitations issued in their honor. Cousin Johnny was on a strict diet. Yet wanting to be no trouble, both he and Cousin Annie refused to reveal any principle of his diet. If he couldn't eat what was being served, he would do without. They made their own beds, washed out their own tubs, avoided using salad forks and butter knives. Upon arriving, they even produced their own old-fashioned ivory napkin rings, and when either of them chanced to spill something on the tablecloth, they begged the nearest Negro servant's pardon. As a result, everybody, including the servants, was very uncomfortable from the moment the old couple entered the house.

Edmund Harper, their host, was most uncomfortable of all. What's more, he had to conceal the fact from his wife, Henrietta, because otherwise he would be accused of "not seeing her through." Henrietta was a planner, an arranger, a straighten-outer—especially of other people's lives. Somehow she always managed to involve Edmund in her good works, and never more so than when it was a matter of relatives from the country. Cousin Johnny and Cousin Annie, for instance, had clearly not wanted to make this visit. In fact, they had struggled valiantly against Henrietta's siege. But they couldn't withstand Henrietta's battering for very long. Henrietta knew that neither of them had ever set foot in the capital city of Nashville; and she couldn't bear the thought of the poor old souls' not seeing Nashville before they died. It ended by Edmund's going with Henrietta in her car to bring the unwilling visitors bodily into Nashville.

Some weeks before the visit, Henrietta had written a letter suggesting that she might enter the old couple's house and do their packing for them—that is, if Cousin Annie didn't feel up to it. And this was what finally made Cousin Annie run up the white flag and pretend to accept Henrietta's terms. Come what might, the old lady's little clapboard Gothic citadel, with its bay windows and gingerbread porches, was *not* going to be entered. In its upright posture on the rockiest hill of Cousin Johnny's stock farm—a farm where the land was now mostly rented out and the stock disposed of, because of Cousin Johnny's advanced years—the house was like Cousin Annie's very soul, and it would be defended at all costs. The morning that Henrietta's new Chrysler car turned through the stone gateposts at the bottom of the hill, the old lady not only had herself and her husband thoroughly packed up, she had them fully dressed for their journey, their hats on their heads, and, with the door to the house already stoutly locked, they were seated side by side on the porch swing—rigid as two pieces of graveyard statuary. As the car pulled up the hill, turning cautiously between the scrub pines and the cedar trees, Edmund Harper saw Cousin Annie rise slowly, in one continuous, wraithlike movement, from her place in the swing. Once on her feet, she stood there still and erect as a sentinel. In the swing, which until now had remained motionless, Cousin Johnny permitted himself a quick, little solo flight, so short and tentative that he must barely have touched his toe to the porch floor. Edmund interpreted this motion as a favorable sign. But then, almost immediately, he saw the old lady's hand go out to one of the swing's chains. The mere touch of her gloved hand was enough to halt the swing, but for several moments she kept her hand there on the chain. And the figures of the two old people, thus arranged, made a kind of *tableau vivant*, which Edmund was to carry in his mind throughout the visit.

For twenty-five years, Edmund had been seeing Henrietta through such plans as the present one. Three country nieces had been presented to Nashville society from the Harper house. Countless nephews had stayed there while working their way through the university—or as far through it as it seemed practicable for them to try to go. And Henrietta scarcely ever returned from a visit back home without bringing news of some ailing connection who needed to see a Nashville specialist, needed a place to stay while seeing the specialist, needed a place to stay while convalescing from the inevitable operation. The worst of all this, for Edmund, was not what he was called upon to do during these visitations but what he was called upon to feel, and the moral support he was expected to give Henrietta. For something nearly always went wrong. Two of the three nieces had eloped with worthless louts from back home before their seasons in Nashville were half over. Most of the countless nephews had taken to a wild life, for which their parents tended to blame the influence of the Harper household more than that of university and fraternity life. Worse still, the convalescents always outstayed their welcome, and Edmund had to support Henrietta in taking a firm hand when it was time for each poor old creature to return to his or her nearest of kin in the country.

In a sense, though, these larger projects of Henrietta's had been less trying for Edmund than the smaller ones—the ones that she had gone in for in recent years. She had turned more and more to brightening the lives of people like Cousin Johnny and Cousin Annie, people whose lives didn't seem absolutely to require her touch. It was three and four day visits from the likes of Cousin Johnny and Cousin Annie that Edmund found it hardest to adjust to—visits from people not really too far removed from his own generation. He found a part of himself always reaching out and wanting to communicate with them and another part forever holding back, as though afraid of what *would* be communicated. And the same seemed to be true for the guests themselves, particularly for the men.

Cousin Johnny Kincaid was not, of course, a real contemporary of Edmund Harper's. There was a twelve-year difference in their ages. Edmund was fifty-eight, and Cousin Johnny was seventy. It was a delicate difference. A certain respect was due the older man, but it had to be manifested in a way that would not offend him and make him feel that he was an old man and that Edmund was not. On the second day of the visit, when the old couple's silence had already become pretty irksome to her, Henrietta telephoned Edmund at his office and said that she had a simple suggestion to make. At breakfast she had noticed that Cousin Johnny seemed to wince every time Edmund addressed him as "Cousin" Johnny. She thought he might be sensitive about his age. She suggested that that night Edmund should try calling him just plain Johnny.

Now, this was the kind of thing that was always coming up. It seemed that every year Henrietta had to dig deeper into the kin and deeper into the country to find suitable objects for her good works. The couples were invariably rather distant kin of his or hers, people Edmund had known all his life but not known very well. Either Edmund couldn't remember what he had called them as a boy or he had literally never called them anything. But the problem had never come into such focus as it did now. On the telephone he didn't dispute Henrietta's point, though it was inconceivable to him that Cousin Johnny had ever in his seventy years winced over a small matter of personal vanity—if that's what it was. Since, at the moment of the telephone call, Edmund's law partner was with him in his office and since the firm's most moneyed and currently most troubled client was also there, Edmund said only, "I'll see what I can do about it tonight." And he wrote the word "Johnny" on the pad of paper in front of him.

"I can tell from your voice that you're terribly busy," Henrietta said apologetically.

"No, not particularly," Edmund said.

"I probably shouldn't have called about something so—"

"Oh, nonsense!" Edmund laughed. And he wound up the conversation in hearty tones meant to convince everybody in earshot of his imperturbability.

But it *was* a serious matter, of course. And when he put down the telephone he still sat for a moment staring rather intently at the instrument. As a matter of fact, he was trying to think the problem through right then and there. It was his habit of mind, as a good trial lawyer, to think any question through and find a positive answer to it as soon as it came up. It wasn't the truth of Henrietta's observation he was debating; he had long since accepted her contention that she was "more sensitive to people" than he was, and so he had to assume that she was right about something like this. Nor was it a question of his willingness to do what she asked of him. It was a simple matter of whether or not he could bring himself to call Cousin Johnny Kincaid just plain "Johnny." Then in a flash he saw he could. He could because—but he didn't go into that at the time. The immediate question was answered, and he was free now to return to his client's urgent affairs.

It wasn't till several hours later that he let himself think again about this silly piece of business that Henrietta had cooked up. He was driving home from work in his hardtop convertible, and the moment he opened the subject with himself, his mind took him back to the previous day. They were making the return trip from the country, with Cousin Annie and Cousin Johnny in the car. It was a seventy-five-mile drive back into Nashville; they had to pass through sections of three counties. Since they were in Henrietta's car, she was doing the driving, and she was providing most of the conversation, too. Cousin Annie, wearing a plain black coat and an even plainer black hat, was in the front seat beside Henrietta. In the back seat of the big car the two long-legged men sat in opposite corners, each with one leg crossed stiffly over the other. They had traveled some twelve or fifteen miles when something made Edmund glance down at Cousin Johnny's foot. He found himself observing with great interest the high-topped shoe, the lisle sock held up by an elastic supporter, and, since it was still early April, the long underwear showing above the sock where the old man's trouser leg was pulled up.

Somehow to be thus reminded that there were still men who dressed in the old style was unaccountably pleasant to Edmund. At the same time it saddened him, too. For here was the kind of old man that he had once upon a time supposed he would himself someday become. And now he knew, of course, he never would. It seemed like being denied an experience without which life wouldn't be complete. It seemed almost the same as discovering that no matter how long he lived he would never *be* an old man. For how could you really *be* old and have it mean anything if you lived in a world where you weren't expected to dress and behave in a special way, in a world where you went on dressing and trying to behave like a young man or at least a middle-aged man till the very end? It was bad enough to be childless and therefore grandchildless, as he and Henrietta of course were, without also being denied any prospect of ever *feeling* or being *treated* like a grandfather, something which Cousin Johnny, also childless and grandchildless, must for a long time now have felt and been treated like. Edmund found the subject absorbing.

The foot gave an involuntary little kick, and Edmund realized that this was probably what had drawn his attention to it in the first place. The twitch was presently followed by another and then, at irregular intervals, by another and another. This was bound to interest a mind like Edmund's, especially in its present mood. With his lawyer's eye he soon made out that the kicks occurred always when the car was passing a field where cattle grazed. He wasn't surprised when Cousin Johnny finally came right out with it: "Seems like the livestock gets fatter every mile we pull in towards Nashville." But as soon as he had said this the old man's eyes narrowed and he bit his lower lip with such vehemence that it was plain he wished it was his tongue he was biting. His utterance had been as involuntary as any of those kicks his foot was giving.

It was as if Fate and Cousin Annie had been waiting together for such a slip from him. The car had just left a fine stretch of low ground where he had seen the herd that brought forth his comment. Now the car was climbing a long, wooded hill, and in a little clearing near the summit Cousin Annie spied a herd of bunched-up, scrawny, and altogether sorry-looking milk cows. For the only time during the long trip, she turned around and showed her face to the two men in the back seat. And it was only the profile of her face, at that. She merely turned and stared out the window, on Cousin Johnny's side, at those cows in the clearing.

"Yes, but—" Cousin Johnny began, exactly as though the old lady had spoken. And then, Cousin Annie having already turned her back to him again, he broke off. That was the whole of the interchange between them. When Cousin Johnny spoke again, which was surprisingly soon, Edmund felt his words had no reference to what had passed between him and Cousin Annie. He said directly to Edmund, "I guess a fellow who's been concerned with cattle as long as I have won't ever see much out a car window but cows, no matter where he goes."

It was some kind of an apology. An apology for what? For a certain boorishness he felt he had been guilty of? An apology for his own narrow interest in life. Or was it, rather, an indication of the old man's awareness of the figure he must be cutting with Edmund?

Edmund's reply to the outburst and the apology was a ten-minute discourse on the history of stock farming in Middle Tennessee. Most of what he said came out of some research he had had one of the young men in his office do for a case he had tried a few years back. He wasn't showing off. He was honestly trying to reassure Cousin Johnny and to draw him out, because already Edmund's interest in this man and his desire to win his confidence and to find a common ground on which they could meet was considerable. But the discourse on cattle farming did not produce a single remark from Cousin Johnny.

A long silence followed. Then there was a period of give-and-take between Henrietta and Cousin Annie about the illnesses and deaths of various relatives. After that, there was more silence. Cousin Johnny's lips seemed to have been permanently sealed. But in the last miles before Nashville, his caution must have been lulled by Henrietta's fresh chatter about the Nashville sights they would be seeing in the days just ahead. When a colossal city limits sign suddenly hove into view at the roadside, Cousin Johnny's mouth dropped open. "Why," he said. "It's a funny thing. When I was just married and was still just a young fellow, I almost came here to work." It was as if until then he hadn't known, or hadn't believed, where it was they were taking him. "In a shoe factory, it was. But my wife and I decided against it. I was to start at the bottom and maybe later go on the road for them."

How different the whole visit might have been if Cousin Johnny had not said that. Because, after that, Edmund Harper would have consented to almost any scheme of Henrietta's to promote understanding between him and his house guest. Why, what wonderful things mightn't they say to each other if only they could talk together man to man! In a flight of fancy that was utterly novel to him, Edmund visualized Cousin Johnny as he would have appeared today had he taken that job at the shoe factory. He saw him now as president of the shoe company after years of working up from the bottom, and saw himself as a country lawyer in Nashville on a visit with his rich relatives. Why, it was *Maud Muller* twice reversed! Moreover, that client Edmund was going to see in his office tomorrow morning and who had been in his office nearly every day for the past two weeks, that richest and currently most troubled of the firm's clients, was none other than the president of a shoe company, probably the very shoe company that Cousin Johnny would have gone to work for . . . *That* was precisely how Cousin Johnny might have turned out. And to think it was only a difference of seventy-five miles.

Cousin Johnny's response to being called just plain "Johnny" was, to say the least, disconcerting. He did exactly what Henrietta said he had done when Edmund called him "Cousin Johnny." He winced. He drew in his chin—almost imperceptibly, though not quite—batted his eyes, and gave his head a quick little shake. And then, as Edmund hurried on to finish the long sentence which he had dropped his "Johnny" in the midst of, Cousin Johnny gazed past Edmund into a fire the houseboy had just now lit in the fireplace. Plainly he was trying to decide how he liked the sound of it—the sound of his Christian name on the lips of this man, this strange kind of man who could come in from work at four-thirty in the afternoon, disappear above stairs to change from a dark double-breasted suit to a plaid jacket and gray trousers, and then reappear and settle down to a long evening, without ever mentioning the work that had kept him all day.

Edmund had carefully waited, before springing that "Johnny" on the old man, till a moment when Henrietta and Cousin Annie were well on the other side of the living room. Afterward, he realized that Henrietta had been conspiring with him without his knowing it. She had lured Cousin Annie over there beyond the piano to see a scrapbook that she kept in the piano bench for just such moments. During the hour since Edmund came in the house, she hadn't mentioned the subject of their telephone conversation. But she knew well enough that he was going to follow her suggestion. And he knew what her attitude would be by now; they were in this together, and she wanted to make his part as easy for him as possible—and as interesting. One quick glance told him that however much he had tried to slur his articulation of the name, Henrietta had heard it. As for Cousin Annie, whose back was toward him, he could not at the moment tell whether or not she heard.

Probably he could not have told if he had had a clear view of her face. And, for that matter, the incident was to pass without his knowing what conclusion Cousin Johnny had reached—whether he did or didn't like the sound of it.

They went into dinner at six o'clock. At first the table talk was livelier than it had been the previous night. Cousin Annie, right away, spoke a number of complete sentences which were not dragged out of her by direct questions. She spoke with enthusiasm of the sights they had taken in that day: the Parthenon, the capitol building, old Fort Nashboro. There was, in fact, every indication that matters had taken a real turn for the better. Edmund found himself wondering if Cousin Annie weren't going to turn out to be like all the other country ladies who had come here in recent years—vain, garrulous, and utterly susceptible to the luxuries of Henrietta's commodious, well-staffed, elegantly appointed house. The bright look on Henrietta's face at the opposite end of the table informed him that she was thinking the same thing. And then, as though conscious of just how far into the woods she had led them, Cousin Annie Kincaid began quietly closing in.

"You mustn't think," she said, "that Mr. Kincaid and I can't dine at whatever your accustomed dinner hour is." This was very much in her usual vein—making known her awareness that they were dining earlier than was normal for the Harpers. Since the houseboy was removing the soup bowls at the time, it might have been supposed that what she said was meant for his ears and that she had phrased it with that in mind. But the old lady wasn't long in finding another occasion to refer to Cousin Johnny as "Mr. Kincaid." She did it a third and fourth time, even. Each time it was as if she feared they hadn't understood her before. Finally, though, she made it absolutely clear. During the meat course, while everyone except Cousin Johnny was working away at the roast lamb and baked potatoes, she drove the point home to her own satisfaction. "It isn't that Mr. Kincaid doesn't like roast lamb," she said, addressing herself to Edmund and speaking in the most old-fashioned country-genteel voice that Edmund had heard since he was a boy at home. "It isn't that he doesn't like roast lamb," she repeated. "It's that he dined alone with ladies at noon and so had to eat the greater share of an uncommonly fine cut of sirloin steak.

He isn't, you understand, used to eating a great deal of meat." Now she turned to Henrietta. "He seldom eats any meat at all for supper . . ." Edmund, remembering the other country ladies who had sat where Cousin Annie now sat, supposed that she would continue endlessly on this fascinating subject. But once she saw that she had the attention of both host and hostess, she suddenly turned to Cousin Johnny and said genially, "You seldom eat any meat at all for supper, do you, Mr. Kincaid?" It was the voice of a woman from an earlier generation than the Harpers', addressing her husband with the respect due a husband. How could anyone call him just plain Johnny after that?

The meat course was finished in almost total silence, but Edmund had two things to think about. After putting her question to Cousin Johnny, Cousin Annie had turned a triumphant gaze on Henrietta, indicating that she recognized who her real adversary was. That was one thing. The other thing was Cousin Johnny's response to being addressed as Mr. Kincaid. There was but one way to describe it. He winced. And there was but one conclusion that Edmund could draw: the poor fellow had lived so long in isolation that he would always wince when singled out in company and addressed directly by any name whatever.

Cousin Annie and Cousin Johnny retired within less than thirty minutes after dinner. As soon as they were safely upstairs, Edmund expected Henrietta to launch into Cousin Annie's performance. She did nothing of the kind. While he was setting up the card table and fetching the cards for a game of double solitaire, she turned on the television set and stood switching aimlessly from one channel to another—a practice she often criticized him for. She seemed to be avoiding conversation. Once they were seated at the table with the cards laid out and the television playing a favorite Western, Edmund said cozily, "*They* disapprove of cards, and *they* detest TV." These were two points that Cousin Annie had made clear the first night.

"I think they're awfully sweet, all the same," Henrietta said gently, smiling a little, and keeping her eyes on her cards.

"Oh, I like them," Edmund said defensively. "Everything they do or say takes me back forty years."

"They have real character."

"Yes," Edmund agreed. "It was pretty marvelous the way she let me have it at the table. She fairly rubbed my nose in it."

Henrietta looked up at him for the first time. "You mean—?"

"I mean the name business, of course. What else?"

"I don't know about that. I suppose she always calls him Mr. Kincaid."

"Well, what else did you think I meant?"

"Didn't you understand what she was saying? Of course I may be wrong."

"What on earth?"

"I'm afraid she was offended because you left Cousin Johnny to have lunch 'alone'—with the ladies. What else could you make of her emphasis?"

"She meant I should have come home to lunch today?"

"I don't know, darling. Maybe not."

"But you think I might come home tomorrow? Or take you all out somewhere?"

She smiled at him appreciatively. "Or better still," she offered, "take Cousin Johnny to lunch with some men downtown. I wonder if he wouldn't like that?"

"But would Cousin Annie let him?"

Henrietta leaned across the table and spoke in a conspiratorial whisper. "We could see," she said.

Edmund was silent. "Well, we'll see about it," he said finally, not promising anything but knowing in his heart that everything was already promised.

At the breakfast table next morning, Edmund sat admiring the graceful curve of Henrietta's wrist as she poured coffee from the silver urn into his cup. He had asked for this third cup mostly for the sake of admiring again the way she lifted the heavy urn and then let the weight of it pull her wrist over in that pretty arc. And the ruffles on the collar of Henrietta's breakfast gown seemed particularly becoming to her, and Edmund admired the soft arrangement of her hair and the extraordinary freshness of her complexion. She really looked incredibly young. She was a beautiful woman in every sense, and nothing about her this morning was more beautiful than the way she had been so right about Cousin Annie. Cousin

Annie and Cousin Johnny had already finished their breakfast, and the old lady had gone back upstairs with her husband to prepare him for his morning at the office with Edmund and his noonday luncheon at the Hermitage Club. Edmund was now waiting for Cousin Johnny to come down in his "other suit" and "good tie."

He wouldn't have thought it possible for it to turn out this way. He was convinced all over again of how much more sensitive to people Henrietta was than he was. And he was so grateful to her. No sooner had he issued the invitation to Cousin Johnny than Cousin Annie became positively affable. And at once Cousin Johnny had begun nodding his head in agreement. Edmund noticed also that the old man began pulling rather strenuously at his lower lip, but all such lip pullings and winces and twitches Edmund was now willing to lump together as meaningless nervous habits. He wasn't at all sure he wouldn't end by having lunch alone with Cousin Johnny in a booth at Jackson's Stable, where they could talk without interruption.

And what a relief it was, anyway, that the thing was settled one way or the other. He had spent his last hour in bed this morning tossing about and wishing that he didn't have to raise the question and yet knowing that he wanted to. Long before the cook came in to fix breakfast, he had heard the old couple stirring in the guest room. It had been this way the day before, too. The monotonous buzz of the two old people's lowered voices seemed to penetrate the walls of the house in a way that no ordinary speech would have done. At that hour they seemed to feel that they must speak in the voice that one normally uses only when there is someone dead in the house or when something has gone awfully wrong. They were hard of hearing, of course, and believed they were whispering! Edmund had to smile at the thought of how carefully they concealed the fact of their deafness in company. At any rate, he woke to the drone of these old country people's voices. And with Cousin Johnny so much on his mind, he couldn't go back to sleep again. He knew that Henrietta was awake, too, and after a while he felt her hand on his shoulder, and he turned his head on the pillow and looked at her. "It's awful to have to lie here quietly like

this, knowing that they're hungry," she whispered. There was
very little light in the room but he could see that while she
spoke she lay perfectly relaxed, with her eyes closed. "I'd give
anything if there were some way they could go on and have
their breakfast," she continued, still in a whisper. "Yet to get
up and offer to fix it myself, or even to suggest they fix it for
themselves, would only make them more uncomfortable, considering how they are . . . What do you think?"

"I just don't know," Edmund said, trying to sound less
awake than he was.

Finally at seven o'clock they heard Cousin Johnny creep
down the steps to fetch the morning *Tennessean* and then creep
back up to the guest room again. (He wouldn't for the world
have made so free as to sit down in the living room to read
the morning paper—not without being expressly asked. It was
a wonder Cousin Annie would let him go down and get the
paper at all.) Edmund knew, from yesterday, that from this
point on the buzz of voices would be only intermittent until
the time should come for the first sounds of activity down in
the kitchen. Then the buzz would begin again and remain
constant until someone knocked on the guest-room door and
announced breakfast. And that was the way it happened. Everything went just the way he knew it would until they were all
four seated at the breakfast table and he had popped the question to Cousin Johnny. From then on everything was different.

Cousin Johnny had gone up to put on his other suit and
his good tie, and Cousin Annie had gone with him. Presently
Edmund, thinking he heard Cousin Johnny coming down the
stairs, rose from the table and went round and kissed Henrietta's cheek. He meant to join Cousin Johnny in the hall
and to take him directly to the car, which had already been
brought up to the side door. But when he went out into the
big front hall, it was Cousin Annie he saw. She had already
come three quarters of the way down the stairs, and when she
saw Edmund she stopped there, with her hand on the railing.
Even before she spoke, Edmund felt his heartbeat quicken. "It's
a pity you've had to wait around," she said. "He's so changeable." Edmund said nothing. Cousin Annie descended the rest
of the flight. At the foot of the stairs she said, "He had already

changed to his good clothes. But he doesn't, after all, want to miss the sights Henrietta and I will be seeing. He's getting back into his other things now."

Henrietta, hearing Cousin Annie's voice, had come to the dining-room door. "Cousin Johnny's all right, isn't he?" she asked.

"Of course he's all right," said the old lady with a shade of resentment in her voice. "It's that he doesn't want to miss that Presbyterian church or Bellemeade Plantation." Then she made her way into the dining room where she had left her coffee to cool.

Edmund went off in the other direction, making *his* way across the hall and into the dark corridor that led to the side entrance. He knew that Henrietta was following him, but he couldn't trust himself to discuss the situation. He hoped to reach the outside door before she caught up with him and merely to wave to her from the car. But he had forgotten his hat and coat. When he was at the entry door he heard a coat hanger drop on the floor of the cloak closet, which opened off the corridor, and he knew that Henrietta was fetching his things for him. He had to wait there and submit to her helping him on with his coat. Still he would have left without saying anything had she not at the last minute put her hand on his arm and said, "Darling, you mustn't mind."

"I think I really *hate* that woman," he said.

"Oh, Edmund," Henrietta whispered, "it may really have been Cousin Johnny's decision. And what difference does it make? Why else do we have them here except to let them do whatever they will enjoy most?"

"Yes, why do we?" he said angrily.

Henrietta removed her hand from his arm and stepped back, away from him. With her eyes lowered she said, "We've been over that." Then she looked up at him accusingly: he wasn't seeing her through.

They had been over it, certainly, some two or three years before this. And he had thought, as she had, that he would never ask this question again. As he raced along the corridor, he had known he would ask it if he let her overtake him. That's why he had made such a dash for the car. He might have reached

into the closet and grabbed his hat—to hell with the coat!—
but he hadn't had his wits about him. And for that you always
had to pay.

Finally, though, he kissed Henrietta goodbye again, and he
waved to her from the car.

All the way to town this morning, he went over and over the
foolish business. It had never been so complicated before. She
had always managed to involve him in her good works among
the relatives—having discovered his weakness there, she had
abandoned most of her other good works—but this time he
was involved in a way or in a sense that Henrietta didn't dream
of. Or maybe she did. He shouldn't underestimate her. Was it
really only a difference in degree this time? In some degree
he was always affected by these country visitors as though it
were something more than a visit from relatives. With them
he had often felt there ought to be more to say to each other
than there ever seemed to be. But never about anyone, before
Cousin Johnny, had he felt: Here is such a person as I might
have been, and I am such a one as he might have been.

Now he could not resist going back to what he considered
the real beginning. It was Henrietta who had urged him to
leave Ewingsburg, the county seat where they had grown up
and where he first practiced law. He hadn't wanted to leave
and had argued against it, and, despite the fine opportunities
offered him by firms in Nashville, she hadn't begun urging
him to go until they had been married for five years and had
learned pretty definitely that there would never be any children. When he used to come home for lunch in Ewingsburg
and would be lingering over his second cup of coffee, it got so
he would catch Henrietta sometimes stealing furtive glances at
him. She suspected him of being bored with his life. And yet
when he talked of buying up more farm land and joining Uncle
Alex and Uncle Nat in their lespedeza venture—aiming for the
seed market—Henrietta thought he would be frittering away
his life. He ought to be in a big place, she told him, where he
could have a real career and be fully occupied.

And so they had gone to Nashville. And Edmund *was* fully
occupied. And perhaps that was the trouble. Who could say
... Not that Henrietta wasn't occupied, too. She was an

enthusiastic joiner of clubs and circles and committees. Why
not? What better way of getting to know people? Edmund was
entirely sympathetic. But she was never satisfied until she had
tried to draw Edmund into each activity, and, since she always
failed, she was seldom satisfied with the activity afterward. In
the early days, she was always finding something new to interest her—and him. Edmund wondered if there would have been
a Nashville for the likes of Cousin Johnny and Cousin Annie
to see if Henrietta hadn't been so active in the work of preserving landmarks and setting up monuments. (Even his refusal to
help iron out the inevitable legal snarls of that work had never
completely destroyed her interest in it. Recently she had had
a hand in preserving the First Presbyterian Church from the
vandals who wanted to pull it down.) For a time she took a
great interest in the home for delinquent girls. Her reports of
the individual cases had interested him hugely, but not enough
to make him consent to join her as a board member. He came
very near to being drawn into her juvenile court work, but
somehow he even escaped involvement there.

Then, after a number of years, she began bringing in those
nieces for the debutante season. Two of the girls were from
his side of the family, one from hers. But that didn't matter.
They were all of them kinfolks from out home—the nieces,
the nephews, the invalids, and finally, after so many years, the
nearly contemporary old couples. They were his responsibility, his involvement as much as hers. There was no getting
around it—not in Edmund's mind. And so they came, and
they came, and they came. Finally, he began to wonder if he
and Henrietta weren't more alike than he had ever imagined.
It occurred to him that she was really fonder of these visitors
and of the people she went out to the country to "see about"
than she was of the friends she had gone to such lengths to
make in Nashville.

One day he spoke to her about it. And he suggested that
perhaps they should think of moving back to Ewingsburg when
the time came for him to retire from his practice. Henrietta had
laughed at the idea. Why, she asked him, should they plan to
bury themselves alive in their old age?

Well, then, he had another idea. (He was only trying to please
her, wasn't he?) Why didn't they invite one of her favorites from

among their not too affluent relatives, or maybe two of her favorites—"It's the kind of thing people used often to do," he said—to come and live with them on a permanent basis? Wouldn't that give her an even deeper satisfaction than doing only a little for this one and that one? (He didn't say: And then the house would always seem itself.) But in reply Henrietta expressed an astonishment just short of outrage. How could he imagine that this would be the case!

"But why not?" Edmund asked impatiently.

Henrietta shook her head bitterly. To think that he understood so little about what her life was like, she said. And then for the first time in years she mentioned her disappointment at not being able to have children. Edmund was confused. Could there possibly be any connection? Was she merely trying to play on his sympathy? He felt his cheeks growing warm, and could tell from the expression in her eyes that she saw his color rising. But looking deeper into her eyes he saw that she, too, was utterly confused. If there was any connection, then she was as confused about it as he was. She knew no better than he what it meant or why she had dragged it in. And he was sure that, whatever it was, they would never understand it now and that, having discovered it so late, they need not do so. Their course together was set, and he had no intention of trying to change it. But he felt a renewed interest in seeing to what strange places it might yet bring them.

Before he reached his office that second morning of the visit, he saw how salutary it had been for him to go over the whole story in his mind again. It was going to allow him to pass the remainder of the visit in comparative equanimity. From then on, it was as if he was an impartial witness to the contest between Henrietta and Cousin Annie. If, afterward, he had had to testify in court and explain why he did not intervene between them, he would have had to say that he thought it only a kind of game they were playing, and that he had had no idea of how deadly serious they were.

There was no telephone call from Henrietta that day. Edmund tried to reach her just after noon but learned from the maid that she and "the company" hadn't been at home for lunch. The maid happened to know the restaurant out on Hillsboro

Pike where they had gone and happened to have the telephone number handy. Edmund could not help smiling as he jotted down the number. Henrietta knew he would be expecting a call from her, and knew that if it didn't come *he* would call— not because he would be afraid she was pouting or because he would feel a need to apologize. She was not a woman who pouted, and she always knew how sorry he was when they had had any kind of tiff. She was wonderful, really. He would find her tonight in the best of spirits. There would be no reference made to their exchange at the side door this morning. It was past, and she had already forgotten it. She was a wonderful woman, and nothing about her was more wonderful than her serenity and the way she was certain to have another suggestion to make to him today or tonight. The only trouble was that he knew what *this* suggestion would be, and it was important that he give her the opportunity of making it as soon as possible. He telephoned the restaurant, but the hostess said that Mrs. Harper and her party had just left.

Not infrequently Edmund stayed home from his office for one day of a visit that wasn't going too well. It was usually the last day. But his staying was by no means a pattern. He could never be certain it was the thing Henrietta wanted, and he always waited for her suggestion. Tomorrow would be the last day for Cousin Johnny and Cousin Annie, and though this was a case in which Henrietta was almost sure to suggest it, it wasn't going to be possible for him to stay. When he came in the house that night, Henrietta was still upstairs dressing. He considered this a stroke of good luck, because it would give her the opportunity he had in mind. Perhaps even it was for this that she happened still to be up there.

Henrietta's dressing for dinner, like Edmund's, consisted not of getting into more formal attire but of putting on something more comfortable and something more youthful than she ever wore away from home. When he came into her room, she was fresh from her bath, still moving about the room in her knee-length slip and her high-heeled mules. And right away she was bubbling with talk about the day's events, proving that she bore him no grudge, even saying the kind of things about Cousin Johnny and Cousin Annie that she had refused to say last night. "Once in the car when we were on our way

out to Traveler's Rest—they were enchanted by Traveler's Rest
and didn't care for Bellemeade or even the Hermitage—once I
said—it was when we were talking about people from Ewingsburg who live here (and whom Cousin Annie has *refused* to
let entertain them or even to see)—I said Bob Coppinger has
gotten to look exactly like Laurence Olivier. 'Like who?' said
Cousin Johnny from the back seat. Cousin Annie was sitting
in the front seat with me and she turned around and said to
him with the utmost contempt for my allusion, 'Some moving
picture star, I think, Mr. Kincaid.' (Yes, she has continued to
call him Mr. Kincaid all day today.) It was as if the old dear
had read my mind. I had been thinking that even though she
disapproves so of TV, we might be able to get them out to see
a Western movie tonight—something real old-fashioned, like
a movie. But after her remark I knew there was no chance, and
that it had been silly of me to think there might be. I even
marvel that she knows who Olivier is. But she knows things.
She knows things you'd never in the world suppose she did.
Let me tell you— Here, give me a hand with these buttons,
won't you?"

While she talked she had gone to her closet and pulled out
the dress she was going to wear. Edmund was marveling more
at the pretty print of the dress material and at the mysterious row of buttons down the back than at Cousin Annie Kincaid's knowledge of movie stars. He realized that the buttons
seemed mysterious because they were at once so unnecessary,
so numerous and so large—each the size of a silver dollar—
and yet were so carefully camouflaged, being covered with the
same print the dress was made of. He found it most absorbing,
and intriguing, and endearing. And suddenly he recognized
the similarity of the whole fashioning of this dress to that of
dresses Henrietta had worn when he was courting her. As he
stood behind her, buttoning those buttons that began at the
very low waistline and continued up to the rounded neckline,
he could not resist, midway, leaning forward and kissing her
on the back of her neck. Henrietta began to give him the day's
itinerary: the First Presbyterian Church, the plantation houses
of Andrew Jackson, John Overton, the Harding family.

"Every place we went," she said, "I had a time making them
get out and see the very thing they had come to see. But what I

was going to tell you was that when we were on our way downtown to see the church, Cousin Annie asked me to point out
the James K. Polk Apartments and Vaux Hall! Could you have
imagined she would have heard of either or remembered the
names? When I told her both buildings had been torn down,
she only said, 'I'm not surprised.' . . . What I think is that those
were places where friends of hers who came to Nashville a million years ago must have had apartments . . . We might have
lived there ourselves if we had come ten or fifteen years before
we did. Do you remember when the Braxtons lived there—at
Vaux Hall?"

But now it was time for Edmund to rush off into his room
and dress. "Well, do make it snappy, dear," Henrietta said.
"Remember I've had them all day. You must have noticed I'm
quite hoarse from doing all the talking."

At dinner, Edmund made a special point of carrying his
full share of the conversation. Cousin Johnny, on the other
hand, was completely silent tonight and ate absolutely nothing.
Cousin Annie was kept busy eating two portions of everything
so that nothing would be wasted on *their* account. It was the
first time Cousin Annie had done this, but then it was the
first time Cousin Johnny had gone without food altogether.
Edmund wondered silently if the old man wasn't hungry and if
they couldn't find him something in the kitchen he could eat.
Yet he couldn't ask. He began speculating on how many other
discomforts the old man might have suffered in the past two
days. He noticed that he had come to the table tonight without his vest. And at some moment last night he had noticed
how the old man's clothes seemed to hang on him and how
he seemed thinner than when he first arrived. The answer
was that he had left off his long underwear. It was the central
heat in the house! *They* weren't used to it. And now Edmund
recalled the scene in the living room when he came into the
house this afternoon. Having been detained at the office to
make last-minute revisions of his brief for the shoe company
case, Edmund had come home a little later than usual, but the
houseboy was lighting the log fire in the living room at the
usual hour. Edmund had, at the time, been scarcely conscious
of one detail in the scene, but subconsciously he had made a

note of it. At the moment of his entrance, the houseboy was on his knees fanning the flames of the fire, and across the room, seated beside Cousin Johnny and with him watching silently the houseboy's efforts, Cousin Annie was fanning herself with a little picture postcard of the Hermitage.

Until these details began to pile up in his mind, at the dinner table, Edmund had thought of Cousin Annie as waging a merely defensive war against Henrietta. Now he saw it wasn't so. She had had the offensive from the beginning and she was winning battle after battle. Every discomfort that Cousin Johnny suffered in silence, every dish he did without, every custom he had to conform to that was "bad for him" was a victory over Henrietta, and gave the old lady the deeper satisfaction just because Henrietta might not be aware of it.

But Edmund had no premonition of how far she might be prepared to go—or perhaps already had gone—until after dinner, when Cousin Johnny and Cousin Annie were going up the stairs together. They ascended very slowly, and Edmund realized that her footsteps were every bit as heavy as Cousin Johnny's. He recalled having mistaken her for the old man on the stair this morning. Very likely it had been she, after all, who had come down to fetch the paper each morning. Was climbing the stairs perhaps bad for Cousin Johnny?—the stairs in this house and in all the landmarks he had been taken to see? And when he went upstairs this morning, had it really been that he *couldn't* come back down and go with Edmund to the office? Suddenly Edmund could visualize the old fellow lying on his back in the bed, or even on the floor, before the old lady helped him onto the bed and made him comfortable and then came downstairs to say that he had changed his mind.

When their guests had gone upstairs for the night and Edmund was setting up the card table in the living room, Henrietta still hadn't mentioned tomorrow and the possibility of his staying at home. But after they had arranged their cards and had begun to play, the suggestion wasn't long in coming. By now, however, his concern for Cousin Johnny had driven that problem out of Edmund's mind, and, because of this, his reply to Henrietta was more abrupt than it might otherwise have been.

"There's one thing I do hope," she had said with considerable force, "and that is that you are going to be able to stay at home tomorrow."

"I can't possibly." That was all he said. For a minute they sat looking at each other across the card table.

"But I've told them you'd be here," she said.

"I wish you had asked me earlier," he said, in a softer tone now.

Her voice was still full of confidence. "I *had* counted on it," she said. "And they have gone up to bed thinking you'll be here."

"Tomorrow is Friday," he said, as if speaking to a child. "I'll have to be in court all day. It's the shoe company case. There's no chance."

"Oh," said Henrietta. She knew that this meant there really was no chance.

"I'm truly sorry, Henrietta," he said. "Fortunately, there will be no court on Saturday. I'll be able to go with you to take them home. But there's nothing I can do about tomorrow."

"Of course there's not. I understand that," she said, smiling at him. She was already recovering from her disappointment. Quietly they began, playing out their game of cards. During the rest of the time they sat there, it seemed to Edmund that Henrietta played her cards as though she were performing some magic that was going to change everything—in her favor. And he couldn't bring himself to tell her about the sudden insight he had had at the dinner table, or about the ridiculous but genuine and quite black apprehension that he wasn't able to rid himself of.

At some hour in the night he heard the old woman's voice distinctly. He tried to think he had only dreamed it and that some other noise had waked him. But then he heard her again and heard Cousin Johnny. The familiar, funereal tones were unmistakable. He only managed to get back to sleep by assuring himself that it meant it must be nearly morning, by reminding himself that he had to have his sleep if he was to have his wits about him in court today.

The next time he woke, he put on the light and looked at his watch. He was sleeping alone in his own room. The two previous nights he had been with Henrietta in her room, but tonight she hadn't suggested it. His pocket watch was lying on his bedside table, with the gold chain coiled about it. It had been his father's watch and had the circumference and the thickness of a doorknob. Before he fastened his eyes on the Roman numerals to which the filigreed hands pointed, he remembered noticing that Cousin Johnny's watch, which the old man took out and wound before going up to bed each night, was almost identical with this one of his father's. It occurred to him that Cousin Johnny's would be resting now on the bedside table in the guest room with its chain coiled around it. This neat coiling of the chain about the watch was a habit Edmund had picked up from his father and one that his father had no doubt picked up from his own father. When finally Edmund focused his attention on the face of the watch, he found the very hour of the night itself alarming. It was half past three. From that moment, he didn't hear Cousin Johnny's voice again; it was only the old lady he heard. He was certain now that the old man was really very sick. He waited, sitting on the side of the bed with the light on. There were silences, broken always and only by Cousin Annie's voice. At last he got up and switched off the light and felt his way through the bathroom into Henrietta's room.

"Do you suppose something is really wrong?" Henrietta said from her bed. He was hardly through the doorway, and the room was pitch dark. Something in the way she said it made him answer, "I suppose not."

"The light's been on in their room for some time. You can see it on the garage roof. Do you think you might just go and make sure—or I could."

"What good would it do? It would only make matters worse, considering how they are."

"Well, what do you think?" she said, meaning, Then why are you here?

"I couldn't sleep."

"Is it that case today?"

"No, but I thought I might sleep better in here." He was sitting on the side of her bed now. "Do you mind?" He didn't know what he would do if she said, yes, she minded. He knew only that he couldn't go back to his own room and bed before

morning. He felt that it hadn't, after all, been the voices that
waked him, and that there *had* been a dream—the kind of
dream that could never be remembered afterward.

"Of course I don't mind, silly," she said. She sounded wide
awake. "I've had a wonderfully funny thought," she said as he
lay down beside her. "You might just go to their door and tell
Cousin Annie that you won't be able to stay home today. Then
maybe she would let *him* get some sleep."

"Can she be that awful?" Edmund said. "You don't suppose
it's anything more than just that?"

"I suppose not," she answered, putting her arm around him.
"You know what an evil influence you are on people." The
touch of her arm was all he had needed. Once again he believed
it was the voices that had waked him, and remembered that he
must have his wits about him tomorrow.

At seven o'clock nobody went downstairs to fetch the paper.
Edmund had left his watch in his room, but neighborhood
noises and a distant whistle told him the time. He slept again,
and next time he waked he knew it was the unnatural silence
in the house that had waked him. He slipped out of bed and
went into his room to dress. It was seven-thirty by his watch.
He dressed hurriedly, but when he went to look in on Henrietta before going downstairs, he found her also fully dressed
and standing with her hand on the knob to the hall door. She
had put on lipstick but no other make-up. She looked pale and
frightened. He crossed over to her and they went out into the
hall together.

The door to the guest room was standing open but the
blinds were still drawn and the room was in complete darkness.
Presently Cousin Annie appeared out of the darkness, wearing
the black dress she had worn on the trip in from the country
and clutching some object in her hand. Edmund and Henrietta
moved quickly toward her. As they drew near, Edmund saw it
was Cousin Johnny's watch she held. When they stood before
her in the doorway, Cousin Annie said, "He's gone."

"Gone?" Edmund echoed, and he almost added, "Where?"
But in time he remembered the euphemism. She spoke as
though they had all been waiting together through the night
for the old man to be released from his mortal pain.

He felt Henrietta lean against him. He put his arms about her, and when she turned and hid her face on his shirtfront, he had to support her to keep her from crumbling to the floor.

"You mustn't," said Cousin Annie. "I did everything anyone could have done. We had known for some time he hadn't long."

Henrietta's strength returned. She drew herself away from him and faced Cousin Annie. "But why—how could you let him come if—"

Edmund felt himself blushing. Was his wife really so shameless?

But the old lady seemed to think the question quite in order. She even completed the question for Henrietta. "If it was unwise for him? Because he wanted so much to come, to see what it was like here . . . Like all of us, he was foolish about some things."

The two women stood a moment looking at each other. Without being blind to the genuine grief in Cousin Annie's countenance, Edmund detected the glint of victory in the last glance she gave Henrietta before turning back into the dark room.

Poor Cousin Johnny, Edmund thought to himself . . . Now Henrietta was following Cousin Annie in there, and now he heard the old lady's first sobs and knew that she had given way, as she had to, and was letting Henrietta see after her. The battle was over, really . . . But poor Cousin Johnny, he kept thinking. Poor old fellow . . . Presently Henrietta led Cousin Annie out into the hall again, and as the two women moved toward the door to Henrietta's room, Henrietta gave him a look that recalled him to his senses and reminded him of his obligations. Already it was time for him to begin making the arrangements. He would be at home after all today. The court would grant a postponement under the circumstances. Cousin Johnny was gone, but *he* was still here to see Henrietta through and make the arrangements.

For a moment Edmund stood there staring into the dead man's room. The door should be shut, he supposed. And when he had done this, he would have to go and telephone a doctor. Cousin Annie didn't realize you couldn't die without a doctor nowadays. While he waited for the doctor to arrive, he would call an undertaker. No, he was being as bad as Cousin Annie.

It wouldn't do to call an undertaker before a doctor had been there. He stepped forward and placed his hand on the door-knob. And then, as though it was what he had intended all along, he went inside the room and closed the door behind him.

He waited just inside the door till his eyes got used to the dark. Then he went over to the foot of the bed where she had the old man laid out. At last they were alone—he and Cousin Johnny. There was only just enough light for him to make out that she had him completely dressed, and with something that must be a handkerchief covering his face. No doubt he was wearing the very clothes—his other suit and good tie—that he would have worn to lunch at Jackson's Stable. And would she have put him in his long underwear? Edmund speculated, not idly, and not, certainly, with humor. And the vest? And the lisle socks and the elastic supporters? Yes, she would have. That was how Cousin Johnny would be taken back to Ewingsburg for burial, was how he would be taken away from Edmund's house where he had died. Suddenly, at the thought of it, Edmund was seized with a dreadful terror of their taking the old man away. Wasn't there some way he could postpone it? But postponing it wouldn't be enough. What if he should lock the door to the guest room and refuse to let them have the body! He had heard of cases in which grief had driven people to such madness, and surely his present anguish was grief—if not exactly grief for Cousin Johnny. What if he should refuse to let them have the old man's body!

He stood peering through the darkness at the white hand-kerchief over the old man's face, the face whose features he already found it hard to remember distinctly. And he was wondering at his own simplicity—indulging in such a fantasy, giving way to such unnatural and morbid feelings! And at such a time. Soon Henrietta or Cousin Annie—or the two of them, even—might come and discover him there. That wasn't likely, but soon he would have to go back to them and he must begin preparing himself for his return. He knew that the first step must be to begin thinking of Cousin Johnny more realistically, not as a part of himself that was being taken away forever but once again as a visitor from the country who had died in his guest room. And, all at once, it seemed to Edmund the most natural thing in the world for him to speak to his dead house guest.

"Well, Cousin Johnny, you're gone," he said. That was all he said aloud. But, placing his two hands on the smooth foot-rail of the bed as though it were the familiar rail of a jury box, he went on silently: "What was it we were going to talk about, Cousin Johnny, in that talk of ours? Was it our wives and their wars within wars and what made them that way . . . We certainly ought to have got round to that. But it wasn't our wives who divided us. It was somehow our both being from the country that did it. You had done one thing about being from the country and I had done another. You buried yourself alive on that farm of yours, I buried myself in my work here. But something in the life out there didn't satisfy you the way it should. The country wasn't itself any more. And something was wrong for me here. By 'country' we mean the old world, don't we, Cousin Johnny—the old ways, the old life, where people had real grandfathers and real children, and where love was something that could endure the light of day—something real, not merely a hand one holds in the dark so that sleep will come. Our trouble was, Cousin Johnny, we were lost without our old realities. We couldn't discover what it is people keep alive for without them. Surely there must be something. Other people seem to know some reason why it is better to be alive than dead this April morning. I will have to find it out. There must be something."

The Little Cousins

To the annual Veiled Prophet's Ball children were not cordially invited. High up in the balcony, along with servants and poor relations, they were tolerated. Their presence was even sometimes suffered in the lower tiers and, under certain circumstances, even down in the boxes. But, generally speaking, children were expected to enjoy the Prophet's parade the night before and be content to go to bed without complaint on the night of the Ball. This was twenty-five years ago, of course. There is no telling what the practices are out there in St. Louis now. Children have it much better everywhere nowadays. Perhaps they flock to the Veiled Prophet's Ball by the hundred, and even go to the Statler Hotel for breakfast afterward.

But I can't help hoping they don't. I hope they are denied something. Else what do they have that's tangible to hold against the grown-ups? My sister and I were denied *every*thing. She more than I, since a boy naturally didn't want so much—or so much of what it was St. Louis seemed to offer us. Having less to complain of myself, however, I undertook to suffer a good many things for Corinna. And she suffered a few for me. We were motherless, and very close to each other at times.

What I suffered for Corinna I suffered in silence. But the grand thing about Corinna was that she could always find the right words for my feelings as well as her own. The outrage I felt, for example, at our being always taken down to Sportsman's Park to see the Browns play and never the Cardinals left me grimly inarticulate. But Corinna would say for me that it seemed "such an empty glory" to have box seats at the Browns' games. "Any fool had rather sit in the bleachers and watch the Cardinals," she said, "than have the very best box seats to see a Browns' game." She phrased things beautifully. At our house we had always to serve Dr Pep instead of Coca-Cola. Of this Corinna said, "It makes us seem so provincial." But we both knew that with a father like ours we just had to endure these embarrassments. According to Corinna, Daddy was "blind to the disadvantage he put us at"—disadvantage, that is, with our friends at Mary Institute and Country Day. What's more, she had divined at an early age what it was that

blinded Daddy: It was always some friend or other of his who
owned or manufactured the product imposed on us. We even
had Bessie Calhoun because of one of his friends—Bessie, from
Selma, Alabama, instead of some stylish, white foreign govern-
ess who might be teaching us French or German. "Except for
Bessie," Corinna said, "we would be bilingual, like the Altvad-
ers and the Tomlinsons."

The year Corinna and I were finally taken to the Ball, the
project was kept a secret from us until the last moment—or
practically. I came in from school at five-thirty, and Corinna
had got home two hours before that, as usual. At the side door,
which Bessie made us use on all days but Sunday in order to
save "her floors," Corinna was waiting for me with narrow eyes
and pursed lips. "You and I are going to the VP tonight," she
said, "but they couldn't permit us the pleasures of anticipation.
Isn't that typical?" The news had been broken to her when
she came in from school and told Bessie she was going down
the block to play. Corinna was already twelve at this time, and
though at school she would never deign to associate with girls
in the lower grades, out of school she spent most of her time
playing with the younger children in our block. The little girls
adored her, and I used to watch her sometimes, mothering
them and supervising their games. She never seemed happier
than then, and she often spoke of the younger children as her
"little cousins." This, I suppose, was in fond allusion to all
the tales we had listened to from Daddy, and from Bessie, too,
about the horde of first, second, and third cousins they each
had grown up among—Daddy in Kentucky, Bessie in Alabama.
At any rate, when Bessie told her she had to stay in and do her
homework that afternoon, Corinna wasn't satisfied until she
had wrung the reason out of her, and then, of course, she was
indignant.

"*Why* didn't you tell me before, Bessie?" she said. "Two
other girls in my class were lording it over everybody else today
because *they're* going."

"That's it," said Bessie. "I didn't want you lording it over
everybody you saw today. That's not the way I'm bringing you
up. And I didn't want you being flighty about your lessons."

Corinna knew that Daddy must have told her not to tell
us. Or she knew at least that Bessie had got his approval. Yet

Bessie always pretended to do everything absolutely on her own authority. And this made life more difficult. This made us forget that she was merely someone hired to take charge of us. It made us try to reason with her about things, made us pretend to be sick sometimes in order to break down her resistance, made us nag at her continually for all kinds of privileges. Bessie's utter disregard for what we considered justice and reason was something else that made us forget who she was, and she never showed any fear of our telling on her or going over her head. Her favorite answer to our "whys" was "Because I said so" or "Because I said to." And if one of us gobbled up his dessert and begged for a share of the other's, Bessie was as apt as not to make the other one share. She was illogical, and she was inconsistent. When we were disobedient, she would hand out terrible punishments—dessertless days and movieless weekends—but then sometimes she would forget, or weaken of her own accord at the last moment. You could not tell about her.

There was her brutal frankness, too. Though she was as blind as Daddy to any need of ours to have our egos bolstered—such as by serving our friends the right drink—and as blind as he to our deep moral and intellectual failings—failings that we ourselves were aware of and often confessed to each other— still she never failed to notice the least sign of vanity in either of us. Corinna was beginning to worry about her looks, and when she asked Bessie whether she thought she would grow up to be as beautiful as a certain Mary Elizabeth Caswell, Bessie said, "Your legs are too thin. You'll have to do a lot of filling out before you can talk about that." I was proud of my drawing ability, and I tried to get Bessie to say she thought I might grow up to be an artist. "Do you like nature?" she said, and I had to admit what she already knew: Flowers and trees had little attraction for me. Bessie only shook her head and gave me a doubting look.

Yet when I was sick in bed with mumps or measles she would often read my palm, and, among other glories, she saw that I would be a great musician. I objected that the singing teacher at school said I couldn't even carry a tune. "What does *he* know about how you may change if you keep trying? I know how little teachers know." It was when we were sick that we discovered Bessie's real talents and saw how indulgent she could be when she had a mind to. This made us sick a good deal; and pretended illness was one of our moral failings that Bessie was blind to. I never knew her to doubt a headache or a stomach-ache or even "a funny feeling all over." When we were sick, she played cards with us, told our fortunes, read to us.

She read to us a lot even when we were well. She had taught school in Alabama before she came north and went into ser-vice, but it wasn't the kind of stories we were used to in St. Louis schools that she read to us. She read "Unc' Edinburg's Drowndin'" and "No Haid Pawn," and her favorites were the *Post* stories by Octavus Roy Cohen. When she read us those stories, she would sometimes throw back her head and laugh and slap her thigh the way she never did about anything else. We loved hearing her read, but we didn't ourselves think the stories were so funny. "Never mind," said Bessie. "*You* don't have to think they're funny."

In conversation Bessie had only two real subjects, and one of them was Mary Elizabeth Caswell. Mary Elizabeth was the bane of Corinna's existence. Bessie had brought up Mary Elizabeth to the age of thirteen. When our mother died, Mr. Caswell had sent Bessie over to us—supposedly for only a few days. I was five at the time and Corinna was eight. Mr. Caswell came to our house on several occasions during those first days and had long conferences with Bessie; it was finally decided between them that she would stay with us. Probably Mr. Cas-well felt that Daddy's need was greater than his own. Though Mary Elizabeth was motherless, too, it was already known that Mr. Caswell was going to marry again within a few months. Besides, not only was Mary Elizabeth a big girl then, but her mother had been of an old family in the city and there was an abundance of aunts and other female relatives to guide her. And so *we* got Bessie, with the result that Corinna had to "spend her life," as she said, listening to unfavorable compari-sons of herself to Mary Elizabeth.

Bessie's other subject was her own family down in Alabama and, more particularly, her half sister, Lilly Belle Patton. Lilly Belle was a saint. Bessie assured us that Lilly Belle was noth-ing like her, had none of her bad temper and selfish ways, was always doing for others and asked nothing for herself. Lilly Belle was the finest-looking, the smartest, and the best-natured of all Bessie's mama's eleven children. Yet she hadn't insisted on going through high school, the way Bessie had, and she hadn't married. Bessie not only went through school and took to teaching afterward but the money she made teaching she spent foolishly—not on her mama, who was pretty greedy about money anyway, but on first one husband and then another. But Lilly Belle was content to stay at home and help Mama, who was certainly never much help to herself. Lilly Belle took in washing and looked after her little half brothers and sisters, of which Bessie was next to youngest, and even "adopted-like" two orphaned cousins. She was a hard church worker, a beautiful seamstress and laundress, she was the best cook in the whole town of Selma, she kept a garden that was the envy of everyone.

Corinna and I never tired of hearing about Lilly Belle, but for Corinna the most interesting part always was Lilly Belle's courtship. Lilly Belle never felt she could go off and marry while the younger children were still at home to be looked after, and by the time the younger ones were up and gone ("gone to the bad, most of them") Mama was too old to leave at home alone. But Lilly Belle had a faithful suitor, who had been waiting for her through all the years. He was, in fact, still waiting, and Lilly Belle wasn't even engaged to him. Sometimes Bessie had letters from a neighbor friend telling her she ought to make Lilly Belle have pity on Mr. Barker. It seems that on summer evenings he and Lilly Belle kept company sitting together on her front porch. Neighbors would hear their voices over there, and sometimes they would hear Mr. Barker break down and cry as he begged her "at least to get engaged" to him. But Lilly Belle knew what was right; she had taken a vow not even to get *engaged* while Mama lived. Sometimes, too, there would be a letter that Lilly Belle had asked the neighbor friend to write Bessie, warning her that Mama was "low sick." Bessie always "reckoned" Mama was really going this time. And Corinna would be on tenterhooks about it for days. She would try to linger in the mornings till the postman came, and she would rush home from school in the afternoon to see if there was any news. "If Mama goes this time," she would ask, "will Lilly Belle really get engaged to Mr. Barker?" And

Bessie would reply, "Of course she will. She hasn't kept him waiting for nothing."

The unfavorable comparisons that Bessie made between herself and Lilly Belle were much more severe than those she made between Corinna and Mary Elizabeth. Yet, quite naturally, Corinna was able to think of Lilly Belle as a heroine of pure romance, whereas she saw Mary Elizabeth as a "pampered, spoiled, stuck-up thing." The worst of it was, Corinna was subject to wearing hand-me-downs from Mary Elizabeth. There was no need for it, of course, but Mr. Caswell and Daddy were that close. Or perhaps Bessie Calhoun was still *that* close to the Caswell family. The dresses would just appear in Corinna's closet and be allowed to hang there for her to ignore until she could resist them no longer. Once she had taken them down and begun wearing them, they became her favorite dresses. She may have managed to forget who it was they had belonged to. Or, without admitting it to me and perhaps to herself, she may have remembered how lovely Mary Elizabeth had looked in them; because Corinna had never lacked opportunity for observing Mary Elizabeth Caswell firsthand. The older girl and Corinna were in the same school together until Corinna was ten. After that, Mary Elizabeth went off to finishing school for two years, but even so she was home for all the holidays, and she and her father and the stepmother would be at our house for meals or we would be at their house. Daddy, during these two years, had begun going about with a very stylish-looking young widow, who was a close friend of Mr. Caswell's second wife. Corinna and I knew this lady then as Mrs. Richards. It was not to be long before she would become our stepmother—a fact that deserves mention only because it explains why our family and the Caswells were now thrown together still more than formerly.

Bessie Calhoun had a clear recollection of every mark Mary Elizabeth ever received in the lower grades at Mary Institute. "Because of Mary Elizabeth," said Corinna, "I have to live in mortal dread of not making the honor roll." At an early age, Mary Elizabeth could cook and sew in a way that promised to rival the arts of Lilly Belle. This information cost Corinna many precious hours that might have been spent with her "little cousins." And because Mary Elizabeth had had a little pansy garden of her own, Corinna was sent "grubbing in the earth" every spring. On the other hand, Mary Elizabeth was almost certainly not the reader that Corinna was, or not the reader of novels—the old best-sellers on the shelves of what had been our mother's sitting room. One day Corinna inquired after Mary Elizabeth's reading habits. Bessie didn't answer right away—something unusual for her. "At your age that child read the Bible, honey." Corinna opened her mouth in astonishment and then she closed it again without saying anything. This was one time when both she and I doubted Bessie's veracity, but Corinna let it pass. There was a limit to what she would undertake. She never raised the question again.

We knew perfectly well why we were being taken to the Veiled Prophet's Ball. This was the year that Mary Elizabeth Caswell was going to be presented. As a matter of fact, Corinna had nagged Daddy about it one Sunday afternoon in the early fall. Since Mary Elizabeth was to be one of the debutantes this year, didn't he think Bessie might take us to watch from the balcony? ("Mary Elizabeth ought to be good for *something* to us," she had said to me in private beforehand.) But Daddy replied, "Don't be silly. You couldn't either of you stay awake that late. You can come downtown and watch the parade from my office the night before. One school night out will be enough." And, of course, we did go down and watch the parade. In fact, we went downtown for dinner with Daddy and Mrs. Richards, and the Caswells and some other grown-ups joined us at the office afterward. They all had a party, with drinks and hors d'oeuvres, while we tossed confetti out the window and watched the floats go by. I hadn't even realized that Mary Elizabeth wasn't present until Mrs. Caswell came over to the window where we were and said, "Mary Elizabeth's out with some of her own crowd, Corinna. But she told me to give you her love and say she would be thinking about you tomorrow night. She's dying for you to see her dress."

Suddenly Corinna leaned so far out the window that I thought she was sure to fall, and I grabbed hold of her.

"Stop it, stupid," she hissed. "Here comes the Prophet's float. The parade's nearly over."

Just below us was passing the last of the countless tableaux representing life in French colonial times and in the days of the Louisiana Territory. We had seen Lewis and Clark, Marquette and Joliet, Indians, fur traders, French peasant girls, river bullies from the days of the keelboat and the pirogue. The parade had begun, for some reason, with Jean Lafitte in the Old Absinthe House at New Orleans, and the final tableau was of Thomas Jefferson signing the Louisiana Purchase. Beyond Jefferson, in his oversized wig and silk knee breeches, I could see the Prophet's float approaching. But I knew that for me the best part of the parade was already over. After so many Indians and fur traders, after the French explorers, after the pirates, the Prophet, with his veil-hidden face and all his Eastern finery, was bound to seem an anticlimax. I stood beside Corinna, hardly watching the royal float go by. As she continued to lean far out over the window ledge, I quietly took hold of the sash of her dress and, without her knowing it, held on to it tightly as long as we remained at the window.

The night of the Ball, we had an early dinner without Daddy. He came in and went up to dress while we were still at the table. After dinner, he sent for us to come to his room, where he said that he wanted us to behave ourselves that night "as never before." He was going out to dinner with the Caswells and Mrs. Richards and some other friends, but he would send the car and chauffeur to fetch us to the Colosseum. He didn't tell us that Bessie wasn't going to accompany us or that we would be sitting with him in one of the boxes downstairs.

And Bessie herself withheld this information till the very last. When it was finally divulged, we had already been so dazzled by another piece of news that the evening before us and these unexpected arrangements seemed of little consequence. When we were both dressed, we went into the sewing room, where Bessie always sat in the evening, to have her look us over.

"How do I look?" Corinna asked.

"You look fine," said Bessie. Then she saw Corinna eyeing herself in the mirror stand, and she added, "But no better than you should."

Corinna went up on her tiptoes and said, "I ought to have on heels."

"Behave yourself tonight, Corinna," Bessie said. "And see that *he* does." She didn't look at me, even. Then leaning back in her chair she said, "I've got something to tell both of you."

"What?" said Corinna.

"I want you to behave yourself next week, too."

"Oh, I thought it was something," said Corinna.

"It *is* something. They've sent for me down home. I'll be gone on the train before you get home tonight."

Corinna stared at Bessie in the mirror. "It's Mama?" she asked, breathless. "*Tell* me, Bessie!"

Bessie nodded. "She's dead. She's been dead for two days. I've just been waiting around here to get tonight over."

Corinna observed a moment of silence. She knew that Mama had been "no pleasure to herself or anybody else" for several years now. Further, she knew that she had never heard Bessie say one good word for her mama, and that no commiseration was expected. But still, the respectful silence would be appreciated and would assure her getting answers to the questions she was bound to ask presently. She sat down on a wooden stool by the mirror and placed her feet, in their patent leather slippers, close together. She sat there smoothing the black velvet skirt over her knees. "Lilly Belle?" she said. "Is she engaged to Mr. Barker yet?"

Bessie nodded again. "She already has Mr. Barker's ring on her finger."

Now it was safe for Corinna to look up. "Will it be a long engagement?" she asked, still restraining herself somewhat.

"I'm going to stay over for the wedding Sunday week."

Corinna sprang to her feet. "Bessie!" she said. "Let me lend you my Brownie so you can bring us some pictures!"

Bessie shook her head. "Never mind about that. Lilly Belle's not going to get herself married to Mr. Barker without some high-type photographer there."

"Bessie, I wish I could go with you! Remember *every*thing."

"When did I forget anything, Corinna? Is there anything I haven't told you about Lilly Belle before this? I'll tell you one thing now. She's going to marry in her mourning, with a black veil to the floor."

Corinna sat down on the stool again, obviously stunned— more by the striking picture in her mind than by the impropriety. But presently she did ask, "Will that be quite proper, though, Bessie?"

"Of course it's proper, if black becomes you like it does Lilly Belle."

Corinna fixed her gaze on the wastebasket in the far corner of the room. "Do you think—" she began, speaking in a tone at once admiring and suspicious. "Do you think maybe she's kept Mr. Barker waiting just so she could marry in black?"

"How can you ask that, Corinna? Do you suppose Lilly Belle's as vain as *you* are?" Then she got up from her chair and said, "It's time for you-all to start downstairs. That car will be here."

It was only after we were out in the upstairs hall that we realized she wasn't going with us. At first, Corinna said she would refuse to go without her. It would be much more fun just to stay at home and talk, she said. "Yes," said Bessie heavily. "I can just see us sending word to your daddy and Mrs. Richards that you've decided to stay home and talk to Bessie."

"Then you'll *have* to come with us," Corinna said. "How can we go by ourselves?"

"Yes, 'have' to come with you," Bessie said. "Can't you just see me in my six-dollar silk sitting down there in the box with you-all and the Caswells." That was the first we knew of where we would be sitting.

We heard Mrs. Richards's voice downstairs; she had convinced Daddy that he couldn't merely have the chauffeur pick us up and have us arrive at the Colosseum by ourselves. And so there Daddy and Mrs. Richards were, waiting for us at the foot of the stairs. As Bessie helped Corinna into her Sunday coat, she said in an undertone, "Behave yourself, Corinna. Don't act silly. Remember this isn't just something gay tonight. I suspect you'll see folks crying. You know, it'll be like a wedding or funeral. There'll be something sad about seeing Mary Elizabeth and all of those other debutantes walking out in their white dresses."

Then we started down, with Bessie still watching from the head of the stairs and Daddy and Mrs. Richards waiting below.

Only a scene as strange and brilliant as that in the Colosseum could have made Corinna forget Lilly Belle altogether. But perhaps the pleasures of anticipation made her begin forgetting in the car. Or it might have been the sight of Mrs. Richards in her furs at the foot of the stairs. I had noticed before that night that with Mrs. Richards Corinna could be counted on to act more grown up than she did with anyone else. As we rode through town to the Colosseum, she and Mrs. Richards conversed, it seemed to me, with wonderful ease. Mrs. Richards had been a Special Maid at the Veiled Prophet's Court when she was a debutante some fifteen years before. She described the excitement of it as though it had been only yesterday—how you waited behind the curtains to hear the herald call out your name, and then how you heard, or imagined you heard, the gasps of surprise from the throngs whose admiring eyes would presently be focused on you as you walked, trembling, the length of the Colosseum, and knelt before the Prophet to be crowned, and then took your place on the dais.

For me, the Colosseum was like the most unreal of dreams. Before that night it had meant to me a wide sawdust arena with metal girders overhead and surrounded by gloomy, often half-empty tiers of seats. It was where I was taken to watch the annual horse show, the radio show, and the Boy Scout Jamboree. Now it had been transformed, by untold yards of bunting and by acres of white canvas on the floor, into a quite cheerful, if rather bathroomy-looking, ballroom. At one end were the thrones of the Prophet and his Queen-to-be, on a raised dais underneath a tasseled canopy, and they were flanked on either side by tiers of folding chairs provided for members of the Court. At the other end were the immense and immaculate white portieres through which the entrances of all persons of the first importance would be made.

After a drill by the Prophet's Guard of Bengal Lancers, the Prophet himself, attired in splendid medieval-Oriental garments and with his face veiled, made his duly ceremonious entrance. I was so bedazzled by the drill of the Prophet's guards and then by the arrival of the pirates and fur traders and Indians I had seen on the floats the night before that I hardly noticed when the Matrons of Honor began filing past our front-row box. These ladies, perhaps forty of them, circled the whole arena and at last took the places reserved for them on the Prophet's left. Even when the debutantes themselves, in white dresses and long white gloves, began to file by, I found it hard not just to sit there peering between them for glimpses of the people in costumes, who now occupied their places in the Court.

It was Corinna who brought me down to earth and reminded me of where my attention ought to be directed. She didn't do it intentionally, with a nudge or a cross whisper, but by her erratic behavior. She was sitting on the edge of her chair and leaning halfway across my lap trying to see the faces of the debutantes, who were now emerging from a small gateway on our side of the arena. I felt that she ought to wait and see them when they passed before our box.

"Stop," I said, trying to push her from in front of me.

"Oh, hush," she said, not budging.

She and I were in the very front row, and I glanced over my shoulder to see if Daddy had noticed her behavior. I discovered that he, along with everybody else in the box, was beaming at her. I was glad they couldn't see her face, or couldn't see it as well as I could, or at any rate didn't know what her narrowed-eyes-and-pursed-lips expression meant. Everything suddenly became clear to me. I knew what all the adults' smiling indulgence meant. Mary Elizabeth Caswell was going to have a place of honor in the Prophet's Court, and they expected Corinna to be thrilled by this. But I knew what tortures Corinna was suffering. Probably she was wishing I had let her fall out of that window last night. For, after this, how could she hope to measure up to Mary Elizabeth? It was hopeless. Now I began watching the faces of the girls as intently as she.

When the last debutante had passed us, Mrs. Richards leaned forward, smiling, and said to Corinna, "I didn't see Mary Elizabeth, did you?" And somehow, probably just because it *was* Mrs. Richards, Corinna managed to give her a very knowing, grown-up smile. When she turned around and faced the arena, she sat staring straight ahead with a glazed look.

After this came the separate entrances of the four Special Maids, each summoned individually to the Court of Love and Beauty by the Prophet's herald, each making her entrance between the great portieres and walking the length of the arena with measured steps and drawing after her a wide satin train. How I prayed each time that the next would be Mary

Elizabeth! But already I knew that Mary Elizabeth would be nothing less than the Queen. Corinna knew it, too. By the time that awful announcement came, Corinna was even able to turn and smile at Mr. and Mrs. Caswell.

"His Mysterious Majesty, the Veiled Prophet, commands me to summon to his Court of Love and Beauty to reign as Queen for one year . . . Miss Mary Elizabeth Caswell." That was all. The Queen's subjects came to their feet. Between the white portieres Mary Elizabeth appeared, arrayed in her white silk coronation gown, its bodice and its wide skirts embroidered all over with pearls and sparkling beads, her slender arms held gracefully, if just a little too stiffly, away from her body and encased in pure white kid so perfectly and smoothly fitted that only the occasional trembling of Mary Elizabeth's hands could suggest there were real hands and arms beneath; and her hair, her head of golden blond hair, fairly shimmering under the brilliant lights that now shone down on her from somewhere up among the panoplied steel girders. The orchestra, perched in a lofty spot directly above the portieres, began to play. To the strains of "Pomp and Circumstance," Mary Elizabeth moved across our vision, with four liveried pages holding up the expanse of her bejeweled train—moved across the white canvas floor of the Colosseum toward her throne.

When the brief coronation ceremony was finished, the Prophet took his Queen's hand and led her out onto the floor for their dance. After only a few measures, the guards broke their formation, each of them going to seek the hand of one of the debutantes as a dancing partner. The Ball had officially commenced.

Very soon, Daddy and Mrs. Richards went out on the floor, with the Caswells, to congratulate the Queen and to join in dancing themselves. Corinna and I were urged to come along, but I rejected the idea even quicker than Corinna did. We would wait in the box and find a chance to congratulate Mary Elizabeth later.

In almost no time, the floor was crowded with dancers. All but those who sat in the balcony were free to participate. Corinna and I sat with our elbows on the rail of the box, staring into the crowd. It was curious to see the Prophet's guards dancing in their heavy shoes, and it was most curious to me to see in how many instances there was a person in costume dancing with someone in ordinary evening clothes. I was seeking among the dancers for Mary Elizabeth and the Prophet.

It was Corinna, of course, who spied Mary Elizabeth first. "There she is," she said in a perfectly flat voice, indicating where with a tilt of her head, being very careful not to point. "She's not dancing with the Prophet anymore."

And then I saw her out there, not twenty feet from us, dancing with a dark-haired young man in white tie and tails. Just as I caught my first glimpse of her, another young man tapped this one on the shoulder, and she changed partners. She was, as Corinna might have phrased it, the cynosure of all eyes.

Corinna was on her feet. She cupped her hands to her mouth and shouted, "Lilly Belle's engaged!"

Mary Elizabeth couldn't hear her above the music. But she stopped dancing and started toward us, leading her partner by the hand. The other dancers respectfully made way for her. When she had come about half the distance, Corinna called out again, "Lilly Belle's engaged!"

"No!" Mary Elizabeth called back, and her voice and her radiant countenance expressed astonishment and delight. "Is it Mr. Barker?"

"None other!" said Corinna in her most grown-up tone. Mary Elizabeth was hurrying toward us now, and I beheld the spectacle of Corinna and Mary Elizabeth Caswell throwing their arms about each other. In that moment all was forgiven— all those splendid accomplishments, and all those unfavorable comparisons: forgiven forever. That which had separated them for so long had now united them.

"But Bessie didn't tell me!" Mary Elizabeth was saying. "She was by, this very morning, to have a close-up look at my dress."

"It's gorgeous," said Corinna.

"Isn't it!" And now another embrace.

"She told me just before I left the house," said Corinna. (Told *me*, not *us*? Before *I*, not *we*, left the house? How selfish that sounded.) "The wedding's Sunday week. And Lilly Belle's going to marry in her mourning veil!"

"Oh no! Stop it!" cried Mary Elizabeth, and she and Corinna shrieked with laughter.

"Bessie's taking the train to Alabama late tonight," Corinna said when she had got her breath again.

"Oh, that wonderful Bessie!" said Mary Elizabeth.

"Isn't she splendid!"

"Have you seen her?"

"Seen her?"

"Up there," said Mary Elizabeth, pointing to the balcony opposite us. "I spotted her a while ago and waved to her."

"Why, she didn't tell me she was coming!" said Corinna. "Isn't that typical?"

The two girls tried to locate Bessie again but soon gave it up. Next, I heard Mary Elizabeth introducing us to her partner, referring to us as her two "little cousins," and realized that Bessie must have talked to her about us. She went on to say how brilliant Corinna was in school and how well I could draw and what "perfect lambs" we both were.

I didn't stop searching for Bessie when they did, and I didn't hear what they were saying any longer. My eyes traveled up one row of the balcony and down the next, searching for Bessie's green silk dress. The crowd up there was thinning out; the poor relations and the children and the servants were going home. Bessie had likely hurried off to catch her train. Already I felt that I might never see Bessie Calhoun again.

But I kept looking for her until I could bear my lonely thoughts no longer. I put my arms on the railing before me, hid my face in them, and commenced to sob.

Instantly all attention was turned toward me, but I wouldn't look up or answer questions. In a matter of seconds Daddy and Mrs. Richards arrived.

"What is it, honey?" I heard Mrs. Richards say.

"He's just tired," Daddy said. "He's not used to being up so late. This is what it means, bringing children to something like this."

Then I was led to a seat at the rear of the box, where I wouldn't be so conspicuous. The Caswells had returned, too, now. I heard Mrs. Caswell say, "Poor little fellow," and this evoked fresh tears and deeper sobs.

"What is it, Son?" Daddy said. "You must try to tell me."

Finally I knew I had to say something—something that would sound reasonable to him. I swallowed hard and lifted my face and found Daddy. I don't know whether or not I knew what I was going to say before I said it. What I said was "Bessie's mama is dead."

"How did you know that, Son?" Daddy asked.

"She told me just before I was leaving the house tonight," I said. Then I hid my face and tried to begin crying again, but I couldn't.

"How awful of her!" I heard Mrs. Richards say, threateningly. "How really unspeakably awful!"

I sat with my face in my hands. After a moment I felt someone's arm go around my shoulder. I didn't know or care whose it was. Probably it was my father's though it may have been Mrs. Richards's, or even Corinna's. Whoever it was, it didn't have the feel I wanted, and I purposely kept my face hidden until it had been removed.

Heads of Houses

I. THE FOREIGN PARTS AND THE FORGET-ME-NOTS

KITTY'S OLD bachelor brother gave Dwight a hand with the baggage as far as the car, but Dwight would accept no more help than that. He had his own method of fitting everything into the trunk. His Olivetti and his portable record player went on the inside, where they would be most protected. The overnight bag and the children's box of playthings went on the outside, where they would be handy in case of an overnight stop. It was very neat the way he did it. And he had long since learned how to hoist the two heaviest pieces into the rack on top of the car with almost no effort, and knew how to wedge them in up there so that they hardly needed the elastic straps he had bought in Italy last summer. He was a big, lanky man, with a lean jaw that listed to one side, and normally his movements were so deliberate, and yet so faltering, that anyone who did not mistake him for a sleepwalker recognized him at once for a college professor. But he never appeared less professorial, and never felt less so, than when he was loading the baggage on top of his little car. As he worked at it now, he was proud of his speed and efficiency, and was not at all unhappy to have his father-in-law watching from the porch of the big summer cottage.

From the porch, Kitty's father watched Dwight's packing activities with a cold and critical eye. Only gypsies, Judge Parker felt, rode about the country with their possessions tied all over the outside of their cars. Such baggage this was, too! His son-in-law seemed purposely to have chosen the two most disreputable-looking pieces to exhibit to the public eye. Perhaps he had selected these two because they had more of the European stickers on them than any of the other bags—not to mention the number of steamship stickers proclaiming that the Dwight Clarks always traveled tourist class!

Yet the exposed baggage was not half so irritating to Judge Parker as the little foreign car itself. The car would have been bad enough if it had been one of the showy, sporty models, but Dwight's car had a practical-foreign look to it that told the

mountain people, over in the village, as well as the summer
people from Nashville and Memphis, over in the resort grounds
and at the hotel, how committed Dwight was to whatever it
was he thought he was committed to. The trouble was, it was
a *big* little car. At first glance, you couldn't quite tell what
was wrong with it. Yet it was little enough to have to have a
baggage rack on top; and inside it there was too little room
for Dwight and Kitty to take along even the one basket of
fruit that Kitty's mother had bought for them yesterday. Judge
Parker pushed himself as far back in his rocker as he safely
could. For a moment he managed to put the banister railing
between his eyes and the car. He meant *not* to be irritated. He
had been warned by his wife to be careful about what he said
to his son-in-law this morning. After all, the long summer visit
from the children was nearly over now.

Busy at work, Dwight was conscious of having more audience than just Dad Parker—an unseen, and unseeing, audience
inside the cottage. Certain noises he made, he knew, telegraphed
his progress to Kitty. She was upstairs—in the half story, that
is, where everybody but Dad and Mother Parker slept—making
sure both children used the bathroom before breakfast. (She
knew he would not allow them time for the bathroom after
breakfast.) And the same noises—the slamming down of the
trunk lid, for instance, and even the scraping of the heavy bags
over the little railing to the rack (the *galerie*, Dwight called it
fondly)—would reach the ears of brother Henry, now stationed
inside the screen door, considerably keeping hands off another
man's work. The ears of Mother Parker would be reached, too,
all the way back in the kitchen. Or, since breakfast must be
about ready now, Mother Parker might be on the back porch,
where the table was laid, waiting ever so patiently. Perhaps she
was rearranging the fruit in the handmade basket, which she
had bought at the arts-crafts shop, and which she was sure
she could find space for in the car after everything else was in
. . . Everybody, in short, was keeping out of the way and being
very patient and considerate. It really seemed to Dwight Clark
that he and his little family might make their getaway, on this
September morning, without harsh words from any quarter.
He counted it almost a miracle that such a summer could be

concluded without an open quarrel of any kind. Along toward the end of July, midway in the visit, he had thought it certain Kitty would not last. But now it was nearly over.

When the last strap over the bags was in place, Dwight stepped away from the car and admired his work. He even paused long enough to give a loving glance to the little black car itself, his English Ford, bought in France two summers ago. Such a sensible car it was, for a man who wanted other things out of life than just a car. No fins, no chromium, no high-test gasoline for him! And soon now he and Kitty would be settled inside it, and they would be on their way again, with just their own children, and headed back toward their own life: to the life at the university, to life in their sensible little prefab, with their own pictures and their own makeshift furniture (he could hardly wait for the sight of his books on the brick-and-board shelves!), to their plans for scrimping through another winter in order to go abroad again next summer—their life. Suddenly, he had a vision of them in Spain next summer, speeding along through Castile in the little black automobile, with the baggage piled high and casting its shadow on the hot roadside. He stepped toward the car again, with one long arm extended as if he were going to caress it. Instead, he gave the elastic straps— his Italian straps, he liked to call them—their final testing, snapping them against the bags with satisfaction, knowing that Kitty would hear, knowing that, for once, she would welcome this signal that he was all set.

He turned away from the car, half expecting to see Kitty and the children already on the porch. But they were still upstairs, of course; and breakfast had to be eaten yet. Even Dad Parker seemed to have disappeared from the porch. But, no, there he was, hiding behind the banisters. What was he up to? Usually the old gentleman kept his dignity, no matter what. It didn't matter, though. Dwight would pretend not to notice. He dropped his eyes to the ground . . . As he advanced toward the house, he resolved that this one time he was not going to be impatient with Kitty about setting out. He would keep quiet at the breakfast table. One impatient word from anybody, at this point, might set off fireworks between Kitty and her mother, between Kitty and her father. (He glanced up, and, lo, Dad Parker had popped up in a normal position again.) Between Kitty and her ineffectual old bachelor brother, even. (He wished Henry would either get away from that door or come on outside where he could be seen.) And if she got into it with them, Dwight knew he could not resist joining her. It would be too bad, here at last, but their impositions upon Kitty this summer had been quite beyond the pale—not to mention their general lack of appreciation of all she and he had undertaken to do for them, which, of course, he didn't mind for *himself*, and not to mention their show of resentment against *him*, toward the last, merely because he was taking Kitty away from them ten days earlier than the plans had originally called for. The truth was that they had no respect for his profession; they resented the fact that his department chairman could summon him back two weeks before classes would begin . . . For a moment, he forgot that, in fact, the chairman had not summoned him back.

As Dwight approached the porch, in his slow, lumbering gait, Judge Parker suddenly rocked forward in his chair. Stretching his long torso still farther forward, he rested the elbows of his white shirtsleeves on the banister railing. Dwight, out there in the morning sun, seemed actually to be walking with his eyes closed. Perhaps he was only looking down but, anyway, he came shambling across the lawn as though he didn't know where he was going. Judge Parker had noticed, before this, that when his son-in-law was let loose in a big open space, or even in a big room, he seemed to wander without any direction. The fellow was incapable of moving in a straight line from one point to another. He was the same way in an argument. Right now, no doubt, he had a theory about where the porch steps were, and he would blunder along till he arrived at the foot of them. But what a way of doing things, especially for a man who was always talking about the scientific approach. It had been, this summer, like having a great clumsy farm animal as a house guest. It had been hardest, the judge reflected, on his wife, Jane. Poor old girl. Why, between the fellow's typewriter and record player, she had hardly had one good afternoon nap out. And, oh, the ashtrays and the glasses that had been broken, and even furniture. For a son-in-law they had the kind of man who

couldn't sit in a straight chair without trying to balance himself
on its back legs. . . . Out-of-doors he was worse, if anything. He
had rented a power mower and cut the grass himself, instead of
letting them hire some mountain white to do it, as they had in
recent years. He had insisted, too, on helping the judge weed
and work his flower beds. As a result, Judge Parker's flowers
had been trampled until he could hardly bear to look at some
of the beds. A stray horse or cow couldn't have done more
damage. All at once, he realized that there was an immediate danger of Dwight's stumbling into his rock garden, beside
the porch steps, and crushing one of his ferns—his *Dryopteris
spinulosa*. Somehow, he must wake the boy up. He must *say*
something to him. He cleared his throat and began to speak.
As he spoke, he allowed his big, well-manicured hands to drape
themselves elegantly over the porch banisters.

"Professor Clark," he began, not knowing what he was
going to say, but using his most affectionate form of address
for Dwight. "Is it," he said, casting about for something amiable, "is it thirty-eight miles to the gallon you get?"

Dwight stopped, and looked up with a startled expression.
He might really have been a man waked from sleepwalking. But
gradually a suspicious, crooked smile appeared, twisting his
chin still farther out of any normal alignment. "*Twenty*-eight
to the gallon, Dad Parker," he said.

"Oh, yes, that's what I meant to say!"

What could have made him say *thirty*, he wondered. Not
that he knew or cared anything about car mileage. It always
annoyed him that people found it such an absorbing topic. Even
Jane knew more about his Buick than he did, and whenever
anyone asked him, he had to ask her what mileage they got.

But he couldn't let the exchange stop there. Dwight would
think his slip was intentional. Worse still, his son Henry, behind
the screen door, would be making *his* mental notes on how ill
the summer had gone. The judge had to make his interest seem
genuine. "That does make it cheap to operate," he ventured.
"And it has a four-cylinder motor. Think of that!"

"Six cylinders," said Dwight, no longer smiling.

The judge made one more try. "Of course, of course. Yours
is an Ambassador. It's the Consul that has four."

"Mine is called a Zephyr," Dwight said.

There was nothing left for Judge Parker to do but throw back his head and try to laugh it off. At any rate, he had saved his fern.

At the steps to the porch, a porch that encompassed the cottage on three sides and that was set very high, with dark green latticework underneath, and with the one steep flight of steps under the cupola, at the southwest corner—at the foot of the steps Dwight stopped and turned to look along the west side of the house. Dad Parker's lilac bushes grew there. Wood ashes were heaped about their roots. Beyond the lilacs was the rock pump house, and just beyond that Dwight had a view of Dad Parker's bed of forget-me-nots mixed with delphiniums. Or was it bachelor's-buttons mixed with ageratum? He was trying to get hold of himself after the judge's sarcasm about the car. In effect, he was counting to a hundred, as Kitty had told him he must do this morning.

For the peace must be kept this morning, at any price—for Kitty's sake. For her and the children's sake he had to control himself through one more meal. And the only way he could was to convince himself that Dad Parker's mistakes about the car were real ones. With anybody but Judge Nathan Parker it would have been impossible. But in the case of the judge it *was* possible. The man knew less than any Zulu about the workings of cars, to say nothing of models of foreign makes. This father-in-law of his most assuredly had some deep neurosis about anything vaguely mechanical. Even the innocent little Italian typewriter had offended him. And instead of coming right out and saying that Dwight's typing got on his nerves, he had had to ask his rhetorical questions, before the whole family, about whether Dwight thought good prose could be composed on "a machine." "I always found it necessary to write my briefs and decisions in longhand," he said, "if they were to sound like much." And the record player, too. The judge *despised* canned music; he preferred the music he made himself, on his violoncello, which instrument he frequently brought out of the closet after dinner at night, strumming it along with whatever popular stuff came over the radio . . . There was not even a telephone in the cottage. That seemed to Dwight the *purest* affectation. Dad and Mother Parker were forever penning little notes to people over in the resort grounds, or at the

hotel. They carried on a voluminous correspondence with their
friends back in Nashville. During the week, they wrote notes to
brother Henry, who had to keep at his job at the courthouse in
Nashville all summer long, and only came up to the mountain
for weekends. In fact, three weeks ago, when the generator on
Dwight's car went dead, Dad Parker had insisted upon writing brother Henry about it. The garage in the mountain village could not furnish brushes and armatures for an English
Ford, of course, but from the telephone office Dwight might
have called some garage in Nashville, or even in Chattanooga,
which was nearer. Instead, he had had to tell Dad Parker what
was needed and let Henry attend to it. Henry did attend to it,
and very promptly. The parts arrived in the mail just two days
later. When the judge returned from the village post office that
morning, he handed Dwight the two little packages, saying,
"Well, Herr Professor, here are your 'foreign parts.'" Everybody had laughed—even Kitty, for a moment. But Dwight
hadn't laughed. He had only stood examining the two little
brown packages, which were neatly and securely wrapped, as
only an old bachelor could have wrapped them, and addressed
to him in Henry's old-fashioned, clerkish-looking longhand.

At the foot of the porch steps, Dwight was listening hope-
fully for the sound of Kitty's footsteps on the stairs inside. He
remained there for perhaps two or three minutes, with his eyes
fixed in a trancelike gaze upon the mass of broad-leaved forget-
me-nots. (They *were* forget-me-nots, he had decided.) Presently
he saw out of the corner of his eye, without really looking, that
Dad Parker had produced the morning paper from somewhere
and was offering him half of it, holding it out toward him without saying a word. At the same moment, out in the rock pump
house, the pump's electric motor came on with a wheeze and
a whine. Someone had flushed the toilet upstairs. It was the
first flush since Dwight came downstairs, and so he knew that
Kitty and the children would not be along for some minutes
yet. There would have to be one more flush.

As he went up to the porch to receive a section of the paper,
the pump continued to run, making a noise like a muffled
siren. That was its *good* sound. It *wasn't* thumping, which
was its bad sound and meant trouble. Probably the low ebb

in understanding between Kitty and her mother this summer had been during the second dry spell in July. Kitty had come to the mountain with the intention of relieving her mother of the laundry, as well as of all cooking and dishwashing. Those were the things that Mother Parker had hated about the mountain when Kitty was growing up. She had missed her good colored servants in Nashville and couldn't stand the mountain "help" that was available. But it seemed that Kitty didn't understand how to operate her mother's new washing machine economically—with reference to water, that is. During that dry spell, Mother Parker took to hiding the table linen and bedsheets, and the old lady would rise in the morning before Kitty did, and run them through the washer herself. No real water crisis ever developed, but, realizing that Dad Parker would be helpless to deal with it if it did, Dwight got hold of the old manual that had come with the pump, when it was installed a dozen years before, and believed that he understood how to prime it, or even to "pull the pipe" in an emergency. Having learned from the manual that every flush of the toilet used five gallons of water, he estimated that during a dry spell it wasn't safe to flush it more than three times in one day. And as a result of this knowledge it became necessary for him to put a padlock on the bathroom door so as to prevent Dwight, Jr., aged four, from sneaking upstairs and flushing the toilet just for kicks.

It seemed that the pump, like everybody else, was trying to make only its polite noises this morning. But just as Dwight was accepting his half of the newspaper, the pump gave one ominous, threatening thump. Dwight went tense all over. There had been no rain for nearly three weeks. There might yet be a crisis with the pump. In such case, brother Henry would be no more help than Dad Parker. It could, conceivably, delay Dwight's departure a whole day. If that happened, it might entail his pretending to get off a telegram to the chairman of his department. Moreover, he would have to do this before the eyes of brother Henry, in whom Kitty, in a weak moment, had confided the desperate measure they had taken to bring the summer visit to an end. It was Henry, lurking there in the shadows, who really depressed him. It seemed to him that Henry had come up for weekends this summer just to lurk in the shadows. Had he joined in one single game of croquet? He had not. And each time Dwight produced his miniature chess set, Henry had made excuses and put him off.

Dwight looked into Dad Parker's eyes to see if the thump had registered with him. But of course it *hadn't* registered. And when the motor went off peacefully, and when everything was all right again, that of course didn't register, either. To Dwight's searching look Dad Parker responded merely by knitting his shaggy brows and putting one hand up to his polka-dot bow tie to make out if anything was wrong there. Everything was fine with the judge's tie, as it always was. He gave Dwight a baffled, pitying glance and then disappeared behind his half of the morning paper.

II. THE GARDEN HOUSE

Dwight sat down on a little cane-bottomed chair and tilted it on its back legs. He opened his half of the paper. His was the second section, with the sports and the funnies. He had learned early in the summer to pretend he preferred to read that section first. Dad Parker had been delighted with this, naturally, but even so he hadn't been able to conceal his astonishment—to put it mildly—that a grown man could have such a preference. To the judge it seemed the duty of all educated, responsible gentlemen to read the national and international news before breakfast every morning. He liked to have something important—and controversial, if possible—for the talk at the breakfast table.

Dwight, tilting back in his chair and hiding behind his paper, was listening for the pump to come on again. He felt positively panicky at the prospect of staying another day, or half day. One more flush of the toilet and he would be free. To think that five gallons of water *might* stand between him and his return to his own way of life! He found that he could not concentrate on the baseball scores, and he didn't even try to read "Pogo." Then, at last, the pump did come on, and it was all right. And again it went off with a single thump, which, as a matter of fact, it nearly always went off with.

Dwight sat wondering at his own keyed-up foolishness, but still he found it irksome that Dad Parker could sit over there calmly reading the paper, unaware even that there was such a thing as an electric pump on the place. It seemed that once the pump had been installed, the judge had deafened his ears to it and put it forever out of his mind. This was just the way he had behaved during the worst dry spell. But Dwight understood fully why no water shortage could ever be a problem for Dad Parker. To begin with, he watered his flowers only with rain water that he brought in a bucket from the old cistern—water that was no longer considered safe for drinking. And Dad Parker, personally, still used the garden house.

The garden house! Dwight was alarmed again. The garden house? Was there any reason for the thought of it to disturb him? There must be. His subconscious mind had sent up a warning. The garden house was connected with some imminent threat to his well-being, possibly even to his departure this morning. Quickly, he began trying to trace it down, forming a mental image of the edifice itself, which was located a hundred yards to the east of the cottage, along the ridge of the mountain. This structure was, without question, the sturdiest and most imposing on the Parkers' summer property. "Large, light, and airy, it is most commodious"—that was how Dad Parker had described the building to Dwight when he and Kitty were first married and before Dwight had yet seen the family's summer place. And Dwight had never since heard him speak of the building except in similar lyrical terms. Like the pump house, it was built of native rock, quarried on the mountainside just three or four miles away; but it had been built a half century back, when masonry work done on the mountain was of a good deal higher order than it was nowadays. Family tradition had it that one spring soon after Kitty's grandfather had had their cottage built, the men of a local mountain family had constructed the garden house for the grandfather free of charge and entirely on their own initiative. It was standing there to surprise "the Old Judge," as the grandfather was still remembered and spoken of locally, when he and the family came up to the mountain that July. The Old Judge had not actually been a judge at all, but an unusually influential and a tolerably rich lawyer, at Nashville, and he had befriended this mountain family sometime previously by representing them in a court action brought against one of their number

for disturbing the peace. They had repaid him by constructing a garden house that was unique in the whole region. Its
spacious interior was lighted by rows of transom windows, set
high in three of the four walls. Below these windows, at comfortable intervals, were accommodations for eight persons, and
underneath was a seemingly bottomless pit. Best of all, the
building was so situated that when the door was not closed,
its open doorway commanded a view of the valley that was
unmatched anywhere on the mountain . . . It was there that
Dad Parker usually went to read the first section of the paper,
before breakfast every morning. And frequently he read the
second section there, after breakfast. Suddenly a bell rang in
Dwight's conscious mind, and the message came through. Dad
Parker had, this morning, already read the first section of the
paper once! From the east dormer window, half an hour before,
Dwight had seen him returning from the garden house, paper
in hand. It was extremely odd, to say the least, for him to sit
there poring over the news a second time. Usually, when he had
read the paper once, he knew it by heart and never needed to
glance at it again—not even to prove a point in an argument.
What was he up to? First he had hidden behind the banisters,
now behind the paper.

Involuntarily, almost, Dwight tilted his chair still farther
back, to get a look at Dad Parker's face. The chair creaked
under his weight. Remembering he had already broken one of
these chairs this summer, he quickly brought it back to all fours.
Another broken chair might somehow delay their getting off!
The chair wasn't damaged this time, but the glimpse Dwight
had had of Dad Parker left him stunned. The old gentleman's
face was as red as a beet, and he was reading something in the
paper, something that made his eyes, normally set deep in their
sockets, seem about to pop out of his head.

By the time the front legs of Dwight's chair hit the floor, the
judge had already closed the paper and begun folding it. As he
tucked it safely under his arm, he looked at Dwight and gave
him a grin that was clearly sheepish—guilty, even.

But deep in the old man's eyes was a look of firm resolve. A
resolve, Dwight felt certain, that *he*, Dwight, should not under
any circumstances see the front section of the paper before
setting off this morning. Dwight couldn't imagine what the

article might be. He had but one clue. He had observed, with-out thinking about it, that the judge had had the paper open to the inside of the last page. That was where society news was printed, and it was one page that the judge seldom read. Dwight realized now that Dad Parker had given him the second section as a kind of peace offering. And while going through the first section again he had stumbled on something awful.

From inside the cottage there came the sound of Kitty's and the children's footsteps on the stairs.

III. AN OLD BACHELOR BROTHER

Henry Parker, just inside the screen door, heard Kitty and her children start downstairs. He pushed the door open and went out on the porch. Through the screen he had been watching his father and his brother-in-law, hiding from each other behind their papers. He believed he knew precisely what thoughts were troubling the two men. He had refrained from joining them because ever since he arrived from Nashville last night he had sensed that his own presence only aggravated their present suf-fering. Each of them was suffering from an acute awareness that he was practicing a stupid deception upon the other, as well as from a fear that he might be discovered. His brother-in-law was leaving the mountain under the pretense that he had been called back to his university. The judge was concealing the fact that there was a party of house guests expected to arrive from Nashville this very day—almost as soon as the Clarks were out of the house—and that an elaborate garden party was planned for Monday, which would be Labor Day. Each man knew that Henry knew about his deception, and each wished, with Henry, that Henry could have stayed on in Nashville this one weekend. Henry couldn't stay in Nashville, however—for good and sufficient reasons—and just now he couldn't remain inside the screen door any longer. Kitty was on the stairs, and his mother was coming up the hall from the kitchen. His lin-gering there would be interpreted by them as peculiar.

Just as Henry made his appearance on the porch, Dwight and the judge came to their feet. They, too, had heard the footsteps of the women and children. It was time for breakfast. Henry walked over to his father and said casually, "Wonder if

I could have a glance at the paper?" The judge glared at him as though his simple request were a personal insult.

"The paper," Henry repeated, reaching out a hand toward the newspaper, which the judge now clutched under his upper arm. The judge continued to glare, and Henry continued to hold out his hand. Henry's hands were of the same graceful and manly proportions as his father's, but, unlike the judge, he didn't "use" his hands and make them "speak." He also had his father's same deep-set eyes, and the same high forehead—even higher, since his hair, unlike his father's was beginning to recede. He glared back at his father, half in fun, supposing the refusal to be some kind of joke. Finally, he took hold of the paper and tried to pull it free. But the judge held on.

"May I just glance at the headlines?" Henry said sharply, dropping his hand.

"No, you may not," said the judge. "We are all going in to breakfast now."

Dwight stepped forward, smiling, and silently offered his section of the paper to Henry. Henry accepted it, but his heart sank when he looked into Dwight's face. Dwight's face, this morning, was the face of an appeaser. Only now did Henry realize that both men imagined he might, out of malice or stupidity, spill their beans at the breakfast table. The judge, it seemed, meant to bluff and badger him into silence; Dwight intended to appease him.

Henry took the paper over to the edge of the porch, leaned against the banister, and lit a cigarette. His mother and sister were standing together in the doorway now, and his father had set out in their direction.

"Breakfast, everybody," said his mother. By "everybody," he knew, she meant him, because he was the only one who had ignored her appearance there. He glanced up from the paper, smiled at her and nodded, then returned his eyes to the paper, which he held carelessly on his knee.

"Henry has taken a notion to read the newspaper at this point," he heard his father say just before he marched inside the cottage.

His brother-in-law lingered a moment. There seemed to be something Dwight wanted to say to Henry. But Henry didn't look up; he couldn't bear to. Dwight moved off toward the doorway without speaking.

"Don't be difficult, Henry," his sister Kitty said cheerfully. Then she and her mother went inside, with Dwight following them.

Henry heard them go back through the cottage to the screened porch in the rear. He knew he would have to join them there presently. He supposed that, whether they knew it or not, they needed him. They were so weary of their own differences that any addition to their company would be welcome, even someone who knew too much.

And how much too much *he* knew!—about them, about himself, about everybody. That was the trouble with him, of course. *He* could have told them beforehand how this summer would turn out. But they had known, really, how it would turn out, and had gone ahead with it anyway; and that was the difference between him and them, and that was the story of his bachelorhood, the story of his life. He flicked his cigarette out onto the lawn and folded the paper neatly over the banister. No, it wasn't quite so simple as that, he thought—the real difference, the real story wasn't. But he had learned to think of himself sometimes as others thought of him, and to play the role he was assigned. It was an easy way to avoid thinking of how things really were with him. Here he was, so it appeared, an old-fashioned old bachelor son, without any other life of his own, pouting because his father had been rude to him on the veranda of their summer cottage on a bright September morning. Henry Parker was a man capable even of thinking inside this role assigned him, and not, for the time being, as a man whose other life was so much more real and so much more complicated that there were certain moments in his summer weekends at this familiar cottage when he had to remind himself who these people about him were. For thirteen years, "life" to him had meant his life with Nora McLarnen, his love affair with a woman tied to another man through her children, tied to a husband who, like her, was a Roman Catholic and who, though they had been separated all those years, would not give her a divorce except on the most humiliating terms. Henry had learned how to think, on certain occasions with the family, as the fond old bachelor son. And he knew that presently he, the old bachelor, must get over his peeve and begin to have generous thoughts again about his father, and about the others, too.

It *had* been a wretched summer for all four of them, and they had got into the mess merely because they wanted to keep up the family ties. His mother was to be pitied most. His mother had finally arranged her summers at the cottage so that they were not all drudgery for her, the way they used to be when she had two small children, or even two big children, in the days when their cottage was not even wired for electricity and when, of course, she had no electric stove or refrigerator or washing machine and dryer. But in making their plans for this visit Dwight and Kitty had completely failed to understand this. Kitty had moved in and taken over where no taking over was needed. Not only that. Because Dwight had to do his writing—for ten years now they had been hearing about that book of his—and because Dwight and Kitty so disdained the social life that Mother and Dad had with the other summer residents, she had forgone almost all summer social life. Henry had it from his mother that the party on Monday was supposed to make it up to Dad's and her friends for their peculiar behavior this summer, and was not really intended as a celebration of their daughter's departure. To have concealed their plans was silly of them, but Mother had been afraid of how it might sound to Dwight and Kitty.

Kitty had to be a sympathetic figure, too, in the old bachelor's eyes. Kitty had written her mother beforehand that they would come to the mountain only if she could be allowed to take over the housekeeping. Yet her mother had "frustrated" her at every turn. She wouldn't keep out of the kitchen, she wouldn't let Kitty do the washing. Further, Henry agreed with his sister that the cottage had suffered at their mother's hands, that it had none of the charm it had had when they were growing up. It was no longer a summer place, properly speaking. It was Nashville moved to the mountain. There was no longer the lighting of kerosene lamps at twilight, no more chopping of wood for the stove, no more fetching of water from the cistern. The interior of the house had been utterly transformed. Rugs covered the floors everywhere—the splintery pine floors that Mother so deplored. The iron bedsteads had disappeared from the bedrooms; the living room rockers were now used on the porch. Nowadays, cherry and maple antiques set the tone of the house. The dining room even ran to mahogany. And, for the living room, an oil portrait of the Old Judge had been brought up from the house in Nashville to hang above the new mantelpiece, with its broken ogee and fluted side columns. With such furnishings, Kitty complained, children had to be watched every minute, and could not have the run of the house the way they did when she and Henry and their visiting cousins were growing up. It was all changed.

As for the lot of the two men this summer—well, he should worry about them. When thinking of *them*, he couldn't quite keep it up as the sympathetic old bachelor who took other people's problems to heart. What was one summer, more or less, of not having things just as you wanted them? Next summer, or even tomorrow, or an hour from now, each of them would have it all his way again. And by any reasonable view of things that was what a man must do. A man couldn't afford to get lost in a labyrinth of self-doubts. And a man must be the head of his house. They were the heads of their houses, certainly, and they knew what they wanted, and they had their "values." Both of them knew, for instance, that they hated lying about small domestic matters, and tomorrow, or the next hour, would likely find them both berating their wives for having involved them in something that was "against their principles." Henry sighed audibly, took out another cigarette, then put it back in the package. If they but knew how practiced *he* was—without a wife—at lying about small domestic matters! If they knew his skill in that art, they wouldn't be worrying lest he make some *faux pas* at the breakfast table.

Finally, Henry bestirred himself. He crossed the porch and opened the screen door. Passing from the light of out-of-doors into the long, dark hall, which ran straight through the cottage to the back porch, he was reminded of something that had caught his attention when he was leaving Nashville, yesterday afternoon. As he was entering a railroad underpass, he glanced up and saw that there was something scrawled in large black letters high above the entrance. He had driven through this same tunnel countless times in the past, but the writing had never caught his attention before. It was the simple question

Have you had yours—with the question mark left off. Perhaps
it had been put there recently, or it might have been there for
years. Some sort of black paint, or perhaps tar, had been used.
And it was placed so high on the cement casement and was so
crudely lettered that the author must have leaned over from
above to do his work. Somehow, as he drove on through the
tunnel, Henry had felt tempted to turn around at the other
end and go back and read the inscription again, to make sure
he had read it correctly. He hadn't turned around, of course,
but during the eighty-mile drive to the mountain the words
had kept coming back to him. He thought of the trouble and
time the author had taken to place his question there. He supposed the author's intention was obscene, that the question
referred to fornication. And he had the vague feeling now that
the question had turned up in his dreams last night; but he
was seldom able to remember his dreams very distinctly. At any
rate, the meaning of the question for him seemed very clear
when it came back to him now, and it did not refer to fornication. The answer seemed clear, too: *He* had not had *his.* He
had not had his what? Why, he had not had his Certainty. That
was what the two men had. Neither of the two seemed ideally
suited to the variety of it he had got; each of them, early in
life, had merely begun acquiring whatever brand of Certainty
was most available; and, apparently, if you didn't take that, you
took none at all. Professor Dwight Clark was forever depending upon manuals and instruction books. (He even had an
instruction book for his little Ford, and with the aid of it could
install a new generator.) And Professor Clark had to keep going
back to Europe, had literally to see every inch of it in order
to believe in it enough to teach his history classes and do his
writing. And the judge's garden, while it contained only flowers and combinations of flowers that might have been found
in any ante-bellum garden, was so symmetrically, so regularly
laid out and so precisely and meticulously cared for that you
felt the gardener must surely be some sweet-natured Franken-
stein monster. And the decisions that the judge handed down
from the bench were famous for their regard for the letter of
the law. Lawyers seldom referred to him as "Judge Parker."
By his friends he was spoken of as "Mr. Law." Amongst his
enemies he was known as "Solomon's Baby." . . . But what was

Henry Parker known as? Well, he wasn't much known. He was assistant to the registrar of deeds. He was Judge Parker's son; he was a Democrat, more or less. At the courthouse he was thought awfully well informed—about county government, for one thing. People came to him for information, and took it away with them, thinking it was something Henry Parker would never find any use for. He had passed a variety of civil-service examinations with the highest rating on record, but he had taken the examinations only to see what they were like and what was in them. He did his quiet, pleasant work in his comfortable office on the second floor of the courthouse. The building was well heated in the winter and cool in the summer. Two doors down the corridor from him, Nora McLarnen was usually at her typewriter in the license bureau. Their summers, his and Nora's, were all that made life tolerable. With *his* parents at the mountain, and *her* two sons away at camp, they could go around together with no worry about embarrassing anyone that mattered to them. Their future was a question, a problem they had always vaguely hoped would somehow solve itself. That is, until this summer.

During past summers, Henry had come to the mountain on weekends for the sake of his parents, or for the sake of making sure his mother had no reason to come down to Nashville on an errand or to see about him. But this summer he had come mostly for Nora's sake. Her older boy was now sixteen and had not wanted to go to camp. He had been at home, with a job as lifeguard at one of the public swimming pools. Nora had wanted to devote her weekends to Jimmy. And by now, of course, the younger boy had returned from camp. For Labor Day, Nora had agreed to attend a picnic with the boys and their father—a picnic given by the insurance company for which John McLarnen was a salesman. All summer it had been on Nora's mind that the boys' growing up was going to change things. In the years just ahead they would need her perhaps more than before, and they would become sensitive to her relationship with Henry. She was thinking of quitting her job, she was thinking of letting her husband support her again, she was wondering if she mightn't yet manage to forgive John McLarnen's unfaithfulness to her when she was the mother of two small children, if she hadn't as a younger woman been too intolerant of his coarse nature. She would not, of course, go back to her husband without Henry's consent. But with his consent Henry felt now pretty certain that she would go back to him. They had discussed the possibility several times, very rationally and objectively. They had not quarreled about it, but they seemed to have quarreled about almost everything else this summer. He thought he saw what was ahead.

He was so absorbed in his thoughts as he went down the hall that when he passed the open door to his parents' bedroom he at first gave no thought to the glimpse he had of his father in there. It was only when he was well past the door that he stopped dead still, realizing that his father was on his knees beside the bed. He was not praying, either. He was stuffing something under the mattress. And Henry did not have to look again to know that it was the newspaper he was hiding. He hurried on back to the screened porch, and, somehow, the sight of Dwight, bent over his grapefruit, wearing his traveling clothes—his Dacron suit, his nylon tie, his wash-and-wear shirt—told Henry what it was the judge had to conceal. There would be an article on the society page—something chatty in a column, probably—about those two couples who were driving up to visit the Nathan Parkers, and even a mention of the garden party on Monday.

IV. THE APPLES OF ACCORD

Kitty was determined that the two children should eat a good breakfast this morning, and she saw to it that they did. Mrs. Parker, who had insisted upon preparing and serving breakfast unassisted, was "up and down" all through the meal. The two women were kept so busy—or kept themselves so busy—that they seemed for the most part unmindful of the men. They took no notice of how long the judge delayed coming to the table, or even that Henry actually appeared before his father did. When everybody had finished his grapefruit, and the men began making conversation amongst themselves, the two wives seemed even not to notice the extraordinarily amiable tone of their husbands' voices or the agreeable nature of their every remark. The only sign Kitty gave of following the conversation was to give a bemused smile or to nod her dark head sometimes

when Dwight expressed agreement with her father. And sometimes when the judge responded favorably to an opinion of
Dwight's, Mrs. Parker would lift her eyebrows and tilt her head
gracefully, as though listening to distant music.

Henry's first impression was that there had not, after all,
been a crying need for his presence. His father and his brother-
in-law, who a few minutes before had been hiding behind their
papers to avoid talking to each other, were now bent upon
keeping up a lively and friendly exchange. The judge was seated
at his end of the table, with Henry at his left and with Dwight
on the other side of Henry at Mrs. Parker's right. Across the
table from Henry and Dwight, Kitty sat between the two
children.

The first topic, introduced by Dwight, was that of the rout-
ing to be followed on his trip. Dwight thought it best to go
over to Nashville and then up through Louisville.

"You're absolutely right, Professor," the judge agreed.
"When heading for the Midwest, there is no avoiding Kentucky. But keep *off* Kentucky's back roads!"

Henry joined in, suggesting that the Knoxville-Middleboro-
Lexington route was "not too bad" nowadays.

"I find the mountain driving more tiring," Dwight said
politely, thus disposing of Henry's suggestion.

"And, incidentally, it is exactly a hundred and fifty miles out
of your way to go by Knoxville and Middleboro," the judge
added, addressing Dwight.

Then, rather quickly, Dwight launched into a description
of a rainstorm he had been caught in near Middleboro once.
When he had finished, the judge said he supposed there was
nothing like being caught in a downpour in the mountains.

But the mention of Knoxville reminded the judge of something he had come across in the morning paper, and his amne-
sia with regard to his hogging and hiding the first section was
so thoroughgoing that he didn't hesitate to speak of what he
had read. "There's an editorial today on that agitator up in East
Tennessee," he said. "Looks as though they've finally settled
his hash, thank God."

"I'm certainly glad," said Dwight. It was the case of the
Yankee segregationist who had stirred up so much trouble. Dwight and the judge by no means saw eye to eye on

segregation, but here was one development in that controversy that they could agree on. "That judge at Knoxville has shown considerable courage," Dwight said.

"I suppose so. Yes, it's taken courage," said Judge Parker, grudgingly, yet pleased, as always, to hear any favorable comment on the judiciary. "But it is the law of the land. I don't see he had any alternative."

Henry opened his mouth, intending to say that the judge in question was known to be a man of principle, and if it had gone against his principle, Henry was sure that he would have . . . But he wasn't allowed to finish his thought, even, much less put it into words and speak it.

"Still and all, still and all," his father began again, in the way he had of beginning a sentence before he knew what he was going to say. "Still and all, he's a good man and knows the law. He was a Democrat, you know." His use of "was" indicated only that it was a federal judge they were referring to, and that he was therefore as good as dead—politically, of course.

"No, I didn't know he was a Democrat," Dwight said, hugely gratified.

Here was another topic, indeed. Dwight and the judge were both Democrats, and it didn't matter at the moment that they belonged to different wings of the party. But Dwight postponed for a little the felicity they would enjoy in that area. He had thought of something else that mustn't be passed up. "I understand," he said, pushing the last of his bacon into his mouth and chewing on it rather playfully, "I understand, Judge, that the Catholics have gotten the jump on everybody in Nashville."

The judge closed his eyes, then opened them wide, suppressing a smile—or pretending to. "They've integrated, you mean?"

The machinations of the Catholic Church was a subject they never failed to agree on. "Not only in Nashville," Dwight said. "Everywhere."

"Very altruistic," said the judge.

"Ah, yes. Very."

"If the *other* political parties were as much on their toes as that one, politics in this country would still be interesting."

Henry felt annoyed by this line they always took about the Catholic Church. Perhaps *he* should become a Catholic. That would give him his Certainty, all right. He grimaced inwardly, thinking of the suffering Nora's being a Catholic had brought the two of them. He realized that he resented the slur on the Church merely because the Church was something he associated with Nora. Silly as it seemed, Nora still came in the category of "Nashville Catholics." She was still a communicant, he supposed, and yet this proved that you could be a Catholic without developing the Certainty he had in mind . . . But he didn't try to contribute anything on this subject. He had already seen that contributions from him were not necessary. Perhaps his father and his brother-in-law were no longer consciously trying to keep him silent, but they were in such high spirits over their forthcoming release from each other's company that each now had ears only for the other's voice. And, without knowing it, they seemed to be competing to see who could introduce the most felicitous subject.

From the subject of Nashville Catholics it was such an easy and natural step to Senator Kennedy, and so to national politics, that Henry was hardly aware when the shift came. Everybody had finished eating now. The men had pushed their chairs back a little way from the table. Dwight, in his exuberance, was happily tilting his, though presently Kitty gave him a sign and he stopped. Neither the judge nor Dwight was sure of how good a candidate Kennedy would make. They both really wished that Truman—good old Truman—could head the ticket again. They both admired that man—not for the same reasons, but no matter.

Meanwhile, Kitty and her mother, having finished their own breakfasts and feeling quite comfortable about the way things were going with the men, began a private conversation at their corner of the table. It was about the basket of fruit, which Mrs. Parker still hoped they would find room for in the car. In order to make themselves heard above the men's talk and above the children, who were picking at each other across their mother's plate, it was necessary for them to raise their voices somewhat. Presently, this mere female chatter interfered with the conversation of the men. Judge Parker had just embarked

on an account of the Democratic convention of 1928, which
he had attended. He meant to draw a parallel between it and
the 1960 convention-to-be. But the women's voices distracted
him. He stopped his story, leaned forward and took a last sip
of his coffee, and said very quietly, "Mother, Dwight and I are
having some difficulty understanding each other."

Mrs. Parker blushed. She had thought things were going so
well between the two men! How could *she* help them understand each other?

"Is the question of the basket of fruit really so important?"
the judge clarified.

Mrs. Parker tried to laugh. Kitty rallied to her support. "It's
pretty important," she said good-naturedly.

Henry hated seeing his mother embarrassed. "I imagine it's
as important as any other subject," he said.

The judge's eyes blazed. He let his mouth fall open. "Can
you please tell me in what sense it is as important as any *other*
subject?"

Dwight Clark laughed aloud. Then he looked at Henry and
said, unsmiling, "Politics is mere child's play, eh, Henry?" And,
tossing his rumpled napkin beside his plate, he said, "Oh, well,
we must get going."

"No," said the judge. "Wait. I want to hear Henry's answer
to my question."

"I do, too," said Dwight, and he snatched his napkin from
the table again as if to prove it.

"We're waiting," said the judge.

"At least theirs is a question that *can* be settled," Henry
said, lamely.

"Oh," Dwight rejoined in his most ringing professorial
voice, "since we can't, as individuals, settle the problems of the
world, we'd best turn ostrich and bury our heads in the sand."

"That won't do, Henry," said Judge Parker. "We're still
waiting."

So they *had* needed him, after all, Henry reflected. A common
enemy was better than a peacemaker. He understood now
that his own meek and mild behavior on the front porch had
assured both men that he was not going to spill their beans.
And in their eyes, now, he saw that they somehow hated him

for it. But, he wondered, why had they thought he might do it, to begin with? Why in the world *should* he? Because he was an old bachelor with no life of his own? He knew that both the men, and the women, too, were bound to have known for years about his love affair with Nora McLarnen. But to themselves, of course, they lied willingly about such a large and unpleasant domestic matter . . . He was an old bachelor without any life of his own! Oh, God, he thought, the realization sweeping over him suddenly that that's how it really would be soon, when he told Nora that she had his consent to go back to John McLarnen. He thought of his office in the courthouse and how it would seem when Nora was no longer behind her typewriter down the corridor. And he realized that the rest of his life with her, the part that had been supposed to mean the most, didn't matter to him at all. He couldn't remember that it *once* had mattered, that *once* the summer nights, when his parents and her children didn't have to be considered, had been all that mattered to him. He couldn't, because the time had come when he couldn't afford to remember it. All along, then, they had been right about him. All his hesitations and discriminations about what one could and could not do with one's life had been mere weakness. What else could it be? He was a bloodless old bachelor. It seemed that all his adult life the blood had been slowly draining out of him, and now the last drop was drained. John McLarnen, who could sell a quarter of a million dollars' worth of life insurance in one year, and whose wife could damned well take him or leave him as he was, was the better man.

While Dwight and the judge waited for him to speak up, Henry sat with a vague smile on his lips, staring at the basket of fruit, which was placed on a little cherry washstand at the far end of the porch. He saw the two children, Susie and her little brother, slip out of their chairs and go over to the washstand. He heard his sister tell them not to finger the fruit. Suddenly he imagined he was seeing the fruit, the peaches and apples and pears, through little Dwight's eyes. How very real it looked.

"The basket of fruit," he said at last, "is a petty, ignoble, womanish consideration. And we men must not waste our minds on such." Intuitively, he had chosen the thing to say that would give them their golden opportunity. But before either of the men could speak, he heard his mother say, "Now, Henry," in an exasperated tone, and under her breath.

V. THE JUGGLER

Judge Parker rested his two great white hands limply, incredulously on the table. "Henry," he said, "are you attempting to instruct your brother-in-law and me in our domestic relations?" He gazed a moment through the wire screening out into his flower garden. He was thinking that Henry always left himself wide open in an argument. Even Dwight could handle him.

"If that isn't an old bachelor for you," Dwight said, rising from his chair. He wished Henry would wipe the foolish grin off his face. He supposed it was there to hide his disappointment. He had observed Henry, all during the meal, trying to work up some antagonism between his father-in-law and himself—about the roads, about religion, about politics.

The judge was getting up from the table now, too, but he had more to say. "While we discussed all manner of things that you might be expected to know something about, you maintained a profound silence. And then you felt compelled to speak on a subject of which you are profoundly ignorant."

"'Our universities are riddled with them,'" Dwight said, savoring his joke, feeling that nobody else but Kitty would get it. "Old bachelors who will tell you how you can live on university pay and how to raise your children. I know one, even, that teaches a marriage course."

"*You* might try that, Henry," said the judge. And then he said, "We're only joking, you know. No hard feelings?" He had thought, suddenly, of the extra liquor that Henry was supposed to have brought up from Nashville for the party. Then he remembered that Jane had already asked Henry. It was locked in the trunk of his old coupé.

"Henry knows we're kidding," Dwight said.

Kitty was helping her mother clear the table. Mrs. Parker was protesting, saying that she had nothing else to do all day. Presently, she said to Henry, "Henry, would you take the famous basket of fruit out front? I haven't given up." She *hadn't* given up. How really wonderful it was, Henry thought. And Kitty, too. She could so easily have agreed to take the whole basketful along, could so easily have thrown the whole thing out once they got down the mountain. But it wouldn't have occurred to her.

"Will you gentlemen excuse me?" he said to the two men, smiling at them. And the two men smiled back at him. They felt very good.

When they were all gathered out on the lawn, beside Dwight's car, Kitty looked at her mother and father and said, "It's been a grand summer for us. Just what we needed."

"It's been grand for *us*," Mother Parker said, "though I'm afraid it's spoilt us a good deal. We shouldn't have let you do so much."

"But we hope you'll do it again," Dad Parker said, "whenever you feel up to it."

"I never dreamed I'd get so much done on my book in one summer," said Dwight, really meaning it, but thinking that nobody believed him. He saw that brother Henry was pulling various little trinkets out of his pockets for the children. He had bought them in Nashville, no doubt, and they would be godsends on the trip. Henry knew so well how to please people when he would. He was squatting down between the two children, and he looked up at Dwight to say, "You're lucky to have work you can take all over the world with you."

"Well, I'm sure it requires great powers of concentration," Mother Parker said. She went on to say that she marveled at the way Dwight kept at it and that they were all proud of how high he stood in his field. As she spoke, she held herself very straight, and she seemed almost as tall as her husband. She had had Henry set the basket of fruit on an ivy-covered stump nearby. It was there to plead its own cause. She would not mention it again.

At breakfast, the children had been so excited about setting out for home that Kitty had had to force them to eat. In fact, even the night before, their eagerness to be on the way had been so apparent that Dwight had had to take them aside and warn them against hurting their grandparents' feelings. Yet now, at the last minute, they seemed genuinely reluctant to go. They clung to their uncle, saying they didn't see why they couldn't stay on a few days longer and let him enjoy the tiny tractor, the bag of marbles, and the sewing kit with them. It seemed to Dwight that their Uncle Henry had done his best to ignore the children during all his weekends at the mountain, but now at the last minute he had filled their hands with treasure. And now it was Uncle Henry who was to have their last hugs and to lift little Dwight bodily into the car. When he turned away from the car, with the two children inside it, Henry took Dwight's hand and said, "I'm sorry we never had that chess game. I guess I was afraid you would beat me." It was as if he had seized Dwight and given him the same kind of hug he had given the children. Probably Henry had really wanted to play chess this summer, and probably he had wanted to be affectionate and attentive with the children. But the old bachelor in him had made him hold back. He could not give himself to people, or to anything—not for a whole season.

When finally they had all made their farewell speeches, had kissed and shaken hands and said again what a fine summer it had been, Dwight and Kitty hopped into the little car, and they drove away as quickly as if they had been running into the village on an errand. As they followed the winding driveway down to the public road, Dwight kept glancing at Kitty. He said, "Let's stop in the village and buy a copy of the morning paper."

"Let's not," she said, keeping her eyes straight ahead.

"All right," he said, "let's not." He thought she looked very sad, and he felt almost as though he were taking her away from home for the first time. But the next time he glanced at her, she smiled at him in a way that it seemed she hadn't smiled at him in more than two months. He realized that this summer he had come to think of her again as "having" her father's forehead, as "having" her mother's handsome head of hair and high cheekbones, and as "sharing" her brother's almost perfect teeth, which they were said to have inherited from their maternal grandmother's people. But now suddenly her features seemed entirely her own, borrowed from no one, the features of Dwight Clark's wife. He found himself pressing down on the accelerator, though he knew he would have to stop at the entrance to the road.

In the mirror he saw his two children, in the back seat, still waving to their grandparents through the rear window.

Presently, Susie said, "Mama, look at Uncle Henry! Do you see what he's *doing*." They had reached the entrance to the road now, and Dwight brought the car to a complete halt. Both he and Kitty looked back. Mother and Dad Parker had already started back into the cottage, but they had stopped on the porch steps and were still waving. Henry was still standing beside the ivy-covered stump where the basket of fruit rested. He had picked up two of the apples and was listlessly juggling them in the air. Dwight asked the children to get out of the way for a moment, and both of them ducked their heads. He wanted to have a good look, to see if Henry was doing it for the children's benefit . . . Clearly he wasn't. He was staring off into space, in the opposite direction, lost in whatever thoughts such a man lost himself in.

Dwight put the car into motion again and turned out of the gravel driveway onto the macadam road, with Kitty and the children still looking back until they reached the point where the thick growth of sumac at the roadside cut off all view of the cottage, and the sweep of green lawn, and the three relatives they had just said goodbye to for a while.

Miss Leonora When Last Seen

ERE IN Thomasville we are all concerned over the whereabouts of Miss Leonora Logan. She has been missing for two weeks, and though a half dozen postcards have been received from her, stating that she is in good health and that no anxiety should be felt for her safety, still the whole town can talk of nothing else. She was last seen in Thomasville heading south on Logan Lane, which is the narrow little street that runs alongside her family property. At four-thirty on Wednesday afternoon—Wednesday before last, that is to say—she turned out of the dirt driveway that comes down from her house and drove south on the lane toward its intersection with the bypass of the Memphis–Chattanooga highway. She has not been seen since. Officially, she is away from home on a little trip. Unofficially, in the minds of the townspeople, she is a missing person, and because of events leading up to her departure none of us will rest easy until we know that the old lady is safe at home again.

Miss Leonora's half dozen postcards have come to us from points in as many states: Alabama, Georgia, North Carolina, West Virginia, Kentucky—in that order. It is considered a fair guess that her next card will come from Missouri or Arkansas, and that the one after that will be from Mississippi or Louisiana. She seems to be orbiting her native state of Tennessee. But, on the other hand, there is no proof that she has not crossed the state, back and forth, a number of times during the past two weeks. She is quite an old lady, and is driving a 1942 Dodge convertible. Anyone traveling in the region indicated should watch out for two characteristics of her driving. First, she hates to be overtaken and passed by other vehicles—especially by trucks. The threat of such is apt to make her bear down on the accelerator and try to outdistance the would-be passer. Or, if passed, she can be counted on to try to overtake and pass the offender at first chance. The second characteristic is: when driving after dark, she invariably refuses to dim her lights unless an approaching car has dimmed its own while at least five hundred feet away. She is a good judge of distances, and she is not herself blinded by bright lights on the highway.

And one ought to add that, out of long habit and for reasons best known to herself, Miss Leonora nearly always drives by night.

Some description will be due, presently, of this lady's person and of how she will be dressed while traveling. But that had better wait a while. It might seem prejudicial and even misleading with reference to her soundness of mind. And any question of that sort, no matter what the rest of the world may think, has no bearing upon the general consternation that her going away has created here.

Wherever Miss Leonora Logan is today, she knows in her heart that in the legal action recently taken against her in Thomasville there was no malice directed toward her personally. She knows this, and would say so. At this very moment she may be telling some newfound friend the history of the case—because I happen to know that when she is away from home she talks to people about herself and her forebears as she would never do to anyone here. And chances are she is giving a completely unbiased version of what has happened, since that is her way.

The cause of all our present tribulation is this: The Logan property, which Miss Leonora inherited from one of her paternal great-uncles and which normally upon her death would have gone to distant relatives of hers in Chicago, has been chosen as the site for our county's new consolidated high school. A year and a half ago, Miss Leonora was offered a fair price for the three-acre tract and the old house, and she refused it. This summer, condemnation proceedings were begun, and two weeks ago the county court granted the writ. This will seem to you a bad thing for the town to have done, especially in view of the fact that Miss Leonora has given long years of service to our school system. She retired ten years ago after teaching for twenty-five years in the old high school. To be sure, four of us who are known hereabouts as Miss Leonora Logan's favorites among the male citizenry refused to have any part in the action. Two of us even preferred to resign from the school board. But still, times do change, and the interests of one individual cannot be allowed to hinder the progress of a whole community. Miss Leonora understands that. And she knows that her going away can only delay matters for a few weeks at most. Nevertheless, she is making it look very bad for Thomasville, and we want Miss Leonora to come home.

The kind of jaunt that she has gone off on isn't anything new for the old lady. During the ten years since her retirement she has been setting out on similar excursions rather consistently every month or so, and never, I believe, with a specific itinerary or destination in mind. Until she went away this time, people had ceased to bother themselves with the question of her whereabouts while she was gone or to be concerned about any harm that might come to her. We have been more inclined to think of the practical value her trips have for us. In the past, you see, she was never away for more than a week or ten days, and on her return she would gladly give anyone a full and accurate account of places visited and of the condition of roads traveled. It has, in fact, become the custom when you are planning an automobile trip to address yourself to Miss Leonora on the public square one day and ask her advice on the best route to take. She is our authority not only on the main highways north, south, east, and west of here, in a radius of six or eight hundred miles, but even on the secondary and unimproved roads in places as remote as Brown County, Indiana, and the Outer Banks of North Carolina. Her advice is often very detailed, and will include warnings against "single-lane bridges" or "soft shoulders" or even "cops patrolling in unmarked cars."

It is only the facts she gives you, though. She doesn't express appreciation for the beauty of the countryside or her opinion of the character of towns she passes through. The most she is likely to say is that such-and-such a road is "regarded" as the scenic route, or that a certain town has a "well-worked-out traffic system." No one can doubt that while driving, Miss Leonora keeps her eyes and mind on the road. And that may be the reason why we have never worried about her. But one asks oneself, What pleasure can she ever have derived from these excursions? She declares that she hates the actual driving. And when giving advice on the roads somewhere she will always say that it is a dull and tedious trip and that the traveler will wish himself home in Thomasville a thousand times before he gets to wherever he is going.

Miss Leonora's motivation for taking these trips was always, until the present instance, something that it seemed pointless even to speculate on. It just seemed that the mood came on her and she was off and away. But if anything happens to her now, all the world will blame *us* and say we *sent* her on this journey, sent her out alone and possibly in a dangerous frame of mind. In particular, the blame will fall on the four timid male citizens who were the last to see her in Thomasville (for I do not honestly believe we will ever see her alive here again) and who, as old friends and former pupils of hers at the high school, ought to have prevented her going away. As a matter of fact, I am the one who opened the car door for the old lady that afternoon and politely assisted her into the driver's seat—and without even saying I thought it unwise of her to go. I *thought* it unwise, but at the moment it was as if I were still her favorite pupil twenty years before, and as if I feared she might reprove me for any small failure of courtesy like not opening the car door.

That's how the old lady is—or was. Whatever your first relation to her might have been, she would never allow it to change, and some people even say that that is why she discourages us so about the trips we plan. She cannot bear to think of us away from Thomasville. She thinks this is where all of us belong. I remember one day at school when some boy said to her that he wished he lived in a place like Memphis or Chattanooga. She gave him the look she usually reserved for the people she caught cheating. I was seated in the first row of the class that day, and I saw the angry patches of red appear on her broad, flat cheeks and on her forehead. She paused a moment to rearrange the combs in her hair and to give the stern yank to her corset that was a sure sign she was awfully mad. (We used to say that, with her spare figure, she only wore a corset for the sake of that expressive gesture.) The class was silent, waiting. Miss Leonora looked out the window for a moment, squinting up her eyes as if she could actually make out the Memphis or even the Chattanooga skyline on the horizon. Then, turning back to the unfortunate boy, she said, grinding out her words to him through clenched teeth, "I wish I could *throw* you there!"

But it is ten years now since Miss Leonora retired, and, strange as it may sound, the fact of her having once taught in our school system was never introduced into the deliberations of the school board last spring—their deliberations upon whether or not they ought to sue for condemnation of the Logan home place. No doubt it was right that they didn't let this influence their decision. But what really seems to have happened is that nobody even recalled that the old lady had once been a teacher—or nobody but a very few, who did not want to remind the others.

What they remembered, to the exclusion of everything else, and what they always remember is that Miss Leonora is the last of the Logan family in Thomasville, a family that for a hundred years and more did all it could to impede the growth and progress of our town. It was a Logan, for instance, who kept the railroad from coming through town; it was another Logan who prevented the cotton mill and the snuff factory from locating here. They even kept us from getting the county seat moved here, until after the Civil War, when finally it became clear that nobody was ever going to buy lots up at Logan City, where they had put the first courthouse. Their one idea was always to keep the town unspoiled, unspoiled by railroads or factories or even county politics. Perhaps they should not be blamed for wanting to keep the town unspoiled. Yet I am not quite sure about that. It is a question that even Miss Leonora doesn't feel sure about. Otherwise, why does she always go into that question with the people she meets away from home?

I must tell you about the kind of lodging Miss Leonora takes when she stops for rest, and about the kind of people she finds to talk to. She wouldn't talk to you or me, and she wouldn't put up at a hotel like mine, here on the square, or even at a first-class motel like one of those out on the Memphis–Chattanooga bypass. I have asked her very direct questions about this, pleading a professional interest, and I have filled in with other material furnished by her friends of the road who have from time to time stopped in here at my place.

On a pretty autumn day like today, she will have picked a farmhouse that has one of those little home-lettered signs out by the mailbox saying "Clean Rooms for Tourists—Modern Conveniences." (She will, that is, unless she has changed her ways and taken to a different life, which is the possibility that I do not like to think of.) She stops only at places that are more or less in that category—old-fashioned tourist homes run by retired farm couples or, if the place is in town, by two old-maid sisters. Such an establishment usually takes its name from whatever kind of trees happen to grow in the yard—Maple Lawn or Elmwood or The Oaks. Or when there is a boxwood plant, it will be called Boxwood Manor. If the place is in the country, like the one today, it may be called Oak Crest.

You can just imagine how modern the modern conveniences at Oak Crest are. But it is cheap, which is a consideration for Miss Leonora. And the proprietors are probably good listeners, which is another consideration. She generally stops in the daytime, but since even in the daytime she can't sleep for long, she is apt to be found helping out with the chores. Underneath the Oak Crest "Clean Rooms for Tourists" sign there may be one that says "Sterile Day-Old Eggs" or, during the present season, "Delicious Apples and Ripe Tomatoes." It wouldn't surprise me if you found Miss Leonora today out by the roadside assisting with the sale of Oak Crest's garden produce. And if that's the case she is happy in the knowledge that any passerby will mistake her for the proprietress's mother or old-maid sister, and never suppose she is a paying guest. In her carefully got-up costume she sits there talking to her new friend. Or else she is in the house or in the chicken yard, talking away while she helps out with the chores . . . It is Miss Leonora's way of killing time—killing time until night falls and she can take to the road again.

Miss Leonora is an intellectual woman, and at the same time she is an extremely practical and simple kind of person. This makes it hard for any two people to agree on what she is really like. It is hard even for those of us who were her favorites when we went to school to her. For, in the end, we didn't really know her any better than anybody else did. Sometimes she would have one of us up to her house for coffee and cookies on a winter afternoon, but it was hardly a social occasion. We went up there strictly as her students. We never saw any of the house except the little front room that she called her "office" and that was furnished with a roll-top desk, oak bookcases, and three or four of the hardest chairs you ever sat in. It looked more like a schoolroom than her own classroom did, over at the high school. While you sat drinking coffee with her, she was still your English teacher or your history teacher or your Latin teacher, whichever she happened to be at the time, and you were supposed to make conversation with her about *Silas Marner* or Tom Paine or Cicero. If it was a good session and you had shown a little enthusiasm, then she would talk to you some about your future and say you ought to begin think- ing about college—because she was always going to turn her favorites into professional men. That was how she was going to populate the town with the sort of people she thought it ought to have. She never got but one of us to college, however, and he came back home as a certified druggist instead of the doctor she had wanted him to be. (Our doctors are always men who have moved in here from somewhere else, and our lawyers are people Miss Leonora wouldn't pay any attention to when they were in school.) . . . I used to love to hear Miss Leonora talk, and I went along with her and did pretty well till toward the end of my last year, when I decided that college wasn't for me. I ought to have gone to college, and I had no better reason for deciding against it than any of the others did. It was just that during all the years when Miss Leonora was talking to you about making something of yourself and making Thomasville a more civilized place to live in, you were hearing at home and everywhere else about what the Logans had done to the town and how they held themselves above everybody else. I got to feeling ashamed of being known as her protégé.

As I said, Miss Leonora is an intellectual woman. She seldom comes out of the post office without a book under her arm that she has specially ordered or that has come to her from one of the national book clubs she belongs to; and she also reads all the cheapest kind of trash that's to be had at the drugstore. She is just a natural-born reader, and enjoys reading the way other people enjoy eating or sleeping. It used to be that she would bedevil all the preachers we got here, trying to talk theology with them, and worry the life out of the lawyers with talk about Hamilton and Jefferson and her theories about men like Henry Clay and John Marshall. But about the time she quit teaching she gave up all that, too.

Aside from the drugstore trash, nobody knows what she reads any more, though probably it is the same as always. We sometimes doubt that she knows herself what she reads nowa- days. Her reading seems to mean no more to her than her driving about the country does, and one wonders why she goes on with it, and what she gets out of it. Every night, the light in her office burns almost all night, and when she comes out of the post office with a new book, she has the wrappings off before she is halfway across the square and is turning the pages and reading away—a mile a minute, so it seems—as she strolls through the square and then heads up High Street toward Logana, which is what the Logans have always called their old house. If someone speaks to her, she pretends not to hear the first time. If it is important, if you want some information about the roads somewhere, you have to call her name a second time. The first sign that she is going to give you her attention comes when she begins moving her lips, hurriedly finishing off a page or a paragraph. Then she slams the book closed, as though she is through with it for all time, and before you can phrase your question she begins asking you how you and all your family are. Nobody can give a warmer greeting and make you feel he is gladder to see you than she can. She stands there beating the new book against her thigh, as though the book were some worthless object that she would just as soon throw away, and when she has asked you about yourself and your family she is ready then to talk about any subject under the sun—anything, I ought to add, except herself. If she makes a reference to the book in her hand, it is only to comment on the binding or the print or the quality of the paper. Or she may say that the price of books had gotten all out of bounds and that the postal rate for books is too high. It's always something that any field hand could understand and is a far cry from the way she used to talk about books when we were in school.

I am reminded of one day six or eight years ago when I saw Miss Leonora stopped on the square by an old colored man named Hominy Atkinson. Or his name may really be Harmony Atkinson. I once asked him which it was, and at first he merely grinned and shrugged his shoulders. But then he said thoughtfully, as though it hadn't ever occurred to him before, "Some does call me the one, I s'pose, and some the other." He is a dirty old ignoramus, and the other Negroes say that in the summertime he has his own private swarm of flies that follows him around. His flies were with him that day when he stopped Miss Leonora. He was in his wagon, the way you always see him, and he managed to block the old lady's path when she stepped down off the curb and began to cross the street in front of the post office and had cut diagonally across the courthouse lawn. It was the street over there on the other side of the square that she was about to cross. I was standing nearby with a group of men, under the willow oak trees beside the goldfish pool. Twice before Miss Leonora looked up, Hominy Atkinson lifted a knobby hand to shoo the flies away from his head. In the wagon he was seated on a squat split-bottom chair; and on another chair beside him was his little son Albert. Albert was eight or nine years old at the time, a plump little fellow dressed up in an old-fashioned Buster Brown outfit as tidy and clean as his daddy's rags were dirty.

This Albert is the son of Hominy and the young wife that Hominy took after he was already an old man. The three of them live on a worn-out piece of land three or four miles from town. Albert is a half-grown boy now, and there is nothing very remarkable about him except that they say he still goes to school more regularly than some of the other colored children do. But when he was a little fellow his daddy and mama spoiled and pampered him till, sitting up there in the wagon that day, he had the look of a fat little priss. The fact is, from the time he could sit up in a chair Hominy used never to go anywhere without him—he was so proud of the little pickaninny, and he was so mortally afraid something might happen to him when he was out of his sight. Somebody once asked Hominy why he didn't leave the child home with his mama, and Hominy replied that her hands were kept busy just washing and ironing and sewing for the boy. "It's no easy matter to raise up a clean child," he pronounced. Somebody else asked Hominy one time if he thought it right to take the boy to the square on First Monday, where he would be exposed to some pretty rough talk, or to the fairgrounds during Fair Week. Hominy replied, "What ain't fittin' for him to hear ain't fittin' for me." And it was true that you seldom saw Hominy on that corner of the square where the Negro men congregated or in the stable yard at the fairgrounds.

Before Miss Leonora looked up at Hominy that morning, he sat with his old rag of a hat in his lap, smiling down at her. Finally, she slammed her book shut and lifted her eyes. But Hominy didn't try to ask his question until she had satisfied herself that he, his young wife, and Albert there beside him were in good health, and several other of his relatives whose names she knew. Then he asked it.

"What does you need today, Miss Leonora?" he said. "Me, I needs a dollar bill."

She replied without hesitating, "I don't need anything I'd pay *you* a dollar for, Hominy." Hominy didn't bat an eye, only sat there gazing down at her while she spoke. "I have a full herd of your kind up at Logana, Hominy, who'll fetch and go for me without any dollar bill. You know that."

She was referring to the Negro families who live in the out-buildings up at her place. People say that some of them live right in the house with her, but when I used to go up there as a boy she kept them all out of sight. There was not even a sound of them on the place. She didn't even let her cook bring in the coffee things, and it gave you the queer feeling that either she was protecting you from them or them from you.

"What do you think you need a dollar for, Hominy?" she asked presently.

"I needs to buy the boy a book," he said.

"What book?" It was summertime, and she knew the boy wouldn't be in school.

"Why, most any book," said Hominy. "I jist can't seem to keep him in reading."

Miss Leonora peered around Hominy at Albert, who sat looking down at his own fat little washed-up hands, as if he might be ashamed of his daddy's begging. Then Miss Leonora glanced down at the book she had got in the mail. "Here, give him this," she said, handing the brand-new book up to that old tatterdemalion. It was as if she agreed with the old ignoramus that it didn't matter what kind of book the boy got so long as it was a book.

And now Albert himself couldn't resist raising his eyes to see the book that was coming his way. He gave Miss Leonora a big smile, showing a mouthful of teeth as white as his starched shirt collar. "Miss Leonora, you oughtn't to do—" he began in an airy little voice.

But his daddy put a stop to it. "Hush your mouth, honey. Miss Leonora knows what she's doing. Don't worry about that none." He handed the book over to Albert, hardly looking at it

himself. Those of us over by the goldfish pool were never able
to make out what the book was.

"I certainly thank you, Miss Leonora," Albert piped.

And Hominy said solemnly, "Yes'm, we are much obliged
to you."

"Then move this conveyance of yours and let me pass," said
Miss Leonora.

Hominy flipped the reins sharply on the rump of his mule
and said, "Giddap, Bridesmaid." The old mule flattened its ears
back on its head and pulled away with an angry jerk.

But even when the wagon was out of her way Miss Leonora
continued to stand there for a minute or so, watching the
receding figure of Albert perched on his chair in the wagon
bed and bent over his book examining it the way any ordinary
child would have examined a new toy. As long as she stood
there the old lady kept her eyes on the little black boy. And
before she finally set out across the street, we heard her say
aloud and almost as if for our benefit, "It may be . . . It may be
. . . I suppose, yes, it may be."

II

School integration is not yet a burning issue in Thomasville.
But some men in town were at first opposed to consolidation
of our county high schools until it could be seen what kind
of pressures are going to be put on us. In the past eighteen
months, however, those men have more or less reversed their
position. And they do not deny that their change of mind was
influenced by the possibility that Logana might be acquired
for the site of the new school. Nor do they pretend that it is
because they think Logana such an ideal location. They have
agreed to go along with the plan, so they say, because it is the
only way of getting rid of the little colony of Negroes who have
always lived up there and who would make a serious problem
for us if it became a question of zoning the town, in some way,
as a last barrier against integration. What they say sounds very
logical, and any stranger would be apt to accept the explanation
at face value. But the truth of the matter is that there are people
here who dislike the memory of the Logans even more than
they do the prospect of integration. They are willing to risk

integration in order to see that last Logan dispossessed of his last piece of real estate in Thomasville. With them it is a matter of superstition almost that until this happens Thomasville will not begin to realize its immemorial aspirations to grow and become a citified place.

So that you will better understand this dislike of the Logan name, I will give you a few more details of their history here. In the beginning, and for a long while, the Logan family didn't seem to want to spoil Thomasville with their own presence even. General Logan laid out the town in 1816, naming it after a little son of his who died in infancy. But during the first generation the Logan wives stayed mostly over in Middle Tennessee, where they felt there were more people of their own kind. And the men came and went only as their interest in the cotton crops required. In those years, Logana was occupied by a succession of slave-driving overseers, as was also the Logans' other house, which used to stand five miles below here at Logan's Landing.

Now, we might have done without the Logan women and without the county seat, which the women didn't want here, but when the Logans kept the railroad out everybody saw the handwriting on the wall. The general's grandson did that. He was Harwell Logan, for many years chief justice of the state, and a man so powerful that in one breath, so to speak, he could deny the railroad company a right of way through town and demand that it give the name Logan Station to our nearest flag stop . . . And what was it the chief justice's son did? Why, it was he who prevented the cotton mill and snuff factory from locating here. The snuff factory would have polluted the air. And the cotton mill would have drawn in the riffraff from all over the county . . . Along about the turn of the century it looked as though we were going to get the insane asylum for West Tennessee, but one of the Logans was governor of the state; he arranged for it to go to Bolivar instead. Even by then, none of the Logan men was coming back here very much except to hunt birds in the fall. They had already scattered out and were living in the big cities where there was plenty of industry and railroads for them to invest their money in; and they had already sold off most of their land to get the money to invest. But they didn't forget Thomasville. No matter how far up in the world a Logan may advance, he seems to go on having sweet dreams about Thomasville. Even though he has never actually lived here himself, Thomasville is the one place he doesn't want spoiled.

Just after the First World War, there was talk of our getting the new veterans' hospital. During the Depression, we heard about a CCC camp. At the beginning of the Second World War, people came down from Washington and took option on big tracts of land for "Camp Logan." Very mysteriously all of those projects failed to materialize. Like everything else, they would have spoiled the town. But what else is there, I ask you, for a town to have except the things that tend to spoil it? What else is there to give it life? We used to have a boys' academy here, and a girls' institute, which is where Miss Leonora did her first teaching. They were boarding schools, and boys and girls came here from everywhere, and spent their money on the public square. It wasn't much, but it was *something*.

The boys' academy closed down before I was born even, and there isn't a trace left of it. The Thomasville Female Institute burned in 1922, and nothing is left of it, either, except the crumbling shells of the old brick buildings. All we have now that you don't see on the square is the cotton gin and the flour mill and the ice plant. We claim a population of eighteen hundred, counting white and colored, which is about five hundred short of what we claimed in the year 1880. It has been suggested that in the next census we count the trees in Thomasville instead of the people. They outnumber us considerably and they have more influence, too. It was to save the willow oaks on the public square and the giant sycamores along High Street that someone arranged to have the Memphis–Chattanooga bypass built in 1952 instead of bringing the new highway through town. It was some Logan who arranged that, you may be sure, and no doubt it gladdens his heart to see the new motels that have gone up out there and to know that the old hotel on the square is never overcrowded by a lot of silly tourists.

To my mind, Miss Leonora Logan is a very beautiful woman. But to think she is beautiful nowadays perhaps you would have to have first seen her as I did when I was not yet five years old. And perhaps you would have to have seen her under the same circumstances exactly.

I don't remember what the occasion was. We were on a picnic of some kind at Bennett's Wood, and it seems to me that half the town was there. Probably it was the Fourth of July, though I don't remember any flags or speeches. A band was playing in the bandstand, and as I walked along between my mother and father I noticed that the trunks of the walnut trees had been freshly whitewashed. The bare earth at the roots of the trees was still dappled with the droppings from the lime buckets. My father pointed out a row of beehives on the far edge of the grove and said he hoped to God nobody would stir the bees up today as some bad boys had once done when there was an outing at Bennett's Wood. My father smiled at Mother when he said this, and my guess is that he had been amongst the boys who did it. My mother smiled, too, and we continued our walk.

It was just before dusk. My impression is that the actual picnicking and the main events of the day were already over. I was holding my mother's hand as we came out from under the trees and into the clearing where Bennett's Pond is. Several groups were out on the pond in rowboats, drifting about among the lily pads. One boat had just drawn up to the grassy bank on the side where we were. My mother leaned toward my father and said in a quiet voice, "Look at Miss Leonora Logan. Isn't she beautiful!"

She was dressed all in white. She had stood up in the boat the moment it touched shore, and it seemed to me that she had risen out of the water itself and were about to step from one of the lily pads onto the bank. I was aware of her being taller than most women whose beauty I had heard admired, and I knew that she was already spoken of as an old maid—that she was older than my mother even; but when she placed the pointed toe of her white shoe on the green sod beside the pond, it was as if that lovely white point had pierced my soul and awakened me to a beauty I had not dreamed of. Her every movement was all lightness and grace, and her head of yellow hair dazzled.

The last rays of the sun were at that moment coming directly toward me across the pond, and presently I had to turn my face away from its glare. But I had the feeling that it was Miss Leonora's eyes and the burning beauty of her countenance that had suddenly blinded me, and when my mother asked me fretfully what was the matter and why I hung back so, I was ashamed. I imagined that Mother could read the thoughts in my head. I imagined also that my mother, who was a plain woman and who as the wife of the hotelkeeper made no pretension to elegance—I imagined that she was now jealous of my admiration for Miss Leonora. With my face still averted, I silently reproached her for having herself suggested the thoughts to me by her remark to my father. I was very angry, and my anger and shame must have brought a deep blush to my whole face and neck. I felt my mother's two fingers thrust under the collar of my middy, and then I was soothed by her sympathetic voice saying "Why, child, you're feverish. We'd better get you home."

I must have had many a glimpse of Miss Leonora when I was a small boy playing on the hotel porch. But the next profound impression she made on me was when I was nine years old. One of the boarding students at the Institute had been stealing the other girls' things. It fell to Miss Leonora to apprehend the thief, who proved to be none other than a member of the Logan clan itself—a sad-faced, unattractive girl, according to all reports, but from a very rich branch of the family. She had been sent back to Thomasville to school all the way from Omaha, Nebraska.

Several hours after Miss Leonora had obtained unmistakable evidence of the girl's guilt and had told her she was to be sent home, it was discovered that the girl had disappeared. Word got out in the town that they were dragging the moat around the old windmill on the Institute grounds for the girl's body. Soon a crowd of townspeople gathered on the lawn before the Institute, near to where the windmill stood. This windmill was no longer used to pump the school's water—the school had town water by then—and there was not even a shaft or any vanes in evidence. But the old brick tower had been left standing. With its moat of stagnant, mossy water around it, it was thought to be picturesque.

The crowd assembled on the lawn some fifty or sixty feet away from the tower, and from there we watched the two Negro men at their work in the moat. The moat was fed by a sluggish wet-weather spring. It was about twenty feet wide and was estimated to be from ten to fifteen feet deep. And so the two men had had to bring in a boat to do their work from.

On the very edge of the moat stood Miss Leonora, alongside Dr. Perkins, the chancellor of the Institute, and with them were several other teachers in their dark-blue uniforms. They all kept staring up at the windows of the old brick residence hall, as if to make sure that none of the girls was peering out at the distressing scene.

Presently we heard one of the Negro men say something to the other and heard the other mumble something in reply. We couldn't make out what they said, but we knew that they had found the girl's body. In a matter of two or three minutes they were hauling it up, and all of the women teachers except Miss Leonora buried their faces in their hands. From where we were, the slimy object was hardly recognizable as anything human, but despite this, or because of it, the crowd sent up a chorus of gasps and groans.

Hearing our chorus, Miss Leonora whirled about. She glared at us across the stretch of lawn for a moment, and then she came striding toward us, waving both hands in the air and ordering us to leave. "Go away! Go away!" she called out. "What business have you coming here with your wailing and moaning? A lot you care about that dead girl!" As she drew nearer, I could see her glancing at the ground now and then as if looking for a stick to drive us away with. "Go away!" she cried. "Take your curious eyes away. What right have you to be curious about *our* dead?"

A general retreat began, down the lawn and through the open gateway in the spiked iron fence. I hurried along with the others, but I kept looking back at Miss Leonora, who now stood on the brow of the terraced lawn, watching the retreat with a proud, bemused expression, seeming for the moment to have forgotten the dead young woman in the moat.

How handsome she was standing there, with her high color and her thick yellow hair that seemed about to come loose on her head and fall down on the shoulders of her blue shirtwaist.

Beyond her I had glimpses of the two Negro men lifting the dead body out of the water. They moved slowly and cautiously, but after they had got the girl into the boat and were trying to move her out of the boat onto the lawn, I saw the girl's head fall back. Her wet hair hung down like Spanish moss beneath her, and when the winter sunlight struck it, all at once it looked as green as seaweed. It was very beautiful, and yet, of course, I didn't feel right in thinking it was. It is something I have never been able to forget.

One day when we were in high school, a girl in the class asked Miss Leonora to tell us about "the Institute girl who did away with herself"—because Miss Leonora did sometimes tell us about the old days at the Institute. She stood looking out the classroom window, and seemed to be going over the incident in her mind and trying to decide whether or not it was something we ought to know more about. Finally she said, "No, we'll go on with the lesson now."

But the class, having observed her moment of indecision, began to beg. "Please tell us, Miss Leonora. Please." I don't know how many of the others had been in the crowd that day when they pulled the girl out of the moat. I was not the only one, I'm sure. I think that everybody knew most of the details and only wanted to see if she would refer to the way it ended with her driving the crowd away. But Miss Leonora wouldn't have cared at all, even if she had thought that was our motive. She would have given us her version if she had wanted to.

"Open your books," she said.

But still we persisted, and I was bold enough to ask, "Why not?"

"I'll just tell you why not," she said, suddenly blazing out at me. "Because there is nothing instructive in the story for you."

After that day, I realized, as never before, that though she often seemed to wander from the subject in class, it was never really so. She was eternally instructing us. If only once she had let up on the instruction, we might have learned something— or I might have. I used to watch her for a sign—any sign—of her caring about what we thought of her, or of her *not* caring about her mission among us, if that's what it was. More and more it came to seem incredible to me that she was the same woman I had gone feverish over at Bennett's Wood that time, which was probably before Miss Leonora had perceived her mission. And yet I have the feeling she was the same woman still. Looking back on those high-school days, I know that all along she was watching me and others like me for some kind of sign from us—any sign—that would make us seem worthy of knowing what we wanted to know about her.

I suppose that what we wanted to know, beyond any doubt, was that the old lady had suffered for being just what she was— for being born with her cold, rigid, intellectual nature, and for being born to represent something that had never taken root in Thomasville and that would surely die with her. But not knowing that that was what we wanted to know, we looked for other, smaller things. She didn't, for instance, have lunch in the lunchroom with the other teachers, and she didn't go home for lunch. She had a Negro woman bring her lunch to her on a tray all the way from Logana, on the other side of town. Generally she ate alone in her classroom. Sometimes we made excuses to go back to the room during lunch hour, and when we came out we pretended to the others that we had had a great revelation—that we had caught Miss Leonora Logan eating peas with her knife or sopping her plate with a biscuit. We never caught her doing anything so improper, of course, but it gave us a wonderful pleasure to imagine it.

It was while I was in high school that Miss Leonora inherited Logana. She had already been living in the house most of her life—all of it except for the years when she taught and lived at the Institute—but the house had really belonged to her grandfather's brother in St. Louis. The morning we heard she had inherited the place, we thought surely she would be in high spirits about her good fortune, and before she came into the room that morning one of the girls said she was going to ask her how it felt to be an heiress. It was a question that never got asked, however, because when our teacher finally appeared before us she was dressed in black. She had inherited the house where she had lived most of her life as a poor relation, but she was also in mourning for the dead great-uncle away off in St. Louis. For us it was impossible to detect either the joy over the one event or grief over the other. Perhaps she felt neither, or perhaps she had to hide her feelings because she felt that it was really the great-uncle's death in St. Louis she had inherited and the house in Thomasville she had lost. Our lessons went on that day as though nothing at all had happened.

But before I ever started going to the high school, and before Miss Leonora went there to teach, I had seen her on yet another memorable occasion up at the Institute—the most memorable and dramatic of all, because it was the night that the place burned down. I remember the events of that night very clearly. It was a February night in 1922. The temperature was in the low twenties, and no doubt they had thrown open the drafts in every one of the coal-burning heaters up at the Institute.

The fire broke out in the refectory and spread very rapidly to the residence hall and the classrooms building. Like any big fire, it quickly drew the whole town to the scene. Before most of us got there it was already out of hand. All over town the sky looked like Judgment Day. On the way to the fire, we could hear the floors of the old buildings caving in, one after the other; and so from the beginning there was not much anybody could do. The town waterworks couldn't get enough pressure up there to be of any real use, and after that girl drowned herself they had filled in the old moat around the windmill.

The first thing that happened after I got in sight of the place was that the gingerbread porches, which were already on fire, began to fall away from the buildings. There were porches on the second and third floors of the residence hall, and suddenly they fell away like flaming ladders that somebody had given a kick to. The banisters and posts and rafters fell out into the evergreen shrubbery, and pretty soon the smell of burning hemlock and cedar filled the air . . . The teachers had got all the girls out safely, and the first men to arrive even saved some of the furniture and the books, but beyond that there was nothing to be done except to stand and watch the flames devour the innards of the buildings. This was very fascinating to everybody, and the crowd shifted from one point to another, always trying to get a better view and to see into which room or down which corridor the flames would move next.

Miss Leonora was as fascinated as any of the rest of us, and it was this about her that impressed me that night. It was not till later that I heard about how she behaved during the first phase of the fire. She had dashed about from building to building screaming orders to everyone, even to the fire brigade when it arrived. She would not believe it when the firemen told her that the water pressure could not be increased. She threw a bucket of water in one man's face when he refused to take that bucket and climb up a second-story porch with it.

I didn't see any of that. When I arrived, Miss Leonora was already resigned to the total loss that was inevitable. On a little knob of earth on the north side of the lawn, which people used to call the Indian Mound, she had taken her position all alone and isolated from the general crowd. The other teachers had been sent off with the Institute girls to the hotel, where my mother was waiting to receive them. But wrapped in a black fur cape—it was bearskin, I think, and must have been a hand-me-down from some relative—Miss Leonora was seated on one of the iron benches that were grouped over there on the mound. Her only companions were two iron deer that stood nearby, one with its head lowered as if grazing, the other with its iron antlers lifted and its blank iron eyes fixed on the burning buildings.

She sat there very erect, looking straight ahead. It was hard to tell whether she was watching the flames or watching the people watch the flames. Perhaps she was fascinated equally by both. It was all over for her. She knew that practically nothing was going to be saved, but still she wanted to see how it would go. Now and then a shaft of flame would shoot up into the overcast sky, lighting up the mixture of cloud and smoke above us, and also lighting up the figure of Miss Leonora over on the mound. Some of the women whispered amongst themselves, "Poor Miss Leonora! The school was her life." But if you caught a glimpse of her in one of those moments when the brightest light was on her, it wasn't self-pity or despair you saw written on her face. You saw her awareness of what was going on around her, and a kind of curiosity about it all that seemed almost inhuman and that even a child was bound to resent somewhat. She looked dead herself, but at the same time very much alive to what was going on around her.

III

When Miss Leonora's house was condemned two weeks ago, *somebody* had to break the news to her. They couldn't just send the clerk up there with the notice, or, worse still, let her read it in the newspaper. The old lady had to be warned of how matters had gone . . . We left the courthouse at four o'clock that afternoon, and set out for the Logan place on foot. None of us wanted to go, but who else would go if we didn't? That was how Judge Potter had put it to us. I suppose we elected to go on foot merely because it would take longer to get up there that way.

It was while we walked along under the sycamores on High Street that I let the others talk me into doing the job alone. They said that I had, after all, been her very favorite—by which they meant only that I was her first favorite—and that if we went in a group she might take it as a sign of cowardice, might even tell us it was that to our faces. It was a funny business, and we laughed about it a little amongst ourselves, though not much. Finally, I agreed that the other three men should wait behind the sumac and elderberry down in the lane, while I went up to see Miss Leonora alone.

Once this was settled, the other three men turned to reminiscing about their experiences with Miss Leonora when they were in high school. But I couldn't concentrate on what they said. It may have been because I knew their stories so well. Or maybe it wasn't that. At any rate, when we had walked two blocks up High Street I realized that I was out of cigarettes, and I told the others to wait a minute while I stepped into the filling station, on the corner there, to buy a package. When I paid for the cigarettes, Buck Wallace, who operates the station, looked at me and said, "Well, how did it go? Do we condemn?"

I nodded and said, "We're on the way up there to tell her, Buck."

"I guessed you were," he said. He glanced out the window at the others, and I looked out at them, too. For a second it seemed that I was seeing them through Buck Wallace's eyes—them and myself. And the next second it seemed, for some reason, that I was seeing them through Miss Leonora's eyes—them and myself. We all had on our business suits, our light-weight topcoats, our gray fedoras; we were the innkeeper, the druggist, a bank clerk, and the rewrite man from the weekly paper. Our ages range from thirty to fifty—with me at the top—but we were every one of us decked out to look like the same kind of thing. We might have just that minute walked out of the Friday-noon meeting of the Exchange Club. In Buck Wallace's eyes, however, we were certainly not the cream of

the Exchange Club crop—*not* the men who were going to get
Thomasville its due. And in Miss Leonora's eyes we were a cut
above the Exchange Club's ringleaders, though not enough
above them to matter very much. To both her and Buck we
were merely the go-betweens. It just happened that we were
the last people left in town that the old lady would speak to,
and so now we—or, rather, I—was going up to Logana and tell
her she would have to accept the town's terms of unconditional
surrender.

"You may be too late," Buck added as I was turning away.
I looked back at him with lifted eyebrows. "She was in here a
while ago," he went on to report, "getting her car gassed up.
She said how she was about to take off on one of her trips. She
said she might wait till she heard from the courthouse this
afternoon and again she might not . . . She was got up kind
of peculiar."

When I rejoined the other men outside, I didn't tell them
what Buck had said. Suddenly I mistrusted them, and I didn't
trust myself. Or rather I knew I *could* trust myself to let *them*
have their way if they thought Miss Leonora was about to leave
town. I was pretty sure she wouldn't leave without hearing
from us, and I was pretty sure they would want to head us back
to the courthouse immediately and send official word up there
before she could get away. It would have been the wise thing
to do, but I didn't let it happen.

In the filling station Buck Wallace had said to me that she
was "got up kind of peculiar," and that meant, to my understanding, that Miss Leonora was dressed in one of two ways.
Neither was a way that I had ever seen her dressed, and I
wanted to see for myself. It meant either that she was got up
in a lot of outmoded finery or she was wearing her dungarees! Because that is how, for ten years now, the old lady has
been turning up at the tourist homes where she stops, and
that is how, if you wanted to recognize her on the road, you
would have to watch out for her. Either she would be in her
finery—with the fox fur piece, and the diamond earrings, and
the high-crowned velvet hat, and the kind of lace choker that
even old ladies don't generally go in for any more and that Miss
Leonora has never been seen to wear in Thomasville except by
a very few—or she would be in her dungarees! The dungarees

are the hardest to imagine, of course. With them she wears a home-knit, knee-length cardigan sweater. And for headgear she pulls on a big poke bonnet she has resurrected from some-where, or sometimes she stuffs her long hair up under a man's hunting cap or an old broad-brimmed straw hat. A queer sight she must present riding about the countryside these autumn nights; and if she rides with the top of her convertible put back, as I've heard of her doing in the dead of winter even, why, it's enough to scare any children who may see her and some grown people, too . . . Here in Thomasville, only Buck Wallace and a few others have seen her so garbed, and they only rarely, only sometimes when she was setting out on a trip. They say she looks like some inmate who has broken out of the asylum over at Bolivar.

But that's how she turns up at the tourist homes. If she is with the two old maids at Boxwood Manor or Maple Lawn, she affects the choker and the diamond earrings. She sits down in their parlor and removes the high-crowned velvet, and she talks about how the traditions and institutions of our country have been corrupted and says that soon not one stone will be left upon another. And, still using such terms and phrases, she will at last get round to telling them the story of her life and the history of the Logan family in Thomasville. She tells it all in the third person, pretending it is some friend of hers she has in mind, and the family of that friend. But the old maids know right along that it is herself she is speaking of, and they say she seems to know they know it and seems not to care . . . And if she is with the farm couple at Oak Crest, then she's in her dungarees. She at once sets about helping with the chores, if they will let her. She talks religion to them and says there is no religion left amongst the people in the towns, says that they have forsaken the fountain of living waters and hewed them out broken cisterns that can hold no water—or something like that. And finally she gets round to telling *them* her story, again pretending that it is some friend of hers she is speaking of, and again with her listeners knowing it is herself. The farm couple won't like seeing an old woman wearing dungarees, but they will catch the spirit of her get-up, and they understand what it means. For they have known other old women there in the country who, thrown entirely on their own, living alone and in desperate circumstances, have gotten so they dress in some such outrageous way. And the two old maids probably still have some eye for fashion and they find Miss Leonora pretty ridiculous. But they remember other old ladies who did once dress like that, and it seems somehow credible that there might still be one somewhere.

When Miss Leonora is at home in Thomasville, it is hard to believe she ever dresses herself up so. Here we are used to seeing her always in the most schoolteacherish, ready-made-looking clothes. After the Institute burned, she changed from the uniform that the Institute teachers wore to what amounts to a uniform for our high-school teachers—the drab kind of street dresses that can be got through the mail-order catalogues. Right up till two weeks ago, that's how we were still seeing the old lady dressed. It was hard to realize that in her old age she had had a change of heart and was wishing that either she had played the role of the spinster great lady the way it is usually played or that she had married some dirt farmer and spent her life working alongside him in the fields.

I even used to think that perhaps Miss Leonora didn't really want to go off masquerading around the country—that it was a kind of madness and meant something that would be much more difficult to explain, and that all the time she was at home she was dreading her next seizure. Recently, however, I've come to realize that that wasn't the case. For years, her only satisfaction in life has been her periodic escapes into a reality that is scattered in bits and pieces along the highways and back roads of the country she travels. And what I hope above all else is that Miss Leonora *is* stopping today at Oak Crest or Box-wood Manor and *does* have on her dungarees or lace choker.

But now I must tell what makes me doubt that she is, after all, staying at one of those tourist homes she likes, and what makes me afraid that we may never see her here again.

I left the other men down at the corner of the lane and went up the dirt driveway to Logana alone. Her car was parked at the foot of the porch steps, and so there was no question about her being there. I saw her first through one of the sidelights at the front door and wasn't sure it was she. Then she opened the door, saying, "Dear boy, come in." I laughed, it was so unlike her to call me that. That was not her line at all. She laughed, too, but it was a kind of laugh that was supposed to put me at my ease rather than to criticize or commend me, which would have been very much more in her line . . . I saw at a glance that this wasn't the Miss Leonora I had known, and wasn't one that I had heard about from her tourist-home friends, either.

She had done an awful thing to her hair. Her splendid white mane, with its faded yellow streaks and its look of being kept up on her head only by the two tortoise-shell combs at the back, was no more. She had cut it off, thinned it, and set it in little waves close to her head, and, worse still, she must have washed it in a solution of indigo bluing. She had powdered the shine off her nose, seemed almost to have powdered its sharpness and longness away. She may have applied a little rouge and lipstick, though hardly enough to be noticeable, only enough to make you realize it wasn't the natural coloring of an old lady and enough to make you *think* how old she was. And the dress she had on was exactly right with the hair and the face, though at first I couldn't tell why.

As I walked beside her from the center hall into her "office," her skirt made an unpleasant swishing sound that seemed out of place in Miss Leonora's house and that made me observe more closely what the dress was really like. It was of a dark silk stuff, very stiff, with a sort of middy-blouse collar, and sleeves that stopped a couple of inches above the wrists, and a little piece of belt in back, fastened on with two big buttons—very stylish, I think. For a minute I couldn't remember where it was I had seen this very woman before. Then it came to me. All that was lacking was a pair of pixie glasses with rhinestone rims, and a half dozen bracelets on her wrists. She was one of those old women who come out here from Memphis looking for antiques and country hams and who tell you how delighted they are to find a Southern town that is truly unchanged.

Even so, I half expected Miss Leonora to begin by asking me about my family and then about what kind of summer I had had. "Now, I know you have had a fine summer—all summers are fine to a boy your age," she would say. "So don't tell me what you have been doing. Tell me what you have been *thinking*, what you have been *reading*." It was the room that made me imagine she would still go on that way. Because the room

was the same as it used to be. Even the same coffee cups and
blue china coffeepot were set out on the little octagonal oak
table, beside the plate of butter cookies. And for a moment I
had the same guilty feeling I used always to have; because, of
course, I hadn't been reading anything and hadn't been thinking anything she would want to hear about.

What she actually said was much kinder and was what anybody might have said under the circumstances. "I've felt so bad
about your having to come here like this. I knew they would
put it off on you. Even you must have dreaded coming, and you
must hate me for putting you in such a position."

"Why, no. I wanted to come, Miss Leonora," I lied. "And I
hope you have understood that I had no part in the proceedings." It was what, for months, I had known I would say, and
it came out very easily.

"I do understand that," she said. "And we don't even need
to talk about any of it."

But I said, "The county court has granted the writ condemning your property. They will send a notice up to you
tomorrow morning. You ought to have had a lawyer represent
you, and you ought to have come yourself."

I had said what I had promised Judge Potter I would say; she
had her warning. And now I was on my own. She motioned
me to sit down in a chair near the table where the coffee things
were. When she poured out the coffee into our two cups, it
was steaming hot. It smelled the way it used to smell in that
room on winter afternoons, as fresh as if it were still brewing
on the stove. I knew she hadn't made it herself, but, as in the
old days, too, the Negro woman who had made it didn't appear
or make a sound in the kitchen. You wouldn't have thought
there was one of them on the place. There didn't seem to be
another soul in the house but just herself and me. But *I* knew
that the house was full of them, really. And there was still
the feeling that either she was protecting me from them or
them from me. I experienced the old uneasiness in addition to
something new. And as for Miss Leonora, she seemed to sense
from the start that the other three men were waiting down
the lane—the three who had been even less willing than I to
come, and who were that much nearer to the rest of the town

in their feelings. Several times she referred to them, giving a little nod of her head in the direction of the very spot where I had left them waiting.

"When I think of the old days, the days when I used to have you up here—you and the others, too—I realize I was too hard on you. I asked too much of my pupils. I know that now."

It was nothing like the things the real Miss Leonora used to say. It was something anybody might have said.

And a little later: "I was unrealistic. I tried to be to you children what I thought you needed to have somebody be. That's a mistake, always. One has to try to be with people what they want one to be. Each of *you* tried to be that for me, to an admirable degree. Tim Hadley tried hardest—he went to college—but he didn't have your natural endowments." Then she took pains to say something good and something forgiving about each of the four. And, unless I imagined it, for each of those that hadn't come up with me she gave another nod in the direction of the elderberry and sumac thicket down at the corner.

"We were a dumb bunch, all along the line," I said, not meaning it—or not meaning it about myself.

"Nonsense. You were all fine boys, and *you* were my brightest hope," she said, with an empty cheerfulness.

"But you can't make a silk purse out of—" I began.

"Nonsense," she said again. "It was neither you nor I that failed." But she didn't care enough to make any further denial or explanation. She set her cup down on the table and rose from her chair. "It's been like old times, hasn't it," she said with a vague smile.

I looked away from her and sat gazing about the office, still holding my empty cup in my hand. It hadn't been like old times at all, of course. The room and the silence of the house were the same, but Miss Leonora was already gone, and without her the house was nothing but a heap of junk. I thought to myself that the best thing that could happen would be for them to begin moving out the furniture and moving out the Negroes and tearing the place down as soon as possible. Suddenly, I spied her black leather traveling bag over beside the doorway, and she must have seen my eyes light upon it. "I'm about to get off on a little trip," she said.

I set my cup down on the table and looked up at her. I could see she was expecting me to protest. "Will it be long?" I asked, not protesting.

"I don't know, dear boy. You know how I am."

I glanced at the traveling bag again, and this time I noticed her new cloth coat lying on the straight chair beside the bag. I got up and went over and picked up the coat and held it for her.

On the way out to the car, I kept reminding myself that this was really Miss Leonora Logan and that she was going away before receiving any official notice of the jury's verdict. Finally, when we were standing beside her car and she was waiting for me to put the bag, which I was carrying, inside the car, I looked squarely into her eyes. And there is no denying it; the eyes were still the same as always, not just their hazel color but their expression, their look of awareness—awareness of you, the individual before her, a very flattering awareness until presently you realized it was merely of you as an individual in her scheme of things for Thomasville. She was still looking at me as though I were one of the village children that she would like so much to make something of. I opened the car door. I tossed the bag into the space behind the driver's seat. I even made sure I did the thing to her satisfaction by putting one hand out to her elbow as she slipped stiffly in under the steering wheel.

Neither of us made any pretense of saying goodbye. I stood there and watched the car as it bumped along down the driveway, raising a little cloud of dust in the autumn air. The last I saw of her was a glimpse of her bluinged head through the rear window of her convertible. When she turned out into the lane and headed away from town toward the bypass, I knew that the other three men would be watching. But they wouldn't be able to see how she was got up, and I knew they would hardly believe me when I told them.

I have told nearly everybody in town about it, and I think nobody really believes me. I have almost come to doubt it myself. And, anyway, I like to think that in her traveling bag she had the lace-choker outfit that she could change into along the way, and the dungarees, too; and that she is stopping at her usual kind of place today and is talking to the proprietors about Thomasville. Otherwise, there is no use in anyone's keeping an eye out for her. She will look too much like a thousand others, and no doubt will be driving on the highway the way everybody else does, letting other people pass her, dimming her lights for everyone. Maybe she even drives in the daytime, and maybe when she stops for the night it is at a big, modern motel with air conditioning and television in every room. The postcards she sends us indicate nothing about how she is dressed, of course, or about where and in what kind of places she is stopping. She says only that she is in good health, that it is wonderful weather for driving about the country, and that the roads have been improved everywhere. She says nothing about when we can expect her to come home.

UNDERGRADUATE STORIES
1936–1939

The Party

S USAN BLEW the stray lock of brown hair away from her face, shook it back into its place with a jerk of her head, and gave the pale butter three more vigorous blows. Then she turned the wooden mould upside down on the plate and pushed out a smooth pat of butter. Wiping the sweat from her forehead with the apron she wore over her best summer organdy, she leaned close to the yellow cake to see if the design on top had come out clearly. She saw that half of the sheaf of wheat was missing and, after a hurried glance at Albert, she tried to scratch the missing half from the inside of the mould.

"You should have let Fanny do it. I told you that'd happen," Albert said smiling and went on scraping the mud off his shoes onto the floor of the porch.

"It might have happened to anyone," Susan answered buntly. She picked up the plate of butter and walked to the icebox at the end of the porch. She opened the top just enough to slip the fresh mould in beside two others and then stepped into the kitchen doorway.

"If there's nothing more I can do, Fanny, I'm going around and sit on the front porch and wait for 'em. They'll begin coming before long."

"Yas'm. Soon as I'm th'ough fryin', my end's ready. Better tell Tom t' come freeze this cream, though, ef he got table sat, Miss Sus'n." Fanny did not take her eyes off her clean, black hands that were covering wings, legs and breasts of chicken with flour, but the tone of her voice was respectful.

"And, Jessie," Susan said to Fanny's half-grown daughter, "as soon as you and little Tom get through cutting those biscuits, you better go out to the house and fix up to serve."

Susan and Albert sat on the front porch rocking and fanning. Tom had finished setting the table in the front yard, and everything was ready for the party. Susan's eyes were glued on the dirt road that led to town and on the dome of the court house four miles away. Occasionally out of the corner of her eye she would steal a glance at Albert who was keeping time to the crunching rhythm of the ice cream freezer with his left foot. The expression on his face was tense and preoccupied. He

609

seemed to be trying to catch the song of the frogs in the pond down by the gate, or hear the howling of the hounds over at the Johnsons' farm, or even discern the sound of a horn down in town.

Bill Hardy pressed down on the horn of his automobile and passed the newer car of John Bradley just before he drove off the paved street of the town onto the dirt road. From the back seat the elder Mr. and Mrs. Hardy waved to the two old people on the rear seat of John's automobile.

Mrs. Hardy glanced down at her white muslin dress. She brushed off a few ashes that had blown back from Katherine's cigarette and tugged at the lace dickey in the low neck of the dress with her white, wrinkled hand.

"It's funny," she said, "Clara Bradley and I always come out in our white muslins on the same occasions."

"What difference does it make?" Mr. Hardy rolled up the window so he could light his cob pipe.

"Now, don't go biting Ma's head off, Father." Bill winked at his mother in the little driving mirror above the windshield.

"Katherine," Mr. Hardy said to Bill's wife, "I remember when the parents or grandparents of every one of the boys that will be here to-night lived on a farm and in a house very much like this house Albert Winston lives in now."

Katherine turned around and settled herself facing her father-in-law. For five minutes she listened patiently to the sound of his sonorous voice. When he leaned forward and pointed to a house straight ahead at the curve of the road, she listened carelessly to what he said.

"And that's the Winston place. Albert's family left the country same as everybody else did many years ago. They had tenants and poor kin folks livin' on it off and on for thirty years till Albert got Susan Blackwell to marry him and come live on it with him. But, of course, Bill's told you all about that."

A little black boy dressed in white came around the side of the one-story white house, ran down the dusty drive, and stood breathless at the gate, holding it open and shooing the mare and mule colt away.

The Hardys drove in, all staring over the round muddy pond, through the grove of big maples and oaks, at the two people descending the wooden steps across the front of the porch. The older couple nodded to little Tom and Mrs. Hardy asked that Bill be careful of the colt. Albert motioned to them to pull up on the lawn beside the magnolia tree and he and Susan came forth to greet the first of their guests.

Albert and Bill shook hands strenuously.

"Well, well, Bill. So you're really back in the old town for once."

"Albert, old man."

"And Susan Blackwell, the most popular girl in the county."

"Welcome back, Bill."

"This is Katherine, the city girl who's come to discover the country."

"I certainly am delighted to know you all," the younger Mrs. Hardy said formally. And there was more handshaking and Mr. and Mrs. Hardy kissed Susan.

Then the Bradleys' automobile appeared in the gateway. And a minute later, as the Bradleys were greeting their hosts, Mac Pilcher drove his new car past the whitewashed gateposts and little Tom closed the gate, for all the guests had arrived.

The voices on the front lawn droned out the crunching of the ice cream freezer on the back porch, but to the ears of Mrs. Johnson, back in the guest room, there was little difference between the sounds. The harsh city voices sounded like the grinding of ice and salt and iron. She smiled at the thought and placed her walking shoes on the floor of Susan's guest room closet. She strolled to the center of the room and looked at her new white pumps in the mirror over the mahogany dresser. There she saw the reflection of Susan and her seven feminine guests.

"I didn't hear y'all coming," she said, as she turned around.

"I know." Susan smiled. "We slipped up on you. We met Mr. Johnson in the hall and he liked to scared me to death. I thought it was Albert's Uncle Syd come back after all these years."

Mrs. Johnson laughed and turned her eyes to the three city girls expectantly.

"This is Katherine Hardy, Louise Bradley and Marcia Pilcher," Susan said, "and I think you know these other ladies." She smiled at her mother and the other three women who had come out from town.

Mrs. Johnson could hardly believe that three country boys from Gibson County had won such beauties when they had failed so utterly with our beautiful Susan. Everyone gave a little noiseless laugh and the eyes of the older women wandered about the room and the elder Mrs. Pilcher said, "Your flowers are lovely this year, Susan."

The young hostess thanked Mrs. Pilcher and thanked the Lord for all the rain in the past week, which had saved the flowers.

When the older women had pushed their unruly locks of hair back under their hair nets and the girls had reddened their lips and their cheeks, Susan led them through the front, square parlor with the walnut parlor-furniture and the family pictures all over the walls, into the hall and out into the yard.

Mrs. Johnson greeted Bill Hardy, John Bradley and Mac Pilcher and spoke to Albert and the three older men more casually, but a little more tenderly.

Tom placed the last two plates of cold food on the table and started to help little Tom and Jessie pour the cool, amber tea. Susan Winston stopped him. "Tom, you go bring in the chicken. The children can pour the tea." Little Tom and Jessie looked at each other silently.

"Now, Albert, you seat the party. It's a man's job."

Albert was standing with the young people beside the little weeping willow tree he had set out last spring. He was pulling leaves off, tearing them up, and listening to reminiscences of a picnic the group had been on in a city park.

"I'll tell you," Mac suggested, "let's let all the old folks sit at this end and the young ones at the far end."

"Anything suits me," Albert answered. But anything didn't suit. He did not like the thought of sitting through a whole meal beside any of these strangers. He was trying to shut out of his mind what the amazement of these three old schoolmates of his must have been when they received his letters inviting them down for the party. It was supposed to be a reunion of old friends, but he knew, and they knew, that Albert Winston had never been really intimate with Mac, John and Bill. They had always thought him queer for reading books, but had thought he was going places in this world. When he quit college after two years and came back to live on the farm his worthless

Uncle Syd had deserted, the whole town turned against him. He had overheard John Bradley say to Susan Blackwell the first Christmas after he quit college, "It's just the same thing as his saying to his Uncle Jack, who's supported him since his mother and father died, that he thought his good-for-nothing Uncle Syd's life was more admirable than Mr. Jack's."

If he were to talk to these people much, they would certainly discover why he had invited them.

"Anything suits me."

"Mama," he said to Susan's mother, who had ridden out from town with the Pilchers, "you sit at this end of the table and I'll sit down there."

He offered his arms to Marcia and Katherine and led them across the grass that looked so much greener after last week's rains and especially so at twilight. The grass and a sudden thought of his garden put him in a better humor. And as Tom was passing the chicken, he talked to Marcia and Katherine of his cabbage, onions, and turnips and of the chickens that Susan had taken off that morning.

He looked at Susan. She seemed far away from the chicken yard and the cabbage patch. Her head was thrown back and she was laughing aloud. He did not like her when she laughed aloud for they never laughed aloud together. They only smiled quietly at Fanny's English, or at Jessie's and little Tom's laziness, or at the hen with the little ducks. This loud laughter was too much a part of the days when he was long-legged and awkward and studious and she was popular and no one knew whether she loved Mac or Bill or John.

"Wait! I want that stuffed egg, Tom," Mr. Johnson said, louder than he meant to. Tom was removing the farmer's dinner plate and placing a dish of chocolate ice cream before him. "How I love these devilled eggs," he said pleasantly to Louise Bradley, who sat on his right. She smiled sweetly and nodded to him, but her ears were listening to Bill's story of the hard times he had when he first came to the city after college: how he was determined to go with the right people and how he had to forget one of the most beautiful things in his life when he married Katherine. He was talking low so his wife, across the table, could not hear him, and Louise was listening intently so she could tell Marcia the next day that Bill has practically confessed marrying Katherine for her money, and having left a country sweetheart behind.

"I think the country agrees with you, Susan," John said to Susan. "You're more beautiful than you were as a girl."

"Agree with her?" shouted Mr. Johnson from across the table. "The country agrees with everybody." He announced this so loud that everyone at the table turned and looked at him. "I'll tell you," he was now addressing the table as a whole, "living on a farm isn't what it used to be. Why, with the coming of the radio, electricity, the automobile and good roads we have all the conveniences of town and country. Why, before long it'll be so we can run up and see our friends in the city and be back in an hour or so. A hundred miles to-day is what ten was—"

"Oh, Mr. Johnson!" Susan burst out. Albert looked at her wildly. Everybody had smelt the old fellow's breath and was naturally amused, but had she so completely gone back to her bold girlhood? Was she going to ridicule these simple people for the sake of entertaining these old sweethearts who had come back to see her with their urbane wives? But, "Now," she continued, "I know why you and Mrs. Johnson came in by the back way. And I'll bet you put Mrs. Johnson up to baking me this cake."

"Ladies and gentlemen," she announced, "the old chocolate cake on your plate is mine but the angel food is a complete surprise to me. It was baked by the competent hands of Mrs. Johnson. This is one part of my dinner that I know will be good."

"How can I ever thank you, honey?"

"What a wonderful neighbor to have!" Mrs. Hardy said from the old folks' end of the table. And from the same end came:

"I wish you'd move to town, Mrs. Johnson."

"If only my wife could make friends like you."

"Oh, it's delicious."

The three young women leaned forward and looked at smiling, blushing Mrs. Johnson and smiled at her. Then they resumed their conversation with the men.

"Your food was mighty, mighty good, Susan," said Mrs. Hardy. She stood by the magnolia tree holding Susan's right hand between her two warm wrinkled hands.

"Those butter beans just hit the spot, old girl. You could tell they were raised in the Winston garden." Mr. Bradley patted Susan gently on the back and moved on a few steps to join in the discussion of who was going to ride to town in the Bradleys' car and who was going to ride in the Pilchers' new Ford.

"It's hard for me to believe that those friers were the same baby chickens that you had so much trouble with this spring," Mrs. Bradley went on.

"Now, Mrs. Blackwell, you come with us in Mac's car," Mr. Pilcher put his hand on the arm of Susan's mother.

"The very same ones," Susan said, shaking her head. "Y'all make me feel so good about my dinner." And she kissed Mrs. Hardy good-night.

"Goodbye, Susan, dear. Tell Fanny how I enjoyed the dinner; and let me hear from you tomorrow," Susan's mother said and she kissed her and climbed into the Pilchers' new Ford.

"Good-night, Tom!" Mr. Johnson called to the Winstons' man servant. Tom and Jessie and little Tom were clearing the dishes from the table, disappearing around the corner of the house, and reappearing to get more dishes. The short fat candles were still burning on the table.

"Good-night Albert and Susan. Best time in years."

"Y'all are so sweet."

"Good-night. Remember I'm having the next reunion."

"Come out to see us."

"Goodbye! So long! Little Tom will open the gate for you."

And the Pilcher and Bradley cars drove down the dusty road to town, taking the old folks to the movies.

A loose shutter banged against the house and Katherine seized Albert's hand and held it tightly. "It's only the wind," he said, laughing. "I must fix that shutter after dinner to-morrow." She still held his hand.

The shifting clouds had hidden the moon and made the night dark. Albert and Katherine and Marcia and John and Mac and Louise were sitting on the porch steps. Susan and Bill were sitting on the lawn in two rockers they had dragged from the porch.

"You must come down to see us soon," Katherine said to Albert.

"I hope I can."

"I think you and Susan are two wonderful people."

"Thank you, Katherine."

"What are you working up to, Kitty?" Mac put in.

"Oh, Mac!" Everyone laughed. "I'm working up to the fact that we must all be going if we're to drive that hundred miles home to-night."

"We certainly must."

"We should have started an hour ago."

Everybody started stretching and pulling himself from his seat.

"I'm afraid this has been awfully dull for y'all," Susan said as she followed the three girls up the porch steps.

"Why, it's been charming, delightful."

"It's been such a change from the ordinary, stupid dinner party."

When they were coming back from the guest room with their hats, Albert was across the hall getting a flashlight from the desk drawer in the library.

"Why, this is a lovely room!" Louise exclaimed.

She and Marcia and Katherine looked in at the book cases, the portrait of the little girl with the round arms and legs, the square piano, and the secretary, from which Albert was taking the flashlight.

"I'm going down to the gate and open it for y'all" he announced as he came forward. Susan had gone out on the porch and was telling the men how much she had enjoyed having them and how much like old times it had been. Albert followed the three girls out. He shook hands with everyone and then hurried down to the gate.

Each of the girls kissed Susan goodbye before climbing into the car. The old folks had taken the other two automobiles to town, so all six of them had to crowd into Mac's sedan.

"Good-night, Susan."

"Good-night, Louise. 'Night, Katherine. Goodbye, Marcia. Goodbye, boys."

"It was really so much fun, Susan."

"Goodbye and thanks."

Mac's car crept slowly down the drive. They all shouted

"Good-night!" to Albert and he playfully shone the bright light in their faces as they drove out the gate.

He shut his gate and started back to the house. It was dark, but he knew every step of the walk back to his house, so he turned off the flashlight.

He dreaded to see Susan. He was afraid that when he looked at her eyes they would say that she couldn't go on with this life. Afraid that they would remind him that she had married him only because the other boys had gone away and met city girls and forgotten her. Remind him that he had known that was the reason. And tell him that he had to let her go now.

He was sorry that he had invited them down. But he could not have stood her silence of the last month any longer. He had to know what she was thinking.

Susan was waiting for him in the library. He stopped in the doorway a minute and looked at her, sitting there on the piano stool. She seemed to be a part of the room, but he wondered if she would be there to-morrow. She was playing an old song.

Susan's eyes followed her own hands across the keyboard. When her fingers touched the keys, there was only the sound of the music. No long, red finger nails kept a metallic rhythm on the ivory notes. Her nails were short, clean, shapely and natural: they did not reach the end of her playing fingers. Tomorrow they would be dirty: but these dancing fingers would be busy. Red nails with white pointed tips would be nicer. But then she could not look at them. They could never dig in the black earth. They could never touch the earth. They could never touch anything. They could only play, and play lightly on polished keys.

She banged loudly and really, a discord on the century old piano that had never been out of that room. She jerked up her hands and looked at her strong, round fingertips. She saw that none of the nails were harmed by the vigorous blows.

She whirled around on the piano stool, held her left fist in the palm of her right hand on the lap of her best summer organdy; and Albert looked into her serious face.

"Well, Susan," he said finally.

"Albert," all at once she seemed eager to talk, "they—Mac, Marcia and them—they're a little shallow."

"But they're like little children," she went on.

"And you'd like to be that free and that happy?" he challenged. He was sweating and trembling all over. He put his hand on the door knob to steady himself. At last, his quiet wife was going to speak her mind. She could not escape him now. There would be a scene and she would go away and there would be no unhappy person in the house.

"Yes," she said softly, "I think I might like to be that happy and that free."

"What are you going to do about it?"

"I'm going to sleep and forget them," she said. She kept staring at the design on the carpet.

"And will it be easier or harder after to-night?" He had to know even if she guessed why he had invited the city people down. The sunny morning he had stood with her before Reverend Thomas in the Methodist church, he had wanted to be near her whether she loved him or not. (He believed she would learn to love him and to read his books and to care for his farm. He wanted her because he loved her. To be near her was all he asked.)

"Will it be easier or harder after, to-night?" he said.

She must not have heard him for the wind was blowing that shutter against the house—

Susan stood up. "Good-night," she said. "I'm glad I told little Tom to shut the baby chickens up to-night. I believe it's going to rain to-night."

Albert climbed into bed ten minutes after Susan did, but she was already asleep. He listened to the frogs singing by the pond, and dog howling over at the Johnsons' house and the eleven strokes of the courthouse clock upon the quiet air of the town.

The Lady Is Civilized

THE RAIN was beating murderously down on the black shingles of every farm house and on the cotton, tomato, strawberry fields in Gibson County. The rain was pounding on the muddy Forked Deer River a mile from the present site of Port Gibson. The rain was beating murderously on the slick shingles of every house top, on the scorched grass of every yard and the dried vegetables of every garden in the dark town.

Every church in town had been praying for rain all through July. And everybody that prayed in private had prayed for rain at his bedside. There had been special meetings in the country churches and in the town "nigger" churches to pray for rain; but the white churches in Port Gibson felt that the regular Sunday and Wednesday night prayers were as much as could be expected of them. The town white folks said that since they weren't dependent on the crops they couldn't be expected to pray as often as the farmers and the town niggers all of whom had cotton or tomato or strawberry patches in their back yards.

But the rain was beating down murderously on the gardens and patches in the town. It wasn't the friendly, slow, constant rain they had prayed for. It was a hard, flaying, murderous rain. It was the kind that beats the turnip greens to pieces and washes the plants up from the ground.

Yet, of course, it was better than no rain at all. Everyone agreed to this, and everyone said so to everyone else. This cloud burst had been coming down for only an hour, but there was only one person in Port Gibson who had not said that it was a shame it had to be this kind of rain or that after all it was better than nothing.

The rain was beating murderously on the grass and on the green roof. Because there was no wind, it was not beating on the window pane. Inside the white remodeled house with the green roof and the new white pillars across its front, Beatrice Gray sat knitting beneath a white ceiling fan. All the windows and shades of the white room had been down all day. Beatrice said she was keeping the hot air out. So, sitting there on the chaise longue beneath the ceiling fan, she hadn't known when the rain started. She had not realized that the temperature had changed. She often boasted that she didn't care what the weather did, that she could always keep perfectly comfortable in the privacy of her home.

The electric clock on the new Italian marble mantelpiece chimed hurriedly that it was eleven o'clock. She dropped the knitting in her lap, rested her head on the chair back, and looked at the face of the clock. The second hand spun round and round and her eyes followed its revolution seven times. Then her eyes lifted to the portrait hanging above the marble mantel. She gazed at the picture she had recently had painted from the old photograph of her father. The portrait was just like that photograph; except, of course, she had asked Mr. Guiozeppe if he didn't think it would be nicer to put a tie on the old gentleman. And Mr. Guiozeppe had very definitely thought so. Yes, she gazed at the portrait and thought not of her father but of what an astutely correct picture it was. After all she had rather have it than the ludicrous thing his cousin Lucius Price had done of him in his grey uniform—the one out at her sister's, in the old house. Hers was much better. It was just like the photograph.

She thought how nice it was to have everything she wanted; how fortunate it was that her father had been such a friend of Mr. West and how nice it was that Mr. West had picked her out of the three daughters to befriend in his last years and to leave his fortune to. She thought of those last years of his life.

She remembered there had been one white letter in the black mail box. She took it out and saw that it was for her and that it was from Mr. C. Ely West, W. 63rd Street, New York City. She showed it to Ernest who was leaving for the office and he asked if it wasn't that old bachelor friend of her father who was such a roué. She said that it was, and Tommy or Mettie, one, said that they had never heard grandfather mention his name before he died. And Ernest winked at his wife. He kissed her goodbye and he and the children started off to work and to school.

Beatrice had sat down on the swing on the little square front porch that had been there before Mr. West died and she had had the house remodeled. She opened the letter and read the big writing of the old man.

The letter had said that since Mr. West had no relations of his own to go back to and be near in his old age, he was going to come back and be near the children of his dead friend.

And two weeks later Mr. C. Ely West had arrived on the midnight in Port Gibson.

The great light of the locomotive made Beatrice hide her eyes behind her white leather purse. The midnight train came whistling and puffing around the bend. It slowed up jerkily and noisily before the station with the one bare light over the door-way. A porter climbed off the last car and another handed him down three bags. And a man in a grey checked suit and a derby stepped down on the white gravel and greeted his friend's three daughters and their husbands. His voice was loud and north-ern, and he had said a lot before the train began to jerk out of the station. When the black locomotive had disappeared and they started for the cars, Beatrice had decided that she did not like him and had reminded herself that he was a very rich man. She took his arm, which he twice raised to twist his tiny dyed moustache, and walked with him over the white gravel to her automobile.

They drove him through the dark town, around the court house square to the Mary Anne Hotel. Soon after he had climbed off the train he had told them that he would not stay at anyone's house and Beatrice realized that Ely West did not intend to become a member of anybody's family. He had not changed since the last time she saw him. And he did not look over fifty. Ernest said that he still had the fifty disease along with the disease of the heart.

Mr. West spent his first day in Port Gibson with Beatrice's sister Jane, out at the old house. The second day he spent with her sister Mettie over on Church Street. And the third day Beatrice asked him to come spend with her. There was so much about old times to talk over. And Mr. West knew a lot of fine things their father had done that he expected they had never heard of.

The children were at school and Ernest had long since left for the office. The house was clean and from the sitting room Beatrice could hear Sana singing as she clattered the breakfast dishes into the sink.

She looked out the open window and saw Mr. C. Ely West strutting up the brick walk outside the iron fence that surrounded the yard. He was whistling, "Sister, Take a Walk With Me." When he had closed the iron gate behind him he stooped to pick a chestnut burr off the grass. He was a young looking man, but it was the careful stoop of an old man with a disease of the heart.

Sana showed the strange man into the sitting room and Beatrice rose from the platform rocker to shake his hand and tell him how good it was to see him. Ely West tossed his derby on the top of the folding bed and wondered when he had seen one of those. Beatrice said she thought it had belonged to Ernest's grandmother, but Mr. West knew the bed wasn't that old and he knew that Beatrice didn't think that it was. She blushed a little when he confronted her with that.

Ely said it was the sweet blush of a school girl and Beatrice asked him if he had ever seen the picture album her father used to keep.

She took the metal-backed album from the lower part of the desk and carried it to the leather couch where her visitor sat. Sitting beside him she looked at the outline of a rose scratched on the back and the name "Thomas Harwood" in the lower left corner. She opened the book to the first picture. It was her mother dressed in light taffeta with a bustle, and a saucy hat with primroses on it, leaning against an iron gate. Mr. West said that she had hated him. Beatrice turned the page. And there were she and Jane and Mettie in the pony cart.

Mr. West took Beatrice's hand in his. He must have felt it stiffen and then relax. For she looked at his pouchy face, his dyed, twisted moustache, his big round stomach. The feel of his moist hand on her own sickened her. Then she thought of something else and the future and the will of Mr. Ely West. And she closed the album.

Sitting there in the redecorated sitting room beneath the ceiling fan a hundred scenes were flashing across the mind of Beatrice. Once she was sitting beneath the chestnut tree with Ely. Then she was driving over to Dyersburg with him to see an old friend who they found had moved away. Again they would be talking in the sitting room. Once they were down at The Lake on the porch of the club house while the others were out fishing. Then they were on the Methodist picnic out at Pea Ridge. Sometimes the children or Ernest were present, but never her sisters.

Then she saw the white, still snow that was on the ground the Christmas Eve before Ely dropped dead on the hotel porch. She saw him coming through the iron gate with the package of presents under his arm. She saw him distributing them before the Christmas tree in the sitting room and then rubbing his moist, wrinkled hands together before the fire and smiling that self-satisfied smile. Then she saw him go out into the gentle snow that had started falling. And clearest of all was the last sight she ever had of him alive; pushing through the gentle fall of snow, with his fur collar turned up all around his ears and his derby almost meeting it.

Before Ely had closed the iron gate Ernest had sent the children off to bed. He waited while from the sitting room window she watched the old bachelor fade into the white speckled night. He seemed to know just how long it would take Ely to get out of sight. For when his wife could see the round figure no longer and felt lost way out there in the snow somewhere, he suddenly drew her back into the bright, warm sitting room. He made her feel the presence of that room and of himself more distinctly than she had ever felt anything. He spoke one word to her. He had spoken it many times before, but always in an affectionate, admiring tone. He had always seemed to be caressing the word as much as herself. But he spoke it now in a tone she had not known he was capable of assuming. It was almost dramatic; as if he had practiced saying it that way for years and years just to get the right effect. He spoke in a deep, resonant voice and threw all of the force into the first syllable.

"Beatrice."

The sound of his voice in that room with the Christmas tree and the wrapping paper and the rocking chairs and the clock with the swinging pendulum had never died in her ears. Whenever she was in that room and there was a silence, she could hear him pronouncing her name as he did that night. No matter how many people were in the room, if there was a moment's silence and her mind wandered she could hear him saying her name, putting all the emphasis on that first "ee" sound. She had had the room redecorated, the whole house redecorated, yet she could still hear his saying it in that bright little room on Christmas Eve.

"Beatrice."

She had whirled around and faced him, smiling fixedly. Determined to tell him before he asked, she produced the diamond pin that Ely had slipped into her hand when he came in the door. She knew Ernest had seen the bungling old man and she knew that at last he suspected. She called Ely a timid old dear and said she had never had an uncle be as good to her. And Ernest just looked silently at the glittering pin. He saw the green, yellow, and red lights on the biggest Christmas tree they had ever had reflected in the diamonds.

He turned his back to her and to the tree and stared at the four black stockings that hung from the wooden mantelpiece. He asked her if she loved Ely. And so there was no use denying what had gone on. She saw that he was not going to leave her, so she had to make him know the truth; that C. Ely West was revolting to her; that she had to be nice to him because of the will. She had never cared for him. But for all she could scream she could not make her voice present in that room as his one word had been.

Then he said in such a quiet voice that she could hardly hear him—for he still stared at the four black stockings—that he believed her, that it had been that that he had feared. He said he would not have minded what she had done to him for the love of another man.

She didn't quite understand what he said, but it was something to that effect. But anyway he went up and tore his stocking down from the mantel and threw it on the red coals in the grate and it blazed up. He watched the blaze die down, and then he went up stairs.

The next morning, of course, there was Ely's awful death, and Ernest was tender and kind to Beatrice for a month or so. But he never touched her and they never talked when they were alone.

The second hand of the electric clock on the marble mantel spun foolishly round and round, but the minute and hour hands told Beatrice that it was a quarter past eleven o'clock.

And Ernest had not come home from the office and Sarah had not come back to stay with her till he got home.

Sarah had gone home after dinner to give Elijah his dinner. She was supposed to come back and stay with Beatrice, however, because when Ernest worked at night on a case he was sometimes twelve or one o'clock getting home. But the rain had set in after dinner, and nobody could have made it from nigger town up to the Grays' house.

But Beatrice was not afraid. In her house she was safe from the weather and the world. She was so unafraid that she grew sleepy when she saw the time, and she got up to go to bed.

She was leaning over her knitting bag putting her knitting away when she heard the voice of a woman somewhere outside calling her name. She straightened up and listened, her head cocked to one side.

"M'ss Be-atrice! M'ss Be-atrice!" it called again. It was Sarah's voice. Beatrice went to a front window of the sitting room and looked out. Sarah waved to her from a model T Ford whose motor was still running.

"Have the do' op'n. I' comin' in."

Beatrice rushed into the hall, laughing. She knew exactly what had happened. Sarah had gotten a ride with someone but she was afraid to wait outside alone while Beatrice came to the door, and Sarah didn't want to pound on the door because Sarah would never pound on a door again after that horrible night the summer after Mr. West dropped dead.

Beatrice flung the door open and looked out into the cold, hard, murderous rain. She gasped for breath. The rain was falling just as it had that night last summer. And then Sarah rushed in past her with the newspaper over her kinky head. Beatrice nearly fainted and she thought Sarah would have, if niggers did faint.

It was so much like that night that neither of them would look at the other, and Sarah ran straight back to her room behind the kitchen. Beatrice sat down on a little hall chair and thought about that night and all that went with it. In her reflective mood she went over the whole thing in her mind.

She recalled that morning when Sana came in to get up the grocery list and said that Irvin had left her. She said it so casually that Beatrice hardly noticed what she had said. But when

Irvin didn't come to work the next two mornings, she asked Sana if he was quitting his job and if she had better get some-one else.

"I gues y' had better, M'ss Be-atrice. They're sayin' he's lef' town. Ain't nobody seen him in three days."

When Ernest came home that night he said from behind his paper, on the front porch, "There's a lot of funny talk going on about Irvin down town."

"Sana says they don't know where he is."

Ernest put his paper down and looked at Beatrice over his reading glasses. "They're saying he's dead, down town."

"What makes them think so?" she asked. She was used to such rumors about niggers.

"That kind of talk's been going round nigger town for two or three days. The sheriff thinks maybe there's something in it. He came over to talk to me about it today."

Beatrice looked up from her knitting. This was the most talkative Ernest had been since Christmas.

"It seems," he continued, "that the sheriff himself saw Irvin as he turned off the square 'bout eight o'clock Monday night and Sana says he never came home."

He sat up on the edge of his chair and whispered. "But the sheriff says he was carrying a new skillet in his hand, and he went down to see Sana last night and there was a new skillet on the stove, and that Jake Roberts was there with Sana. He thinks Jake's living with Sana now."

Sarah, who was the house girl then, stepped out on the porch and said that dinner was ready.

"I only told you, so that whatever happens won't be such a shock to you," he added abruptly as they went in to dinner. Beatrice understood that she was not to think this little con-fidence meant he was going to be like he had been before Mr. West came.

But a week went by and Sana quit mentioning Irvin, and everybody knew she was living with Jake. Jake quit his job and stayed around her house to answer questions that people came and asked.

The sun had beat down on Port Gibson without rest during that July. The nigger churches were all having special meet-ings to pray for rain and for Irvin Thomas. One congregation offered to come over and work his cotton patch for Sana. But she had thanked them and the next morning set Jake Roberts to working the patch.

He finished working it about noon just when the sky began to cloud up a little. It began drizzling about two o'clock and rained a little off and on all afternoon.

Sana came in about seven o'clock and said that Sarah had come home early and fed Elijah his supper and was going back and do the dishes and stay with Miss Beatrice while Mr. Ernest was at his office. The rain started pouring down in a little while. It seemed to get harder and harder. Everyone said it was a cloud burst, but it lasted too long for that.

It poured and beat and poured until eleven o'clock. Then it suddenly stopped short, without gradually drizzling off the way rain does. Ernest had come home earlier, so Sarah decided to try to make it to her house before the rain started again. She took a newspaper with her and the jar of sweet pickles Beatrice had given her.

As Sarah turned off the square toward nigger town a few drops of cool rain began to fall and she started running. She decided that it would be shorter to cut through the backs of the houses on Pierce Street and go in the back way of her own house.

By the time she got in back of Aunt Easter Sellars' old cabin the drops were falling steadily, so Sarah hurried still faster over the fence stile into Sana Thomas' cotton patch. The rain kept falling harder and she was running against the rows of cotton. Suddenly she stumbled over something. And she fell in the mud there in Sana's cotton patch. She was wet and dirty and tired and she reached for a cotton stalk to raise herself up by. Her hand hit on human flesh.

She looked beside her and saw that she held in her own brown hand a black foot and leg. Then she saw the half burned head of Irvin Thomas. The rain was beating fiercely down on her and on the parts of the body.

Pulling her newspaper over her head, the soaked, shaking little nigger headed back for Mr. Ernest's house through all the murderous rain.

"M'st' Ernest! M'st' Ernest!" came the desperate cries to Beatrice's half sleeping ears. And there was pounding, pounding,

pounding on the wet front door. She was down stairs in ten seconds and had flung the door open. Sarah rushed in past her, still holding the paper over her head, and threw herself at the feet of Ernest, then standing at the foot of the stairs.

"I found Irvin Thomas," she wailed. "I found his legs and his arms and his body and his haid in Sana's cotton patch. All cut up! The rain, the rain's done washed 'im up." And she lay there on the floor weeping and beating on the floor and praying while Ernest went up stairs and put his clothes on over his pajamas. And he went out in that rain and cranked the car and drove to the sheriff's office.

The rain was beating murderously down on the slick black shingles of Sana's unpainted house. A wind had blown up from the north and the hanging baskets of Wandering Jew on Sana's porch were swinging in the wind. Sana's house was dark and there was only the sound of the rain thumping on the roof.

Ernest and the sheriff and three other men hopped out of the Ford with the black curtains. Ernest and the sheriff ran up the wooden plank walk to the porch with the hanging baskets. The three other men who wore long, black rain coats and rain hats and carried shovels trotted in the mud around the side of the house. All of the men held great, strong flashlights that shone through the thick falling rain.

"Sana Thomas, open this door in the name of the law!" the sheriff called out in his robust voice. He thought the rain would drown it out from the ears of the neighbors. But the lights in all the houses in that end of nigger town began to flicker on and off like lightning bugs in the rain. And half-dressed niggers swarmed the mud street beneath umbrellas and rain coats and newspapers.

The latch on the thin door broke easily under the pushing shoulders of the two white men. Ernest fell forward and the ray of his light lit on a glazed two-color print of Judas Iscariot selling out to the chief priests. He turned the light about the hall between the two rooms of the house. It now lit on a glazed two-color print of Judas hanging over a cliff from the bough of a tree. He turned it still again and it lit on the third print. This was Jesus forgiving the woman taken in adultery.

The sheriff's robust voice was commanding again. He stood in the doorway to Sana's bedroom shining his white light in their black faces. Ernest stepped in the doorway beside him and shone his light on the piteous couple.

Jake was propped up on his elbows and the white sheet had slipped down and exposed his broad, black, hairy chest. The muscle in his big left arm quivered and he chewed on the right side of his lower lip.

Sana lay on her stomach hugging Jake's left arm. Her face was hidden in the pillow. She was crying and praying softly and monotonously. Ernest thought she sounded like his Catholic grandmother the day she died. He could not hear what she was mumbling, but he knew she was praying.

"I reckon maybe y'all better get somethin' on and come along with me," the sheriff said casually.

Sana looked around over her brown shoulder at the blinding light. She could not see who was with the sheriff. He handed Ernest his pistol, went over and dragged her from her bed with Jake and wrapped a dirty wool kimono around her.

"Ernest, you bring Jake, will you?" he said.

The face of Sana Thomas had been fixed and resigned. But when she heard the name "Ernest" every muscle in it seemed to break loose and she broke loose from the tall white man and ran toward her master. The sheriff did not understand her move. He followed her and held her arms behind her while she screamed up into Ernest's face.

"Mist' Ernest, I ain't a bad nigger. You know that. Jake and me had to have each other. We just had to. White folks don't know what that means. But honest to Gord we did—we had to. Irv wouldn't let us. He said he'd kill us if he found us together—and he would 'ave. So we killed him with that ax and tried to burn *him*, but we couldn't so we buried him out there!"

She looked out the back window and saw the flashlights of two of the men in the cotton patch.

Ernest motioned to the sheriff to let her arms go.

"It was us or him, Mist' Ernest! Jake and me was gonna have each other. We had to."

Ernest looked into her big twitching eyes. "What do you want me to do, Sana?"

"Deefend us! Don't let 'em hang us," she screamed, and she took hold of his left sleeve.

The sheriff smiled and told Jake to get his clothes on. Ernest looked out into the hall. One of the other men had come in and lit the kerosene lamp. Ernest looked at the picture of Judas Iscariot selling out and at that of the woman taken in adultery being forgiven.

Beatrice didn't go to the trial at all. But of course there was so much talk about it that she knew everything that went on, though Ernest would never discuss it after her begging him not to take the case. Her friends would come to her and ask why her husband had defended that low-down pair. Beatrice would gossip with them about it and say she didn't understand it and say what a good nigger Irvin had been. Most of the women were indignant and said that Ernest was almost condemning all of the virtuous black and white women in the town, that it was really a reflection on Beatrice. But Beatrice only smiled vaguely and said she didn't think it was that serious and that Ernest had just gotten interested in the case was all.

The Life Before

ON THE corner of two of those old streets down town that have never been widened but on which street cars and motor busses clank and barely manage to turn the corners without scraping the parked automobiles the great, square "Hotel Hensely" was still standing with its eight story plaster facade of Gothic arches now the shade of a grey alley cat. This part of town had not sunk to the status of a slum section. People would just say that there was nothing down there anymore. On the corner diagonally across from the hotel was what was once known as the Confederate Bank Building, now, with all the white marble torn out, a wholesale poultry store. On one of the other corners of the intersection was a Jewish costumer's shop. The little store space on the fourth corner changed occupants so often that it would be laborious to ascribe any particular business to it. And up each street ran a row of second hand book shops, restaurants, and cheap clothing stores.

"Hotel Hensely," or The Hensely House as natives, despite its electrical sign reading "Hotel Hensely," still called it with some affection and pride, had seen its last day of fashion nearly twenty years before when the new hotels over on the capital square had climbed fifteen and sixteen stories into the skyline. Now old men in shirtsleeves and galluses filled the green benches on the sidewalk before the hotel, and the doorman was a negro in similar attire. Through the lobby moved weary strangers carrying their own shabby baggage, and the clerk at the desk was a fat, bald-headed man that welcomed the guests with no smile, often pointing out to them with his pen a notice that read: Advance Payment Preferred.

Around the lobby ran the colonnade of stout marble pillars, and half way up was the little used and ill-lighted gallery. At five in the afternoon the transient guest in the lobby might notice the unfriendly clerk gazing up at this balcony. Finally he could see him nod at the figure of a woman who came out of the shadows up there and took her seat by the balustrade. And so generous a smile would come over his face that it seemed he had been hoarding something in his nature to give it all to this smile. It wasn't the sort of smile that he gave to the new girls in the pool room at the end of the lobby. It was the sort that a guest could never suspect his hard physiognomy capable of softening into. And there was but one other time at which this smile could be seen on the face of the clerk. That would be some ten or fifteen minutes later when a soft featured man in his fifties, wearing a black felt hat and a dark suit, would appear in the doorway of the lobby where he waited for the woman on the gallery to join him. When the couple had passed through the revolving door out into the street, the smile would fade from the face of the clerk; and he would again be the merciless clerk pointing to the notice: Advance Payment Preferred.

When the couple would return at seven or eight in the evening, their presence in the lobby was the cause of no such metamorphosis in the night clerk's face. He was a younger man, and he gave up the key to Room 416 as impersonally as he would any other key and answered with abruptness the gentleman's usual question as to whether or not there were a package for Mr. or Mrs. Powell.

If there were a package for Mr. or Mrs. Powell, it was always a book or perhaps two books together in a publisher's mailing box. And the couple would leave the desk examining together the new book which one of them would review on the literary page of the Sunday edition of *The Herald-Democrat*. Sometimes they would laugh over the book. Again one would read the first page aloud to the other as they waited for the elevator. Sometimes they would bring the book back to the desk and together plot a curt, sometimes saucy note for the Sunday Editor and leave a dime with the night clerk, asking that a bellboy return the book to the *Herald-Democrat* office "the first thing" in the morning.

Mr. and Mrs. Powell had the old Governor's Suite on the fourth floor. Beside the little vestibule with the straight chair and the old-fashioned card table with one leaf propped against the wall their apartment consisted of three square rooms and a bath. One, the corner room, was their parlor. The other big room was their bed room, and the small room was furnished as a study, a room which they never used. The apartment had stood in disuse for a decade before it was assigned to the Powells by the clerk. He had assigned it to them as a surprise, as a wedding gift, at the time when Mr. Powell had brought his bride to The Hensely House.

Mr. Powell had lived, a bachelor, at The Hensely House for ten years before his marriage. And, excepting his year of courtship, he had kept, as a bachelor, approximately the same hours that he and Mrs. Powell now kept and entertained as few friends in his room. He had come here to live as a young man in his early thirties when The Hensely House was only beginning to "slip." He had come back then, not to his native city but to the largest town in his native state, from a six-year stay abroad. He had set up at The Hensely House because, being of a well-to-do Southern family, he had never thought of stopping at another place; and until the time of his marriage he simply never thought of moving out.

During his first ten years there he might have watched, had he been one of the guests who spent his evenings in the lobby, a continuous decline in the quality of the patronage that the old hotel received. As it was, the changes came to him as a series of shocks. They would be brought to his attention by incidents in the elevator, by the appearance of characters especially typical of their level of society, and finally by a fight between two salesmen in the lobby over a woman who he was told was "upstairs." And the decline would be brought to his attention by notices in the newspaper of the hotel's changing hands again and again.

Several years before his marriage he noticed what he believed to be the last step in the degradation of the hotel. It lay in the appointment of a man who had once carried trunks in the hotel and later been in charge of the pool room to the position of manager and clerk. Heretofore the hotel had retained, if not the old-fashioned obsequious, at least a moderately courteous clerk at the desk. Now management and clerkship in the hotel required physical force; and Mr. Powell knew from where the new power had been drawn. As he came and went through the lobby he could but notice the rough treatment that guests received, and he one day saw the new clerk personally eject a drunken couple and order their luggage to be locked in the storage room. Therefore he carefully avoided any conversation with the former porter.

One afternoon, however, he had been forced to ask the clerk to call his room the moment a package came from *The*

Herald-Democrat. And the clerk had replied so courteously that Mr. Powell, who had fixed his eyes on the elevator, quickly looked at the man before him and said with real gratitude, "You're very kind."

The clerk had not let it go at that. He told Mr. Powell that this was no service at all and that any service that the management could do him was a pleasure. And he took that opportunity to ask Mr. Powell if he remembered him around the hotel through the years. It delighted the clerk that Mr. Powell recalled that he had carried his trunk the day he moved to the hotel. To make amends for his negligence of the clerk whom he had thought so inhuman he told him that he was due respect for having risen from the bottom to the top "in the establishment."

"I'm afraid not," said the clerk. "When I was a boy around here I used to think I would push myself up to the running of this hotel. That is, when it was full of the likes of you. But it's more like 'the establishment' has come down to my size," he said.

Mr. Powell smiled sympathetically, shook his head and started slowly toward the elevator. But the clerk moved behind the counter along with him. He was still talking, and talking as though it were his one chance to speak this. Mr. Powell stopped, and the clerk told him that his presence sometimes made it possible to imagine that he hadn't "missed the boat, after all."

Half an hour later Mr. Powell's books were delivered to his room; and though the clerk never spoke his feelings to him again, by his very smile Mr. Powell was never allowed to forget the difference between himself and the other guests at the hotel.

Mr. Powell's enquiry regarding larger quarters in the hotel was answered with courtesy and without show of surprise at the desk. But the night he brought home Mrs. Powell they both recognized their apartment as the famous old Governor's Suite with the fourposter bed and the green drapes. They very easily reached the agreement that there was nothing to do but to accept their "sumptuous" quarters. They had considered several other places in town within their price range but had at last decided on The Hensely House as the most convenient to their pursuits in life and as, what was of admittedly great importance to each, the most private. Consequently they settled there to what Mrs. Powell's spinster sister and her only at-all-intimate friend together described as "an obscure, if comfortable, old age" before either was yet forty-five.

The callers that the couple generally received in the first years of married life were five. There was first Mrs. Powell's spinster sister who died a few years after their marriage, thus adding a little to their small income. There was the elderly state librarian and his wife; but the librarian, too, had died, and they soon lost contact with his aging wife. The Sunday Editor of *The Herald-Democrat*, a comfortably-fixed Jew, called several times a year and promised to bring his wife with him the next time, and his daughter who was an artist. And finally and always there was the one intimate friend that Mrs. Powell had at the time of her marriage, a tall red-headed woman who managed the city's only large auditorium, still called The Opera House. She was the most infrequent caller of them all (though she lasted through the years), but she always sent to them complimentary tickets to whatever performance was at her Opera House.

Most of Mrs. Powell's mornings were spent in the New City Academy of Art where she was allowed space for her work. Some, however, she spent in the City Library doing her research. When she had first met Mr. Powell she had told him that she was the missing link between the days of heraldry and these days of machinery. "I dress myself," she had said, "on the money I make discovering and copying the ancient coats of arms for those on top in town each year." Then with her hand and her smile she had called his attention to the simple dress she wore as evidence of the very modest returns of her business. He had looked with honest approval at the dress and remarked on its pleasing pattern and the taste with which she wore her jewelry.

Her jewelry had later become a subject for much discussion, for she and her sister had a great store of their mother's stones set in gold clips and rings, and after her sister's death she had felt that perhaps she should "dispose" of some of it. But it was one of her vanities to take pleasure from ornamenting her simple, dark dresses with a brooch or clip of some sort at the V-neck, or from wearing a necklace of very white pearls and perhaps a pair of old-fashioned ear rings. And it became one of his pleasures to see her in these jewels.

So after some months of discussion it was decided that she should keep the jewelry.

In the afternoons from one until nearly five Mrs. Powell was in her room resting by order of her doctor, whose medicine she took before meals and whose office she visited monthly. Her illness she and her husband had agreed never to mention at her promise to take every possible care of herself and to visit her specialist once a month. And she had learned to administer medicine to herself that had formerly required the aid of her sister. At five she dressed and awaited on the gallery the appearance of Mr. Powell in the doorway. Then perhaps they would stroll in the formal, treeless park before the capitol or through The Arcade to purchase Mr. Powell a few handkerchiefs or Mrs. Powell a yard of ribbon. In their restaurant after dinner they would chat over their black coffee often for as long as an hour. Occasionally they would talk of some book which they were reading, or incidents from the day's work, or they might observe some girlhood friend of Mrs. Powell who would happen in.

But the subject for conversation which most consistently presented itself was the personality and the opinions of Benton Young, a mutual friend of their youth. Of whatever matter they talked at length sooner or later his opinion was recalled, or at least something he had said that would throw light on the subject. Sometimes his personality would be suggested by a character in a book or by some person whom they had run across during the day. At last this had happened so often that it became a joke between them, and each would laugh at himself or at the other when he began to tell that something had reminded him of Benton Young. At other times one would for no reason "just think" of Benton Young, of some trait of his, of some incident of his friendship with him.

Later, walking home, they might continue discussion of him. Or there were evenings when they would talk of him late in the night as they lay in bed.

Mrs. Powell's friendship with him had come twenty-five years back when she was hardly twenty years old. It came at a time when she needed it. She met Benton Young at the reception for a young musician after his first concert. She and her sister had but a year before lost their parents, and a few years before that a family fortune. She was presented to Mr. Young by the young musician himself who introduced him as his very dear friend and benefactor. From this one evening spent in his company she knew that the musician meant that Benton Young was his benefactor because he allowed him to be his friend. And she determined then that she too must be Benton Young's friend.

The friendship which had followed was a result of her persistence in placing herself near him. He was twenty years her elder and a professed bachelor in the town, so she could make advances in their friendship that might otherwise have been impossible. And in their two years of association it was always she who sought him. And even until the time of their separation when he left his native city for Europe he gave her no direct advice on any matter. All she gained from him she took from observation of his way of living and his expression of objective opinions of things.

What Mrs. Powell got from him was somewhat different from what Mr. Powell received. It came a few years later when he knew him as a fellow expatriate in Paris. Benton Young was a writer, a critic of the arts of a sort, author of two novels which caused "no stir," and he called himself "a *prosateur*." To the girl whom he had befriended with his acquaintance back in the states he had given a serious attitude toward the arts to which she had formerly only been "sensitive." He had shown her that she could really take them into her empty life. To Mr. Powell he had shown that such things could *really* mean something. He met Powell in Paris as a young man with "good background" and enough money to get started on. Enough money to get started on a Career as a writer. He found him a young man set only upon that Career, whose interest in ideas and ideals amounted to something like the disinterested curiosity of a journalist. In place of this interest he gave him a real love for the best in the art of writing of which he professed to be enamored. And as Benton Young said when they met for the last time in Paris, he perhaps gave him his failure in his Career; for when Mr. Powell's income began to dwindle a few years later he had not pushed himself in the world enough, and yet had found that he was not a writer himself. So he returned to the largest city in his native state where his family connections found him "something in his line to do," and his small income carried him along.

And so for the ten years he lived alone in The Hensely House. Each morning he went to the State Library at the capitol and took notes for his weekly column in *The Herald-Democrat*: "Forgotten Paragraphs in Southern History." (Eventually his column was carried in other newspapers over the state, and he would receive letters from relatives and descendents of the senators and governors whose characters he would elucidate. One letter from the most eminent woman historian of the South wished to know why "he thought" he was fitted for his position; and her letter set him wondering for several days. (His answer to it in his column gave only the qualification that he could write a good English prose sentence.) After an hour's note taking he would go to the City Library and "do his reading." He read Clarendon and Gibbon and Newman and the novelists of the nineteenth century. At first he had thought, of course, he'd some day write something critical on the great prose writers; later doing his reading seemed only his religious worship. He read to save his soul. During the afternoons in an upstairs room of the City Library he worked on his column or on the book reviews which he did for the Sunday Editor. After his marriage his daily life went along in the same way but that he left his pursuits a few minutes earlier to meet Mrs. Powell at their restaurant for lunch and a few minutes earlier to meet her in the lobby before dinner.

In their parlor they read to each other on winter evenings. They read the new novels which they received from the Sunday Editor. Or they listened on their radio to campaign speeches (criticizing the rhetoric, not the politics) and to music and sometimes half way through a radio drama. They played Russian Bank—or Rummy when Mrs. Powell was very tired. Through the fall and early winter they would go to The Opera House regularly just to be seen by their friend the manager who was kind to them. When the performance was especially good they would stay through the second act, or its equivalent. But Mrs. Powell was careful of the hours she kept, and the Powells were never heard later than ten-thirty in their descants and little fits of laughter as they came down the wide, carpeted hallway to their apartment at night.

The Augusts of their first two summers together they spent in a little denominational mountain resort a hundred miles east of the city. But they found only inconvenience in their work and the bother of being entertained by Mrs. Powell's girlhood acquaintances who would entertain them at tea with some visiting churchman, knowing, the Powells decided, no other way to entertain "so peculiar" a couple. The third summer, therefore, they agreed that the city's heat was preferable to the bother of the resort. Consequently their other seven Augusts they had braved the heat with after-dinner and all-Sunday-afternoon street car rides and a ceiling fan in their bed room.

Mr. Powell was proud of Mrs. Powell's beauty and of her taste in dress. Though these were the days of short skirts, she wore her dresses nearly to her ankles. And though even the librarians' hair was now bobbed, she wore her hair long and stacked on the top of her head. He enjoyed walking through the hotel lobby or through The Arcade with her wearing a plain, dark dress with a diamond brooch or belt buckle or cuff buttons and perhaps tiny gold ear rings on the lobes of her ears. Her hats, of a soft shade of green or blue malines, sat rather high on her head; in the evening she wore one with a broader brim. And the shape of her long and narrow feet was exaggerated by the low heeled pumps with the single straps that buttoned. Mr. Powell was six inches taller than she, and his greying hair could always be seen over her hat as they came through the revolving door at night, and his hand over her shoulder pushing the door for her. At every corner his white hand was at her elbow, and his narrow eyes, wrinkled at the corners, seemed solicitous of the comfort of her every step. When they had closed the door of their apartment at night, she would often take off her hat and rest her head on the blue serge cloth that covered his chest; and he would put his arms around her and hold her there, knowing that she was tired.

Then, too, Mrs. Powell would laugh at him for many of the conventions that he observed. Once a month he wrote a letter to the Sunday Editor to thank him for the good books that they had received to review or to "be perfectly candid" about other books that did not deserve a review in a first rate publication. This, he said, made it plain "on just what grounds" he stood with the Jewish editor. At the end of each month, too, he went in detail over the bill at the restaurant at which they ate their meals, and he gave the proprietor at Christmas a "present which he could not really afford." And this was all to make plain "on just what grounds" the restaurant proprietor stood with him. Mrs. Powell laughed at him for the regularity with which he arose each morning at seven-thirty and polished his own and her long, narrow, black shoes.

But, as conscientiously, she arose five minutes later each morning and bathed and applied the great quantities of powder to her body that she did and drew his bath for him. And when he returned from his bath, she would have his blue serge suit and what clean linen she thought he needed laid out on the bed for him.

It was, in fact, the absence of his clothes from the bed that stopped him in the center of the room as he returned from his bath one morning. His clothes had not been laid out, and he found Mrs. Powell standing, in her lavender dressing robe, by one of the tall windows. In her heelless slippers between the long drapes her height seemed that of a child of nine or ten years. He spoke to her, and she turned to him smiling. But she had not powdered her face, and with the green draperies and her lavender robe her complexion seemed a mixture of those colors.

"I'm not going to go over and work today," she said, still smiling at him. Her appearance, at first childlike, now suggested a very old woman. She wasn't yet fifty-five.

He took a step toward her. Then, as if recalling a tacit agreement, he said calmly, "You'd better get back to bed, dear."

"When you have gone, I think I shall," she said.

"No," he told her, and he went to her. "Now." He helped her out of her robe, and she climbed between the covers of the bed.

When the doctor was leaving, two hours or so later, Mr. Powell stopped with him in the vestibule. And he was told that "it might be a week, it might be a month before the end."

He was out of the apartment only for an hour at meals after that. He thought that she might need that much rest from the sight of him. The nurse slept on a cot in the little study that they had never used. She slept there in the day time, and he slept for a while at night. He read to his wife and talked with her and would sit for hours while she rested or slept.

During the first week the red-headed manager of the Opera House came twice. Each time she wept as she talked to Mr. Powell in the vestibule. The Sunday Editor came once and sent flowers the next day. After this the nurse left instructions at the desk that no visitors should see either Mr. or Mrs. Powell. Mrs. Powell even wanted to let the nurse go, and she asked the doctor not to come back.

Indeed, the doctor could do little for her and so would often not see her or Mr. Powell but would only enquire from the nurse. The nurse sat in the parlor mostly with the bed room door half open, and Mr. Powell sat by his wife's bed holding her hand. She would drop off to sleep in the afternoons; and he would sit by her, gazing out the window at the old Confederate Bank Building. He was thinking one afternoon, as he gazed out there, of that letter of introduction to Mrs. Powell which he had once received from Benton Young. He had called on her, and she too had had a letter. It was the last either had ever heard from him and after many failing attempts to communicate with him to tell him of their marriage they had supposed him dead in some obscure village in central Europe. For there, a vague rumor had come from one of her performers through the manager of the Opera House, he was supposed to have been seen—aged and in failing health.

It was not the first time that Mr. Powell had sat by the window during his wife's illness and thought of the man that had directed the life of each and finally brought them together. And they had, of course, together talked of him for many hours since the morning she had had the first warning of the end as she stepped from her bath. Today by the window Mr. Powell was only wondering what had become of those letters of introduction.

His back was to the bed, and his eyes were vaguely on the owner of the poultry store, who was closing up his store for the day. He heard his wife stir in the bed and turned to see her half sitting up, resting on one elbow. Her eyes shone and she was smiling at the doorway.

"Benton Young," she said.

Mr. Powell looked at his wife and then at the half opened door. He turned back to her and sat on the bed beside her. "My darling," he said.

But she waved him away and kept looking through the half open doorway. "There's Benton Young in the parlor," she said in seemingly real amazement. "He's coming in to see us." Mr. Powell stood up and turned to call the nurse. And he beheld Mr. Benton Young stepping into the room.

Mr. Powell's head was swimming, and he took hold of one of the strong posts of the great bed in which his wife was lying.

"Benton," his wife said in nearly a whisper, "you haven't changed. You haven't aged a day." Mr. Powell saw their old friend take a few steps forward, and he saw in the dim twilight that he appeared no older than he had been over twenty years before when Mr. Powell had left him in Paris.

He saw Benton Young take another step forward and heard him address Mrs. Powell and himself by their given names. He heard him telling them that knowledge of their marriage had brought him great satisfaction and that he hoped the function of his acquaintance with them had been only to prepare them for the ten years of happiness that they had had. Then Mr. Powell was conscious of a soft cry from his wife's bed, and as he turned to her he called aloud for the nurse. He held the hand of the faded woman tightly and kissed her sallow forehead, and now he saw that she had lost consciousness.

Before he thought of Benton Young again it was eight o'clock, and the doctor and the nurse had sent him out to breathe the cold night air and to get himself a cup of coffee. But by the time he had finished half a cup of coffee he had forgotten the strange appearance of the man in his apartment that afternoon. He returned to the hotel and sat by his wife's bed all that night.

In the middle of the next morning he was by her side looking at her weary features when his wife's eyes opened and looked at him. She smiled feebly, and he came close to her.

"I've something to tell you," she whispered.

"Are you sure that you want to," he asked, "that you're up to it?"

She nodded to him and then told him that he knew all that she was going to tell him but that she wanted to say it to him before she died. "We're two peculiar old people, dearest. The things we've wanted no one else has seemed to value. The strangest things either ever wanted were the other and a life centering around this old hotel." He tried to stop her, protesting that he *did* know all of this and that she mustn't use her strength. "But it's about our lives before that I want to tell you," she continued. "It seems that it was nothing but a preparation for these ten years. I could have asked for no more. I could never have guessed there might be this much for someone as small as I. In those years before I knew you I often wanted to whip myself into a commoner mould." She hesitated for what he knew would be her last sentence. "I'm only glad that I kept myself peculiar through those years for our marriage."

In the afternoon Mrs. Powell lost consciousness again, and in the old hotel on that twilight she drew her last breath.

In a few days Mr. Powell stopped at the desk and asked the manager and clerk if a Mr. Benton Young had enquired at the desk for his room number during Mrs. Powell's illness. The bald-headed clerk was certain that he had not. And he told his favorite guest that he had never left the desk before midnight during Mrs. Powell's illness. Mr. Powell then saw him write down the name of Benton Young on his white pad as he said that he would keep an eye out for him and notify Mr. Powell immediately if Mr. Young called. Mr. Powell didn't question the nurse, for he could consider the doctor and nurse only as the mechanics of death. And he did not enquire at the desk again, and he felt no urge to seek further knowledge of his old friend. He was not interested in the physical fact of whether Benton Young was alive or dead.

Chronology

1917   Born Matthew Hillsman Taylor Jr. on January 8 in
        Trenton, Tennessee, the fourth child and second son of
        Matthew Hillsman "Red" Taylor and Katherine Baird
        (Taylor) Taylor. (Before Red and Katherine's wedding,
        in 1908, the two Taylor families were unrelated. His were
        the "West Tennessee Taylors," based for generations in
        Trenton, the seat of Gibson County, a city of twenty-
        five hundred about a hundred miles northeast of Mem-
        phis, in what was then cotton country; hers were the
        "East Tennessee Taylors," based along the Nolichucky
        River, in the Blue Ridge Mountains, near the border
        with North Carolina. Red Taylor, b. 1884, a former All-
        Southern tackle for the Vanderbilt Commodores, was
        junior partner in Taylor & Taylor, his father's Trenton
        law firm. In 1909, at the age of twenty-four, Red was
        named the youngest speaker in the history of the Tennes-
        see House of Representatives, which he served through
        1915. He then became attorney general of the Thirteenth
        Judicial District. Katherine Taylor, b. 1886, a graduate of
        the Belmont School, in Nashville, was a skilled musician
        and a charismatic raconteur. She was the daughter of the
        late Robert Love Taylor [1850–1912], a luminary of the
        Democratic Party remembered throughout Tennessee as
        "Our Bob." Bob Taylor was three times the governor of
        the state, in 1887–91 and in 1897–99, and then a U.S.
        senator from 1907 until his death. He was also a popular
        lecturer on the Chautauqua circuit.) Matthew Jr., born at
        home, is nicknamed "Pete" by a next-door neighbor, and
        the name sticks. His sisters are Sarah Baird "Sally" Taylor
        (b. 1910) and Mettie Ivie Taylor (b. 1912); his brother is
        Robert Love "Bob" Taylor (b. 1915). The family resides
        in a Queen Anne cottage at 208 High Street, the first
        of three Trenton houses that Taylor will live in during
        his first seven years. They worship together, at Red's
        insistence, at the city's First Methodist Church, where
        Katherine, a convert from the Disciples of Christ, is the
        organist.

1924   After his father's death, Red decides to sell the family law
        practice and seek greater fortune in Nashville, about 125
        miles east of Trenton. In spring, he accepts the position

of chief corporate lawyer to Rogers Caldwell, a finan-
cier then known as the J. P. Morgan of the South. By
September the family has settled on Hogan Lane, in a
hilltop house they call the House of the Seven Gables.
Pete is enrolled in the first grade at Robertson Academy,
a private elementary school.

1926   In January Caldwell & Company acquires the Missouri
State Life Insurance Company, headquartered in St.
Louis, and Rogers Caldwell appoints Red vice president
and chief executive. That summer the family moves into
a modern manse on Lenox Place, in St. Louis's fashionable Central West End. Pete enrolls at Miss Rossman's
School, a private elementary school.

1929   When Missouri State Life acquires the title to 5 Washington Terrace, a twenty-year-old Beaux Arts mansion
furnished with European art and antiques, Red, now
president of the firm, arranges to make it the Taylor
family home. (Established in 1902, Washington Terrace is
a private enclave of fifty houses and a self-governing community of several of the wealthiest families in the Central West End.) The immense, many-bedroomed house,
which features a third-floor ballroom and a detached
two-story stable, is staffed by five African American servants, all originally from the Trenton area. Housekeeper
Lucille Rogers, who had attended college at Memphis's
historically black Le Moyne School, becomes Pete's
closest companion, the person to whom he confides his
dreams and aspirations. ("I had more conversations with
her than with my mother on those subjects," Taylor told
The Paris Review, "and of course far more than with my
father. Lucille had more influence on me when I was a
child than any other adult.")

1930   Enrolls at St. Louis Country Day School, a private academy for boys in grades seven through twelve. Begins to
write and direct plays starring his classmates, which he
stages in the ballroom at home. When not conceiving
plays he is sketching or painting; he will harbor a dream
of becoming an exhibiting artist well into early adult-
hood. In November the banking branch of Caldwell &
Company, which after the Crash of 1929 had merged

with BancoKentucky, enters receivership, precipitating
the closure of 120 banks in seven states.

1931   An audit of the books at Missouri State Life, conducted
as part of a government investigation into the bank collapse, reveals that Caldwell & Company has mortgaged
many of the insurance company's assets and transferred
the monies to other Caldwell holdings. Though Red
denies personal knowledge of the matter, the board of
directors of Missouri State Life demands his resignation.
On December 1, days after Rogers Caldwell had reneged
on an oral promise to defend him before the board, Red
resigns. Family legend has it that from that day forward
the name "Rogers Caldwell" was never again uttered by
Red Taylor.

1932   On New Year's Day the family moves into an apartment
on Waterman Avenue, near Washington University. The
contents of 5 Washington Terrace are auctioned and the
mansion sold. In October Red, unemployed and living
on savings, moves the family to Memphis, Tennessee,
where both he and Katherine have family. The Taylors
lease a house at 79 Morningside Park, in the exclusive
Central Gardens neighborhood. Pete enrolls at Central
High School, the largest public school in the city.

1933   In June the family moves a few blocks west to a rented
house at 1583 Peabody Avenue. Red opens a Memphis
law practice and slowly rebuilds fortune. Pete begins his
junior year at Central High as an honors student, a favorite of the English and Latin faculty, and a reporter for the
school's biweekly paper, the *Warrior*.

1935   In the winter of his senior year Pete is named editor
of the *Warrior*, for which he writes a regular humor
column, "Lord Chatterfill'd's Letters to His Son." In
April he is awarded a two-thousand-dollar scholarship to
Columbia University, where he intends to study literature
and art, but father forbids him to accept it. Red instead
offers to send him to Vanderbilt, his alma mater, to study
law. Though tempted by the prospect of a new life in
Nashville, declines the offer, and, through a connection
made by his brother-in-law, Sally's new husband Millsaps
Fitzhugh, finds work as an errand boy for the Memphis
Commercial Appeal. (Fitzhugh, a well-read attorney, will

become very close to Taylor, introducing him to books by Tolstoy, Chekhov, and other Russian masters.)

1936 Living at home with his parents, takes Saturday painting classes at the newly established Memphis Academy of Arts. In the spring enrolls as a special student at local Southwestern College (now Rhodes College). Peter Hillsman Taylor, as he now calls himself, takes two English classes, one a freshman composition course taught by Allen Tate, a thirty-five-year-old poet, critic, and biographer already well-known to followers of Southern writing as a member of the Fugitive group and a contributor to *I'll Take My Stand: The South and the Agrarian Tradition* (1930). (Taylor will remember Tate as an "electrifying" instructor and as the authority figure who gave him permission to become a writer. "He made literature and ideas seem more important than anything else in the world," Taylor said in a 1986 interview. "You wanted to put everything else aside and follow him.") In the summer he takes two more courses with Tate, one in modern fiction, with an emphasis on Henry James, and the other in creative writing. For Tate he writes his first short stories, "The Party" and "The Lady Is Civilized," both of which are enthusiastically received. Taylor is devastated when Tate and his wife, the novelist Caroline Gordon, announce they have accepted teaching positions at Woman's College, in Greensboro, North Carolina, for the coming academic year. Tate recommends that Taylor continue his studies at Vanderbilt under his mentor, the forty-eight-year-old poet and critic John Crowe Ransom, a plan that Red Taylor readily agrees to—so long as Peter also prepares himself for a career in law. After spending the fall trimester living in a Nashville rooming house, joins the Phi Delta Theta fraternity. There he meets master's candidate Randall Jarrell, a brilliant young poet and critic who will become a lifelong friend and, in Taylor's view, the most perceptive reader of his fiction. At Christmastime his two short stories are accepted by *River*, a literary monthly being planned by Dale Mullen, an undergraduate at the University of Mississippi at Oxford.

1937 In March "The Party" is published in the first number of *River*, followed in April by "The Lady Is Civilized." At the end of the spring trimester, Vanderbilt puts Taylor on

academic probation. (Although he had received three A's
from Ransom, he had failed botany, algebra, trigonometry, and physical education.) Returns to parents' home
in Memphis, and in the fall resumes classes at Southwestern College. His evenings and weekends are spent
not in the library but in the company of four bohemian
classmates—two young men and their girlfriends—who
together explore the West Tennessee "demimonde" of
roadhouses, rent parties, and open-air "gin picnics."
They call themselves the Entity, and their favorite dive
is the Jungle, a juke joint in Proctor, Arkansas, some
twenty-five miles west of Memphis. At Christmastime,
his interest in both school and the Entity fading, Taylor
begins to look for a full-time job.

1938   In February accepts position as a sales representative for
Van Court Realtors and immediately withdraws from
Southwestern. Spends evenings writing unpaid book
reviews for the *Commercial Appeal.* In March hears
through a Vanderbilt acquaintance that Ransom, now
at Kenyon College, in Gambier, Ohio, has established
a full-tuition scholarship in creative writing and hopes
that Taylor will apply. When, in May, Kenyon admits
Taylor, his father, despite his continued misgivings about
Taylor's pursuing a writer's life, does not object. During
the summer Taylor writes "A Spinster's Tale," which
he will later consider his first mature short story. (Over
the next two years he will repeatedly try to place it in
a national magazine.) At Kenyon is assigned a room in
Douglass House, a decrepit Carpenter's Gothic residence
just off campus. His housemaster is Randall Jarrell, now
an instructor of freshman composition; his housemates
include the young poet Robert Lowell, who will become
for Taylor a kind of "second brother," and the future
book and magazine editors David McDowell and Robie
Macauley. In October "The Lady Is Civilized," one of
the *River* stories that helped win him his scholarship, is
reprinted in *Hika,* Kenyon's undergraduate monthly.

1939   Reviews Allen Tate's novel, *The Fathers,* for *Hika,* and
during July visits the Tates in Monteagle, a mountain
resort town southeast of Nashville that will become a
lifelong summer haunt. Poem "The Furnishings of a
House" appears in the third number of Ransom's newly

established quarterly, *The Kenyon Review* (Summer 1939); it is the first piece of writing for which Taylor is paid. In the fall contributes several new stories to *Hika*, including "The Life Before" and "Middle Age." Presiding over his creative life, as well as those of Jarrell and Lowell, McDowell and Macauley, is the calm, benign, and nurturing figure of John Crowe Ransom. ("I suppose it really was a sort of idealized father-sons relationship," Taylor would write in 1985. "He was the father we had not quarreled with, the father who was not a lawyer or businessman, and was the man we wished to become. [And] I am absolutely certain he had a parental love for all of us.")

1940   In his final semester at Kenyon publishes the story "Winged Chariot" in the graduation number of *Hika*. Travels home to Memphis, bringing with him, as houseguests, Robert Lowell and his new wife, the young writer Jean Stafford, both on their way to jobs at Louisiana State University. (Lowell is to be a teaching assistant to Ransom's former pupils Cleanth Brooks and Robert Penn Warren; Stafford is to be an editorial assistant at Brooks and Warren's literary quarterly, *The Southern Review*.) Through the agency of Lowell, Stafford, Ransom, and Tate, "A Spinster's Tale" is placed in *The Southern Review* for Autumn 1940. (Within a year the journal will also publish "Sky Line" [a revised version of "Winged Chariot"] and a new story, "The Fancy Woman.") Impressed by his fiction, Brooks and Warren offer Taylor thirty dollars a month to grade freshman papers for the academic year 1940–41. In August he moves to Baton Rouge, rents a room in Warren's apartment, and enrolls at LSU as a postgraduate student. Come Thanksgiving week he withdraws from the program to devote more time to writing. (Taylor, though he will spend most of his life on university campuses, will never consider himself an "academic." He regularly tells his colleagues and students that he is not an intellectual but rather "someone who writes stories and lets his intelligence come out *that* way.") He will remain in Baton Rouge through the end of the school year.

1941   In April returns to Memphis, and in May is drafted into the U.S. Army. Is stationed at Fort Oglethorpe, in

Catoosa County, Georgia, just across the border from Chattanooga, Tennessee. Serves as a clerk in the transportation section, an office position that allows him time and privacy for writing. Engages Diarmuid Russell, of the New York firm of Russell & Volkening, as his literary agent "for the duration." On December 7, Japanese aircraft attack Pearl Harbor, Hawaii, and America enters World War II.

1942   Promoted from PFC to corporal, and then to sergeant. Becomes head clerk of the transportation department, and travels with deployed troops to embarkation points in California, Florida, and the District of Columbia. "The Fancy Woman" is selected for *The Best American Short Stories 1942*, the first of nine stories by Taylor that will appear in the series through 1980.

1943   During Easter furlough travels to Monteagle to visit the Tates. There he meets Eleanor Lilly Ross (b. 1920), the Tates' favorite student at Woman's College and now a master's candidate in English at Vanderbilt. The connection between Taylor and Ross, one of a family of artists and writers in rural Norwood, North Carolina, is instant and profound. Six weeks later, on June 4, the couple is married by Father James Harold Flye, at St. Andrew's School Chapel, near Sewanee, Tennessee. (The Tates stand in for the parents of the bride; Robert Lowell is the best man, and Jean Stafford is Ross's bridesmaid.) The newlyweds rent a small apartment in Chattanooga, where that summer Taylor, who commutes by bus to Fort Oglethorpe, writes the story "Rain in the Heart." Starts work on a novel, a study of the relationship between an only child and his wealthy, complicated stepmother that he calls "Edward, Edward."

1944   In January is ordered to Camp Butner, near Durham, North Carolina, to train for overseas duty. In February his outfit—Headquarters Company, Twelfth Replacement Depot—transfers to Fort Dix, near Trenton, New Jersey. ("When we do go across," Taylor writes his mother, "our function will be the handling of other men as they come over. We'll remain from fifty to one hundred miles behind the lines and continue to send replacements up. So we'll be comparatively free from danger.") In March Taylor and his company sail on the

Ile de France for Northern Ireland. During a prolonged stay in Somerset he makes a friend of local business-man Charles Abbot, who introduces him to the work of Anthony Trollope, which will become a lifelong plea-sure. By late spring his company is established at Camp Tidworth, in Wiltshire, in southwest England, where Taylor will serve for the rest of the war. In the summer, through arrangements made by an army chaplain, he is welcomed into the Anglican Communion by William Wand, the Bishop of Bath and Wells. Throughout the year he works on "The Scoutmaster," which will win third prize in a "novelette" contest sponsored by *Partisan Review* and the Dial Press.

1945   In the weeks following V-E Day, completes the stories "Allegiance" and "A Long Fourth" and makes repeated visits to London, eighty miles northeast of Tidworth. Ten days after V-J Day, travels to Paris and—by accident, on the street—encounters Gertrude Stein, who invites him to her Left Bank apartment for a spontaneous, pri-vate, two-hour conversation. (They talk of writing, the Jameses, Trollope, and the antebellum South, and Taylor finds her "sensible," "witty," and "warm.") In the fall teaches American literature in a U.S. Army school, his first experience as a classroom instructor. On December 9, sails from Southampton as one of 11,500 American troops aboard the *Queen Mary*. Arrives in New York on December 15, and five days later is demobilized, at Camp McPherson, in Atlanta. After a reunion in Chattanooga, he and Eleanor spend Christmas with his parents in Memphis.

1946   In February leases a house in Sewanee, Tennessee, where, under a two-book contract with Doubleday (negotiated by Diarmuid Russell), he assembles a collection of seven short stories. In March, Doubleday declines to pub-lish the book until he also delivers his novel "Edward, Edward." In April, at the urging of the Tates, Taylor accepts a teaching position at Woman's College for the academic year 1946–47. In the meanwhile, he and Elea-nor will live in New York City, where Tate has secured Taylor a summer job as reader for Henry Holt & Com-pany and an apartment, at 224 West Tenth Street. At Woman's College continues to work on "Edward,

Edward," completing the first draft during Christmas break.

1947   In the spring organizes annual arts forum at Woman's College, enlisting Robert Penn Warren, now the author of the best-selling novel *All the King's Men*, as the key-note speaker. In attendance are Robert Lowell—whose first trade collection of poetry, *Lord Weary's Castle*, had just been published—and Lowell's editor, Robert Giroux, of Harcourt, Brace & Company. After the forum, Giroux proposes that Harcourt buy Taylor's contract from Doubleday and publish his collection of stories immediately. Giroux suggests the book's title, "A Long Fourth and Other Stories," and commissions an introduction from Warren. Taylor renews his con-tract with Woman's College, and persuades the English department to hire Randall Jarrell as an instructor beginning in fall 1947. In July, Taylor and Jarrell jointly buy a duplex at 1924 Spring Garden Street, Greensboro. Taylor dismisses Diarmuid Russell as his literary agent, and rewrites "Edward, Edward" throughout the fall.

1948   In January accepts offer to teach creative writing at Indiana University for the 1948–49 academic year. In March *A Long Fourth* is published by Harcourt, Brace. Robert Penn Warren's introduction, which Taylor con-siders "exactly perfect," praises both the author's choice of subject matter—"the contemporary, urban, middle-class world of the Upper South," which is "his alone"—and his "natural style, one based on conversation and the family tale, with the echo of the spoken world." The book is reviewed widely and well, and, in response, Katharine S. White, fiction editor of *The New Yorker*, asks to read Taylor's future work. He sends her a revised version of his *Hika* story "Middle Age" (later retitled "Cookie"), which appears in the number for November 6. Signs a first-refusal agreement with *The New Yorker*, which will publish three short stories and an excerpt from his novel during the coming year. Daughter, Kath-erine Baird "Katie" Taylor, born in Bloomington on September 30.

1949   "The Death of a Kinsman," a one-act play, appears in the winter number of *The Sewanee Review*. Miserable at the University of Indiana, where neither housing nor office accommodations are satisfactory, decides to return to Woman's College in the fall. Spends summer with Jarrell on Spring Garden Street, then, in September, buys a house in Hillsborough, forty miles east of campus. Delivers the final draft of his novel, now titled "A Woman of Means," to Robert Giroux.

1950   Eleanor, who had written prose as an undergraduate, enrolls in Jarrell's creative writing class and begins to write poems, two of which soon appear in *Poetry* magazine. In May, *A Woman of Means* is published by Harcourt, Brace to mixed reviews. (The New York *Herald Tribune* finds it a "work of very solid merit" but "not, however, the fully realized novel for which a reader of Mr. Taylor's excellent short stories could wish.") When awarded a Guggenheim for the academic year 1950–51, Taylor arranges for Robie Macauley to teach his classes at Greensboro. Writes three stories during his paid year off: "Two Ladies in Retirement," "What You Hear from 'Em?," and "Bad Dreams." "Their Losses," first published in *The New Yorker*, is reprinted in *Prize Stories 1950: The O. Henry Awards*, the first of seven stories by Taylor that will appear in the series through 1982.

1951   In the fall, Jarrell leaves Greensboro, and he and Taylor sell the duplex. Taylor accepts an invitation to teach as a visiting professor at the University of Chicago in the spring of 1952.

1952   The Taylor family is unhappy in their crowded quarters in Chicago's Plaisance Hotel, at 1545 East Sixtieth Street, opposite Jackson Park. In the spring Taylor is awarded a writing grant of a thousand dollars by the National Institute of Arts and Letters. Soon afterward he is approached by Kenyon's new president, Gordon Keith Chalmers, to become an associate professor of English and dramatic literature at the college. In the summer the family moves to Gambier, Ohio, and Taylor rents the house of a faculty member on one-year leave. Renews his acquaintance with John Crowe Ransom, finds a good friend in drama professor James E. Michael, and soon involves himself in the affairs of both Ransom's *Kenyon Review* and the college's theater department.

1953   Assembles a second volume of short stories and resolves to write a new, almost novella-length story to cap the collection. (This story, "The Dark Walk," will occupy most of his working hours from February to September.) In the summer leases a substantial brick house from Kenyon College. (The eleven-room house, on Brooklyn Street, was built in the 1830s and, he tells Katharine White, is "just to our taste.") In the fall becomes obsessed with every detail of James Michael's staging of Chekhov's *Uncle Vanya* at Kenyon's Hill Theater and resolves to write a full-length stage play.

1954   On April 29 *The Widows of Thornton*, comprising eight stories and the play "The Death of a Kinsman," is published by Harcourt, Brace. The collection is dedicated to Allen Tate and Caroline Gordon. (Orville Prescott of *The New York Times* writes that "Taylor's precise artistry, his skill with dialogue, and his insight into what makes a traditional Southern reaction to life slightly different from a non-Southern one are all admirable. [These stories] are all in the general tradition of Chekhov's ironic melancholy and static action [and] all of them are good.") In June, Taylor is awarded a three-thousand-dollar fellowship from the Rockefeller Foundation, allowing him to teach half time at half his salary during the 1954–55 academic year. Begins work on a four-act stage play based on childhood memories of Washington Terrace.

1955   Son, Peter Ross Taylor, known as Ross, born on February 7. In April Taylor is named a Fulbright Scholar to the United Kingdom and France for the academic year 1955–56. Family spends July and August in Oxford, where Taylor lectures in creative writing at the Fulbright-sponsored Conference on American Studies. They then settle in Paris, where they rent a six-room flat at 20 boulevard St.-Michel, their home through the following April. Completes and copyrights a draft of his play, "Tennessee Day in St. Louis."

1956   Kenyon classmate David McDowell, now an editor at Random House, negotiates a three-book contract with Taylor—a play, a novel, and a third collection of stories. From May to August the family lives at the Villa Gemma, in Rapallo, Italy. In the fall family returns to Kenyon where Taylor is to teach creative writing and playwriting.

1957   In February *Tennessee Day in St. Louis* is published by Random House. On April 27 the play is given its premiere in a Kenyon student production directed by James Michael. In the fall, during the months following the sudden death of Taylor's good friend President Chalmers, Kenyon's acting president, Frank Bailey, terminates the Taylors' lease on their Brooklyn Street house, repurposes the property, and, among other reforms, moves to cut the budget of *The Kenyon Review*. Taylor, feeling betrayed by Bailey, accepts a better-paying position as professor of creative writing at nearby Ohio State University, where he will be required to teach during spring semesters only. In summer purchases house at 25 Bullitt Park Place, in Bexley, a southeastern suburb of Columbus. In October Katharine White retires from *The New Yorker*, and William Maxwell is named Taylor's new editor at the magazine. David McDowell leaves Random House to cofound the publishing firm of McDowell, Obolensky, and invites Taylor to follow him there.

1958   In January travels to Memphis for his parents' fiftieth wedding anniversary, which they celebrate with a party for two hundred guests, and then begins teaching at Ohio State. ("Columbus is an O.K. place," Taylor will tell Robert Lowell. "It is exactly as though I'd gone back to Memphis to live—but without my past to haunt me.") The Taylors summer in Bonassola, a beach town in the Italian Riviera. (Also vacationing in nearby Levanto are Randall Jarrell and the poet and translator Robert Fitzgerald.) They spend the fall at 20 via Montevideo, in Rome, often in the company of Robert Penn Warren and his wife, the writer Eleanor Clark.

1959   "Venus, Cupid, Folly and Time," published in *The Kenyon Review* during the previous spring, is awarded the O. Henry First Prize and is also included in *The Best American Short Stories 1959*. Taylor's third collection of stories, *Happy Families Are All Alike*, is published by McDowell, Obolensky on November 25. (*The New York Times* calls the book's appearance "a literary event of the first importance," and the Sunday *Times Book Review* says that these ten recent stories, "like all fine works of art, are beautifully wrought . . . full of imaginative subtlety . . . [and] insure the author very heavily against oblivion.")

1960   When William Maxwell takes a sabbatical from *The New Yorker* to complete a novel, Taylor is reassigned to fiction editor Roger Angell. The Taylors spend the summer in Monteagle, Tennessee, renting the same cottage in which they had honeymooned seventeen years earlier. The Ford Foundation, which in February had granted Taylor the opportunity to spend a year "in a close working relationship with a theatre company" in the U.K. or the U.S.A., assigns him to London's Royal Court Theatre. In late July the family leases a flat at 25 Kensington Gate, in southwest London, and Taylor begins his tenure with the English Stage Company, attending all of their workshops, rehearsals, and performances. (The company's fifty-year-old artistic director, George Devine, is known as an advocate for contemporary British playwrights, including Edward Bond, Christopher Logue, John Osborne, and Arnold Wesker.) In October Eleanor's first collection of poems, *Wilderness of Ladies*, is published by McDowell, Obolensky. (She will publish five further collections, the last in 2009, and receive several honors for her work, including, in 2010, the Poetry Foundation's Ruth Lilly Prize.)

1961   George Devine reads Taylor's plays and tells the author that there is "no place for them in the modern theatre." Taylor, deeply hurt, cuts short his tenure with the English Stage Company, returning to Ohio in May rather than July. The family enjoys the first of many summers in their own Monteagle cottage, which Taylor had financed at the end of the previous summer. On September 6 "Delayed Honeymoon," a New York Theatre Guild adaptation of Taylor's story "Reservations," is broadcast live on CBS television's *United States Steel Hour*. Taylor complains to Roger Angell that the screenwriter, Robert Van Scoyk, and the lead actors, Elinor Donahue and Larry Blyden, had reduced his story of wedding-night anxieties to mere "situation comedy."

1962   Taylor is promoted to full professor of English at Ohio State. In the fall, Andrew Lytle, editor of *The Sewanee Review*, publishes a special Peter Taylor number of the

quarterly featuring Taylor's story "At the Drugstore,"
two essays on his fiction, and a consideration of his plays.

1963   In February Randall Jarrell, who had lately returned to
the faculty of Woman's College, informs Taylor that in
1964 the school will reincorporate and expand as the
racially integrated, coeducational University of North
Carolina–Greensboro. By late spring Taylor has negotiated a teaching contract with Greensboro and made an
offer on a large clapboard house at 114 Fisher Park Circle.

1964   On February 28 Taylor's fourth collection, *Miss Leonora
When Last Seen*, is published by Ivan Obolensky, Inc.
The volume comprises six recent stories and ten others
reprinted from *A Long Fourth* and *The Widows of Thornton*. ("The condition of Mr. Taylor's art," says *The New
York Times*, "gives rise to real people meditating actual
problems. . . . These stories multiply their meanings.
They have enduring interest.") Obolensky, who had
broken with McDowell at the end of 1960, pressures
Taylor for the novel that McDowell had signed up in
1956. At the end of the summer, with the family in need
of ready cash, Taylor reluctantly sells the Monteagle cottage. In the fall serves as visiting professor in creative
writing at Harvard University. He lives in a bachelor
apartment on the eleventh floor of Leverett House,
overlooking the Charles River, while Eleanor remains in
Greensboro with fifteen-year-old Katie and nine-year-
old Ross. Renews old friendships with Robert Lowell
and Robert Fitzgerald, and makes new ones with poet
Adrienne Rich and playwright William Alfred. Students
include future novelists John Casey and James Thackara
and filmmaker James Toback, all of whom will become
friends for the rest of Taylor's life.

1965   Returns to Greensboro to find Jarrell suffering severe
depression and the manic side effects of Elavil. Taylor
works on a novel, "The Pilgrim Sons," and completes a
draft of a new stage play, "The Girl from Forked Deer."
On October 14 Jarrell steps into the path of a car on a
highway near Chapel Hill, an act that Taylor will come
to accept as a suicide. Brother-in-law Millsaps Fitzhugh,
at age sixty-two, dies on October 7, and his father, at
age eighty-one, on November 13. In a year-end letter to
a friend, Taylor writes: "It was Millsaps who introduced

me to Tolstoy and Chekhov, Randall who taught me how to read them, and Father who made it possible to understand a good deal of the subject matter. I loved all three of them."

1966   On February 28, at Yale University, Taylor, Robert Penn Warren, Robert Lowell, and others speak at a memorial service for Jarrell. Robert Giroux, who had edited Jarrell at Harcourt, Brace, is so moved by their words that he invites the three friends to coedit a tribute volume, *Randall Jarrell, 1914–1965* (Farrar, Straus & Giroux, 1968). Renewed acquaintance with Taylor leads Giroux to buy the contract for "The Pilgrim Sons" from Obolensky. A grant from the Rockefeller Foundation allows Taylor to take a leave of absence from Greensboro for the 1966–67 academic year. In the fall he is promoted to Alumni Distinguished Professor of the University of North Carolina–Greensboro.

1967   Works on his novel and revises his play throughout the winter and spring. On March 19 sister Sally Taylor Fitzhugh dies, in Memphis, at the age of fifty-six, after a long bout with emphysema. ("The loss of Randall and Dad was hard," Taylor tells Lowell that summer, "but with Sally [the sadness] won't go away.") Taylor accepts an invitation from the University of Virginia, Charlottesville, to join the English faculty as head of the creative writing program. Signs a one-year lease on a four-bedroom clapboard house—the largest yet, and the best for entertaining—at 1101 Rugby Road, near the main campus. Over the next sixteen years he will make many close friends among the university's students and faculty, including Ann Beattie, Fred Chappell, James Alan McPherson, Breece D'J Pancake, and Alan Williamson.

1968   Struggles with his novel "The Pilgrim Sons," two chapters of which, "A Cheerful Disposition" and "Daphne's Lover," are placed in *The Sewanee Review*. Play, retitled "A Stand in the Mountains," is printed, with a long preface by the author, in the spring number of *The Kenyon Review*. The preface is an extended historical gloss on the play's social milieu—that of the summer community in Monteagle, especially the subset of reactionary intellectuals who, in the 1930s and '40s, saw the mountain resort as a "last stand" for fading Southern agrarian virtues.

In April returns to Kenyon for an eightieth-birthday celebration for John Crowe Ransom. In Gambier, he reunites with his old Douglass House friends and meets Ransom's editor, Judith Jones, of Alfred A. Knopf, Inc. After vainly attempting to purchase 1101 Rugby Road in Charlottesville, buys a two-story brick house about a block away, number 917, which had been previously owned, from 1959 to 1962, by William Faulkner. In September Robert Giroux agrees to contractually substitute a volume of collected stories for the novel "The Pilgrim Sons." In December, after a long series of rejections from Roger Angell, Taylor declines to sign his first-refusal agreement with *The New Yorker*, ending his twenty-year relationship with the magazine.

1969   In February Taylor is informed that, in May, he will be inducted into the National Institute of Arts and Letters. He is unable to attend the ceremony, however, as his mother is in failing health. On May 18 she dies, in Memphis, at the age of eighty-two. A contest over her will precipitates a permanent break between the Taylor siblings. (Peter and his surviving sister, Mettie Taylor Dobson, will never forgive brother Bob for making grasping legal maneuvers as executor of their mother's estate.) By the end of the summer Taylor makes a down payment on Brooks House, a century-old house on Main Street, Sewanee, near the campus of the University of the South. On August 28 *The Collected Stories of Peter Taylor* is published by Farrar, Straus & Giroux. The volume of twenty-one stories is dedicated to his late mother, "Katherine Taylor Taylor, who was the best teller of tales I know . . ." (The reviews range from the respectful to the ecstatic. "[Taylor] writes stories that are more than neatly crafted," writes Joyce Carol Oates in *The Southern Review*. "They are both hallucinatory and articulate, the violence of [his] vision being bracketed by, even tamed by, the intelligent and gracious voice of his narrators. . . . This *Collected Stories* is one of the major books of our literature.") In October, James Michael mounts a Kenyon production of *A Stand in the Mountains*, which Taylor thinks "works" more successfully than *Tennessee Day in St. Louis*. Turns away from fiction to write a series of one-act plays centering on ghosts, both real and imagined.

1970   In the spring four of his ghost plays are published in literary journals (three in *Shenandoah*, the other in *The Virginia Quarterly Review*). His mother's estate finally settled, he pays off the mortgage on 917 Rugby Road and for the first time becomes a homeowner. In the fall he also makes a down payment on yet another property—a log farmhouse in Advance Mills, Virginia, that he calls Cohee and imagines using as his summer writing studio. Taylor urges Farrar, Straus to publish "The Collected Plays of Peter Taylor," but Giroux refuses until at least one of the plays receives a major production. Giroux sponsors Taylor for membership in The Players, a private society for New York theater professionals founded in 1888. Once a month The Players' clubhouse, at 16 Gramercy Park, becomes Taylor's weekend home, its library a place of study and its membership a window on Manhattan's theatrical world.

1971   Writes four further ghost plays, three of which will be published in *The Sewanee Review*, the other in *Shenandoah*. On May 28 "A Stand in the Mountains" is given a semiprofessional production by the Barter Theater Company of Abingdon, Virginia, courtesy of artistic director Robert Porterfield, an acquaintance from The Players. In June, Taylor receives an honorary doctorate in letters from Kenyon. After the ceremony, at the college's Hill Theatre, Taylor is delighted by an evening of three of his ghost plays staged by his old friend James Michael.

1972   In January informs Robert Giroux that he has abandoned "The Pilgrim Sons" and offers in its place a collection of ghost plays. When Giroux demurs, Charles P. Corn, a former assistant at *Shenandoah* now an editor at Houghton Mifflin, acquires rights to the volume and also to a future collection of stories.

1973   On February 14 *Presences: Seven Dramatic Pieces*, dedicated to his Kenyon colleague James Michael, is published by Houghton Mifflin Company. An eighth dramatic piece, "The Early Guest," appears in the Winter number of *Shenandoah*. In early summer Taylor divests himself of all his properties—the Faulkner house, Brooks House, and Cohee—in order to purchase Clover Hill, a large eighteenth-century farmhouse in Albemarle County, about ten miles from Charlottesville. In September Peter and Eleanor, their children now grown, take a furnished apartment at 19 Ware Street, in Cambridge, Massachusetts, as Taylor begins a term as visiting professor at Harvard. Their social circle that fall includes Robert Lowell, his new wife Caroline Blackwood, Robert Fitzgerald, Octavio Paz, and Elizabeth Bishop. At Christmas they return to Clover Hill, their possessions still in boxes and moving crates there.

1974   In the winter begins to write fiction for the first time in five years. The new stories are short and concentrated, and their sentences are arranged on the page like verse. (Taylor calls them *story-poems* or, jokingly, *stoems.* "They *look* like poems," he tells Robert Lowell. "I don't kid myself that they *are* poems.") In May, while helping improve the nine acres at Clover Hill, he suffers a near-fatal heart attack. During the six long months of his recuperation he decides to sell Clover Hill and purchase 1101 Rugby Road, Charlottesville, which has at last come on the market. At the advice of his heart surgeon, Dr. Richard Crampton, he stops smoking, abstains from liquor, and waters his wine. He experiences several brief but intense episodes of depression, yet continues to work on his story-poems. John Crowe Ransom dies, at age eighty-six, on July 3. In the fall Taylor accepts an invitation from Harvard to teach every spring for the next four years.

1975   Spends three winter weeks in Key West with Eleanor and finds that, in the Florida climate, he "feels fifteen years younger." By the summer, five of Taylor's story-poems have been completed and have begun to appear in literary magazines. The sixth and most ambitious, "A Fable of Nashville and Memphis," evolves into "The Captain's Son," his first prose fiction in more than six years. In September, he sends the story to William Maxwell, who, unbeknownst to Taylor, is on hospital leave from *The New Yorker.* It is read in Maxwell's absence by Roger Angell, who immediately accepts it for the magazine. The story is edited by Maxwell, who will retire from the magazine at the end of the year, and by Maxwell's assistant, Frances Kiernan.

1976   Again engaged with fiction, Taylor resigns from Harvard and reduces his workload at Charlottesville. When

"The Captain's Son" appears in January, Jonathan Coleman, a recent graduate of Virginia now a junior editor at Knopf, asks Taylor if he might publish his next collection. Through the agency of Timothy Seldes, his first literary representative in thirty years, Taylor returns his unearned advance to Houghton Mifflin and signs a contract with Knopf. In July he completes a long story, "In the Miro District," and mails it to Frances Kiernan, now a fiction editor at *The New Yorker*. It will appear in the magazine the following February.

1977 In January begins to renovate his new Key West property, 1207 Pine Street, a tree-shaded, white-clapboard island cottage purchased sight unseen during the previous summer. (It will be the Taylors' winter residence, from January through April, for the next six years.) On April 14, Taylor's sixth collection of stories, *In the Miro District*, is published by Knopf. The book is dedicated to Taylor's heart surgeon, Dr. Crampton, "in appreciation for an extension of time." (Stephen Goodwin, in *The New Republic*, finds these eight new stories, four of them in verse, "varied and innovative, even rebellious," and written in a new "risk-taking" voice that is prepared "to withhold nothing, to disguise nothing, to speak all that it knows.") In June the Taylors downsize to a smaller principal residence—their last—at 1841 Wayside Place, Charlottesville. In the late summer a special number of *Shenandoah* is published in honor of Taylor's sixtieth year. On September 13, Robert Lowell, also sixty, dies of a heart attack in New York City. At the funeral, in Boston, Taylor reads Lowell's poem "Where the Rainbow Ends," from *Lord Weary's Castle*. In October he is diagnosed with adult-onset diabetes, the medical condition that had shortened the life of his father. After Christmas he receives news that, in May, he will be awarded the Gold Medal for the Short Story by the American Academy of Arts and Letters.

1978 Allen Tate dies, at the age of seventy-nine, on February 9, and Jean Stafford, at sixty-three, on March 26. On August 1 completes a long story, "The Old Forest," and mails it to Frances Kiernan.

1979 "The Old Forest" is published in the May 14 number of *The New Yorker*. Despite its length—nearly twenty-five thousand words—it is selected for inclusion in both *The Best American Short Stories 1980* and *Prize Stories 1980: The O. Henry Awards*. In the wake of the critical success of *In the Miro District*, Farrar, Straus reprints *The Collected Stories* in hardcover and paperback.

1980   Greatly enjoys the winter social circle in Key West, which includes John Ciardi, John Hersey, Ralph Ellison, Alison Lurie, James Merrill, Richard Wilbur, and James Boatwright, the editor of *Shenandoah*. In September Frances Kiernan accepts another short story, "The Gift of the Prodigal," which will appear in *The New Yorker* the following June. In August signs a contract with Judith Jones of Alfred A. Knopf for a novel and a collection of short stories. Spends the fall sketching out three long stories, one of which, the tale of a middle-aged New York book editor's reluctant return to his childhood home in Tennessee, seems to be the germ of his next novel.

1981   Suffers diabetic nerve damage to legs and feet, which makes sleep nearly impossible. Painkillers help but interfere with his writing. Still he makes good progress on his novel, which he calls first "The Duelists" and then "A Summons to Memphis."

1982   Stuart Wright, a book collector and fine-press printer in Winston-Salem, North Carolina, prints a chapbook edition of Taylor's play "The Early Guest," limited to 140 hand-sewn copies. Taylor assembles the typescript of "New and Selected Stories," an omnibus conceived as a companion to *The Collected Stories*. The book, which comprises "The Old Forest," "The Gift of the Prodigal," and twelve stories from out-of-print collections, is submitted to Knopf by his agent, Tim Seldes. Judith Jones, remarking that Knopf had contracted for a volume of previously uncollected stories, regretfully declines publication.

1983   In May is inducted into the American Academy of Arts and Letters, the fifty-member inner circle of the National Institute of Arts and Letters. In June teaches his final class at the University of Virginia. Accepts an invitation to teach the fall semester at Memphis State University (now the University of Memphis), partly to research the Memphis sections of his novel-in-progress, partly to observe the filming of a one-hour television film based on "The Old Forest." The film, directed by Steven John Ross, is a coproduction of the Department of Theater and Communications Arts of MSU and Humanities Tennessee. *A Woman of Means*, Taylor's novel of 1950, is reprinted in hardcover by Frederick C. Beil, New York. Tim Seldes, after unsuccessfully submitting "New and Selected Stories" to Farrar, Straus, places the book with Allen Peacock of The Dial Press.

1984 In spring gives a reading at the University of Georgia–Athens, where his host is Hubert H. McAlexander, a young professor of English with an interest in Southern fiction and biography. In August is awarded a Senior Fellowship in Fiction from the National Endowment for the Arts. While working on proof of "New and Selected Stories" changes the title of the book to "The Old Forest."

1985 On February 8 Taylor's seventh collection of stories, *The Old Forest*, is published by The Dial Press. (The reviews are the best and most numerous of his career. Anne Tyler, writing in *USA Today*, calls Taylor "the undisputed master of the short story form. In *The Old Forest*, as in all of [his] writing, there is a quality that makes the reader feel satisfied, even honored. I believe the word for it is integrity.") The collection, which is reprinted four times, will sell more than twenty thousand hardcover copies and, in the following year, receive the PEN/Faulkner Award for American fiction. In October Steve Ross's film *The Old Forest*, featuring voice-over narration by Taylor, receives both its premiere at the Chicago International Film Festival and the first of many showings on the fledgling A&E television network. In the fall is visiting professor in creative writing at the University of Georgia, where his deepening friendship with Hubert H. McAlexander will eventually result in three collaborative book projects, *Conversations with Peter Taylor* (1986), *Critical Essays on Peter Taylor* (1993), and a posthumous biography, *Peter Taylor: A Writer's Life* (2001). In November delivers his novel "A Summons to Memphis" to Judith Jones. The book, about a grown man's enduring struggle to find himself—and his calling—in the shadow of a strong father and damaged, bickering adult siblings, is, he tells Hubert McAlexander, his way of posing the question, "How successful are we ever in understanding what has happened to us?"

1986   On March 2 Taylor's estranged brother, Bob, dies at the age of seventy. In May a limited, slipcased, hardcover edition of Taylor's play *A Stand in the Mountains* is published by Frederick C. Beil. (The frontispiece is a photograph of Taylor, at the age of twenty-six, taken in Monteagle by Father Flye.) On July 24 suffers a stroke that leaves him temporarily paralyzed on his right side, the recovery from which will be slow and only partial. On October 6 *A Summons to Memphis* is published by Knopf. Taylor is gratified by the critical response, especially a front-page piece by Marilynne Robinson in *The New York Times Book Review*. ("*A Summons to Memphis* is not so much a tale of human weakness," she writes, "as of the power of larger patterns, human also, that engulf individual character, a current subsumed in a tide.")

1987   In spring *A Summons to Memphis* receives the Ritz Paris Hemingway Award and then the Pulitzer Prize in fiction. Works on a new novel, "To the Lost State," a companion piece to *A Summons to Memphis* that draws on his memories of his mother and his maternal grandfather, the colorful Tennessee politician Robert Love Taylor. In the fall, a substantial "composite" interview with Barbara Thompson Davis, conducted in annual sessions over the last six years, is published in *The Paris Review*. Frances Kiernan, his editor at *The New Yorker*, leaves the magazine at the end of the year.

1988   Stuart Wright, working closely with Taylor, completes a descriptive bibliography of Taylor's work and brokers the sale of his literary manuscripts to the Vanderbilt University Library. The Taylors buy a summer property in Sewanee, the same house Peter had leased in 1946, and purchase a plot in the university cemetery, near the grave of Allen Tate. In September Taylor is hospitalized for a bleeding ulcer. "Something in Her Instep High," an episode from "To the Lost State," appears in the Fall number of *The Key West Review*.

1989   Hires an "amanuensis," or combination typist and personal assistant, and begins dictating his correspondence and, later, his fiction. In this fashion he and his young helper, Brian Griffin, produce the manuscript of a long story, "The Witch of Owl Mountain Springs." In November, when *The New Yorker* declines to publish his new story, he decides never to submit to the magazine again. In the late fall is incapacitated by a second and more severe attack of diabetic neuropathy.

1990   By spring he is feeling well enough to dispense with his amanuensis and resume work at the typewriter. "Cousin Aubrey," a second episode from "To the Lost State," is published in the Winter number of *The Kenyon Review*. Begins work on another long story, "The Oracle at Stoneleigh Court," which he hopes to publish as a stand-alone short novel.

1991   "The Witch of Owl Mountain Springs" is published in the Winter number of *The Kenyon Review*. In June, during a conversation with Christopher Metress, a doctoral candidate at Vanderbilt writing his dissertation on Taylor's work, learns that among his papers in the Vanderbilt library are three unpublished stories from the 1960s. Upon rereading "At the Art Theater," "In the Waiting Room," and "The Real Ghost," decides that they, together with "The Witch of Owl Mountain Springs," will form the core of his next book, a collection of short works, old and new, addressing themes of death, the past, and the supernatural.

1992   Hires a second amanuensis, Mark Trainer, and resumes work on "To the Lost State." "The Oracle at Stoneleigh Court" is published in the literary annual *New Virginia Review*. Taylor decides that it is not a stand-alone novella but instead the title story of his new collection, now comprising ten works of short fiction, "Cousin Aubrey," and revised versions of three ghost plays from *Presences*.

1993   On February 16 Taylor's eighth collection of stories, *The Oracle at Stoneleigh Court*, is published by Knopf. The book is dedicated to his wife, Eleanor. (The reviews are mixed, but Jonathan Yardley, writing in the *Washington Post*, calls it "quintessential Taylor: wry, leisurely, intimate . . . He is, in his seventy-sixth year, the best writer we have.") In April receives the PEN/Malamud Award for his lifetime contribution to the art of the short story. In November, completes final draft of "To the Lost

State," for which Judith Jones suggests the title "In the Tennessee Country." Immediately begins adapting his play "A Stand in the Mountains" into a novel, a work he alternatingly refers to as "Call Me Telemachus" and "The Brothers Taliaferro."

1994   On August 16 *In the Tennessee Country* is published by Knopf. (John Bayley, writing in *The London Review of Books*, calls it "a revelation . . . an immaculate piece of fiction, and a subtly unpretentious work of art. The Henry James of *A Small Boy and Others* would have adored this book.") In mid-October Taylor suffers a final, paralyzing stroke, and soon slips into a coma. He dies at home, in Charlottesville, on November 2, at the age of seventy-seven. Three days later, after a funeral service at All Saints' Chapel, in Sewanee, he is buried in the cemetery at the University of the South. He is survived by his wife, Eleanor Ross Taylor (1920–2011); his sister, Mettie Taylor Dobson (1912–2000); his daughter, Katherine (1949–2001); and his son, Ross (b. 1955).

Note on the Texts

This volume contains twenty-nine short stories that Peter Taylor wrote from the summer of 1938, when he was twenty-one, to the fall of 1959, when he was forty-two. All first appeared in American books or periodicals from 1940 to 1960. The volume also contains, in an appendix titled "Undergraduate Stories," three stories written from 1936 to 1939 that Taylor published in little magazines and undergraduate monthlies but did not later revise or collect in book form. A companion volume in the Library of America series collects thirty of Taylor's later stories, written from 1960 to 1992.

Most of the stories reprinted here also appeared in the following hardcover collections by Peter Taylor:

A Long Fourth and Other Stories, with an introduction by Robert Penn Warren (New York: Harcourt, Brace & Company, 1948). (First U.K. printing: London: Routledge & Kegan Paul, 1949.)

The Widows of Thornton (New York: Harcourt, Brace & Company, 1954).

Happy Families Are All Alike (New York: McDowell, Obolensky, 1959). (First U.K. printing: London: Macmillan, 1960.)

Miss Leonora When Last Seen and Fifteen Other Stories (New York: Ivan Obolensky, 1963).

The Collected Stories of Peter Taylor (New York: Farrar, Straus & Giroux, 1969).

The Old Forest and Other Stories (Garden City, N.Y.: The Dial Press, 1985). (First U.K. printing: London: Chatto & Windus, 1985.)

Because it was the author's usual practice to revise the texts of his short stories slightly every time he collected them, the latest book version of each is used here.

The stories are arranged here in the order of composition as determined by correspondence between Peter Taylor and his editors at *The New Yorker* magazine preserved in The New Yorker Records at the New York Public Library, supplemented by information contained in Hubert H. McAlexander's biography *Peter Taylor: A Writer's Life* (Baton Rouge: Louisiana State University Press, 2001).

Taylor wrote "A Spinster's Tale" at the home of his parents, in Memphis, Tennessee, in 1938. The story was begun in February, shortly after he withdrew from the program at local Southwestern College (now Rhodes College), and was completed in July or August, just before he began the fall term at Kenyon College, in Gambier, Ohio. Although Taylor had been writing short fiction since the summer of 1936, he would always think of "A Spinster's Tale" as his first mature story—the first "worth sending out" to *The New Yorker*, *The Atlantic*, and other national magazines. After nearly two years of unsuccessful submissions, it was accepted by Robert Penn Warren and Cleanth Brooks for *The Southern Review*, a literary quarterly published by the University of Louisiana at Baton Rouge, and appeared in the number for Autumn 1940. It was reprinted in *A Long Fourth* (1948), *Miss Leonora When Last Seen* (1963), and *Collected Stories* (1969). The text from *Collected Stories* is used here.

"Cookie" was written at Kenyon during the fall of 1939. It first appeared, as "Middle Age," in the December 1939 number of *Hika*, the college's undergraduate monthly. In April 1948, following the publication of the collection *A Long Fourth*, Katharine S. White, chief fiction editor of *The New Yorker*, invited Taylor to submit future work to the magazine. Taylor immediately responded with a revised version of "Middle Age," which White published in *The New Yorker* for November 6, 1948. It was reprinted, as "Cookie," in *The Widows of Thornton* (1954), *Miss Leonora When Last Seen* (1963), and *Collected Stories* (1969). The text from *Collected Stories* is used here.

"Sky Line" was written at Kenyon during the winter and spring of 1940. It first appeared, as "Winged Chariot," in the June 1940 number of *Hika*. A revised version appeared, under the present title, in the Winter 1941 number of *The Southern Review*. It was reprinted in *A Long Fourth* (1948) and *Miss Leonora When Last Seen* (1963). The text from *Miss Leonora When Last Seen* is used here.

"The Fancy Woman" was written in a rented cottage in Monteagle, Tennessee, during the summer of 1940. It appeared in the Summer 1941 number of *The Southern Review*. It was reprinted in *A Long Fourth* (1948), *Miss Leonora When Last Seen* (1963), and *Collected Stories* (1969). The text from *Collected Stories* is used here.

"The School Girl" was written at the home of Taylor's parents, in Memphis, Tennessee, during the spring of 1941. It was accepted by *The Southern Review*, which in the winter of 1941–42 suspended publication due to the war. Cleanth Brooks and Robert Penn Warren then placed the story, as well as others in *The Southern Review*'s unpublished inventory, with Paul Engle, editor of *American Prefaces*, the literary quarterly of the University of Iowa. It appeared in the special "Southern Number" of *American Prefaces* dated Spring 1942, the source of the text used here.

"A Walled Garden" was written at Fort Oglethorpe, Georgia, just across the state line from Chattanooga, Tennessee, in the fall of 1941.

It appeared, as "Like the Sad Heart of Ruth," in *The New Republic* for December 8, 1941. (Taylor, who was then a private first class in the U.S. Army, engaged Diarmuid Russell, of the New York literary agency Russell & Volkening, to represent his work "for the duration." This was Russell's first sale on Taylor's behalf.) It was reprinted, under the present title, in *Happy Families Are All Alike* (1959) and *The Old Forest* (1985). The text from *The Old Forest* is used here.

"Attendant Evils" was completed at Fort Oglethorpe in the early months of 1942 and was submitted unsuccessfully to *The New Yorker* on March 25 of that year. It appeared in *A Vanderbilt Miscellany, 1919–1944* (Nashville: Vanderbilt University Press, 1944), a hardcover anthology, edited by the English professor Richmond Croom Beatty, representing the best poetry, fiction, and essays produced by members of the Vanderbilt community between the two world wars. The text from *A Vanderbilt Miscellany* is used here.

"Rain in the Heart" was written in the summer of 1943, shortly after Taylor and his new wife, the former Eleanor Lilly Ross, had moved into their first apartment, in Chattanooga, Tennessee. Taylor worked on the story at home and at his desk in the transportation department at Fort Oglethorpe. It was accepted by Allen Tate and Andrew Lytle for *The Sewanee Review*, and appeared in the number for January–March 1945. It was reprinted in *A Long Fourth* (1948) and *The Old Forest* (1985). The text from *The Old Forest* is used here, except for the correction of an editorial error at 111.17, where the words "*September of '63*," used in the versions of the story printed in *The Sewanee Review* and *A Long Fourth*, have been substituted for "*December of '62*."

"The Scoutmaster" was written while Taylor was stationed in Somerset, England, in the spring of 1944. Taylor's agent, Diarmuid Russell, submitted the story for the 1944 *Partisan Review*–Dial Press Novelette Award, open to unpublished works of fiction of between ten thousand and twenty-five thousand words. It won Third Prize, one hundred dollars, and publication, as "The Scout Master," in the *Partisan Review* for Summer 1945. It was reprinted, under the present title, in *A Long Fourth* (1948) and *The Old Forest* (1985). The text from *The Old Forest* is used here.

"Allegiance," begun in 1944, was completed at Camp Tidworth, in Wiltshire, England, in the spring of 1945, shortly after V-E Day. It was accepted by Taylor's friend and mentor John Crowe Ransom, editor of *The Kenyon Review*, and appeared in the *Review* for Spring 1947. It was reprinted in *A Long Fourth* (1948), *Miss Leonora When Last Seen* (1963), and *The Old Forest* (1985). The text from *The Old Forest* is used here.

"A Long Fourth," begun in 1944, was completed at Camp Tidworth in the summer of 1945. (It was the last story for which Diarmuid Russell served as Taylor's agent.) It appeared in *The Sewanee Review* for July–September 1946. It was reprinted in *A Long Fourth* (1948) and *The Old Forest* (1985). The text from *The Old Forest* is used here.

"Porte Cochere" was written in Bloomington, Indiana, where Taylor taught creative writing in 1948–49, and was submitted to *The New Yorker* on October 13, 1948. (It was the first short story Taylor sent to Katharine S. White after her acceptance of "Cookie" and his subsequent signing of a first-refusal contract with the magazine.) It appeared, as "Porte-Cochère," in *The New Yorker* for July 16, 1949. It was reprinted, as "Porte-Cochere," in *The Widows of Thornton* (1954) and, as "Porte Cochere," in *The Old Forest* (1985). The text from *The Old Forest* is used here.

"A Wife of Nashville," written in Bloomington, Indiana, was submitted to *The New Yorker* on May 24, 1949, and appeared in the number for December 3 of that year. It was reprinted in *The Widows of Thornton* (1954), *Miss Leonora When Last Seen* (1963), and *Collected Stories* (1969). The text from *Collected Stories* is used here.

"Their Losses" was written in Greensboro and Norwood, North Carolina, where Taylor enjoyed the summer of 1949. It was submitted to *The New Yorker* on August 5, 1949, and appeared in the number for March 11, 1950. It was reprinted in *The Widows of Thornton* (1954), *Miss Leonora When Last Seen* (1963), and *Collected Stories* (1969). The text from *Collected Stories* is used here.

"Uncles" was written in Hillsborough, North Carolina, where Taylor kept a home while teaching at Woman's College, Greensboro, in 1949–51. It was submitted to *The New Yorker* on October 17, 1949, and appeared in the number for December 17, 1949. The text from *The New Yorker* is used here.

"Two Ladies in Retirement" was submitted to *The New Yorker* on July 15, 1950, and appeared in the number for March 31, 1951. It was reprinted in *The Widows of Thornton* (1954) and *The Old Forest* (1985). The text from *The Old Forest* is used here.

"What You Hear from 'Em?" was submitted to *The New Yorker* on December 10, 1950, and appeared in the number for February 10, 1951. It was reprinted in *The Widows of Thornton* (1954), *Miss Leonora When Last Seen* (1963), and *Collected Stories* (1969). The text from *Collected Stories* is used here.

"Bad Dreams" was submitted to *The New Yorker* on March 20, 1951, and appeared in the number for May 19, 1951. It was reprinted in *The Widows of Thornton* (1954), *Miss Leonora When Last Seen*

(1963), and *The Old Forest* (1985). The text from *The Old Forest* is used here.

"The Dark Walk," a nearly novella-length story, was conceived by Taylor for first publication in his collection *The Widows of Thornton*. It was written from February to September 1953, in Gambier, Ohio, where Taylor taught creative writing at Kenyon College from 1952 to 1957. In compliance with his first-refusal agreement with *The New Yorker*, he submitted it to the magazine on September 10, 1953, simultaneously with his delivery of the manuscript of *The Widows of Thornton* to his publisher, Harcourt, Brace & Company. *The New Yorker* demurred due to its length. By December 1953, the rights department at Harcourt, Brace had placed the story with *Harper's Bazaar*, which published an abridgment, approved by Taylor, in the number for March 1954. The complete text of "The Dark Walk" first appeared in *The Widows of Thornton*, which was published on April 29, 1954. The text from *The Widows of Thornton* is used here.

"1939" was submitted to *The New Yorker* on November 15, 1954, and appeared, as "A Sentimental Journey," in the number for March 12, 1955. It was reprinted, under the present title, in *Happy Families Are All Alike* (1959) and *Collected Stories* (1969). The text from *Collected Stories* is used here.

"The Other Times" was submitted to *The New Yorker* on August 1, 1955, and appeared in the number for February 23, 1957. (It was the last story of Taylor's to be edited by Katharine S. White before her retirement from the magazine.) It was reprinted in *Happy Families Are All Alike* (1959) and *Collected Stories* (1969). The text from *Collected Stories* is used here.

"Venus, Cupid, Folly and Time" was submitted to *The New Yorker*, as "In a Bower of Paper Flowers," on February 28, 1957, and was rejected by Taylor's interim editor, Robert Henderson. Taylor quickly sold the story to John Crowe Ransom and revised it through November 1957. It appeared, under the present title, in *The Kenyon Review* for Spring 1958. It was reprinted in *Happy Families Are All Alike* (1959) and *Collected Stories* (1969). The text from *Collected Stories* is used here.

"Promise of Rain" was completed in Bexley, Ohio, a suburb of Columbus, in the summer before Taylor began his tenure at The Ohio State University, where he taught from the spring of 1958 through the spring of 1962. It was submitted to *The New Yorker*, as "The Public School Boy," on August 15, 1957, and appeared, as "The Unforgivable," in the number for January 25, 1958. (It was the first of Taylor's stories to be acquired and edited by William Maxwell, who remained his *New Yorker* editor through 1960.) It was reprinted, under the present title, in *Happy Families Are All Alike* (1959) and *The Old Forest* (1985). The text from *The Old Forest* is used here.

"Je Suis Perdu," inspired by the Taylor family's eight months in Paris (September 1955 to April 1956), was completed in the summer of 1957. It was submitted to *The New Yorker* on September 30, 1957, and appeared, as "A Pair of Bright-Blue Eyes," in the number for June 7, 1958. It was reprinted, under the present title, in *Happy Families Are All Alike* (1959) and *Collected Stories* (1969). The text from *Collected Stories* is used here.

"A Friend and Protector" was completed while Taylor was vacationing with his family in Bonassola, Italy, during the summer of 1958, and was unsuccessfully submitted to *The New Yorker* on August 3 of that year. It appeared, as "Who Was Jesse's Friend and Protector?," in *The Kenyon Review* for Summer 1959. (This story was edited by Taylor's Kenyon classmate Robie Macauley, who in 1958 succeeded Ransom at the *Review*.) It was reprinted, under the present title, in *Happy Families Are All Alike* (1959) and *The Old Forest* (1985). The text from *The Old Forest* is used here.

"Guests" was completed while Taylor was vacationing with his family in Rome, Italy, during the fall of 1958. It was submitted to *The New Yorker* on November 14 of that year and appeared in the number for October 3, 1959. It was reprinted in *Happy Families Are All Alike* (1959) and *Collected Stories* (1969). The text from *Collected Stories* is used here.

"The Little Cousins," also completed in Rome, was submitted to *The New Yorker* on November 25, 1958, and appeared, as "Cousins, Family Love, Family Life, All That," in the number for April 25, 1959. It was reprinted, under the present title, in *Happy Families Are All Alike* (1959) and *The Old Forest* (1985). The text from *The Old Forest* is used here.

"Heads of Houses" was written in Monteagle, Tennessee, and Bexley, Ohio, during the winter of 1958–59. It was submitted to *The New Yorker* on April 13, 1959, and appeared in the number for September 12, 1959. It was reprinted in *Happy Families Are All Alike* (1959) and *Collected Stories* (1969). The text from *Collected Stories* is used here.

"Miss Leonora When Last Seen," written in Bexley, was submitted to *The New Yorker* on November 10, 1959, and appeared in the number for November 19, 1960. It was reprinted in *Miss Leonora When Last Seen* (1963) and *Collected Stories* (1969). The text from *Collected Stories* is used here.

Under the rubric "Undergraduate Stories" are collected three stories that Peter Taylor wrote from the summer of 1936, when he was nineteen, to the summer of 1939, when he was twenty-two. They were published in *River: A Magazine in the Deep South*, a short-lived literary monthly edited and published during 1937 by Dale Mullen, then a twenty-one-year-old senior at the University of Mississippi, Oxford, and in *Hika*, an undergraduate monthly founded in 1933 at Kenyon College.

"The Party," Taylor's first completed story, was written at his parents' house, at 1583 Peabody Street, Memphis, during the summer of 1936. (In interviews, Taylor repeatedly claimed it was composed in longhand entirely on the family's porch swing.) It was written for Allen Tate, the teacher of a summer class in creative writing offered by local Southwestern College. During the following fall, Tate unsuccessfully submitted both it and Taylor's second story, "The Lady Is Civilized," to *The Southern Review*. Taylor sent the story to *River* when a call for contributions was published in a number of little magazines at the end of 1936. It appeared in the premiere issue of *River*, dated March 1937, the source of the text used here.

"The Lady Is Civilized," like "The Party," was written at Taylor's parents' house in Memphis during the summer of 1936. It appeared in the second issue of *River*, dated April 1937, and was reprinted, in a slightly revised version, in *Hika* for October 1938. The text from *Hika* is used here.

"The Life Before" was written at Taylor's parents' house in Memphis during the summer of 1939. It appeared in *Hika* for November 1939, the source of the text used here.

This volume presents the texts of the original printings chosen for inclusion but does not attempt to reproduce features of their typographical design. The texts are presented without change, except for the correction of typographical errors. Spelling, punctuation, and capitalization are often expressive features, and they are not altered, even when inconsistent or irregular. The following is a list of typographical errors corrected, cited by page and line number: 8.8, anixety; 73.25, "Get's; 50.7, week end.; 64.34, stair,; 81.17, mirrow; 92.11, lot"; 93.10, week's; 160.2, has—Then; 171.38, blonde; 182.25, near by; 216.24, Dunbar's; 246.32, Op'rater!"; 279.1, factory town.; 335.38, landloard,; 372.6, Moore.; 377.12, Pierce; 419.1, coveralls The; 478.28 (and *passim*), *perdu!*; 535.27, second and; 537.18, was bane; 609.14, foor; 610.3 (and *passim*), Johnson's; 610.26, sonorus; 610.33, that; 610.38, Hardy's; 611.13 (and *passim*), Bradley's; 612.13, parlor-funitue; 612.38, throught; 613.11 (and *passim*), Pilcher's,; 613.30, farmers; 614.37, Your; 615.17, Winston's; 615.23, Y'all; 616.36, boys.; 616.37, Susan,"; 617.32, fingerstrips.; 618.12, starting; 619.37, lounge; 620.32, roue.; 625.8, Gray's; 626.4, ""I guess; 626.7, porch.;

627.11, harded; 627.39, "M'st; 628.8, weaping; 628.33, two color; 630.4, adultry; 631.30, colonade; 631.32, loby; 631.35, ballustrade.; 632.30, *The*; 633.11, aboard.; 636.14, capital; 637.24, acquaintence; 638.5, capital; 638.10, who; 640.4, went,; 640.21, heeless; 642.20, acquaintence.

Notes

In the notes below, the reference numbers denote page and line of this volume (line counts include headings but not section breaks). No note is made for material included in standard desk-reference books. Biblical quotations are keyed to the King James Version. For reference to other studies, and for further biographical background than is contained in the Chronology, see Hubert H. McAlexander, *Peter Taylor: A Writer's Life* (Baton Rouge: Louisiana State University Press, 2001), and, as editor, *Conversations with Peter Taylor* (Jackson: University Press of Mississippi, 1987). James Curry Robison, *Peter Taylor: A Study of the Short Fiction* (Boston: Twayne, 1988), includes memoirs of Taylor by Stephen Goodwin, Mary Jarrell, Allen Tate, and Robert Penn Warren, and interviews with Taylor by Mr. Goodwin (1973), J. H. E. Paine (1986), and Mr. Robison (1987). C. Ralph Stephens and Lynda B. Salamon, editors, *The Craft of Peter Taylor* (Tuscaloosa: University of Alabama Press, 1995), includes memoirs of Taylor by Madison Smartt Bell, Cleanth Brooks, David H. Lynn, and Robert Wilson, and "An Oracle of Mystery: A Conversation with Peter Taylor" (1993), by Christopher Metress. Ben Yagoda, "The Oracle of the South" (*Washington Post Magazine*, May 9, 1993), is a late profile of Taylor. For further bibliographical information than is contained in the Note on the Texts, including lists of textual variants, see Stuart Wright, *Peter Taylor: A Descriptive Bibliography 1934–87* (Charlottesville: Bibliographical Society of the University of Virginia/University Press of Virginia, 1988).

COMPLETE STORIES 1938–1959

6.11–14 Miss Hood and Miss Herron . . . Belmont School] On September 4, 1890, Ida E. Hood (1863–1940) and Susan L. Herron (1862–1902), two progressive-minded educators from Philadelphia, opened the Belmont School for Young Women in Nashville, Tennessee. The school, which offered high school and junior college classes "preparing girls for lives of purpose," was located in the city's West End, on the grounds of Belle Monte, the antebellum estate of Colonel Joseph and Adelicia Acklen. In 1913, upon the retirement of Misses Hood and Herron, Belmont College merged with the nearby Ward Seminary for Young Ladies (founded 1865), forming the Ward-Belmont School. In 1951, Ward-Belmont entered into a financial relationship with the Tennessee Baptist Convention (TBC), under which all future members of the school's board of directors were to be members of the Southern Baptist Church. Ward-Belmont then abandoned its high school program and reorganized, in 1952, as Belmont College (now Belmont University), a private, four-year, coeducational institution. The university ended its relationship with the TBC in 2005.

7.15   drummer] Traveling salesman; one who drums up business.

14.15   Black Maria."] Police van.

16.10–11   *Tales of ol' Virginny*, by Thomas Nelson Page] Page (1853–1922), a lawyer and diplomat as well as a writer, was well-known for his local-color romances of post–Civil War plantation life, often told in what he called "the dialect of the Negroes of Eastern Virginia." His best-selling book was *In Ole Virginia; or, Marse Chan and Other Stories* (1887), here remembered colloquially as *Tales of ol' Virginny.*

18.28   Centennial Park] Public park in Nashville's West End, established by the city in 1884. Originally called West Side Park, it was renamed when, in May 1896, it was designated as the site of the Tennessee Centennial and International Exposition (May–October 1897). Among its notable features is a full-scale stucco replica of the Parthenon in Athens, which was built to serve as the arts pavilion of the Tennessee Expo. In 1931, the basement rooms of the Parthenon were redesigned to accommodate two art galleries, one for the James M. Cowan Collection of American Painting and the other for temporary exhibits.

30.4   'corporosity'] Southern slang: one's body and, by extension, one's physical health.

55.29–30   *nity, with anxiety, and with pity. . . . wild with delight.*] From *The Crime of Sylvestre Bonnard* (*Le Crime de Sylvestre Bonnard*, 1881), a novel by Anatole France (1844–1924), translated from the French, and with an introduction, by Lafcadio Hearn (New York: Harper & Bros., 1890).

58.27   Dyersburg] City in northwest Tennessee, eighty miles north of Memphis.

59.36   floorwalker] Salesman who assists customers and manages junior staff in a department store.

66.30   "Louisville Lady"] Song composed in 1933 by Peter DeRose, with words by Billy Hill, and popularized by several recordings released during that same year, including sides by the orchestras of Isham Jones, Anson Weeks, and Dick Robertson. The male singer moans for his late Louisville Lady, who drowned herself after learning that he had two-timed her. ("I was her man. / Why did I do her wrong?")

72.9   'If love were like a rose.'] Cf. "A Match" (1862), by English poet Algernon Charles Swinburne (1837–1909), whose opening line is "If love were what the rose is . . ."

80.7   Miss Hood] See note 6.11–14.

81.6   Belmont at Nashville] See note 6.11–14.

84.25–28   League work . . . Chest Drive] From its founding in 1922 through World War II, the Junior League of Memphis, a young women's volunteer group, raised money for the Memphis Community Chest Federation, the predecessor organization of today's United Way of the Mid-South.

88.2   Orange Mound] Historically black community, founded in the 1890s, some seven miles southeast of downtown Memphis, Tennessee.

89.16   shotgun house] Narrow, rectangular, one-story residence, seldom wider than twelve feet, with connected rooms arranged one behind another, and with doors at the front and the back. It was the most common style of low-income housing built in the American South from Reconstruction through the 1920s.

92.17   Morningside Park] Exclusive residential subdivision of midtown Memphis, Tennessee, developed in 1908.

95.4–7   Peavine Ridge . . . seven miles to the west.] This story is set during World War II in and around Fort Oglethorpe (1902–46), in Catoosa County, in the extreme northwest corner of Georgia. (Fort Oglethorpe was home to the U.S. Army's 6th Cavalry Regiment from 1919 to 1942.) Peavine Ridge, above Peavine Creek, is seven miles southeast of Missionary Ridge, in urban Chattanooga, Tennessee.

96.9–17   "Yes, she jumped in bed / / right in beside her."] From a bawdy folk song sometimes called "The Wayward Boy," sung to the tune of the late-eighteenth-century English marching song "The Girl I Left Behind Me."

96.27   WAC] Member of the Women's Army Corps (1943–78), the former women's branch of the U.S. Army.

97.31   Midway] Shopping and entertainment district of the city of Fort Oglethorpe, Georgia.

108.39–109.1   "I have never seen the Federal dead . . . the sunken wall at Fredericksburg."] From Daniel Harvey Hill, "Chickamauga—The Great Battle of the West," a contribution to *Battles and Leaders of the Civil War*, volume 3, edited by Robert Underwood Johnson and Clarence Clough Buel (New York: The Century Co., 1887). D. H. Hill (1821–1889) was lieutenant general of the Confederate Army of Tennessee at the Battle of Chickamauga (September 18–20, 1863).

120.3–5   . . . you're turning night into day . . . / / . . . sleepy time gal.] From "Sleepy Time Gal," song (1925) by Richard A. Whiting and Ange Lorenzo, words by Joseph R. Alden and Raymond B. Egan.

120.12–13   "I'd Climb the Highest Mountain" or "Three O'Clock in the Morning."] "I'd Climb the Highest Mountain (If I Knew I'd Find You)," song (1926) by Lew Brown and Sidney Clare; "Three O'Clock in the Morning," waltz ("Las Tres de la Mañana," 1919) by Argentinian composer Julián Robledo, words (1921) by Theodora Morse (a.k.a. Dorothy Terris).

120.21–25   Every cloud must have a silver lining. / / . . . I shall be melancholy too.] From "My Melancholy Baby," song (1912) by Ernie Burnett, words by George A. Norton.

128.36   Russian bank] Competitive form of solitaire for two players, each using his own deck of cards.

129.1   Decoration Day] Original name for Memorial Day, in use from the late 1860s through the early years of the twentieth century. Before 1968 the holiday was traditionally observed on May 30, not, as it is today, on the last Monday in May.

149.22–23   Nell Gwynn . . . London park.] Nell Gwynn (1650–1687), the witty young mistress of Charles II, was, after 1670, housed by the king at what is now 79 Pall Mall, in Westminster, London, across from St. James Park. She was so popular with the public that, according to legend, flowers "could not grow in the park" for passersby picking them and leaving them on her doorstep.

163.23   Miss Hood's school] See note 6.11–14.

172.22   "Barbara Allen,"] Traditional Scots ballad (Child 84) concerning a young woman, Barbara Allen, who callously refuses to comfort a longtime male acquaintance who is apparently dying from unrequited love for her. When Barbara Allen hears the tolling of the young man's funeral bells, she is overcome with horror and grief and tells her mother that she, too, shall soon die of heartbreak.

177.31   those fellows at the University in Nashville.] That is, the so-called Agrarians, twelve Southerners who together published a collection of original essays titled *I'll Take My Stand: The South and the Agrarian Tradition* (New York: Harper & Bros., 1930). The group, whose members included such then-emerging writers as Donald Davidson, Andrew Lytle, Allen Tate, Robert Penn Warren, and Stark Young, had for its guiding spirit the then-forty-two-year-old poet and critic John Crowe Ransom (1888–1974), a professor of English at Vanderbilt University. In the unsigned introduction to *I'll Take My Stand*, the Agrarians described their book as an argument for the "Southern way of life" over "what may be called the American or prevailing way. . . . An agrarian society is hardly one that has no use at all for industries, for professional vocations, for scholars and artists, and for the life of cities. Technically, perhaps, an agrarian society is one in which agriculture is the leading vocation . . . a form of labor that is pursued with intelligence and leisure, and that becomes the model to which the other forms approach as well as they may. . . . The theory of agrarianism is that the culture of the soil is the best and most sensitive of vocations, and that therefore it should have the economic preference and enlist the maximum number of workers." The book's detractors attacked agrarianism as an exercise in nostalgia and a romantic, reactionary defense of the ways of the Old South.

178.8   *The Decline of the West*] Two-volume work (*Der Untergang des Abend-landes*, 1918, 1922–23) by the German historian and philosopher Oswald Spengler (1880–1936), first published in English in 1926. It outlines the cyclical rise and fall of history's great civilizations, concluding with a pessimistic vision of the inevitable demise of the Western tradition in political thought and culture.

179.24   parlor pink] American slang of the 1920s to 1940s: a female "pinko," or communist sympathizer.

189.16   Chucky Jack Sevier] John "Nolichucky Jack" Sevier (1745–1815) was a frontiersman, Revolutionary soldier, and politician who, in 1796, became the first governor of the state of Tennessee.

189.16   Judge John Overton] Overton (1766–1833), a banker, lawyer, and jurist in early Tennessee, was a legal and political advisor to Andrew Jackson.

189.17–19   Andy Jackson . . . and Chucky Jack met in the wilderness] In 1801, John Sevier relinquished the office of governor of Tennessee, having served the constitutional limit of three consecutive two-year terms. His elected successor was Archibald Roane, a close friend of Andrew Jackson. When, in 1803, Sevier mounted a gubernatorial challenge to the incumbent Roane, Jackson, in a bid to ruin his chances, falsely accused Sevier of bribing auditors who had allegedly uncovered improprieties in his personal finances. Despite Jackson's treachery, Sevier won the election—but the insult rankled. After an angry face-to-face encounter on the steps of the Knoxville courthouse, during which Sevier called Jackson an adulterer, Jackson challenged him to a duel, which Sevier repeatedly declined. On October 16, 1803, Jackson and a party of supporters, hoping to force a confrontation, followed Sevier into the wilderness while he and his associates were on their way to a conference with Cherokee leaders. What happened next is unclear, but all eyewitnesses testified that, while both Jackson and Sevier stood their ground and drew their pistols, no shots were fired.

201.20   Vaux Hall] Exclusive Romanesque Revival apartment building (c. 1897–1930s) in downtown Nashville that, after the Crash of 1929, slowly declined into a budget-rate hotel. It was razed in 1952.

207.18   Centennial Park and the Parthenon] See note 18.28.

209.18   Hermitage Club] Private men's club (c. 1866–1935) in downtown Nashville whose members included many of the city's most prominent businessmen.

210.38   *How We Cook in Tennessee*] Regional cookbook (1906) compiled by and printed for the Silver Thimble Society of the First Baptist Church, Jackson, Tennessee.

214.28   Russian bank] See note 128.36.

215.25   Brownie] Inexpensive box camera (fl. 1900–1980) manufactured by the Eastman Kodak Company, Rochester, New York.

216.35   Neil Hamilton] American character actor (1899–1984) who, in his youth, was first a nationally known shirt-and-collar model and then a leading man in silent pictures.

216.36   Irene Rich] American silent-film actress (1891–1988) who survived the transition to talkies to become the female sidekick of Will Rogers.

216.36–37   Edmund Lowe] American character actor (1890–1971) who, in his youth, played the dark, suave, self-contained hero in dozens of silent films.

227.13–14   "We were at Ward's together after I was dismissed from Belmont.] See note 6.11–14.

230.35   Toddle House] Southern short-order restaurant chain (1930s–80s) with an all-day breakfast menu featuring fluffy "Toddle House Eggs"— scrambled eggs "made with cream, not milk, and fried in real butter."

233.29–30   Union Planters."] Memphis-based Union Planters Bank (now absorbed into Regions Bank of Alabama) was, from 1906 to 2004, Tennessee's largest financial institution.

235.1   Stoneleigh Court] Throughout the first half of the twentieth century, the Beaux Arts–inspired Stoneleigh Court Apartments (1905–65), at L Street and Connecticut Avenue, NW, were home to many of Washington's political and cultural elite.

235.13   Maxwell House] From 1869 to 1961, the Maxwell House Hotel, built and managed by John Overton Jr. (see note 189.16), was the premier hotel in downtown Nashville.

235.18–19   séance at Mr. Ben Allen's house."] Benjamin Bentley Allen (1855–1910), a gentleman of leisure and self-styled occultist, lived at 125 Eighth Avenue South, in downtown Nashville, from 1880 until his death some thirty years later. During these years, he and his companion, the spiritual medium Miss Sue Perkins, held celebrated midnight séances at the house, during which they conjured "The Thing," described in memoirs and press accounts as a mischievous force that levitated Allen's parlor table, rattled the china, and brushed unseen against the legs of the assembled guests.

239.37   Gracie Allen] American comic actress (1895–1964) who, together with her husband and straight man George Burns, was a star of vaudeville, radio, film, and early television. Her persona was that of a ditzy blonde who doggedly pursues an illogical line of reasoning to its logical and always benign end.

240.3   Gypsy Rose Lee] Burlesque artist, chanteuse, and raconteur (1911–1970) who counted among her friends and admirers H. L. Mencken, Carson McCullers, W. H. Auden, and other writers, artists, and intellectuals.

241.36   carroted fur] Animal fur that has been treated with mercury nitrate, which imparts a bright orange-yellow color.

243.12   Statler] The thousand-room Statler Hotel, at 800 Washington Street, was from 1917 to 1954 the premier hotel in downtown St. Louis. Today, after several changes in ownership, it is known as the Marriott St. Louis Grand Hotel.

243.24   John Burroughs School] Private, coeducational, nonsectarian day school, founded in 1923 in St. Louis, Missouri.

246.35   Little Dixie] Regional nickname for central Missouri, especially those counties just west of St. Louis along the Missouri River.

247.34   Vandervoort's] Colloquial name for Scruggs, Vandervoort & Barney, a leading St. Louis department store from 1850 to 1969.

249.4   Home-Run King] Baseball player George Herman "Babe" Ruth (1895–1948).

260.30–31   membership in the Colonial Dames of America] According to the bylaws of the National Society of Colonial Dames of America (founded 1891), "The Corporate Societies [i.e., the forty-four state and local chapters of the CDA] shall be composed entirely of women who are descended in their own right from some ancestor of worthy life who, residing in an American colony, rendered efficient service to his country during the Colonial period, either in the founding of a State or Commonwealth, or of an institution which has survived and developed into importance, or who shall have held an important position in a Colonial government, or who by distinguished services, shall have contributed to the founding of our nation."

280.5   Piggly Wiggly] Piggly Wiggly Inc., founded in Memphis in 1916, is a chain of inexpensive self-service grocery stores serving the South and the Upper Midwest.

289.11   Bell Witch] According to legend, the family of one John Bell, a settler in Robeson County, about forty miles north of Nashville, was haunted by "Kate," a malicious female ghost, from 1817 to 1821. The Bell Witch, as she came to be called, had for a medium Bell's adolescent daughter, Betsy, and in the girl's presence moved objects, sang hymns, and quoted scripture. Over the years, Kate—an invisible yet physical presence—began to verbally abuse Mr. Bell, advise Betsy in her life choices, and comfort Mrs. Bell and the family's youngest member, Jack Jr.

289.11–12   General N. B. Forrest . . . saved the cotton] In 1862, Nathan Bedford Forrest (1821–1877), of Bedford County, Tennessee, was a brigadier general in the Confederate States Army. In December of that year he led a series of raids in western Tennessee whose objective was to destroy the Mobile & Ohio Railroad between Jackson, Tennessee, and Columbus, Kentucky, thereby disrupting the supply chain of Ulysses S. Grant. On December 20, ten days into the campaign, he and some eighteen hundred troops reached the occupied city of Trenton, Tennessee. There they quickly seized the railroad depot and took about seven hundred Union soldiers prisoner.

316.13 Ward-Belmont School] See note 6.11–14.

322.28–29 before the Baptists finally took over Ward-Belmont).] See note 6.11–14.

342.36–39 Bonnie Kate Sherrill . . . Fort Loudon.] Catherine "Bonnie Kate" Sherrill (1754–1836) was, after 1780, the wife of John Sevier (see note 189.16). According to legend, the couple first met in 1776 when Kate, a resident of Fort Watauga (not, as Taylor has it, Fort Loudon), was accidentally locked out of the fort during a Cherokee attack. Sevier, a visitor at the fort, witnessed her plight and, risking his own life, pulled her over a fence to safety.

351.25 Hollins College] Small, private women's college in Roanoke, Virginia, founded in 1842.

366.38 National Academy] The National Academy, a combination museum, school, and institution for American advancement of the visual arts and architecture, was founded in New York City in 1825. In 1939, its school was located at 109th Street and Amsterdam Avenue.

367.8–9 Bard College or Black Mountain or Rollins] Four-year American liberal arts colleges that in 1954, when this story was written, were noted for their *au courant* fine arts and performing arts curricula.

369.23 Middle Path] Ten-foot-wide paved footpath that runs north–south through the center of the Kenyon campus.

371.29 Bexley Hall] Founded simultaneously with Kenyon College, Bexley Hall was for nearly a century and a half the college's Episcopal seminary. In 1968, the seminary disassociated itself from Kenyon and relocated to Rochester, New York. The main building of the former seminary, a Gothic Revival structure built in 1839–58, is still known as Bexley Hall and today houses Kenyon's administration offices.

371.37 Bishop Philander Chase] Chase (1775–1852), who in 1819 had been ordained as the first Episcopal Bishop of Ohio, founded Kenyon College and Bexley Hall Seminary in Gambier, Ohio, in December 1824.

371.38–372.10 The first of Kenyon's goodly race / / spanked the naughty freshmen well.] According to *Songs of Kenyon* (New York: Hinds, Noble & Eldredge, 1908), compiled by Alfred Kinsley Taylor (class of 1906), the words to the song "Philander Chase" (1903) were written, to the traditional English tune "The Pope," by the Reverend George Franklin Smythe, DD (1852–1934). Smythe, who from 1902 to 1920 was Colburn Professor of Homiletics and Religious Education at Bexley Hall (see note 371.28), was also the author of *Kenyon College, Its First Century* (New Haven: Yale University Press, 1924).

372.6 Hannah More] More (1745–1833), an English poet, playwright, and Evangelical Protestant reformer, was an acquaintance of Philander Chase and an early benefactress of Kenyon College.

372.14–15 new president of the college . . . famous and distinguished poet] In 1937, Gordon Keith Chalmers (1904–1956), president of Kenyon from that year until his death, hired poet John Crowe Ransom (see note 177.31) as teacher of creative writing and founding editor of the quarterly *Kenyon Review*.

373.1–3 *The Wings of the Dove . . . The Cosmological Eye* and *The Last Puritan* and *In Dreams Begin Responsibilities*.] Four notable American books of the modern period: a novel (1902) by Henry James (1843–1916), a collection of short fiction (1939) by Henry Miller (1891–1980), "a memoir in the form of a novel" (1935) by George Santayana (1863–1952), a collection of short stories and poetry (1938) by Delmore Schwartz (1913–1956).

374.1 "verdurous glooms and winding mossy ways."] From "Ode to a Nightingale" (1819), by English poet John Keats (1795–1821).

379.12 Mary Institute] Private girls' school in St. Louis, Missouri, founded in 1859 by William Greenleaf Eliot (1811–1887), a cofounder of Washington University, and named for his late daughter, Mary Rhodes Eliot (1838–1855), who died at the age of seventeen. The school later formed close social and academic ties with a neighboring boys' school, St. Louis Country Day School, founded in 1917. The two schools merged in 1992, forming Mary Institute & St. Louis Country Day School.

386.13 *Partisan Review*] Prestigious literary quarterly founded in New York City in 1932. By 1939 its aesthetics were high modernist, its politics anti-Stalinist. It ceased publication in 2003, shortly after the death of its co-founder and longtime editor William Phillips (1907–2002).

386.26 New Directions anthologies] *New Directions in Prose and Poetry* (1936–91) was a series of roughly annual literary anthologies edited by James Laughlin (1917–1997) and published by New Directions Publishing Co., New York. Early numbers included new work by Henry Miller, Ezra Pound, Delmore Schwartz, Wallace Stevens, Dylan Thomas, and many other modern writers.

387.31 Shelley Poetry Prize] The Shelley Memorial Award, administered annually since 1930 by the Poetry Society of America (founded 1910), is a cash prize given to a living American poet "with reference to his or her genius and need." Recipients are chosen by a jury of three poets—one appointed by the president of Radcliffe, one by the president of the University of California at Berkeley, and one by the PSA Board of Governors.

387.32–33 *Crimson . . . Advocate*] *The Harvard Crimson* (founded 1873) is the daily student newspaper of Harvard University, *The Harvard Advocate* (founded 1866) the college's student literary quarterly. Both are staffed and edited by Harvard undergraduates.

389.13–22   Today while we are admissibly ungrown, / / For him bringing manliness to light.] Cf. "For the School Boys," by Peter Taylor, published in *Hika* 6.4 (February 1940), page 10:

> Today while we're admissibly ungrown,
> Now when we are each half boy, half man,
> Let us examine ourselves half with half
> And exploiting our feminine intimacy
> Scramble the halves of all, and each regard
> In what manner he has not become a man.
>
> Before the old attachment to ten rooms
> Of carpenter's gothic fails to undo pride,
> To release in midnight confidences whims
> And yens we want to weed or recognize
> At least, let us expose, and count it good,
> What is mature. And childish peccadillos
>
> Let us laugh out of our didactic house—
> The rident punishment one with reward
> For him bringing lack of manliness to light.
> Oh, we shall find variety enough
> For the interest of all. And we'll pour forth
> All manner of malediction and polemic,
>
> Being boys. And sympathize and profit,
> Being men. It is unpredictable
> Whether one sanguine person here shall find
> So blind an alley as the prodigy's,
> But our number, small enough for chats, is large
> Enough for that worst tragedy of the mind.
>
> What we've to learn our hundred little quarrels
> Each should reveal some part. And every heart
> Opened here would find a bitter failing—
> Though I should only look from my dormer
> At gingerbread about our eaves and say
> I have not loved enough this gingerbread.

389.26–28   Now that we're almost settled . . . / / . . . in th' ancient tower . . .] The opening lines of "In Memory of Major Robert Gregory" (1918), by W. B. Yeats (1865–1939), from his collection *The Wild Swans at Coole* (1919).

389.31–36   She had told him—Janet Monet had . . . could not entertain him alone . . .] A parody, through close imitation, of the late style of Henry James. Cf. the opening sentence of *The Wings of the Dove* (see note 372.38–373.2): "She waited, Kate Croy, for her father to come in, but he kept her unconscionably, and there were moments at which she showed herself, in the glass over the mantel, a face positively pale with the irritation that had brought her to the point of going away without sight of him."

390.4–5   She knew that he knew . . . / / . . . what a life he had led—] Cf. "Go Ask Father," a folk poem of the early twentieth century:

>"Go ask Father," she said, when I asked her to wed.
>She knew that I knew that her father was dead.
>She knew that I knew what a life he had led.
>She knew that I knew what she meant when she said:
>   "Go ask Father!"

403.23   "Temptation"] Torch song (1932) by Nacio Herb Brown, words by Arthur Freed. In the M-G-M musical *Going Hollywood* (1933), it is crooned by Bing Crosby to the actress Fifi D'Orsay as they flirt and sip tequila in a Tijuana nightclub.

424.30   Bronzino's "Venus, Cupid, Folly and Time."] *Venus, Cupid, Folly and Time* (c. 1540–45) is an allegorical painting by the Florentine Mannerist master Agnolo di Cosimo (1503–1572), also known as Bronzino. The complex, swirling composition depicts a nude Venus sitting on the ground and holding, in her right hand, one of her son Cupid's arrows, and in the other hand, the golden apple that she was awarded by Paris. Cupid, standing to the right and slightly behind his mother, kisses her on the lips and fondles her right breast. Folly, pictured as a preadolescent boy, rushes up behind them from Venus's left, ready to surprise them with a shower of pink rose petals. Looming above all is the figure of Time, an old man bearing a dark blue mantle symbolizing age, or death, or the oblivion that will soon cover them all. The oil-on-panel painting, measuring 57 × 46 inches, now hangs in the National Gallery, London.

444.24   Wave] Member of the women's branch of the U.S. Naval Reserve, 1942–48.

444.31–32   Earl of Chatham . . . Pitt County] William Pitt, 1st Earl of Chatham (1708–1778), also known as William Pitt the Elder, was a British statesman during the reign of George III. As prime minister during the French and Indian War (1754–63), he became intimate with colonial American affairs and grew deeply sympathetic with the revolutionary cause. Later, as a member of the House of Commons, he endeared himself to the American colonists by arguing against the Stamp Act (1766) and other instances of punitive British taxation.

457.32–33   three-point-two draft beer] In March 1933, nine months before the end of Prohibition, President Franklin D. Roosevelt signed the Cullen-Harrison Act, which permitted U.S. manufacture and sale of low-alcohol beer and wine (alcohol content not to exceed 3.2 percent of weight). Throughout the 1930s, and in some states for many decades after, so-called three-point-two beer (or "near beer") continued to be sold legally in grocery stores, short-order restaurants, and other establishments without liquor licenses.

467.2   "A Message to Garcia."] Inspirational essay on self-reliance, personal initiative, and civic responsibility (1899), written (and self-published as a best-selling pamphlet) by American writer-entrepreneur Elbert Hubbard (1856–1916).

471.1   *Je Suis Perdu*] French: "I am lost," "I am confused," "I am at a loss."

471.2   L'ALLEGRO] Pastoral poem (published 1645) by John Milton (1608–1674), addressed to a female personification of Mirth. The title is an Italian word meaning "The cheerful man."

473.25   *chauffage central*] French: central heating.

474.37   L'École Père Castor] Exclusive, experimental private nursery school ("Father Beaver's School," 1941–61) on the boulevard Saint-Michel, in the Latin Quarter of Paris. It was founded by writer, illustrator, and educator Paul Faucher (1898–1967), creator of the Père Castor series of books for young readers.

477.22   *"Je regrette."*] French: "I am sorry."

480.15   IL PENSEROSO] Pastoral poem (published 1645) by John Milton, written as a companion piece to "L'Allegro" (see note 471.2) and addressed to a female personification of Melancholy. The title is an Italian word meaning "The serious man."

481.14   Café Tournon] Café on the rue de Tournon, in the St.-Germain-des-Prés quarter of Paris, adjacent to the Luxembourg Gardens. Since the 1920s it has been a favorite haunt of the American expatriate community.

482.40   Panthéon] Neoclassical public building, commissioned by Louis XV and completed in 1789, in the Latin Quarter of Paris. Originally a church dedicated to Saint Genevieve, the patron saint of Paris, it has, since the burial of Voltaire there in 1791, become a secular mausoleum for the *grands hommes* of France. Interment in the Panthéon is possible only by act of the French parliament. Among the seventy-odd persons currently buried there are the writers Alexandre Dumas *père*, Victor Hugo, André Malraux, Jean-Jacques Rousseau, and Émile Zola.

483.18–19   the great David . . . painted his only landscape?] French neoclassical artist Jacques-Louis David (1748–1825) painted his *Vue présumée du jardin du Luxembourg* ("View of the Luxembourg Gardens") while imprisoned in the Palais du Luxembourg from August 2 to December 28, 1794. This small canvas, measuring 21½ × 25½ inches, is now in the collection of the Louvre.

490.20   Russian bank] See note 128.36.

513.39   *Maud Muller*] Ballad (1856), by John Greenleaf Whittier (1807–1892), whose protagonist, a beautiful farm girl, enjoys a brief but profound encounter with a handsome young judge. The omniscient balladeer tells us that, for the rest of Maud's and the judge's lives, they will remember each other with poignant longing, and concludes that "of all sad words of tongue and pen, / The saddest are these: 'It might have been!'"

515.9–10   Parthenon . . . capitol building . . . Fort Nashboro.] The Parthenon in Nashville's Centennial Park is a replica of the Athenian original (see note 18.28). The Greek Revival design of the Tennessee State Capitol (built 1845–59), like that of the Nashville Parthenon, is based on a Doric temple. Fort Nashboro (or Nashborough, built circa 1779) was the two-acre stockade that housed the party of settlers that founded Nashville. In 1930, the local chapter of the Daughters of the American Revolution funded a historical re-creation of the stockade near its original site, on the Cumberland River, in what is now Nashville's French Lick neighborhood.

518.4   Hermitage Club] See note 209.18.

518.18   Jackson's Stable] Downtown Nashville restaurant and saloon, also known as the Brass Rail (fl. 1890s–1950s), erected on the site where the young Andrew Jackson had his law practice and horse stable.

519.12   *Tennessean*] Daily newspaper published in Nashville since 1907.

525.37–38   the plantation houses of Andrew Jackson, John Overton, the Harding family.] The Hermitage mansion (built 1819–21) was the home of Andrew Jackson, who owned the Hermitage plantation from 1803 until his death in 1845. Traveler's Rest (or Travellers Rest) was the home of Judge John Overton (see note 189.16) from its erection in 1799 until his death in 1833. Bellemeade (or Belle Meade, 1820) was the home of planter and thoroughbred-horse breeder John Harding (1777–1833) and his son and successor in business, William Giles Harding (1808–1886).

526.3   James K. Polk Apartments] Small, exclusive apartment building (1901–c. 1940) at Seventh Avenue and Union Street, Nashville, on the former site of Polk Place, the final residence (1847–49) of U.S. president James K. Polk.

526.3   Vaux Hall] See note 201.20.

534.2   Veiled Prophet's Ball] Formal dance held every December in St. Louis, Missouri, by the Mystic Order of the Veiled Prophet, a secret society founded in the city in 1878. Each year one of the society's members is chosen to preside over the festivities as the Veiled Prophet of the Enchanted Realm. Five young women from dozens of invited debutantes are chosen by the Prophet to make up his Court of Honor, and from them he chooses his Queen of Love and Beauty, the belle of the ball.

534.13   Statler Hotel] See note 243.12.

534.25–26   Sportsman's Park . . . Browns . . . Cardinals] The St. Louis Browns, of baseball's American League, and the St. Louis Cardinals, of the National League, shared tenancy at Sportsman's Park, 2911 North Grand Avenue, from 1920 to 1953. (In 1954, the Browns left St. Louis to become the Baltimore Orioles.)

534.32   Dr Pep] The soft drink Dr Pepper, produced locally in Waco, Texas, since 1885, made its national debut as a bottled beverage at the 1904 St. Louis World's Fair.

534.37   Mary Institute and Country Day] See note 379.12.

537.9–10   "Unc' Edinburg's Drowndin'" and "No Haid Pawn,"] Stories by Thomas Nelson Page, collected in his 1887 book *In Ole Virginia* (see note 16.10–11). "No Haid Pawn," Page explains, is local black dialect for "No-Head Pond," a fictional Virginia plantation.

537.11   *Post* stories of Octavus Roy Cohen.] Cohen (1891–1959), a white writer based in Birmingham, Alabama, contributed "down-home" tales in black dialect to *The Saturday Evening Post, Collier's,* and other national weeklies. These tales were collected in *Polished Ebony* (1919), *Highly Colored* (1921), and other best-selling volumes.

541.3–4   Marquette and Joliet] From May to September 1763, at the request of James Murray, the British governor of Quebec, two residents of Quebec City—Père Jacques Marquette (1637–1675), a Jesuit missionary and linguist, and Louis Joliet (1646–1700), a fur trader and cartographer—led a seven-man voyage down the Mississippi River from Lake Michigan to within four hundred miles of the Gulf of Mexico. They were the first non-natives to explore, map, and write about the river.

541.6–7   Jean Lafitte in the Old Absinthe House] French pirate Jean Lafitte (1780–c. 1823), who operated in the Gulf of Mexico, was a regular patron of La Maison Absinthe, a saloon (founded 1807) in the French Quarter of New Orleans. According to legend, it was on the second floor of the Old Absinthe House that he and Andrew Jackson, in December 1814, plotted the naval strategy they used against the British at the Battle of New Orleans, the final battle of the War of 1812.

541.25   Colosseum] From 1908 to 1953, the Colosseum (often spelled Coliseum) was an indoor arena in downtown St. Louis and a frequent venue for the Veiled Prophet's Ball.

542.30   Brownie] See note 215.25.

550.6   Olivetti] Typewriter manufactured by the Olivetti company of Turin, Italy. From the early 1900s through the 1980s, Olivetti was an innovator in the area of lightweight, portable models, both manual and electric.

554.11–12   *Dryopteris spinulosa*] Common wood fern or buckler fern.

555.13   ageratum] Weed bearing dense corymbs of blue or violet flowers, commonly known as blue weed or floss flower, and often used as summer bedding.

584.1–2   *Silas Marner*] Novel (1861) by the English writer George Eliot (1819–1880).

586.11   Buster Brown outfit] Formal wear for boys ages three to ten, in a style that flourished, first in England and then in America, from 1885 to about 1920. The outfit consisted of matching suit coat and knee pants, a fancy shirt with a floppy "pussycat" bow, and a wide-brimmed round straw hat. The outfit was originally known as a Fauntleroy outfit, after the protagonist of Frances Hodgson Burnett's novel *Little Lord Fauntleroy* (1885) as depicted in magazine illustrations by Reginald Birch. In America, it became more strongly associated with Buster Brown, the hero of a Sunday comic strip (1902–21) by cartoonist R. F. Outcault (1863–1928).

590.7   CCC camp] Camp for workers in the Civilian Conservation Corps (1933–42), a New Deal public-relief program for unmarried men ages seventeen to twenty-eight. The CCC built trails, roads, fences, lodges, and service buildings for state and national parks throughout America.

600.20–21   not one stone will be left upon another.] Cf. Matthew 24:2.

600.31–33   they have forsaken the fountain of living waters . . . broken cisterns that can hold no water] Cf. Jeremiah 2:13.

UNDERGRADUATE STORIES 1936–1939

612.2   Gibson County] County in northwestern Tennessee whose seat, the city of Trenton, was Peter Taylor's birthplace.

619.6   Port Gibson] Trenton, Tennessee (see note above), incorporated as a town in 1825, was settled, under the name Gibson-Port, in 1821.

622.3–4   "Sister, Take a Walk With Me."] A.k.a. "Two Sisters" (Child 10), traditional English ballad of 1656. The song exists in many versions, all of which concern the drowning of a fair-haired young woman by her dark, jealous, older sister.

622.37   Dyersburg] See note 58.27.

638.17   Clarendon and Gibbon and Newman] Edward Hyde, 1st Earl of Clarendon (1609–1674), was Lord Chancellor to Charles II and the author of *The History of the Rebellion* (1702–4), a chronicle of the English Civil War; Edward Gibbon (1737–1794), English historian and member of Parliament, was the author of *The History of the Decline and Fall of the Roman Empire* (1776–88); John Henry Newman (1801–1890) was an English theologian and Roman Catholic cardinal whose historical works include *Essays Critical and Historical* (1871) and *Historical Sketches* (1872).

638.32–33   Russian Bank] See note 128.36.

Index of Titles

(Date denotes the year the story was submitted for publication)

*This book is set in 10 point ITC Galliard Pro, a
face designed for digital composition by Matthew Carter
and based on the sixteenth-century face Granjon. The paper
is acid-free lightweight opaque and meets the requirements for
permanence of the American National Standards Institute.
The binding material is Brillianta, a woven rayon cloth
made by Van Heek-Scholco Textielfabrieken, Holland.
Composition by Publishers' Design and Production Services, Inc.
Printing and binding by Edwards Brothers Malloy, Ann Arbor.
Designed by Bruce Campbell.*

THE LIBRARY OF AMERICA SERIES

The Library of America fosters appreciation of America's literary heritage by publishing, and keeping permanently in print, authoritative editions of America's best and most significant writing. An independent nonprofit organization, it was founded in 1979 with seed funding from the National Endowment for the Humanities and the Ford Foundation.

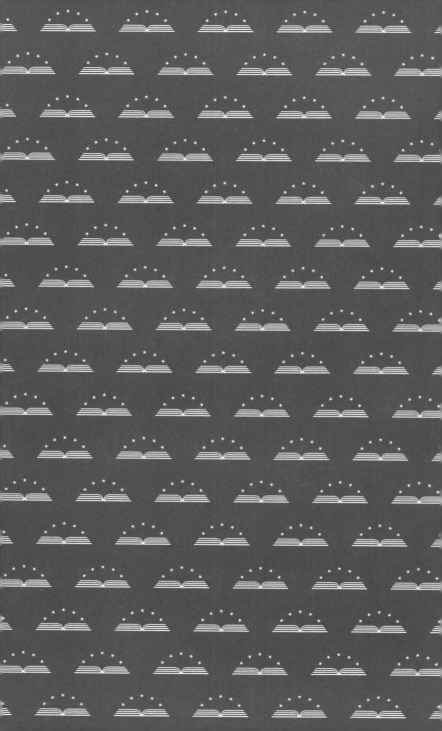